April Witch

April Witch

A   N O V E L

Majgull Axelsson

TRANSLATED BY LINDA SCHENCK

Villard / New York

This is an entirely fictional account. Although there is both a neighborhood health center and a nursing home in Vadstena, as well as an Institute of Space Physics in Kiruna, none of these institutions is identical to the ones described in this novel. The characters and events are also the products of my imagination—although I am grateful to Ray Bradbury, who got me thinking about the whole business of April witches several decades ago.—Majgull Axelsson

English translation copyright © 2002 by Random House, Inc.

This work was originally published in Sweden, as *Aprilhäxan*, by Prisma Publishers, Stockholm, in 1997. Copyright © 1997 by Majgull Axelsson.

Grateful acknowledgment is made to the following for permission to reprint previously published material:
Houghton Mifflin Company and McClelland & Stewart Inc.: Twelve lines from "A Sad Child," from *Morning in the Burned House,* by Margaret Atwood. Copyright © 1995 by Margaret Atwood. Rights throughout Canada are controlled by McClelland & Stewart Inc., *The Canadian Publishers.* Reprinted by permission of Houghton Mifflin Company and McClelland & Stewart Inc.
Alfred A. Knopf, a division of Random House, Inc: Seven lines from "Cosmic Gall," from *Collected Poems 1953–1993,* by John Updike. Copyright © 1993 by John Updike. Reprinted by permission of Alfred A. Knopf, a division of Random House, Inc.
Sony/ATV Music Publishing: Excerpt from "Heartbreak Hotel," by Mae Axton, Tommy Durden and Elvis Presley. Copyright ©1956 (renewed) by Sony/ATV Songs LLC. All rights administered by Sony/ATV Music Publishing, 8 Music Square West, Nashville, TN 37203. All rights reserved. Reprinted by permission of Sony/ATV Music Publishing.

Library of Congress Cataloging-in-Publication Data
Axelsson, Majgull.
    [Aprilhäxan. English]
    April Witch / Majgull Axelsson.
      p. cm.
    ISBN 0-375-50517-2
    I. Title.
PT9876.1.X44 A5713 2002
839.73'74—dc21   2001035867

Villard Books website address: www.villard.com

Printed in the United States of America on acid-free paper

9 8 7 6 5 4 3 2

FIRST U.S. EDITION

Book design by Joseph Rutt

Waves and Particles

Neutrinos they are very small
They have no charge and have no mass
And do not interact at all
The earth is just a silly ball
To them, through which they simply pass
Like dust maids down a drafty hall
Or photons through a sheet of glass . . .

John Updike

"Who's out there?" asks my sister.

She's more perceptive than the others, the only one who ever senses my presence. She looks like a bird right now, standing there craning her neck, staring out across the backyard. She's wearing nothing but a gray bathrobe over her white nightgown, and doesn't seem to notice last night's frost hanging in the air. Her robe is open, the belt untied, dangling from one single loop. Like a slender tail feather, it trails behind her down the steps from the kitchen.

She swivels her head sharply, listening in the direction of the yard, awaiting a response. When none is forthcoming, she repeats her question, now in a shriller, more anxious tone of voice: "Who's out there?"

Her breath forms small white plumes, very becoming to her ethereal type. Like mist, I thought the very first time I ever saw her. It was a hot August day many summers ago, long before I had moved into assisted accommodation. A medical conference was about to begin in the auditorium of the nursing home, and Hubertsson had gotten them to roll my wheelchair out and park me in the shade of the big maple tree. He orchestrated a coincidence in which he bumped into Christina Wulf in the parking lot and got her to walk across the big lawn where I was sitting. The heels of her pumps went right through the soft grass, and when she reached the graveled yard she stopped for a moment to make sure there was no dirt stuck under her shoes. That was when I noticed she was wearing panty hose, despite the heat. A neat blouse, a calf-length skirt, and panty hose. All in shades of white and gray.

"Your elder sister is one of those ladies who washes her hands in chlorine bleach," Hubertsson had said before showing her to me.

On the surface, that was a good description. But not completely adequate. Now that I could see her in the flesh, she seemed to me so ambiguous in both shape and color that the laws of physical matter failed to apply to her. She should be able to seep like smoke through closed windows and locked doors. For one instant as he reached out to support her, I thought Hubertsson's hand was going to pass straight through her arm.

Which wouldn't have been so strange, really. We often forget that what we consider laws of nature are actually nothing but our ignorant ideas about a highly complex reality. For instance, the fact that we are living in a cloud of particles with no substance: photons and neutrinos. Or the fact that all matter—even that of which the human body is composed—is primarily emptiness, a vacuum. The distance between the particles in the atoms is just as great as the distance between a star and its planets. What gives rise to surface and solidity is not the particles themselves, in other words, but the electromagnetic field that binds them. Quantum physics also teaches us that the very smallest elements of matter are not just particles. They are also waves. Simultaneously. For the duration of a microsecond the electron tries out its potential positions, and for that instant all its possibilities are equally real.

So everything is in flux. As we know.

Seen in light of this there is nothing particularly peculiar about the fact that some of us are able to violate the laws of physics. But when Hubertsson's hand reached Christina as she stood there on one foot examining the sole of her shoe, she turned out to have contours just as solid as those of any other human being. His hand grasped her arm and remained there.

She hasn't become less transparent over the years; she still looks like she might dissolve at any moment and drift away in a jumble of waves and particles.

But, of course, this is simply an illusion. Christina is actually a solidly coherent lump of human matter. Extraordinarily coherent, even.

And now her electrons have decided to change position. She blinks and forgets me, tightens her bathrobe around her body, and walks, her rubber boots squelching, along the slushy gravel path in the direction of the mailbox and the morning papers.

The letter is at the bottom of the mailbox. When she catches sight of it a tiny wave of horror wafts like a breeze through the yard. *Astrid,* she thinks, just as she remembers that Astrid is dead, that she has, in fact, been dead for three years. That is some comfort. She stuffs the papers under her arm and starts toward the house, all the time twisting and turning the envelope. She's not watching her step.

That's why she trips over the dead seagull.

AT THAT VERY instant my second sister opens her eyes in a hotel room in Göteborg, gulping for air. That's how she always wakes up; for one instant she is terrified, before she remembers who she is and where. When her morning panic subsides, she starts to fall back to sleep, then halts herself and stretches toward the ceiling. Jesus! She doesn't have time to lie around! This is the day she is going to spend a perfectly ordinary Thursday retracing her own footsteps. A walk down memory lane. She's been that way before, but not for a long time.

Margareta sits up in bed, fumbles for a smoke. The first puff gives her the shivers, she feels as if her skin rises and hovers a fraction of an inch above her flesh. She looks down at her arms. They are naked, pale and goose-bumped. She forgot her only nightgown at Claes's place . . .

For a confirmed smoker Margareta is surprisingly addicted to fresh air. Covering her nudity with the blanket, she walks over to the window and opens it wide. She stays there in the cold air, staring out at the late winter day, gray as lead.

Nowhere in Sweden is the air as ugly as in Göteborg, she thinks. It's a habitual, familiar thought, the one she uses to console herself when the northern darkness of Kiruna presses her to the ground. She's been lucky after all. Had it not been for a coincidence, she might very well have had to live her whole life under the metallic Göteborg sky. A coincidence in Tanum . . .

Margareta inhales deeply, letting the smoke seep out from a satisfied smile. She's going back to Tanum today. For the first time in more than two decades, she's returning to the place that determined her adult destiny.

She had just turned twenty-three, and was studying archaeology, when it happened. She'd been on a dig there all summer, sifting and brushing her way through the sand of the heather-covered heath in an attempt to reveal yet another ancient rock drawing. All the time, a string inside her had oscillated with expectation. That string was vibrating for Fleming, a Danish visiting professor with a deep voice and slitlike eyes. Even in those days Margareta had already had, to put it mildly, some experience of middle-aged men, and now she was using all the tricks and wiles she had in her bag. She lowered her gaze and drew her hand quickly through her hair when he looked at her, she let her breasts protrude and her hips sway as she walked, laughed softly and cooed at his jokes during the coffee breaks.

Initially, he'd been more intimidated than flattered. Although he did often seek her out, smile and laugh back, he took no initiative. Instead he would mention—increasingly often and out of context—his wife and children, his age and obligations. But Margareta didn't release her grip. She was fanatical by nature, then as now, and the more he flaunted his signals and evasions, the more intently she would lock eyes. She wanted him!

The problem was that she didn't really know what she wanted him for.

They would go to bed together. Naturally. At night in her tent she would often fantasize about how he would embrace her waist with one arm while undoing his fly with the other hand. He would tremble and fumble, but she would not aid him. On the contrary, she would exacerbate things by pressing her crotch to his, rotating it slowly. Once his fly was open, however, she would allow her own hand to find its way in, cupping his sex, which would rise, throbbing and erect, out of the shapeless lump under the white cotton weave of his briefs, after which her fingers would wander on, light and flitting, like butterfly wings.

But sleeping with him was only the means. Not the end. Margareta had a feeling all she would be able to see was the mirror image of her own desire in his, and she really didn't mind. A different void in her was waiting to be filled afterward, she knew, as they lay in the heather surrounded by the summer's night. That was when Fleming would say or do something—she didn't know what—but something that would forever fill every empty cavity in her body. From that moment on, she would live in satisfaction. Forever filled to overflowing.

And at last it happened. One evening Fleming put his arm around her waist while his other hand fumbled with his fly. Margareta's hand embraced his sex and her desire burst into pure anticipation as she sank under him into the heather. Shortly afterward Fleming exploded. After which it was over, because once Fleming's cock had slackened he turned out to have nothing with which to fill her. His weight, which had been solace and a promise such a short time ago, was now stifling, threatening.

Gasping for air, she heaved him aside. He reacted not at all, simply grunted and changed position, sound asleep in the flowering heather.

To this day Margareta has no idea what made her get up and go. It would have been more her style to stay put, snuggling in his armpit, more like her to be content for a few months with the crumbs he had to offer, rather than immediately to begin to dream of larger ones. But the bitter taste of disappointment in her mouth moved her to pull on her shorts and leave. She walked intentionally in the wrong direction, away from the dig and the archaeologists' campsite, toward something different . . .

"Oh, honeybunch," Margareta consoles herself, standing at an open window twenty-five years later. She reaches out with one hand from the blanket in a floundering gesture, as if she wanted to reach through time and touch the empty girl wandering across the heather at Tanum. But at the same instant she realizes what that gesture implies about her perception of reality, and stops herself in mid-movement, changing the direction of her hand. It grasps her cigarette instead, and stubs it out.

Margareta is a physicist and, as such, slightly intimidated by contemporary physics. Sometimes she has the impression that concepts like time, space, and matter are dissolving right in front of her eyes, and then she has to stop herself, rein in her bolting imagination, and persuade herself that, from the human point of view, nothing has changed. Here on earth, matter is still solid, and time is still a river running through the world from the beginning of life until its end. It is only in theory, she tells herself, that time is an illusion. To people, time is real, and therefore it is a signal of human madness to try to reach through it, for instance to try to console a twenty-years-younger edition of oneself.

She shuts the window hard, pulls the curtains, and lets the blanket fall to the floor. She stretches. Now she'll shower and make herself beautiful, and then she'll bounce off in Claes's old jalopy, first to Tanum and then on to Motala and, eventually, Stockholm. The boring conference she has just suffered through in Göteborg filled its function. A whole week away from Kiruna and her goddamn dissertation! In the shower, the memory comes over her again. Suddenly she sees Fleming before her, recalls his anxious smile the next day, and his eager whispers. Wasn't it wonderful? And wouldn't it be wonderful that night, again? And in the fall he would arrange to be her adviser . . .

The older Margareta lifts her face into the spray and shuts her eyes.

Behind them she sees the young Margareta smile softly and bend deeper over the task at hand.

"Sorry," she says. "Sorry, Fleming. I don't think so . . ."

"Why not?"

She turns her head and looks up at him. "Because I've had enough of archaeology. I'm gonna do physics in the fall. Made up my mind last night."

The older Margareta allows herself a dry snicker at the memory of the look on his face.

MY THIRD SISTER is lying on a mattress, blinking. Otherwise she is completely immobile.

Birgitta has no bed. She doesn't even have a mattress cover; she's lying right on the filthy foam rubber. Her arms are out from her sides; a thin trickle of saliva is running out of the left corner of her mouth . . .

She looks terrible. Crucified bread dough.

And yet she is thinking about beauty, she's remembering when she was fifteen and the milk white Marilyn Monroe of Motala. On the floor beside her is Roger, a skimpy little shrimp of a guy with greasy hair and ash gray stubble. It's because of him Birgitta can't sleep, because of him she has to force herself to remember the days when she was pretty. And now she's almost there. She sees Hound Dog glide out of his car, shut the door, and look around. The parking lot is silent; all you can hear is Cliff Richard's voice gushing out of a portable record player. Everyone's eyes are glued to Hound Dog; the girls' desire flutters toward him on butterfly wings, the boys' helplessness is transformed to stunned silence.

Birgitta knows he is moving toward her, she knows he is moving toward her even before he starts to move. Here he comes, yanking open the car door and grabbing her wrist.

"You're my girl now," he says. Only this. Nothing more.

Like in a movie, Birgitta thinks for the thousandth time in her life. It was just like at the movies. And the film rolls on, the chorus and strings fill the space as she recalls how he bent her over the hood of a car and leaned down to give her a first kiss . . .

But Roger moves in his sleep and breaks the sequence; the film cracks and the image disappears. She turns her head and looks at him; a slight odor of ammonia makes her nose prickle. His bleached blue jeans have a dark stain spreading from the fly down over his left thigh . . .

Birgitta is exhausted, but had she had any energy left she would have thrown herself over that worm of a man and smothered him with the weight of her own flesh. She doesn't, though. She can't even cover her ears with her hands to keep out his voice. And it wouldn't help anyway. The words are already out, his comment etched into her cerebrum for eternity: "Jesus Christ," he says in her memory, covering her face with his hand. "Jesus Christ. It's enough to shrivel a man's dick."

Birgitta blinks and gasps for breath, searches her memory for the chorus and strings, for Hound Dog's huge hands and the Marilyn Monroe of Motala. But the film has snapped, the reel rattles disconsolately round and round, the stump of the film fluttering and all the pictures gone.

She shuts her eyes tight, squeezes them to two thin lines, trying to force the comforting memory to resurface. When she fails, she peers out of half-open eyes down at Roger. Today she'll finally toss the bastard out.

Driftwood

It's spring, Cecy thought. I'll be in every living thing in
the world tonight.

Ray Bradbury

JUST BEFORE DAWN, all the sounds in the corridor change, the whispers and muffled steps of the night shift are punctuated by clacking heels and crystal clear voices. The day shift. Kerstin One's day shift today, no less. You can feel it in the very air, which buzzes with energy and activity even before she arrives. When it's Kerstin Two's day shift the air hovers heavy, and smells of coffee.

It's Wednesday. Maybe I'll get a shower. I haven't had one for a whole week, and the sweet-sour scent of my body is beginning to overpower me. It disturbs my concentration. There's definitely nothing wrong with my sense of smell. Unfortunately.

I breathe a long, focused breath into my mouthpiece, and the monitor above my bed flickers.

"Do you want to save this text before shutting down? Yes/No?"

Short puff. Yes, I want to save the text. The computer hums and puts itself to sleep.

Not until now do I realize how tired my eyes are. A burning sensation under my eyelids. I need to rest in the dark for a while. Moreover, the safest thing is to pretend to be asleep in case Kerstin One should decide to make her morning rounds. If she discovers I've been up all night, she'll preach one of her little sermons on the importance of a normal day-and-night rhythm. She might even order her training patrol to bolster me up in a wheelchair and roll me out to one of the everlasting idiot competitions in the dayroom. Concentration for five-year-olds. Or Picture Bingo. The first prize is always an orange, and the winner is expected to smile and stop drooling—each according to his ability—for the award ceremony. That's why I never win no matter how many I answer right. Kerstin One fixes the results, and patients with attitude problems—as she says in her Americanized social worker jargon—simply aren't allowed to win. That would be a waste of the therapeutic value of idiot competitions. My attitude problem is that I pretend I'm unable to smile. I drool and grimace and pretend to be desperate to make the corners of my mouth turn up when the training patrol entices me with the orange of victory, but I cannot. Ever. And Kerstin One—who knows I am lying and playing a role— is equally indomitably furious every time. But she still can't get herself to accuse me openly; she cannot reveal to the nurse's aides that, in fact, I once smiled at her.

It was a month ago, on my first day on the ward. I'd been hearing her voice in the corridor for hours—one moment babbling cheerfully, the next moment bleating tenderly—and it had given me gooseflesh. It reminded me of far too many other voices. Hers made them burst into a chattering cacophony in my ears: they included Karin from the cripples' home; sunny Ruth, who wanted a foster child (but not one like *her*!); German Trudy at the neurology clinic and her successors: Berit, Anna, and Veronica. They all had those encouraging birdsong voices, and they all behaved like hookers. They smiled and chattered and caressed for a price. But their hands were icy cold, and the price they demanded was outrageous. A halo.

In my assisted accommodation I was surrounded by fairly indifferent women with warm hands and voices that never promised too much. Then, a few years ago, I got my own special apartment for the disabled with round-the-clock caregivers. They spanned the spectrum, from young men to elderly women fleeing unemployment, through tired young mothers with very little education and middle-aged artists whose dream of the big breakthrough was beginning to fade. They fed and washed and clothed me without demanding that I express my gratitude by loving them. They were implacably unruffled and good listeners; if I groaned or tightened an unexpected muscle in pain they would instantly release their grip and try to find a gentler way.

But those days were now past. My convulsions grew more and more frequent. Often, I was close to gliding over into status epilepticus, the never-ending epileptic seizure. And one day Hubertsson was at my bedside, explaining, with eyes lowered as if ashamed, that this couldn't go on. I couldn't manage with just home caregivers, I required constant monitoring by medically trained personnel, at least for a few months, at least as long as it would take to find and regulate the dosage of a new medication. And therefore I would have to go back to the nursing home from which he had once liberated me. And the voice out in the corridor revealed that this place was under the management of a person who would break a leg, if necessary, for the cause of goodness.

In spite of which I did try to behave civilly. When Kerstin One came into my room she found a polite greeting on the screen, and I was just about to introduce myself when she bent over my bed, pushing the monitor aside, and said, "You poor thing," extending a hand to stroke my cheek.

I cannot control my spasms, but this time I was lucky. My head jerked and twisted to the side, as it always jerks and twists to the side, and I found myself at precisely the correct angle to grasp her thumb. I clutched. And I bit. I bit so hard that I could feel my front teeth cutting her white skin and penetrating to the bone before the next spasm tore my head aside, forcing me to let go. That was when I smiled. A warm, open, heartfelt smile. The only smile I will ever bestow upon Kerstin One.

With the next spasm I managed to grasp the mouthpiece again and started to blow. I couldn't see the monitor—she had shoved it too far to the right—but I was still able to make myself understood: "No one calls me a poor thing!"

She bumped the screen and ran from the room with a dry sob, her left hand cupping her right thumb in an extremely reproachful gesture. For one second I wanted to rejoice in my victory until, an instant later, I glimpsed the text flickering over my head. *No one calls me a poor thing!* Well, jeez. Arnold Schwarzenegger couldn't have put it better.

And yet it needed to be said. Because there is no state of being that has worn out so many names as this one; every decade for the last century has spit out some bitter old word and found a new, sweeter one. Thus the cripple became maimed and the maimed soul lame and the lame an invalid, the invalid a handicapped person, the handicapped person disabled, and, finally, the disabled became the developmentally challenged.

Underlying each of these expressions is a wild desire. And believe me, I share it. No one wants more than I do for us to find the enchanted word one day, the perfect word that will cause scarred brains to heal, that will give bone marrow the ability to repair itself, and enable atrophied nerve cells to rejuvenate. But so far we have not discovered it. And if you sum up the words used thus far, I would say the total comes to exactly what Kerstin One had just bleated over my head.

Pending the appearance of the perfect word, then, I choose to stand aside from the prevailing descriptions. I know what I am. A piece of driftwood. A leaky piece of wreckage, the flotsam and jetsam of a distant time.

"I'll be damned if it wasn't this century itself that smashed your body to pieces," Hubertsson said one New Year's Eve at my place when he'd had too much to drink. That line brought the heat to my cheeks, although I left my monitor vacant. Because what could I have answered? Alas, do let me be human to you, my beloved, not a monument? You can't say things like that. Particularly not when your legs are forever locked in the fetal position while your arms and head are in constant spastic motion, your face grimacing, and your hands fluttering like underwater flora. In which case you avoid words of love like the plague and pretend you don't hear.

But I do hear. I see. And I feel.

I see and hear and feel despite the fact that what is a whole unbroken chain to others is fragmented and broken to me. Only a few thin threads now unite the real me with what is my body. My voice consists of three sounds: I sigh with well-being, I groan with pain, or I bellow like an animal at the slaughter when I am suffering. These things I can control. I can also blow short and long puffs into a mouthpiece, puffs that are transformed into text on a computer screen. Moreover I can still—although only with extreme difficulty—grasp a spoon with my left hand, move it down to a plate and up to my mouth. I can chew and swallow. That's it.

For a long time I tried to convince myself that the chaos that is my body still contains the very core of being human. I have my free will and my sound mind, a heart that beats, a pair of lungs that breathe, and—not least—a human brain with so many remarkable abilities that I tremble to consider it. But these cheerful catchphrases didn't help. In the end I was still forced to admit that I am trapped in the spider's web of terms and conditions the Almighty Trickster has spun across our world. In the past month, that insight has been reinforced. Sometimes I even imagine that Kerstin One is his messenger, that she is the little spider of God who will one day come crawling across the web to dissolve the flesh and marrow from my bones with her sour saliva, and suck me dry.

Indeed. That would be logical. But it mustn't happen yet. I still have two missions to accomplish.

First I need to know which of my sisters stole the life that was intended for me.

After which I want to follow my beloved to his grave.

Only then will I be prepared to allow myself to be drained.

*   *   *

Now I hear him. No one opens the ward door as gently as he, no one shuffles so sleepily through the morning corridor. He's slightly hesitant today, possibly afraid that Kerstin One will suddenly appear to block his way. K-One, he calls her. As distinguished from K-Two. "She's hopeless," he says, "with that streamlined appearance of hers and all those white surfaces. I'll be damned if she's not molded in vanilla ice cream. Warm her up and her color and shape will melt away."

He isn't much for silky skin and taut tendons nowadays. It might have something to do with his own aging, of course. His face has become elongated and fatigued in the last few years, his eyebrows gray and bushy, his double chin enlarged, and the bags under his eyes swollen. In the same process, his shirts have become increasingly stained and the seats of his trousers baggier. Some of the nurse's aides in Kerstin One's training patrol call him sickening. Kerstin One finds it sufficient to mark out her personal space. If he gets too close she quickly pulls back and runs her hand through her long hair, as if to rid herself of his touch.

I'd never do that. If I had a creamy vanilla body with taut tendons and the ability to move it, I'd want to touch him often. He is the only human being whose touch I have ever liked. That may be because he touches me so seldom. Once a month or so he gives me a formal examination, but then there's always a nurse present and his hands are objective and impersonal. Only once did he ever conclude the examination with a caress. That was when I had my fourth bout of pneumonia in a year. He cupped my hand in both of his and drew me close, pressed my cheek to his chest. "Pull yourself together," he said. "You're not gonna die on us this time either."

The woolen sweater under his white coat was rough against my cheek. And he smelled like almonds . . .

Oh well, that was eleven years ago, and it never happened again.

Sometimes—when we're alone—he sits on the edge of my bed and strokes my blanket with one hand, but most of the time he sits at a distance, not even looking at me. He settles into the deep bay window, clasps his hands around his knee, looks out as he speaks, and glares intently at the monitor when I answer. To him I am more present through my words than through my body.

In fact, he is the one who gave me the power of words. And not only that. He is responsible for having given me a sense of smell and taste, the memory of cold and warmth, the name of my mother, and pictures of my sisters. He is the one who prized out a donation of handwoven linen sheets for my bed from the local craft guild in exchange for a lecture on how the tubular fibers in linen prevent bedsores. He got the Rotary Club to subsidize my computer and the Lions Club to pay for my TV, and once a year he stuffs me into a specially constructed vehicle for the disabled and conveys me to the Stockholm Technical Museum to show me the diffusion chamber. Once we get there, he lets me sit in the dark room for hours and, all by myself, consider the dance of matter.

Hubertsson has given me everything. Everything.

I WAS EXHAUSTED and investigated to pieces fifteen years ago, when the neurosurgeons in Linköping gave up on me and had me moved to the nursing home at Vadstena, where I had to be on an IV drip for the first several weeks just to keep me alive. I seldom opened my eyes, and didn't move voluntarily. After just a couple of days I could feel the bedsores budding and blossoming on my hips, despite the fact that they turned me over every couple of hours. There was plenty of staff in those days. Ambitious staff, too. One of those nurses found an old clipping from the local newspaper and hung it on my wall. It was a photo of me, bolstered upright in a wheelchair with my mortarboard on my semibald head. *The most amazing graduate of the year!*

"Look at that," the nurses would say as they turned me toward the wall. "Do you remember how smart you are? You graduated from high school."

In those days I was still able to make certain sounds reminiscent of ordinary speech, but the very thought of forcing an answer over my lips wore me out. I wanted nothing more than for them to take that awful photo away, but I didn't have the energy to say it.

Hubertsson came on the third Thursday; he'd been away on vacation. He stepped into my room and grunted as a nurse read him my records. I didn't open my eyes to look at him. A doctor is a doctor, what was there to see?

He bent down over my bed and inspected the clipping on the wall before examining me, but without a comment. Instead his rough hands felt my body, probing and touching me just as a hundred other doctors had probed and touched. It wasn't until he was leaving the room that I realized he was different. He stopped in the doorway and said: "Get rid of that clipping, please. Put it someplace where other people can read it, but don't make her . . ."

That very afternoon an assistant nurse brought in a roll of tape and did as he had said. When she was done she extended a glass of juice in my direction just in case, and for the first time in three weeks I managed to open my mouth and drink.

A couple of days later he entered my room with a six-inch-thick document binder in his hands. He walked straight over to the bed and took my left hand. "Are you planning to speak when you're spoken to today?"

I looked lethargically at him, but didn't answer.

"Forget it," he said, pressing my hand. "One for yes, two for no."

This was a signal system I remembered well. The very first one. From the cripples' home.

"You've been thoroughly examined and diagnosed. As you may know. But do you know anything else about yourself?"

I withdrew my hand. That was none of his business.

"Don't get uppity," he said. "Do you know where you were born? Or to whom? Yes or no?"

He'd grasped my hand again, tighter. "Well? Yes or no?"

I gave up, shut my eyes, and squeezed his hand twice. He immediately let go and walked over to the window, sat down in its deep niche, and clasped his hands around his knee.

"It's goddamned incredible," he said. "Here you lie, driving yourself half mad with contemplation about astronomy and elementary particle physics and other abstractions—I've read your papers!—but without so much as a single scrap of knowledge about yourself . . ."

He sat silently, turning the pages of the binder. I fixed my eyes on him, but without really seeing. It was late autumn, and the afternoon was already growing dark; he was nothing but a contour to me. After a while he got up and returned to my bed.

"There's a reason for your being as you are," he said. "An explanation. There is always a reason and an explanation. I can give it to you. But the question, of course, is, Do you want to know?"

I managed to grab at his hand and squeeze it as hard as I could. Twice.

"All right," he said. "Your call. But I'll be back tomorrow."

He could have added: and every morning until the end of time.

* * *

NOW HE OPENS the door, allowing a little fan of light from the corridor to spread across the floor. "Hey, lady," he says, as he's been saying every morning for fifteen years. "How's tricks?"

I respond with a quotation: *"O Captain! my Captain! . . ."*

He grins and shuffles over to the bay window. "Come on, I'm not dead yet. How're your sisters?"

By the time he's settled in I've puffed my answer. It's flickering at him on the screen: "About as well as they deserve to be."

He laughs. "I believe that! Now that those poor creatures have ended up in your vise grip . . ."

THERE WAS A time when I believed that he was the one who made my waking dreams. That was what I called them. That other word— hallucinations—was much too upsetting.

One evening shortly after we'd met for the first time, a seagull landed on the ledge outside my window, a perfectly ordinary gull with gray wings and yellow legs. But this was a dull November evening, and the seagull shouldn't have been there. He should have been hovering over the sea off the coast of Gibraltar. Nor should I have been able to leave my own body and burrow under his feathers. But suddenly there I was, deep inside and surrounded by the softest down.

At first I didn't realize what had happened; I was simply astonished and bewildered as I sank down into the miracle that was the gull. The membranes under his feathers glittered like mother-of-pearl, his liver was shiny, moist, and blood red, the bones of his skeleton hollow and brittle, as if the Almighty Trickster had decided to carve himself a flute, only to become bored and transform his creation, with a little grin, into the most screeching, least sonorous of birds. Not until I looked down and saw the ground below me did I realize where I was. I was sitting inside the black eye of the gull.

Never will I forget my horror, the trembling din that bore me back to my own body in an instant. I roared. My mouth was wide open and spewing forth a guttural gruel of hysterical vowels. Footsteps were running along the corridor, heels clapping against the floor, followed a moment later by other clattering feet. Three women in white were crowded in my doorway, but just as they opened the door the seagull rose and vanished.

That evening was followed by others.

To begin with I was terribly frightened. If a fly walked across the ceiling I shut my eyes fast and told myself I had to keep a grip on my reason, which was my only possession worth owning. Sometimes it helped, but not always. Suddenly I might find myself suspended upside down from my own ceiling regarding hundreds of images of the being in the bed below me through the prismatic eyes of the fly. At which point I'd start to scream while I was falling back into myself.

"She's having nightmares," the nurses would complain to the doctor on duty. "She wakes up in the middle of the night screaming, every night . . ."

"Aha," Hubertsson would say. "Good. Excellent." But when he saw their expressions he changed his tune and prescribed a mild sedative.

In those days he was still a good-looking man, although not with the decaying beauty he possesses today, just good-looking. And he knew how to use it. Every Thursday he would check in to the Standard Hotel in Norrköping, and every Friday morning when he arrived to see me, much later than usual, his eyes reflected satisfaction. The girls on the ward were seldom indifferent to his charms; there was always someone who would let her eyes lock with his for a moment longer than necessary. When they bathed me or made my bed, their quiet conversations were almost always about him and the women he had bedded. At least at first. Once they realized he came to see me almost every morning, a little circle of silence spread around me. An astonished and quite affronted silence.

I was equally astonished myself, had no idea what he was after. Well, I had encountered interested physicians before, particularly during the years I was an intelligent idiot who was likely to finish high school, but none of them was ever like him. He just kept coming. Day after day, morning after morning. Sometimes he said not a word, sometimes he would speak nonstop for an hour or more. He shared his views on politics and the state of the world, his opinions on the decline of the scientific community and the narrow-mindedness of the specialist system, as well as the occasional poignant detail about people he had gone to school with or his colleagues. None of which interested me.

Sometimes he scared me. If he came early, before it was light and before I was really awake, certain childhood memories might burst open in my mind, and I could briefly feel panicky. The shadow! But my heart would stop pounding when he headed for the bay window. The shadow of my childhood never strayed so far from the bed; he wanted to be close to the helplessness that made his sexual organ hard. Hubertsson, however, never desired my incapacity. What he wanted was something else, something no one had ever desired.

By the time winter was over I was acclimatized, and had forgotten all about his first visit and the questions he had asked that time. But one April morning he brought the thick binder with him again, set it at the foot of my bed, and reached for my left hand.

"Your mother's name is Ella Johansson," he said.

I retracted my hand as angrily as I was able, but he wouldn't let go.

"You were born in the maternity ward of Motala Hospital on the thirty-first of December, 1949. One minute to midnight."

My convulsions intensified, as they always do when I'm upset. I tried to shut my eyes to close him out.

"She never had any more children. In spite of which you have three sisters."

I opened my eyes; he noticed and knew he had me hooked.

"Ella was the one to name you Desirée. Which means 'the desired one.' "

I glowered at him. I'd discovered the irony of my name years ago.

"There is every indication that you were a healthy fetus."

Thank you very much. Cold comfort.

"But as a newborn you developed jaundice. A serious case. And in those days they hadn't yet learned to give babies blood transfusions. That was what caused your cerebral palsy."

He sucked his bottom lip for a moment and turned the page.

"In addition to which you suffered some brain damage at delivery. That explains your epilepsy and aspects of your paralysis. You may also have had a slight cerebral hemorrhage shortly after you were born. Ella had had rickets, which deformed her pelvis, but they let her go on for thirty hours. That's how it was in those days, they almost never did C-sections . . ."

Did she die in childbirth? Was that why I was abandoned? Suddenly I wanted to know. I tugged at Hubertsson's hand to get him to realize I wanted to ask questions. But I hadn't had anything to say for months, and it took time for me to find my voice. Nothing but moans and grunts came out. Hubertsson appeared to believe my sounds and nonspastic waving were protests. He gripped my hand even harder, pressing it to the pillow, his eyes still glued to his documents.

"Your head was quite deformed, but you were apparently born to the caul . . ."

So what? That wasn't what I wanted to know. Now I was furious, so irate and confused I tried to spit in his face. It wasn't a successful effort; I misjudged the rhythm of my jerky movements and the blob hit the wall. But that was enough to get him to let go of my hand. He straightened up, took one step back, and looked at me. "I was born to the caul, too," he said. "It's infallible protection against drowning, you know."

He frowned briefly, then allowed his expression to turn into a wry smile. "We're a special breed, you and me. A specially fortunate breed."

He stopped talking and looked away, out the window, then went on in the same ironic tone: "I'm actually not supposed to tell you this, but it so happens I knew your mother. Ella, I mean. She was my landlady once upon a time, and nowadays she happens to be my patient. What's left of her, that is . . ."

"CALLING, CALLING," HE says now. "Do you read me? Are you all right?"

I blink and return to the present. He's standing at the foot of my bed, a shadowed figure enclosed in late winter dawn light. It's not flattering, voids his face of all color, making it look like parchment. I puff a quick answer: "I'm okay. How about you?"

He lets the question hang on the monitor for a while, unanswered. I am forced to repeat it: "What's with you? How are your levels?"

He shrugs his shoulders. "Don't bug me . . ."

But I insist, I'm concerned, and blow so hard into the mouthpiece that my spelling goes awry: "I'm srerious. Have you checked?"

He sighs deeply. "Yes, I've checked my levels. They were about as expected. So I've done what needs to be done . . ."

"Extra insulin? Today again?"

"Uh-huh."

"You really ought to be more careful!"

He puts his hand quickly to his forehead, then looks me straight in the eye. "Cut it out now."

But I don't intend to cut it out. I snap at the mouthpiece and blow an instant answer: "Your levels might be better if you didn't drink so much."

I don't know what's gotten into me. Never in all the years since that

New Year's Eve when he drank himself into a stupor at my place have I indicated my awareness of his longing for the repose of intoxication. That's
been a condition, article number one of the unspoken contract that governs our relationship. I have the right to be both facetious and impertinent, but I must not be intimate. Never. So fear flutters in my stomach.
I've violated the pact; he's going to leave me!

But he doesn't go. He just freezes up in surprise and then snaps an answer: "Jesus! I'll be damned if this isn't starting to be like a long marriage."

He walks back to the bay window and settles down. I lose my grip on
the mouthpiece. A long marriage? He's never said that before. Never so
much as alluded. Of course I have to admit that I have had fantasies
of that kind, that I've dreamed the Almighty Trickster came striding
down the hall, dressed like a costumed Zeus in a deep blue cape and a
diamond-studded crown, to transform me into Hubertsson's bride. He'd
lay his healing hand on my body and my legs would straighten right out
and become muscular—perfectly shaped muscles—my hands would lie
still and my face would be smooth. The leathery pouches that are my
breasts would swell into real lily puffs and be ornamented with lovely little nipples, rosy wild strawberries in a bowl of cream. And the sparse tufts
of hair on my head would be turned at the very same moment into a shock
of waves. Chestnut brown, maybe. It would be just too much to crown all
that beauty with a blond mane. Hubertsson might be overwhelmed and
turn tail long before the wedding night. And I would never want to
frighten him; I'd just sit there on the edge of my bed in my wedding dress,
radiant, when he arrived for his last morning visit. Like a real-life Cin-
derella.

"What're you laughing at?"

I snap at the mouthpiece and then prevaricate, like a true wife: "I'm
not laughing."

He snorts and turns his back on me again. Outside it's getting very
light; the gray dawn hour is over. Looks to be a nice day; the corner of sky
I can glimpse behind Hubertsson is icy blue. But the new light doesn't
help. His face is still ashen, and the lines in his skin as dark as ever. I ache
when I see him. My husband? Maybe so, in a sense.

Not that I know much about marriage—all I have to refer to is a few
thousand novels and countless TV series—but there is a strong resem-
blance between what I've read and seen and the relationship between the
two of us. We've been circling each other for fifteen years, always in the

same orbit, like a pair of lost electrons with the same charge, incapable of really fusing, equally incapable of separating. We have spoken for days and weeks, months and years, and yet we have remained silent about the things that have burned the deepest holes in us. That's why we have often delved deeply into my childhood while barely scratching the surface of his. And that's why I know more about his job and his patients than about the short marriage he had long since left behind when we met. Similarly, we've consistently given a wide berth to the most important aspects of my reality. The look in his eyes was an early warning to me not to talk about my gift. So I have to pretend it's a game. I play Scheherazade; he has to play at being a doctor amused by a peculiar patient with storytelling skills. This is how we hide from each other in the Chinese boxes of what we allege to be our common sense.

Sometimes I grieve for the fact that, even with all his uniqueness, Hubertsson is such an ordinary man. He suffers from theophobia, dreads the very idea of not understanding. And so he must refuse to have anything to do with issues relating to the nature of matter and the universe, yawns demonstrably when I happily account recent discoveries in elementary particle physics, and looks nervous when I amuse myself thinking about the idea that when the universe ceases to expand and begins to contract, time will go backward. He isn't amused. He does, however, love the fact that I am able to make up so many truly credible stories about my caregivers and the staff here, so credible they are gradually confirmed in reality, one after the next. He calls me a keen observer. Sometimes he even goes so far as to call it intuition.

Now he's stopped being grumpy. "Did anything happen last night?"

There is hope of forgiveness. I snap ingratiatingly at the mouthpiece. "Oh yes. I killed the seagull."

He looks surprised. "Why?"

I wished I could tell him the truth, that I killed the seagull because I saw Christina dreaming. As I puff my fabricated answer the true memory flutters past; I see the windows of Christina's house shining in the dark, see the gull on the ledge outside her bedroom window, myself in its eye. Christina's dreams swept like pale mist over her bed. At first they were blurred and incomprehensible, later a clear image took shape: three girls in a cherry tree. And there came Ella across the lawn with a tray of juice, her glasses slipping down her nose, her eyes looking cheerily over the edge of her frames.

That was all. But it was enough.

My wrath burst forth like a sea anemone. I saw it, a blood red toxic creature stretching its tentacles in every direction, toward Ella, my betrayer, toward Christina, Margareta, and Birgitta, those fucking thieves. Suddenly I was furious with the whole world, the seagull included, and I pulled him up into the air and forced him to fly screeching in wide circles into the wind until his wings were exhausted and he began to tremble. Then I turned him around and made him dive from his great height down to Song Street, straight into the red wall of my sister's home.

But Hubertsson would interpret the truth as insanity and madness. So I just give him a one-sentence reply: "That seagull was only making things difficult . . ."

Hubertsson's brow creases. "Are you chickening out again?"

I don't answer. My vacant monitor makes him get up and come back to the bed. He stands at the foot, inspecting me through narrow slits. "Are you all right? Did you get scared? Just because it's about those three?"

My hand slaps the bars in a particularly violent spasm. He sees it but doesn't react.

"I don't get it," he says. "All those other stories just run right out of you, but this one is taking years. Why are you so scared of making up a tale about those three? And don't you see that that's exactly why you need to do it?"

I snap at the mouthpiece. "Playing shrink with me now?"

He just snorts and walks over to the table, stroking the black binder with one hand. "Do you need more material?"

I make a sound that should be interpretable as a no. I do not need more material. He supplied me with that binder years ago. It's full of medical records, photos, and press clippings about my mother and sisters. I know most of it by heart.

"What was that?"

I snap at the mouthpiece again and start blowing into it. "No, I don't need any more. It's coming along nicely this time, I know it's going to work."

"May I read it?"

"Nope. Not yet. Not until it's done."

He turns his back on me, silently scrutinizing one of the paintings on my wall—a banal IKEA reproduction—his hands deep in his pockets. When he stands with his back to me I get anxious, feel the need to plead.

I'm blowing so hard that a pool of saliva collects in the mouthpiece. "Listen, I'm not giving up this time. Promise."

He hears my puffing stop and turns around, reads and smiles.

I am forgiven.

"Good."

It grows quiet between us, our eyes meet. That's when I see there's something missing: the little gleam that has always been there, underlying the look in his eyes. I know what that means; anybody who has lived life in a hospital knows what that means. There's no time to lose.

My jaws lock, clamping the mouthpiece. At the same time my head is torn so hard to the side that the rubber hose stretches to a dirty yellow line in the air. Hubertsson walks over and carefully works the mouthpiece out of my mouth. His skin still smells of almonds. And that scent has a color. The whole room suddenly sparkles, bathed in rosy morning light.

No excuses will do anymore. Time to put my sisters in motion. Though not quite yet. First I want to shut my eyes and luxuriate for a moment in the aroma of almonds.

Elsewhere

The past and future light cones of an event P divide
space-time into three regions. . . . The elsewhere is the
region of space-time that does not lie in the future or
past light cones of P.

Stephen W. Hawking

WHAT A STRANGE letter; she's never seen anything like it. The envelope is a used one, opened and taped closed, the name of the previous
recipient crossed out in ballpoint pen with sharp, vertical lines, Christina's own name written alongside. The handwriting looks unnatural,
like a poor forgery. The letters slant haphazardly; some have been scrib-
bled rapidly, others are elegantly ornamented. At the top right-hand corner a stamp has been pulled off, and three new ones adding up to far too
much postage are stuck in an uneven line at the top left. But there's no
postmark—the mailman wasn't the one who put this letter in Christina's
mailbox.

Astrid, she thinks, and the ground trembles under her feet until she remembers that Astrid is dead, that she has actually been dead for three
years. She can feel, though, that her body isn't convinced, despite the fact
that she went out of her way to see it with her eyes and feel it with her
hands, hands even paler than Astrid's at the time. Still, her muscles,
bones, and nerves don't believe her; her body reacts as if Astrid were still
alive: the small of her back tightens up and cramps, the pain spreads and
settles in across her hips like a lead belt.

Although she is a physician—or perhaps *because* she is one—Christina
knows no other way to manage pain than to ignore it. She pushes her
glasses up over her forehead, leans myopically over the envelope, and
tries to make out to whom it was originally addressed. But the gray morning isn't light enough; she can only deduce a few letters—an *A,* an *E,* and
an *S*—under the blue lines. Then she tries to wedge a finger in and open
the envelope, but that fails, too. The tape is too thick. She needs a pair of
scissors.

Not Astrid, she thinks, walking toward the house, turning the envelope
over in her hands. Birgitta then. Of course, Birgitta. In which case I will

have to phone Margareta, who'll bawl me out because we haven't seen each other in years. . . . Do we really have to go on pretending we're sisters forever?

The bird causes her to forget the letter; she trips over the dead body, and as she's regaining her balance she unconsciously stuffs the envelope into the pocket of her bathrobe. She retreats, sees the gray film that's developed over the black eyes, and draws her top lip back in a grimace of disgust.

With her local morning paper and a national one, too, hugged tightly to her chest, she rushes to the back door, her rubber boots flapping. Erik's in the kitchen slicing bread for breakfast, his cheeks rosy after a shave and his ginger hair dark and damp after a shower. He turns his pale blue eyes on her as she removes her boots, and for one uneasy moment she sees herself as he sees her: ash blond, thin, in a wrinkled nightgown with night-rumpled hair. A ruffled house sparrow. She hastens to tighten the belt on her robe, it's been trailing behind her outside. She ties it, trying to make her voice as cool and matter-of-fact as possible. "There's a dead bird out in the yard. A gull."

He walks over to the back door and looks out, knife in hand. "Where?"

He cranes his neck and rises to his toes; she presses in close behind his back to get the same angle of vision. There's a soft scent of soap about him, and she represses a sudden impulse to throw her arms around him, dive deep down into that scent. It would take us too far, she says to herself. We don't have time.

The white bird is difficult to see from a distance, camouflaged in dirty snow and shiny gravel.

"Over there," says Christina, extending her arm below his elbow. "In front of the lilac bush. See it?"

Now he sees: the head twisted at an unnatural angle, the spread wings, and the half-open bill. He says nothing, just nods and picks up a plastic bag.

Out in the yard he pulls the bag over his hands, grasping the bird through the plastic, then reversing the bag and tying it.

"Heavy one," he says on his return. "Want to feel it?" He lifts the bag, weighing it in his hand, already developing a theory.

"Broke its neck. Must have flown straight into the wall. I thought I heard a thud around four-thirty this morning, decided it was the wind. . . . Didn't you hear anything?"

Christina shakes her head mutely.

Erik looks first at her and then at the bag. "There must've been some-thing wrong with it. A healthy bird wouldn't fly right into a house. It shouldn't be inside, in any case. I'll go dump it in the trash."

Afterward he washes his hands thoroughly in hot water, holding them under the faucet so long his whole hands turn the color of his freckles.

CHRISTINA'S PROFESSOR. THAT'S Margareta's usual description of Erik. In fact he's not actually a professor but has been treading water as a senior lecturer for years. Still, there's more than a grain of truth to Margareta's description. Erik looks exactly the stereotype professor. His shoulders are narrow, his skin pale, and once his hair has dried after his shower it stands in a disheveled ring of red curls around the almost bald spot at the top of his head. "His Einstein hairdo"—Margareta laughs, somewhere in Christina's memory—but today Christina doesn't want to laugh at Erik, so she purses her lips and refuses to join in.

Not that Erik would notice if she smiled at him across the breakfast table. He is deeply immersed in the paper, fumbling absentmindedly with the butter knife over the tabletop, unaware of what he's doing. There have been mornings when Christina has swept the butter in wide circles and just let him grope in vain, wondering with interest how long it would be before he looked up. His record's eight minutes.

In those days they lived in Linköping, and their twin daughters were in the midst of the most miserable adolescence. They sat on either side of the table—Åsa by Mamma and Tove by Pappa—following the meander-ings of the butter in silence. When Erik finally looked up with confused eyes, Christina would dissolve in giggles, while Åsa's forehead wrinkled and Tove snorted. They'd get up as one, push their chairs to the table with scornful scrapes, and burst out in chorus: "God, when are you two going to *grow up?*"

Now Christina wonders herself. We are babyish. At least Erik is. He's childish in the best sense of the word; the world still amazes him. At some point in early puberty, most men stop being surprised by the world, and spend the rest of their lives trying to vanquish it. But Erik is still curious. He's fighting not for glory but for knowledge.

TODAY, THOUGH, HE is leaving. Up in the bedroom his gaping suit-case waits to swallow the last shirt. He's going away for five months, during which Christina will be on her own. This is the first time; in the past the girls have always been at home. But they're grown up now, students at Uppsala University who just flit through Vadstena for the occasional visit at intervals of many months.

Christina isn't displeased. On the contrary. She did put on a suitably dejected air when Erik guiltily informed her that he was going to be a visiting researcher again, but deep inside she felt a little quiver of satisfaction: she'd be left in peace.

She smiles to herself, thinking of the many solitary breakfasts she has to look forward to. She'll have black coffee. Fresh-squeezed orange juice. And little hot white rolls with cheddar cheese and whiskey marmalade. She'll throw his oat flakes and muesli away the minute she gets back from the airport. Maybe she'll even get a cat. . . . As always when she dreams of flight and freedom, he seems to sense it. He lowers the newspaper, looks at her, and says, "Why don't you take a couple weeks' vacation in May and come over?"

Christina smiles deceptively. She intends to spend May sitting in the yard on her own watching the lilacs burst into bloom, not sweating on some dusty university campus in Texas. "We'll see. Depends on what happens with Hubertsson. If I need to cover for him I don't think so."

That's enough to put him off. He nods and raises the paper again. Hubertsson's sickness disturbs him, he doesn't want to hear about it. A physician who doesn't take care of his own diabetes, who guzzles and gluts himself to the very verge of amputation, makes reasonable people upset and worried. And Erik is a reasonable person.

But still, when Christina sees how his forehead creases over the editorials, she finds herself filled with the same shamefaced tenderness as so many times before. He's my husband, she thinks. And more as well. He's my rescuer and my protector. He's never been anything but good to me, and yet here I sit dying for him to be gone.

She gets up impulsively and goes around the table, bends over and kisses the almost bald spot at the top of his head. "I miss you already," she says.

There's an instant of reluctance; his muscles go rigid only to melt just as quickly. He gets up, puts his arms around her, and kisses her neck, her cheeks, and her ears. That's how it's always been. She gives him one kiss and gets many in return. Too many. She never has enough love to give, his sweeps right over hers and drowns it. Now she has to restrain her impulse to put her hands on his chest and push him away. The very thought is a threat to their peace of mind for the coming months. Neither of them would remember her kiss, or forget her rejection.

Now he's calmed down, stopped kissing her, just holds her close, and his embrace finally becomes real. "I miss you, too," Erik says at last, caressing the top of her head.

Christina frees herself, puts her hands in her pockets. Then she remembers. The letter! That weird letter.

"Look at this," she says, extending the envelope. "I found it in the mailbox when I went out for the papers."

But Erik has already sat down again and dipped back into the daily news; he casts an absentminded glance at the envelope. "Who's it from?"

Christina shrugs her shoulders and gets the scissors. "Dunno . . ."

She pinches the envelope as she carefully cuts a minuscule strip off the top edge. It's thick. Must be a long letter.

But when she pulls out what's inside, she thinks at first that she was mistaken, that there's no letter at all, just a little package with pink crepe paper, carefully wrapped around something small and valuable. But nothing valuable falls out when she has opened the wrapping paper on the kitchen table. At first it seems completely empty. It takes her a while to notice the text in the middle, a few minimal lines in pencil, not a single letter taller than a fraction of an inch.

Christina pulls the lamp closer, holds it at a right angle to the pink paper, and reads:

> *I'm the desired one*
> *I'm the one who didn't come*
> *I'm the forgotten sister.*

And a little way farther down, in an uneven mini-scrawl:

> *I was in Aunt Ella's cherry tree, too*
> *But no one noticed me!*
> *Aunt Ella, tantarella, tarantula*
> *Spider or dance?*
> *Spider!*

*   *   *

"DISGUSTING," CHRISTINA SAYS an hour later, shifting into over-drive. "Sick, disgusting, and neurotic, that's what it is. What kind of drama is she directing now? I thought we were done with all that, I thought she'd exhausted her repertoire. We've already seen Poor Birgitta gets a bad reputation and Innocent Birgitta unfairly accused and driven to drug addiction, not to mention a whole series of performances on the theme of Heroic Birgitta detoxes only to encounter difficulties and re-lapse! I'm so tired of her. And I'm sick to death of Margareta. Why in God's name do I have to go on playing big sister, little sister with strangers at almost age fifty? All right, so we lived together for a few years, but Mar-gareta and Birgitta didn't mean a thing to me. Just Aunt Ella. Nowadays I have absolutely nothing in common with them. Nothing! *Nada!* Zilch!"

Erik puts his hand on her arm. "You're speeding, slow down. Don't worry about it, just throw the letter away and put the answering machine on so you can hear who's calling. Sooner or later they'll have to realize you're not interested."

"Ha!" says Christina. "I'd like to see Birgitta pick up on that kind of hint. Or Margareta for that matter. It's going to require the heavy artillery, I think. Neither of them has ever shown the least comprehension of the subtleties of existence . . ."

Erik laughs, and his familiar chuckle eases her anger. She turns toward him and sees his hair glistening like reddish gold in the sunlight. The gray morning has brightened into a glistening late winter day, the sky huge and bright blue above them, the sun sparkling on the patches of snow in the fields, where the earth is black and moist.

SHE'S TAKEN THE day off to drive him all the way to Arlanda, the Stockholm airport. They've got plenty of time, his flight doesn't leave for hours. She downshifts and lowers her speed. There's no need to hurry, they can take their time and enjoy their last few hours together.

But Erik isn't in enjoying mode. As soon as they got on the highway he seemed impatient with sitting still and being driven. He's speaking sar-castically now. "Do you have any major plans for the Post-Industrial Para-dise in my absence?"

Christina sighs and swallows a curt reply. She's been living with his whiny jealousy for twenty-three years now. For a long time she imagined it would fade as the years passed. The last thing she'd ever expected him to turn it on was a house.

But that's how it is. Erik is jealous of their house. And however irritated she might feel, Christina has to admit he has his reasons. She loves the Post-Industrial Paradise, there's no denying it.

When the girls moved to Uppsala, Erik was happy to acknowledge that their house in Linköping was too large, and that it was very much his turn to be the commuter, since she'd been commuting between the house in Linköping and her job in Vadstena for all those years. But when she showed him the red eighteenth-century house, it turned out he had other plans. Actually, he had said, he was ready for apartment living. And there were any number of fine, centrally located apartments in Linköping, of good quality and practical, and just the right distance from the University Hospital. Wouldn't it be better for Christina to take a job in Linköping instead? The recent reform of the GP system meant lots of job opportunities . . .

Throughout their marriage, Christina had tiptoed around Erik, always on her guard so as not to upset and irritate him. Arguments and angry voices frightened her. A curt reply was enough to set panic butterflies fluttering in her stomach. So she had complied, and adapted to his needs in an uncomfortable combination of anxiety and indifference. Where was she supposed to get the energy to fight and argue about the trivialities of everyday life? She barely had the energy to get out of bed in the mornings; all her efforts went into carrying around the terrible secret that was her fear and her wearisome burden.

And still, she was ashamed of her behavior. Her constant adaptation was a kind of deception, a means of manipulating him. Erik, however, didn't seem to have noticed. His field of vision was as narrow as most men's, and he found it perfectly natural that she always wanted what he wanted. It was the only sensible thing.

But once Christina had the opportunity to buy the old house on Song Street in Vadstena, she became a different person. If the choice had been between Erik and the house, she would've chosen the house. And he seemed to realize it. When he saw her with the old-fashioned handmade key in her hand, he stopped talking about apartments in Linköping and admitted defeat. All he could give her by way of punishment was a weak threat: it was all right with him if they bought the old place, but—and he truly hoped she knew he meant it—he did not have time to devote to home repairs. They were her problem.

And Christina tackled that problem. With Erik holed up in the

Linköping house, she spent all her free time for several months scraping paint and pulling down wallpaper, tearing out filthy wall-to-wall carpeting and sanding old floors. She directed plumbers, electricians, carpenters, and roofers, all the while painting cupboards and doors with egg-and-oil tempera. Bit by bit she reversed the damage of modern times, and out of the chaos there gradually emerged the perfect compromise between traditional craftsmanship and contemporary comfort. And it was more hers than his. She had conquered the house with her physical input. For the first time in her life, Christina felt as if she owned something, and for the first time in her life she realized what a pleasure ownership can be.

But it was Erik who gave the house its name. The living room was just finished, but not yet furnished, still empty. Christina had lit a fire in the tile stove and opened the double brass doors wide to show him the beauty of the shadows from the fire on the pearl gray walls. The room surprised him; he halted in midstep and stood stock-still on the doorsill. Then he said: "It's like looking back on another time . . ."

His hands in his trouser pockets, he took three long strides across the big floor tiles, turned slowly full circle, inspecting every detail, and then turned to her with a gentle laugh. "Congratulations, Christina. You've created the post-industrial paradise. In this room you'd never know there had been a twentieth century, it could just have been an unfortunate parenthesis."

His joke had thrown her off, embarrassed her. Suddenly she felt like the vulgar girlfriend of a purveyor of stolen goods, a con man displaying stolen jewels. For weeks afterward his words rang in her head. She tried to analyze why they had upset her.

It was no news to Christina that she had a neurotic relationship to history. It made her feel hungry and undernourished, bitter and jealous. Erik couldn't understand it. He shrugged his shoulders at all the old clergymen and physicians who peopled his genes, sighing with irritation over all the old books and antique parsonage furniture he and his sisters had inherited and were expected to polish and exhibit. What did he want with all that old stuff? He was a medical researcher, not a curator, and he knew perfectly well who he was and where he came from without having to carry all that old furniture around with him.

Christina had never managed to make him understand how she felt about herself—as if she belonged to a family of Christinas with no navels, born to no one, hatched like birds or lizards out of big white eggs. He just waved his arms and dismissed her with his impassive common sense. She knew perfectly well that Astrid was her mother. And if she wanted more, wasn't it easy enough to have a look at the census registry? And if she was bothered by the fact that she hardly remembered anything that happened to her before the age of seven, *tant pis!* He knew she remembered the hospital as well as the orphanage, her years at Aunt Ella's, her adolescence with Astrid. And if she wanted to know more, all she had to do was request her early medical records and the files of the child welfare authorities.

"You just don't get it," she had once said dejectedly. "It's not my own history I want. It's someone else's."

And that was what the Post-Industrial Paradise had given her. When she bought the house, she also bought into history, she got what she wanted as people today get whatever they want. Her front door was dated 1812. The house itself was even older, and in the antique bookshelf in her newly furnished living room was a little booklet from the Old Vadstena Society stating that the first building on this site had been constructed as long ago as the late fourteenth century. That's about as much history as a historyless person can buy.

Moreover, love doesn't require rational explanations to justify its existence. Christina loved the Post-Industrial Paradise in spite of any insights she might have about it. When she was home alone she sometimes found herself doing the strangest things: leaning her cheek against a window, caressing a wall, or standing stock-still in a corner of the living room for twenty minutes or more just to watch twilight creep in and settle like angel hair over the pale colors. Once she got her fingers caught trying to embrace a door. When Erik got home that night she felt as guilty as if she'd spent the afternoon with a lover, as if her bruised fingers were just as revealing as a love mark on her neck might have been. Erik had known it, and had been unnecessarily rough on her aching fingers when he bandaged them.

My husband, she had thought that time, as so many others, stroking his cheek impulsively. My husband.

ÅSA AND TOVE are waiting for them outside the international terminal. Erik sees them from a distance and shouts in surprise. Christina finds it touching to see how moved he is. He didn't expect their daughters to make the trip from Uppsala to Arlanda airport just to say good-bye to him. He tumbles out of the car with open arms, embracing them both before Christina can even turn the engine off. When she gets out of the car they are standing, heads close together, like football players in a pregame huddle. The Foxes, she thinks. The Fox team, or else the annual meeting of the society of redheads. To which I don't belong.

She takes the time to be sure the car is locked, then walks over to them.

THE NEXT COUPLE of hours are a flurry of voices and motion. Erik flutters from the check-in counter to the newspaper stand, while the girls chatter hungrily about lunch at Sky City. It takes nearly an hour for them to make their way to the restaurant, though, with the girls going into every single store on the concourse. Erik smiles and pays up in an unusual spurt of generosity. New purses? Sure. Real Louis Vuitton. A new sweater each? Why not? Hand-knitted folklore. New gloves? All right, a shopping spree's a shopping spree.

Afterward, when the plane's taken off and the girls are back on the bus to Uppsala, bags tightly in hand, Christina walks toward the parking lot on light feet. It's breezy, and she raises her face in pleasure into the wind, her hair streams. For one moment she feels as if she could take off and fly on her own. Free as a bird. No appointments, no one to make dinner for, no children or patients waiting. For the first time in over twenty years she is her own mistress. She presses the accelerator, revving the engine to a cheerful growl before she pulls out of her parking space.

THE DEPRIVATION HITS her suddenly. She's stopped along the roadside for a cup of coffee, and leaving the cafeteria she has a sudden memory of Erik's rough cheek against her own, and then the silky cheeks of the girls. It feels like real physical loss, a heavy, engorged pain in the gut: my family! Four hours ago we were having lunch and all talking at once, now the silence is so penetrating it is as if none of them had ever existed . . . but I want them here, I want them with me and around me!

She stops in the parking lot, takes a few deep breaths. Dusk has begun to fall, the air is cold and damp. Over by the truck and bus parking lot a grove of trees is on guard, like a cohort of Roman soldiers waiting for their marching orders. But no orders are forthcoming. The world is perfectly still: no wind, no movement, for one instant there isn't even any traffic noise. Christina sweeps her cape close around her, looking at the sky. It's lilac, empty, cloudless, starless, even airplaneless.

They're all gone, she thinks. They no longer exist, nor do I for them . . .

A solitary man crosses the parking lot, and his eyes force her to pull herself together. With exaggerated impatience she starts digging around in her purse for the car keys. Once inside, she turns on the light and inspects her face in the rearview mirror. Erik's eyes had been glazed over when they parted, Åsa had sniveled, and Tove wept openly, while she had just stood there, feeling nothing.

"What kind of a woman am I?" she asks her reflection, repeating the question right away and louder, as if she were speaking to a hearing-impaired patient: "What kind of a woman am I?"

A FEW HOURS later her car is bumping along the cobblestones of Song Street. The Post-Industrial Paradise is silent as a promise in the sheen of a solitary streetlight, safely shadowed by the old red tower on the other side of the street. When she has parked and closed the door, she stops for a moment, standing absolutely still, head tilted, as if listening for something. The town around her seems perfectly silent at first; suddenly a gentle but potent wind blows in from Lake Vättern, blowing and singing and bearing a scent of spring and clover bloom despite the winter chill. Christina feels as if it is settling in behind her back, driving her forward despite her hesitation, in the direction of the mailbox. She opens it, fearing the worst, but finds nothing but one bill and a flyer from the local supermarket.

She walks through her nocturnal garden before going inside. She stops by the lilac bush, kicking gently at the gravel, as if wanting to bury the memory of the dead bird. She doesn't notice the glow of the cigarette, doesn't see the person sitting watching her from the back steps. So she jumps when the sudden rough voice startles her.

"Hi there, Christina," it says. "Did you get mail today, too?"

SWEET JESUS WHAT a petit bourgeois soul, Margareta thinks. Three-quarter-length loden green cape and leather gloves. Not to mention the Hermès scarf she undoubtedly has hiding under all the external elegance . . . with chains and horses' heads and all that shit. Lordy Lord!

She gets up, tosses her cigarette butt into the gravel, crushes it under her heel, grinding both the tobacco and the filter beyond recognition. Moving closer, she sees the look on Christina's face. Her mouth is open, her top lip drawn back, teeth exposed.

"Did I scare you? Sorry. I didn't mean to . . ."

Christina's hand flutters up to her collar, she squints nearsightedly from behind her thick lenses. "Margareta? Is that you?"

Rhetorical question—she knows perfectly well who it is. The husky voice, the exaggerated nonchalance of posture, the element of shock—it couldn't be anyone but Margareta. She sounds a little perkier: "Goodness, how nice to see you. Have you been waiting long?"

"Actually, for hours. I was just beginning to wonder if you were on night duty."

"Wow—you must be freezing!"

"I'm all right. I dress for the frozen north, you know. I've had quite a pleasant time, in fact."

MARGARETA IS LYING, of course. Although she hasn't, in fact, been freezing—she almost never freezes, her whole body is wrapped in a slightly too thick layer of insulating subcutaneous fat—she hasn't been having a good time, either.

Actually, she's had one hell of a bad day, her sojourn into the landscape of the past. And during the hours she's spent alone in Christina's yard,

Margareta has been forced to admit to herself that she had known in advance what it would be like.

Some experiences just need to be left in peace, they're as fragile as a cobweb and cannot tolerate either thoughts or words. You just have to be satisfied with letting them flicker in a corner of your awareness now and then.

That's how her time in Tanum has always been: damp as the dew and transparent, it has gleamed in a corner of Margareta's consciousness, and she has been extremely cautious upon approaching it. Only once had she tried to put the experience in words: once in the soft relaxation after lovemaking she had tried to tell Claes how she had happened into physics. Whispering and fumbling, she'd described herself, young Margareta crossing the heath, in the pale predawn light exactly the same pale rosy shade as the heather, how heaven and earth had merged and the North Star gleamed, only to be extinguished by the morning light.

"At that very moment I climbed a little hill . . . and when I got to the top and looked out over the heath I caught a glimpse of three huge white bowls. Three satellite dishes, but I didn't know that at the time—hardly anybody knew what a satellite dish was in those days. I'd never seen anything like it, but I assumed it was something extraterrestrial. . . . And it made me so happy! I was so extraordinarily happy that they were so big and so beautiful and that, well . . . just that they were there!"

Claes had lain quietly on her shoulder while she was talking, but now he freed himself, sat up, and let his naked feet hit the wooden bedroom flooring. His voice was filled with fake concern: "Good grief, Margareta! Have you worked that experience through?"

And of course she laughed back, got up like he had, and let her own feet hit the floor. She nudged him. "Aren't you the one who's always saying it's all right to be a little nutty?"

He smiled. "Right. But even nuttiness has its limits!"

Afterward she'd been annoyed with herself. Why had she started babbling? It would have been better to keep that experience private, accept that it couldn't be shared. Not with anyone, not even a reliable friend and lover. It was a product of the spirit of its times, and now they lived in a time when the eternal was off-putting.

There might, in fact, be words to describe what she had felt, but not acceptable words, not words that Claes, man of the present that he was, could take in. If she'd said that her heart swelled when she saw those dishes, that they made her think of shipwrecks and desert islands, it would have embarrassed him. If she'd gone on to say that what she'd had was a religious experience, he would have been outright turned off. Reasonable people did not have religious experiences. Not these days.

But that was the truth. Her heart had, literally, swelled that morning, and for the first time in her life she had felt the presence of God. The satellite dishes were more enormous and more awe-inspiring than any of the old cathedrals and temple ruins she had visited as a student of archaeology. And suddenly she had felt like a Robinson Crusoe who, after an entire lifetime of waiting, finally saw a ship on the horizon.

"Oh yes," she had said aloud, but without really knowing what she meant. "Oh, yes."

The colors of the heath deepened as the sun rose, a hundred thousand heather blossoms were divested of their anemic night nuances, darkening to purple, the silver threads of trembling grass were transformed to gold, and in the enormous bowls above her all the colors of the rainbow shot out for just one instant before merging and paling once more. Suddenly the white bowls ceased to be sails and became voices. The voices of longing, calling to the universe: *"Over here! Over here! Save us!"*

But now it was all gone. Even the memory. Today she had trampled the cobweb to pieces. Now she would never again recall a young woman sinking to her knees in the heather, her eyes glued to the dishes, without the simultaneous memory of a middle-aged woman parking her car along the roadside and getting out. Her eyes narrowed, her soul trembling with anticipation, as if she wished to extend the pleasure by looking elsewhere at first; she didn't want to see the three white bowls until she was standing in just the right spot, over by the door on the passenger side. Once there, she opened her eyes at last, they were wide open and clear, prepared to be filled . . .

But they did not fill. Margareta blinked and knew that although the heath, the heather, and the satellite dishes were all still there—that twenty-five years was no longer than a single breath—she herself had changed. And in the head of that new Margareta tens of thousands of trivial facts drove the sense of awe to flight. She looked at the white bowls, trying in vain to call up the memory of cathedrals and temple ruins, shipwrecks and white sails; she failed. She was so familiar with this kind of sight there was no leeway for imagery: those satellite dishes were not beckoning to the heavens, they were receiving transmitted signals. With the best will in the world, one might think of them as ears. But Margareta was incapable of calling forth a single religious feeling about ears. Eyes might be fires, but ears are and will remain perfectly banal funnels. Important, functional, but about as likely to inspire devotion as calluses.

"Asshole," she said aloud to herself, kicking at the grass along the roadside ditch. "Idiot! Dumbbell! Hippie relic!"

For one single moment her head spun: what would have become of her if she hadn't walked away that night? She would've long ago had her Ph.D. No graduate student in archaeology takes more than four or five years to finish her dissertation, while a physicist may need ten or fifteen. Archaeologists also jet over to Greece for seminars and conferences, and have wine and love affairs in the evenings. Physicists sit all by themselves in drafty cabins in the frozen north making instrument readings. At least that's what half-brain physicists like Margareta do, physicists who do not have the intuition that characterizes the really great talents and takes them to work at CERN in Switzerland.

Right, thought Margareta once she was back in the car, flooring it, time for me to accept that I'm nothing but a half-brain talent . . .

Her hand groped over the passenger seat looking for her cigarettes, found them, and lit one. The smoke from the first puff burned her eyes and brought tears to them; she blinked and a tear fell. But it didn't clear her vision. Her eyes were just full of new tears.

Margareta sniffled, wiping her nose in irritation. Was she really sitting here crying? Margareta Johansson—the mistress of the art of bitching? Not her; she hadn't cried in fifteen years and had no intention of starting now. The car was just too smoky. . . . She rolled down the window. The wind only made her hair blow, and her eyes filled again.

All right then. Sure. She could perfectly well admit to herself that she was a little depressed, that she'd been slightly depressed for quite a while. Ever since she realized that nothing in her life was more than half: she was a half-young talent with a half-written thesis, a half-decent financial situation, and a bunch of half-sisters. Or whatever you wanted to call them. For most of the year, moreover, she was the woman missing the lower half of her body: Claes lived in Stockholm and she lived in Kiruna.

In addition to which Claes had made it clear that he had no more to offer her than friendship and physical contact. Half a relationship, in other words. Margareta stubbed out her cigarette and made a face: maybe she had a future as a sideshow attraction. Come see the half-woman! Only half price!

By the time she was approaching Uddevalla, she'd shaken off her self-pity. She stopped at an intersection to have a look at the map. Yes, this was where she'd have to turn off toward Jönköping. It was a bit of a detour if she was really heading for Stockholm, but there was one more place she had to stop on her journey down memory lane.

She had already decided before leaving Kiruna that she wouldn't stop in Vadstena, despite the fact that she knew Christina's new address by heart. She just planned to putter on past that self-satisfied little town with its self-satisfied little doctor and go right on to Motala, where she intended to light a memorial candle on Aunt Ella's grave and take a discreet look at the old house before she went on to Stockholm. Not that there was any great hurry—Claes was going to be in Sarajevo for a few more days—but she was really glad to have a chance to be alone in his apartment. She had no direct desire to root around in his private possessions, but if a drawer or a cupboard door just happened to be open, well . . .

She stopped for lunch at the Golden Otter, sitting for half an hour or more in the empty cafeteria staring out over the blue-gray winter waters of Lake Vättern before returning to the car. A short while later it happened: there was a rattling sound, and suddenly Claes's old Fiat sounded like a battalion of armored tanks. Margareta turned into a side road and pulled to a stop, got out of the car, and walked slowly around it once, inspecting for damage but without locating the problem. She started the car again, but it sounded even worse. She didn't dare drive it back out on the highway, just went slowly and carefully on in the direction it was facing.

And so she did end up in Vadstena in spite of herself, driving at a snail's pace through all the narrow little streets in a car that sounded like a rolling disaster. And of course the garage she eventually found couldn't promise her a quick repair. The old exhaust system had packed it in. They might be able to get one from Linköping, if she was lucky.

"Tomorrow," said the mechanic in his rural drawl. "You'll have it tomorrow afternoon. Not a chance before that."

Perspiring with stress, Margareta pulled her hand through her bangs. "Is this gonna be an expensive repair?"

He lifted his cap and looked aside. "Can't really say yet. Time will tell . . ."

And when she walked out into the parking lot, there was a letter under the wiper.

BY THE TIME she arrived at what had to be Christina's house, she was trembling and disconcerted, and the fact that no one answered the door-bell only added fuel to her fire. She circled the house a few times, bang-ing at the back door and ringing the bell again and again, but after a while she realized she was behaving hysterically. The house could very well be as empty as it looked. There was no rational reason to believe that Christina was hiding someplace behind those dark, shiny windowpanes refusing to let Margareta in. She just wasn't home. It was as simple as that.

In the end, out of breath but relieved thanks to this momentary insight, Margareta sat on the back steps, prepared to wait. For a while she kept touching the envelope, turning it over and over, running her index finger across the opening, but after some time her muscles began to relax, she grew pleasantly warm, her hands fell to her lap, enclosing the letter. She no longer held on to it, it just lay there on her jeans-covered thigh.

This could have been a time to relax and enjoy, if some stubborn voice in her head hadn't been incessantly repeating the closing line of the let-ter: *"Shame on you! Shame on you! Nobody wanted you!"*

AT SOME POINT during her interminable vigil, Margareta stretched her legs, her boots dragging through the gravel on the path. She'd bet any-thing Christina raked the gravel path fastidiously once a week, just like Aunt Ella had taught them. Every Saturday the girls had been equipped with rakes and expected to do their chores. Christina's was the path from the gate to the front door, Margareta's the gravel driveway, and Birgitta's the graveled area behind the back door.

If Margareta had ever thought of embroidering a runner with the words of wisdom that had permeated her life, this Saturday lesson would have been the motto: *As thou rakest, so shalt thou live.* It had been true for the three of them: as they had raked, they had indeed lived.

As soon as Aunt Ella was out of sight, Birgitta would set down her rake in the grass and creep up against the wall of the house, well hidden from the kitchen window. She would sit there glaring out from under her bangs, chewing at her already bitten-down fingernails until they bled at the quick.

Margareta held this attitude in contempt. Instead of trying to get out of her chore, she wanted to do a really beautiful job. She'd sweep the gravel into neat semicircles, draw flowers and circus horses and princesses in them with a stick, only to burst into dejected tears when she surveyed the results. No one would even be able to tell she'd done her very best! You couldn't see the driveway had been raked at all.

Only Christina raked like she was supposed to. Where she had been working, the gravel was in neat, systematic rows. She'd do her own part first, then go on to Margareta's, and finish off with Birgitta's. She never complained; in fact she seemed to be concerned about what would happen if she got caught, and kept glancing worriedly up at the kitchen window, hurrying as fast as she could to finish her sisters' chores.

Well, not sisters exactly . . .

Margareta shifted her weight and felt in her pockets for cigarettes. In the last few years Christina had completely shut her out—was never the one to be in touch and never had time to meet. Last Christmas, Margareta had optimistically lifted the receiver every time the phone had rung, hoping Christina might get herself together and invite her for the holidays like she used to. But all she got was a season's greetings card by a local artist: From the Wulfs. That was the ultimate proof: Christina didn't want to be her sister. *Shame on you! Shame on you! Nobody wanted you!*

And suddenly she wondered how she could possibly be sitting there waiting. She lit a cigarette with trembling fingers. Why in God's name was she forcing herself on someone who so explicitly didn't want anything to do with her? Margareta had spent her whole life being the one to leave rather than be left. She should do it again, should get up and go find a little hotel. She could slap her credit card down and have a nice dinner— she was really hungry—with a glass of wine, and then crawl into bed between clean, white sheets . . .

Or maybe she should rent a car and drive straight to Stockholm. However, she couldn't leave the Fiat in Vadstena forever, Claes would be livid if it wasn't there when he got back. And there was the letter thing, too. She had to relieve the burden of that damn letter somehow, and unfortunately Christina was the only person who would understand what it meant. Something was going on. But there were only three people in the world who could know it, and one of them was the author herself, on whose shoulder Margareta wasn't about to go crying. That might even be

dangerous: no one could know what might be going on in such a demented brain.

And yet, why should she let the whole thing bother her? Could a low-
life junkie from Motala possibly do Margareta Johansson any harm?
Maybe she should just take this letter, along with all the others that were
likely to arrive in the next few weeks, and flush them down the toilet.
Why should she be intimidated?

"I shouldn't," she said to herself, starting to rise. She'd ignore the whole
stupid story, go find the nearest hotel, and take a room. Birgitta could go
to hell. Christina, too, for that matter . . .

At that very moment a car pulled up outside, and Margareta froze in
mid-motion. Now it was too late to flee. She sat there, immobile, listening to her sister's light footsteps enter the yard. Funny, she was stopping
by the lilac bush, kicking at the gravel . . .

Margareta realized she was invisible, and that triggered her penchant
for drama. She sank back down onto the step, inhaled deeply at her cigarette, and then said, in her rawest voice: "Hi there, Christina. Did you get
mail today, too?"

NOW THEY ARE standing, some distance apart, hesitant, Christina
with her feet close together and her hands clasped virtuously over her
pubis, Margareta bowlegged, hands deep in her pockets. Suddenly she
feels completely in control. The evening air has cleared her lungs and
rinsed all the sludge from her circulatory system; she feels strong, clean,
and purified.

"Sorry to have kept you waiting," Christina says gravely, moving toward
the back door. "I had to take Erik to Stockholm today. He's off to be a visiting scholar in Texas for a new project. It's fascinating, really, on the subject of older primiparas and . . ."

She's very good at concealing the fact that an uninvited guest wasn't
precisely what she had in mind. Her voice is inviting, kind, and modu-
lated, absolutely unlike the voice Margareta recalls from their childhood.
For the first few months after she came to Aunt Ella's, Christina had only
whispered. Sometimes she almost seemed to be hissing. When she finally
started talking normally, it turned out she spoke with a very strange dialect, some kind of distorted southern drawl. Most people from southern Sweden gradually lose their diphthongs but retain their rolling r's.
Christina, though, who wasn't even born in the south, not only rolled her

r's but also couldn't get a single vowel out right. Not until several years later, when blue-fingered Astrid—that witch who was Christina's real mother—came to demand her daughter back, did anyone understand why. Astrid talked that way, too. But by that time Christina had completely adopted the local dialect and wasn't about to change back again. She hid behind Aunt Ella's chair and screamed at the top of her lungs every time Astrid approached.

Christina puts the key in the lock and opens the back door, glides inside, and turns on the light. Margareta follows on her heels, removing her jacket as she inspects the kitchen. Makes sense, she thinks. They've hidden their megafreezer and superfridge behind wooden doors. Couldn't hide their top-of-the-line stove, though. Which must be why there's a copper bowl with strawflowers on the wood-burning range. To distract the eye. Sweet Jesus! It's not hard to figure out what kind of game they're playing in this house.

"Nice," she says, hanging her shearling-lined leather jacket over the back of a chair. "Nice new house you have here. Or new old house."

For an instant Christina stands still in the middle of the kitchen floor, her fingers on the top button of her cape, as if reluctant to open it and reveal the silk scarf that almost has to be underneath. Without unbuttoning her cape she walks in the direction of the hall closet, saying over her shoulder, "If you want, I'll show you around as soon as I get my things off."

Margareta, however, has no intention of waiting in the kitchen; she saunters on in. Passing the hall mirror, she catches a glimpse of Christina that confirms why she was in such a hurry to go right to the closet. She's pulling her scarf off as if it were a shameful secret, stuffing it into the drawer of an old bureau, and running a hand through her hair. The hand flutters on down to the string of pearls under her suit jacket. Is she going to pull it off as well? There isn't time. At that very instant Margareta appears at the door, leans against the opening, and smiles an acrid smile. "Nice pearls," she says. "Present from the professor, I presume?"

That seems to be all Christina needs for her adolescent stubborn streak to come back to life. With a twist of her neck she signals that she has absolutely no intention of removing her necklace, whatever Margareta may think. "Yes," she says, running her hand over the pearls. "They are nice. Antique. They've been in Erik's family for generations. I inherited them from his mother."

Margareta raises her eyebrows. "Ingeborg Anxiety? She died?"

Christina nods. "Uh-huh. Last year."

Margareta goes silent, examining her own reflection in the mirror alongside Christina's. Suddenly she's tired. Who is she to be sarcastic about Christina's scarf and pearls, anyway? Isn't she something of a stereotype herself, with all the conventional trappings of an unconventional middle-aged woman? Black denim pants, expensive top, squared-off pageboy, and eye makeup. The leather thong with ceramic beads around her neck is so obviously from a craft shop that that suddenly seems a poor excuse for its lack of elegance. What kind of message did she think she could send by wearing it?

Christina turns toward her and looks. "Tired?"

Margareta nods. "Haven't been sleeping very well lately."

"Why not?"

Margareta shrugs. "Don't know. Maybe prescience."

Christina reacts with a little doctor's frown; prescience isn't part of her worldview. Then suddenly she recalls: "Didn't you say something about mail?"

Margareta takes the envelope out of her pocket and extends it, but Christina doesn't take it, just sticks her hands into her jacket pockets and bends over to inspect it. They raise their eyes at the same instant, looking right at each other. Margareta makes a face and looks away rapidly. The lump in her throat she's been trying her best to ignore swells up and pops like a slimy soap bubble. She has to purse her lips hard not to burst into tears.

But Christina sees. "It's all right," she says, anxiously patting Margareta on the arm. "Take it easy, Margareta. . . . What did she write that upset you so much?"

Margareta extends the envelope once more, and this time Christina has to take it. She handles it as if it were infected, her fingers forming a pair of tweezers she inserts carefully into the envelope, pulling out a wrinkled piece of paper she places carefully on top of the bureau. Then she straightens her glasses, giving Margareta a grim look before beginning to read aloud in her well-modulated voice:

Three women had babies.
Ow, cried Astrid, ow, cried Ella, ow, cried Gertrude.
Ow.

The midwife turned her back.
Ploploploplop!
Four babies came.
One fell to the floor. Whose was the ugly babeling?
Shame on her! Shame on her! Nobody wanted her!
Shame on you! Shame on you! Nobody wanted you!

There are a few silent minutes. They don't look at each other. Christina smoothes the letter. Then she appears to make a decision. She opens one of the drawers and withdraws a package of tissues. "Blow your nose," she says. "Then we'll have something to eat."

Margareta does as she's told, but in the middle of blowing, while her nose and mouth are still buried in the tissue, she says in a thick voice: "I could kill her! It's all her fault. My whole damn life's Birgitta's fault."

THE PROMISE OF spring had been an empty one. Now that night is falling, winter has come in for the final attack. A harsh wind is blowing and it's begun to snow. A soggy little drift has already started to form on the windowsill. Margareta shivers at the kitchen table. A bush outside the window brushes it regularly, alternating between gentle swipes at the glass and sharp little blows, like the duster of an angry cleaning woman.

Margareta's read Christina's letter, snorting with indignation. If she overreacted to what was really just incomprehensible nonsense in it, it was probably to keep herself from bursting into tears. And now she was long past crying, despite the balled-up tissue still in her fist. The lump in her throat is gone, and her eyes are dry and glued to Christina's movements at the kitchen counter.

She moves comfortably among her shiny kitchen gadgets, at the same time somehow looking like an intruder in her own home. She walks surreptitiously, arms close to her body, quickly turning down the tap so the water won't run too hard, suddenly stopping the refrigerator door from swinging closed. Then she takes a deep breath—apparently completely subconsciously—seizes the door with both hands, and shuts it in perfect silence.

The light in the kitchen reinforces the clandestine impression. The only light Christina has turned on is over the table—a designer lamp that couldn't have cost less than a decent winter coat, Margareta reflects—while Christina makes dinner in dusky light over at the counter. Her machinations, however, are promising: she's decanted a bottle of wine, moved a loaf of home-baked bread from freezer to microwave, and has a lump of soup defrosting on low heat on the stove.

"Should I do anything?" Margareta asks.

Christina looks up in surprise, almost as if she's forgotten Margareta's presence. But only for an instant. "No thanks," she says reassuringly. "I'm almost done. You just relax."

"Do you mind if I smoke?"

Christina shrugs her shoulders. Margareta takes a cigarette out of her pack and leans over her lighter. "Want me to light the candle, too?"

"Sure," says Christina indifferently. "Fine."

Margareta recognizes the candleholder. It's from Peru. She bought it herself, and a memory of that day flutters quickly past: sitting on a beach in Lima late at night. Just a few hours earlier, she'd seen that child for the first time, a boy thin as a stick and wrinkled as a prune, with black eyes. He lay like a newborn, hands over his head, staring at her unblinking. The look in his eyes made her speechless for several hours. Without a word to anyone she walked to the beach, sat down in the sand, silent and still, staring out over the Pacific. It's perfectly logical, she thought. We abandoned children are a species apart, we have to look out for one another . . .

As she walked back to the hotel she was smiling from deep inside, like a woman who'd just become a mother, and when she passed a street vendor with hand-painted candlesticks she bought five of them, on impulse. One had been on Aunt Ella's nightstand at the nursing home, another had found its way to this kitchen table in Vadstena. But God only knows, she thought, where the most beautiful one is now, the one I set on the floor next to the child's cot . . .

Christina sets a bowl of steamy soup in front of her; Margareta recalls the sourish scent. "Oh, Aunt Ella's soup?" she asks hungrily, seizing her spoon.

Christina smiles for the first time all evening. "She gave me tons of recipes the year before she died. . . . I make her stew, and her raspberry cake, too . . ."

Margareta smiles greedily over her soup. "Mmm, you'll have to give me the raspberry cake one. . . . Remember?"

She needs to say no more. Christina laughs a soft, cooing laugh, sounding like a distant echo of Aunt Ella herself. Her hand vibrates at the same frequency as her laugh when she pours the wine.

"That time you really got caught with your fingers in the cookie jar. You were in terrible trouble! Even I was scared to death."

Margareta smiles back. "Holy shit! I was in her bad books for ages after that."

Christina passes her the bread. Her movements have relaxed, the ice between them is almost broken now.

"Have you been to the cemetery lately?" Margareta asks, helping herself to a slice of the hot bread and knowing the second her fingers feel its consistency that this, too, is Aunt Ella's old recipe.

Christina shrugs. "I was there on All Saints' Day. Sneaking around. I'm not really comfortable in Motala anymore."

Margareta stops in surprise, the butter knife in midair. "What's the problem? You haven't bumped into her, have you?"

"No, but—" She stops, her eyes glued to the wall behind Margareta.

"What?" asks Margareta impatiently. "But what?"

"I always feel like I'm being observed. It's as if everybody recognizes me. Since the time she stole my prescription pad and the police kept calling me in for questioning. And then to appear in court. It was in the papers and on the radio. Disgusting."

"You were never mentioned by name, though, were you?"

Christina responds with a wry little smile. "Makes no difference. Everybody knows everybody around here. Take what happened last spring. I drove to Motala to pick something up and decided to try a new place at the market for lunch. Nothing special, a regular self-service lunch. After a while, I realized the owner of the place kept finding reasons to pass my table. She was banging around, clattering dishes and glasses, and in the end I just had to look her way. At which point the woman says: 'Aren't you Dr. Wulf from Vadstena?' I couldn't deny it. She reacted with a look that was supposed to be compassionate, I guess, and said: 'Well, I just want you to know that we gave your sister a chance here as a dishwasher. I do what I can for people. But it didn't work out.' "

Margareta smiles awkwardly. "So what did you say?"

"What could I say? Should I have asked her why it didn't work out, whether she stripped down in front of the lunch line, or pulled the customers in behind the counter for a fuck, or injected the potatoes with amphetamines? Thanks anyway. I just stood up and told her the truth. That I don't have a sister."

That's hitting below the belt, but Christina doesn't seem to notice

Margareta's heightened complexion, how she gradually blushes. She just raises her glass and says: "Here's looking at you . . ."

But Margareta doesn't respond. Hands clasped on the table, she refuses to participate in the toast. "Sorry," she says. "I shouldn't have let you pour me wine. I'm driving back to Stockholm later, so I'd better not drink."

And I'm never coming back here, she goes on to think. Never, never never. Count me out, bitch!

Christina lowers her glass in surprise. "No way you can drive tonight. Not in this weather. . . . And your car's in the shop, besides."

Margareta glances out the window. It's blustery out there, but far from a snowstorm so far. "I'll rent a car," she says. "Work to do, you know. I have an important meeting at the physics department the day after tomorrow to prepare."

"But we need to talk," says Christina. She's more solemn now, may have realized how she offended her.

"We can talk over dinner."

Christina lowers her eyes and takes a deep breath. "Margareta, please! We haven't spent any time together in so long. If I ask nicely?"

Margareta gives her a steady gaze, but Christina's looking down, her white pincer-fingers picking nervously at a few crumbs on the tablecloth.

"Please?" she asks, eyes still lowered, this time sounding almost intimidated. Silence between them.

Margareta's thoughts flutter wildly. She doesn't really want to leave tonight, but she has absolutely no desire to stay here. Either way she's been humiliated. Then she finds a sudden out: "All right," she says, grasping her wineglass. "I guess I can get it done if I leave in the morning. And pass through Motala as well, to visit the cemetery, since nobody's been there with flowers for ages . . ."

"WELL, WHAT ABOUT Birgitta, then?" says Christina when they've finished their meal and are sitting quietly in front of the fire in the tile stove in the living room. "What're we going to do about Birgitta?"

"Kill her," says Margareta, taking a deep draft from her liqueur glass. Christina's poured her an amaretto; it's sweet and brings a taste of almonds to her palate, only to burn like fire one second later as it goes down. She's feeling good now. Christina has treated her to a piece of the good life, the life she never takes the time to live herself. It demands attention to detail, and Margareta's never thought she had time for detail. In puberty she always went around with her underwear riding up and her slip a rim around her hips, because she never bothered to take twenty seconds to straighten her clothes. And she's gone on like that. She's begun every day of her adult life standing at the kitchen sink with a smoke and a quick cup of instant coffee. She's stood there burning her tongue and with some vague longing for a real breakfast at a set table. Every day she's promised herself that tomorrow morning will be the first day of her new, better life. The life in which she'll stop smoking and start the day with morning exercise and breakfast; she'll put up kitchen curtains. . . . But not today, today she has lots to do and if she doesn't do it right now death will catch up with her and it will never get done.

Christina doesn't have a liqueur herself. She seems to drink just as little now as when she was young. All she had at dinner were a couple of circumspect sips from her wineglass. Now she's sitting stiff as a ramrod in her high-backed easy chair, legs crossed, coffee cup in hand. Her fingers are stiff and spread, as if her cup were suspended between her fingertips. When she drinks, she bends her taut neck down over the cup, just touching the edge gingerly with her lips.

"I mean it," says Margareta, resting her head against the back of the armchair. "I think we ought to just do her in."

Christina smiles an oblique little smile. "Don't think I'm not tempted. But it's too late."

Margareta blinks hard. "How so, too late?"

Christina takes a little swallow of her coffee and permits her smile to narrow. "We should've done away with her a long time ago, after that business with Aunt Ella. If we had, no one would ever have suspected. But as things stand now, we've reported her to the police a few times too many, and given too much information to the investigating officers. . . . The cops know what we think of her. We'd be locked right up. At least I would."

Margareta smiles uncertainly, sitting up straighter in the armchair. "Well, I was only joking . . ."

Christina's gray eyes are crystal clear; she looks Margareta straight in the eye before taking another sip of her coffee. When she has swallowed, she smiles again. Her ordinary, friendly smile. "Me, too," she says. "I was just joking myself. . . . So what *are* we going to do?"

Margareta lights a cigarette and shrugs. "Don't ask me. Right now I guess we can't do very much. Except try to anticipate her next move."

"And what would you guess?"

"No idea . . . that's the worst thing about all this. She might do anything. A dead cat on the hall rug. Or an appearance on a television talk show. *Ricki Lake*. Or *Forgive and Forget,* or whatever it's called."

Christina surreptitiously slips off her neat little pumps and pulls her legs under her. "Arggh!"

"Or a bag of excrement on your office desk."

"Too late there, too. I've already had one. And she never repeats herself."

Margareta sighs and shuts her eyes for just a moment, but she's unstoppable. "Or an anonymous letter about you in the local paper . . . no real journalism, just gossip. Or a little arson. . . . You do have a smoke detector, don't you?"

Christina nods dumbly. Margareta finishes her drink bottoms up, bangs the glass onto the tabletop. Silence. Christina's huddled up like a ball in her easy chair. Her feet are concealed under her skirt, her hands in the sleeves of her blazer. "But that's not the worst thing," she says at last, looking down into her lap.

Margareta doesn't answer. I know, she's thinking. I know. The worst thing is that she knows everything there is to know about our weaknesses. *Shame on you! Shame on you! Nobody wanted you!*

"Could I have another amaretto?" she asks.

AN HOUR LATER she's sitting listlessly on the edge of the bed in Christina's guest bedroom. The room is small and overfurnished. Christina's really outdone herself here: a cast-iron bed frame, an old chest of drawers, an antique desk and chair. And a replica of old-fashioned wallpaper.

Margareta can hear Christina brushing her teeth in the bathroom. Probably with an antique toothbrush. Hand-carved and from 1840 or so. Plus she probably brushes with Elmer's glue so her mouth will stay firmly shut all night and no unintentional spontaneous comments fall out . . .

Their talk didn't end up amounting to much. So what had she expected? For Christina to have a solution to an insoluble problem? Or for her to offer sisterly cooperation to somebody she seems to regard more as a difficult acquaintance? She'd been idiotic to come at all. And tomorrow she'll get going as early as possible—she can pass some time in town while her car's being finished—and from now on she'll really show Christina she's learned her lesson. No contact, no matter what . . .

"Okay," Christina calls from out in the hall. "Bathroom's all yours, Margareta."

Margareta fumbles for her towel and her toiletries bag, but just as she's getting up the phone rings and she freezes in mid-motion. In the mirror over the bed she sees her own face: eyes narrowed to slits, forehead creased.

"Yes," Christina's saying out there, "yes, but . . ."

Nothing for a few minutes.

"Well, that's true," says Christina, "but . . ."

She's been interrupted. The other person seems to be speaking non-stop.

"How bad is it?" Christina asks.

The mumble at the other end rises an octave. A patient, Margareta thinks. It must be something about one of her patients.

"Yes, I know. I happen to be a doctor myself," Christina finally says. "All right, I suppose we'll come. Okay."

She hangs up without saying thank you or good-bye. For one moment the house is perfectly silent. Margareta doesn't move a muscle from where she is standing at the guest bedroom mirror, and Christina seems to be equally immobile out in the hall.

"Margareta," Christina finally says. Her voice is low. "Margareta?"

Margareta sighs deeply and walks out of the bedroom. She stops in the hall, towel and toiletries bag in hand. "Was it her?"

"No," says Christina. "It was the women's shelter in Motala."

"What did they want?"

Christina sighs, pulling her hand through her hair. Suddenly she looks less anxiously tidy; her nightgown is wrinkled, her hair ruffled, her bathrobe untied.

"They say Birgitta's been battered. Battered and assaulted. She's in Motala Hospital and they thought we'd better go down . . ."

"Whatever for?"

Christina sighs dejectedly, but her voice is dry and objective. "Because she's dying. They said she was dying . . ."

"YOU OLD LUSH!" somebody shouts from afar. "Puking in bed, you filthy, disgusting hooker . . ."

Puking? In bed?

The voice fades into a mutter. Birgitta doesn't know who shouted and doesn't have the energy to look. What difference does it make? Still, she seems to be in a bed someplace . . . a bed with dirty sheets. Little black grains of something greasy and grubby stick to her fingertips when she runs her hand over the fabric. She's seen those little grains in so many beds she doesn't even need to open her eyes to know what they are. The only way a bed can get like that is if the linens haven't been changed for so long the filth can't even penetrate the ply of the weave. In addition to which she recognizes the smell, the sweet brown smell of tobacco mixed with the sour odor of vomited beer.

Right. He was right. The old wino has thrown up in bed. And then apparently lain right down in her own sick. It's drying, and feels a little stiff against her cheek. Still, she's too tired to change positions, her body is too heavy, too warm. All she can do is lift her hands, unfathomably slowly, clasp them, and put them under her cheek. Gertrude once told her she looked like the angel on a bookmark when she lay like that. A real little angel.

Now everything's quiet again, and she can put her mind to what she really wants to think about. Those snobby bitches!

Her thoughts roll out into a familiar landscape. A huge landscape. She has a tommy gun under her arm and is sneaking quietly, like a sniper, from one hilltop to the next. There, one round for Margareta. And there, the next for Christina. She lets the bullets rain down on her knees, stomach, breast, and neck. Ha! That'll make ground meat of the stupid asshole . . .

Birgitta never gets tired of hunting down snobs. However deep she is in DTs or withdrawal, however high she is, however low she falls in her alcoholic stupors, she always plays the same game. This is her only secret, she's never tried to explain it to her gang or her social worker. Otherwise she's good at words, she can talk their own language to the down-and-outs, can speak Latin with the authorities. In court she can even sound like the official record. But what could she possibly say about this? The accused admits having, on 8,673 occasions, mentally mauled the plaintiffs, Margareta Johansson and Christina Wulf, to ground meat. Well, what of it? It's not an unlawful threat. It's nothing she's ever said or done.

Now the pain and nausea roll over her again, as if someone were pounding her insides in a mortar, up and down, up and down. Her intestines cramp, her stomach burns with acid. But this time she doesn't really throw up, nothing comes out of her mouth but a thread of wet, acrid mucus. Shit. She can't drink at all anymore. In the old days she could do two hits and put away a whole bottle on top of it, and feel great. Nowadays she can't keep even one little beer down.

Oh, for a beer. If only she had a beer.

Her arm is like lead, but somehow she manages to lift it and pull herself up in the bed. She groans and the world spins, she feels as if her brain were a loose sponge in a rolling sea. Her stomach cramps, but she is determined to get up, at peril to her life.

Now she is sitting, but she hasn't yet opened her eyes, doesn't yet know up from down. She tries wiggling her toes a little; they touch an icy floor and a piece of cloth. She looks between her parted legs. There's a green patterned shirt at her feet. The floor is gray, and there is a burned spot just behind her heel.

Slowly she lifts her head and looks around. She's not at home, she's elsewhere. The room is little. To the left, three black windows fill the entire wall. Someone's tried to cover one of them with a blanket, but it has fallen down and is just hanging by a corner. Under the radiator a knocked-over table lamp is on. It must be night. Or early morning.

Whose place is this?

It looks just like all the other places, at once familiar and anonymous. The furniture's from the social services, a rickety table covered with burns and rings, a bed—she's sitting on it—and two mattresses on the floor. Two wooden chairs, one standing, the other thrown over.

The air is thick with smoke and human smells. There must've been one helluva party: the ashtrays are overflowing with butts, and the table is covered with bottles, cans, and glasses. Birgitta leans forward very carefully, shakes a can, and knows it's almost half full. She grasps it greedily in both hands and drinks; the mallet in her stomach strikes from below and tries making her guts turn inside out, but she resists, sitting straight up with her eyes shut tight, fighting the nausea. When the first cramps settle she tries taking quick little sips of the flat beer, not opening her eyes until it's all gone. The lamp on the floor seems brighter, and all the contours are in better focus.

Now she sees she's not alone. There are four—make that five—sleeping bodies along the walls. None of them is Roger's. But in the far corner a very blond girl is sitting, staring straight ahead but seeing nothing. She looks weird, like an illustration in a book of fairy tales. Little Princess Rosebud has slipped out of her story.

Birgitta grabs the edge of the bed and pulls herself up with a groan. There she is again, that old woman who keeps taking more and more liberties with her thoughts and movements. She sneers at herself. So this is what's happening to her, she who always said she'd die young and be a lovely corpse.

What the hell? She needs to use the toilet now, anyway. Knees like jelly, reeling, she heads for the door and then finds herself in a narrow hallway. The bathroom door's wide open; the light is on in there, and her own reflection squints back at her, lips gray, hair stringy.

A drunken bitch.

A fat lush. So ugly that . . .

The shame burns suddenly, but she's prepared and dodges it. She covers her face with her hands and sinks to the toilet seat, ceasing, for a while, to exist altogether.

SHE WAKES UP with someone pulling her hair, shaking her by the head in a rough grip, but the pain is clean and clear and burning. Almost enjoyable.

"Ow," she protests in a thick, sleepy voice. "What the fuck are you doing?"

"Shove over, bitch. I gotta piss."

The person standing above her is a big man with a hoarse voice and a double chin. He's strong, and he knows what he wants. He lifts her by the hair and tosses her out into the hall. She bumps down to the floor, after first sliding over a pile of clothes.

"Fucking asshole!" she shouts.

He doesn't reply, just stands at the toilet, legs wide apart and an arm on the wall in front of him. He may not even hear her: he has that mute, shut-off look of a person in a cosmos of his very own. She's bothered by the fact that she doesn't recognize him. He's obviously a longtime junkie, and she thought she knew the whole Motala gang. But she's never seen this one before . . .

Now he starts talking to the bathroom wall; without turning around he mutters a long string of obscenities. His voice is soft and monotonous, and difficult to decipher at first. After a while, he raises it and she can distinguish certain words: "Murder every single goddamn woman, turn all those fucking hit-whores inside out and let them drown in their own stinking cunts . . . come-cunts, come-come-come-come-cunts . . ."

Instantly, Birgitta's mind clears; she's heard that kind of shit before and knows precisely what it is a prelude to. She fumbles through the pile, searching for her winter jacket and, finding it almost immediately, starts pulling it on as she crawls toward the door. At that very moment he comes back into the hall, sees her sneaking away, and helps her out. In one long stride he is at the door, opens it wide, grabs her by the hair again, and lifts her. Before she knows what's happening she's hanging by her hair, and with her full weight suspended she feels as if she's being scalped. The white-hot pain blinds her. It's all over very quickly though. One second later he lets go of her hair and kicks her in the ass with one bare foot. Not very roughly, just hard enough for her to land on the floor in the outside hall.

"Filthy hooker," he says in a nearly normal conversational tone. "Get out!"

Birgitta knows exactly what degree of submission is required to avoid a beating. She looks down at the floor as she crawls away, as far out of sight as she can get. Had there been stairs she would have slid right down them as fast and invisibly as a snake in tall grass, but there is no flight of stairs. . . . A flutter of panic, no stairs! Then she sees the elevator. The minute he closes the door she has to get to it.

It's a few minutes later, and the gray dawn light floods the courtyard as she hears the building door close behind her. There's a little new snow, and it's still very cold. Birgitta shivers and pulls her jacket close. In mid-motion she catches sight of her feet. They're in a pair of black heels she's never seen before. High black heels. She looks like she's got Minnie Mouse's shoes on.

Slowly, she raises her head and looks around her. This is a totally unfamiliar courtyard. She's standing outside a tall gray apartment building she's never seen before, and on the other side of the lawn are some equally unfamiliar three-story buildings. Recently renovated. Somebody's dumb idea to improve on concrete by painting it pale pink. It looks ridiculous. Overkill.

Birgitta shakes her head and starts off, wobbling on the high heels across a lawn and past a playground, looking everywhere for a clue to where she is. But she doesn't see any clues. Just buildings. Big buildings and small buildings, gray buildings and pink buildings. Interspersed with various winter-weary bushes, more or less vacant parking lots, slushy snowdrifts, and ugly graffiti.

Where is she?

Bewildered, she rotates 360 degrees in the middle of a parking lot. It's all alien to her, there's nothing she recognizes. And it's cold. Her cheeks are already burning, and her toes are going dead. Which isn't surprising, because her feet are soaking wet. Suddenly she imagines herself, wheelchair-bound after foot amputations—an enticing and terrifying idea at once. She imagines the snobs standing in the doorway of her hospital room, their guilty consciences showing. They have heavy coats on, she's wearing nothing but a pale blue hospital robe, the white collar of her nightshirt folded neatly at her throat. Her hair's been washed and is as shiny and sweet-smelling as when she was young. She'll pretend at first not even to notice the snobs. Leave them standing there for ages in the doorway, fighting back tears. Then, slowly, she'll lift her head and look at them with her big, black eyes . . .

Aw. She shakes off this dream image and turns full circle once more. This is nuts. She's standing here in an unfamiliar world in somebody else's shoes, slowly freezing to death. . . . If only she at least had a beer. She's got to get home; she has millions of caches and there must still be a beer in at least one.

She hears a car engine in the distance, a solitary dawn vehicle. Crossing her arms over her chest, she walks in that direction, an endless migration past an infinite number of concrete buildings somebody's covered in makeup, past lawns and playgrounds, but now she has a destination, and she hugs herself to keep warm and walks fast. If she could just get to a main road she'd know where she was. She's lived her whole life in Motala and there isn't a main thoroughfare she wouldn't recognize, even dead drunk. And as soon as she knows where she is, she'll make her way home and have a beer. And a sleep. A real sleep. In her own bed. For one instant the thought is so real she can almost shut her eyes and fall asleep as she walks . . .

Shit! Why won't those pictures that plague her brain ever let up? They're perilous, they're magical and bewitching, and they mess with reality. Nothing ever works out like in a dream, so the best thing to do is put all those pictures in a little black bag at the back of your brain and never give in to the temptation to open it. She's known that since she was a kid. She must have seen herself moving out of Old Woman Ella's house and back in with Gertrude a million times. And what happened? Gertrude went and died. And then, when she was older, she fantasized so intently about playing happy families with Hound Dog that now she remembers the dream better than reality. They'd have a two-bedroom apartment in a new building, with frilly kitchen curtains. And what came of that? A wood-burning stove, no hot water, and an outdoor privy until Hound Dog left her and they took her baby away.

So now she'd better wake up, not imagine getting back home, because if she does she'll never see home again. And if she thinks about sleep she'll never sleep again. Think about what you're doing, Aunt Ella always said. And there was something to it. The only sensible words that viper ever uttered over all those years . . .

There's the main road. Her stomach seizes up when she realizes she doesn't recognize it, either. It's a wide road, much wider than any Motala street, a divided highway with an island in the middle. On the other side she can see another housing complex: tall gray buildings with black windows. She's never seen them before.

What the hell is going on? Where is she?

Birgitta shuts her eyes and takes a deep breath, then opens them again and tries to think about what she's doing. Birgitta Fredriksson is standing in the middle of some lawn, wearing somebody else's soaking, freezing shoes and her own quilted jacket. She has no idea where she is or how she got here, but she knows she'll be warmer if she pulls up her zipper.

However, that's an impossible project; her fingers are already so stiff with cold that she couldn't do it if she tried.

In front of her there's a sidewalk with patches of icy snow on the black pavement. She has to step through a snowdrift to get there. The hard snow crackles and gives way under her feet; she gets little lumps of ice in her shoes. But she's across and on the sidewalk. At a distance there's a woman staring at her. Birgitta runs her hand through her hair and tries to look like an ordinary Mary Smith on her way to work. She sticks her hands in her pockets so as not to wave them around like a drunk, and walks in the direction of the woman with little, careful steps. Oh, now she sees. It's a bus stop.

"Excuse me," she says, hearing how raw her voice sounds. She clears her throat while trying to persuade herself that even an ordinary Mary Smith could have slightly rusty pipes first thing in the morning. To be on the safe side, she speaks in a higher-pitched voice. "Excuse me, I'm lost. . . . Could you please tell me where we are?"

The woman's an immigrant, with short black hair and a thin coat, too tight across the behind. She stares at Birgitta, her brown eyes wide, and responds with a little, extremely ambiguous gesture that might mean anything. *"Don't you try anything with me, bitch!"*; *"Don't bother me, I don't speak Swedish"*; *"I'm not here and neither are you."*

"Listen," says Birgitta, trying a smile at the same time she recalls that her mouth is her caste mark. No ordinary Mary Smith would walk around with a gaping black hole where her teeth had been. Every time she smiles she shows her real self: a junkie who's retrained as a wino late in life. She slams her jaws shut and extinguishes the smile.

At that very moment, the bus arrives. There's something wrong, though, and it takes Birgitta a few seconds to realize what. It's the digital destination display at the front.

This bus is going to Vrinnevi? Vrinnevi's in Norrköping!

Suddenly Birgitta remembers where she is.

THE BUS DRIVER doesn't flinch, just lets the engine idle and growl impatiently, while he stubbornly repeats the same phrase. If you don't have the fare you can't ride. No exceptions.

Birgitta clings to the pole by the door, pleading: "Jeez, man, have a little human decency. It's freezing out here. . . . I'll send the money later, I promise. Just give me an address and I'll send your fucking bus company the fare the minute I get home. Please!"

The driver just glares straight ahead, saying nothing. "Jeez," Birgitta begs once more. "Goddamn it. Show a little Christian generosity!"

"Get off the steps," the driver says, still staring straight ahead. "This bus is leaving now, I'm closing the door."

The door hisses gently, but nothing happens. And Birgitta has no intention of giving in so fast.

"Come on. Please? Some asshole took off with my wallet, but I've got some cash at home and I promise to send the fare the minute I get there. I just need to get to the police station first and file a report. Oh come on. Fucker!"

"Get off. Door's closing."

The driver closes the door partway, threateningly, but doesn't dare finish the job.

Birgitta climbs up the next step. "Come on! I won't even take up a seat, just stand in the aisle and hang on to a pole. And I'll send the fare! I swear it!"

"Get off," says the driver. His lips are pursed now, and he's straightened up. Birgitta steps farther into the bus. Now she's right by him. "Please?" she asks, trying to smile without opening her mouth. "Just this once, be a nice guy and help a girl in trouble . . . ?"

Girl! Somebody behind her repeats the word, snorting. She twists around. Two teenagers are sitting at the front of the bus. One is holding her scarf to her mouth to suppress her giggles, the other's covering hers with both hands. Neither dares to look up. Birgitta sizes them up and turns her back again. She's allergic to giggly teenagers; more than anything they remind her of what's become of her. Once she, too, had the power to giggle the world away. But there's no time to be bothered by them now.

"Off," says the driver again.

"Come on," says Birgitta. "I might even have a little change in my pocket. That thief didn't clean me out completely, I can pay. Look, here's one coin. And two more. What's the fare, anyway?"

Now the driver turns the engine off and gets out of his seat. She's not scared, he's just a spineless skinny-bones like Roger. Typical mamma's boy who feels important only because he's in charge of one whole bus.

"You'll have to get the next bus," he says. "Get off."

Birgitta continues to go through her pockets. "You can pull out now."

"Are you deaf? Get off, I said."

Those teenagers are still snorting behind her back. From farther back in the bus a man speaks up, softly but firmly: "Throw her off, then. We're going to be late."

"Right," says another passenger. "Some of us have jobs. We haven't got all day."

"Shut up," says Birgitta. "Just shut up and mind your own business."

At that very moment she sticks her hand in the back pocket of her jeans and feels something unexpected. A bill? Of course! When she's drinking she always puts the last of her money in that pocket. For one second she forgets how she's supposed to be on guard against her dreams, and an image crosses her mind, a picture of her triumph as she slaps a twenty-crown bill down in front of that little turd of a bus driver. And that little image does it. Looking down at her hand, she sees that it's happened again. Her dream has messed up reality. She's not holding a bill. She's holding a letter. A weird little letter.

"FUCKING GESTAPO!" SHE shouts, tumbling down to the sidewalk. She loses her balance for a second but doesn't fall, just twirls around and tries to get back on the bus. But the driver's faster. He shuts the door with a contemptuous hiss, and there's nothing for her to grab on to. The bus rolls slowly away from the stop, and the passengers watch her impotent arms flailing.

"Fucking Gestapo!" she shouts again, aiming a kick at the back tire. "Goddamn Hitler pig! I'll sue you for assault and battery . . ."

But by the time she's shouted this the bus is already far gone, and all she can see are the red lights on the back, slowly vanishing into the dawn.

NOT UNTIL SHE'S walked quite a way does she remember the odd letter she's still holding in her hand. It brushes her cheek when she tries to wipe her nose with her hand. Her nose is running, her eyes are tearing, but she can't tell if she's really crying or if it's just the cold.

She stops under a streetlamp and looks at the letter. It's in an old envelope, used. Somebody's struck out the old address and written her own alongside. Miss Birgitta Fredriksson. Miss! What kind of an asshole would call her Miss?

Her fingers are so cold she has to rip the envelope to get the letter out.

For a moment, when she sees that what's inside is a little piece of folded yellow paper, a wild hope flares. Somebody's sent her a prescription: maybe Valium or, wishful thinking, roofies. Her hands tremble and fumble so in the end she has to use her mouth to open the folded paper.

It really is a prescription form. It's even got her sister's stamp on it: CHRISTINA WULF, M.D. But the familiar text on the paper is written in red Magic Marker with big, awkward letters:

Oh, if I were in Birgitta's shoes
I'd fill my cunt with sticky glues
And travel all over, far and near
Screwing for nothing, there and here.

And at the very bottom, in smaller letters:

And she did it!
She did it!
She did it!

A claw rips at her stomach lining. The pain takes her by surprise. She bends over, clutching her abdomen.

AFTERWARD SHE CAN'T really remember where she was heading. She's been walking for an eternity along the same street. The gray sixties concrete is behind her now, replaced by yellow-brick fifties apartment buildings on her right and smug single-family homes on her left. Lights are on in a few apartment windows, but it's still dark in the houses.

Birgitta is looking for Old Lady Ella's house, doesn't really know what year it is, all she knows is that she has the letter with that horrid old rhyme stuffed down her bra. She feels the crumpled paper chafing against her skin; its scratching and rubbing fuels her fury.

That stupid ass! Ella and the snobs! Now she's really going to kill them, now she's done imagining, now she's fed up. Lies and slander. Police reports and malicious testimony. Even when she was on the right track, when she'd gotten herself together and was working her life out, even then they harassed her with their accusations and reports. They've only made things worse for her, never helped her. And all because they're so fucking jealous. Just as jealous today as the first time they saw her. Because she had Gertrude, a real mamma who loved her. Christina didn't have anybody but crazy Astrid, a mother who'd actually tried to set fire to her own kid! And Margareta had no mother at all. Found in a laundry room. What the hell kind of a mother would leave her newborn kid in a laundry room? Useless shit mothers they had. While she had Gertrude. And none of them could take that—neither Ella nor the snobs. Old Lady Ella always wanted to be the only one, the biggest and best. Swedish motherhood medalist! Right! As if nobody knew what she was really like.

Birgitta sniffles and wobbles down from the sidewalk to the street. The sidewalk's icy and slippery, but the street's been plowed and there are wheel ruts all the way to the asphalt, places where there's so little slush that even the soles of patent leather Minnie Mouse shoes get a grip. She kicks a frozen lump of ice and gravel along as she walks. It's a big, hard one, bigger and harder than even Hound Dog's fists, and he did have the biggest fists she'd ever seen on a man. Oh, Hound Dog. He was the other cause of their damn jealousy. Never, ever would she forget the look on Margareta's face that evening. Her face glaring from behind the window of a car, literally green with envy. Hound Dog had chosen her. Every single girl who was anything in Motala—not Christina and the other wallflowers, of course—had been there, and every single one of them was wishing it had been her. That was it. It happened to only one person. And she, Birgitta, was that person.

She stops in the middle of the street and lets it happen again. She's out at Varamo beach, it's the sixties and pale blue June dusk. She and Margareta are sitting around in a car with Little Lars and Loa, listening to Cliff Richard's new record on a portable record player, when Hound Dog pulls into the parking lot in his Chrysler. It's a red one with enormous fins and a whole array of lights on the back. He sits behind the wheel for a moment, allowing himself to be observed, engine idling. Maybe he knows he's gorgeous, maybe he knows his shiny black hair is gleaming and the nylon shirt under his leather jacket is as blindingly white as his forehead.

But his beauty isn't the most enticing thing. It's knowing that he's dangerous—he's stolen cars, been to reform school for a couple of years, worked one summer for a traveling circus—that suddenly gives the parking lot a spicy aura that makes the girls lower their eyes and moisten their lips.

"Hound Dog," says Little Lars, a prickly vibrato in his voice, bending forward to turn the key in the ignition of his pappa's new Anglia. Little Lars looks like his father's car. He has pointy angles in unexpected places.

"Don't," says Birgitta. "Don't start the car."

Little Lars has learned obedience. He's been obeying his father for nineteen years, in addition to which he obeyed his schoolteacher for eight, and he's been obeying the foreman at the Luxor plant for the last four. Now he obeys Birgitta, for the first and last time.

Hound Dog slides out of his seat, shuts the car door, and looks around. Except for Cliff Richard's voice, the parking lot is silent. Everyone's eyes are on Hound Dog: the girls' dreams flutter toward him like butterflies, the other young men's helplessness takes the shape of an abrupt hush.

Birgitta knows he's coming to get her, she knows she is the one he is going to approach even before he moves in the direction of Little Lars's Anglia. Little Lars knows it, too. Beads of perspiration break out on his brow, but he says nothing, just leans forward, lifting the record player off her lap and onto his own. At that very moment Hound Dog jerks open the car door and grabs Birgitta by the wrist.

"You're my girl now," he says. Nothing else. That's it.

Like a movie, she thinks. This is just like at the movies . . . and she imagines she can hear the soundtrack rise to jubilation as he pulls her out of the car, a chorus and strings moving toward a crescendo as he bends her back against the hood of the Anglia for a first kiss. Out of the corner of her eye she sees Little Lars in the car, hands over his eyes; behind her she catches a glimpse of Margareta's green face. Her eyes are slits, her teeth bared. She looks like a monster, thinks Birgitta, closing her own eyes. Hound Dog's tongue tastes bitter, of beer; this is the first time she's experienced that taste, that smell. All the other guys had tasted of just Vicks or Lucky Strikes.

He never holds her hand, never once will he hold her hand. Instead, he takes her wrist and holds it like a prison guard, and she trips willingly along behind him to the red Chrysler. While she gets comfortable, he starts the engine and then pushes a button. The top folds back and down. It's a convertible! Her joy knows no bounds! She's sitting in a Chrysler convertible with the toughest guy in Motala. Everything this town has put her through suddenly seems endurable. There was a point. And the point was this very moment . . .

He has to drive across the whole parking lot to get out. This is Birgitta's triumphal procession. She is the chosen one. Chosen. The Lady of Lake Varamo on display for the plebeians. But at the very instant the car exits the parking lot, she hears the shrill voice of a boy shout from behind: "Oh, if I were in Birgitta's shoes."

She'll never forget that scornful laughter, despite the fact that she'll never be absolutely sure she really heard it. But she does know she really sees Hound Dog glance quickly down at her and ask: "What the fuck was that?"

"Aw," she says, "nothing."

What can she say? That they were shouting a rhyme that had been haunting her since she was thirteen? A rhyme that was on public toilet walls and in phone booths? A rhyme shouted in the school yard and mumbled behind her back when she started working at the Luxor plant? She can't tell him that, that would bring the whole thing to a quick conclusion. And he'd hear about it soon enough, anyway . . .

"Great car," she says instead, running her hand across the vinyl seat.

Which actually earns her a smile.

BRAKES SQUEAK BEHIND her, an engine growls. Birgitta turns halfway around with a deprecating gesture: cool it. But the driver presses the accelerator again, revving the engine. Birgitta decides to ignore him, turns her back, and walks intentionally along the black wheel rut in the asphalt at a snail's pace, kicking the big lump of ice ahead of her. She doesn't hear him. He can rev his engine as much as he pleases, she still has no intention of hearing him.

There's a white house across the street. Old Lady Ella's house was white, too. Maybe that's it, though it doesn't look quite right. Maybe Ella has remodeled, planted new bushes, and put the windows in different places just to confuse Birgitta. She wouldn't put it past her. Someone turns on a kitchen light, and she sees a silhouette moving around in there. It must be her, waddling from table to stove as ever, her saggy old breasts slapping under her bathrobe. Breasts like fuzzy woolen mittens. Oh, Jesus, what a sickening bitch!

She might have staggered across the street in the direction of the white house if the driver of the car behind her hadn't put his hand on the horn and honked. But he did, three provocative toots.

Birgitta stops in her own footsteps, frozen. "Shut up!" she shouts, as if the car were a living being who could hear her. But she's standing with her back to it, and her shout resounds in the wrong direction. "Shut up! Leave me alone!"

He just honks again. So Birgitta turns around. She wobbles as she turns, but regains her balance and can see that there are three cars lined up behind her now, headlights beaming. The front one is still moving: rolling implacably toward her, growling and threatening, the driver opening his window and leaning out. "What do you think you're doing?" he cries. "Come on, lady, get up on the sidewalk!"

Just one glance tells Birgitta what kind of man he is. Shiny car, short haircut. Glasses, shrill voice, white shirt, and tie. A snob.

Birgitta despises snobs. So she bends forward reflexively, picks up her big lump of ice, and raises it over her head, swinging it with one single, strong motion right at his face. He screams, his engine stalls; his hand seems glued to the horn.

THUS THE MORNING silence bursts into a cacophony of sounds. Shouting, honking, two other cars braking, their doors opening, two men getting out and slamming their doors behind them, a dog barking and, one second later, a gray-haired old man opening the door of the white house. He totters slowly down the steps, both hands on the railing, not seeming to notice he's barefoot. Birgitta is silent and immobile as an animal on its guard in the middle of the street, following every movement around her attentively. When the barefoot man sets his naked foot on his front path, she is triggered into action and starts walking backward. After a moment she turns around and runs. She's out of sight before he even reaches the sidewalk. But he saw her. He and the others. If they had eyes, they saw her.

There are no hiding places. The yards are too small, and all the hedges are leafless, black and sharp. The courtyard behind the apartment building on the other side of the street is big and desolate, there's not even a bike shed to huddle up in. Birgitta hears her own footsteps, her own panting, and sirens in the distance. Already? Could the cops really be on their way?

She shakes the doors to a couple of apartment buildings, tries the keypads and fails, nothing but a series of little red lights. The sirens are getting closer, she's got to run, and she's got to get away . . .

* * *

THEY FIND HER on some cellar stairs, she's slid down the icy steps, scraped her hand and turned her ankle. She's been fruitlessly pulling and kicking at the door for ages, has even tried to break the glass with one of her Minnie Mouse heels. She couldn't. Couldn't even crack it. Solid plate glass.

She gave up when she heard the sirens go off and the car come to a halt on the street, sitting heavily down on the cold cement and pulling her jacket over her head. She was still there when a rosy-cheeked young police officer bent down over the railing from six feet up.

"Here she is," he shouts. "Found her." He's got that disgusting local dialect, and a German shepherd who's barking triumphantly.

Penal Expeditions

I call myself a *benandante* because four times a year, at the four changes of season, I turn out at night along with the others to wage the invisible war against the spirit, while our bodies remain.

auctioneer Battista Moducco to the Cividale inquisitors on June 27, 1580

GOOD. GREAT.

I've finally set my sisters in motion. Now I've got them precisely where I want them.

Christina is sitting in a car outside the Motala women's shelter, ashen with exhaustion, and Margareta is coming out through the door. She closes it carefully and checks to be sure it has really locked behind her, having seen all the signs in the hallway, warnings of the proximity of adrenaline-overcharged males of the species. She stops to light another one of her eternal cigarettes. Christina opens the car door for her and gestures an indication that she's prepared to tolerate the smoke to find out what's been going on.

"They never called," says Margareta, shaking her head as she settles in. "There were only three women in, one volunteer and two who needed protection. None of them had called, they swore it."

"And you believed them?"

"Completely. She, the volunteer, even took me aside to tell me that Birgitta's been blacklisted there. She's wrecked their furniture once too often."

"Oh my God," Christina says dully, starting the car. "She's even got herself blacklisted from the women's shelter . . . quite an accomplishment, I'd say."

"What now?" asks Margareta.

"Breakfast," says Christina. "I have to be at work in a couple of hours."

BIRGITTA BEGINS TO curse. And not just a single oath. She doesn't leave a single saint untainted; she neglects neither angels nor devils. She, too, has gone pale now: her hair's straggly, her complexion dull, her pores huge, her lips just half a shade darker than her skin.

Oh, well. Such is life. Even for the former Marilyn Monroe of Motala.

The young policeman, by contrast, is a knockout. Right out of the fashion posters: blond, blue-eyed, and enormous, with peachy pastel skin stretched across muscles of iron and a frame of steel. Young men haven't always looked like this: this is the postmodernist, fin de siècle variety. Yet young men today needed neither enormous jaws nor iron muscles. It would have been far more logical if they had grown pale and thin, and wilted like fragile lilies of the valley instead of developing into mighty oaks.

Birgitta, too, has a well-developed jaw musculature, but for very different reasons than the young officer. For over twenty years her molars have incessantly ground against one another in the tooth grinding so typical of amphetamine addicts. But now there is silence in her head. She's not got much in the way of teeth left to grind, in addition to which she now abuses other substances. She pretends that it was a choice, that she dispensed with amphetamines of her own free will after having seen them kill too many of her contemporaries. But if the truth be told, it wasn't Birgitta who abandoned amphetamines, it was the amphetamines that abandoned her. They stopped working, left her to drown her sorrows in booze. That's what sets off the sensitive nostrils of the young police officer as he walks down the cement stairs. Birgitta smells. And not of roses and jasmine.

She's still huddled down with her jacket over her head, refusing to move even when he tells her time and again to get up. Not until he grabs her arm and drags her up the steps does she come to and start swearing. She spits on his arm, bellows that he's abusing an innocent woman, and sends a kick in the direction of his German shepherd. The dog bares its teeth, preparing to attack, but the fashion model–cum–policeman stops him with a snort. This is about his dignity. No one's going to claim he needs a dog's help to arrest a lush swearing a blue streak. He can manage her himself.

Birgitta, by contrast, has never felt much of a drive to preserve her dignity. She has been drawn to humiliation as if she thirsted for it. There isn't a store in Motala where she hasn't shoplifted and been caught; there isn't a street where she hasn't been arrested, shouting and thrashing; there isn't a clinic where she hasn't lied and been exposed. I've seen her throwing up in rubbish containers in the town square on a Saturday afternoon, of course, when the square was full of people, and then bending stiffly forward with smelly diarrhea running down her legs. I've seen her sitting in a snowdrift, dead drunk and soaked in her own pee late one evening, encircled by a gang of mocking teenagers. I've seen her spread her legs for one man after the next: even men like Roger, who have covered her face with their hands so as not to have to look at it. And in the middle of it all, I have seen her arrogance, that incomprehensible pride in her own decay.

The injured driver is inside a little circle of people on the sidewalk. He's got his hand over one eye, a drop of blood suspended like a tear from his cheek. The other two drivers surround him like bodyguards; they turn their pale faces to stare at Birgitta, wide-eyed. An older police officer is in front of them, somehow strangely present and absent at once. He may be an angel, a worn-out guardian angel who has seen so much in his day that he no longer sees anything at all.

The barefoot man's got shoes on now. He's standing next to the distracted policeman with one arm raised when the poster boy herds Birgitta across the street, sometimes shoving, sometimes pulling. "That's her," he shouts, waving his brown-spotted hand. "She did it, I saw her!"

"Shut up, old man!" Birgitta says automatically.

That's the straw that breaks the camel's back for the fashion model, whose aging parents brought him up to show respect for the elderly. He gives her a hard rap on the neck, so hard she's unable to make so much as a sound. That's the moment when it hits her that she's no spring chicken, either.

CHRISTINA AND MARGARETA have gone silent, too, sitting in the car on the way back to Vadstena. They resemble communicating vessels, my sisters. When one is angry or upset, the other grows anxious, flattering, pleading, and smiling, only to become grumpy and irritable the minute the other is finally placated. That's how they've always been, at least when Birgitta is out of sight. As soon as she turns up, the other two are in deadly consensus. Truly deadly.

But now, in the tired dawn light, they've achieved some kind of silent equilibrium. The night that's just ended has been so full of words they're all used up. The sisters have spoken incessantly, first in respectful whispers when they thought they were on their way to a deathbed, then in objective, muted voices at the emergency ward, then in sharp, suspicious tones when it turned out that no Birgitta Fredriksson had been admitted that night. Christina was the more upset; her reserved, superficial attitude eroded quickly, leaving her raw and vulnerable. Her heels clattered angrily against the floor as she inventoried the entire hospital, marching from ward to ward, her physician's voice so strict and authoritative that one of the nurse's aides curtsied to her in sheer terror. And when Christina was transformed, so was Margareta. Her self-confident surface cracked, she fluttered anxiously behind Christina in her fashionable rubber-soled shoes, babbling nervously. "Come on now, she's not here, let's go, just come on . . ."

But Christina was implacable; she searched systematically through every single ward in the huge gray building, from pediatrics to geriatrics. When—after more than an hour of pounding the corridors—they finally gave up and were in the elevator to the ground floor again, she was pale with fury. This was the last straw. Now she was going to get Birgitta locked up for good, and she'd be the one to throw away the key.

"There are hopeless cases," she said, holding the outside door open. "I just have to accept it. There are people who can't be helped. . . . It's genetic. She's just like her mother. Hopeless!"

A cold wind ruffled Margareta's hair as she groped in her pockets for cigarettes. "God, Christina. You should know better than anyone else not to go around shouting about genetics."

Christina turned on her, fixing her with a black glare. The color had come back into her cheeks; even her dull blond hair seemed to gleam in the glow of the streetlight. "If you're implying that I'm anything like Astrid, all I can say is that I assume I had a father, too."

Margareta cupped her hand around the flame to light her cigarette. "I guess Birgitta did, too."

"Sure," said Christina. "Some old drunkard. Some other hopeless case."

"And what do you know about your father, if I may ask?" said Margareta. "Or I about mine? Me, I don't even know who my mother was. What can people like us know about their genes?"

"Enough. Our lives bear witness to them. And if there's anything I'm sick and tired of it's your damn humanism. First you whine and curse about her, but then you don't dare take all the consequences. 'Kill her,' you say. But when push comes to shove, it's poor Birgitta here and poor Birgitta there. I've seen it before, don't forget."

Margareta blew an angry plume of smoke into her face. "So are you trying to tell me that your exemplary genes account for the decent life you live? Does it have nothing to do with the fact that you were Aunt Ella's pet?"

Christina snorted. "Pet? Me? You were her pet, if anybody was! You were the charming one, the funny one. I was just the good girl, and if I wasn't good I was nothing. Nonexistent. And Birgitta lived with Aunt Ella, too, don't forget. Sometimes she even liked Birgitta better than me. Like when she got a job at the Luxor plant. That made her very special. A real working-class girl. That was worth far more than my good grades and prizes."

Margareta reached out a hand to touch Christina's cape, trying to find her arm. But Christina pulled back roughly. That made Margareta aware of how very upset she was.

She lowered her voice. "But don't you see? You intimidated her with all that success. It was alien to her. Birgitta's factory job was normal, recognizable. And that was all she aspired to for us: a normal life. A regular job, a regular husband, and a few regular kids . . . which is what you attained. You always got everything she wanted for us, of course, just a cut or two above her wildest dreams."

But Christina only turned her back and headed for the parking lot. "Stub it out now," she said. "Put it out and let's get going."

Margareta inhaled on her half-smoked cigarette, running behind. "What's the hurry?"

"We need to go to the shelter. We have to work this thing out, once and for all."

Oh, Jesus, as if anything were ever going to be worked out.

"BREAKFAST TIME," CHIRPS an assistant nurse from the doorway. She sounds like a perky parakeet. "Yogurt or oatmeal, Desirée?"

The question's nothing but a formality. She knows I want yogurt. Not that I like it, I prefer oatmeal with applesauce, but when Kerstin One's on duty I don't get to feed myself the oatmeal. I drip it on the sheets, so I have to be fed. And if it's a choice between yogurt through a straw and imposed physical contact with the training patrol, I choose yogurt. Always.

I don't know that girl's name, I still haven't got the names of all the nurses and nurse's aides on the day shift down pat, whereas she talks to me as if we were childhood friends. It's Desirée this, Desirée that. Kerstin

One is always instructing her underlings about the fact that people cooperate more readily if you address them by their given names. Her husband's in sales.

The nameless girl sets my tray on the nightstand, chirping all the while: "Let me puff up your pillow, Desirée. And we'll raise the back, so you can sit up better. Then you won't spill. You do want coffee, don't you? The girls say you're a real little coffee klatcher! Ha, ha ha. And have you and Dr. Hubertsson had your little morning meeting yet? Or should I bring in a cup for him as well?"

Go sprain your ankle, I think. Or do yourself in.

For one instant it crosses my mind that I could really get inside her head and make her fall down hard on her ass. But I stop at the thought. Nowadays I can afford neither the time nor the risk associated with penal expeditions.

Things used to be different. The first summer after I discovered my gift, I have to admit I was dumb enough to take almost any risk because I was so hungry for experience that I showed no consideration for those around me. I couldn't see them as anything but possible conveyors: the hospital chaplain, the physiotherapist, the nurse's aides and the doctors, other patients' visitors and next of kin. Impatient, urging, I drove them out that summer and then instantly abandoned them when I found other, far better, carriers. There were so many things I had never been, and now I wanted to be everything at once. I was constantly shifting from shape to shape: in the morning I was a girl in high-heeled sandals with the summer sun on my neck, at lunchtime a young man sitting on the beach at the lake with sand running between my fingers, at dusk a middle-aged woman bending over royal blue monkshood inhaling the fragrance into every single cavity of her cranium.

I learned a lot that summer: what it's like to kiss and be kissed, how dancing can moisten the driest genitals, and how it feels when you let your nose and mouth slide across the downy head of a newborn.

And other things.

But as fall approached, as the days grew shorter and the trees stood out like black etchings against the sky, everything changed. I became acquainted with the *benandanti,* listened to their warnings, and, all on my own, discovered that my outings exacted their price. After every time I'd been away, I grew increasingly tired; sometimes I lay semiconscious for hours. But at that point I was sufficiently saturated with experiences to settle down. I began to be interested in events on the ward again. That was when I started getting under the skin of my caregivers. Which was how I learned that the gentlest of them, the ones who smiled the kindest smiles at the head of my bed, were the ones to fear most. Psychopaths. Potential killers, every one of them.

"What kind of life is that?" they whispered to one another in the coffee room and the corridor.

"She can't talk properly, she can't even walk."

"And that head . . ."

"God, yes. She looks like an alien. I was actually scared of her at first."

"Not to mention her bedsores. I saw right down to her hipbone yesterday. And Hubertsson fusses about linen sheets. As if that would help."

"She must be suffering . . ."

"She must. It's inhuman. She's been lying here convulsing for thirty years, is it right to let her go on for thirty more? Or longer! Better to put her out of her misery."

That fall, the staff occupational-injury rate on my ward skyrocketed. One person stumbled down the steps and broke a foot. Another got boiling water over her hands. A third happened to self-medicate with my antiepileptic. A fourth cut right through her fingertip slicing bread. Et cetera.

Well, maybe I was a bit rough on them, but personally I think my judgments were fair. I was just punishing their artificial compassion, a sentiment with a human voice but no human heart. I left the soft-spoken older nurses and the timid young girls in peace; I even learned to tolerate their blunt endearments. I let them ruffle my hair and stroke my cheek without snapping at them. But their silence was a prerequisite. Because true kindness doesn't speak. Its evidence takes many other shapes, but not words.

Which explains why I detest that nameless girl who's now setting up my breakfast on my nightstand. Her mouth is so full of words they dribble like drool down over her chin. And still I know that when she leaves my room she'll ask that same question: *What's the point of living if you're like that? It's so meaningless.*

Don't misunderstand me. She doesn't really think I'd be better off dead—though I think so myself, sometimes. It's her self-importance I can't stand, her blatant assumption that my life has even less meaning than hers. What makes her life so precious? That she can breed? Or spend decades of evenings in front of the TV with some morose man? Or have the pleasure of traipsing out onto the cobbled streets of Vadstena for the occasional shopping trip?

She'd be dumbstruck if I asked. I know it. Because every single ambulatory individual—including Hubertsson—finds it very easy to talk about the meaningless, but equally difficult to discuss the opposite: meaning. The very word brings out the Salvation-Army-officer-in-a-brothel side in every one of them. They suffer from such a combination of embarrassment and temptation that they just blush and look in the other direction.

They say it's Isaac Newton's fault, that his mechanical worldview has alienated Western man from the concept of meaning for the last three hundred years. And it's true: if the universe just ticks as smoothly as a Newtonian clock, and the human being is a random microbe, the word *meaning* is nothing but an embarrassment. And in such a universe a biologically imperfect microbe—like myself—is utterly extraneous. The clockwork will operate perfectly smoothly without it. It might even tick better. This makes the existence of such a microbe less meaningful than that of biologically perfect microbes.

But today we know that Newton was only scratching the surface of reality. The universe is not a perpetuum mobile, it is a heart. A living heart that expands and contracts, that grows infinitely before shrinking beyond recognition. And like all other hearts it is full of secrets and mysteries, riddles and adventures, changes and transformations. There's only one thing that never changes: the quantity of mass and energy. That which once was will be for all eternity, although it may shift in form.

Every particle in the imperfect lump that is my body is therefore just as eternal as the universe itself. But what makes this particular collection of particles unique is that it is aware of its own existence.

I possess consciousness. This does not distinguish me from any of the other human beings around me, the ones who can walk and speak. But I am convinced that the meaning is concealed in that very factor: consciousness. I know nothing of its form or content—I do not know whether meaning is an equation or a poem, a song or a saga—but I know that it exists. Somewhere.

And therefore I dare assert that my life contains as much meaning as the life of that nameless girl, the one who is in the process of cutting my bread and butter into pieces the size of postage stamps. Yes, I am sufficiently arrogant even to dare to contend that my life is more meaningful than hers. Because she will always be where she is. Never elsewhere.

But I can be where I am not. Precisely like an electron before it makes a quantum leap. And like the electron I, too, leave tracks. Even where I haven't been.

April witch, the *benandanti* call me. You're almost like us, but not one of us. I allow my conveyor—a seagull or a magpie, a crow or a raven—to spread its wings and take an ironic bow. I know. I'm almost like them, but not one of them.

Some of them envy me. I have more abilities and can span larger areas. But that's only fair. A *benandante* always has a well-functioning body, leads a normal life in the normal world. Most of them withdraw from their bodies only on the special occasions four times a year. Some of them don't even know what they are. When the seasons change and they wake up one morning after having been out all night in the Procession of the Dead, they have nothing but vague memories of pale faces and gray shadows. They tell themselves they were dreaming.

An April witch is different. She knows who she is. And once she's acquainted with her abilities, she can see through time and hover in space, she can hide in drops of water or insects just as easily as she can take possession of a human being. But she doesn't have a life of her own. Her body is always thin, imperfect, and immobile.

There aren't many of us. To tell the truth, I've never met another. Four times a year I faithfully attend the Procession of the Dead in the hope of meeting one of my kind, but it hasn't happened yet. The Vadstena central square fills up with all kinds of beings, but I've never met another April witch there. I have to make do with *benandanti*, those minor figures of the shadow world.

Still, sometimes minor figures are also useful. Thanks to them, I've become more careful than I was in the early years. The *benandanti* have taught me that if anyone should address my empty body while I was away, I'd never be able to enter it again. I'd become a formless shadow that took shape only during the Procession of the Dead.

When I had my own apartment I was safe; people left me in peace except when I requested help. If I appeared to be sleeping, my assistants would just quietly shut the bedroom door until I woke up. Here things are different: whoever wants to look in is free to do so at any hour of the day or night. And nothing seems to provoke Kerstin One and her training patrol more than a patient who drops off to sleep in broad daylight. They would be sure to talk to any patient who even dared to think about dozing off.

So during the day I have to keep guard over my body, be content with observing from a distance without intervening. I might permit myself a hasty outing, such as snatching a bird on the wing and making it take a letter to a certain address.

But the nights are mine. As long as I have a private room, they will remain mine. And different night shifts. I've learned to be cautious with these women, too. Early at night I mostly leave them in peace; they're busy then and difficult to control. I never ask them for anything while I'm still in my body, just let them get me ready for bed and turn off the light before I ride a seagull or a magpie. Seagulls are best, with their wide wings and the resilience in flight that magpies lack. In addition to which, they're less sensitive, never seem to notice another consciousness flying through their own. Magpies, by contrast, tend to get upset. When they sense something alien behind an eye, it triggers their anxiety. Almost like people.

Because I don't want to alert the women on the night shift to anything alarming, I almost never possess them. When I do, it's only during the quiet hour between two and three in the morning, when the patients are sound asleep and they are able to relax in the coffee room and let their thoughts wander. I'm systematic about distributing my favors, too; I allow my consciousness to flow slowly through them, one after the other. I whisper words of comfort to the sad ones, paint flowery dreams for the young ones, and sing little snippets about still water for the worried ones. Once they are all resting in that narrow borderland between sleep and waking, I choose one of them to serve me.

One night several weeks ago, then, I had Annika write a letter for me in this way, with tiny letters on pink crepe paper, and then carry it through the corridors to my room and hide it in my pillowcase. The next night I let Marie-Louise write another letter and make the same pilgrimage. A few nights later still, it was pale Ylva's turn to find a yellow prescription pad, and stamp it with the stamp Dr. Wulf had left behind. But when I whispered Birgitta's poem into her ear, it made her so sick she dropped the pen. Then I had to expand my self, let it fill her whole head, make her hand seize a thick red marker and move it awkwardly across the paper as I dictated. When Hubertsson came in that morning, I was so worn out I didn't even have the energy to speak when he spoke to me. But by the next night I was strong enough to have black-eyed Tua dig up three used envelopes and address them. And last night, once the stone had been set in motion, I drove Lena into the nurses' office early, made her shut the door very quietly, dial a number, and claim she was calling from the Motala women's shelter . . .

And I did all that for Hubertsson's sake, because he had been waiting for the story of my sisters for so long.

Still, no matter how important he is to me, I cannot give him what he wants without giving him what he doesn't want at the same time. The story of the life that was left for me.

THE BEGINNING OF that story was actually a gift from Hubertsson to me.

"You are the ultimate victim of the ultimate starvation," he once said. And perhaps one can see it like that; the story of each of our lives is also a story of those who preceded us.

Thus my story begins more than thirty years before I was born. It's a November day toward the end of World War I, and a little girl sits weeping in a room in Norrköping with a wood-burning stove. "Not turnips, Mamma," she whimpers, her throat swollen with tears. "Not turnips!"

But her mother doesn't answer, just bends down and adds a log to the fire, watching the birch bark catch before closing the door and allowing the fire to pick up.

Everything about the little girl's face—her eyes, her lips, her chin—is wet and pleading. Everything about her mother—her resolute mouth, her clenched fists, her rejecting back—is dry and determined.

"Please, Mamma, not turnips again today!"

But her mother has swallowed her compassion, can no longer remember why the girl's tears are such torture to her. The child gathers herself for a new effort, opens her mouth to beg once more. But at that very instant her mother turns around and looks her right in the eye. The child is suddenly silenced. Although she's not yet four years old, she knows what she's seeing in her mother's eyes. Things are going to get worse.

"All we have is turnips," her mother says. The child doesn't answer, just sits in silence while her mother dries the tears from her face with her apron. The cloth is soft from many washings, but that same water has hardened the hand underneath.

Later, as fall matures into winter and things really do get worse, the little girl doesn't cry anymore; she grows silent as the hunger eats its way into her body. It kneads the soft bones of the child and reshapes them; her legs bend and become bowed, her ribs bloom with outgrowths just where the bone ends and the cartilage begins, and her pelvis is invisibly remolded into a new, different form.

The child bears her exhaustion like a hump on her back. In the mornings, when her mother has gone to the factory, leaving her alone with the fire burning in the stove, she curls up to spend the day in a corner of the wooden settle that is also their trundle bed. She doesn't play. She's already forgotten the days when there was hot oatmeal with milk in the morning and she was able to play. But one day, when she finds some crumbs under the mattress, the memory resurfaces. She happens to insert her hand beside the mattress and run her index finger along the wooden slats. Suddenly there's something hard. Crispbread crumbs. Once, long long ago, somebody lay in this bed eating crispbread. The girl dampens her finger and runs it through the depths of the trundle bed again. The crumbs stick to her finger, and she puts them in her mouth. Although she's so little, she recognizes the taste—that slightly nutty flavor of burned crispbread edges. At that very moment her nose begins to bleed, suddenly and inexplicably.

The girl will bleed throughout her life. Her blood vessels are as delicate as soap bubbles: the slightest breeze and they break. And it only gets worse with time. Her body seems to refuse to accept reality, that the lean years end, that her mother is able to put potatoes, pork, and onion gravy, dark bread and aromatic apples on the table, that she herself grows up and learns to bake sweet rolls with lots of butter and to culture full-fat milk and ladle it, quivering, from the bowl. She goes on bleeding, and her skeleton is permanently misshapen.

The doctor who examines her when she's in labor has no idea about rooms with cast-iron stoves or hunger, and so he doesn't bother to measure the conjugate axis of her pelvis. For thirty hours my soft skull rubs those deformed bones, for thirty hours we suffer while an ancient hunger barricades the route to life. Not until we are both close to death do they put her to sleep and section her womb.

"What is it?" Ella whispers when she comes to.

What can they tell her? What is there left to say?

The midwife turns her back in silence. Everyone is silent.

I, though, reach my hand through time, whispering: Driftwood. It's a piece of driftwood, Mamma.

BUT PERHAPS I'LL spare Hubertsson that particular story. He already knows all about Ella's delicate vascular walls and her crumpled skeleton. In contrast to myself, he has actually both known her and cared for her.

What he wants from me is different: a story with an ending. He wants the close of that story that began one June day more than thirty years ago, when he found the stroke-ridden body of his landlady on the floor.

Again and again he has told me about how the three girls reacted: Christina standing there paralyzed in the doorway with both fists to her mouth, Margareta sitting on the floor beside Ella, holding her hand, and Birgitta backing into the wall, whining: "It's not my fault, not my fault . . ."

He rode in the ambulance with Ella. And late that evening when he returned home, the house was empty, just a note on the door to inform him that the girls had been taken into the custody of the child welfare authorities.

Since then he has only been able to observe them from afar. Well, Christina is his colleague, but she keeps her distance. She is happy to talk about her work, even has him over for dinner occasionally, but whenever he mentions Ella and what happened that day, she goes silent and looks away.

"I wonder," he says now and then. "I can't help but wonder what happened before I got home that day . . ."

And one time I was foolish enough to say: "Let me write you that story."

I had second thoughts almost instantly.

HUBERTSSON THINKS I'M scared, that that's why I'm taking so long over the story, why I keep starting over. But that's not it. I'm not afraid of my sisters, I just don't want to get too close to them. The truth is I don't want to get too close to anybody. Except possibly Hubertsson.

The worst part of my predicament—both the external one and the internal one—is that I am unable to defend myself. For nearly fifty years now other people have constantly been at my body: shampooing my hair and rubbing my skin with creams, brushing my teeth and cleaning my nails, changing my shitty diapers and replacing my bloody sanitary pads. And all this—a pleasure when I was a child and tolerable when I was young—is now a daily torment. It's as if every single hand leaves a hole in my body, and my self is slipping through those holes. Soon I will be nothing but a bag of skin surrounding a rattling pile of bones; the rest will have run out onto the linoleum floor of this public health facility and been mopped up by the cleaners.

With my secret powers, it should actually be the other way around. An April witch should be able to press the self of her carrier into a thin membrane against the white walls of the cranium and exploit the body for her own purposes. But I lose myself far too often in the heads of others, merge and allow myself to become mixed in. So suddenly there I am, laughing and crying, loving and hating on their terms rather than my own. I am consumed by my carriers. Despite the fact that I don't want it that way, that it's wrong.

So nowadays I choose to enter only animals and indifferent strangers. There, I can remain at the surface, I need never fear death by water. That's also why I am so especially careful not to crawl into the people who are important to my life for better or for worse: never Kerstin One and never Hubertsson. And never, ever my sisters.

One of the three of them is living the life that was intended for me. And I want to know which one, every bit as badly as Hubertsson wants to know what happened that day so long ago.

But I just want to know it. I don't want to experience it. I want to see but not be involved.

And yet. I've promised Hubertsson an answer to an old question, and a promise is a promise. That's why I am in several different places at this very instant. I am reclining on my bed groping resolutely for a piece of a salami sandwich at the same time as I am both hovering near the ceiling of the jail cell where Birgitta's been tossed to sleep it off and standing on the front steps of the Post-Industrial Paradise watching Christina rummage around in her handbag for her keys. Margareta is standing behind her, biting her lip.

"I'm just going to have a shower," she says. "Then I'm off."

Christina's too tired after the long night of running around to pretend hospitality. She shrugs her shoulders.

Margareta's voice takes on a pleading tone: "Maybe I'll get a couple hours' sleep first, though. If that's all right with you. They said the car wouldn't be ready until early afternoon."

Christina shrugs her shoulders again and opens the door. Her silence makes Margareta even more nervous.

"But I can fix breakfast, if you want. While you shower and get dressed."

Christina hangs her cape neatly on a hanger. Margareta tosses her jacket on an old trunk and raises her voice. "Yes, that's the plan. I'll fix breakfast while you get ready for work. Want tea or coffee?"

Finally Christina answers. "Coffee," she says, inspecting her face in the hall mirror. "Black coffee."

BIRGITTA LIES, MOUTH open, on the slanted floor of the drunk tank. She's asleep but not dreaming, even in her sleep she knows you have to be on guard against your dreams.

Nobody's bothered to question her. When she refused to give her name, they just tossed her in the cell without further ado. She didn't scream, didn't even swear. Just lay down on her side with both hands under her cheek. Like an angel. A real little angel.

Oh, Jesus! Was this what she abandoned me for?

Yes, it was. Ella abandoned me. Three healthy, needy little girls were given a good home in 1950s Motala because a few years earlier a severely disabled, spastic, epileptic baby with cerebral palsy had been put away in a cripples' home and forgotten.

From a utilitarian point of view, this was a good decision; the happiness of three purchased at the expense of the fourth. And Ella lived in utilitarian times, times when suffering and imperfection were intolerable. In the early days of the welfare state, things were supposed to be clean and orderly, so all the nuts and the deformed were institutionalized. In homes where the white coats of the doctors smelled fresh as a breeze, where the floors were scrubbed daily with sudsy water, where the halls were so quiet you could hear the starched uniforms of the nurses rustle as they walked. All that disturbed the perfection were the abandoned children, the drooling, blind heads of children with water on the brain, the whining club-footed ones, the whimpering humpbacks, the screaming, stuttering epileptics and spastics.

In many ways Ella was a child of her times; as one of the very first trained home helpers in Sweden, she was a member of the hygiene brigade. As a teen she had learned to fear the compulsive, claustrophobic nature of factory work, and had fled the textile industries of Norrköping for Motala. There she was dressed in something resembling a nurse's uniform, and she cycled across town daily, making meals for solitary elderly people, washing and wiping the noses of the children of ill women, reminding trembling, newly delivered mothers of their obligations so they would not allow themselves to be consumed by postnatal psychoses.

She was a gem. Everyone, on both the social and child welfare boards, said so. Cheerful and dutiful, neat and tidy, competent and reliable. Not to mention a good cook. So no one was particularly surprised the day Hugo Johansson, the first construction worker ever to be elected to the Motala town council, began to court her in his blunt fashion. They were made for each other: solid, conscientious, honest, and industrious. It was a good thing, too, that Hugo was twenty years her senior and a widower, because it meant he already had a home to offer his young bride.

Somewhere in Hubertsson's documents there is a picture of Hugo, a touched-up portrait from the forties of a middle-aged man with eyes beyond his years and a plain face. I find it difficult to accept that he really was my father; his eyes don't speak to me.

Maybe that's not so strange, though. Because Hugo was never really anything more than my mother's sperm donor. By the time they put Ella on the delivery table in a nearby ward, Hugo was already battling his cancer.

I STOP CHEWING my mouthful of sandwich and perk up my ears. The heels of the training patrol are clattering in extra-efficient swirls out in the hall, but their voices are subdued, in the register that means there's an extremely sick patient.

I wonder who it is.

I don't know all that many of the other patients. In fact, I outright avoid them. Most are elderly, and their presence torments me in various ways. The other day I saw one of them—an old man—sitting alone in the dining room when one of Kerstin Two's girls was rolling me along the corridor. It took my breath away to glimpse him through the half-open dining room door, and the girl who was pushing me halted in midstep. For one moment we were frozen in position, eyes locked: the nurse, the old man, and myself.

Just like me, he sat bolstered up in a wheelchair. But the top strap had come loose, and his torso was slumped forward. His left cheek was resting on the tabletop. His false teeth were falling out. Both his arms hung slack at his sides. He didn't have the strength to use them to heave himself up. His shoulders rested heavily against the sharp edge of the table. It must've hurt.

He wasn't saying anything, wasn't even moaning. Slowly, though, he raised his eyebrows. At that instant, time thawed. The nurse released my wheelchair and put both hands to her mouth. "Oh God, no!" she said.

I was glad she left it at that. She was one of the girls in Kerstin Two's shift, so she didn't talk baby talk with him, just took a couple of swift steps across the floor and helped him up. "Would you like to go to your room, Folke?" she asked.

He shut his eyes and nodded. Suddenly I was seized by the most tremendous desire to go to him, to get up out of my own wheelchair, grasp him in my strong arms, and carry him far from this humiliation to a better place. . . . But all I could do was avert my eyes when he was rolled past me, just like, thousands of times, others have averted theirs from me.

Folke may be the one who's decided to die now. That's what they do, the old ones who are strongest. Decide to die. Of course, they can't control what illnesses will strike them, but once they have been afflicted they do seem to have power over their own deaths. They simply let go: one day they open the hand that's been gripping their lifeline and let go.

Personally, I'm still clutching my lifeline tight. Mostly because of my sisters and Hubertsson, but also because I know what happens to people who die before their time. But Folke has nothing to fear. His life is finished, he'll never need to wander in the Procession of the Dead.

The door bangs; the girl with the parakeet voice opens it with her hip. "Done with breakfast, Desirée?"

I snap at the mouthpiece and puff. "Yes, and I'd like a shower today. All right?"

Her face takes on a hesitant expression as she reads my text on the screen. She shrugs her shoulders. "Don't know. I'll have to ask . . ."

"I haven't showered for over a week."

She's using silence now to impose her will on me. I'm making demands, I must be spoiled. Every patient who's lived in a place of her own with assisted care is regarded as spoiled. And I am particularly spoiled because Hubertsson backs me up. People like me think they can make all the decisions. Even about when and how often they get showers. With no consideration whatsoever for the workload of the staff or the cutbacks in the health care sector.

I haven't let go of the mouthpiece. "I really need a shower today. I stink. Not to mention that I get bedsores if I don't shower a couple of times a week. As you know."

Now she's stopped chirping, her voice is a whole octave lower as she swishes out the door, tray in hand. "Well, I said I'd ask! What else can I do?"

She's going to report me straight to Kerstin One. But Kerstin One will postpone her reaction.

I smile to myself and prepare to wait.

OVER AT THE Post-Industrial Paradise, Christina sits down to break-fast, suppressing a sigh. This was supposed to be the first breakfast of her time to herself, a breakfast she'd been dreaming about for ages. But somehow there's no whiskey marmalade, no cheddar cheese, no little white rolls. And definitely no peace and quiet.

Her egg looks strange, semisoft-boiled, semipoached. The shell must have cracked while it was boiling; the white's run out and is hanging on the outside like foam at the mouth. That egg looks like it has rabies. In addition to which, in an attack of misguided overambition, Margareta has made eight slices of toast. They're in the breadbasket, cold and obviously scraped.

"I prefer to make my toast at the table," says Christina with a cautious smile. Margareta shrugs her shoulders; making breakfast has turned her sullen, and just now she doesn't give a flying fuck about Christina's veiled criticism of her culinary skills.

"So, are you going to stick around for a few hours' sleep?" Christina asks, spreading a thin layer of butter on her fresh toast. The butter is full of black spots. Margareta's just buttered one of the scraped slices.

Both of them gaze silently down into the sooty butter until Margareta finally answers. "Yes, if you don't mind. But I'll be leaving around midday."

Christina nods gravely. "I'll give you a key then, so you can lock the door when you leave. You can leave it in one of the conch shells in the yard."

Margareta grimaces. "The ones by the back door?"

"Right. I bought them a couple of years ago when Erik and I were in Bali. They were a job to get home in one piece."

Margareta gives a tiny snort. "You mean they're real?"

Christina looks up, shocked. "What else would they be?"

Margareta sneers, reaching for her cigarettes, her half-eaten toast on her plate. "How do you like that?" she says, clicking her lighter. "I was sure they were plastic."

And at that very moment, when it is finally Christina's turn to be sarcastic, the phone rings. She is needed at the nursing home. Right away.

KERSTIN ONE COMES more quickly than I'd expected. She's wearing rubber-soled sandals, so I don't hear her approaching, either. The door of my room just blows open, and there she is.

The extraordinary thing about beautiful women is that they don't actually have faces. Think of how they're portrayed in advertisements, for instance. The loveliest of the lovely has no facial features at all, she's just a set of freely hovering eyes and a hint of a mouth.

That applies to Kerstin One as well. Although she does have a nose, cheeks, and a chin, her bright eyes and her perfectly shaped lips dominate her face so fully that you don't see anything else. Now she raises her lovely arched eyebrows in my direction and glues her shining gaze to my wretchedness. "Have you got new bedsores?"

I snap at the mouthpiece. "No, not yet."

"I thought you told Ulrika you had bedsores."

"Who's Ulrika?"

"The nurse's aide who brought in your breakfast. She said you were complaining about bedsores."

"I never said that. What I said was I get bedsores from not showering."

"We're too understaffed to do any showers today."

"But I haven't had a shower in a whole week!"

"Sorry about that. But I can hardly be blamed for the fact that we're underbudgeted. However, what I can do is see to it that you get taken out to the common room. Being in your wheelchair is the best way of preventing bedsores. And it's Picture Bingo day besides. Plus a visiting choral society."

My convulsions redouble; my head jerks so hard I can hardly keep the mouthpiece between my lips. Still, I manage to puff out a choppy protest:

"I couldn't care less about Picture Bingo. Nor am I interested in hearing a chorus. I want a shower!"

Kerstin One waits patiently till I'm done blowing. Then she smiles. "You'll enjoy yourself once we get you out there. Maybe you'll even win the orange today. Besides which, we need to change your room around. We're going to give you a little change of scenery!"

The mouthpiece glides out of my mouth and slips aside. I'm struggling against my spasms and trying to snatch it back at the same time. But Kerstin One is in no hurry, just stands at the edge of my bed with that cordial smile on her face watching me snap at thin air, time after time.

When I finally get a grip on the mouthpiece, I'm too tired to puff more than the essentials: "Change of scenery?"

Kerstin One's smile broadens. "Right. You're going to move in with another patient. Won't that be fun?"

I blow a long puff: "No!"

Kerstin One's voice deepens as she leans forward and tucks in my covers. "What a shame. I thought you'd be glad to have some company."

She straightens up, crossing her arms over her chest. "I'm really sorry, then. But there's nothing to be done about it. We have to rearrange the ward so Folke in two gets a private room. He's not well at all, and his whole family is going to arrive soon. So we're giving him your room and putting you in with little Maria."

I'm biting the mouthpiece now, knowing very well that I might chomp a hole in the pipe, in which case I won't be able to speak until Kerstin Two and her shift come on duty. Or maybe not even until Hubertsson comes in tomorrow morning. I panic at the thought, but I'm completely unable to open my jaws and let go. I puff: "With whom?"

My words blink on the monitor. Kerstin One looks quickly up on her way out the door. With one hand on the handle she stops, waving with her other. "You know, little Maria. The girl with Down's syndrome. She's such a sweetie, mongoloids always are. The salt of the earth, you know. Always kind and gentle. You could learn a lot from her!"

White flashes blind me, a cramp that is more than spastic inscribes my body. I close my eyes. It's dark over at the horizon. The storm is approaching and I have no choice but to surrender to its force.

Pump Twin

. . . and said to yourself in the bathroom,
I am not the favorite child.
My darling, when it comes
right down to it
and the light fails and the fog rolls in
and you're trapped in your overturned body
under a blanket or a burning car,

and the red flame is seeping out of you
and igniting the tarmac beside your head
or else the floor, or else the pillow
none of us is;
or else we all are.

Margaret Atwood

"Nursing home?" says Margareta. "I thought you worked at a community health center."

Christina's flapping around the kitchen looking for her keys. She's already got her cape on. "I do. But in my capacity as GP I have nursing home patients, too."

She finds the key ring on the counter by the stove and starts to ease a key off. But her fingers won't do as she wishes, and she grows blood red with effort.

"Give it here," says Margareta from the kitchen table. "I'll do it."

Christina buttons her cape while she waits for Margareta to coax off the key. It takes only a second.

"There you go." Margareta returns the key ring to Christina, putting the back door key on the table. For one moment they both look at it, Aunt Ella's voice echoing in their heads: *Never put keys on the table! It's bad luck.* Margareta grabs the key and stuffs it into her jeans pocket with a smile.

"Okay," says Christina, in less of a hurry suddenly, almost reluctant. "Okay. Be well, then. We'll be in touch, I guess . . ."

Margareta makes a little face. "Yeah, I guess so. You take care of yourself, too."

"Are you going to the cemetery?"

Margareta nods. "If I can get there before dark."

"What about Birgitta?"

"Well, I guess she's had her fun and games for this time."

There's a moment of silence; then Christina clears her throat. "All right then. I'll be in touch. Got to get going now . . ."

Suddenly she looks as if she's about to take a step in Margareta's

direction, to touch her. But Margareta halts her by shooting a huge puff
of smoke her way.

"ERIK," CHRISTINA SAYS to herself as she turns the key in the ignition. No response. She often finds herself saying his name aloud, not because she misses him but because the thought of him steadies her. And
just now she needs steadying. It's as if the events of the past day and night
have moved a curtain aside—an iron gray velvet curtain, a billowing iron
curtain—and revealed the past. She'd forgotten this when she was happy
Erik was going away, that he's her curtain man, the person who helps her
live as if there were no past. In his proximity, what is over and done with
is dead; when he is out of reach, it begins to live and breathe.

But this time she doesn't intend to comply. She's no longer a child, no
longer an adolescent, and the past is past. The Christina Wulf who is here
today has nothing to do with the old Christina. Her birth took place at
Lund University, at the very second in late 1960s world history when the
world itself jolted and changed gears. Someone rolled an egg into a dormitory room, and a few hours later it began to hatch. By the middle of the
night the shell was cracked all the way around and it split open. A young
woman stepped out.

From the very first moment she was what she was meant to be: a serious, focused individual who sat down at the desk and opened her books
at the stroke of eight every morning. Very occasionally she would set her
books aside late in the afternoon, pull out a sheet of pale blue stationery,
and write a letter to a foster mother she once met in a different life. It
always said the same things: I'm fine and saving money so I can come
see you at Christmas. She seldom received an answer, but there were
other letters in her mailbox. They were often postmarked Norrköping.
She crumpled those letters up and threw them in the wastepaper basket
unopened. She didn't know anybody in Norrköping. She was newly born
and living in Lund.

"You can choose your life," she often said to herself in those days. "You
don't just have to take what you get."

But now she's been grown up for a long time, has made her choice and
lives in Vadstena. She's a person with obligations and responsibilities,
who has neither the time nor the freedom to poke around in the past. She
turns the key in the ignition again. The engine responds only with a half-
hearted cough. Two red lights on the dashboard come on. The oil and the

battery. Christina runs her hand through her hair. She's perspiring, and her glasses are suddenly fogging up.

"Relax," she says aloud to herself, forcing her eyes to close. She turns the key once more, and the miracle occurs: the engine responds with a friendly putter. It's working. She casts a quick glance at her watch. Seven minutes have passed since the phone rang. It will take her another eight to get there. She'll make it in time.

Of course Christina knows Folke in the nursing home is dying. She cannot save him. He's developed his final case of pneumonia, that fatal pneumonia that releases everyone with senile dementia sooner or later. Folke isn't actually demented, though, just sick unto death of old age. When all the energy in his body was gradually draining away, he just shut down his senses voluntarily, no longer wanting to see, hear, or speak. There's nothing Christina can do about that, except to wish him bon voyage.

In fact, she doesn't really have to go to the nursing home at all. She could have settled on prescribing morphine over the phone and gone back to the breakfast table. Other doctors do it that way. But Christina is unable to; she knows that if she did she would spend the rest of the day battling her guilt-ridden fantasies about Folke's last hours of suffering. That's what's worrying her about not getting there in time, too. She is afraid of the way his family will look at her, not to mention that blond ward nurse, the one who phoned. Kerstin One, they call her. She makes Christina nervous, gives her the feeling that she realizes how uncomfortable Christina is in her professional role.

Yes, that's the truth. She's not happy with her profession. She made the wrong choice. And she's known it for ages. Ever since the day she saw Erik for the first time, in fact.

She just happened into a talk he was giving. He was a freckle-faced Ph.D. student, noticeably unaccustomed to public speaking. To begin with he was on edge; his eyes were jumpy and he kept falling silent. Gradually, though, his fascination with his subject vanquished his discomfort. *Agenesia cordis!* An extremely rare disorder, only one case in every 35,000 pregnancies.

Christina was only listening with one ear. Nothing he had said up to this point had triggered a feeling in her that this was important. Interesting, possibly, but nothing a newly certified GP needed. Moreover, she wasn't used to sitting still anymore; she'd spent the last few months running from patient to patient, from night to day duty, from hospital ward to community health center, from nursing home to geriatric facility.

Her astonishment, that sense of surprise she had had for the entire first year over the fact that she'd made it, had begun to fade. That she, Christina Martinsson, was actually a registered M.D. When she caught a glimpse of her own reflection—a gray little woman in a white coat with a stethoscope in her pocket—in some shiny black winter window, she was no longer surprised. On the contrary, she'd begun exchanging ironic little glances with herself. Right you are! Here comes the doctor.

But there were fewer and fewer moments of triumph. She'd begun to realize how naïve she had been. Year after year she'd plowed deep into her textbooks, passionately focused on what she wanted. Her studies had followed her into sleep, and she'd often woken up in the night from wild dreams about mysterious patients. But that was only normal. In the mornings she had just washed those dreams right out of her hair and dived straight into the facts for the new day. One morning, she used to think, I'll wake up and be a doctor and everything will be different. Above all, she would be different. All the quicksand inside her would dry up and become solid; she'd be firmly molded, invincible, strong as a concrete pillar.

And that morning did come, but the miracle refused to happen. Twelve months of mornings had come and gone since, but there had been no transformation. And Christina had begun to realize that it was not until now—after eleven years of study and training—that she had to choose her profession. She'd had to become an M.D. first, in order to know whether or not she really wanted to be a doctor.

But why? What had made it so important?

It was Astrid, of course. And Ella. She'd become a doctor for both her mothers.

Christina let her head fall forward, completely ignoring the young speaker. Yes, that was the truth. Not that Astrid or Ella had ever imagined she could possibly succeed. Ella had been hesitant, expressed deep concern during her long illness over the fact that Christina had decided to study medicine, and Astrid had been openly sardonic. The first time Christina dared mention it to her, she'd just snorted and mumbled that pride goeth before a fall. In spite of which Astrid was one of the reasons. In her world doctors—all doctors—possessed magical powers, in the face of which she was altered into a perfectly ordinary little old lady, an anxious old woman who smiled ingratiatingly and watched her tongue. And that was how Christina wanted to see her. Never any other way. Only like that.

This profession was an escape, a way of getting away. But Astrid wouldn't let her go. She'd planted a little seed in Christina, a little seed of loathing that secretly took root during her years of medical school, and burst into full bloom when she got her first job. Now she had to hide her disgust with the bodies that paraded past her: hairy thighs and pasty stomachs, women's sagging breasts and old men's wrinkled rumps, stinking unhealed wounds and foul-smelling genitals.

The flesh is its own castigation. But a physician is freed, clean and uncontaminated; she hovers over the imperfections of others, so high that the decay can never reach her . . .

Oh, yes. Once again, Christina looked up at the young lecturer. She'd remain a doctor. Because of the hovering. And because of Aunt Ella, because she'd smiled that distorted smile of hers, painstakingly placed both her hands over Christina's hand the first time Christina stood at her bedside in the nursing home in her white coat, stethoscope poised.

The young speaker was fumbling nervously up at the podium, pulling down a screen, and readying a slide projector. Christina straightened up like a schoolgirl with a guilty conscience, trying to look attentive. The lights in the lecture hall dimmed, it got dark, the first slide came up on the screen. A placenta. The vascular tree had been filled with methylene blue, and the pointer fluttered over the slide, hunting for the artery.

"The etiology is still uncertain, but one theory is that it may be a vascular deformity early in pregnancy which leads to the weaker twin's being supplied with already circulated blood via the umbilical cord. . . . But this supply reaches the lower half of the body first, which accounts for its being—as we'll see in a moment—somewhat better developed . . ."

He activated the next slide. It sent a silent chill through the hall. At first Christina couldn't figure out what she was seeing. She blinked and straightened her glasses, then found her hand involuntarily and ever so unprofessionally covering her mouth. She forced it down to her lap, to turn the page of her notebook as if she were preparing to write something very important, although she wrote nothing at all.

The slide was of a tiny body attached to an umbilical cord and with skimpy, incomplete growths instead of legs. An infant with neither head nor arms, a little lump of flesh with ruddy skin. There was no question

but that it was human. But only half a human being. The top half was perfectly smooth, soft and gently rounded where the neck and head should
have been.

The speaker stood alongside the slide projector, letting the picture sink
in before continuing: "In the literature, the phenomenon has been referred to as the *acardiac* monster, the heartless monster. That's quite correct in that there is no heart, in fact, but it's a term I prefer to avoid
because I think it sounds a bit—well—sensationalist."

He went on to the next slide, which showed the same creature from a
different angle. Now a virtuous little flap of skin appeared between the
two growths that should have been legs. The pointer fluttered over it.

"The deformed child and the able-bodied twin are always the same
sex. Usually girls, although the reason for that overrepresentation is not
known. Pump twin mortality rates are high, because as the pregnancy
continues the demands on the blood supply increase, which also poses
problems for the pump twin . . ."

Many years later, when their own twin girls were already school age,
Christina realized one night that she must have misunderstood Erik. Impulsively, she reached out a hand and gave him a shake, in violation of the
sacred nature of his sleep, which had always been a feature of their
marriage. "Erik," she whispered in the dark bedroom. "Erik!"

It took a while for him to answer; he grunted and turned away. But
Christina went on shaking him by the shoulder. "Hey, I just need to ask
you something."

He opened his eyes and turned sleepily toward her. "What's wrong?"

"Do you remember the lecture where we met? When you were talking
about the heartless monster? Remember?"

"Mmmm. What about it?"

"You talked about the *pump twin,* didn't you? But which twin did you
mean? The able-bodied one? Or the other thing?"

He concealed his irritation under a little laugh. "My God, Christina,
what a thing to ask in the middle of the night. I was talking about the
able-bodied fetus, of course. You can hear it in the name: the pump twin
pumps blood into the deformed one."

"Oh," said Christina. "I see. Thanks. You go back to sleep now."

"What made you ask?"

"Never mind, it just came into my mind. The term itself. I've always
imagined the other one as the pump twin."

He was half asleep now, but still infallibly polite and interested. "How could you?"

Christina retracted her hand and crawled deeper under the covers, shutting her eyes tightly to drive away that old image.

"Aw," she said, "I always thought it looked like a pumpkin."

"Sleep tight," he said.

"You, too," said Christina.

ASTRID HATED THE way they talked to each other, the fact that they said *thank you* and *after you* and *sleep tight* and *be well*. When she arrived, uninvited, for her first and only visit to their home, she made her opinion perfectly clear. "You put on airs," she said in her heavy southern Swedish accent. "You sound so damn highfalutin and uppity. Why don't you just say what you mean, straight out? Do you really have to act so stupid? Aren't you a married couple? Why don't you talk like one?"

Christina had expected this open hostility, she'd been preparing her reaction for months and years. Her line was well rehearsed and on the tip of her tongue, yet she was completely silent for a moment. Instead of saying anything, she just clamped her mouth into a tight little minus sign, whisking away her mother's half-full coffee cup. Silent and rigid, she carried it over to the kitchen sink.

"Hey, miss," shouted Astrid behind her back. "I was still working on that coffee."

Christina froze, turned back around, cup in hand, staring wide-eyed at her mother.

Astrid was gesticulating with her cold blue hands. "Have the blinking courtesy to put my cup back down in front of me and provide me with an ashtray, thank you."

"You can't smoke in here. Erik won't have it."

"Aha," said Astrid, lighting up. "His Majesty the Great Thinker hath commanded. . . . Well, you can just open the window, you know."

Her floppy breasts were sagging under her like half-full bags of marbles as she reached across the kitchen table. She worked at the hooks long and demonstratively, opening the window wide, then falling back awkwardly into her chair with a little huff. She inhaled deeply and pleasurably on her cigarette, then banged the spot on the table where her coffee cup had been.

Christina slammed the half-full cup back down in front of her and took a deep breath. Her voice had to be steady when she delivered the Reply. "It is no more honest to shout and scream at people than it is to speak kindly. But you've always thought there was only one real feeling: anger."

Christina had clearly underestimated her opponent. Astrid gave her a look that smashed the Reply to smithereens. "Kiss my ass!" she said. "You sound like a refrain straight off the damned hit parade, do you realize that? *'Say sweet words of love, dear, and saaaay them with a smile'!*"

Christina just stood there by the kitchen table, still erect and firm, but with the old fear fluttering in the pit of her stomach.

Astrid bent forward and, quick as a salamander, grabbed her wrist with those blue fingers, giving it a tight little twist, not hard but just enough to really hurt without leaving a trace. Her breathing was shallow, her voice clear, but softer than usual, almost a whisper: "And don't you get on your high horse with me, girl. You could never have become a doctor or a fancy wife if I hadn't let you—"

At that very moment Erik opened the front door and shouted hello. Coat hangers rattled in the hall.

He's hanging his jacket up, Christina thought.

Astrid's grip tightened. Something hit the floor.

He's taking off his shoes. Oh, Erik, get in here, please!

Paper rustling, he was checking the mail. Astrid twisted a little harder, rubbing her daughter's skin against her wristbones, attentively examining her reaction. Eyes glazed. But no resistance. Christina had displayed resistance only once in her life, and what happened that time had taught her never to do so again.

"Hello?" shouted Erik again. "Hello, anybody home?"

He moved in the direction of the kitchen. Christina blinked, looking her mother straight in the eye. Astrid snorted deprecatingly, but she was the one who looked down. She let go and pushed Christina's hand aside with a childishly sullen gesture.

"Hi," said Erik from the kitchen door. He was smiling, he hadn't seen.

Astrid stubbed her cigarette out quickly, wiped her brow, and looked away. Christina's eyes flickered as she looked from one to the other, narrowing in triumph when she looked at Astrid, widening and glittering when she smiled at Erik. "Goodness, hello, dear. I didn't hear you come in."

My husband, she thought, relaxing into his embrace. I actually have a husband.

*　*　*

SHE'S NEVER TOLD him he's the only man she's ever been to bed with, in fact the only man she's ever kissed. When he sat down beside her at dinner at that very first conference, she stiffened, and a few weeks later, when he phoned and asked her to the theater, she had to go into the bathroom and throw up after she'd said yes. Not because he was distasteful, but because it was such an enormous thing to be noticed by a man.

Throughout that spring, with its dinners, concerts, and plays, her hymen became thicker and less penetrable. Ten years earlier it would have been acceptable, five years ago slightly comical, now it was something to be ashamed of. This was a new age, an age in which a woman was considered defective if she had never given herself to a man and was almost thirty.

The night before Midsummer's Eve, she burst into anxious tears as she was packing her new leather suitcase full of carefully ironed summer clothes. What good would it do her that her best cotton dress smelled of the wind and the seaside? What good would it do that her newly polished nails were shiny as mother-of-pearl and that she'd had her hair cut in a new, very becoming style? This was the time it was meant to happen, she knew it. Otherwise, Erik would never have invited her to celebrate midsummer at his parents' vacation home in the archipelago.

Much of what she knew she was in for, she was also prepared to tolerate: the condescending way in which people who had been born into money treated a newcomer, the tactful questions his sisters would ask about her family, the way his parents would raise their eyebrows at her curt answers. At those times, Erik would be at her side, she knew it; he had already begun to tell ironic little jokes about his mother's nervous way of mentioning "Christina's worrisome background." But would he be able to tolerate her virginity? Or would it put him off, make him shy away and recoil? Or even turn his back on her in contempt?

Afterward, she thought about it as her body's having made an independent decision. Her right hand suddenly reached out and pulled down the blinds, her feet carried her over to the dresser, where her right hand picked up her hand mirror and her left hand undid her skirt, letting it fall to the floor. One hand shoved her suitcase aside, the other drew down her panties. Her right leg rose of its own accord, her foot setting itself on the edge of her bed, and the three middle fingers of her right hand shaped themselves into a surgical instrument. Her eyes allowed themselves to shut.

Afterward she reached for the hand mirror and looked between her legs. It was like examining the genitals of a strange woman and, yes, there appeared to be every indication that this woman had had some—probably limited—sexual experience. There wasn't much blood. A quick wash would remove every trace. And what she had just done would never have happened.

On her way to the bathroom she happened to look at the fingers of her right hand. There were thick lines of red blood around her cuticles and in the creases on her knuckles. She reeled with nausea, nearly losing her balance. She caught herself on the wall, used it to take the few steps to the bathroom, shut the door without turning on the light, groped in the darkness for the cold-water tap, and rinsed and rinsed and rinsed her fingers until they were so cold they were numb.

And still somehow, when Erik parked outside her building the next morning, she ran lightly down the steps. It was a gorgeous day: the sky above Vadstena was as blue as the Virgin Mary's gown, the birches gleamed in the sun, the air was easy to breathe.

"You're looking awfully cheerful," Erik said suspiciously, embracing her on the sidewalk. "What's going on?"

Christina hurried to reduce her smile to a more appropriate size. "Nothing special," she said, in her usual reserved tone of voice. "I'm just feeling really good today is all."

Because I have a man, she thought for the first time in her life. I've paid the price and now I actually have a man!

No one at Aunt Ella's, including Christina, ever expected Christina to get herself a man. In puberty, she bore the burden of her femininity with a grimace, attempting at regular intervals to shed it. Christina was the one who was nauseated and in terrible pain when she had her period, who rolled on the floor in agony once a month, and who then, clammy and trembling, had to be tucked in under a layer of blankets with a hot-water bottle. Margareta and Birgitta just teased their beehive hairdos and prepared to conquer the world as only young women can.

It was a terrible time. Christina would lie in bed on lovely summer evenings trying to warm her icy hands on the hot glass bottle wrapped in a heavy woolen sock Aunt Ella had filled and put under her covers, eyes tightly closed, trying to recall better days: the last day of school in first grade, when she brought home her first award, downy Sunday mornings in the kitchen, the butter melting on Aunt Ella's home-baked breakfast rolls, playing in the cherry tree in the yard on quiet summer evenings.

Being a little girl at Aunt Ella's had been easy. Simple, calm times. All you had to do was eat your meals, do as you were told, and allow yourself to be looked after. In that order. None of these things was difficult for Christina. She liked the taste of Aunt Ella's cooking, she understood how she was supposed to behave, being looked after was a pleasure. Whereas Birgitta screamed protests when Aunt Ella insisted on scrubbing her face before dinner, Christina leaned longingly toward Aunt Ella when her turn came. Birgitta used to complain that Aunt Ella was rough, but Christina liked being held firmly. At the children's home one of the nurses had been very gentle when she touched the children, and Christina had screamed hysterically the minute that nurse approached her: she screamed and shouted until the nurse finally lost patience and grabbed her roughly. That was when Christina would let herself be washed. But she would go on screaming, just to be on the safe side.

That was one of the few things she remembered from the home, that and a large room with tall windows and rows of beds. In her memory, everything was white: the walls, the beds, the light filtering in through the branches of the trees outside. On occasion, however, an instant snapshot would flash through her mind: a little boy hugging his one-legged teddy bear, a little girl in a coat and boots turning around to look at Christina as she walked out the door, a toddler crying because someone had taken her security blanket. My blanket, my blanket, I want my little blankie. But these were pointless, incomprehensible memories, nameless, contextless, and unvoicable.

That was true of the hospital, too. All she could remember was the rustle of whispering voices, and white fingers inserting the hypodermic needle into the vial. Oh, yes, she also remembered one complete person, a single one of the other patients on the public ward where she ended up. That was a heavy old woman who talked incessantly, and who was in constant motion, walking from bed to bed, commenting loudly on the state of health of the other patients and their treatments. She was particularly interested in the five-year-old child with the burns.

The worst part was the thirst. There were shots to dull the pain, injections that allowed Christina to hover high above the hurt, but there was nothing to cure the thirst. The nurses in their white uniforms at the edge of reality said the drip would make her feel better, but it didn't. Her tongue grew thick, and was covered with heavy mucus, her lips cracked, and her throat swelled so every breath became a hiss. In the end, her thirst plagued even those who had to see her, and drove them to place a bowl of water at her bedside. A bowl of water with bits of gauze. The idea was for Christina to wipe her lips with the compresses, to ease her suffering. But time and again the white-clad creatures would bend down over her, urging: *You may wet your lips, but you mustn't suck the water. Whatever you do, don't suck at it.*

Of course she did. But she sucked ever so quietly, so no one would notice. She seized a compress with her able hand and wiped her mouth just like the nurses had told her to do, but she also clandestinely opened her lips under the gauze, searching the loosely woven compress with the tip of her tongue. And suddenly it became a living thing, a greedy little animal with a will of its own, forcing her to suck every single drop of water out of it.

An instant later something stinky and yellow rose up from her innards, her body contracted in cramps, the fire in her burns began to flame anew. But when she opened her eyes to air the pain, the fat woman was standing over her bed, wagging her index finger. "I saw you," she said. "You were sucking on it. It's your own fault."

Christina's mouth clamped shut, and she swallowed her tears.

"That's right," the woman repeated. "I saw you do it. I know it's all your fault."

And deep inside Christina's mind, a shrill voice joined in. "You see, you damn kid? It's your own fault. Whatever happens it's your own fault."

THE BLACK IRON gate creaked as Sister Inga closed it behind her. "Come along," she said, reaching for Christina's hand. She had bright blue mittens on, exactly the same shade as her coat. Christina, by contrast, was wearing a light brown coat with pea green mittens. She could see it was ugly; during their long, silent walk, the colors had grown hard and sharp-edged, they hurt her eyes as if she had dust in them. If only she had known how to make the world as black, white, and gray as a photograph, she would have done it.

"Come on, don't be shy," Sister Inga said, reaching for her hand again. "She's my sister-in-law, you know. And she's very, very nice."

But Christina's soft, pliant hand wouldn't stay in Sister Inga's. It was too soft to hold. The little girl was like an ice sculpture on the gravel path leading up to the house, and she didn't seem to hear. Because now it had finally happened, she had stepped into that photograph. This garden looked exactly, in every detail, like the black-and-white world she had created in her mind. Everything was correct: the vague light, the white haze, the black branches of the fruit trees against the gray sky, the melting glaze of frost icing the lawn. This was a yard for girls like herself. A garden for ice princesses.

Sister Inga took her hand firmly and pulled her along. "Come on, now. There's nothing to be afraid of."

The steps up to the door were huge. And of stone. Not at all like the wooden stairs leading up to the porch in front of the children's home. These steps didn't creak when you stepped on them; they were heavy and implacable, like a mountain waiting to be climbed. Freshly shoveled, too. There was a layer of new snow on the red roof tiles, but it had been removed from the steps.

Sister Inga rang the bell and opened the door at the same time, shepherding Christina ahead of her into the little vestibule. It was of stone, too, the floor gray and shiny, the walls pale green and porous. It looked like a hospital, a little stone hospital.

Sister Inga quickly slipped off her galoshes, the thin layer of rubber that had protected her high-heeled dress shoes against the impending winter outside. Just as quickly, she helped Christina out of her rubber boots. Then she knocked firmly on the brown wooden inner door and opened it.

"Hi!" she called into the apartment. "Hi there! Anybody home?"

The sounds coming from inside made Christina's spine tingle. The radio signal indicating the beginning of the hour, and the hissing of something in a frying pan. Both were sounds she had learned to detest in the tiled kitchen of the children's home, nervous, rushed noises. Sounds as saturated with unhappiness as lumpy powdered milk in a stainless steel institutional mug.

Here, though, someone turned the radio right off and lifted the frying pan from the burner. Here there was room for human voices.

"SHE EATS LIKE a bird," said Sister Inga, lifting a strand of hair off Christina's face, opening her barrette and clasping it again. "Doesn't say much either. Hardly makes a sound except to weep."

The woman across the table looked for a split second straight into Christina's gray eyes. "Never mind," she said. "There's quite enough talking in this world already."

The girl sitting next to her lay her cheek for one moment against her upper arm. "You talk, Aunt Ella. You talk all the time."

Ella gave the tip of her nose a little tweak. "Oh my," she said. "That nose of yours is in other people's business again, Margareta!"

The little girl giggled and took a deep draft from her glass of milk.

She'd eaten eleven meatballs, Christina had counted. Eleven! And there was still a whole mountain of meatballs left in the serving dish over on the counter. She herself had eaten only one single meatball, then set her fork aside with as much determination as ever, preparing to counter Sister Inga's attempts at coercion. On one point, though, she had conceded: she'd drunk her glass of milk almost to the dregs. Because this was real milk, you could tell, not that awful powder mixed with tap water.

"I hope you don't mind," said Sister Inga, "our turning up uninvited like this. There were only four children who didn't get taken out for Christmas, so we thought we might just as well take them home ourselves and close the place for the holidays. The matron took two and Brita and I one each. . . . It was the only way we could get to celebrate Christmas ourselves this year."

She stopped, stroking Christina's brow once more. "And she's so sweet. She won't be any trouble."

Ella smiled gently from across the way, in her flowery housedress, her doughy arms heavy on the tabletop. "No trouble," she said. "I don't mind at all."

LATER THAT DAY Christina was alone in Aunt Ella's living room. The nubbly sofa cover rubbed her thighs slightly, she didn't have any woolen bloomers to cover the area between where her panties ended and her stockings began.

The house was perfectly silent. Sister Inga and Margareta had gone to the market square to buy a Christmas tree. They'd begged Christina to come along, but she had shaken her head stubbornly, going all limp. Sister Inga had been unable to force her into her coat.

"Let her stay here with me, then," Aunt Ella had finally said, and after a steady stream of criticism and excuses, Sister Inga had given in.

So now she was sitting bolt upright on the couch looking around. She liked this room, where the colors harmonized rather than fighting and screeching and trying to do one another in. The pale yellow curtains gently complemented the deep gray sofa; the full golden nuances in the rug played against the brown of a low sideboard along the wall. Above the sideboard hung a big painting, portraying a forest in autumn colors. She was tempted by it. Perhaps she'd wander into the painting and become an autumn princess instead of an ice princess. . . . No, she wanted to stay in this room, in this house, in this silence that seemed only to be deepened by the steady ticking of the clock on the wall.

Suddenly there was Aunt Ella in the arched doorway, still wearing her flowery housedress. The face under her dark hair was broad and square, pale arms crossed over heavy breasts. Her glasses had slipped down her nose, and there was a white ball of cotton in one nostril.

"Candy?" she offered, squinting over the tops of her frames and pulling a bag of sweets out of her pocket.

"Silk pillows," she said, as if that explained something, sinking down next to Christina in an armchair. Christina bent carefully forward, look-ing down into the bag. The pieces of candy did look like silk cushions: shimmery and shiny in pale satin tones. Pink, lilac, baby blue.

"Help yourself," said Aunt Ella, shaking the bag.

Christina formed a tongs of her thumb and index finger and put her hand carefully into the bag. The silk pillows were a little sticky, and she had to pry loose the prettiest one. It was pale lilac.

"Have a few," said Aunt Ella, shaking the bag again. "Get in the Christ-mas spirit!"

Christina put her hand in again; this time a whole lump of candy came up out of the bag. Four sticky silk pillows. She held her breath, her eyes glued to Aunt Ella's face. Would she shout at her now?

But Aunt Ella didn't shout, she didn't even look at the lump of candies, just closed the bag and put it back in her pocket. Then she leaned back in the high-backed armchair, gazing at the painting across the room. For one moment she looked as if she, too, was considering going into the for-est of the autumn princess.

"Oh me, oh my." She sighed. "Life can be tough."

At that very moment the thin shell on the silk pillow in Christina's mouth broke. Creamy sweetness spread across her tongue. Oh, yes. Now she remembered. This was the taste of chocolate.

OUTSIDE, DARKNESS WAS falling, and dusk crept inside, too. It wasn't going to be a white Christmas; the snowy haze of the morning had turned more or less into rain. It didn't matter. Christmas was coming, and she could just as well wait for it sitting quietly in Aunt Ella's living room, silently watching the raindrops run down the panes of the shiny black windows.

She didn't talk. That was what made her so unusual: never before had Christina met an adult who could sit still for a long time and say nothing. All the other grown-ups were so busy talking that they never took time to think, but here was a woman who just sat where she was, with one nos-tril stuffed with cotton and her mouth agape. But she wasn't sleeping: her gray eyes were clear and wide open.

Then, suddenly, there were the sounds of Sister Inga's laughter and Margareta's voice out in the vestibule. The apartment door opened, and in tumbled Margareta, her feet in thick woolen socks and her coat but-

tons undone. Aunt Ella put both hands on the armrests and heaved herself up, extended her arms toward Margareta, and helped her out of her
coat, laughed at her babbling and ruffled her hair.

Christina turned away and looked out the window, following its shiny
surface. A thought fluttered past and struck her with astonishment. Everything would have been different if I had been able to speak.

It was the first time. She'd never had that thought before.

BUT HER VOICE didn't come back instantly just because she willed it
to do so, nor had it vanished because she had willed it to. Such things like
that happen in their own way.

Margareta, though, didn't seem to notice that Christina didn't talk. She
filled the house with her own voice, the words flowed out of her mouth
like drops of mercury, rolling across the floor and disappearing into the
corners before you knew it.

When they had decorated the tree, she took Christina with her. Finally,
she was going to show her the whole house: the dark basement with its
cement gray laundry room and pale green bathroom, the stone steps and
the upstairs hall, the brown door to the apartment upstairs where Aunt
Ella's lodger lived. And the attic, of course, the most important place of
all. Christina took a deep breath when she stuck her head up through the
trapdoor; it smelled good up here. Dust, wood chips, and planks.

"It's instead of a playhouse," Margareta said, approaching a little set of
furniture over by the window along the gable side. "Uncle Hugo planned
to build a playhouse, but he died before he could even get started . . .
though he did make the furniture."

Suddenly Margareta and Christina seemed to have become giants. The
furniture was too small for them; their buttocks overflowed the edges of
the wooden chairs, and they couldn't get their knees under the table.

"He made this furniture for some really little kid," Margareta explained. "But it's mine now."

A LITTLE WHILE later they were back down in the apartment. Aunt
Ella had a three-bedroom apartment, and Margareta had a name for each
room: the big room, the little room, the dining room, and the empty room.

However, the empty room wasn't really empty: there was a bed and a
chest of drawers in it. Margareta didn't go in, just opened the door a

crack, never releasing the handle. "This is actually my room," she said. "Or it will be. When I start school . . . I sleep in Aunt Ella's bedroom now. In the little room."

Christina made a face. She'd never want to sleep in the same bed as a grown-up.

"Not in the same bed, of course," said Margareta, as if she were a mind reader. "It's a double trundle bed. There's a bed underneath Aunt Ella's, and we trundle it out at bedtime."

But there was no evidence in the little room that it was Margareta's room, too. The bed and an armchair, a linen cupboard and a sewing box, but not a single toy or storybook. At the children's home each child had a little cupboard to keep clothes and other things in. That wasn't what it was like here; Margareta's clothes were hanging in Aunt Ella's closet out in the hall. She'd seen that with her own eyes when Margareta had shown her around, big dresses and little ones on the same rod, all mixed up.

But Margareta didn't appear to be bothered by the fact that their things were all mixed up in the closet or that her presence in the little room was so invisible. She fluttered on out into the kitchen and opened another door. "The broom closet," she shouted. "This is where my toys are."

Christina took a cautious step forward and peered in. The broom closet wasn't a proper closet at all; it was a little nook with a white light-bulb suspended from the ceiling and an old rag rug on the floor. There was a sharp smell that Christina recognized. It was the same smell as at the children's home the days the floors looked all shiny. Floor wax.

It didn't take her long to know she liked being in the broom closet, sitting on the floor making Margareta's dolly bed while the grown-up women were doing things out in the kitchen. Aunt Ella wasn't making meatballs now, but something else was simmering in the black cast-iron skillet. Something that smelled of cabbage and vinegar.

Dinner wasn't even ready yet when bedtime came around. Christina and Margareta were served individual little plates of cocktail sausages and meatballs at the kitchen table, with Ella still at the stove and Sister Inga preparing homemade mustard. She was sitting with a bowl on her lap, and at the bottom of the bowl was a cast-iron ball that rolled heavily over mustard seeds, crushing them. The vapor made her eyes tear.

"You know, this is a real cannonball," she sniffled to the girls. "It belonged to Hugo's and my grandmother. We only use it to make the Christmas mustard, a family tradition."

Aunt Ella smiled awkwardly and extended a handkerchief. "Here, blow," she said with a little laugh. "You're dripping in the mustard!"

Christina listened with attentive fascination to that laugh that kept pouring out of Aunt Ella. It sounded like she must have a dove nesting in her throat, a little dove cooing with satisfaction as it settled down in the nest. She was so busy imagining the dove she forgot to think about what she was eating and had suddenly consumed everything on her plate: three cocktail sausages, four meatballs, and almost a whole slice of bread with cheese on it. Chewing the last bite, she was suddenly overcome with nausea. She opened her mouth and let the masticated bite fall to her plate. At that very instant the alien voice in her head woke up again: "You little brat, spoiled rotten. How can you spit out your dinner?"

Christina shut her eyes, waiting for the fire. But it didn't come. For the first time ever, her scars didn't flare up at the moment the voice appeared. She waited a moment more, then very carefully opened her eyes just the tiniest bit and peeped out. Sister Inga was wiping her eyes on the handkerchief, she hadn't even noticed. Margareta was gaping at Christina but not saying anything. And Aunt Ella set her hand very softly on Christina's head, running it gently over her hair, while her other hand was silently dropping the unswallowed bite of bread into the pocket of her housedress.

Sister Inga blew her nose and looked around. "Good heavens," she said. "I do believe Christina's joined the clean-plate club!"

And that was the end of the first day.

ON THE MORNING of the next day the rest of the family began to arrive. First there was Selma, Aunt Ella's aging mother, a bony woman in her best dress, as smooth and black as her face was white and wrinkled. She tipped up Margareta's chin, inspecting her dryly, then released her without a word and turned to Christina. "A new one?"

Sister Inga crossed and uncrossed her legs behind Christina's back. "Oh no, she's at the children's home where I work. We're just here for the holidays."

Selma shrugged. "Oh, all right then. Mind you, I don't have anything against children. As long as they behave. Otherwise they know where they can go—"

Sister Inga opened her mouth as if to comment, but at the same moment new voices were heard in the vestibule. Here they were: the main characters. The most important visitors of all.

Stig stood in the doorway with open arms, and one moment later there was Gunnar behind him in precisely the same pose. They had both unbuttoned their overcoats, exposing slightly yellowing shirtfronts in the latest nylon. Their voices thundered, filling the whole house.

"Here we are," bellowed Stig.

"Merry Christmas," hollered Gunnar.

Behind them flocked their families: each one's wife—Bitte was Stig's and Anita was Gunnar's—with a total of five sons with wet-combed hair in varying sizes. They all had those names ending with *e* that were so popular at the time, and slippery-sounding: Bosse, Kjelle, Lasse, Olle, and Ante.

"How nice to see you," said Aunt Ella.

Christina's eyes fluttered up toward her. Aunt Ella not only had exchanged her housedress for a dressy gray dress with a lace collar but also seemed to have changed to a voice in the same color and fashion.

Sister Inga had been transformed as well, but in a different way. She blushed eagerly as she reached out a hand toward Stig: "Hey, big brother. It's been ages . . ."

Stig shook her hand hastily and began working his way out of his coat. "Great to see you. How're things?"

"Fine, fine. And what about you? How's local politics?"

Stig quickly straightened his suit jacket. "Haven't you heard the latest? They made me chairman of the child welfare board in October."

Sister Inga's hand flew to her mouth, and now her transformation was complete. No longer a strict nurse in charge of the children at the home, now she was nothing but a little girl. "No kidding. That's amazing. Congratulations!"

Stig put his arm around Gunnar, pushing him toward Inga.

"And here we have the soon-to-be chairman of the Luxor local trade union. Next year they're sending him on a three-month union officials' training program, after which he'll be a shop steward before you can blink an eye, count on it."

"Aw," said Gunnar, jostling his brother playfully. "It's gonna take more than a training course before my mouth runs on like yours, anyway."

"We'll see about that," said Stig. "If I know you, you'll be a fast learner."

"Ooooh," said Sister Inga breathlessly. "Hugo should have seen you now! He would have been so proud."

*   *   *

CHRISTINA WOULD NEVER forget that first Christmas dinner at
Aunt Ella's. Nothing special really happened, nothing that would not
come to be tradition from one Christmas to the next or from one family
gathering to the next. Enormous quantities of food appeared as if by
magic and were consumed: herring, anchovy and potato casserole, spareribs and headcheese, meatballs and cocktail sausages, cheeses and pâtés,
ham and red cabbage. Malts and ales were passed from hand to hand
along both sides of the adults' table, and Stig—growing redder and redder
in the face and already down to his shirtsleeves and to having loosened
his tie—agreed to be in charge of pouring the schnapps. No bottles were
passed around at the children's table, however. Instead, next to each
child's plate was a whole bottle of Christmas cola. Christina was unable
to eat at all, but there was an alibi meatball and a single cocktail sausage
on her plate throughout. Not that she needed an alibi, she was barely visible during this first party at Aunt Ella's. That suited her perfectly. She
could watch without being observed, listen without being heard.

Actually, she wouldn't have been able to make herself heard even if she
had been able to speak. How could any little girl make herself heard
above the din arising from the collective vocal cords of this loud family?
She shut her eyes and listened. Over at the adults' table, Gunnar was
telling some story in an inebriated Saturday night voice. Selma cackled at
him with her piercing laugh. Stig joined in, pounding the table with a fist
and gasping for breath—*aaiih, aaiih, aaiih!* he sounded like a stuck pig—
as Bitte, Anita, and Inga released silver peals of laughter that rose toward
the ceiling like a flock of swallows. The boys at the children's table were
laughing, too, though none of them could possibly have heard the joke
or known what was so funny, and for one second Margareta's shrill voice
cut through the hubbub: "What was so funny? Come on! Tell us what
he said!"

Aunt Ella's little dove-coo was the only absent laugh. But she was
there: when Christina opened her eyes she could see Aunt Ella standing
in the doorway inspecting her guests. Christina's eyes were drawn involuntarily to Inga, Anita, and Bitte, their colorful dresses and glittering
hairdos, their shiny eyes. Aunt Ella was different, with her square face
and gray dress.

Now she cleared her throat, trying to attract their attention in all the
noise: "Hey, everybody! Listen up! Would you please go into the living
room now?"

After a lot more noise and laughter, Stig and Gunnar, leaders that they were, got up and put their arms around each other's shoulders. Like one big four-legged—if slightly reeling—creature, they approached Ella, separated wordlessly, and embraced her, sandwiched between them. The three of them stood there as if welded together, Hugo's widow and his younger brothers. A unit, a family.

"Best meal ever," said Stig.

Gunnar nodded in drunken gravity. "Fantashtic! Couldn't have been better . . ."

Aunt Ella giggled. "Right. And I thank you. Now get on out there and have some coffee and something from the sweets table."

She sounded just like she always did: secure, firm, and kind, but if you looked closely you could see her upper lip trembling just slightly. She looked strange. As if she were the visitor in the house.

THROUGHOUT HER ADULT life, Christina would wonder about the actual negotiations, what kind of clandestine meeting must have taken place at Aunt Ella's house sometime during those first Christmas holidays. The question she has asked herself so many times surfaces again as she swings into the parking lot: Who took the initiative? Was it Aunt Ella? Sister Inga? Or Stig?

She hopes it was Aunt Ella, wishes Aunt Ella had whispered into her brother-in-law's ear that this particular child was the one she wanted: this silent, skinny little girl with the ash blond hair. But that probably wasn't what happened. Aunt Ella was always on her guard about asking Hugo's relatives for anything. She suspected they felt that she'd already been given quite enough, that her marriage to Hugo had been too short, in reality, to justify her being the beneficiary of both his house and his life insurance policy.

It probably hadn't been Sister Inga either. She was too young at the time: far too young and blond and self-centered to be seriously interested in anyone else's destiny. She was never truly present, half of her was always elsewhere. Every now and then she would lose it altogether and take a few dreamy steps to a waltz no one but she could hear, allowing the wide skirt of her children's home uniform to sweep around her like a ball gown.

No, it had probably been Stig's idea for Christina to move, as it was a few years later for Birgitta.

"Pike-jowled Stig." Birgitta laughs somewhere in Christina's memory. Christina gives a little smile as she carefully wedges her car between two others in the staff lot. She's surprised that she hasn't thought about Birgitta's nickname for Aunt Ella's more prominent brother-in-law for so long. But suddenly she remembers it, and remembers as well Margareta's shrill laugh when Birgitta coined it. All she had done at the time was smile a pinched little smile that wouldn't expose her teeth. Christina never dared to laugh out loud when Birgitta called people by the nicknames she invented for them; she had every reason to suspect that somewhere at the back of her mind Birgitta was harboring a sarcastic nickname for her, too.

Well, pike-jowled or not, if Stig hadn't been a local politician, Christina would have ended up somewhere else. Probably with some Nonconformist church family in a rural village. Or on some muddy country farm. That was where kids from the children's homes usually eventually found themselves, back in the fifties. If they got taken in by a foster family at all. Some of the children had to spend years at the home, until a wild-eyed or tubercular parent could collect them.

Astrid was the wild-eyed variety, and had it not been for Stig she would have collected her daughter when the girl was only twelve. And that—Christina clamps her jaws tight in conviction—that would have cost her her life. Because not until she was taken in by Aunt Ella did her determination to live even awaken, and without a strong sense of determination, no one could survive in Astrid's proximity. So, in fact, it was no exaggeration to claim that pike-jowled Stig had saved Christina's life. "So even if he was laughable in some ways," she says aloud to herself as she unbuckles her seat belt, "he was admirable in more."

Over the years his admirable ways declined, however, and he grew slightly pathetic in his endless desire for importance and power, his need to be even more dignified than his dear departed brother. He never realized he was his own worst enemy. He drank too much, talked too much, and was far too partial to grandiose gestures ever to resemble Hugo.

So giving Aunt Ella a child in return for the fine Christmas dinner was a gesture very much in his style. Widows were permitted to take in foster children only in exceptional cases, but as chairman of the child welfare board, pike-jowled Stig would only have had to snap his fingers to make it happen. Not many other men in Motala could have done the same. And pike-jowled Stig—despite all his fine words about collective spirit and solidarity—did love to do things he knew no other man in Motala would be able to accomplish.

At some point during adolescence—when Ella was already at this very nursing home in Vadstena, in a hemiplegic state, and Christina herself had been banished to Astrid's concrete apartment in Norrköping—she realized for the first time that what was true of Birgitta might also have been true of her. Perhaps Aunt Ella had never really wanted to take her in, perhaps she had had no choice but to do Stig's bidding. It might very well be true. Aunt Ella had often sighed deeply over decisions made by pike-jowled Stig, but she never openly opposed them.

That idea struck her so suddenly and so physically she instinctively bent over her plate and let the bite of sausage she was chewing fall out. A little thread of saliva hung from her bottom lip for a moment. Astrid looked up from across the table, where she sat leafing through an old *Ladies' Home Journal*. "Sweet Jesus," she said softly, raising her blue fingers to remove her cigarette from the corner of her mouth. "You can be pretty damn disgusting. Do you know that?"

Christina shakes her head to drive away the picture of Astrid, but the curtain's wide open now and won't allow itself to be shut, so instead she finds herself remembering how Margareta was standing eagerly on the steps, in nothing but a dress and rain boots, the next time the black gate closed behind Christina's back. Margareta was obviously cold without her coat; she was hugging herself with bare arms, swaying at the knees as she stood there. "Come on, Christina, come on! We get to sleep in the empty room. Aunt Ella's got it all arranged, but she wouldn't let me move my things in until you got here. So come on! Hurry!"

But Christina wasn't listening, didn't even see her. She was looking in a different direction. It was a late February afternoon this time, and the sun was angling in over the yard. There were colors, even though it wouldn't be spring for ages yet, or leaves on the trees. The black-and-white photograph was now a watercolor, with the fallen leaves like brown scabs on the grass. Behind Christina, Sister Inga was laughing at Margareta, and already had her coat unbuttoned.

"My goodness, you are in a hurry . . ."

Margareta ignored her. "Christina, come on! Hurry up!"

A few minutes later Christina could see the transformation of the empty room with her own eyes. Now there were twin beds along the walls, and a little table by the window. The chest of drawers was gone, and Christina felt a shiver down her spine at the thought of that topsy-turvy closet out in the hall. Would her clothes be stuck in, too, amongst Margareta's and Aunt Ella's dresses?

"Can I move in now, Aunt Ella? Christina's here now, so I can move in, too, right?"

Aunt Ella was laughing her soft dove-coo somewhere in the background. "She's been beside herself for days now, could hardly wait."

"Christina, too." Sister Inga nodded. "She's been ever so excited."

Christina turned her head, looking up at Sister Inga's face. What was she lying for?

ONLY A FEW days later, Christina's clothes began to smell different. It was a complex scent, with many traces, and in the mornings when she was getting dressed she would try to separate them. Strong detergent. Fried food. Sour body odor. Christel talcum powder. Aunt Ella's scents.

She didn't know what had brought her to Aunt Ella's or how long she would stay. All she knew was that one day Sister Inga had taken all her clothes to the laundry, and the next day she had packed them neatly into a brand-new valise. Then there had been the half-hour train ride to Motala. And from there the bus ride—on a gray-blue bus perfectly matched to this gray-blue industrial town—to the far side of Motala. During the holidays Christina hadn't noticed that Aunt Ella's building was the last one on the road, but now she realized it was both in town and in the countryside. There were other buildings to the left, farmland to the right, and woods on the other side.

The road was the main road to Vadstena, and it was dangerous. They were absolutely not allowed to go near it without Aunt Ella, but in the yard they could do as they pleased. Except break branches off the fruit trees, of course. But they were allowed to climb the cherry tree, if they stayed on the thickest boughs.

In the early days, however, no one climbed the trees in Aunt Ella's yard. Christina was too timid and Margareta wasn't interested. After the first week, Margareta became like a different child, whiny and easily upset, always crying about real and imagined injustices. And she refused to eat, too.

"What's gotten into you?" Aunt Ella would sigh, lifting her up into her lap day after day, trying to feed her as if she were a baby. "Take a bite now. You're usually such a good eater."

But Margareta pursed her lips and shut her eyes tight, leaned into Aunt Ella's bosom and closed off all the world. Her crankiness made the little dove in Aunt Ella's throat fly away. And it seemed to be only Margareta who could bring it back; nothing Christina did helped. Aunt Ella was always sure to praise Christina when she dried the dishes, and she smiled when Christina went and got the dustrag to show her willingness to help with the cleaning, but she never laughed that cooing laugh.

Margareta's refusal to eat made Christina start eating, despite her continued inner reluctance. After every meal she also carried her own plate and milk glass over to the sink, and then curtsied politely and said thank you. She did all this with a shard of cold calculation in her glance. She was well aware that when Aunt Ella praised her, Margareta would howl worse than ever.

Eyes wide and innocent, she would cross the kitchen floor again, carry her cutlery to the sink, rinse her scraped plate with hot water, and then turn around to curtsy to Aunt Ella.

"What a good girl," said Aunt Ella in a worn voice. "Excellent, Christina."

And what do you know? It worked. Now Margareta was screaming at the top of her lungs, flailing wildly like an infant on Aunt Ella's lap.

How did she ever get through those first few weeks with us? Christina wonders, pulling the hand brake and glancing quickly at herself in the rearview mirror. She's slightly pale from being up all night, but nobody ever expects Christina Wulf to look very bright-eyed and bushy-tailed anyway. *Dull* is the word people have always used about her appearance, as she knows. Your classic wallflower. Not to mention the name Birgitta finally made up for her. *The Louse.* Margareta had laughed then, too.

"Well, that's what I'm like," she says to her reflection. "Christina Wulf the Louse. 'Take me as I am, or leave me be.'"

Now she no longer seems to be in a rush. She crosses the parking lot slowly, as if to postpone her inevitable entrance. She doesn't like walking into the nursing home. Yet she does burst into gentle protests and consolations every time some elderly person for whom she's arranged a bed there weeps and calls it the waiting room of death. She tells them not to look at it that way. Certainly not. The door of the building is both an entrance and an exit, the facility is mainly one for rehabilitation. In reality, though, she knows just as well as her patients that this isn't the truth. The nursing home is death's waiting room, and the only people who come out of there alive are the ones born under a very lucky star.

But it's not the label that makes her dislike the nursing home. It's the way everything in there has grown ugly. The staff was given a free hand, and apparently, just like nature, staff abhor a vacuum. Consequently this perfectly nice building from the 1940s, with its pale yellow plaster and its pleasing proportions, has been turned into one great big family room, a family room decorated with little pine shelves and pink-plastic-potted plants, cheap brass candlesticks and paintings of wide-eyed children with tears running down their cheeks. Not to mention a number of store-bought, plastic-framed embroidered samplers with proverbs about finding happiness in the little things in life and appreciating our mothers.

All these things not only make the building shrink but also make the people in it more diminutive than they really are. Why should a man like Folke—who worked as a gardener in his day, and who spent his whole life making seeds sprout and plants bloom—have to die surrounded by plastic geraniums? It would have been better to carry him out in the woods, or to place his bed in the center aisle of a church, so that he could spend his last hours of life enjoying the things that make this world tolerable: the color of the sky and the beauty of the earth.

Erik and the children used to tease her about having oversensitive eyes. "Girls, your mother is an aesthete," Erik would say, rolling his eyes. "Let her have her way."

All right. It was true. Her years at Aunt Ella's had made her an aesthete. But when she said that to Erik, he just gave a wry smile and changed the subject. She could imagine what he was thinking: that good taste requires education, and Aunt Ella was anything but an educated woman. *Simple* was the word he used: "Christina grew up in the home of a simple woman."

His condescension always astonished Christina, the way he seemed to consider Aunt Ella somewhat less human than—for instance—his own mother. Ingeborg Anxiety grew up in a rural parsonage rather than in a room in Norrköping with a wood-burning stove; she went on to secondary school when Ella was already in domestic service; she drank tea from English bone china while Ella drank coffee in robust Swedish cups; and in Erik's view all this made his mother somewhat truer and deeper than Ella. But Ingeborg Anxiety never knew the first thing about beauty: she simply arranged the attributes with which she had been endowed as she was expected to, just as all through her life she behaved, thought, and felt exactly as she was expected to. An obedient soul.

Of course Christina could see that Erik's disdain was rooted in ignorance, in the fact that although he had met people whose lives had been shaped by scarcity, he had never really known such a person. If she reminded him that life wasn't equally easy for everyone, he would only be annoyed. Anyone with a bit of gumption could make his way in the world, and the rest of mankind had to be looked after, one way or another. However, Christina didn't remind him too often about it, because the words tended to get stuck in her throat and silence her. There were no words to describe what Aunt Ella had meant to her, at least no words of which Erik would approve. Her gratitude posed another obstacle to enunciating these things. What would her life have been without Erik and his family? They were the ones who had raised her to the status of full-fledged human being.

And so she had never told Erik how it upset her to hear him equate simple with simpleminded. How would she be able to make him understand the very different connotations the word had for her, that it described the sense of caring that permeated life in Aunt Ella's home? That home in which every object had its beauty and its place, the stiff, mangled linen tablecloths Ella had woven herself, the neatly labeled kitchen towels, one for drying glasses, the other for plates, the fragile, gilt-edged coffee cups that had been a wedding present. Not to mention the fact that Aunt Ella was a minimalist: when the geranium was in bloom, she set it all on its own in the kitchen window, in its full glory.

Then, as the fifties drew to a close and women like Bitte and Anita began to fill their homes with one set after another of frilly curtains and flowery lampshades, Aunt Ella kept strictly to solid colors and refused to become a throwaway consumer. And so, for as long as she lived there, her home remained a frozen image of the forties. And in that house the days merged, any day was every day, they broke like waves on the beach. The rhythm was comforting; the very repetition muffled all anxiety and calmed all fury. And so things soon fell into place: Margareta hopped off Aunt Ella's lap and started eating again, Christina grew accustomed to all the smells and was no longer aware of them. They went into the broom closet together to play, coming out only at mealtimes.

In Aunt Ella's house, nothing was more important than eating, and no other work was more important than preparing meals. Every Monday a truck from the nearby textile mill delivered fifty semifinished women's blazers, on which Aunt Ella was to scallop the edges before the end of the week, but she would sooner have sat up all night with her sewing than to have neglected the preparation of meals by day. And the same applied to all the other domestic chores. It was more important to make the horseradish sauce for the boiled cod than to scrub the stairs. It was more important to steam the cabbage leaves for stuffed cabbage than to clean the living room. And it was more important to dry out leftover bread in the oven for bread crumbs to dip the pork chops in so they'd be nice and crisp than to do the pile of ironing that was waiting down in the laundry room.

Aunt Ella's chubby hands were never idle; work flowed like a river between them. And yet she never seemed to rush, she was always humming, and always had time to let her little dove-coo laugh purl out if something was funny. And now Margareta wasn't the only one who could entice it forth. When Christina sucked on a strand of her hair, Aunt Ella clucked at her, pulling the damp strand out of her mouth with "That can't be very tasty, silly."

Silly was an important word. Christina understood what it meant: you'd done something wrong but it didn't matter. Doing something wrong at Aunt Ella's wasn't awful; she'd figured that out when she heard Margareta giggle with pleasure when Aunt Ella growled cheerfully at the sloppy way she made her bed. Still, she couldn't be absolutely sure that the same rule applied to all silly girls. There was probably something special about Margareta, so she'd better make her own bed neatly anyway.

Only once did Aunt Ella ever try to lift Christina onto her lap as she was always doing with Margareta. But when she felt Christina go rigid, she set her right down. She didn't turn her back, though, but stayed over her for a moment, opening her barrette and clasping it shut again around that strand of hair that was always coming out, giving her a friendly pat on the behind when she was done. After that, she touched Christina only when she wanted to help her with something. She washed her face and hands, combed her hair, and helped her on with her coat despite the fact that Christina was really big enough to do all those things herself. And Christina never protested, she was perfectly happy to allow herself to be treated like a little girl. And down in the cold bathroom in the basement, she would even allow Aunt Ella to run her index finger across the scars. They were completely healed now, and seldom hurt. Only the big patches of thin, pink flesh remembered, while Christina herself had almost entirely forgotten.

Aunt Ella didn't seem bothered by the fact that Christina couldn't speak, never shook her head and whispered to other women as the sisters at the home had done. She just let it be: fixed her gray eyes on Christina's mouth to see if she was shaping her lips into a silent yes or a no. That was all. And when little sounds began to emerge with the lip movements, she said nothing about that, either.

At Midsummer there was another family party with herring and schnapps. Christina's job was to chop chives. She did her work very carefully, the tip of her tongue protruding, trying to get every little piece of chive to be exactly the same size.

Sister Inga came up behind her and watched. "You certainly are a serious chopper, young lady," she finally said.

"Thank you," said Christina with a little curtsy.

Sister Inga spun round, staring at Aunt Ella. "Did you hear that? She spoke! She can talk!"

Aunt Ella didn't even look up from where she was standing at the kitchen table arranging the herring fillets on a glass platter. "Well, of course she can talk," she said. "She's going to start school in the fall."

OH, THAT SUMMER . . . , thought Christina, moving quickly up the nursing home stairs. That was the summer of all summers. Not that the weather was anything special. On the contrary, it started to rain in the middle of June and went on nonstop for six weeks. But that didn't matter. Christina liked the rain, it raised a sort of barricade between Aunt Ella's house and the rest of the world. The mornings were perfectly silent in the kitchen. Aunt Ella would do her piecework while the girls sat drawing at the kitchen table. Now and then Christina would look up and listen to this mute concentration, but all she could hear was the rain spattering on the windowpane.

Despite the weather, however, they did have to get some fresh air. Every afternoon Aunt Ella would get out their raincoats and boots and send the girls to the yard. They would always stand on the steps for a few minutes, reluctant to go out in the rain, but soon they would run right out and allow it to embrace them. One day they made a slug farm behind the currant bushes: Christina hunted for slugs while Margareta drew roads and houses in the soft, wet soil. One day they went on an outing to Vadstena. Aunt Ella's bag was heavy with two thermoses—one with coffee, the other with cocoa—plus twelve sandwiches, three sticky buns, and six apples. They ate almost the whole picnic on a damp park bench down by Lake Vättern, then walked up to the castle, laughing. But when a nun cycled past them with her wimple flying about her ears like a raven's wings, they went silent and just stared. Aunt Ella, too.

For Christina, though, Vadstena was never a town full of nuns, because from the very first moment it was the town of pale women. As soon as they got off the train, on their walk up Castle Road, she had noticed it, and later, when they walked down the High Street, she leaned back to look up at every approaching face. Yes, it was true. In Vadstena all the women were pale. Christina liked it; she imagined the women with the pale faces must also have whispering voices. She made up her mind right away. When she grew up she was going to live in a city where people just whispered to one another . . .

Aunt Ella had a mission on their trip. She wanted to buy a new lace-making pattern. It wasn't an easy task. She went in and out of the shops, examining patterns with gravity. When she finally made up her mind, she gave a guilty sigh. Lace making was an expensive hobby. Far too costly for something you didn't really need, something that was just for pleasure.

Lace making was Christina's first triumph as well, her first victory over Margareta. Every time Aunt Ella sat down with her lace-making pillow, Christina would be right there beside her, staring at her hands. At first it looked impossible: like dragonflies shooting aimlessly through the air when Aunt Ella shifted the bobbins. Soon, though, she learned to see the pattern in the movements, and some time later she could reach out over Aunt Ella's shoulder and point to the next bobbin to be moved. At that point Aunt Ella went up to the attic and brought down an old pillow for Christina, and she helped her to set it up for herself. As the August evenings grew dark they would sit opposite each other at the big dining room table, their lacework growing inch by inch. Mother dragonfly and her grown-up daughter. And out in the kitchen sat little sister dragonfly, moping because she wasn't allowed to bring her watercolors into the dining room. Served her right.

But she doesn't have time to be thinking about that right now; she should be scaling the steps two at a time to get to her office and put on her white coat. Sixteen minutes have passed since the phone rang. Please let Folke still be alive . . .

KERSTIN ONE IS sitting at her desk in the nurses' office. Every time Christina sees that woman it gives her a little shock. She's so terrifyingly perfect, so intact, all the way from her ivory nails to her golden coiffure.

"Hi," says Christina with exaggerated intimacy in her voice, trying to appear more amicable than she feels. "I'm here. Is Folke still in two?"

Kerstin One fixes her big blue eyes on Christina, holding her answer in for a fraction of a second too long, just to highlight her criticism. She consistently demonstrates a critical attitude toward all the doctors at the nursing home. Matter of principle, apparently. "Yes, for the moment," she says. "But we're emptying another room for him. We're a bit full up right now, but I think we can work it out. Rather, I know we'll work it out. Some people will just have to make room for others."

Christina nods, quickly grasping the file Kerstin One extends.

"Should we change his antibiotics?" Kerstin One asks, raising her eyebrows.

Christina sighs. She's already tried three, and none has worked for Folke. Neither will a fourth. "I think not," she says curtly, turning her back.

DEATH HAS BAD breath. Christina smells the acrid odor before she even enters the room, and when she does, it's overpowering. All she needs to do is glance at Folke to know his time has come. You can see it in his face; his jaw has dropped, his mouth is a gaping cavity, the skin on his cheeks is thin, tight over the edema that's a result of his long illness. There's nothing she can do. Still, for the sake of appearances, she puts on her stethoscope and palpates his chest. The sound is exactly as she had expected, muted and muffled. His respiratory capacity is reduced, and his left lung makes a little wheezing sound. But Folke's stubborn heart goes on ticking in there, weak and choppy, perhaps, but with a grave determination in each beat. There had been no great hurry. Folke's heart will be struggling to achieve the impossible for hours yet.

On the other side of the bed is a gray-haired woman, holding Folke's hand in hers. For an instant, Christina wishes she didn't have to do this: there's nothing worse than having to tell weeping wives and glassy-eyed adult children it's time to pull the plug.

"Shall we go out in the hall for a moment?" she asks softly. But the woman doesn't answer, just tries and fails to blink back her tears; they run down her wrinkled cheeks.

Christina hesitates. Perhaps the woman didn't hear her. "Excuse me," she says. "Could I have a quick word with you in the hall?"

But the woman just shakes her head. "I don't want to leave him."

"Well, there are a few things we need to discuss."

"It's all right. I'm familiar with the procedure."

Christina says no more. Dying has its liturgy, and she has all the ritual phrases on the tip of her tongue—there's nothing more we can do, but at least we'll be sure he doesn't suffer—and when she's denied the opportunity to voice them it paralyzes her. She stays by Folke's bedside, watching his wife cry, and sighing involuntarily. What a day that woman has ahead. She's going to sit there holding Folke's hand and watching him traverse the various stages of the death process for fifteen to twenty hours. The thirst. The pain. The labored breathing and the rattling chest. There ought to be an easy exit from life, an open door, a welcoming . . .

And yet Christina feels not only compassion but also a kind of envy of the way the old woman can take her grief for granted. She's never been able to weep that way, not even when Aunt Ella finally died in the terminal care facility after fifteen years. Margareta could do it. She bent over Ella's dead body and embraced it, blackening the white hospital gown with her runny mascara, speaking slurred, meaningless words of solace to the dead woman: "It's all right, little Ella, it's all right, everything's going to be all right now . . ."

Christina had been furious. It was as if Margareta stole her own grief when she was flooded with tears like that. Heels clattering, she ran from the room, along the corridor and down the stairs, out under the huge maple tree on the nursing home lawn. It was winter, but she didn't care, she fought her way through the knee-high snow, ignoring the way it was filling her shoes and freezing her feet. And when she finally made it, she threw herself at the tree, kicking, hammering her white fists against its bark.

"Goddamn it," she shouted, swearing for the first time in many years. "God fucking damn it to hell!"

Later that night, when Aunt Ella's body had been taken away, she and Margareta had crossed the parking lot to the community health center and sat in Christina's office. Once they were ensconced there and each had a steaming cup of tea between her cold hands, after a long silence, Christina asked: "Do you believe it's possible to live without love? To survive?"

Margareta sniffled and wiped her nose with her hand. "Well, of course it's possible," she said. "Some people have no choice."

That was when Christina started to cry. Not because Aunt Ella was dead, but because Margareta had already forgotten so much.

*   *   *

FINALLY SHE MANAGES to ask the old woman a few physician's questions, and then she goes out into the hall. She needs to speak to Kerstin One about Folke's liquid balance and his morphine. Sometimes she has a feeling that that woman becomes stingy with the painkillers the minute the doctors are out of sight. She's known nurses like that before, women who seem to be seized by a sense of omnipotence in the proximity of death. Once, just out of medical school, Christina had seen an elderly, religious ward nurse bend over a moaning dying man and hiss: "But do you really want to meet the Lord with a body full of poisons?" Kerstin One's motivation must be different, however, because she's never alluded to the deity.

Christina leans against the doorframe at the nurses' office and clears her throat. Kerstin One looks up from her papers. Neither of them manages to say a word, however, because one of the nurse's aides comes running. "Hurry!" she says. "Seizure in six. Worse than usual!"

"Maria?" asks Kerstin One.

"No, no. It's Desirée."

Kerstin One gets up slowly and smoothes the wrinkles from her white tunic. They vanish as if by magic, and in the wave of a hand she looks newly ironed. Christina observes this with fascination before realizing she ought to do something. She has no idea what patient they're talking about, can only just connect the names to the faces of all her own nursing home patients. But she says, "Do you need me?"

"Doubt it," Kerstin One answers.

WHEN CHRISTINA ENTERS the health center, a mild scent of coffee tickles her nostrils, and looking into the lunchroom, she finds Hubertsson sitting there reading the morning paper.

"Hi," she says. "Aren't you early?"

"I'm always here early. Didn't you know?"

No, she didn't. Why would she know that? The truth is, she tries to avoid Hubertsson whenever possible. It wasn't a conscious decision, just an instinct, the instinct that applies to everyone who ever knew any Christina other than the one who's a GP at the Vadstena community health center. Hubertsson was Aunt Ella's lodger from the time Christina was fourteen, so he knows the schoolgirl she once was. The one with the Scotch plaid skirt and the duffel jacket like all the other girls had, but who never succeeded in being really like the others. Her duffel jacket had wooden buttons instead of bone ones, and her skirt was blue plaid instead of the requisite red. Aunt Ella made both the jacket and the skirt herself, but Christina still didn't blame her; she had picked out both the buttons and the fabric. However, it would hardly have mattered if she had made the right choices; she would still have retained her given place in the class hierarchy, at the bottom. She shared the rank with two girls who were also so flat-chested and uninteresting that the others could hardly be bothered to speak to them. On the way home from school Christina used to clear her throat again and again so no one would notice how rusty and unaccustomed to being used her voice was. She didn't always succeed. One afternoon when she came home and found Aunt Ella in the living room with a new lodger, she croaked out a "How do you do?" Ella had served him coffee in her best cups and had beads of perspiration under her nose and a dark red ball of cotton in one nostril. Her nose always bled when she was nervous.

"He's a doctor," she whispered to Christina a few minutes later, when she closed the door behind Hubertsson. Christina nodded gravely. They stood there for a few moments, listening to him walk up the stairs to the apartment at the top, unlock the door, and lift his valises inside. Christina observed Aunt Ella. The nervous tension in her stance was a sign of respect Christina had never seen her display before. It surprised her. People with degrees didn't usually impress Aunt Ella; in fact a gleam of disdain often flickered in her eyes when Christina spoke in hushed tones of her secondary school teachers and their educational backgrounds. Aunt Ella didn't think too much book learning was good for a person. It could turn your head, she said, and it was her impression that this was precisely what had happened to some of Christina's teachers. Obviously, that rule didn't apply to doctors of medicine. Their knowledge was awe-inspiring, not something to make fun of. And although Hubertsson came to be a familiar face in the household as the years passed, and Aunt Ella's friend, she never quite managed not to exude an air of subservience in his presence.

At that time, he had just become a divorcé. That was why he had come to work in Vadstena and to live in Motala, to get as far away as possible from his old life as a ward doctor at a Göteborg hospital. But Aunt Ella never mentioned that. It was Birgitta—of course—who snooped around and found out.

He's still a divorcé, never remarried. It's a shame, he could have used a wife. Especially now, when he's ill and aging.

"Is there enough coffee for me?" Christina asks.

"Sure," says Hubertsson, turning the pages of his paper. "Have a seat."

But Christina starts by going over to the fridge and rooting around. She's got some butter and a piece of cheese in there. Could there be a slice of bread, too? No luck.

"Would you mind if I snitched a piece of your bread?"

Hubertsson sets the paper on the table. "Go ahead. Just help yourself."

"Sure you don't mind?"

He laughs. "There's a white roll at the bottom of the bag. Take it."

He observes her as she splits the crumbly bread in two.

"And what brings you rushing into work, out of breath and having skipped breakfast?"

"Nursing home," says Christina, laconically settling in at the table. "But I did have breakfast, actually. Just not a very nice one."

"Oh," said Hubertsson. "Why not? Did you burn your cereal?"

"Margareta," says Christina, quickly taking a bite of her sandwich so as not to have to go into details.

Hubertsson leans forward, clearly curious. "Your sister? She's in town?"

Christina chews and swallows before answering. "My foster sister."

Hubertsson gives an ironic smile. "Right," he says, lifting the paper back up. "Your foster sister. I remember."

Christina's forehead creases; she suspects he's going to start pestering her about the old times again. But Hubertsson says nothing more, just goes on turning the pages of his paper. The question is whether he can read any farther down than the headlines. He ought to be half blind by this point, considering how badly he's handled his diabetes over the years. The truth of the matter is that Hubertsson is sicker than most of his own patients. And today he looks worse than usual. Quite ashen.

Christina leans forward, touches his arm to make him look up. "And what about you?" she asks. "Are you all right?" Hubertsson gets up and shuffles toward the door. "I'm absolutely fine," he says over his shoulder. "Great. Never better. Very well indeed. Any other questions? Or can I go read my paper in peace now?"

Christina makes a face at his back. Grumpy old fart.

As the morning rolls on she gets involved enough in her work to forget all about Hubertsson and her sisters; only a strange weakness in her elbows reminds her that she's been up all night. Today she likes working, not because she loves her profession any more than she used to but because there's security in routines, in the repetition of words and phrases she's said a thousand times before. In addition to which she has simple, straightforward patients all morning: a slight case of gastritis, a few little streptococci, a five-year-old with hives who's had his last orange. The risk that there might be a tumor lying in wait behind any of those symptoms is minimal. When the next patient comes in the room, she feels even easier. All she needs to do is glance at the slits that pass for this adolescent's eyes to know what's wrong. Pinkeye.

Still, of course, she examines him thoroughly, even being so considerate as to turn off the ceiling light when he lies on the examining table so the sharp light won't hurt his eyes. She feels a kind of tenderness for him; his shoulders are as narrow as Erik's, and his chin is covered with bright red acne. Not exactly in with the in-crowd, this one. Not a bit like the young males, bulging with testosterone, whom Åsa and Tove used to bring home during their teenage years.

"I'll prescribe some ointment for you," she says after the examination. "And I think you'd better stay home from school for a couple of days."

Usually Christina's restrictive about prescribing bed rest. She knows that the national health authorities keep statistics on how many people doctors put on sick leave, and that if you're overly generous they get critical. But this kid's too young to be included in the statistics. And his entire pathetic appearance bears witness to his need to have a few days off from the world.

He sits up but remains on the examining table, his legs hanging down. Christina halts herself as she's about to rise from her shiny, stainless steel stool to go and write him a prescription. "Anything else?"

At first he doesn't say anything, just lets his head sink and sighs.

"Hey," says Christina softly. "Did you want to talk about something?"

He looks up at her out of his red slits, his eyelashes sticky with pus. "What's the point of living?" he asks hoarsely.

Christina's hands fall to her lap, and she turns her palms up instinctively. The gesture says, Don't ask me. But her mouth says nothing.

"You're a doctor, so shouldn't you know? What's the point in being alive?"

Suddenly her tiredness overwhelms her, and she can't find a single pat phrase. "Well," she says, "no, I don't have an answer. I don't know myself. I just go on doing it."

He remains in the same position, his legs still dangling, a little hole in the toe of one of his white tube socks. "And what if you don't want to live? What do you do about it?"

"Don't you want to be alive?"

"No."

"Why not?"

"I just don't, that's all."

And then she does exactly what she's not supposed to do. Reaches out a hand and strokes his hair, just wanting to console him . . . But in midmovement her phone rings, and automatically she rises to answer. One second later she realizes she shouldn't have, and when she answers she's annoyed. "Hello, this is Christina Wulf. Can I help you?"

The voice at the other end of the line is thin and anxious. It's the nurse at the desk, and she knows she's not supposed to call the doctor when she's with a patient. "Christina, I'm awfully sorry, but it's the police and they won't wait, they say it's urgent, and I haven't been able to put them off . . ."

Christina glances across the room; the young man is still in the same position, but his feet are no longer dangling. "All right. Put them through."

There's a click on the line, and a new voice. A woman. "Excuse me, is this Dr. Wulf?"

"Yes."

"I'm phoning from the Norrköping police station. We're holding some-one here who's given your name . . ."

Christina sighs with impatience. One of the fairly small number of chronic alcoholics in Vadstena must have gone to Norrköping and ended up arrested for D & D. What's she supposed to do about it?

"Her name is Birgitta Fredriksson—"

Christina interrupts. "Has she been assaulted?"

"Certainly not. More the other way around."

"What do you mean, the other way around?"

"She's here on suspicion of battery. We brought her in early this morn-ing. But we can't hold her any longer, and she hasn't got the money for a bus ticket back to Motala. She says you'll be willing to be her security, if you see what I mean. If we lend her the bus fare, that you'll guarantee we get the money back. Is that all right? Can you agree to the arrangement? You're her sister, aren't you?"

Somewhere in the background she hears a familiar voice. "Jesus Christ, just make her do it, will you? Tell her she fucking owes it to me . . ."

Christina's fury is pure white; it glistens in front of her eyes and burns in her throat. "Not on her life!"

"Excuse me, Dr. Wulf," says the voice of the police officer. "Are you still there, Dr. Wulf?"

Christina takes a deep breath, and when she speaks her voice is metallic. "Yes, I'm right here. But I'm sorry to say I cannot be of assis-tance. There must be some misunderstanding, because I don't have a sis-ter."

"Oh, well, that's what she said."

"She's lying."

"She has a prescription with your name on it."

Christina feels the fear climb her spinal column. "A medical prescription?"

"No, just the form. There's some kind of obscene poem on it, and a stamp with your name. Christina Wulf, Vadstena District Health Clinic . . . That's you, isn't it?"

Christina runs her hand through her hair, with some idea of what that poem might be, since none of them has ever been able to forget it. But she's not playing this game. Never.

"Nothing strange about that. If you check your records you'll find that the person you're holding stole a prescription pad from me a few years ago. She's been convicted of theft for it."

The police officer hesitates, you can almost hear her scratching her head. "Oh, I see. . . . Well, I don't know what we're going to do now."

"I imagine you'll have to call the welfare people."

The line crackles, Christina hears a little shout of surprise in the voice of the police officer, and suddenly that familiar voice rings so loudly in her ear that her eardrum vibrates: "You fucking goddamn bitch, you listen to me," Birgitta roars. "You've never done anything but make life miserable for me, but this time you're just going to have to give me a hand. I never thought you'd fall so low. How could you write me an anonymous letter? It's revolting. You make me sick, you're fucking disgusting, so vicious—"

Christina slams the receiver down and buries her face in her hands. Her insides have gone liquid, like quicksand. She's slick as an inflatable toy, and she'll never be able to stand on two legs again. For at least a minute she can't even look up, just hears the ticking of her watch and then a soft voice in the background. Oh, my God, that kid! She forgot all about him.

She turns her chair 180 degrees, taking a sharp breath. "I'm so sorry. This kind of thing isn't supposed to happen. Where were we?"

The boy looks at her, his infected eyes nothing but black lines. "You were going to give me a prescription."

"Yes, but . . ."

He slides off the examining table, suddenly sounding like a full-grown man. "The eye ointment," he says. "We were at the eye ointment."

WHEN HE'S GONE she remains in the dim room, unable to get up and turn on the light. The next patient will just have to wait; she needs a few minutes to settle down, for her innards to congeal again. She turns her desk chair to look through the window and sees the young man crossing the parking lot diagonally. His posture worries her; his shoulders are slanted, his arms drooping at his sides, his head down. He ought to be cold, slipping along in the frozen slush, but he hasn't buttoned his jacket, and he's not wearing mittens or a scarf. A standard checklist question from medical school crosses her mind: Suicide risk? Yes. He's definitely a suicide risk.

And suddenly she has a hasty vision of the interplay between his life and her own, how difficult and complex and awful everything is if the fact that she was an abused child who ended up in a foster home once upon a time results in the suicide of a young man who is a complete stranger to her forty years later. If there had never been a Birgitta in Christina's life, the telephone would have been silent on her desk when he was just starting to open up, and it would have stayed silent until he was finished with what he had to say.

"If wishes were horses then beggars would ride," she hears Astrid's scornful voice saying in her memory. Astrid. Yes, it's her fault, she's the one who turned Christina's life into what it is. And she is so powerful that long after her own death her dirty fingernails can scratch at other people's wounds. Unconsciously, Christina opens the bottom drawer of her desk and pulls out an envelope. It's brown and slightly wrinkled, and has been at the bottom of her desk drawer for years.

Erik has no idea she possesses this envelope, has no idea that fifteen years ago she had done what he so often recommended she do. She sent for her childhood medical records. And not only that. She also got hold of the emergency service report from the fire department, the preliminary investigation made by the police, and—with the aid of her professional authority as a physician and a few white lies—some of Astrid's medical records from the Sisters of St. Birgitta Hospital here in Vadstena.

Her own medical records are at the top. She raises the yellowing sheet of paper toward her desk lamp, rereading the familiar words. *Five-year-old girl. Arrived at 10:25 P.M. by ambulance. Unconscious. Second- to third-degree burns on abdomen, chest, left upper arm, and right palm . . .*

She can't believe it. She is equally reluctant to believe these records every time she looks at them: it can't be true, it just can't be true. Yet of course she knows every single word is true, if for no other reason than that she still has the scars. Some spots on her skin will always be thinner and glossier than others: her abdomen, her chest, her left upper arm, and her right palm.

In addition to which she has the preliminary report from the police, and the testimony of Herr and Fru Pettersson, the neighbors she cannot remember, no more than she can recall the apartment where she and Astrid lived in the house on St. Peter's Street in Norrköping. And yet she imagines she can hear Fru Pettersson's broad local dialect as she leafs through the police report: "Well, we were quite used to hearing the child cry, but mostly she just sobbed softly. . . . This time, though, she was screaming at the top of her lungs. It hurt to listen . . ."

The rest of the details were in the summary at the bottom of the first page of the report:

Herr and Fru Oskar and Elsa Pettersson stated that at about half past nine on the evening of March 23, 1955, they noticed a persistent smell of smoke. Fru Pettersson went out into the hall and was able to establish that the smoke was emanating from the apartment next door. So she urged her husband to phone the fire department, and then tried the door of the neighboring apartment and found it to be unlocked.

Once inside, she rushed into the kitchen, then into the front room, but was unable to find the source of the fire, or Fröken Astrid Martinsson, whose apartment it was. When she tried the door of the bedroom, however, she found that it was locked, but that the key was in the lock, on the outside of the door. She unlocked the door and went inside. There were flames coming from the crib. Fru Pettersson extinguished the fire with a rug.

While she was doing this, Astrid Martinsson appeared, and slashed her twice in the back with a kitchen knife. Herr Pettersson entered the room shortly. A tumult ensued when he attempted to take the knife from Fröken Martinsson, and a kerosene lamp fell to the floor, starting a second fire. Fru Pettersson was also able to extinguish this flare-up with the rug, during which time Herr Pettersson overpowered Fröken Martinsson and held her down . . .

Christina stuffs the papers back into the envelope. She doesn't really need to read them, she knows it all by heart. Particularly the record of the questioning with Astrid. To begin with, she claimed that the fire started when her little girl overturned the kerosene lamp. When confronted with the statement of the ambulance driver that the child's arms and legs had been tied to the crib and he had had to cut her loose, Fröken Martinsson became violent.

There were also the diagnoses of Astrid from the Sisters of St. Birgitta Hospital, one after another and all with doubtful question marks in the margins: Endogenous psychotic? Paranoid schizophrenic? Manic-depressive? Psychopathic with outbreaks of psychosis? Her treatment also seems to have been permeated by this uncertainty. During her seven years at the hospital, Astrid was treated by being strapped down and with long baths, with Seconal and Librium, electroshocks and insulin coma treatment, and then, finally, the miracle medicine of her day: Thorazine.

CHRISTINA KNOWS ALL this but can recall none of it. And the strange thing is that she knew it all without remembering it even as a child, even the time Astrid appeared at Aunt Ella's to demand the return of her daughter.

It was a cold day in early January, one of those clear days when the air is so sharp with frost that it scratches your lungs, and the light is so white it cuts your eyes. But Aunt Ella's kitchen was cozy and nice-smelling; she was baking sweet rolls. Christina and Margareta were on Christmas vacation and had been out in the snow playing all morning, but now they were sitting around doing nothing at the kitchen table, waiting for their snow pants to dry. A shivering sparrow landed in the bird feeder outside the window, picked listlessly at the last of the dry bread crumbs, then fluffed up and went immobile.

"May we crumble a roll for the sparrow?" Margareta asked.

Aunt Ella was just bending down to take a baking sheet from the oven, using the edges of her apron as pot holders. "Well," she said, "not a fresh one, anyway. But there are still two from last week in the bread box . . . you can have them."

Both girls rose at the same instant. It looked as if Margareta would be the first to reach the bread box, she took two giant steps to pick up speed and then slid along the linoleum in her thick knitted socks.

But Aunt Ella stopped her with an outstretched arm. "Cut it out, silly. You walk normally or you'll wear holes in your socks from all that sliding."

That was enough to give Christina a head start. By the time Ella let go of Margareta, Christina had removed the two old rolls from the bread box and was holding one in each hand with a triumphant grin.

"Oh, Aunt Ella!" Margareta whined.

Ella didn't even need to look to know what had happened, she knew exactly what was going on. With her back to both girls she said, "One each. And no fuss."

That was when someone knocked on the door.

FOR THE REST of her life, Christina would know that time is a relative concept, that an instant and eternity are equivalent. An image flew through her brain: a stone plopping into dark water, wide rings spreading over the surface. That was time. The stone was the present, the rings the past and the future. She knew everything that had happened and everything that was going to happen, yet she was equally unable to remember either past or future. In the space of one single breath she had time for a thousand thoughts: Who'd come here and not bother to ring the doorbell at the front? Why didn't we hear the front door close before we heard the knocking on the apartment door? Why is the hair on my arms standing on end?

Aunt Ella and Margareta behaved as if it were perfectly normal for someone to be knocking at the door. Margareta snatched one of the stale rolls and moved toward the kitchen window. Aunt Ella wiped her hands on her apron and went to open the door.

The voice out in the hall sounded strange, a southern Swedish drawl that wasn't really southern bounced at Aunt Ella and interrupted her before she could even introduce herself. "I've come to get her," the alien voice said.

Aunt Ella's voice suddenly went shrill. "Who? Who do you mean?"

"She's mine. I'm taking her."

There was a thud; Christina shut her eyes and knew it was the stool under the little shelf with the telephone on it that had tipped over. Nosebleed, she thought. Aunt Ella's gonna have another nosebleed. And, quite right, the next moment Aunt Ella was standing in the kitchen doorway holding a corner of her apron to her right nostril. She gestured brusquely to Christina: get away!

Afterward she was able to think, and knew she should probably have hidden in the broom closet, but it never occurred to her at the time. During the past year, with Christina in fourth grade and Margareta in third, the broom closet had lost its significance; they were now too big to shut themselves into a closet all day and play. So the broom closet had returned to being just that, the home of the vacuum cleaner and the bucket and rags, with the duster on a hook and a stiff cloth pouch next to it. Christina had helped Aunt Ella embroider the words on it, which sounded like the first words of a song or a nursery rhyme: bags and corks and twine, shop receipts and laundry line. Suddenly her eyesight sharpened; it was as if she could see right through the walls. Now every little detail in their otherwise invisible everyday routines was distinct. The brown linoleum. The pattern on the oilcloth. The little sparrow still outside the window. I'm going to petrify you all with my gaze, Christina thought. No one is allowed to move without my permission.

But she had evidently moved without her own permission, because she suddenly found herself by the kitchen table. How did she get there? She couldn't recall. Nor could she recall having pushed Aunt Ella's chair aside and placed herself behind it. But there she was, wedged between the back of Aunt Ella's chair and the wall.

"Where is she?" asked the voice in the vestibule.

Aunt Ella let go of the corner of her apron; a little wreath of blood appeared like flower petals around her nostril. She turned toward the hall. "This just won't do," she said in her sharpest tone of voice. "What on earth do you mean by barging in here?"

Aunt Ella used that tone of voice only in exceptional circumstances, but when she did the whole world, not only the girls, stood at attention. Christina had seen it happen with the grocer and the tenant upstairs. But this person wasn't about to budge, she could tell. And so it was; an arm was extended and shoved Aunt Ella to the side. And there she stood. Astrid.

She actually looked like a witch. Maybe that was because she was so tall and stooped, so thin and with such a pointed nose. Or else it was her weird clothes. A black raincoat and sou'wester. In January? Not to mention that she had the sou'wester on backward: the wider brim was hanging down over her forehead, blocking her eyes.

"Chrissstiiina!" She hung on to each syllable as if reluctant to let go of the name.

"My little giiiirl!"

Astrid opened her arms and took two steps forward. Someone cried out; it might have been Christina herself, she thought it was, although she never felt that shrill monotone leave her mouth.

"Don't you believe them," said Astrid. "It's nothing but bold-faced lies."

Out of the corner of her eye, Christina saw Margareta gaping from the other side of the table. She was still holding that stale roll. And over by the kitchen door Aunt Ella was paralyzed. She might have been a photograph of herself had it not been for the dark little trickle of blood running slowly down from her right nostril. Christina opened her mouth again, and this time she could hear the shrill, tremulous scream.

"Stop shouting," said Astrid, talking very fast now, sounding almost breathless. "There's no need to scream, it's nothing but lies and inventions. They've made it all up. We were happy, Christina."

Her eyes flickered behind the shadow of the sou'wester; it was as if Astrid's skin was so sleek that no matter how hard Christina tried to stare at her, her eyes glided elsewhere. Her arms were still open, her hands a little shaky, her fingers so pale they looked blue.

At medical school Christina would learn that this trembling was the primary side effect of Thorazine. The secondary one was sudden blood pressure drops. Sensitivity to light the third. Grotesque grimaces the fourth. Drops in body temperature the fifth. So in medical terms it was easy to explain what at the time looked like witchcraft and wizardry.

But when it happened there was just something magical about it. A shimmering white ray of sun found its way in through the kitchen window, touching Astrid first and then expanding to encompass Ella over by the door. She blinked, and that involuntary reflex appeared to awaken her; she took a deep breath, then crossed the kitchen floor in one huge step, swerved around Astrid, and placed herself in front of Christina with her arms spread to protect her. Astrid twirled around, trying to seize Christina, but it was too late, her blue fingers were grasping at thin air. A grimace distorted her face; her top lip drew back, exposing her teeth and gums, her tongue seemed to fall out and hang down over her chin, her right eye shut, then opened again. One second later she reeled, her legs gave way, and she fell to the floor, unconscious.

AFTERWARD, WHEN AUNT Ella had phoned pike-jowled Stig and the people from the Sisters of St. Birgitta had collected Astrid from her very first home leave, nothing was the same. It was as if Astrid, by coming to Aunt Ella's, had broken something, a glass partition or a wall of ice or an enormous soap bubble. Every sound was sharper. Suddenly the cars on the road outside roared, the winter wind etched its way into the roof tiles, the heels of Hubertsson's silent predecessor started to clatter on the stairs. The very air changed; the house was chilly and raw, Christina was cold and had to go around inside in a heavy sweater and thick woolen stockings. The cold made her fingers stiff and thick, they wouldn't obey her as they always had. Impatiently, she threw aside her embroidery when her stitching began to look as childish as Margareta's. She no longer had the peace of mind to spend the evenings sitting beside Aunt Ella with the radio on; instead she wandered listlessly around the house, disturbing Margareta, who spent almost all her time reading on her bed in the empty room, went from window to window picking dead leaves off the house-plants and staring at her own reflection in the shiny black glass. Sometimes she practiced endurance. How would it feel if a thin, white face suddenly appeared outside the windowpane? How would it feel if Aunt Ella died? How would it feel if she had to leave Aunt Ella's house one day?

A black hole. That was what it would feel like. That was what it felt like.

AUNT ELLA ALSO changed after Astrid's visit. She raised her eyes of-tener from her own piecework, following Christina with her gaze, but not smiling or commenting. She also changed her habits: she no longer let the girls answer the phone or run out to get the mail. Aunt Ella did those things herself now. Beyond which she stopped out in the yard and opened some of the envelopes even though it was still winter and cold outside. Christina could see her from the kitchen window: Aunt Ella tearing an envelope open, her brow creased, skimming the letter and then going straight to the garbage can and throwing it away.

The only one who didn't change was Margareta. She seemed not to no-tice that things were different, that there were suddenly secrets in the house. She still rubbed around Aunt Ella's legs like a cat whenever she had the chance, she still bored Christina with the details of the plot of every single book she read. She didn't even appear to notice how much more often pike-jowled Stig dropped by, or that it always happened to be at the girls' bedtime.

But Christina noticed. Night after night she lay in her bed in the empty room, wide awake, listening to him harping on at Aunt Ella down in the kitchen. He talked incessantly, but Aunt Ella almost never re-sponded.

Persuasion. That was what it had to be. Pike-jowled Stig was trying to persuade Aunt Ella to do something she didn't want to do. The thought drove a wave of nausea through Christina, and suddenly she had to find out what it was, no matter how. Very cautiously she put her bare feet down on the floor of the empty room, then stood up and pattered quiet as a mouse out into the hall.

"What we need is a long-term solution," said Stig after a little swallowing sound that revealed he was drinking Aunt Ella's coffee. "And the children's home is no long-term solution. Not in her case."

Christina caught her breath. Were they sending her back? Suddenly she realized she had to pee, badly. She was about to wet herself. She tried hard to hold it in but was unable, and a little rivulet began to make its way down her left thigh. She rushed in the direction of the bathroom, but couldn't stop to shut the door behind her.

It was still open when Aunt Ella and pike-jowled Stig came out into the hall a moment later to see what the noise was. Christina shut her eyes against the embarrassment. She didn't want to be seen on the toilet, her flannel nightgown up over her knees, but she couldn't get up and close the door without wetting the entire bathroom floor.

"What are you doing up?" Aunt Ella asked in amazement.

And behind her Christina glimpsed Stig's smiling face.

"Hey, Margareta," he said. "How'd you like another sister?"

"Pardon me, but that's Christina," said Aunt Ella.

THE NEXT DAY Birgitta was on Aunt Ella's doorstep.

Christina couldn't make up her mind whether the new little girl was cute or ugly—she was somehow both. Her hair was pale blond and curly, her eyes perfect orbs, and her pouting mouth had a very clear Cupid's bow. She would have looked like a doll if her body hadn't been so clumsy. Her legs were straight as arrows, not even the slightest curve at the calves, her belly protruded, her hands were chubby and thick-fingered. The shade of the skin on her neck was different from that of her face. Grayer. In addition to which a little rivulet of mucus ran from one of her nostrils, and the fingertips around her bitten-down nails were so red and swollen you could just feel how much they hurt.

"I want to live with my mamma," said Birgitta. A babyish line, but not said in a childish tone. Her voice was deep and rasping, quite manly.

"I know, my dear," said the woman from the child welfare authorities who had brought her. "But you know your mamma needs to rest up."

"She won't be able to rest if I'm not with her. I'm the one who looks after her."

The child welfare woman smiled listlessly, bending forward to unbutton her jacket. "All right, little one, I know that's what you think. But now your mamma needs to get some real rest, that's why she asked us to look after you for a while."

Birgitta gave her a suspicious glare, sniffled, and wiped her nose with her index finger. That motion caused the woman to pull her own hand back, and a second later Birgitta had buttoned her jacket up again. For one moment there was perfect silence in Aunt Ella's vestibule. Everyone—Margareta and Christina, the child welfare woman, and Aunt Ella—just stared at her buttons. Birgitta glared back at them, shifting her eyes from one face to the next. When the inspection tour was complete, she shut her eyes and exhaled; it sounded like a deep sigh. Unable to control themselves, Christina and Margareta repeated this sigh, and for a second it sounded as if a wind were rippling through Aunt Ella's vestibule.

The next instant, Birgitta opened her eyes. There was a gleam; she twirled and headed for the door.

THERE'S A KNOCK on Christina's door, an anxious little tap-tap-tap that makes her believe for one moment that the freezing cold little sparrow from Aunt Ella's bird feeder has flown through time and landed in the hallway of the District Health Center. Her body, though, knows better, and immediately arranges the alibi she requires. One quick sweep and she's shifted the desk lamp and turned her chair so it looks like she's making entries in her patient records. "Yes," she says, in her most contained tone of voice.

" 'Scuse me, Christina," says a hesitant voice. It's Helena, one of the nurses.

"I'll see the next patient in a second," says Christina, not raising her eyes from the monitor.

"That's not the trouble," says Helena. "You're only five minutes behind schedule . . ."

Christina twists her chair all the way around and looks in the direction of the door. "So what is it?"

"Hubertsson . . ."

"What about him?"

"He seems really weird. And they called from the nursing home, too. One of his patients has apparently had a particularly violent epileptic seizure . . ."

"And?"

"Well, Hubertsson . . . I kind of can't reach him."

Christina adjusts her eyeglasses. "Has he been drinking?"

Helena's positively contorted with discomfort, she's the strongest advocate for Hubertsson at the whole center, his counsel for the defense, a mother hen with no chicks, prepared to put up with all his idiosyncrasies and moodiness for the sheer pleasure of spreading her wings to protect him when he's unwell. "No, I don't think so. He's just not really with it."

Christina rises, stuffing her hands deep into the pockets of her white coat. She's annoyed. This isn't the first time Helena's thought Hubertsson was behaving weirdly, but she still stubbornly refuses to accept

Christina's theory that the explanation for this strange behavior must be that he keeps a bottle of whiskey hidden someplace. Unless, of course, he's highly allergic to sugarless cough drops: whenever Helena thinks he's at his weirdest Christina's noticed he smells strongly of a combination of alcohol and menthol. At times like these Christina has to see not only her own patients but his as well.

"Where is he?"

"In his office."

On her way through the waiting room Christina takes a head count: there are three patients, one of whom must be hers, the two others Hubertsson's. That means no lunch for her today.

Hubertsson's door is ajar. Just as Christina had recently done, he's turned out all his lights, and he's sitting there just like Christina was a few minutes ago, staring out the window. But he's not looking at the parking lot; his eyes are glued to the yellow brick facade of the nursing home. Christina grasps the back of his desk chair, twirls him around, then bends down and looks him right in the eye. "Are you all right?"

His face is even more ashen than it was this morning, his brow is beaded with perspiration. Christina raises her voice. "Are you okay?"

He makes a parrying gesture but doesn't answer.

"Have you been drinking?"

His eyes fade in and out of focus; he shakes his head. She leans in closer, inhales as he exhales. There's no smell at all, neither whiskey nor menthol, not even a hangover.

"Had anything to eat today?"

He responds with a little sound that could mean anything.

Christina feels his forehead. It's not just damp, it's drenched in perspiration. "What about your insulin? Did you take it?"

He grunts something incomprehensible; his eyelids flutter. Suddenly she knows exactly what he's having. A hypoglycemic reaction. She's amazed. Although he doesn't practice what he preaches to his diabetes patients, he's usually quite good at fending off hypoglycemia. He never leaves his apartment without a handful of sugar cubes in his pocket.

"Quick," Christina says over her shoulder to Helena. "I'll need a blood glucose. Get a needle ready."

She senses Helena's palpable relief. Nurses are almost always like that. Nothing makes them feel more secure than not having to make a decision and being asked to prepare a hypodermic needle. She puts Hubertsson's big hand in her own and pricks his fingertip, then presses the little test strip to it. The answer is instantaneous: his blood sugar level is extremely low.

Now the two women work in silent concentration, neither seeing nor speaking to each other. Helena bends over Hubertsson, slipping one of his arms out of the white coat, rolling up his right shirtsleeve, tightening a tourniquet just above his elbow. Christina snaps her fingers in the crook of his arm to make the blood vessels surface. Hubertsson exhales as he feels the entry of the needle. And when Christina very slowly presses the content of the vial into his vein, he opens his eyes and says, quite distinctly, "Desirée."

"BIRGITTA, MARGARETA, AND Christina," said the child welfare woman, laughing her little visitor's cackle. "If you only had a little Desirée, you'd be just like the royal princesses."

"Desirria, diarrhea," said Birgitta. She'd sat herself down in the middle of the kitchen floor the minute the lady dragged her in from the front steps and refused to move. Christina's stomach fluttered with anxiety: the new girl should have known she was too big to sit on the floor. Not to mention that she should have stopped blurting out dirty words like a baby who didn't know any better, that she should have gotten up and sat on a chair at the table, she should have had her soft drink and sweet roll just like Christina and Margareta.

"Desirria, diarrhea," said Birgitta. "Princess Poopa and Farta, Count Diarrhea von Turdman . . ."

Margareta giggled, but Christina looked anxiously up at Aunt Ella. It was worse than she had imagined: Aunt Ella's face was absolutely pale, her pupils huge and black. The usually imperceptible wrinkles at the corners of her eyes deepened, as if someone had painted a big, black spider's web around each of her eyes. Aunt Ella sat staring at Birgitta, immobilized. Christina knew the new girl must realize she had Aunt Ella's eyes on her, no question about that, yet she didn't look back, just sat there as if she were stuck, her legs spread wide on the kitchen floor. She had a hole in the knee of her tights, her gray-blue cardigan was too small, and she kept pulling at the sleeves as if to lengthen them.

The woman from the child welfare authorities glanced at Aunt Ella, then put her hand to her throat and said, "Birgitta, just cut that ridiculous behavior out right now."

"The Countess Diarrhea von Shitfart . . ."

Once again Margareta giggled. Birgitta looked up from the floor, glanced quickly at her, a smile trembling at the corners of her mouth for a split second.

The lady got up and stood firmly in front of her. "Birgitta, I want you to get up. And then to go over to the table and sit down and drink up, like the other girls are doing!"

But Birgitta just looked back down at the floor again. "I never drink anything orange."

"Why on earth not?"

" 'Cause orange drinks taste like piss."

After which it took only an instant. Aunt Ella, hitherto immobilized, got up, took two determined steps over to Birgitta, and pulled her to her feet. Birgitta's legs were completely slack; she dangled like a rag doll from Aunt Ella's arms.

"There's one thing you need to know, young lady," said Aunt Ella very softly. "Those words that just popped out of you are words I dislike very strongly. And in this house I make the rules. For your information."

She dragged Birgitta over and set her down on the empty chair at the short end of the table, then pulled over the glass that had already been waiting for ages for Birgitta and filled it with orange drink. "Drink up," she said, crossing her arms over her chest.

Margareta laughed out loud, apparently not realizing what was going on, as usual. "It's homemade orange drink. Aunt Ella made it herself. We've been saving orange peels all this fall."

Christina said nothing, but she glared straight at the new girl and simultaneously lifted her own glass to her lips, drinking every drop in a few big swallows. But Birgitta didn't copy her. She just sat there mute and still, staring at the orange liquid.

Aunt Ella bent over her, still speaking softly but very clearly. "Drink up," she said. "You just drink it up right now."

The kitchen clock ticked in the background, its little red second hand jerking from numeral to numeral. As it reached the twelve, Birgitta extended a hand toward the glass, and by the time it got down to the six she had finished her orange drink.

And a new era had begun.

*   *   *

STARTLED, HUBERTSSON BLINKS and shakes his head like a bear who's been hibernating, as Christina and Helena lead him over to his own examining table by the wall.

"You just rest for a while," Christina instructs him. "We'll do a new test in fifteen minutes and decide whether you need to go to Motala."

He mutters something, and a couple of seconds pass while Christina decodes it. The nursing home. Oh yes, they'd called from the nursing home. She turns to Helena, who is covering Hubertsson with a yellow honeycomb blanket, smoothing it with exaggerated solicitousness over his shoulders. "Who called from the nursing home exactly?"

Kerstin One.

"All right. I'll call her back."

She uses Hubertsson's phone, drumming her meticulously filed nails on his blotter as it rings. It takes some time to get an answer, but when someone finally picks up it's Kerstin One's metallic voice. Christina can practically hear its clink, notwithstanding the fact that Kerstin One sounds perfectly relaxed.

"Well, the only reason we called, really, is that Hubertsson insists on knowing every time this particular patient has a seizure. First there was a seven-minute one, then a thirty-minute respite, and then a new one that lasted nearly forty-five . . ."

Christina bites her lip. A forty-five-minute episode is right on the border of status epilepticus, a seizure that never ends.

"Is it all over now?"

"Uh-huh. I gave her four Valium suppositories, ten milligrams each."

Christina gasps. How did she dare? A dose of that size would knock out a horse.

"What's the patient's weight?"

"About eighty-five pounds."

Christina feels her fist cramp. Is the woman out of her mind?

"Male or female?"

"Female. Hubertsson's pet, you know."

No, she didn't know.

"Was Hubertsson the one who prescribed such a high dose?"

Kerstin One sighs impatiently. "No, ordinarily he comes over and puts her on a drip when a seizure lasts so long, but I couldn't get hold of him today. . . . Don't worry, though, she's strong as an ox. She's paralyzed and doesn't speak, has cerebral palsy, epilepsy, and is spastic, but she's not about to give up the ghost. She's over forty-five and has been institution-alized her whole life, but like I said, she isn't much for dying."

Christina feels her mouth go dry. "I'm coming over there."

Kerstin One sighs again. "There's no need, she has seizures on a daily basis, sometimes more than one a day. We generally just notify Huberts-son, and then she sleeps for a few hours. She's a great sleeper, so it's all right with everybody."

Christina clears her throat. "I'm coming anyway."

She almost hears Kerstin One shrugging her shoulders. "Well, if you don't have anything better to do on your office hours, suit yourself."

THIS TIME SHE'S gritted her teeth and steeled herself for the shock, but she's still taken aback when she sees Kerstin One. She looks like a shampoo ad; her long blond hair's glittering as if the Milky Way were in it as she helps a patient along the hall. Her pantsuit is sparkling white, the socks on her feet look soft and fluffy, her white sandals as if they'd just been removed from their shoe box. All this perfection is anything but flat-tering to the woman at her side, however. Her hair has no luster, hangs heavy and dull around her head. She's dressed in a washed-out jogging suit and is shuffling along in a pair of bedroom slippers with the backs bent in. Maria has Down's syndrome, severe epilepsy, and a smile that looks like a clemency application.

"Hi, Maria," says Christina, despite the tremor of impatience that courses through her. She knows Maria can feel miserable for weeks when someone neglects to say hello to her. "How're you doing today?"

"Not so well," says Maria, shaking her head. "Not so well at all . . ."

Christina is startled. Maria never complains, always just shoots a smile in the direction of the person who asks, assuring her that everything is terrific, even if she's on the verge of collapse.

"Well, goodness, what's the matter?"

"Not allowed to be in the angel room," says Maria, hangdog.

"Never mind," says Kerstin One, squeezing Maria's hand. "You know it's only temporary."

Christina knows that Maria's room is sacred to her. It reminds Christina of a shrine, a temple to naïveté, while the rest of the nursing home is more like one big community center. Maria's room is all deco-rated with angels: chubby china cherubs on the windowsill, handmade seraphs dangling from the ceiling, glittering bookmark angels and colorful magazine angels covering the walls from floor to ceiling. Maria makes them and sticks them to the walls, sometimes even with Elmer's glue. The director of the nursing home, a practical woman with no illusions about paradise, tends to sort of glaze over every time Maria's room comes up for discussion. They say she has nightmares about what's going to happen when the local officials discover it. But she's never once tried to deprive Maria of her angels. She knows that roomful of angels is what gives Maria the will to go on living. When she comes to after one of her eternal attacks, she always looks around uneasily until she's sure her angels are still there, and then she's all right.

"What's keeping Maria out of her room?" Christina asks, but without looking Kerstin One in the eye. A little prick of fear makes her look at Maria instead.

"It's really a shame, but we had no choice," says Kerstin One. "Folke needs a room of his own, and since we can hardly put him in with the angels, we've had to move Hubertsson's little pet. And since she's sleeping right now and needs not to be awakened for some time, we thought Maria had better spend a few hours in the dayroom."

Maria tries to shoot a pleading smile in Christina's direction, but she doesn't succeed and the corners of her mouth turn downward instead. That makes her look like she's about to burst into tears. Christina runs her hand through her bangs; she's starting to feel slick and liquidy again. What a day! And it's not even noon yet . . .

"Isn't there any other way to work it out?" she asks in a tone of resignation.

"Not really," says Kerstin One. "We considered various options. But we're having Picture Bingo today, you know, so it's going to be lots of fun."

SOMETHING BRUSHES THE top of Christina's head as she enters Maria's room. She raises a hand instinctively, as if to ward off a bird on the wing, and for a split second she recalls the dead seagull on the path in her yard. But these aren't bird wings, they are the soft yarn-feet of an angel touching her head. Maria's latest creation is hanging from a string just inside the doorway, an eighteen-inch-tall angel with a Styrofoam head and gold tape curls, wrapped in an old towel marked COUNTY HOSPITAL PROPERTY. The same words are visible under the sparse collection of feathers on the angel's paper wings. Maria's stock of cardboard and colored feathers seems to be waning, so she's managed to whine her way into possession of some of the old things from the days before responsibility for the nursing home was transferred to the town council.

The hundreds of angel pictures on the walls seem to absorb all the light, making the room darker than it needs to be. Although it's still morning out there in the world of human beings, in Maria's and the angels' room, endless night prevails. But there's something different about the room today. The table, usually over by the window, where the light is strongest, has been pushed aside. Scissors, feathers, rolls of tape, and cut-up magazines have been gathered into a pile in the middle.

The other patient's bed is along the wall over by the window. Her belongings look tenuous and alien here in Maria's treasure house: a binder and a few books are at the foot of her bed, a computer on a steel stand is at the head. A yellow hose with a nozzle at the end is suspended from the computer; it makes Christina realize which patient this is. Right, she's heard about this one, the woman at the nursing home who can communicate only by computer. Just now, though, the monitor has no words on it; the patient is beyond words and thus also out of reach by computer. But the screen saver is appropriate here in Maria's room. It's outer space and a galaxy, and when Christina looks at it she is momentarily dizzied— she feels for an instant as if she were being transported through the universe at the speed of light. She blinks, lowers her eyes to the patient's record. Desirée Johansson, d.o.b. December 31, 1949. Cerebral palsy, spastic, and severely epileptic since birth.

She looks like a baby bird, a naked little baby bird who hasn't got feathers yet. She's so thin she hardly appears to leave an imprint on her mattress, so emaciated every bone and ligament appears to be visible through her skin. The fingers on one of her hands have stiffened into what looks like a claw. She's lying in a strange position: on her back with her legs pulled up and crossed like a fetus. Her face is heart-shaped, her chin sharp and pointed. The skin on her eyelids is so thin you can see the blue delta of blood vessels under it.

So this is our Hubertsson's pet . . .

Christina's hands tremble slightly as she bends over the patient and puts the stethoscope to her chest. She glances once again at her records: it's obviously true that the woman has seizures on a daily basis, and the attacks of the last few years appear to have exacerbated her brain damage. Right now, however, she is resting calmly, her heart ticking as comfortingly and rhythmically as the clock in Aunt Ella's living room, and her breathing is steady, with no ambient noise. Christina puts her stethoscope back in her pocket and tests the patient's arm and leg reflexes. Everything seems fine, she finds no residual cramps. Finally, she opens the patient's mouth very carefully and shines her little flashlight inside. No, she does not appear to have bitten her tongue or the insides of her cheeks. There are no problems here, or at least as few problems as a person in this state can be having. Christina turns out her flashlight and inspects the sleeping patient. The poor tiny little thing . . .

The woman in the bed jerks and opens her eyes; for one instant Christina looks straight into her clear blue gaze, before her eyelids slowly shut again. Christina steps back, her heart pounding. In a split second it's all over. After a couple of breaths the patient appears to be sound asleep again and Christina's heart recommences beating at its normal, slightly stressed rate.

She straightens the striped top sheet on the patient's bed and tucks her in. This causes one of the books at the foot of the bed to fall to the floor, and Christina bends down and picks it up. She raises her eyebrows at the title: *Einstein's Dreams*. She takes a look at the other books on the bed. *The Quark and the Jaguar* by Murray Gell-Mann, Ray Bradbury's *Golden Apples of the Sun*, *The Benandanti: The Good Witch Masters* by Carlo Ginzburg. *Witches and Witch Trials* by Bror Gadelius. Plus a copy of Stephen Hawking's *Universe: The Cosmos Explained* that's been read so hard it's falling apart.

Christina shrugs. All that new physics business is Margareta's department, she's never had the energy to get involved. Margareta's harangues about matter and antimatter just give Christina a headache. The Big Bang and the expansion of the universe, quarks and strings and all that. There's a scent of New Age about it all, and that's a perfume Christina can't abide.

She piles the books neatly on the nightstand. She finds it touching to see such a worn copy of the Hawking. For a woman like this, he must be next to godly. The question is what she admires most about him, his brain or his fame? Or maybe even his love affairs?

A LITTLE WHILE later, crossing the parking lot, Christina discovers that she suddenly feels much better. The cool air is perking her up, and her heels clatter cheerily on the shiny, wet asphalt. Reflexively she sets her hand at the back of her head and lifts her hair, allowing the fresh lake-side wind to caress her neck. She suppresses a sudden impulse to open her arms wide and spin around; no GP in her right mind would be jubilant in a parking lot over the simple fact that the sky is blue and cloudless, the sun bright and sparkling, and the buds on the chestnut tree over there on the lawn bursting with life. It's this feeling of spring in the air that makes her so happy. Tomorrow's the equinox.

At Aunt Ella's, special rites and rituals surrounded every change of season. The coming of spring meant getting the summer clothes down from the attic, the fifteenth of September meant taking them back up again, irrespective of temperature or weather. If the girls complained that it was too hot or too cold, Aunt Ella responded with one of her endless store of proverbs: In like a lion, out like a lamb.

Christina smiles gently. In many senses, Aunt Ella's old-fashioned way of doing things was funny. For instance, she firmly believed that girls still wore pinafores to school in the fifties, just as she had in the twenties, and so she had made Christina a checkered cotton dress and an embroidered pinafore for her first day of school. But Aunt Ella was adaptable, too. She looked closely at the other little girls when she walked Christina to school, and when she saw how they were dressed, she simply bent down over Christina, untied the pinafore, and put it in her handbag. Which was actually a shame. It was a pretty thing, monogrammed with Christina's initials on the bib and a little border of birds at the bottom. Christina still has it, in a plastic bag in the Post-Industrial Paradise, along with other handmade items she got at the auction after Aunt Ella's death. Once in a while she opens one of the carefully taped plastic bags to take in what she recognizes as Aunt Ella's smell: strong soap and Christel talcum powder. But the scent dissipates a little every time, so she opens them sparingly.

She likes thinking about them, though, knowing they're there. That they belong to her. No one but her.

CHRISTINA WAS THE one who had to give up the most space when Birgitta moved into the empty room. Margareta had always lived in her bed—that was where she did her reading and drawing, where she played with her dolls and did her homework—while Christina used her bed only to sleep in. She did her reading and her homework at the table by the window. But there was no room for the table now, the new bed had to go there. Aunt Ella took the table out into the hall, but that was no good, it was too dark there. And now they weren't allowed to sit at the dining room table, either. By just her third day there Birgitta had managed to break one of the china figurines in the dining room, so all three girls were banished from there. All that was left was the kitchen table. But it had changed, too; now that Margareta and Birgitta had to sit there as well, it was impossible to concentrate. They talked all the time, giggling and whispering secrets.

Things were never really calm in the house again after Birgitta's arrival. She was almost electrified: she emitted sparks, and if you got too close you risked a shock. Every time the phone rang she grabbed it off its hook and shouted, *Hello!* before Aunt Ella could even turn around, and when the doorbell rang she rushed out like a fury. She never wanted to sit still and read like Margareta or sit and embroider or make lace like Aunt Ella and Christina. Her games were noisy whirlwinds, and when she wasn't playing a game she was making trouble. She never even hesitated to break Aunt Ella's rules: one day she opened the black cast-iron gate and wobbled out onto the road on Aunt Ella's bicycle; another day she ran away and was gone for hours before Aunt Ella found her in the middle of town at her old address; on a third occasion still she stole four crowns out of the pin money. And when Aunt Ella told her she'd have to spend two whole days in the empty room as punishment for her theft, she stuck out her tongue and shouted: "You old hag! You're not my mamma! You're not in charge of me."

Christina placed her hands firmly over her ears and shut her eyes tight when that happened. But Aunt Ella didn't notice right away, she had her hands full forcing Birgitta, kicking and screaming, into the empty room and locking the door. When she returned to the kitchen, there was blood under her nose. As she moved toward the sink, she glanced quickly in Christina's direction, saw that she remained stiff at the kitchen table and hissed: "Why are you still sitting there? The world's not coming to an end!"

A few minutes later, however, when Christina was on her knees throwing up into the toilet, Aunt Ella was her old self again, holding one hand on Christina's brow and patting her back with the other. "It's all right," she whispered. "Everything's going to be all right . . ."

But Aunt Ella had been wrong about that. Nothing was ever quite all right again. The first spring Birgitta wore them all out, each in a different way. With Margareta at her heels, she careened through the house and yard, conquering one square foot at a time. Margareta sometimes laughed, sometimes gasped, daily running the gauntlet between fear and fascination. Nothing was what it had been; now the attic was a witch haunt, the basement a ghost hideout, the garden a dangerous jungle. At bedtime Margareta burst into tears like a toddler, not letting Aunt Ella turn out the light. Aunt Ella wasn't allowed to leave the empty room while the girls were still awake, either. She had to sit at the side of Margareta's bed and hold her hand until she was fast asleep.

Aunt Ella's nose bled constantly. More and more often when the girls came home from school in the afternoon they would find her sitting in the living room, eyes shut, mouth hanging open, a wad of blood-red cotton in each nostril. Her lace-making pillow lay on the dining room table, untouched, and one day she even served those abominable, newfangled instant mashed potatoes for dinner. And still she just barely got her finishing work done that week, and only by sitting up until two in the morning the night before the van from the factory was to arrive.

Still, the very worst thing of all was that Aunt Ella didn't look at Christina the way she used to. All right, she did smile and say thank you as usual when Christina helped her with the dishes, quizzed her on her homework as she always had, and helped her when she had to count squares in her cross-stitching, but Christina now felt invisible the moment she stepped out of Aunt Ella's sight. Aunt Ella didn't follow her with her eyes as she used to. Had she, she would have seen that there were things worth noticing. That Christina was standing up straighter, for instance. Because now Christina was a girl who had to be constantly on the alert.

She couldn't figure out what had made Birgitta decide that she, of all people, was her worst enemy. But she had. Starting the very first week, Birgitta's eyes had narrowed when she looked at Christina. The next week Christina found her doll with no arms or legs, the week after a page was ripped out of the library book she'd borrowed. Soon she learned to be especially cautious about playing in the yard. Suddenly she'd be shoved from behind and fall flat on her face and rip both the knees of her stockings. The worst thing that could happen was that she ruined her stockings but didn't hurt herself, because then she'd get a lecture from Aunt Ella about how she ought to be big enough to know that stockings didn't grow on trees. Christina never dared to tell her she'd been pushed, because she knew that the moment she did, Birgitta would turn up at the edge of her field of vision, eyes more slitlike than ever. In addition to which, Aunt Ella had her principles, and one of them was that children should never tell tales. A stocking with a hole in it was almost always the fault of the person whose leg had been in that stocking. So it was much better if she scraped her knee, too. Then there would be no recrimination, just a Band-Aid, a cookie, and some words of comfort.

However, everything became somewhat easier once Birgitta had conquered the cherry tree. It had always been there, in the middle of Aunt Ella's yard, enticing them with promises of what awaited the person who first dared to climb to its highest branches. Christina and Margareta had often allowed themselves to be tempted, but neither had ever been daring enough to go any higher than the very bottom limbs. Birgitta dared to, though. Huffing and puffing, she pulled her awkward body from one branch to the next, higher and higher, ignoring the big scratches the bark was making on the insides of her thighs. Margareta began trying to climb after her but made it only to the middle, then just ended up hanging on to the trunk for dear life. Christina got no higher than she ever had. She just climbed onto one of the lower branches and stayed there, craning her neck desperately to look up at Birgitta and Margareta.

"Careful," she shouted.

But Birgitta wasn't careful: she laughed her throaty laugh, grabbed the next branch over her head with both hands, and pulled herself up to standing. Christina shut her eyes. She didn't know if she hoped or feared that Birgitta would lose her grip. All right, she hoped so. But the next time she looked Birgitta was sitting on her branch again. She hadn't fallen.

Birgitta's being such a good tree climber was what made Aunt Ella accept her, in the end. For the first few months she never laughed at anything Birgitta said or did. On the contrary, her voice went all rough and commandeering the minute Birgitta was in sight. But that June evening when she came out in the yard and saw the three girls poised in her cherry tree like fruit, her face brightened up with an enormous smile. "Good heavens a mercy," she said, looking over her eyeglass rims. "Nice climbing, Birgitta!"

She was carrying a tray. She set it down in the grass so hard the glasses of juice clinked against one another. She said, "Hold it right there, girls. I'm going to get the camera."

She managed to take a picture that had all three girls and the whole tree in it. It came out very well, so well that Aunt Ella had it both enlarged and hand-tinted. But the photographer made a mistake with his paints. Birgitta's dress came out pink and Christina's green, instead of the other way around. Birgitta was delighted with the switch: from the moment the framed photo took its place atop Aunt Ella's linen cupboard, she considered pink her very own color.

"Starting right now, everything that's pink is mine," she declared that night when they were all in bed in the empty room.

"And everything that's yellow is mine," said Margareta. "Because I'm wearing a yellow dress in the picture."

Christina twisted toward the wall in her bed. She could hear by the anticipation in their breathing that they were just waiting for her to speak. It was quiet for several minutes, until Margareta could stand the suspense no longer. "What about you, Christina?" she whispered. "Green or blue? Or red?"

Christina didn't answer. Pink was the only color she had ever liked.

HELENA IS WAITING for Christina in the doorway of the health center. "I rebooked one of Hubertsson's patients," she says. "But you'll have to see the other. And you're half an hour behind on yours."

"How many patients did Hubertsson have for this afternoon?"

"Six, but we're calling around to try to reschedule them."

Christina glides into the staff locker room and begins to take off her boots. "How's Hubertsson doing?"

"I tested him a few minutes ago. His blood sugar's rising. He's asleep at the moment."

"Okay, we'll see how things go, then."

"Oh, and your sister phoned."

Christina inhales sharply. "My sister?"

"Yeah. She wanted to say good-bye before leaving, but when I told her what was going on she said she'd call you when she got to Stockholm instead."

Christina relaxes. Over the last few hours she'd more or less forgotten having left Margareta at the Post-Industrial Paradise that morning.

"She asked to be remembered to Hubertsson, too," Helena adds with a smile. "I didn't know you had known him since you were kids."

"Well, we have."

"Amazing," says Helena. "I had no idea."

ACTUALLY, CHRISTINA ISN'T surprised Margareta had sent greetings to Hubertsson. She undoubtedly had wonderful memories of him. After all, he'd been her first love. Just before her fourteenth birthday Margareta had stopped rubbing against Aunt Ella like a cat and begun instead to puff up with yearning the minute Hubertsson was around, which was at dinner every day. Because after just six months in the apartment upstairs from Aunt Ella's, Hubertsson had abandoned all pretense of cooking his own meals.

"If I have to eat the contents of one more can I'm sure to develop scurvy," he declared, offering Aunt Ella a sizable sum of money every month in exchange for one hot meal a day. Plus the same amount again if she would do his washing and cleaning.

Aunt Ella needed only a minute to think about it. She certainly had the time. Christina and Margareta were now in secondary school and were away all day. Birgitta was working at the Luxor plant and was away even longer. And Ella needed the money. The house was sorely in need of various repairs, and hand-finishing for the textile mill didn't pay as it once had. Not to mention that the girls cost more and more to maintain. The extra cash would really come in handy.

Still, there would also be expenses associated with accepting Hubertsson's offer. No one could expect a real doctor to eat his dinner on an oilcloth from the Coop. So one day Aunt Ella took the train into Linköping to do some shopping, because in Motala you couldn't buy an oilcloth with a fancy Viola Gråsten pattern. And all the other ladies in her sewing circle said Viola Gråsten it had to be. Aunt Ella attended the circle regularly, although she was not one of the more voluble members. While she was in Linköping she also bought a can of varnish for the kitchen chairs, and material to make both table napkins and new kitchen curtains. Plus five natural pine napkin rings.

The napkin business posed a problem. One year in the forties—just before she became a home helper—Aunt Ella had been in domestic service for an architect and his family, and she had learned a thing or two at that job about the symbolic value of the napkin. This was a modern family, so Ella had her meals with the family on weekdays and, like everyone else, a clean linen napkin once a week. The difference between the gentry and the servants was marked most subtly: each member of the family had a personal napkin ring, while Ella was supposed to fold her napkin into a square and set it right on her plate.

In Aunt Ella's household there were no napkins except on special occasions. If you got sticky during a meal, you went to the lavatory afterward and had a wash, and that was fine. At Christmas, Midsummer, and when there were family parties, Aunt Ella bought thin little tissue napkins, but mostly because they looked nice. Now, however, things would have to be different, because she was certain Hubertsson was accustomed to both napkins and napkin rings. And wouldn't it look strange if he were the only one at the table with a napkin to open onto his lap?

Christina and Aunt Ella worked very hard one whole evening getting the kitchen in order. They sanded and varnished the kitchen chairs, hemmed the napkins, and hung the curtains. Birgitta mocked their zealous efforts, turned up the collar of her suede jacket, and went out on her Saturday adventure. Margareta hung around the kitchen door commenting and criticizing but never being any help. In the end Aunt Ella got sick of her and put her to work, making five woolen tassels in different colors for the napkin rings, so they all would know which was theirs. She let her pick the colors herself. Of course she gave Birgitta a pink one and herself a yellow one, while Christina got a white woolen tassel, and Aunt Ella a baby blue one. But for Hubertsson's napkin ring, she made a bright red satin bow.

Her cheeks were a matching shade of red when Hubertsson came down from his little apartment on Sunday evening for his first dinner in Aunt Ella's kitchen. "Your seat's at the end of the table," Margareta said boldly, thus marking the fact that she was no longer a little girl who spoke only when she was spoken to and called men Uncle. Hubertsson watched her in amusement. He was intelligent enough to realize what was making her eyes as bright as the newly varnished kitchen chairs. But he wasn't the least bit interested in being a wolf among the lambs. What interested him was a nice joint of beef with parsley potatoes, peas and carrots, rowanberry jelly, and pickled cucumbers. Over all of which he poured the creamy gravy, the scent of which hinted at vinegar and anchovies, bay leaves and black pepper, and had permeated every nook and cranny of the house at least an hour before.

So there they sat, the five of them, with their new napkins on their laps, at Aunt Ella's kitchen table eating in silence. Birgitta with her blond beehive hairdo and her kohl-blackened eyes, Margareta with her ponytail and rosy cheeks, Christina with her new glasses halfway down her nose, Hubertsson with a curl in the middle of his forehead, and a tense Aunt Ella with cheeks flushed from an afternoon at the stove. She wasn't able to relax until Hubertsson dug in for thirds.

"Pardon me," he said. "I don't normally eat so much. But this is absolutely delicious."

Everybody laughed. Even Birgitta.

* * *

OTHERWISE, THESE WERE years when Birgitta didn't laugh very often. Although she seemed to have grieved away all the sullen childishness in her nature when her mother died, she still didn't behave like the others after her first deep misery passed. She never flailed or screamed anymore, but her top lip was perpetually drawn back in a grimace of utter contempt.

Toward the end of her spring semester in seventh grade, she was transformed into a virtual pillar of determination. Evening after evening she sat at Aunt Ella's kitchen table repeating the same sentence: nobody can make me go to eighth grade! She was old enough to choose not to go to school, and only seven years were compulsory. In addition to which, Uncle Gunnar had promised to get her a job at the Luxor plant if she wanted one. She snorted when Aunt Ella tried to tell her factory work wasn't all that much fun. Fun? Who the hell went to work because it was fun? You went to work to make money. And at the Luxor plant even fourteen-year-olds like her earned good money.

From the very outset Christina was astonished to see what respect Aunt Ella showed for Birgitta's job. Suddenly it was more important to get Birgitta's lunch box ready than to quiz Christina and Margareta on their homework in the evening. And although Christina was three months older and Margareta just eleven months younger than Birgitta, Birgitta now seemed to have grown up, while the two of them were still just girls.

Aunt Ella didn't even protest about Birgitta's getup. She lent her the sewing machine willingly, to take in yet another pair of jeans or a skirt. In the end Birgitta had several skirts that were so tight you could follow the contours of her pudenda through the cloth. Which suited her perfectly, as you could see from her satisfied smile when she examined the results in the hall mirror. That was precisely how she wanted to look: protruding breasts in front and bottom at the back, and the indication of a triangle in the middle of her skirt.

She devoted a lot of time to her hair, to teasing and spraying it, to trying out new hairstyles and ways of brushing it. But when she was ready to go out, she always looked just the same: a huge pile of cotton candy atop her head, lips painted white and eyes black. A girl who hung around with the guys with the souped-up jalopies, no little scaredy-cat who didn't dare show what she was.

Christina found Birgitta disgusting. It was revolting, all that abundant white flesh and her ever-lowered eyelids. Not to mention the sour smell that always surrounded her and that now filled the empty room, even when Birgitta was out. However, Christina could find something disgusting about almost anyone nowadays. Hubertsson had disgusting fingers, pike-jowled Stig a disgusting mouth. Sometimes Christina even thought Aunt Ella had become a little disgusting. When she made breakfast in the mornings in nothing but her nightgown and bathrobe, her body emitted a sharp little odor that permeated the kitchen. That smell caused Christina to alter her own habits. Now she would never come to the kitchen table until she had washed and dressed and done her hair, and when Aunt Ella's scent got too overpowering she would just lift her newly washed hand to her nose and inhale the aroma of soap. It tickled her nose.

Margareta was actually the only one who was never disgusting. She didn't even get disgusting when Birgitta tried to make her into her own image, because no matter how Birgitta struggled with her teasing comb and her hair spray, her lipstick and mascara, she never managed to transform Margareta for very long. Just half an hour later Margareta looked like a raccoon somebody'd pulled up out of the well: her teased hair was straggly, her lipstick licked away, her mascara rubbed into black rings around her eyes. Aunt Ella would laugh and tell her to go wash up. *"Silly!"*

Sometimes Margareta even got to go along with Birgitta on her adventures. On those Saturday nights they'd push and shove at the hall mirror, with Aunt Ella standing in the kitchen doorway inspecting them over the rims of her glasses. She seldom commented, never preached or criticized. She seemed to have abdicated, seemed not to feel she had the right to have any opinions about this new, incomprehensible phenomenon known as the teens.

Nobody ever asked Christina to come along at times like that. It was Birgitta who settled it, without a word. Her open hostility toward Christina, however, had dissipated into indifferent contempt. Birgitta simply closed Christina out, became unaware of her existence, never addressed her except to fire a scornful comment, and seldom responded when Christina spoke to her. Moreover, she had developed a special look for Christina and Christina alone: a quick glance followed by an even quicker blink. *"Louse,"* that blink said. *"Don't even imagine I'd notice you!"*

Yet Christina knew everything Birgitta was up to, in the most minute detail. Margareta quite simply couldn't keep it to herself: every morning she spent their half-hour walk to the secondary school confiding in Christina everything Birgitta had confided in her. In the early days she was full of giggles: her eyes glittered as she whispered the name of the first boy Birgitta ever allowed to remove her bra, and the nickname of the one who had put his hands down her panties at the same time. But as the months passed, her smiles became more and more forced. One morning when she opened the door of a phone booth and pointed to the rhyme someone had written on the wall inside, there was no smile at all. Christina pushed her glasses to the bridge of her nose and read the first line out loud: *"Oh if I were in Birgitta's shoes . . ."*

"Hush!" cried Margareta, hand to mouth.

Christina stared at her, eyes wide. The moment she realized what was on the wall she knew not to read any more of it out loud. How could Margareta ever even have imagined she would say those horrible words?

Hands trembling, she began groping around in her schoolbag for her pencil case, fished out her best ballpoint pen—the one she otherwise used only to write the final drafts of her essays—and crossed out the graffiti on the wall as firmly as she could. What kind of an idiot had written those lines?

Margareta was crying. She leaned against the wall of the phone booth weeping as disconsolately as a child and sinking slowly to the ground. Her voice was thick, but she couldn't keep it inside anymore, had to tell the very worst part. "And at school I heard she went all the way with three different guys last Saturday. . . . But when I asked her she said she couldn't remember, had been too drunk to remember. And then she laughed!"

Panic fluttered in Christina's stomach. She pressed her pen even harder to the wall, drew another thick line through the graffiti, although she knew there was no point. Those words would never be effaced. Never ever.

The certainty sank like a stone in her body. She'd always known this day was coming. And here it was.

Disaster.

HELENA IS STANDING in the hallway to catch her as she says goodbye to the fourth patient.

"How's Hubertsson?" Christina asks, voice lowered.

"Out of danger," Helena answers just as softly. "I just went out and got him a couple of sandwiches. Bought one for you, too. Come on."

Christina casts a glance at the cubbyhole with the patient records outside the office door. There appear to be two patients in the waiting room. "Do I have time?"

"You have to take a break and eat something. Come on now."

Hubertsson's sitting at his desk, but with his back to the computer and his chair facing the middle of the room. Christina's never noticed his screen saver before, but now she sees it's a galaxy full of stars. She raises her eyebrows. Hubertsson wouldn't give a screen saver to just anybody. Kerstin One may be right when she calls that patient his pet.

"I checked on Desirée Johansson," she says tentatively. But Hubertsson doesn't react: he's busy inspecting the contents of the bag Helena has extended to him. He appears to fall for the ham sandwich, but makes a face at the sparkling water. "I would've liked a beer instead," he says.

Helena smiles understandingly, as if at a mischievous little boy. "Oh no, no beer for you for a while."

"Can't a poor fellow at least have a cup of coffee?"

"I was just going to get it," says Helena, gliding happily out through the door.

Christina bites into her own sandwich so as not to make a face. She must have seen a thousand nurses pandering to male doctors in the course of her career, and it irritates her anew every time. But really she has less reason to be annoyed with Helena than with most of them. Helena's not the kind of nurse who refuses to get records or test results for female doctors while running herself ragged for the men. But when it comes to Hubertsson, she sure makes a fool of herself.

Hubertsson, however, appears to take Helena's dedication entirely for granted. He looks pleased as he leans back in his desk chair and takes a swallow of his mineral water.

"So how are you feeling now?" Christina asks.

He gives her a crooked grin as he puts the bottle down. "No problems. Perky as a teenager."

Christina snorts. "A teenager who knows how to get into trouble, then."

He smiles widely and changes the subject. "I heard Margareta called and particularly asked to be remembered to me. How long will she be in town?"

CHRISTINA TAKES A swallow from her own bottle to postpone answering. He's been absolutely impossible for the last few months; the minute he gets a chance he tries to turn the conversation back to Margareta and Birgitta and Aunt Ella. And he does it on purpose, he knows it infuriates her.

"She's gone," she replies curtly. "She was just passing through. Incidentally, as I just mentioned, I had a look at one of your patients while I was at the nursing home. Desirée Johansson. Kerstin One had put four Valium suppositories up her, ten milligrams each."

But Hubertsson's stopped listening, he's sitting perfectly still, staring out the window. Christina follows his gaze: there's a bird on the windowsill. A gull. It stares intent at Hubertsson and then, with an ironic, elegant movement, sets one yellow webbed foot in front of the other and lowers its white head. Very slowly it opens its wings; they are gray and white and enormous, and nearly cover the lower half of the window. The bird seems to be bowing. No, more than that, to be genuflecting.

"My goodness," says Christina.

Her voice seems to penetrate the pane of glass; the bird rises with a jolt. Christina gets up, too, crosses to the window, and follows the gull, watches it hover over the parking lot. "Very strange," she says. "And yesterday . . . Aren't gulls migratory birds?"

"Certainly not," says Helena, setting a tray of coffee on Hubertsson's desk. "Some stay the winter. What makes you ask?"

Christina glances at Hubertsson; he's no longer sitting still, has angled his chair to reach for a cup of coffee. "There was this weird gull out there. And yesterday we found a dead one in our yard."

Hubertsson stops in mid-motion, the cup halfway to his mouth. "Oh?"

"That's right. Broken neck. Erik said it must have crashed right into the side of the house."

Helena says with a laugh, "Must be mad gull disease. We'd better notify the local bird-watching society."

She doesn't notice the suspicious look that's come over Hubertsson's face. But Christina does. The bizarre thing is that he looks like Aunt Ella. Her face had gotten that very look when, after several days of hesitation, Christina had finally told her what she knew about Birgitta. And that was the very shade of gray her face was the next afternoon when she lay on the living room floor, no longer able to move or speak.

"The child welfare authorities have taken the girls into custody," pike-jowled Stig had written on a note he'd thumbtacked to Hubertsson's door.

All three of them stood pale and silent in Aunt Ella's hall. Out in the kitchen the stuffed cabbage was still on the stove, its aroma permeating the air; the table was set for dinner, but it hadn't occurred to any of them to put the dinner dishes away and the stuffed cabbage in the refrigerator.

"Got everything you need?" asked Stig with a voice exuding authority. "Toothbrushes? Nightgowns? Schoolbooks?"

No one answered, but Margareta nodded numbly.

Outside, the first snow of winter was falling, dusk lay gray over the yard, transforming it into a black-and-white photograph.

"We're all going to my house now," said Stig, locking the front door. "For a few days anyway, until we know whether or not this is going to be a long story."

Bitte had set them up in the recreation room, a dark little corner of the basement in their newly built home. Stig had put up seaweed green wallpaper, and Bitte had decorated the room with a set of commemorative china plates. She looked anxiously at Birgitta, who was pulling off her cardigan with large, sweeping movements, and said: "Collectors' plates are very expensive, so I'd appreciate if you'd keep an eye . . ."

At dinnertime they crowded around the kitchen table: Bitte's boys—well, they were her boys, almost exclusively hers—took up a lot of space with their enormous adolescent hands and their long legs. Christina and Margareta had to share one end of the table, and Birgitta and Bitte were cramped in at the other. The only ones who said anything at all were Bitte and Stig.

"So they took her to Linköping," said Bitte, shaking her head and drinking some of her milk. "She must have been very bad off, then . . ."

"You never know," said Stig, glancing at Christina. "That's not necessarily true. They have the best doctors in Linköping. The specialists. They'll have her up and around again much faster than the doctors here in Motala would."

Bitte shook her head. "But a brain hemorrhage . . ."

Stig banged his milk glass down on the table. "We're not even sure it *was* a brain hemorrhage."

"Well, didn't Hubertsson say . . ."

"Hubertsson!" spat Stig contemptuously, wiping his mouth with the back of his hand.

THREE WEEKS LATER, on Sunday, he was opening the door of his Volvo Amazon and telling the girls to be quick. Christina settled into a corner of the backseat, carefully placing Aunt Ella's big hibiscus on her lap. When she'd gone to Aunt Ella's after a week to straighten up and water the plants, it had been bone-dry and lost a lot of leaves, but now it had recovered and had three big buds. She wanted Aunt Ella to see when it bloomed, from her hospital bed in Linköping. Margareta sat next to her, pressing to her tummy the framed photo of the three girls in the cherry tree. Birgitta sat in the front seat, empty-handed.

They weren't talking. They'd barely exchanged a word since it had happened. Margareta didn't even talk in the mornings when she and Christina were walking to school, nor did she speak in the evenings. She didn't even bury her nose in a book, as usual. When she had dutifully written her vocabulary lists and done the math problems that were her homework, she lay on her air mattress in the rec room, staring at the ceiling.

Christina was more active. After the first week she went to Aunt Ella's house daily, took in the mail and sorted it, watered the plants and dusted. Now and then she vacuumed, not because it was necessary but because she found the sound of the vacuum cleaner comforting. She never went up to Hubertsson's, just put his mail on the bottom step and shut the door silently behind her.

She hardly ever saw Birgitta, who left for work early in the morning and never came home for supper. Every night, though, Christina would wake up when Birgitta tiptoed down the stairs to the rec room, shoes in hand. Perhaps she sensed that Bitte's boys were ashamed to have her in the house. Their flirtatious smiles and hungry looks were extinguished the day one of Kjelle's classmates whispered that rhyme to him. Everyone in Motala knew it now. It had flown all over town like a bird on the wing.

Stig inspected them when they got out of the car at the Linköping county hospital. "Ready?" he asked in his military voice.

Margareta nodded, Christina whispered a yes. But Birgitta suddenly took a step backward. "I don't want to come in," she said.

"Don't give me any trouble now," said Stig, shutting the car door.

Birgitta shook her head so hard her beehive trembled. "I really don't want to."

Stig grasped her by her upper arm, his voice falling an octave: "Cut it out right now."

With a single movement, Birgitta tore loose, so violently the bobby pin holding her blond bangs up from her forehead fell to the asphalt. She turned around and began to run, as fast as her tight skirt and high-heeled shoes allowed. Halfway across the parking lot she turned around and cried out in a piercing voice: "I'm not going in there! Are you deaf, you old fart?"

Stig shrugged and stuffed his car keys into the pocket of his Sunday suit jacket. "Let her run away, then, the little tramp."

"YOU LOOK LIKE Captain Hook," said Margareta, laughing through her tears. Aunt Ella smiled her new, lopsided smile, raising her trembling left hand to the black patch covering her right eye.

"She can't blink," the woman in the next bed informed them. "That's why the patch. Otherwise her eye would dry out."

For a split second Christina was sure this was the same woman who had hovered over her own hospital bed ten years earlier, and she swiveled her head and gave her such a hostile look the woman got right up out of bed and started shuffling toward the door. It wasn't the same woman, of course, Christina realized a moment later, but she was still glad to see her leave the room. The bold stares of the other four patients on the ward were quite enough.

Aunt Ella was still unable to speak. When she tried, nothing passed over her lips but a little saliva froth. Still, both Christina and Margareta knew what she wanted. Margareta sat on the edge of her bed, lifted Aunt Ella's hand to her own cheek. Christina sank to her knees at the head of the bed, laying her head on the pillow alongside Aunt Ella's.

None of them spoke. There was nothing more to say.

THAT AFTERNOON THEY gathered in Stig's living room. He stood next to the big table, his shirtsleeves rolled up, while the girls sat on the new, flowered couch: Christina on the left, Birgitta on the right, Margareta the shock absorber in the middle. Stig didn't dare look right at them, but kept his eyes firmly glued to three neat piles of documents from the child welfare board on the table in front of him, as he painstakingly searched his breast pocket for cigarettes and a lighter. It took him an eternity to pull a Chesterfield out of the pack and light it.

"All right," he said, exhaling a cloud of smoke. "I'm sure you all realize, now that you've seen her."

He paused briefly, his eyes still stubbornly lowered. "This is what we've arranged," he said. "The board has organized a little studio apartment for Birgitta and a new foster family for Margareta. And Christina will be moving in with her mother in Norrköping."

A FEW HOURS later, when the white, late winter day has just begun to be shrouded in the pink silk of sunset, Christina catches a glimpse of Hubertsson. He's crossing the parking lot in his old overcoat, briefcase in hand. So he must be on his way home, he never puts his coat on just to walk over to the nursing home. He must be tired of hearing Helena's chatter. No, he doesn't seem to be walking to his old Volvo . . .

Christina glances at her watch; they're still way behind, despite her best efforts to be quick with each patient. The next one was born in 1958. That's good. Men of that age don't usually want to pass the time of day.

Just as she's getting up to beckon him in from the waiting room, she looks out the window again and sees Hubertsson stop. He's turned in the direction of the health center and is obviously speaking to someone. Christina gives a little grin. Helena must have seen him through the window and be giving him a piece of her mind for not going straight to his car . . .

But Hubertsson doesn't like being told off; he raises his bushy eyebrows and responds, then turns abruptly around and heads for the nursing home. Christina hears the window of the nurses' office slam shut. Hubertsson hears it, too. He raises his briefcase dismissively in response.

She's seen that gesture before. Once, thirty years ago.

IT WAS AT that time of day, on Saturday afternoon, when all Swedish towns went silent, the shops were shut and the people withdrawn into their homes. A damp dusk lay heavily over Norrköping, the dark facades of the buildings had just begun to be illuminated with yellow squares of light, and the streetlamps had started to develop halos.

Christina stopped for a moment after she closed the hospital door behind her, standing on the steps, slowly putting on her gloves. She was in no hurry. She was never in a hurry when it was time to go home from her weekend job at the hospital.

There was a bit of a gap between where the sleeve of her duffel jacket ended and her mitten began. She'd grown a couple of inches in the year she'd been living in Norrköping, and most of her clothes were getting too small and worn out as well. The underwear was the worst. When her class had gym she always tried to hide behind a locker door so no one would see the holes in her panties or the grayness of her only bra.

It had never occurred to her to ask Astrid for clothes money, but she set aside a little of the money she made at work every month, stuffing a couple of worn bills inside her math book cover. It would take time to save up for a new duffel jacket, but maybe that was just as well. She couldn't imagine how Astrid would react if she suddenly saw a new coat in the hall.

So for the moment Christina would have to go on pulling up the ends of her mittens, or sticking her hands deep into her jacket pockets. But next week she would get herself a new bra. And some panties. Astrid would never notice them.

She pulled up her hood to protect her hair from the drizzle and crossed the shiny asphalt on the diagonal, not looking up until she was out on the South Promenade. There she stopped for a moment; there was a trolley at the stop, and she considered treating herself to a ticket. Then she changed her mind. Better to save the money and take a little longer to get home. If she walked she wouldn't be there for another hour.

That was when she saw him. It took her a second to realize who it was, and it brought a gasp to her lips; the whole world seemed to shift slightly sideways, as if she'd been shoved. The next moment her whole body was joyous. There he was! It really was him getting off the trolley in front of Norrköping hospital!

"Hubertsson," she shouted. "Hubertsson!"

His eyes ran along her at first, not finding anything to lock on to, and for a second it looked as if he thought he'd heard wrong and was just going to keep on walking.

Christina panicked, rushed over and grabbed him by the arm. "Don't you recognize me? It's me, Christina!"

He took one step back, inspected her. "Oh, right. It is you."

The words tumbled out of her: "How's Aunt Ella?"

Hubertsson made a little face. "Status quo."

"Does she get my letters?"

"Yes."

"Are they going to keep her at your nursing home?"

"It's not my nursing home. But yes, I suppose so."

"Is it all right to visit her?"

"Of course it's all right. And how are you, by the way?"

Christina shrugged.

"Aha," said Hubertsson. "Aha."

There was a moment's silence, then he cleared his throat and turned impatiently. "I must run along. I've got an appointment. . . . Be well."

Christina nodded, all her joy dissipated; she found herself standing there awash in disappointment. It was as if Hubertsson's indifference had severed the last silver thread that tied her to the past. But maybe it could be repaired. If she didn't buy that new underwear. The thought caused her to call out to him once more: "Hubertsson!"

He turned around without stopping, kept walking backward as she asked her question.

"How much is a train ticket to Vadstena?"

"Thirty crowns!"

He turned back around, raising his briefcase in a dismissive farewell.

THAT WAS ALL. As if she didn't exist.

However, that was nothing new. Ever since she'd arrived in Norrköping it was as if she had become a glass figurine; people didn't notice her until they happened to bump into her. Beyond the teachers at school, there were only three human beings with whom she spoke: Astrid, Margareta, and Sister Elsie.

Sister Elsie seemed almost to like her. On their Saturday morning coffee breaks, she always asked how the math test that week had been, and when Christina reported she'd gotten another A, Sister Elsie would nod with such satisfaction her double chin wobbled.

But she wasn't always equally pleased. Now and then she would tilt Christina's chin between her thumb and index finger and scrutinize her face. Was she really eating as she should? Getting enough sleep? A healthy teenager should have rosy cheeks, not big bags under her eyes. And although she was a very good student and a good girl to have a weekend job, too, and undoubtedly a great help to her mother, wasn't she overdoing it? Shouldn't she spend the weekends getting rest and fresh air instead?

Christina was always ashamed when Sister Elsie raised her chin. It was as if her pale face were lying. That job was, in fact, the only restful thing she did. At the hospital she didn't have to be constantly on her guard; here it sufficed to be polite and respectful, and to do as she was told. But there was no way she could say that.

Nor could she tell Sister Elsie that she was one of the factors that made it restful here, that Christina's tense neck muscles always relaxed the minute she heard Sister Elsie's voice and smelled the scent of soap and rose water that encircled her round little body. She wore a tight girdle under her pale blue nurse's uniform, soft but composed, precisely like Christina herself wished to be. But instead Christina was turning slowly, day by day, into an ice sculpture: hard and frozen stiff on the outside, although still mushy and viscous inside.

Sometimes she fantasized that Sister Elsie would ask her if she'd like to become apartment mates. Her apartment would turn out to be in one of those English-style town houses along the South Promenade, and Christina would have her own bedroom there, with roses on the wallpaper. Every evening she would do her homework at a little nineteenth-century lady's secretary while Sister Elsie was out in the kitchen making their evening tea. Then they'd sit side by side in the little living room listening to a play on the radio. . . . But of course Sister Elsie never asked her anything of the kind. As far as she knew, Christina lived with her mother and wanted to go on doing so, like all other high school girls.

Once Christina had seen Sister Elsie shudder with aversion when she heard the other nurses talking about Hageby, and from that day on she inspected her rubber boots carefully before entering the hospital grounds. There mustn't be any mud around the edges, because it was their filthy shoes that identified the inhabitants of Hageby, the newest housing project in Norrköping. The first tenants had moved in over a year ago, but the area was still not much more than a muddy construction site.

Astrid had been one of those first tenants. She'd been on the waiting list for a new apartment for years and finally had a one-bedroom apartment at the very top of a tall, cement-gray building. Even now, a year later, she still commented daily on her good fortune and complained at length and with the greatest of contempt about the old wooden building with no conveniences she'd left behind. Christina was always careful not to say a word about the apartment that could be interpreted as criticism, not a word about the muddy site outside, but when she was elsewhere she was equally careful not to mention her address. Not that anyone would ever ask, not that she had any friends.

There was no one in her class she could talk to, but she didn't find that surprising. The others had been classmates since childhood, Christina was the new girl. In addition to which she didn't really have the energy to extend herself to try to make friends. Between classes she'd take some homework out to the school yard and find a spot where she could prepare for the next lesson in peace. There were other pale girls around the periphery of the school yard as well, but there was something overwhelming about the idea of trying to spark a conversation with one of them.

Margareta had turned up quite soon, after the first Christmas vacation. She'd run up to Christina in the school yard, so unexpectedly that Christina hadn't even had time to react before she was being showered with Margareta's regular waterfall of words. Did Christina know Aunt Ella had been moved to Hubertsson's nursing home in Vadstena? Margareta had been there to see her the week before she moved to her new foster home in Norrköping. Now she was an only child, with a room of her own and piles of new clothes. Why didn't Christina come with her one day after school and have a look?

The bell rang before Christina could get a word in edgewise, and the next time she caught sight of Margareta she was already over in the corner where smoking was allowed, flirting with a boy a year older than them. She'd never repeated her invitation, and nowadays they just said hi and how are you when they passed in the halls. They didn't have much in common. Or perhaps it was that Christina had so much not to tell, perhaps that Margareta had her hands full transforming herself into the perfect teenager. After just a month she looked as if she had been cut right out of the latest issue of *Seventeen*. It was difficult to believe that this was the same girl who had allowed herself to be made up to look like she was going out with a guy from the motorcycle gang just one year earlier. Now she had the pageboy haircut that was in fashion, and wore a scarf that hung all the way to her knees. She was in with the in-crowd, no doubt about it. While Christina was a nothing. Well, a bookworm, of course.

*   *   *

DURING THE FIRST few weeks after she moved back in with Astrid, Christina had made three decisions. One: she was going to get her diploma, whatever the price. Two: she was not going to think about the past. Three: she was not going to cry.

This third decision was actually the prerequisite for the first two. And that made it the most difficult one. Sometimes she wondered if she was turning out like one of those Pavlovian dogs she'd read about in school. She didn't go around feeling unhappy. In fact, she didn't feel much of anything, but still her eyes filled with tears every afternoon when she put the key in the door of Astrid's apartment. It was as if there were a crying machine in her body. The minute she shut the door her body was trembling with sobs, her eyes overflowing, her mouth opening involuntarily and emitting inarticulate moans. Trying to fool herself by hanging her duffel jacket neatly on a hanger didn't help. It was as if she were standing outside her own body, watching her own hands fumble and drop her jacket to the floor. Calmly, with the greatest of discipline, she bent down and lifted it up, her mouth still moaning and whimpering, howling, and roaring.

"Why did you have to tell?" the crying machine whined. "Why couldn't you just keep quiet?"

What could she say to that? Nothing. What was done was done.

Her tears always stopped just as suddenly and inexplicably as they'd started; the machine jolted and stopped. Christina gasped for air, sniveling, and looked at her watch. The crying machine was as punctual as ever. Astrid would be home in twenty minutes. She rinsed her face in cold water and started peeling potatoes. And as one brown knob after the next turned white in her hands, she swore to herself once more that she would never weep again. She just had to stop, it was as logical and as necessary as the answer to a math problem. Because if she didn't stop crying she wouldn't have time to do her homework properly, and if she didn't do her homework her grades would be worse, and if she got worse grades Astrid would force her to drop out of school. She might even force her to the very worst possible fate: working at the textile mill.

Anything else she could take. But not that.

DURING THE FIRST Christmas vacation, just a month after Christina's arrival in Norrköping, Astrid had arranged a job for her at the mill. She'd made it sound like she was doing Christina a tremendous favor: thanks to the fact that she herself was so well liked by both the foreman and her fellow workers, her daughter was given one of the few sought-after vacation jobs. In the weaving mill, nonetheless.

The mill was Astrid's universe. Every day when she got home from work she sat down heavily on a kitchen chair, rubbed her swollen feet, and gave a detailed account of the events of the day. The quality controllers, those stuck-up bitches, were demanding a nickel an hour more than the weavers. One of the dumb Finns out in the yarn stockroom had got his leg caught in a door, which served him right, clumsy bastard. Birgit was going to be a grandma, though she was only thirty-four. Nothing strange about that, since both she and her daughter had always been real easy lays, Maud and Monkan agreed with her about that . . .

Maud and Birgit, Monkan and Babs; the names flew past Christina, who had no idea what faces went with them. But her mind quickly came to paint its own picture of the mill, beyond Astrid's tales. It was the most up-to-date textile mill in all of Sweden. So it should be shiny with stainless steel. All the floors were parquet, which was necessary for the machinery. So the floors must gleam, too. The looms were fully automated. Thus the huge rooms housing the looms should be virtually free from human beings.

Reality was a blow. When the foreman opened the door to the loom hall where Christina was to sweep her way through Christmas vacation, she felt as if someone had been boxing her ears. What a dark place! And so ugly! The looms were pale grasshopper green, and the parquet floors were so cracked and worn the place looked like a bomb site. But that wasn't the worst part. The worst part was the dull growl she'd noticed in the background since the minute they walked through the gates of the mill; it grew to a roar when the doors to the loom hall opened. It was a wild scream from a creature capable of anything imaginable, a madman who beat her up and lashed her body. The giant, she'd thought, before she stopped thinking. The giant's shouting for more meat for his grinder . . .

That was what made her dare to dial the number to the personnel office of the hospital, with a trembling hand, when summer vacation began to approach. A few quick questions, and it was settled. She had a job from the first day of summer vacation. She could even work on the last day of school if she wanted. They were desperate for nurse's aides.

Until then there had been an armed truce between herself and Astrid.

She'd moved in on a Sunday, and Astrid had welcomed her with coffee, pastries, and a hesitant smile, but only a few hours later her voice had roughened. By bedtime, when the time had come to make up the convertible sofa in the living room, Christina hastened to say that she could do it herself, it was no trouble. But she didn't do it immediately. When Astrid left the room she walked straight over to the balcony door and opened it wide. She stood still there for a moment, taking a deep breath to rid her lungs of Astrid's cigarette smoke. A dubious optimism welled up in her. Maybe it wouldn't be so bad. Maybe pike-jowled Stig had been right when he frowned at her tearful face and called her prejudiced. He'd preached a long sermon to her before she left Motala. Didn't Christina know that the mentally ill had been left in the shadows of society for far too long? These were new times, mental illness was no longer incurable or shameful, there were drugs and constructive social policy. Christina's mamma was, in fact, an outstanding example of the kind of progress there had been. She was perfectly healthy now, fully capable of caring for and supporting her own daughter. There was nothing for Christina to worry about. What had happened in Aunt Ella's kitchen when she was eleven was an expression of an illness long since cured. It would not recur, pike-jowled Stig guaranteed her.

Christina walked over to the sofa bed and opened it out. It was a particularly ugly piece of furniture, nubbly brown, heavy as a tank. All the furniture in the room was heavy and brown. And Astrid appeared to have something against corners. Nowhere could you see where two walls met; the furniture was angled to hide the corners as if they were a shameful secret. And the teak ledge by the balcony door was covered in a thick layer of dust . . . she'd run the vacuum and dust the surfaces after school tomorrow, maybe that would soften Astrid's voice up a little.

As Christina began to unfold the bottom sheet, she heard Astrid emerge from the bathroom. She must have felt a little puff of the evening air, because one second later she was in the living room doorway, in her bra and panties. "What the hell are you up to?" she asked Christina, wide-eyed.

Christina grabbed the sheet tight. "I'm making my bed."

"Don't be an idiot. What's the balcony door doing open?"

"I wanted to air the room out."

"Air it out? What for? Jesus, it's winter you know, the whole place will be freezing cold in no time."

Astrid crossed over to the balcony door and slammed it shut, fumbled with the blinds, pulled them down and twisted them closed. When she turned back around her eyes were slits and her voice was muffled. "Are you one of those girls who likes to show her body off?"

Christina blinked and felt faint, as if her legs would give way under her, but she forced herself to remain upright.

Astrid grinned. "Oh, I get it. Of course you are. You're just one of those girls who likes undressing in front of the open window, showing off her boobs to every dirty old man passing by."

Christina opened her mouth to explain that she was, in fact, still fully dressed, that she had had every intention of closing the blinds as soon as she had made the bed, and that in addition no one could look into the windows of a twelfth-floor apartment, but she couldn't get a single word out of her mouth. Her body had made up its mind. Words were no good.

"Don't stand there staring at me," said Astrid. "Get to bed. And remember that I will not have any goddamn tarty types. If you want to live with me, you'll behave."

STILL, FOR THE first few months Astrid seemed almost normal, if a bit unpredictable. She got up when her alarm clock rang in the morning, put on the kettle, washed and brushed her teeth, woke Christina, and put out the breakfast things. In the evenings she watched TV in the living room while Christina sat out in the kitchen doing her homework. Every now and then she'd shout out a brusque order: she wanted a cup of coffee or her foot basin or a new pack of cigarettes, and Christina would scurry to get the coffee, fill the basin with water, or run down to the shop. But she never hung around the living room afterward. The minute she'd satisfied Astrid's need she'd mutter something about her homework or a test and withdraw to the kitchen table.

Talking too much to Astrid had its risks. It was impossible to know what words, what subjects of conversation, would bring that gleam to her eye, that cold little gleam that inevitably forced Christina to lower her eyes and not say another word. The word *crazy* was taboo, even when one of the teachers Astrid held in such contempt had done something really crazy. Nor was she allowed to mention Aunt Ella or Motala or ask any questions about Astrid's past or the man who had once made her pregnant. Beyond which there was a total ban on any conversation that might lead to the subjects of medications, fires, or little children.

It wasn't very difficult to keep quiet, though. The difficult thing was to see to it that Astrid never felt criticized. If Christina did the dusting and the vacuuming too often, or emptied the overflowing ashtrays when Astrid was looking, she might have an episode. Once she poured all the cigarette butts and the used coffee grounds out onto the living room rug; another time she rubbed her own dirty panties in Christina's face to punish her for having been so impertinent as to pick them up off the hall floor. But these were exceptions. Most times she just gave Christina a piece of her mind. And that was enough. It was quite sufficient for her to raise her voice, letting it get just a little shrill, to make Christina go pale and drop her dustcloth or the vacuum hose. The truce came to an end on the day, after weeks of terrified anticipation, when Christina broke the news to Astrid that she'd arranged a different summer job for herself than the one Astrid had in mind.

Astrid's initial harangue took longer than usual, which wasn't a good sign. She made it sound as if Christina was displaying disdain for the mill by taking a job at the hospital, and now she was going to show her that Astrid could be contemptuous, too, in case she doubted it. She paced the living room floor, chain-smoking and talking nonstop. Working at the hospital was a prissy job if she'd ever heard of one, but Christina *was* a real little priss, wasn't she? Spoiled rotten and so uppity it was disgusting. But there was one thing she should understand very well, if she was going to be a little lady, which was that room and board cost just as much for ladies as for regular people. So she would damn well see to it that she paid precisely as much for her room and board during the summer as she'd done at Christmas vacation, irrespective of how little she made emptying bedpans. She couldn't expect Astrid to subsidize her lady's ways because, as opposed to that Ella woman, Astrid wasn't being paid to look after Christina. And if she wasn't satisfied with the arrangements she could just move out: Astrid had fended for herself from the age of fourteen, living in rented rooms. Christina had already been allowed to finish ninth grade, which was more than anybody had ever let Astrid do, although she had been at the top of her class, best student at the school, truth be told. And forget finishing high school, that was just one more of the ways in which she was above her station. She supposed it was that damn Ella who had given Christina ideas, just as she'd filled her mind with all kinds of lies about Astrid. Was Christina such a birdbrained idiot that she thought Astrid didn't know it? Well, probably. Stupid and lazy, those were the words. It sure was one helluva lot easier to sit your behind down at a desk like an upper-class kid than to take an honest job and start paying your way . . .

The lavender sky outside the living room window seemed to be moving toward dusk. Christina felt she could sink right into it at the same time as she sat stiffly, hands in her lap, in Astrid's living room. A flock with hundreds of black birds flew toward the sunset, then turned in instantaneous formation and changed direction. One moment later Christina focused her eyes on Astrid, for the first time without recoiling, and inspected her. Her tall, bony body was so unlike Christina's own, as different as her long, pointed chin and hooked nose were from Christina's. A thought crossed her mind: this isn't my mother. We're not even related. It's all a ridiculous misunderstanding.

Astrid had stiffened.

"What the hell are you staring at? Are you even listening?" Her hands trembled as she raised them into fists before Christina's eyes. There was a froth of saliva at the left-hand corner of her mouth. "Have you heard one single damn word I've said? I'm telling you I won't pay your way any longer!"

Christina pushed her aside and got up, suddenly icy calm. "How much do you want?"

Astrid's fists opened out, her hands fell to her sides. "What?"

"How much do you want?"

"What do you mean?"

"How much do you want me to pay a month to live here?"

Astrid gaped. Christina's mind started working it out, she'd always been good at math problem solving. "I gave you a hundred and twenty-five crowns for Christmas vacation. That was three weeks. So the price of room and board in this house must be one sixty-six a month. I'll be able to afford that for the summer, too, I'll even have twenty-five left for myself. And in the fall you'll get my student grant, four hundred twenty-five, in which case I'll still owe you two hundred thirty-nine a semester, which makes fifty-nine. Let's round if off to sixty. I'll see that you get it, I promise."

Walking erectly, she exited the living room and went into the kitchen, turned on the water, and got a glass from the cupboard. What a feeling! Her mind was as clear and cool as the water flowing into her glass. But she was thirsty, God she was thirsty . . .

She'd just raised the glass to her lips when Astrid kicked her. It flew from her hand, landing on the green-striped rag runner but not breaking, just rolling down to the linoleum and under the kitchen table.

"Let me tell you one thing," said Astrid, groping with her blue fingers to get a solid grip on Christina's hair. "When somebody kicks me in the ass, I kick back."

Christina shut her eyes and emptied her mind. This must have happened before. Otherwise, why could she already taste blood?

CHRISTINA TURNS OUT the ceiling light when she's closed the door after the last patient of the day, and sinks down into her chair. She just needs to rest her eyes for a few minutes, they're so tired. All of her is tired, really: the long, sleepless night suddenly rolls in over her like a tidal wave . . .

She leans back and extends her hands, surveying her long, thin fingers in the afternoon light from the window. They're straight and strong; nothing about their shape reveals that they conceal five fractures that have healed without medical attention, two on the fingers of her left hand, three on her right. In fact, she didn't even realize she was walking around with healed fractures until she was at medical school. In one class she had been asked to put her hands into an X-ray machine, and when the image was projected in front of the group of medical students, a hiss of interest filled the air. There was no way she could get out of the bone density scan the teacher then insisted on, but when the results proved to be perfectly normal she did manage to fend off his questions. She had no idea when or how she had fractured those fingers. Maybe trying to catch herself with her hands after a fall on the ice one winter. Oh, the X ray indicated the fractures had occurred on different occasions. How odd. Did they hurt? No, she had no recollection of ever having aching fingers . . .

Her eyes smart as she recalls the pain. The fingers were always Astrid's finale. At that point she was bleary-eyed with euphoria and her lips were wet with saliva. She pushed Christina to the floor, set her knee against her rib cage, and forced out a finger from her clenched fist. The second before it happened the apartment was always so quiet you could hear a pin drop: Astrid raised her head a little and took a deep breath, Christina gasped for air and tried to stifle the scream she knew was about to come . . .

But not the last time. Not the day before she graduated from high school. That time she shouted, loud and shrill: "It doesn't matter what you do to me. I'm going to be a doctor anyway. I'll be a doctor someday no matter what you do!"

"You prissy, stuck-up bitch," Astrid whispered. "You snotty little shit! You'll never be a doctor, you'll end up in the nuthouse."

Her grip on Christina's ring finger tightened, she forced it farther and farther back.

The pain glowed, white, but Christina still managed to get her words out: "That's what you think! But it's not congenital."

Now it was going to happen. Soon. Any second. She bit her lips. If she let out so much as a sound even more of her would shatter.

And she had no intention of giving Astrid the satisfaction of being right. Never would she let Astrid be right.

CHRISTINA LOWERS HER hands. That's quite enough. She has no desire to remember any more.

"I can't wait to get home," she whispers to herself, with a little smile. The Post-Industrial Paradise isn't very far away. All she has to do is get up and put on her cape. She can leave her car in the lot and take a nice walk through Vadstena in the blue twilight, and when she gets home she can light a fire in her tile stove, throw a shawl around her shoulders, and drop into an armchair with a cup of tea and a good book. It will be so quiet all around her that she will be able to pretend the rest of the world is empty, that she's as secure as only the very last person on earth could be . . .

That's what she thinks. But she doesn't get up, doesn't get her cape, just goes on sitting there in her desk chair. And she'll still be sitting there when the phone rings.

The Mentally Retarded Smile

All we have is each other
Each other Each other Each other

We are a double scream

Lars Forssell

I DON'T WANT to wake up. Don't want to know.

More and more frequently, my seizures cost me an ability or two. My epilepsy is an autumn storm and I a solitary tree. It tears at me and shakes me so leaf after leaf falls to the ground. Soon there will be nothing but the naked branches.

Last week I lost the feeling in my right foot. I don't want to know what I lost today.

BUT IT ISN'T even autumn. Tomorrow's the spring equinox. The first day of spring and the last day of winter.

The *benandanti* feel it as an itch all over their bodies. They can hardly sit still at the dull banks or shops where they work; they're imagining fennel and sorghum instead of debit and credit, their eyes can hardly focus, they don't listen when they're spoken to. They just want to get away, knowing that those who died early are already gathering, preparing for that night's procession.

Other people—people like Hubertsson and Christina, Margareta and Birgitta—know nothing about this. Most of them don't even remember the spring equinox, and of those who remember, fewer yet know that this was a sacred day in other times. Every year, ever since Tiamat and Marduk were the gods of Mesopotamia, winter and spring have battled; in the Inuit culture a man born in the winter has had a wrestling match with a man born in the summer; in ancient Sweden there was a tournament between the Count of Winter and the Count of Summer; in Germany men and animals were lashed with budding twigs. But the real battle has been a secret one. For centuries, *benandanti* have fought against witches in covert night struggles on the spring equinox, first in medieval Italy, later up in the Nordic part of the world. In the South they were armed with fennel stalks while the witches had branches of sorghum; in the North it was budding branches of leafy trees against the coniferous branches of the witches. But everywhere the object of the battle was the same: the next season's harvest. The *benandanti* protected mankind against starvation.

I bear the secret insignia of a witch, the *stigma diaboli*: I am unable to cry. I have never been able to cry. Still, I turn deserter and join the *benandanti* each spring at the equinox. But no one minds. There are very few witches today to accuse me. There are very few witches at all. And for this reason the nature of *benandanti* ceremonies has changed. Nowadays they are mainly the callers in the Procession of the Dead four times a year. They hardly notice a black bird hovering over them, screeching about the starvation of the olden days. Which isn't strange. The *benandanti* are human beings, living in their own time, and like all other human beings today they have forgotten what starvation is. They no longer know its long fingers, or that it can rip deep into times of fullness with its claws.

But I know. That's why I screech. That's why I'll be shrieking tonight.

I CAN'T POSSIBLY get up yet, though. Kerstin One has pumped me so full of Valium I'm lying heavy as a boulder in my own body. My heart is pounding slowly, every beat sends a tremor through my rib cage. My thoughts tremble to the same rhythm, soon I won't be able to hang on to them anymore.

In this condition, I can barely watch my sisters from a distance, let alone push them around. But that's all right, by this point the story is self-propelling. It will roll on irrespective of my will or my intention.

Margareta's just figured something out and it frightens her; that's why she's standing in front of the bathroom mirror in the Post-Industrial Paradise with her teeth chattering, trying to wrap her naked body in a bath towel. She's not doing very well, keeps losing her grip and dropping it. Again and again she has to bend down, pick the towel up off the floor, and start over. She's in too much of a hurry, as usual. If she took the time to really dry off after a shower, she'd be less cold and it would be easier for her to get the towel in place. But she never takes the time, instead she tucks the corner of the towel in around her chest and rushes out into the upstairs hall, runs down the stairs with wet feet, unaware of the puddles she's making. Christina won't like it, she doesn't like wet footprints on the floor. In fact they will scare her. She will, of course, try to convince herself that the footprints are only Margareta's and a perfectly logical result of having a sloppy houseguest, but she'll fail. For weeks a little voice inside will threaten her, warn her: Watch out! You may not be as alone in the house as you think, there may be someone hiding in a corner, someone or something that likes to play with matches. . . . Poor Christina! She won't get a really good night's sleep for weeks. When all she wants is a little peace and quiet.

Birgitta couldn't care less about peace and quiet. Since they let her out of the D & D cell, she's managed to drive one female police academy trainee to tears, make a free phone call by sneaking into an empty office, sneak into the staff room and be discovered, and annoy two young police officers by complaining about the coffee she shouldn't have been drinking in there. Now they've managed to get her out of the detention area. But she refuses to leave the building, has made her way to the desk by the door, and is standing there, waving her arms and declaring loudly to the exhausted victims of crimes waiting their turn to file a report that in her humble opinion the Norrköping police station is just about as high-class as some old Gestapo lair, and that it is her intention to report at least seven of its officers for interference in judicial matters.

Oh, yes. She's in fine fettle today. But perhaps not as receptive as she should be. She doesn't realize her audience isn't exactly perfect. People who have just had their windows smashed, their stereos stolen, and their cars hot-wired are seldom inclined to sympathize with loud middle-aged women whose faces and language bear witness to the fact that they've been around. Nor does she see the two young policemen approaching her from behind, two extremely debonair young policemen with eager gleams in their eyes. Now she's really got to go. The lush.

KERSTIN ONE GIVES me a hard slap on the cheek and forces me to look her in the eye. Her eyes glitter like gems. "Right," she says, pulling off her disposable gloves. "We'll have to change the sheets now, the bed's all wet. And let's get a clean nightgown on her, too."

"Not day clothes?" Ulrika asks tentatively.

"No, not when she's had so much Valium. She'll sleep for hours."

Although I still don't dare take stock of my abilities, I move my mouth slightly to indicate I have something to say and am asking for the mouthpiece. Kerstin One sees but pretends not to. Maybe she's afraid I'm going to ask for a shower again. Instead, she draws one hand across my brow while she pushes my computer stand aside with the other. Now the mouthpiece and the yellow hose dangle far out of reach. I won't be able to speak until someone decides I should.

Not until now have I noticed the walls. I blink. It can't be real. It's not real.

"Look," says Ulrika. "She's noticing the angels."

Kerstin One frowns and corrects her. "Don't talk *about* the patients, talk *to* them. Hearing tends to be the last thing they lose."

My hearing's perfect, and she knows it. Still, she raises her voice and nearly shouts into my ear. "See the angels, sweetie? They're Maria's angels. You're in Maria's room. Aren't they lovely? And Maria's such a nice girl, I'm sure you two are going to hit it off."

She raises her head and shouts in the same cutting tone: "Maria, come say hello to Desirée."

I can't see her, but I can hear what an obedient soul Maria must be. At the very instant Kerstin One shouts her veiled order, Maria drops some metal object, letting it fall to the tabletop, pulls out her chair, and shuffles into my line of vision. For one minute I imagine I recognize her, then quickly realize my mistake. This Maria has green eyes, without the threatening yellow and brown stripes Tiger-Maria's had.

"Aren't you going to say hello to Desirée?" asks Kerstin One.

"Hi, Desirée," says Maria, shooting me one of her pleading smiles.

FOR MANY YEARS I lived alongside just such a smile. I know them well. They are the only defense of the retarded against the world: a penance, a beggar's smile. In the end, Tiger-Maria spent every waking minute smiling.

Personally, I started refusing to smile early on, believing that if I didn't smile like that, the rest of the world would understand I wasn't mentally retarded myself, I only looked that way. But I hoped in vain. Dr. Redelius, the senior physician, had established from the very outset that I was so retarded it wasn't even any use to talk to me. And from then until I was nearly twelve, he repeated his diagnosis every time it was my turn to pass muster on his weekly rounds. It made no difference that there was a stack of books on my nightstand. I just turned the pages, he said. It was mechanical behavior, imitation.

"The politicians can go right on imagining that anyone irrespective of disability can become a professor," he said, pausing for breath. "But in my view it's better to face facts. A child like this has to be fed three meals and washed twice a day, beyond which there's nothing we can do for her."

The ward nurse at his side nodded and pretended to note something down. She always pretended she was taking notes on what he said, and although anyone could see she was just moving the pen through the air a fraction of an inch above the patients' records, Redelius himself never seemed to notice. On the contrary, he seemed flattered by the movements of the pen: every now and then he would pause artificially so she wouldn't miss anything.

"As supervisor of this facility," he went on, slowly and clearly, "I have a responsibility not only in relation to the patients but also"—pause—"in relation to our principals, better known as the taxpayers." Long pause. "And in fact we must realize that it's a wiser use of our taxes to invest them in children and young people with a future"—pause—"than in creatures who cannot possibly be trained to a higher level than that of a chimpanzee." New pause. "Like this one."

That was it for me. He turned away and went on to the next bed, where Tiger-Maria lay at attention. She was thirteen at the time and had just begun to figure out one or two things about herself and her environment. That day she was tied down in bed.

Redelius inspected the straps. "Has Maria been a bad girl?"

The ward nurse pressed the pile of records to her chest. "She tried to run away."

Redelius shook his head as if he had suffered a great loss. "Oh, Maria, Maria, Maria! What have you done?"

Tiger-Maria burst into tears: loud, sobbing, childish tears that wet her entire face instantly: tears down her cheeks, perspiration all over her forehead, saliva down her chin. My spasms accelerated, I wanted to tell them Tiger-Maria hadn't been trying to run away at all; she was just planning to limp down to the sweetshop. Her mamma had sent her a whole ten-crown bill in an envelope for her birthday, and Tiger-Maria wanted to treat us all to candy. She'd forgotten that you couldn't go out past the gates without asking the matron, but wasn't it only human to forget? Particularly if you were a thirteen-year-old with Down's syndrome and a short-term memory that had been subjected to hundreds of epileptic seizures? In addition to which, Maria would never ever be able to run away; her hip joint injury made it impossible for her to move more than a couple of hundred yards at a time, didn't they know that?

But no words came out. At that point I was able to make myself anywhere near understood only if I was perfectly calm and if the person listening had all the time in the world. And now there was no one listening. All I could produce was frothy saliva and a few inarticulate sounds. Redelius didn't notice my spasms becoming more violent, he just looked at Tiger-Maria and sighed. "And when was this?"

The ward nurse put down her pen and looked gravely at him. "Yesterday."

"And what have Sister and Matron decided?"

"Bed rest for three days, no outdoor play on the fourth and fifth."

Redelius nodded. "So you see, Maria. Rules are there to be followed. And I do hope you will have learned something from this experience."

"Yeeeessss!" sniffled Tiger-Maria, smiling her beggar's smile behind the tears. "I'll learn-earn, I prom-om-ise, I'll learn-earn . . ."

And I shut my eyes, suddenly absolutely furious with Tiger-Maria.

There were four girls in our room: Tiger-Maria and myself, Elsegerd and Agneta. Each of us had a bed and a chest of drawers of our own, and we shared a little table with two chairs. Outside our window was a huge oak tree, outside our door was a long hall with eight brown doors. One flight up was an identical hall, and the same went for one flight down. At the end of each hall was a little nurses' office. The children weren't allowed in there; if you wanted something you were supposed to knock on the door and wait for Sister to open. We didn't mind. Most of us would never have been able to navigate the doorsill anyway. We were all developmentally challenged, some more seriously than others.

What made our room special was that all four of us had epilepsy in addition to our disabilities. That meant we had to wear helmets twenty-four hours a day. Well, not really helmets, but sort of quilted caps that snapped under the chin. To Elsegerd and Agneta these caps were detested caste marks, while Tiger-Maria and I bore it all with equanimity. We were pariahs in any case.

You see, there was a clear hierarchy among the children at the cripples' home: the less disabled you were the higher your rank, and if you were both motorically dysfunctional and mentally retarded you were at the very bottom of the totem pole. And there was nothing more important to the

children who were not retarded than to keep the line of demarcation between themselves and the idiots perfectly clear. This was a purely pre-
cautionary measure. Everyone knew that outside the gates we all ran the
risk of being regarded as idiots, and that was hazardous, because if you
were considered an idiot you would somehow be inclined, in the end, to
live up to the part. And epilepsy must be some kind of mental disability.
If you weren't an idiot you'd never consider writhing around on the floor
at intervals, foaming at the mouth and wetting yourself.

Elsegerd and Agneta would have been high up in the hierarchy if it
hadn't been for their epilepsy. Elsegerd had a clubfoot and only needed
one crutch, Agneta had spina bifida, and although she did have to use a
wheelchair, this was compensated for by the fact that she was so cute. A
cascade of blond curls flowed out of her quilted helmet, and when her little doll's face burst into a melancholy smile, it was enough to bring tears
to anybody's eyes. At the Christmas parties she was always the one who
got to sing, "I saw mamma kissing Santa Claus . . ." That could make even
Redelius shed a few silent, grimacing tears.

Agneta really had a mamma. And a particularly devoted mamma at
that. The minute there was anything even vaguely resembling a holiday
she would turn up at the home and take Agneta walking all around Stockholm and in and out of the shops. She'd be wheeled back into the room
in the evening with a huge pile of bags and packages on her lap. Who
wanted to see? A new blouse! A puzzle! A bar of perfumed soap! And on
all the long holidays she even got to be at home or at her family's country
place, just as if she'd been a regular boarding school student.

Elsegerd and Tiger-Maria had mammas too, but they weren't quite as
fortunate. Elsegerd's parents were missionaries in darkest Africa and
came home just once every three years. Tiger-Maria's mamma was a
widow with four children and lived way up north in Vilhelmina. She
couldn't come even as often as the missionaries. But once a week she sent
Tiger-Maria a card, which the Sisters would read aloud at lunch and
which Tiger-Maria then put into a shoe box. When the other girls were
doing their homework, Tiger-Maria would pull a chair up to my bed and
spread the postcards out on my cover. Which one did I like best? The
snow scenes? Or the sunset over Lake Malgomaj? I always voted for the
snow scenes, but the decision was in Tiger-Maria's hands, and she always
chose the sunset over Lake Malgomaj.

After they'd done their homework, my classes began. Elsegerd was my teacher, Agneta my pen holder, Tiger-Maria my fan club. I needed them all, not least Tiger-Maria.

It began as a game, a game Elsegerd wanted to play because ever since she was in first grade she'd known she wanted to be a teacher when she grew up. The table was her lectern, the chairs served as desks. To begin with she tried to get Agneta and Tiger-Maria to be her pupils, but they quickly grew bored, Agneta because she already knew everything Elsegerd had to teach, Tiger-Maria because she couldn't keep up. They giggled and chattered, wanting to play something else. And when they'd left the room, Elsegerd started teaching me, for want of a better pupil. I was so eager I started to drool. There was nothing I wanted more than to learn to decode the little symbols in books. It must be like listening to the radio with your eyes, and listening to the radio was my favorite occupation.

"O," said Elsegerd, waving her reading book. "O mother, an ocean."

"Uuuuuh," I said.

"No, no," said Elsegerd. "Come on, try! It's O. *O!*"

"Ouuuuh!"

"Right! Well done! I'm giving you a star for that. This is an *M*. Can you say *M?*"

"Uuuuum!"

"Yes! Perfect! Here's another star for you, Desirée. Class is over for today. We're going to sing a song and say a prayer."

"Uuuuum!"

"Oh yes we are. If you don't want to pray to God you must be a very bad girl."

She folded my resistant hands, intertwining my fingers, then rushed through "Our Father who art in heaven" so fast my convulsions didn't have time to tear my hands apart.

"Amen," she concluded breathlessly.

"Ohmn!" I said, causing Elsegerd's pale little face to burst into a wide smile. "My goodness," she said. "I think I'll have to give you an extra star for that one!"

This was my primary schooling: a road paved with Elsegerd's stars. Sometime later Agneta sat down next to Elsegerd to help me hold my pen and learn to write. Tiger-Maria lay on her own bed, gaping with astonishment at my progress. When we were done with the reading book we moved into the country of multiplication, then on to the landscape of science, with its fields and birds and trees, each of which had a name and none of which I'd ever seen. We held our breath with King Gustav Vasa when he hid in a hay cart, and together we flew over every country in the atlas. Elsegerd was a brilliant pedagogue, sometimes slightly too brilliant. She told the story of Christian the Tyrant and Valdemar Dayback with such empathy that Tiger-Maria became virtually phobic about the Danes. And when Redelius took a three-month sabbatical to study in the United States and his substitute turned out to be Danish, she went into a spin.

Preben was his name. He shocked us by coming into our room all by himself, unaccompanied by Redelius's usual entourage of nurses and nurse's aides, almost as if he were our guest. He moved from Elsegerd's bed to Agneta's and then on to mine, introducing himself and shaking hands. But when he arrived at Tiger-Maria's bed he got a surprise: where was child number four?

The other girls were quick to formulate a defense tactic: Elsegerd limped up to him, curtsied again and again, and apologized in general terms for Tiger-Maria, Agneta turned on her charm and blinked her glittery eyes, as she explained how Tiger-Maria was hiding under her bed in terror.

"Is she schcared of doctorsh?" Preben asked in his spongy Danish accent.

"No," Agneta answered. "She's scared of Danes."

Preben looked crestfallen but was quick to recover, kneel down, and peek in under the bed. "Hello there," he ventured.

Tiger-Maria screeched and covered her ears with her hands.

"What makesh you schcared of Danes, young lady?"

Tiger-Maria screamed even louder. Elsegerd got worried and scurried over and shut the door. Preben was even more confused. "Why are you shutting ush in?"

At this point Elsegerd was so upset she was at a loss for words, but Agneta cocked her head and smiled her most enchanting smile. "She closed the door so Matron and Sister won't hear Maria screaming."

"Aha," said Preben, settling down cross-legged on the floor. "And will you pleashe now exschplain to me what makesh Maria so schcared of the Danes?"

"Valdemar Dayback," said Agneta.

"Christian the Tyrant," said Elsegerd.

Preben chuckled and got up, brushed off his white coat and sat down on the edge of Tiger-Maria's bed. "Well, well, Valdemar Dayback," he said. "Do you know what that name means?"

We all knew, even Tiger-Maria. But it was Elsegerd who answered, sinking slowly onto the edge of her own bed. "Valdemar Returns the Day."

"Yes," said Preben. "Exactly. And why was he given that name? Because he liberated Denmark from the darkest night."

We recognized that tone of voice. It was just like story hour on the radio.

HE PROVED TO be an even better teacher than Elsegerd. For an hour and a half he sat on Tiger-Maria's bed telling us how, with a brilliant combination of wiles and weapons, Valdemar Dayback defended Denmark when it was being squeezed between King Magnus of Sweden and the Holsteins. The room went very still. Very soon I could see Tiger-Maria's hand, relaxed on the floor. She had uncovered her ears and was listening just as attentively as the rest of us. A few days later, when Preben returned to our room on his regular weekly rounds—this time with Redelius's whole entourage in attendance—she remained quietly in her bed, lying as if at attention, just as the ward Sister had instructed us to do. He stopped at her bedside and smiled. "Hello there," he said. "Remember me?"

Maria lowered her eyes and smiled her penitent's smile. "You're the Dane."

The ward nurse gasped and would have corrected Tiger-Maria instantly if Preben hadn't halted her with a gesture. "Yes, but do you know my name?"

"Uh-huh," said Maria. "You're Valdemar Dayback."

MARIA WAS RIGHT. Preben was Valdemar Dayback. He brought us back the light, initiated us to the fact that things didn't necessarily have to be as they had always been. He saw to it that Elsegerd received vocational counseling, that Agneta got physical therapy for her atrophied leg muscles, and that Tiger-Maria was given a new Sunday dress. She needed it. For years Tiger-Maria had gone around dressed in washed-out hand-me-downs and other girls' outgrown blouses. Now she glowed on Sunday mornings as she entered the chapel and walked down the aisle, like a rectangular little bride, in a thick navy blue cotton creation with a collar of real machine lace. Mine was the best gift of all, though. A referral to a speech therapist at the Karolinska Hospital.

I was thirteen by then and had lived in Stockholm as long as I could recall, without ever having seen the city. When the other children were taken on outings—which happened at least once a year—kids like Tiger-Maria and me didn't get to go along. There was no point, of course, since we couldn't make sense of what we saw.

But now at least I got to go to Karolinska. All by myself. In a taxi.

I'll never forget it. One of the nurse's aides dressed me in a dress that had been Agneta's when she was seven, carried me down the stairs, and set me in the backseat of the cab. When we arrived at the red-brick building, the driver carried me in to the speech therapist's. Her name was Fru Nilsson; she was an elegant little woman in high heels and with her shirt collar turned up. Her lips glowed with cherry lipstick, her nails were polished in the same shade, her hair carefully combed and teased in a very fashionable hairdo. But what fascinated me most was her peculiar smile: instead of the corners of her mouth moving outward, she pursed her lips into a tiny circle, so three little slanted lines appeared on either side of the crease under her nose. She looked as if she had whiskers, as if she were a happy little mouse in a comic book.

Soon, however, I would learn she was no ordinary mouse but a lion in disguise, a lion whose roars drew one word after the next out of my own mouth. Clear sounds she wanted, no growls and moans! But when Redelius returned from the United States, still intent on saving the taxpayers' money, she proved to be even stricter with my governor than she was with me. First she uttered a series of long growls, followed by a roar that caused him to yield in fear and trembling. I would be allowed to continue traveling to Karolinska once a week for speech therapy. This may have had something to do with the fact that Fru Nilsson was the wife of one of the most prominent neurosurgeons at Karolinska: like all authoritarians, Redelius was a dog deep inside. He lay on his back and exposed his throat the moment he scented a power greater than his own.

Nor was anything else as it had been for Redelius. When he left for the States, he was still the regent of his own kingdom; when he returned he was a sleazy dictator whose days were numbered. It was as if his replacement had made a hole in the wall surrounding the institution, and through that hole flowed light and air and new ideas.

It's possible, of course, that the hole had been made thanks to the efforts of others beyond Preben. A radio reporter with a pleasant voice described the reality in which we lived in a way that made the entire nation begin to doubt that what we needed most was military rigor and religious services. A few courageous parents cared enough to make clear objections: was it really necessary to train all children in wheelchairs to be basket makers and bookbinders? Did they even have to be cared for in homes just to get an education? Wouldn't it be both better and less expensive to put wheelchair ramps in the ordinary schools and let them go on living with their families? And in his office with the walnut wainscoting, the minister for social affairs rubbed his chin and thought out loud: Wasn't it high time, now that the superstructure of the welfare state was in place, to invest a little money in the very last stepchildren, the retarded?

At that point in time we were all teenagers, and we laughed maliciously at the cloud that was shading Redelius's brow. Three of us also knew the name of the cloud: Karl Grünewald and his draft bill on care for the disabled. Even Tiger-Maria and I were going to have the right to go to school! And it was going to be prohibited to strap children down in bed and to put Tiger-Maria in a straitjacket when she was homesick.

How we loved those days! The walls of our room were painted bright yellow, and the nurses' office was turned into a dayroom. The parents' association applied for a grant to buy us a TV, and once we had one they convinced Matron to change our bedtimes. Now everyone over the age of ten was allowed to stay up all the way to nine o'clock every single night! On the ground floor they made a playroom for the little ones, with yellow and blue and green educational toys. A play lady came in on Thursdays, and she let the seven-year-olds strip down to their underpants and spend an hour in the shower room doing whatever they wanted with some big jars of finger paint. At the end of the hour she lined them up in the shower and rinsed them off. That was all you had to do, she explained when Matron expressed her dismay. Finger paints were water-soluble, and the kids had to get clean anyway, didn't they? And surely nobody minded if the wheelchairs got a little wet?

The big news for us older children was the book trolley. The librarian's name was Barbro, and she showed her big white teeth when she laughed during her story hours, for which we all gathered in the dayroom. She always sat on for a while afterward with those of us who read most and smiled a secret smile at each child as she gave him or her a book for the week: Agneta got *Pippi Longstocking,* Elsegerd got *The Wizard of Oz,* and—with a wink that showed she knew what kind of a person I was—there were *The Treasure* and *The Driver* by Selma Lagerlöf for me.

But nowadays it was difficult to have undisturbed reading time. Suddenly the whole building had come to life. Parents and siblings started turning up at all hours. People who, just a few years ago, had curtsied and bowed and kowtowed now just snorted disdainfully when Matron or the nurses complained about their not respecting the visiting hours. Didn't a mother have a right to see her child at any time she chose? Was this some kind of prison, perhaps? Was there no one at all here with the most elementary knowledge of what children needed or how they developed?

The light streamed into our rooms.

Nobody thought about the fact that in the very lightest places you can also find the very darkest shadows.

A BREATH. THAT was how it began.

The other three girls had already fallen into such deep sleep their breathing was no longer audible. I was the only one awake, staring out into the dark. This was the best hour of the day or night, the only one that was entirely my own. Now my thoughts could flow freely, without ricocheting off the chatter of the girls and the routines of the nurses.

I lay there thinking about Stefan. He was a year older than I and lived in the room above ours. In fact, his bed was exactly on top of mine, Agneta had told me. As opposed to myself, she had been upstairs. I'd never seen either his room or his hall, but I saw Stefan himself every day when they wheeled us out into the park. He was blond with a light olive complexion, like a boy all dipped in gold. His bangs were long and rebellious, but not so long as to conceal the fine edges of his swallow-shaped eyebrows.

Stefan wrote poetry. Everyone knew it, just like everyone knew that once his desperation had flared up and driven him to thrash wildly around the workbench in the bookbindery with one of his crutches, sending paper, glue, and spools of thread flying to the floor in chaos. The teacher and the most mobile students fled, and once they were gone Stefan blocked the door handle with another student's cane. He stood there, barricaded, for over an hour, and not even the eventual appearance of Redelius on the other side of the door, threatening punishments now nearly forgotten, such as the straitjacket and the leather straps, could make him open the door. The custodian finally had to climb in through the window and wheel him away from the door. At that point, however, Stefan had stopped shouting and buried his face in his hands.

All the girls at the home were in love with Stefan. Without exception. I wasn't dumb enough to imagine he would ever so much as look in my direction, but I liked having him to think about. Sometimes I allowed myself a little dream in which there were two wheelchairs alongside each other under the big oak tree, where Stefan was reading his latest poem to Desirée, his hand seeking hers and the wind murmuring in the leaves above . . .

It was at one of those moments I heard it for the first time. The breathing of a stranger.

I hadn't heard the door open or close, hadn't heard any footsteps on the linoleum, hadn't even heard that vague whispering rustle the sleeve of a shirt makes against the shirt itself. There was just the one sound: a deep breath. Almost a sigh.

The room was dark, but not so dark that you couldn't make out a shadow or a contour. Still, it took some time for me to get a grip on the new shadow over by the door. It was perfectly motionless, yet there was no doubt that it was the contour of a living being. A most attentive living being.

It was as if it could sense that I was looking at it. At the very moment I noticed the shadow, it knew I was awake. But it didn't recoil, didn't withdraw into the darkness. Instead, it took one step forward and let me hear it breathe again. It breathed heavily, huffing.

Now I wasn't the only one awake. I could hear Elsegerd's sheets rustling and a stifled noise from Agneta's bed. Only Tiger-Maria was still sleeping, but not as deeply as before. She twisted and turned, and her breathing revealed that she was in the process of waking up.

That was what the shadow wanted. It glided from bed to bed on padded feet, as if to assure itself that we were all prepared to see and hear what was about to happen for the first time and would go on happening every night for many months to come. It stopped first at the foot of Elsegerd's bed, then Agneta's, and then mine. It laid its hand on the bars at the side of the bed, giving a gentle rattle so the whole bed trembled. That was a threat, a warning. I didn't dare move, but I peered out between half-closed eyes; I simply tried to see as much as I could. In vain: there was no face to see. What stood before me was nothing but a shadow.

Now, though, it turned its back on me, approaching Tiger-Maria's bed, stopping at the edge and raising one hand, as if in benediction. "Oh, Maria," a voice whispered in the darkness. "My angel, my little tiger lily! My slut. My sticky little pussy!"

AFTERWARD, WHEN THE door had closed and the shuffling footsteps out in the hall were no longer audible, we lay silent for an eternity, staring out into the darkness. Just one sound could be heard, a soft squeal coming from Agneta's bed. It was a high-pitched screeching sound that burst my eardrums and drove like a nail through my head. In the end it was intolerable. I tried pressing my hands to my ears, but my spasms pulled them away and the sound was still there. Suddenly I could hear myself joining in, my own throat producing the same shrill sound as Agneta's.

It was Elsegerd who finally did the amazing thing, the most forbidden. She turned on the light, groped for her crutch, and got out of bed. A most severely punishable action. At night there were no visitors at the home, and the old rules still applied.

I'll never forget her standing there, wobbling and tottering on her crutch, pulling her ash blond bangs off her forehead. Suddenly Elsegerd was beautiful; her face white, her eyes black and deep. Without a word she limped over to Tiger-Maria's bed, lifted the twisted top sheet and gave it a shake, turned it, smoothed it over Tiger-Maria's immobile body, and tucked her in.

I craned my neck and could see Tiger-Maria. She was lying there, rigid as a mannequin, staring up at the ceiling with a smile.

One day many years later, several years after I had moved from the assisted accommodation to my own apartment, there was a strange woman at my door. She was wearing a cinnamon brown coat, and I remember being surprised by the color. I'd never realized brown could glow. But this coat glowed so brightly I couldn't see who was in it.

"Hello, Desirée," she said. "Don't you recognize me?"

I blinked doubtfully in her direction. Elsegerd?

"I was sure you'd remember me," she said, taking a few steps into my living room. She still had a limp, but all she needed these days was a slim cane.

"We were roommates at the cripples' home . . ."

I was amazed. It had never occurred to me that I would ever encounter

Elsegerd or Agneta again. When we parted it was forever, since people like ourselves were never allowed to make our own decisions. Agneta vanished even before Tiger-Maria died, Elsegerd immediately afterward. She wasn't even able to attend the funeral. Although she was actually too young, she had gotten a place at a rural junior college. She reeled from tears to laughter those last few days, one moment joyous over the freedom she was going to have, the next dissolved with grief about Tiger-Maria.

And now here she was in my living room, in the beige armchair I'd recently bought so my visitors would have somewhere to sit. My apartment. My armchair. My guests.

"Wow," said Elsegerd, looking around as she took off her coat. "What a great apartment. It's so pretty, and so light!"

It was a sunny winter day, the kind when the dust particles glittered in the rays of sun over the parquet floor and my flowered curtains looked even nicer than usual. I often sat there admiring my own curtains in those days. Sometimes I even wondered if I was becoming a curtain fetishist. In fact, it was a room full of beautiful things: my birch table, my red couch, my overfilled bookshelves. My handwoven rag runner, of course, the one I'd gotten a good price on thanks to Hubertsson's connections with the ladies at the craft guild.

I was so busy admiring my own lovely living room that at first I didn't notice what was revealed when Elsegerd took off her coat. When I did see it, I gasped: a high, white collar and a black shirtfront. In those days I was still able to reach out for my mouthpiece. I stuck it in my mouth and blew into it: "You're a minister?"

Elsegerd lowered her eyes and ran her hand over her skirt in a girlish gesture. "Uh-huh. I was ordained last year. That's what brings me to Vadstena. The ecumenical conference, you know. But I decided to play hooky today, to come see you."

I extended my hand as well as I could, touched her lightly. "I'm glad you came."

She glanced quickly at my monitor and smiled. "Me, too. I thought we could have a belated birthday celebration. I bought Napoleon pastries."

I laughed and puffed into the mouthpiece. "Oh, you remember. That's what I used to ask for every year."

"Yeah. Wasn't it kind of Agneta's mother to arrange four birthday parties a year?"

"Remember the time Tiger-Maria asked for a princess crown for her birthday?"

Elsegerd's eyes glazed, and she looked away. "Want me to make some coffee?" she asked. "Or can you do it yourself?"

I started the motor on my wheelchair and rolled out into the kitchen.

NOT UNTIL SEVERAL hours later, when dusk was beginning to fall, was Elsegerd ready to talk about Tiger-Maria.

"I think about her almost every day," she said, playing with the fabric of her skirt. "It was my fault . . ."

I refrained from puffing an answer.

"I mean—you couldn't have done anything, or told anyone—and Agneta was too weak, you couldn't have expected anything of her. I was the oldest and the healthiest of us, I should have realized it was going to kill her . . ."

I allowed a few comforting words to flutter across the screen: "But you did try. I know you spoke with Matron, though she never talked to the rest of us."

Elsegerd made a face. "She accused me of having a dirty mind. Can you believe it? She saw Tiger-Maria refuse to speak and then to eat, saw her walk around smiling her hollow smile day after day . . . but she could still claim it was all in my dirty little mind!"

I sighed so deeply my words ended up at the bottom of the monitor: "That's how it is. Still. People like us aren't the ones who set the rules for what's reality."

Elsegerd sniffled. "But I should've been like that Stefan. I should've blocked the door to keep that creature out. I should've shouted and screamed so the night nurse would have had to come in."

"It wouldn't have helped. She was almost always down looking after the little kids. And even if she'd heard us, she would have been too far away to do anything. He would have gotten away, and no one would have believed us."

Elsegerd leaned forward and grabbed my hand. "But you know, don't you? You remember him and what he did? Even though we never dared to talk about it? Even though we just sat there and didn't tell anyone?"

"I remember."

Elsegerd exhaled, her face bright as silver in the twilight. "Thank you."

I retracted my hand. "What are you thanking me for?"

Elsegerd didn't answer, and after some time I deleted my words from the screen. I guess I knew what she was thanking me for.

We sat there silently for a long time, remembering Tiger-Maria.

HE'S COMING. I can hear him on the stairs, muttering to himself. But I don't want him in here. Not yet. Not until I've taken stock of my abilities.

And yet, the minute I hear him push the door open and shuffle into the room, my exhaustion abates, withdraws like the ebb of the tide, leaving the beach free. I open my eyes.

"Where the hell have you ended up? In heaven?"

Hubertsson is standing in the middle of the floor, pushing an angel's white terry-cloth dress off his bald spot.

I move my lips to indicate my desire to speak. Hubertsson lumbers over to the bed, pulls my computer close, and inserts the mouthpiece into my mouth, saying, "And how can you possibly be awake? Those four Valium suppositories ought to have knocked you out for the night and all day tomorrow."

Puffing an answer is difficult. "You don't look so great yourself. How're you doing?"

"Well, I had a touch of hypoglycemia. But I'm all right now. I'll go have a good lunch, then rest at home this afternoon."

Take care, I want to say. Watch out for yourself. No wine with lunch, please, and check your insulin levels once an hour! But I'm on my guard, remembering the first commandment. No intimacies.

"Just thought I'd look in on you first. After all that Valium . . ."

"Christina was here."

Hubertsson glances at the screen, and says, "Yes, I know. She told me. But I think she thought you were asleep."

I don't say I was awakened by her thoughts: *the poor tiny little thing . . .* That one's going to cost her. Sooner or later.

"I was dozing."

Hubertsson clears his throat and looks away. "Life is full of coincidences. . . . She found a dead gull yesterday. In her yard."

I don't reply, just look at him. He doesn't dare look back, taking me by the wrist instead, looking at his watch, checking my pulse. That's unusual. He tends to leave my pulse to the nurses. His hand is light as butterfly wings, his fingertips warm. "Hmmm," he says, letting go. "I guess you're tired."

Quick puff. Yes.

"I'll have to have a word with K-One. She's overdone it. Four Valium suppositories!"

I don't answer. Don't have the energy. The tide is rolling in toward the beach again. Hubertsson looks around, looks for a seat. But he can't sit on the window ledge in this room, my bed's in the way. So he just stands there by the bed, uncertain, eyeing the thousands of angels on the walls. My eyes follow his, and although I am beginning to drown in exhaustion again, I realize that the last time I opened my eyes, all I had seen was a fraction of the whole. Maria's angels are crowding and pushing one another in layer upon layer on the walls, curious cherubs peeking over the shoulders of seraphs, enormous white men's wings bumping into soft, rounded women's wings, tiny winged putti fluttering around, trying to get some air under their glittering little appendages . . .

"This is some weird room," says Hubertsson.

He's right. It sure is weird. But the next instant I'm grateful to Maria for her obsession. Because if the walls weren't covered with her paper angels, Hubertsson wouldn't have been overwhelmed. And had he not been overwhelmed, he would not have moved my hand to make room to sit down on the edge of my bed. And had he not gone on being overwhelmed, he wouldn't be sitting where he is now, my hand still in his.

An egg in its nest. A pearl in its oyster shell.

My hand in his. Where it belongs.

ONLY THE MOST ignorant still believe, like Saint Augustine, that time is a river. We others know it is a delta: that it branches out and seeks new routes, that it rejoins itself only to seek a thousand new courses. Some may be waterfalls, some no more than little stagnant pools passed by the tide, forever still . . .

This is one of those times. A pool. I sink down in it. I want to stay forever in this water.

HE'S NEVER HELD my hand before.

Well, maybe once. Though I'm not sure it really happened, whether it's a memory or a dream.

But if it really happened, it was very long ago, long before the nursing home was renovated, long before I had moved into assisted accommodation. It may have been the same day he told me her name. I don't know. Don't remember.

But I do remember him carrying me down an ugly yellow hall. The ceiling panels rushing past, pale stars that had abandoned all hope of vanquishing the darkness. In Hubertsson's arms I played that game with the light I always played when I was a child. I squeezed my eyes shut, allowing the white to deepen to red, then blinked so hard the whole world began to shimmer, shut my eyes so tight again that the memory of the light was reflected in green on the insides of my eyelids . . .

Those were the days before his illness. He was a strong, healthy man. I seemed to weigh nothing in his arms; he walked in long, bounding strides, almost running up the narrow stairs that separated my ward from hers. We encountered only one person on the way, a solitary nurse's aide who smiled an anxious smile at Hubertsson. He nodded quickly in response, not slowing down, not indicating any intention to explain what he was doing carrying a patient between the wards. Afterward, the memory of her face made me smile triumphantly—they must really have wondered, she and the other women, they must have speculated and gossiped about it all afternoon. But when it happened, I saw her without noticing her.

After an eternity, Hubertsson stopped outside a door. "I know she can hear what you say," he says. "And I believe she can see. So try to be quiet. Don't make any noise."

Suddenly I was frightened. My left hand grasped the lapel of his white coat, tore at it, and my head reeled involuntarily from side to side, in increasingly violent convulsions. I didn't really want to see her after all! What difference could it make? She'd disposed of me as you would throw away a broken glass, she'd handed me over to Redelius and the cripples' home, and they, in turn, had turned me over to the researchers at the neurology clinic. None of this could be undone, time has no holes through which we can pass to change things that have already happened . . .

I tried to explain all this to Hubertsson, but I was too upset and he was unable to interpret my grunts. "Shhh," he just said, pushing the door open with his elbow.

I recognized the room: it could have been mine. Gray morning light and pale green walls. Orange nylon curtains, a concession to a fashion just gone out of style. A worn plastic chair with little cracks in the seat cover. A table next to it. The standard county council nightstand that seemed to be the only constant on the planet. Striped sheets and a yellow honeycomb blanket.

I blinked. No. Upon closer scrutiny there were lots of things in this room I didn't have in mine. There was a stout candlestick on the table, and a whole row of photos on the windowsill. An aerial shot of a white two-story house with a summer garden in full bloom, two high school graduation photos of girls in gold frames—one serious, one smiling—and a color-tinted enlargement of what appeared to be a black-and-white snapshot from the early sixties. Three girls sitting in a cherry tree; their faces painted a shade of pale pink, their dresses pink, yellow, and green, but the leaves on the tree all around them as gray and colorless as in the original shot.

Hubertsson took a few more steps into the room; I shut my eyes and turned my face to his chest. His breath was warm on my cheek as he whispered, "It's all right. She's asleep."

The first thing I saw was her hands. The skin hung, and was so thin it looked blue; her nails were filed to perfect ovals and polished to a sheen. Someone had even gone to the trouble of pushing her cuticles down so far that the white semicircles were perfectly visible. That surprised me: my experience of manicures in the public hospitals was limited to straight cuts. So she was obviously getting special treatment.

My curiosity overpowered my fear, and I raised my eyes to her face. It was just as pale as her hands, the skin oddly smooth, with the thin violet lines of a burst vascular net on her cheeks. Her hair was the angel hair of an elderly woman: thin, white, and curly.

"Cerebral hemorrhage," Hubertsson whispered. "She's been lying here, hemiplegic, for fourteen years. Now she's developed pneumonia."

She lay there, her mouth open, like a dying woman. And yet I couldn't hear her breathing. The room was perfectly still: only her chest rose and fell slowly.

AFTERWARD, WHEN I was back in my bed, either just awakened or just brought back by Hubertsson, he took my hand and placed it in his own, cupping his other hand over it like an eggshell. Not until that moment did I dare to ask the question I had never had the courage to ask before, the question I had hardly even dared pose to myself. My voice was perfectly clear, each word tumbling from my mouth like a glass marble: "Why did she abandon me?"

Hubertsson didn't reply.

BUT HE WOULDN'T be the person he is if he'd left a question unanswered. The next day he was prepared, although at that point I'd changed my mind and was saying I didn't want to know. I hissed at him and criticized him for harping on it. I even tried to cover my ears with my hands— though the results were negligible.

His address opened on the subject of time. Ella's time.

" 'Why?' you ask. 'Why did she abandon me?' Well, because that was what people did in the fifties. No aberrations were tolerated, particularly not by the medical corps. When I was doing my residency in Göteborg there were still plenty of old geezers who took it completely for granted that a deformed body always contained a deformed soul. At my clinic there was one senior physician who always advised the parents to put babies with deformities into a home and forget about them. Even if it was as small a matter as a clubfoot."

He grew still, frowning.

"When it comes right down to it, I don't know what was in his mind, whether he actually believed that every child with a clubfoot was mentally retarded, or whether they just disturbed his sense of symmetry. He was a very orderly person, a great believer in conformity. I believe he mainly thought it would be messy and disruptive to have a lot of lame, disfigured people out on the streets. A far better thing to have them put away in institutions. They didn't live all that long in those days, anyway."

He turned in my direction, and I seized the opportunity to stick my tongue out at him. It's a credit to his powers of perception that he could tell this was intentional, despite the intensity of my spasms.

"You may stick your tongue out if you like," he said. "But if you don't learn about those times, you will never understand Ella, either. And don't imagine you know what life was like back then, you were too little to have any insight into all the bowing and curtsying and currying favor with those higher up the ladder, or all the kicking and spitting and holding those lower down in contempt. And the health and medical care system was worst of all. Sometimes I think it was a damn sight worse in the hospitals than in the army."

He turned away again, standing at the side of my bed and pulling a piece of paper out of the binder full of my records he'd put at the foot end, drumming his fingertips on it and raising his voice.

"The person who passed judgment on you was a neurologist, a Dr. Zimmerman. He examined you during your third week of life and immediately knew everything about you. It says here in black and white that you are so severely disabled you cannot possibly develop the ability to learn. . . . You'll never even be able to acquire the most elementary skills, such as mastication or eye contact. We can also assume that this meant that in his considered opinion you would never develop an emotional life."

He let go of the paper, and it floated down onto the bed. He cleared his throat.

"I haven't spoken with Ella about any of this. She doesn't even know that I know you exist. And now it's too late. She's too ill. To the best of my knowledge she's never mentioned your name to a single soul in all these years. People knew, of course, that she and Hugo had a child, but I have no idea how she explained it, whether she claimed you had died or what. . . . In those days people didn't talk about these things very much; it was considered best to forget it and go on."

His voice fell. "You must bear in mind that Hugo had cancer, and that he died three months after you were born. She must have sat by him throughout. In her medical records it says that she got out of bed and snuck off the very day after her delivery. That was bold of her. In those days women who'd given birth were warned to remain horizontal for at least a week or they might die of a blood clot. And you got sent to Stockholm because of your epilepsy and your cerebral palsy. You needed special care, of course. Do you know you spent the first two years of your life in the children's hospital?"

He glanced my way, not really looking. It didn't matter. I had no intention of revealing that he was forcing another piece of the puzzle on me now.

"Damn it, I'm not even sure they let her see you at all. Or maybe just through a pane of glass. Though I doubt it, actually. They really preferred to keep babies apart from their parents in those days . . . particularly if something had gone wrong."

He turned back toward the window, staring out at the gray sky.

"And if you wonder why she never came to see you, the answer is in Zimmerman's letters to her, of which there are copies in your records. Do you want to see them?"

I snorted out an answer: "No!"

His posture caved in just a little. "No. I can understand that. They don't make great reading. . . . In fact, they're nothing but variations on the same theme: This kid's not worth investing in. Can't learn anything. Not to walk. Not to speak. Not to understand."

The memory of Redelius fluttered through my mind. Chimpanzee. *Hey hey, we're the Monkees* . . .

Hubertsson looked as if he were just standing there daydreaming, the hands that had been gesticulating fell slack at his sides. For some time he stood without moving, then he blinked and went on.

"Well, anyway . . . Ella's letters aren't part of the record, but she appears to have written Zimmerman quite frequently. He answers that it would be absolutely impossible for you to be cared for at home. And he advises her not to visit you, as it would only upset her. Not to mention that you wouldn't know the difference. You were being given everything you needed, fed every four hours and changed between feedings . . ."

But she still had some responsibility for me, I wanted to say. No one could have prohibited her from coming. She should've realized she had obligations to fulfill, she should have been able to recall that I was her child and that I was also a human being, beyond my disabilities. But I was too tired to speak at that point, just closed my eyes, pleading with Hubertsson to shut up. But he didn't, he went on talking, rapping his knuckles on the marble windowsill.

"Yes, you were well looked after, according to Zimmerman. Ella and her husband ought to think about the future instead, have another baby."

He laughed out loud. "The damn fool had forgotten she was a widow!"

He was quiet for a few minutes, and his body language began to signal his imminent departure.

"Well," he said in the end. "I suppose that accounts for how Margareta came to be Ella's foster child . . ."

MY FATIGUE IS so all-embracing I'm not even sure whether or not my hand is still resting in Hubertsson's. I don't even care. It's been there.

But I'm still in a body of water. It's green and clear as glass. I can see a great distance. All the way to my sister Margareta.

She smiles as she sits in Claes's old car listening to his voice on the radio. Margareta is never so contented as when she is in transit between one place and the next, driving so fast she can convince herself no one could ever catch up with her. And at this moment she's extra content; first because she's putting the miles between herself and Christina—that nutcase—and second because she's on her way to Norrköping, where Birgitta is. Now she's figured it all out and is off to do her good deed for the day. She's a true-blue Girl Scout, my youngest sister.

Birgitta, by contrast, has no plans to do any good deeds at the moment; she's walking the North Promenade in Norrköping in high heels that are too big for her, trying to figure out how she's going to get back to Motala. There's no way she can take the bus, but the train might work. She's stowed away in the toilets on trains before. But before she does so she wants a smoke, and she has only loose change in her pocket. How can she get cigarettes without any money? What do you say? Can anybody answer that?

Their circles overlap, they're moving slowly in the same direction. Everything's working out fine. I can sink more deeply into the water.

I'M DROWNING!

Water's filling my mouth and my throat, water's running out of my open mouth and down over my neck and chest. I cough, but I don't open my eyes, all my energy is going into it. Coughing, panting for breath . . . Help, I'm drowning!

Someone raises the head end of my bed so fast my head tips forward.

"Jesus," a voice mutters. "All I meant to do was give her a little juice, I had no idea . . ."

"It's not your fault," says Kerstin One. "Just give me a hand now, bend her forward!"

My head droops, I don't even try to control it. Because now I know what I've lost, what that last seizure cost me.

I can't swallow. I'll never be able to swallow again.

Cherry Princess

Put your hand in mine to love's tone
I'm not one who'll stay
To devour love's marrow, skin, and bones.
I'm one who'll turn up but then run away.

A seductive folk song
Lured me from home
I'm just a stone rolling along
Put your hand in mine to love's tone.

Hjalmar Gullberg

MARGARETA STUBS OUT her cigarette the minute the door closes behind Christina, leans back in the old rib-backed kitchen chair, and stretches. She should probably clear the table right away to be on the safe side. Wouldn't want Her Majesty coming home early from work and going apoplectic because the breakfast things were still out.

It's always surprised Margareta that Christina, who has so systematically mastered all the other rites and signals of the intellectual, moneyed class, hasn't figured out that there's no status attached to good housekeeping. Grooming and clothes are one thing. The order of the day is a freshly scrubbed body and clean clothes, but a messy house. Corners free from dust bunnies are petty, as in petit bourgeois. Or worse still: a sign of the inferiority complex of the proletariat. Only people with something to hide need everything in its place.

Well, in that respect, at least, she's been better than Christina at adopting the lifestyle of the social class to which they now both belong. Her apartment back in Kiruna is the embodiment of chaos. However, because her only conceivable visitors are other physicists, it couldn't matter less. They'd chime right in with an empathetic laugh when she voiced her usual apologetic statement: "Entropy's on the rise. My place is empirical proof."

Still, she wouldn't actually have anything against a home like Christina's. It's nice to sit and watch the morning light sift through crystal clean windowpanes, to have a kitchen floor with wide, white tiles hygienically scrubbed and a rag runner so clean that you can see every nuance in the multicolored rags. But it's so much work! Not to mention the fact that Erik—or at least his inherited fortune—must be one of the prerequisites for Christina's being able to have a home like this. Personally, Margareta's always preferred to keep her men, even the ones with full piggy banks, at a bit of a distance. The problem with most men is that they consider themselves the main characters not only in their own dramas, but also in their women's, and Margareta has no desire to be the supporting actress in her own story.

Anyway, now she can take a look at one or two things in the house. Last night she noticed a cupboard out in the living room that interested her. It looked like a little altar with a white cloth, pewter candlesticks, and an old photo of Ella when she was young and had pudgy cheeks. There's every reason to suspect there are secrets in that cupboard. Interesting secrets.

After doing the dishes, Margareta wipes her damp hands on her jeans and opens one of the French doors to the living room. It creaks softly. Out in the kitchen the morning sun is shining in, but it's still gray dawn in the living room. She stands looking around for a minute, then shakes her head slowly. Now she sees what she hadn't noticed yesterday. Christina's made her living room into a shrine for St. Ella. Her relics are everywhere if you can just read the signs: a little tablecloth with lace edging, the simple cut-glass fruit bowl Ella used to have on her own living room table, the shelf of rust red volumes from the forties: the collected works of Martin Andersen Nexø. Not to mention the silver-framed icon over there on the altar. That photo.

But Ella requires no temple. She wasn't a saint, just a woman with an unusual flair for motherhood. And one who could also cut the girls dead, in a tone of voice that would curdle milk and make the flies on the kitchen window pass out and fall down. In addition to which she had a parsimonious streak. Drawing pads and crayons were special gifts of grace for Christmas and birthdays. The rest of the year you were expected to draw on old paper bags and wrappers with a pencil. But that didn't matter so much. The really bad part was her jealousy: the toxic little green gleam that came into her eyes about only one thing: schooling.

That gleam flared up while Christina was waiting to hear whether she'd been accepted to secondary school. She was twelve at the time and looked like she was expecting a death sentence. Every morning she would stand right inside the door, pale and grave, while Aunt Ella went out to the mailbox. And as the days passed she grew thinner and thinner. It was as if the long wait sucked all the stuffing out of her, as if she would be unable to get out of bed in the morning if she didn't find out soon.

When the envelope finally arrived, Aunt Ella had already opened it before she got back in from the yard, was holding it up as she walked through the door.

"What does it say?" Christina whispered.

Aunt Ella looked right past Christina at the wall above her head, very serious. "Bad news . . . You didn't get in."

Christina's face went ashen, she looked as if she might faint. She took a few steps backward, sinking onto the stool by the telephone shelf. "I knew it," she said.

Aunt Ella chortled, and waved the letter high. "Oh come on—I was only joking! Of course you got in, with your grades."

But Christina just sat there, unable to force herself to smile.

AT THIS POINT in her own life, Margareta understood how Aunt Ella could have been so envious of their schooling, but she still could not accept it. Because even if Aunt Ella grieved for the fact that she herself had been born at a time when the out-of-wedlock child of a woman working in the textile mills couldn't dream of going to upper secondary school and then teacher training seminary, she should have been adult enough to take pleasure in her girls having chances she had never had.

Christina refused to recall that episode at all. Once, when Margareta brought it up on the phone, her voice had gone sharp and shrill. Lies and slander! No one in the world could have taken more pleasure in the good fortune of others than Aunt Ella, she had said, then hung up on Margareta and broken off diplomatic relations. It took months for Margareta to work her way back into Christina's good graces.

Margareta makes a face. Is it slander to remember Aunt Ella as she really was? Did she love her less for it? Of course not. Aunt Ella—with all her strengths and weaknesses—was the best mother Margareta ever had. Not that there had been much competition . . .

The altar to Aunt Ella is actually a handcrafted cupboard from 1815. The year is painted on the front. She has to turn the key three times to get the door to open, and at first sight she's disappointed by the contents. There's hardly anything in there at all: just a few assiduously taped plastic bags on the top shelf and a brown paper bag on the bottom one. That's all. But whatever there is, she needs to inspect it.

She sits cross-legged on the floor, reaching for the bags. She already knows what's in them. Things Aunt Ella made. Christina must have been selective at the auction; there can't be a fraction of all Aunt Ella's handiwork here, but what there is is exquisite. She doesn't even dare open the first plastic bag for fear of damaging the contents: it's an artistic lace creation, a bird pattern mounted on blue velvet. Margareta smiles. Aunt Ella was hardly able to conceal her triumph when she showed it to the ladies in her sewing circle. They began exclaiming about exhibits and museums. And it really is impressive: like an engineering project, the result of many months of patient calculation. She also remembers the little hemstitched runners: it took two months to finish one. But here's something unfamiliar: a pinafore in checkered cotton with a border of little birds and a cross-stitched monogram: CM. Christina Martinsson, in other words. Funny. She can't recall ever having seen Christina in it. And here—oh—a little baby shirt in the softest batiste. Now that must have been hers, she was the only one who was still a baby when Aunt Ella took her in . . .

Carefully Margareta opens the tape and gently lifts out the little shirt.

The front's no bigger than the palm of her hand. Could she really have been this tiny when she came to Aunt Ella's? How big is a four-month-old baby anyway?

Margareta smoothes the plastic bag on the floor, laying the little shirt on it carefully. It's completely handmade, with finished seams, invisible hemming, and white embroidery on the ruffled collar. Only a really longed-for baby would have clothes that were such a labor of love. You could tell. Somebody really *had* wanted Margareta.

"I guess some angel noticed how sad and lonely I was," Aunt Ella would say when Margareta was still a little girl and the only child in the house. "So she tipped a cloud over and let you fall down to me."

"Did I make a hole in the roof?" Margareta would ask.

"Not that time," Aunt Ella answered. "You had the wisdom to land in the cherry tree. I found you there one day when I went out cherry picking."

"Had I been eating them?"

"You'd had your fill. You've always been a glutton. There were pits all over the ground. That year I couldn't make any cherry pies, there wasn't enough fruit left. But I didn't mind. I had you instead."

Margareta was five years old, and smart enough to know this was a story. Still, she crept higher up in Aunt Ella's lap and chuckled with satisfaction.

*   *   *

TONGUE BETWEEN HER lips, Margareta folds the little shirt along the ironed creases. She's glad Christina has it: it will be safe in her cupboard for years and years, and when she dies one of her daughters will be sure to keep it. That's what this family's like: they save things and look after things and put them away for posterity. And when the collection of miscellaneous particles that is now Margareta Johansson has one day dissolved and become part of thousands of other collections of particles, this shirt will still be there as testimony to her existence. She will have a batiste gravestone.

Good grief, is she sitting here waxing sentimental? She doesn't have time for that, she needs to concentrate on putting the plastic bags back exactly as she found them. If Christina discovers Margareta's been going through her cupboard she'll be furious in her ice-cold, chip on the shoulder way. And Margareta doesn't want that: Christina's normal arrogance is quite sufficient.

Smiling, Margareta reaches for the bag on the bottom shelf, but the moment she touches it her smile freezes. She opens it and peeks inside. Yes, she was right. This bag contains a high school graduation cap. Christina's.

Never in her wildest dreams would she have imagined Christina wanting to save it.

CARS DECORATED WITH birch sprigs. Funny posters. Lots of noise.

Margareta was standing in the crowded school yard, waiting for a first glimpse of the graduates. But in vain. She was too short to see, even on tiptoe. If she'd had really high-heeled shoes she might have, but of course she would never have been allowed to leave the house in high heels. Margot kept very good track of teenage fashions, and high heels were definitely out. Only Doris Day types wore heels nowadays. And, Margie dear, you wouldn't want to be a Doris, would you?

No, she wouldn't want to be a Doris. And most of the time she liked the clothes Margot bought her: short skirts and flats, low white boots and op-art-patterned dresses. And the ones she didn't like she would wear anyway. Things were easiest that way, she'd learned.

Today she was wearing white open-toe boots and a perfectly straight little orange minidress. She was gorgeous! Just beautiful! The guys would fall for her like autumn leaves. Margareta snorted. Margot's way of mixing up idioms drove her crazy. She could claim that it was sunning cats and dogs and that the floor was slippery as an adder.

Just never mind! She had hours and hours to herself now, Margot would probably even be upset if she came home early. She'd given her quite a lot of money to spend on flowers—buy a rose for everyone you know who's graduating, Maggie! Don't skip a single one of them—Margot's underlying assumption being that she would be asked to one party after the next at the homes of the graduates she gave flowers to, and wouldn't be back until midnight.

If the truth be told, though, Margareta had decided to concentrate on one single graduate: Christina. It was a kind of penance: she'd been going around with a guilty conscience about her sister for long enough. They hadn't spent one single after-school hour together since they'd moved to

Norrköping, just stopped in the hall for quick talks about Aunt Ella. Christina had met Hubertsson outside the hospital one time, and Margareta called him in secret once a month. They told each other about that. But they never talked about themselves, or about what had become of Birgitta: this was an unspoken pact between them.

Christina didn't look well. She hadn't looked well for the past year. Pale as a specter, with big circles under her eyes, she'd stood in a corner of the school yard with her nose in a book every single recess. Margareta hung out in the smokers' area, laughing and chatting and flirting. Now and then she'd cast a quick glance in Christina's direction, but Christina never looked back. It was as if she had no idea there was a world beyond her books, as if she had no idea she was standing in a school yard full of potential adventures.

Come to think of it, she'd seemed to be living in a world of her own even at Aunt Ella's. She never left the yard with Birgitta and Margareta to see what was happening at one of the nearby playgrounds, didn't want to come along when they went swimming at Varamo in the summer, or to the meetings of the Social Democratic youth group with Margareta in the winter, and she'd never had a best friend like other girls. She just sat there, like a pale little replica of Aunt Ella, devoted to her lace making and her embroidery. Aunt Ella must have gotten quite tired of having her hanging on her apron strings year after year.

Today, though, Margareta was going to help make Christina's graduation an occasion for her to remember. She'd bought three yellow roses to hang around her neck, and a book of Karin Boye's collected poetry she intended to confer upon her at her reception. She wasn't quite sure where Christina and her mamma lived, or how she'd get there, but she could ask Christina when she gave her the flowers.

Where was her mother, anyway? Margareta looked around. She knew she'd have no trouble recognizing the witch. Her one visit to Aunt Ella's had made an indelible impression. But there were so many people in the school yard she just couldn't find her.

A buzz passed through the crowd: here they come! From afar high-pitched voices could be heard singing the school song. A solo trumpet joined in for a few bars, then the singing shifted to shouts of joy. The graduates flooded the school yard; the crowd divided to let the procession pass.

Margareta had always been a sucker for emotional occasions, and now she found herself at the front of the crowd, hopping with excitement. How dumb of her not to have bought flowers for lots of the kids she knew! There was Anders with the big ears, she could at least give him a hug. And there was Leif! And Carina, in the most gorgeous graduation suit anyone had ever seen! Hugs and kisses all around, and lots of congratulations!

She was hot and pink-cheeked by the time she had pulled out of Anders's embrace and began to look around. Where was Christina? Had she already been driven home in one of those cars with birch sprigs on the bumpers?

No, no. There she was! That was Christina, wasn't it, marching determinedly across the school yard? She looked as resolute and pale as ever, yet somehow not quite herself. She had raised her left hand in front of her face like a shield, was pushing total strangers aside with the palm of her hand, shoving her way between proud mothers and their joyous graduating sons, elbowing an old lady in the back and propelling her aside.

What was with her? Was she out of her mind?

"Christina," Margareta shouted, forcing herself in her direction. "Congratulations, Christina, congrats!"

Christina halted for a moment, letting her hands fall, only to resume her passage. She was almost all the way out on the sidewalk by the time Margareta finally caught up with her.

"Wait, Christina, wait up!"

Christina whirled around, stared at her with unseeing, gray eyes, blinked a few times, and returned to herself again. Margareta hung the roses around her neck. They dangled, alone, over a cheap white synthetic blouse. Her straight white skirt looked like something from a bargain basement, too. Her shoes were a pair of old pumps that had been given a coat of polish for the occasion. It hadn't helped much: the polish had cracked in the old creases and exposed the leather. Tan. Christina watched Margareta examine her, and for a moment they both stared at the cracks.

Margareta blushed. "Congratulations," she said, looking up. "And good luck."

"Thanks," said Christina.

"Where's your reception going to be?"

Christina gave a little laugh, it sounded like someone clearing a dry throat, but before she could answer a chubby little lady turned up alongside them. "There you are, Christina! Congratulations, my dear!"

Christina's cheeks suddenly took on some color; she curtsied and dipped her head gracefully as the woman hung a bouquet around her neck. Lilies of the valley.

"Where's your mother, sweetheart? I'd love to meet her. She must be so proud of you today."

Christina curtsied again. "She couldn't come, Sister Elsie. She fell ill last night."

The plump woman's hand flew to her mouth. "Oh, how awful! Today of all days. Nothing serious, I hope?"

Christina curtsied again; she seemed to feel the need to curtsy every time she addressed this woman. "No, I don't think so. But she had a really high temperature. A hundred and four last night. So unfortunately we've had to cancel my reception."

Sister Elsie frowned. "A hundred and four? My, if that fever doesn't break you'll have to be sure she sees a doctor."

Christina curtsied again. "Yes, I'll do that. And thank you ever so much for thinking of me."

Sister Elsie patted her cheek. "The pleasure was all mine, honey. It's so nice to know there are still good girls around."

The minute Sister Elsie was out of sight, Christina started walking. Margareta rushed behind her. "What a shame your mother's sick, Christina. Do you have to go right home, or would you like to get something someplace? I've got enough money to treat you."

"She's not sick."

"What?"

"Astrid's not sick, she's at work. I made that up."

"So you're going to have a reception?"

"No, no reception."

She took long strides, Margareta had to strain to keep up. "Could I take you out for something, then? To celebrate?"

"No, I can't."

"Why not?"

" 'Cause I don't have time. I've got a train to catch."

She turned the corner into Queen's Street. Margareta's toes were sliding forward into the slits in her boots. She had to stop for a minute and slide her feet back. By the time she got around the corner Christina was half a block ahead, and she really had to run to catch up. Her toes slid forward again.

"Wait," she puffed. "What train? Where are you going?"

"To Vadstena," said Christina. "I've got a summer job at Aunt Ella's nursing home."

CHRISTINA MUST HAVE gotten everything ready that morning. Her suitcase was packed and deposited in a locker at the station, her ticket was safely zipped into a pocket of her wallet. She seemed to calm down once she got her suitcase out. She set it between her feet and glanced at the station clock. "We're early," she said. "There's half an hour until train time."

But all she wanted to do was go out and wait on the platform. Lifting the suitcase brought a scowl to her face, but she refused to let Margareta carry it, just switched hands. They sat on a bench staring out at the empty tracks.

"Free," said Christina.

"What?"

"Oh, nothing."

"Where will you live? At the nursing home?"

Christina giggled. "No, at the cloisters, in the guesthouse. They hardly charge anything. And if you help out in the kitchen it's even cheaper."

Margareta hesitated. "Are you religious now?"

Christina laughed again; she seemed to have come to life now that they were on the platform. "No, I'm not becoming religious. But I need a little peace and quiet. And I guess a cloister's as good a place as any."

"What does your mamma say about it?"

"Astrid? She hasn't been told."

"She doesn't know where you're going? But what if she reports you to the police? You're still a minor, you know."

Christina shrugged. "Dream on. She'd never dare to go to the police station. Anyway, I think she'll be perfectly happy to be rid of me."

"You think so?"

"Mmmm-hmmm," said Christina. "Maybe she'll get a cat instead. And run it through the spin cycle."

Margareta's mind boggled. She leaned forward and looked at her toes;

they were bright pink against the white leather boots. They looked ridiculous. What dumb boots. "Has it been that bad?" she finally said.

"Yes," said Christina. "It really has been that bad."

SHE STAYED ON the platform until the train pulled out. Christina hung out through the window of her carriage, her hair flying behind her, waving her graduation cap, suddenly looking as if she'd been drinking champagne. Margareta waved back halfheartedly. Anxiety had begun to creep under her skin, slimy insects with sharp jaws dug tunnels in her stomach, fat flies crawled up and down her arms, spiders climbed right up her whole body and gathered at her larynx. She could hardly breathe.

She walked back through the waiting room and asked at the ticket window for change so she could make a call. The phone booth was occupied, and by the time it was her turn she was so agitated she could hardly get the coin into the slot.

A woman answered. An adult woman. Margareta put on a childish voice: "Good afternoon, my name is Margareta Johansson. I'm a student of Herr André's. May I speak with him?"

"One moment please!" The woman put her hand over the receiver and shouted: "Bertiiil! Telephone. It's a student."

He came to the phone almost immediately. There was a note of impatience in his voice. "Hello?"

"It's me."

He gasped, then lowered his voice. "Are you crazy? What are you doing calling me at home?"

"Oh, please, André," Margareta whispered, staring straight into the Masonite in front of her, poking with her little finger in a hole, enlarging it. "Don't be angry with me! I just miss you so much. . . . Couldn't you see me tonight?"

ON HER WAY home, just after midnight, she invented someone's cousin from Stockholm. She'd bumped into him at Anders's party. No, she had better have met him at Rasmus's, since Margot didn't know Rasmus. His cousin's name was Peter, and he was almost too good to be true. A blond type with a Beatles haircut. Blue-eyed and suntanned. A tennis player. His father had a car showroom, and he wanted to be a lawyer. Sign: Scorpio. Favorite color: blue.

Margot bought him from head to toe where she sat on her living room couch, in a pink dressing gown over her girdle and with a towel in precisely the same shade twisted like a turban around her head. "Did he kiss you?" she asked, placing her pudgy hand over Margareta's.

"No. He tried, of course, but I refused. I let him give me a peck on the cheek, though."

"Good girl. Mustn't give in too easily. Will you see him again?"

Margareta nodded and smiled. "Yeah. We're going to the movies tomorrow night. And I promised to show him around town in the afternoon."

Margot drew up her shoulders, cooing with pleasure. "Wonderful! What're you going to wear?"

Somewhere deep inside, Margareta sighed. She was tired and confused, her genitals ached, but she had no choice. She had to pay for her room and board somehow. "I can't decide," she said, cocking her head coquettishly. "Can you help me pick something out, please?"

Margot giggled. "At this hour?"

Margareta nodded.

They tiptoed up the stairs, Margareta with her white boots in her hand, Margot in pink bedroom slippers. How many pairs of slippers did that woman own? She had pink ones, powder blue ones, turquoise ones, red ones . . . and a robe to match each pair. Color coordination was important. People who didn't understand about matching just had no style.

Margareta's room was perfectly color-coordinated. Sometimes she thought of herself as nothing but an accessory, one of the details that contributed to the perfection of the interior design. A girl's bedroom requires a girl. Margot had bought the wallpaper, curtains, and bedspread in London over a year before Margareta had come into their home; they were simply irresistible. Imagine having the same roses on the walls as on the curtains and the bedspread. That was the kind of thing you could find only in London. It would never make its way to this dull socialist country. Margot had always wanted a daughter: a sweet little teenage daughter who would sleep in a bedroom with flowers on the wallpaper, and when she saw that wallpaper she knew the time had come. It had all gone very smoothly. All the social worker from the child welfare office had to do was take a quick look around their house to know it was the ideal foster home. A place any girl would give her right arm to live. But higher forces had undoubtedly been involved as well. We all have our guardian angels, and Margot's was really on her toes. His name was Astor, had she said that?

They were in the upstairs hall now. The even snores they had attuned their ears to as they walked up the steps suddenly went silent. Margot froze to ice. "Shhh," she said, finger to her lips. They stood stock-still for a moment, until they could hear Henry snoring again.

Margot giggled. "I was afraid he was waking up. That would've been terrible."

Margareta smiled and nodded her head.

"Sometimes we girls need a little time to ourselves," said Margot, opening the door to Margareta's room. "Okay, sweetheart, let's see what we can find in this closet of yours . . ."

HALF AN HOUR later, they still hadn't found what they really wanted. Margareta pulled on dress after dress, pirouetting in front of the mirror. Margot sat with her chin in her hand, looking more and more upset. "Nope," she said. "This just won't do. We'll have to get up early in the morning and go shopping. I saw such a cute little outfit in that boutique down on Queen's Street. Yellow and green. How do you say it, anyway? *Boooooutik? Boatik?*"

Margareta nodded and smiled, knowing you have to mix sugar with salt. "But I have classes tomorrow morning . . ."

"Oh, forget that," said Margot, with a dismissive gesture. "I'll write you a note. It won't take us long, you won't miss much, and it's the end of the year anyway."

"But we're doing something really important tomorrow morning, I'm afraid."

"Who cares? Honestly, you take school far too seriously. A girl doesn't really need a diploma, you know. And if you know what's good for you, you won't tell Peter what program you're in. It might put him off. Boys don't like overintelligent girls, you know."

Before Margareta could answer, the door opened and Henry was there in his striped old man's pajamas. The pants were bulging; he had a huge erection. "Margit, are you coming to bed?"

Margot got up, annoyed. "Call me Margot. Margot, not Margit. Honestly . . ." She glanced at herself in the mirror, licked her lips, and prepared to obey.

* * *

As Margareta scurried back to her room from the bathroom after a quick swipe with the toothbrush, she covered her ears with her hands. It didn't help. Henry made love noisily. She couldn't block out his grunts.

She knew it was no good stuffing her ears with cotton. The only way to keep Henry's noises out was to fold the lobes of her ears up and hold them over the openings with her index fingers. That did work, though, and she was able to get into bed and pretend there was nothing special going on in the house.

The problem was that she couldn't fall asleep while she was holding her ears. At Aunt Ella's house she'd always fallen asleep on her back with one arm over her head. This was her favorite position. In it, she fell right asleep, but nowadays she seldom had the chance, which was a shame. She far preferred her dreams to her nocturnal ruminations, and there was no way she could keep from thinking when she lay there awake. Night after night she interrogated herself. Who was Margareta Johansson? What was she? A person with shameful secrets. A person with a double life. A liar. A hypocrite.

She couldn't, however, see that she had any choice. She didn't see how she could survive in this house without lying. If she came clean with them now they'd treat her just like that troublesome poodle Margot had had put to sleep last winter. Not that Margot would take her to the veterinarian—that would be a solution entirely devoid of style—but she would certainly have her sent away. And God only knew what kind of a place her next foster home would be. Not to mention her next school.

And she didn't actually dislike Margot. She drove her crazy sometimes, of course, but mostly Margareta just felt sorry for her. There was something pathetic about her, waddling around in her forever matching but ever so unbecoming clothes. She would never let anyone see her real hair; when she wasn't wearing one of those synthetic wigs of hers she had a towel twisted into a turban around her head. She didn't seem to be bald, though. Now and then a thin strand of hair would hang out of the turban. She just seemed to be as unwilling to display her hair as she was to display her body. She never removed her girdle, even wore it under her dressing gown when she was pretending to be a soft little woman stretching out on the chaise longue after her bubble bath. Last summer when it had been almost a hundred degrees, she'd still walked around in her wig, her girdle, and her nylons. That was when Margareta realized she was ashamed. She obviously felt she had a great deal to hide.

Aunt Ella had never concealed anything and had never worn stockings in the summer. She had sat in the yard with her legs in the sun, not minding the blue lines of her varicose veins in her white skin. But Margareta didn't let herself think about that, she never let herself think about Aunt Ella when she was alone. She let herself think about Aunt Ella at school sometimes, or when she was at a café with some of the other girls in her class. Whose fault was it? Why had it happened? She didn't let herself think about that, either.

Margot didn't like her talking about Aunt Ella. Most of the time, she didn't even want Margareta to remember she was a foster child; Margot wanted them to pretend they were really mother and daughter. In the beginning, she'd tried to get Margareta to call her "little mamma," but when she heard how stiff and unnatural the words sounded every time Margareta said them, she stopped asking her to use that name. She could call her Margot. Lots of parents now let their children call them by their given names, she'd read it in *Women's World*. Or maybe it was in *Vogue*. Or *McCall's*.

Women's magazines were Margot's only friends. They were her companions when Margareta had left for school in the mornings and Henry had gone to his business. At dinnertime you could tell from her vocabulary which magazine had arrived that day. If it was *Cosmopolitan* she called things "charming," if it was *Vogue* they were "chic." When Margareta came into their lives, she also took out subscriptions to *Seventeen* and *Women's World,* which made things "neat" some days and "cute" others.

Henry appeared to find it perfectly normal that his wife lived in a dreamworld. Now and then he'd shake his head and call her nuts, but mostly he put up with it. When she asked him for money—as she did nearly daily—he opened his wallet and muttered cheerfully about women and their madness. Margareta suspected that Henry was of the opinion that she, too, was one of Margot's mad ideas: an expensive whim, along the lines of a new fur coat or Persian rug, something his little wife could take an interest in, as long as she didn't get too difficult to handle. Personally, he couldn't care less. He hadn't shown the least bit of interest in Margareta, hadn't been a foster father to her for so much as an instant; he hardly ever even noticed her. He had his business to think about, of course, the company he had built up from a simple joinery to a furniture plant with over three hundred employees. Now he could afford both a crazy wife and a spoiled foster child, but he most certainly didn't have any time to devote to them. Except at night, of course, when Margit— or Margot, as that crackpot of a wife of his insisted on calling herself nowadays—was expected to do the only thing women are any good at.

No, in this household there was no choice but to lie. Margot demanded that she pay her keep in intimacies, and only intimacies of the proper kind. Margareta's mandate was to make Margot's magazine world real, so she had no choice but to invent ideal boyfriends and platonic relationships. And of course there was some kind of divine justice in it, it was a logical punishment. She'd needed to be taught to keep her big mouth shut sometimes, to no longer let every thought in her head slip over her tongue.

She began to learn a thing or two about the world, stuff she'd never realized before. Like the fact that everything has its price, that there's no such thing as a free lunch. That was why she had to accept being a toy, being a dress-up doll for at least another year, until her own graduation day. Assuming she could really graduate; her grades weren't what they used to be. Margot was concerned for all the wrong reasons; there was no risk whatsoever that potential suitors would be put off by Margareta's studious mind.

But when push came to shove Margareta wasn't interested in any suitors, anyway. She didn't even want a boyfriend. A musty odor of flesh and lust clung to every single boy in the school yard, and that smell frightened her. But she was still unable to resist them more than halfway. She spent her breaks flirting wildly in the smokers' corner, shooting glittery glances and witty lines in every direction, but the minute one of the guys laid a hand on her, she had a smooth way of slipping out of his grip. That wasn't what she wanted. She wanted a man. A great big man, so big he would fill heaven and earth . . .

She lifted one of her index fingers carefully from her earlobe. Was it over? Yes. There was Henry, snoring again, so she could safely turn onto her back and throw one arm over her head.

Doing so, she could feel how she ached down below. She sighed: yes, everything had its price. And this was the price of having a man. A huge man so big he filled heaven and earth.

*　*　*

ANDRÉ. THAT WAS what she called him, although it was actually his surname. But she couldn't make herself call him Bertil, which was a name that might do for a workhorse or a bank teller but was completely inconceivable for a lover.

And he was her lover. She was seventeen years old and had a real lover.

She wasn't quite sure whether she was ashamed or proud of it. When she sat at a café table gossiping with her girlfriends, he sometimes entered her mind and brought tears of humiliation to her eyes—a dirty old man! Jeez, she was going all the way with a dirty old man! But when she bumped into him in the hall at school, she felt the blood rise to her cheeks and could barely conceal her triumph. That's my lover! He knows it, I know it, and no one else in the whole world knows it.

Still, she was glad he wasn't one of her teachers. Only once—not long after she'd come to Norrköping—had he substituted in her class. That was when it began, the moment he set his worn old satchel on the desk at the front of the room and said: "Hello, brats. Sit down and shut up."

Their chairs scraped against the floor; the atmosphere in the classroom suddenly brightened with expectation. Herr André. You knew what a man called André must be like.

"New girl in class?" he asked, examining the register. "Margareta Johansson. Make yourself known."

She gave a little wave of the hand; he stood up and sauntered down between the rows, hands deep in the pockets of his flannel trousers. He was tall and solid, with dark, thick hair. He looked a little like that American actor, oh, what was his name? . . . Dean Martin. Right. Hubertsson had looked like Dean Martin, too.

"From Motala? Do they teach you any geography in Motala?"

The class giggled. Margareta liked it, it was a friendly, interested sound. She smiled. "Sure. Quite a bit."

He sat on the edge of her desk, his thigh only inches away from her hand. "Oh yes? Can you spell the name of the longest river in the United States of America, then?"

The class laughed. Margareta moved her hand away, quickly checking in her head that she remembered the rhyme.

"I PP I SS I SS I M . . ."

A roar of laughter ran through the classroom. Margareta blinked and blinked. What was so funny about that? André just sat there on her desk until the last little ripple of amusement had gone silent.

"Excellent," he said, standing up. "Particularly the I pee pee part. And backwards!"

"Ooooh!" said Margareta, her hand moving involuntarily to her mouth.

AFTER THAT DAY he always smiled when they passed in the hall. And Margareta smiled back, but more hastily and furtively with every passing day. That gleam in his eye . . . she pressed her books tighter to her chest and rushed on.

"What're you blushing about?" the girl at the desk next to hers asked as they sat down for their next class.

"Blushing? Me?"

"Come on. You can't fool me . . ."

She fantasized about him all summer, such intense fantasies that in the end she was also dreaming about him. Strange dreams, though. Night after night they wrestled in the school yard, huffing and puffing.

She had no desire to wrestle with André, however. She just wanted him to kiss her.

HE WAS ONE of the staff chaperones at the first school dance of the fall. She was a student council representative, so it was only natural for them to stand and talk that evening, even for him to reach out and grab her by the wrist when she started to turn away. And his asking her to dance, well, that could be interpreted as a polite gesture toward the student council: a dance with one of the organizers. It could also have been a joke: one of André's gentle little gags. Because when he put his hands on her waist, the whole gym burst into a universal smile: Look! André's dancing with Margareta!

He held her at a safe distance, didn't press her to him or squeeze her like the guys did: just led her firmly around the dance floor, his eyes glued to hers throughout. When she happened to brush against his sex, his eyes narrowed. His lips parted and, for an instant, she saw his teeth. Margareta liked him looking at her, holding her gaze with his own, but what she was really preoccupied with was his hands, his left hand intertwined with hers, his right hand open along her back. They really were huge: she felt she could fit her whole self into the palm of one of them, could curl up there and go to sleep. She wished he would lift her up, carry her in those enormous hands, press her tightly to himself and spin.

He thanked her for the dance by allowing his cheek to touch hers for a single instant. That touch made her head spin, and she was unable to concentrate on the words he whispered.

"Pardon?" she asked, but without looking at him, she just stared down at her own arm. The hair was standing on end. As if she were cold.

He leaned down over her and repeated: "You're a hot little tease, aren't you?"

AFTER THE LAST dance, he put on his coat and seemed to be leaving, but somehow he was still hanging around nearly an hour later when Margareta and the rest of the student council had straightened up. When they were finally ready to leave, he stood at the door, holding it open so they had to crouch under his arm, one at a time, to get out.

Margareta was last. She stood in the middle of the gym floor, her hands clasped in front of her. She hoped she looked appealing, for the first time in her life she consciously thought: I hope I look all right.

"Come here," he said.

This is going to be it, she thought, putting one foot in front of the other. It's happening. It's real.

He took the Lord's name in vain when he penetrated her.

AFTERWARD, THEY CROSSED the school yard together, he with his huge strides, she stumbling and rushing to keep up. In the car he lit a cigarette before turning the key in the ignition. His lighter made dark shadows play across his face. "Why didn't you tell me you still had your cherry?"

She shrugged, reaching for his cigarettes.

"Did it hurt?"

She shook her head. It hadn't hurt. It had been good. But different for her than for him: not for a single instant had she been tempted to shout, or speak in tongues. And now she wanted to remain in her silence. As long as she didn't speak, she was still enclosed, embraced, enveloped. What had happened had happened in a place beyond all words, and only for as long as she didn't speak could she still feel his skin on hers, only as long as her lips were sealed could she retain his taste in her mouth.

"Answer me! Did I hurt you?"

She put her hand on his, suddenly wishing she knew sign language, although she had no idea what her fingers would say even if she did.

"THAT SHIT!"

With tears in her eyes, Margareta stuffs the graduation cap down into the paper bag and pushes it back into the cupboard. She still can't think about André without getting angry. If he were here she would punch him! But what would she be punching nowadays? A corpse. Or a trembling old man at some geriatric home someplace. But she can at least indulge herself in wishing gout upon him. Or some other really uncomfortable ache or pain.

He had taken advantage of her. All right, so she did fall into his arms of her own free will; all right, so she did sneak into the staff room and rummage through the coats to leave a little note in his pocket; all right, so she did stand around in the school yard waiting for him every afternoon. But still: she was sixteen going on seventeen when it started, and how old was he? Forty. Or forty-five. He was a father of three and a teacher at her school; he knew that she was an orphan and a foster child, that she bit her nails and often had stomachaches. He should have known the only thing she needed was to be noticed. But what did he give her? A crash course in Lolitaism.

Though she hadn't realized it until she was over forty herself. Instead, she had gone around for more than twenty years feeling inferior because her sexuality was different from other women's, because it was cryptic and clandestine, because it roved around on the flip side of other people's marriages, because it was rooted in deceits and lies and pretense. What difference did it make that she put a brave face on it, joking with her reflection about bad girls not being worst? Deep down inside she was still convinced of her worthlessness. And it was André who had ruined her, he was the one who made her believe she had to spread her legs in compensation for any nice word. For people like Margareta Johansson, sex was the price to be paid for the right to exist.

If André had let her be, she might have met a boy her own age, some little bookworm with a pimply chin and sweaty palms. Everything would have been different. They could have been in love rather than just making love. They could have quarreled and made up, slept in each other's arms, trusted.

She slams the cupboard door shut. What had Moa Martinson written: "Trust a man? You deserve a good strapping, then!" Now she would put the key in its place and have a shower. And forget that she had really loved him, that she had actually never been able to love another man without thinking about André.

That shit.

THE PHONE RINGS as she's heading upstairs and, halfway up, she can't figure out whether to take it upstairs or down. By the time she gets moving again it's too late, she can already hear Christina's formal message coming from the answering machine in the downstairs hall. Margareta heads down, thinking it may be Christina herself on the line, in which case she could turn the answering machine off and pick up.

And it does turn out to be her sister, she can hear that from the very first syllable. But not the right sister. The wrong one.

"You fucking stuck-up bitch," Birgitta slurs. "How could you be so damned mean, refusing a person a measly bus ticket? And how could you write the kind of crap you put in that letter? Huh? Tell me that! What kind of a mind do you have? You just better watch out is all I can say, I'm gonna—"

Margareta automatically lifts the receiver; every cell in her body knows she's going to regret it, but she does it anyway. "Hello? Birgitta?"

An instant of silence.

"Margareta?" Birgitta's voice asks. "Is that Margareta?"

"Yes."

"Jesus, I thought you were up there with the frigging Lapps. Or in Africa."

"Africa?"

"Yeah, you worked in Africa at some point—"

"No, no. That was South America. And I was just there for three months years and years ago."

"Same shit. What're you doing at the Louse's place?"

You ought to know, Margareta thinks, saying nothing. Suddenly she's a little scared. *Shame on you! Shame on you! Nobody wanted you!*

"I'm just passing through," she says stiffly, though she really wants to say something very different: Thanks a lot for writing, and for costing me a night's sleep, my sweet sister. But don't forget we're in the same boat: nobody wanted you, either. Not even your beloved little mother dear.

"Have you got a car?"

"Yes, but . . ."

"Jeez, that's great. Do you think you could come get me? I'm absolutely stranded."

Dream on, Margareta thinks. At the same time she hears herself say, "Hang on. Where are you?"

"In Norrköping."

"Norrköping? What're you doing there?"

"Well, it's a long story. I'll tell you later. How long will it take you to get to Norrköping? An hour? Listen, I'll be waiting outside the police station in an hour—"

"Hold it!" Margareta shouts, but too late. Birgitta's already hung up.

WHAT'S A PERSON to do? Margareta laughs in resignation at her reflection in the bathroom mirror. What does a well-mannered woman do when her sister is in need?

Pays no attention. That's what she does.

The very thought gives her a twinge of guilty conscience. But Birgitta's an adult, in fact, and should have learned by now that she can't just order people around. And if she's managed to get to Norrköping, why can't she get herself back home?

Birgitta must have extended her territory lately. They've been in only sporadic touch, and over the last ten years she seems to have stayed in Motala most of the time. However, this might be nothing but another one of her usual put-ons. Birgitta has no idea, of course, that Margareta knows she's had her little outings. To Vadstena, for example, to deposit a bag of excrement on Christina's desk and steal one of her prescription pads. Or to the women's penitentiary for a few months. But when she's going into rehab she usually phones Margareta to tell her the good news. This time she's really never going to drink or take drugs again. Straight and narrow.

For the first few years after Aunt Ella's stroke, Birgitta often went to

Norrköping. Margareta had known it at the time, too. One evening when
she and André were driving around looking for a place to park where no
one would see them, she had seen Birgitta down in Salt Flats.

"Stop!" she said, covering his hand with her own. He put on the brakes
in sheer surprise, then pressed the accelerator again. "What, here? Don't
you know what kind of neighborhood this is?"

Well, of course she did. It was the last remaining slum in Norrköping,
maybe the last one in Sweden. People still had outhouses here, and only
cold running water inside. This was where the illegitimate, unacknowl-
edged stepchildren lived, the ones for whom the doors to the great big
happy Swedish family of the welfare society had never opened. In the
evenings, flashy cars rolled slowly down the streets of Salt Flats, and men
seeking refuge from their all-too-orderly lives glared through their wind-
shields with hawk eyes.

Birgitta was standing under a streetlight in the classic pose. It was her,
wasn't it? Oh, yes. Definitely. Margareta even recognized her old suede
jacket. It was unbuttoned, and under it she was wearing a white blouse
that pulled tight across the bust. Birgitta had grown. Birgitta, too.

"Wait," said Margareta again. "I know her . . ."

"Who?" said André, applying the brakes again. "The one under the
streetlight?"

"That's my sister."

"What? You don't have sisters!"

"Oh yes, I do, in a way. Back up a little. I want to talk to her."

"No way," said André. "She's a hooker."

THE WATER IN the shower's too hot. It feels good but makes her limp
with exhaustion, makes her thoughts transparent and garbled. She doesn't
even have the strength to lather herself, just stands there, face upturned.
Maybe she should sleep for an hour or two first so she won't be a danger
on the roads. Then she can pick up the car and head for Stockholm. She
wonders what the new exhaust system's going to cost. And how much she
has left in the bank this month. Probably not much. She's applied the
same principle of accounting for ages: best to spend your money on something before it runs out.

She turns around, lifts up her hair, lets the water run down her neck.
Not that the money business worries her. This is the one area in which
she's always felt secure. She's like a silkworm: if she runs out of thread all

she has to do is spin a little more. She can always pull together an article on the aurora borealis or sun storms for a Sunday supplement (under a pseudonym, of course), or take a few hours of substitute teaching at some high school. It always works out. Not to mention that she intends to make Claes pay for half the exhaust system. That's only fair. He's going to make more use of it than she is. She wonders if he's called from Sarajevo. Will the answering machine on the old, unfinished set of drawers in his hall in Stockholm be blinking? She hopes so. She likes hearing his voice on the answering machine . . .

Suddenly a heavy thought detonates under all these light ones: How could Birgitta have known that Margareta was going to turn up in Vadstena yesterday? She hadn't even known it herself. How could she have known what garage she'd leave the car at? How could she have hidden in the right place at the right time to deliver that letter during the few minutes Margareta had been inside arranging for the repair?

There's no explaining it. A mystery. Why hadn't the problem occurred to her earlier?

Suddenly, the hot water runs out. Margareta hugs herself. She's freezing.

MARGARETA DOESN'T LIKE mysteries. But she's had to learn to live with them.

She was found in the laundry room of a building in Motala, a perfectly ordinary laundry room for its time. It was on the side of an apartment building from the forties, with concrete steps down from the courtyard and a white door, in the middle of which there was a pane of rough, frosted glass. Inside the laundry room there was a soaking tub along one wall and a cylindrical stainless steel washer on the other. The floor was tiled, there was a red hose, coiled like a serpent, running from a tap on the wall to the floor drain. She knows all this, she remembers it. Because the week after she graduated from high school she lied her way to some time out of Margot's sight and went to see it.

It was early summer, but already very hot. The laundry room door was wide open, white sheets were hanging still on a line in the courtyard, and some children were playing in a nearby sandbox. Margareta descended the steps slowly, stood at the open door, and looked in. The place was cloudy with steam, and at first she saw nothing but her own shadow, cast on the white tile floor.

"What d'ya want?" A woman emerged out of the mist. She was wearing a housedress and rubber boots, had her hair up on her head, but not under a turban, just a kerchief. She was a big, heavyset woman, beads of perspiration clung to her forehead. Margareta extended a hand and curtsied, to be on the safe side. The woman stared at her for a moment, then wiped her own hand on the housedress and shook Margareta's. "What d'ya want?" she repeated.

Suddenly, Margareta was dumbstruck. How could she explain?

"I just wanted to look," she finally said.

"Look? At what?"

"This laundry room."

The woman frowned and put her hands on her hips. "You wanted to look at the laundry room? Are you nuts? Get out of here now."

"But—"

The woman waved her arms. "Go on, shoo. Just be off!"

Margareta stumbled backward, hit the steps, and lost her balance. She managed to grab the railing, but she still slammed her tailbone on a stair. It was so painful she couldn't control herself: tears came to her eyes and rolled down her cheeks. Suddenly she was weeping and moaning, like a child. Once she started she was unable to stop; suddenly she was crying about everyone and everything: Aunt Ella's brain hemorrhage; André, who couldn't love her; Christina's fears and Birgitta's sins; Margot, poor Margot and her color-coordinated wardrobe. But most of all she was crying about herself: because she was all alone in the world and wasn't even allowed into this laundry room.

The woman looked frightened. "Hurt yourself?"

Margareta looked up at her, sniveling. "All, all I wanted to do was look. At the laundry room. It was where they found me . . ."

"Found you? Is that you? The baby in the basket?"

HER NAME WAS Gunhild, and she was sixty. She was a widow now, but she still lived in the one-bedroom apartment she and Eskil had moved into after the war. She waddled from the kitchen counter to the table, setting out coffee, sticky buns, and seven kinds of cookies. She hoped Margareta would help herself to the little she had to offer, she said. She was so pleased to have her there, had wondered so often what had become of her.

Gunhild wasn't the person who actually found her, that was Svensson, the caretaker, but he'd been dead for many years now. However, they had put Margareta on the very same couch she could still see in the sitting room over there. Svensson had carried her up here, because Gunhild and Eskil were the only people in the whole building who had a telephone in those days. She hadn't been there for long, though, because the police had arrived in about fifteen minutes, and in less than an hour someone from the child welfare agency had been there. She'd brought a bottle and clean diapers, which was lucky because Margareta was screaming at the top of her lungs.

"What did I have on?"

Gunhild frowned, thinking hard.

"Well, to tell you the truth you weren't wearing any clothes. She'd wrapped you in rags, and in an old towel of mine I'd left down in the laundry room. The umbilical cord was still there. It looked really strange . . . but she'd washed you, there was no blood on you, none of that gooey stuff."

Margareta dipped a third cookie in her coffee and braced herself for the most important question: "Do you know who she was?"

Gunhild sank down in her chair and crossed her arms over her ample bosom. The kitchen was in shadow; the air was cooler than outside, but her pale forehead was still beaded with sweat. "No, dear, I don't. I honestly don't."

Margareta looked down into her cup; there were some crumbs floating in her coffee. "But what did you think? Was there anybody here in the building you suspected?"

"No," said Gunhild. "People did talk, of course, I can't deny that, but not about anybody in this building."

"Cross your heart?"

Gunhild appeared to realize the gravity of her answer, looked Margareta right in the eye, and put both her hands in full view on the tabletop. "Yes," she said. "Cross my heart."

They sat quietly for a few minutes. The tap was dripping: it sounded like a heartbeat, as if someone were hiding over there, eavesdropping on their conversation, but unable to keep down the beating of his heart. Margareta stirred her coffee, scraping the spoon along the bottom of the cup to drown out the rhythmic sound.

Gunhild looked distressed. "I don't know, no one knew. . . . She might have birthed right there and hosed up the mess. The floor must have been wet anyway, because Svensson's shoes left big prints on my living room floor. I had to wax it afterward."

At once Margareta could visualize him: a wiry little man in blue overalls standing in the middle of Gunhild's living room. How could she know he was wiry? Well, she was sure of it, but she wasn't sure about anything else. She couldn't remember which way the sun was coming from, from the kitchen side or the living room side.

"What time of day was it?"

"It was morning. Eskil had just left for work."

"How did she get into the laundry room?"

Gunhild stopped, about to bite into a cookie. She set it down on the flowered china plate. "I've wondered about that too, but I don't know. Maybe there was something about it in the papers. . . . Oh, good grief. How could I forget the scrapbook? Have another cookie while I hunt for it."

Margareta was left alone in the shady kitchen. The window was ajar, and she could hear the children playing in the courtyard. Their voices were cool despite the heat, cool and bright white. The tap dripped.

"Here." Gunhild waddled back into the kitchen, her scrapbook in her arms. She wiped a few crumbs off the oilcloth with her chubby arm, pulling her chair closer to Margareta's before she sat down.

"Let's see here," she said, opening the big brown album. "This was Eskil's scrapbook, so most of it's about soccer. He went to school with Gösta Löfgren."

Margareta nodded. She'd been raised in Motala and could hardly have missed Gösta Löfgren. Even Aunt Ella knew who he was. Gunhild turned the pages, running quickly through his progress toward the national team.

"There we are," she finally said, pointing to a headline with her pudgy index finger: BABY GIRL FOUND IN LAUNDRY ROOM.

It had never occurred to Margareta that there must have been newspaper coverage, but now she could see that the events surrounding her birth had been big news, although the headlines were somewhat smaller than those describing the victories of the Motala soccer team in the top league. A national evening tabloid had run a photo of her: a grave infant staring right into the camera, with the headline: MAMMA, WHERE ARE YOU? Another had used the same theme. Margareta made an embarrassed face and looked on. The two local papers and the big national morning paper were less gushy, but they had also covered her, with long reports.

She leafed dully through the scrapbook, skimming the headlines but not actually reading. Suddenly she regretted having come. Neither Gunhild's scrapbook nor her laundry room was going to provide any answers. Finally there was a picture she had to squint closely at. Caretaker Vilhelm Svensson was, indeed, a wiry little man. For one moment her nostrils knew how he smelled. Of smoke and summer sweat.

Gunhild poured them a second cup of coffee. She, too, suddenly seemed tired. Perhaps this meeting with the person who had once been that baby hadn't exactly been what she'd imagined, either.

"You must try to forgive her," she said. "I'm sure she had no choice.

Things are different today, but in those days it was a disgrace to have a baby if you weren't married. A terrible disgrace."

She stirred her coffee, watching the concentric circles for a moment before repeating: "It was such a disgrace . . ."

BACK ON THE bus, Margareta felt a little carsick and bloated from all Gunhild's cookies. The heat was heavy on the farmlands, the diesel fumes from the bus exhaust came back in through the open windows, making her gag.

Aunt Ella was very surprised to see her. She reached out with her good hand and smiled her lopsided smile. She was able to speak again now, though her voice was slow and slurred, but she didn't say much, using body language and gestures most of the time to indicate what she wanted. Now she wiped her brow. The heat didn't agree with her.

Taking Aunt Ella on a walk through Vadstena was a new experience. During all the time Margareta was living at Margot's, she had only twice managed to lie her way to the money for a bus ticket and a free Sunday, and on both these occasions there had been snow. Today, however, she could easily roll the wheelchair along the sidewalk and they could have a long walk, much longer than Margareta had originally intended.

They strolled the streets leisurely. Margareta stopped at the windows of the various handicraft shops, and Aunt Ella leaned forward and regarded the lacework, sighed and gestured dejectedly with her good hand. The town rested quietly all around them, so quietly that Margareta lowered her voice and spoke in a hush without even knowing it, as if Aunt Ella were napping in her wheelchair and shouldn't be bothered. Yet they were only talking of everyday things: the heat, Hubertsson, and the fact that Christina was coming to Vadstena again. She was going to work at the nursing home this summer, too, and would be arriving from Lund in a week.

The park down by the lake was nearly empty; it wasn't tourist season yet. The shadows under the tall trees were gentle and green, occasional sunny spots dotted the newly cut grass, and the castle hovered like a shadow along the edge of the park. Margareta applied the wheelchair brake and sat down on a bench. They sat there for a long time in silence, looking out at Lake Vättern, inhaling the scent of mown grass, listening to the crying of the gulls.

"I went to Motala today," Margareta finally said. "To that laundry room."

Aunt Ella turned her head to look at her, but Margareta continued to stare at the lake. Her thoughts went spinning off in some other direction, as they tended to do when she had something important to say. *I always thought that business about water being blue was a myth,* she was thinking. *Usually, it's gray. But today it's really blue. As blue as midnight blue ink.*

"It's really weird," she went on. "When we lived in Motala it never occurred to me to go over there. I knew exactly what street it was, and what building, but I didn't sort of believe it. It wasn't real. It was almost easier to believe you had really found me in the cherry tree . . ."

Aunt Ella smiled a quick smile.

Margareta lowered her eyes and looked at her hands. "But you know what I actually did believe when I was little? I believed you were my real mamma, but you were keeping it a secret."

Aunt Ella extended her hand, and Margareta took it.

"That was how it felt. And that meant I never had to think about her, the other one, because she didn't exist. Not until I moved to Norrköping did I start thinking about her, not until then did I realize that what you had told me was really a true story. That I'd been found as a baby, that I was an orphan."

Aunt Ella squeezed her hand, but Margareta withdrew hers and started rummaging around in her purse. She put a cigarette between her lips, leaning slightly forward to light it, then glancing quickly back over her shoulder.

"Margot would die if she saw me," she said, exhaling a puff of smoke. "Nice girls never smoke out of doors."

Aunt Ella shrugged and turned toward the lake, following a seagull with her eyes as it dived into the glittering water, only to rise into the sky a moment later with a fish, glittering like a silver ornament, in its beak.

"Why did she abandon me?" Margareta suddenly asked, tossing the half-smoked cigarette to the ground. "Do you know? Can you imagine how anyone could abandon a newborn infant?"

Aunt Ella didn't answer, just sat in her wheelchair, unmoving, staring at the seagull.

"No." Margareta sighed. "Of course you can't."

*   *   *

PHYSICS WAS HER solace. Far more comforting than archaeology.

This is the most human of predicaments, she would tell herself during the first few years of her physics studies. We know nothing about our origins. God abandoned us in a laundry room and went away.

She wasn't so foolish as to say it out loud. She was quick to realize that the conventions of natural science required a certain reserve in regard to both the microcosmos and the macrocosmos. Only the acknowledged geniuses were permitted to indulge in the existential sides of this pure science, while little run-of-the-mill physicists were required to show moderation in thought, word, and deed. Those who did not ran the risk of being regarded as belonging to the faculty of philosophy or—God forbid— theology. And that rule is still in force. A mediocre Ph.D. student in physics on the outskirts of the habitable world is not allowed to consider God. That's the preserve of people like Albert Einstein and Stephen Hawking. And only barely. Hawking's relationship to God contains far too much vanity and self-flattery to win the true respect of his colleagues and, in certain respects, Albert Einstein serves as an object lesson.

"God does not play dice," he said. But God does. If there is a God, he is a notorious crap shooter, as the quantum physicists have proven. Matter is in a constant state of hesitation, unable to decide whether it consists of waves or particles. That decision is in the eye of the beholder. Moreover, some particles are also able to be in more than one place at a time, which may, in turn, indicate that there is more than a grain of salt to the theory of multiple universes. Somewhat oversimplified, this assumption implies that the ability of particles to be in more than one place at a time is circumstantial evidence of the fact that reality is continually being split, that the universe multiplies by division.

God must be pulling our collective leg, Margareta sometimes thought. He's messing around with us, teasing us. But we're on to him, and it's no good throwing new mystifications in our path. We'll poke his creation apart, examine every detail, search for and find the missing part of antimatter down to the smallest little positron, calculate the precise weight of the neutrino, because the only reason he pretends the universe is without mass is to be able to mock our attempts to compute it. We'll capture the Higgs particles in a tin can and laugh till we cry as we rattle it mockingly in his face. He can't fool us.

She kept such thoughts to herself, though, spending the days glued to her monitor like a good girl, devoted to her magnetic storms: that aspect of reality she can embrace with both emotion and reason, while the other, the mysteries, is one she doesn't speak of.

Still, she wondered in silence whether other physicists were able to mobilize sufficient brain power to understand reality, rather than merely to calculate it. For example, the fourth force of nature. Gravity. Like everyone else, Margareta knew how to describe it, how to calculate it, but she didn't know what it really was. She wasn't alone in that, either, of course. No one seemed to know what gravity is. But she seemed to be the only one who was bothered by not knowing. Now and then she looked around the cafeteria at the Institute of Space Physics at lunchtime and thought: Now I'm going to do it. I'm going to stand up and ask. She could imagine the scene, the others putting down their cutlery and stopping eating, the dead silence.

"Well," she'd say. "Excuse me for interrupting your lunches, but does anyone besides me believe that gravity is God? Or at least the hands of God?"

Right. She could see the next scene, too, some weary colleague lifting her by the collar of her blouse and the seat of her pants and tossing her out into a snowdrift. Fini Margareta Johansson. That one wouldn't be hired when she finished her thesis. If she finished her thesis. A straight shot to the loony bin instead.

So Margareta sat there like a good girl, on her chair in the cafeteria at lunchtime, drinking her skim milk and masticating her meatballs. Only occasionally did she close her eyes for a moment and reflect on her longing. She wanted someone. A friend. A child. A sister. Someone to share her ruminations.

No TIME FOR a bathrobe. Wrapped in nothing but a towel, she hurries down the stairs and out into the hallway, shivering, to rummage through her jacket pockets. The slip is crumpled, but she can still read the phone number.

Her teeth are chattering as she dials, but she manages to keep her voice steady. "Hello," she says. "I brought in a Fiat yesterday. Is it done? Great. I'll be there in ten minutes."

Where's the phone book? She pulls out the drawers in search of it. Damn. A thousand silk scarves and cashmere shawls, but not a single phone book. She'll have to call directory assistance. She needs two numbers. One for a taxi, the other for Christina's health center.

Afterward she takes the stairs in three long strides, wanting to get dressed and out of this madhouse as fast as possible.

Christina is just as much of a nutcase as her mother. No doubt about it.

WHEN SHE'S GATHERED her belongings together and zipped her suitcase, she takes a deep breath. She needs to sound calm and indifferent when she speaks to Christina; she has to say a completely relaxed thanks and good-bye, as if she still had no idea, still didn't understand at all.

"May I please speak with Dr. Wulf?"

"She's not in," says a tired voice. "I'll put you through to the nurse."

Not in? What if she's on her way home?

"Nurses' office, Helena speaking!"

Hale and hearty type.

"I'm trying to reach Christina Wulf. But apparently she's not in."

"That's right. Can I help you? Did you want an appointment?"

"No, not at all. This is her sister. I've been visiting and I just wanted to say good-bye and thank you before I left."

Sister Helena's voice is just a little softer now, more confidential. "Oh, I see. Well, I'm very sorry Christina's not here to take your call. . . . She had to run over to the nursing home."

"Would you please tell her I called? And that I'll be in touch from Stockholm?"

"Yes, of course."

Margareta's about to hang up, then she remembers: "Oh, doesn't Hubertsson work at your health center, too? Is he in?"

"Yes, he's in, but I'm afraid he's unable to come to the phone just now, either."

"Oh well, please send him my regards, too. We haven't seen each other in years, but I think he'll remember me. Margareta. Christina's little sister."

Helena's interest is obviously kindled. "So you and Christina have known Hubertsson since the old days?"

Margareta smiles to herself. Typical of both Christina and Hubertsson not to reveal to their colleagues how they actually know each other. Well, it will be a pleasure for her to puncture their shabby little secret. "That's right. He rented a room from us for years."

"Amazing," Helena says dreamily.

MARGARETA TAKES NO great pains to hide the back door key when she sets it in Christina's conch shell and heads for the sidewalk. She prefers to wait outside for the taxi just in case her hostess turns up.

Out of her mind. Totally blown away. Several screws loose.

Birgitta probably never put that shit on her desk. Maybe she never even stole Christina's prescription pad. . . . And she certainly lacks the resources, discipline, and willpower to implement such a complex operation as Margareta was subjected to last night. But Christina possesses them.

She must have invested ages in this little scheme. She must first have found out that Margareta was going to Göteborg, then have gone there herself for the express purpose of shadowing her. Then, when Margareta stopped to have coffee and enjoy the view at the Golden Otter, she must have crawled under the car and messed up her exhaust system . . .

The very idea stops her in her tracks and fills her with suppressed

laughter. How absurd! Christina couldn't possibly have set down her little handbag on the asphalt in the parking lot and crawled on her stomach
in her loden green cape and her painstakingly ironed Hermès scarf under
the car, only to turn carefully over on her back and start picking apart the
chassis . . .

It doesn't make sense. That can't be what happened. If for no other
reason than that it would have meant Christina getting her hands dirty.
And Christina can't stand having dirty hands. It makes her sick. Literally.
Makes her throw up.

Maybe she's the one who's going mad.

Who cares? She has to get out of here anyway. As fast as she can.

TRUST. CONFIDENCE. SOLACE. Comfort. Safety. Security. Protection. Words.

Maybe they mean something in some other universe.

If she had been a sensible sixteen-year-old—or a more sensible person
at all—things would never have turned out like this. If she had known
enough to restrain and control her own anxiety, if she had known enough
to keep her mouth shut, if she had never opened the door of that phone
booth, everything would have ended up the way it should have.

Aunt Ella would still be living in her house in Motala. Maybe she
would have needed home help a few hours a week, and who would her
home helper have been if not Birgitta? Because Birgitta would have settled down, of course: at some point as she was nearing twenty she would
have met a Bill or a Leif or a Kenneth who was a solid factory worker or
garage mechanic or construction worker. And when she had had two children by him—boys, of course, there was no question of anything else in
Birgitta's case—she would have decided not to go back to work at the factory but to be an at-home mother for a few years in their two-bedroom
apartment, wiping the boys' noses and making them porridge, grieving for
her mother and her illusions, gathering her strength and pulling herself
together, while Bill or Leif or Kenneth did as much overtime as he could
to scrape together the down payment on that little house they dreamed
about. And once they had the house, Birgitta would have started as a
home helper—part-time, of course—in order to help with the mortgage
payments. Her posture would have straightened up and all her old sense
of shame run off her. With a smile on her relaxed face she would have
biked around Motala just like Aunt Ella used to do. Here comes Birgitta

Fredriksson (or whatever her name would be), her bike wheels whizzing! The honest wife of an honest workingman. A perfectly ordinary person.

And when Aunt Ella was feeling under the weather—she'd have been over eighty by this time, after all—Birgitta would have phoned her older sister Christina. Who was a doctor. And Christina would have gotten into her little car at the end of her working day and dropped in on Aunt Ella, taken her blood pressure, checked on her doses, and urged her to be nice to herself. But, of course, as soon as she'd left, Aunt Ella would have phoned Margareta and grumbled a little rebelliously: there would be no keeping her away from the annual meeting of the Association of Retired Persons, no matter what Christina said! And Margareta would have laughed and cheerfully supported this subversive stance.

When Christmas came around they would all have gathered at Aunt Ella's. Birgitta would bring her Bill or Leif or Kenneth and their sons, two enormous young men with hands as big as toilet seat covers and gleams in their eyes. They'd put their arms around their chubby mother's shoulders and give her a little hug, call Aunt Ella Grandma, and turn her head with technical details from the factory that was their infinitely secure workplace. Yes, Birgitta's boys would be safe, immunized with education against raging unemployment; they'd be, quite simply, indispensable.

Just like in the old days, they'd have to set a little extra table for the young people in Aunt Ella's dining room, where Birgitta's boys would sit along one side and Christina's girls—Åsa and Tove—along the other. Because although he was a mixed bag, of course Margareta would never wish Christina's professor and her girls out of her life. And at one short end there would be room for the fifth child. Hers.

He would have been the boy she had noticed at the orphanage in Lima. Margareta and her son would have made Aunt Ella the head of an unending lineage of orphans; children who extended a hand, generation after generation, and took in other lost children. But on this particular occasion he would be far from lost. He'd sit there—an Indian, a copper-skinned young man, handsome and mysterious as a figure in an Andean myth—at Aunt Ella's Christmas dinner, regarding his cousins through narrow black eyes, with a little smile always at hand under his serious surface. And in the middle of the meal he'd catch Margareta's eye, lift his glass of Christmas cola in a toast, and say: *"Por la vida, Ma!"*

And Margareta would smile back, lift her own glass, and return the toast. *Por la vida!* To life, to trust, and to the solace that filled Aunt Ella's home.

THE TAXI'S TAKING forever. Margareta sinks down on the front steps of the Post-Industrial Paradise, chin in hand. What's wrong with me? she thinks. What's wrong with the three of us? Why are we always ready to believe the worst about one another? How did we ever become so damned underhanded and suspicious?

Things should've been different. After all, we grew up in the era of security, in the era when every sunrise was a victory over the day before. Everything evil that could happen had already happened, the past had been survived and endured and put behind them, all that remained was an endless line of bright tomorrows . . . and they knew it. Everybody knew it.

But perhaps solace isn't actually anything but naïveté, and maybe they're right, the cynics who run the world today, when they claim that naïveté is simpleminded by nature. Because although Margareta was a naïve young woman who was comfortable in an age of naïveté, that is not a complete description of the young woman who opened the telephone booth door for Christina. She was simpleminded as well. An idiot. Practically a moron.

Although it must be said that naïveté was not her only side. She did know the world was full of specters. Some of them occasionally made themselves palpable at the perimeters of her existence, only to vanish, like her own mother and Birgitta's; others bided their time threateningly, like Christina's mother. Sometimes the shadows could even be glimpsed on Aunt Ella's face. When she thought no one was looking she'd drop into a kitchen chair, resting her head in her hands on the tabletop, and when it emerged, there were furrows from nosebleeds and weeping.

The specters appeared elsewhere as well, not only at Aunt Ella's. One girl in Margareta's class told them, with jittery, flashing eyes, about a place called Auschwitz, where her mother had lain outside a gas chamber for two days and two nights anticipating death, until she was rescued by a white bus. And one day she had gone home after school with another of her classmates, Susanne, who had opened the linen closet to show Margareta a secret hidden under a pile of white pillowcases. It was a picture. A photo of a little girl wearing a pink sweater. Her eyes were closed.

"This is my sister," Susanne whispered. "Her name is Daisy."

Margareta looked at the girl in the picture for a moment, then whispered back: "Why are her eyes shut?"

"She's blind."

Margareta felt the world spin, then tried to find something nice to say. "She's pretty anyway, really pretty."

"She was. Not anymore," Susanne whispered, putting the picture back under the pillowcases. "She's got water on the brain."

"What's that?"

"Her head just keeps growing and growing, it's full of water. . . . We went to see her three years ago, and it was just huge. . . . Like a balloon. Her head was so heavy she couldn't sit up."

"Can't she ever come home?"

Susanne shut and locked the linen closet door. Suddenly she was talking in a normal voice again, as if there was no reason to go on whispering now that the closet was closed. They were all alone at home; Susanne's mamma and pappa were out and there were no other siblings. "No. She just can't. We don't even visit her anymore."

"Why not?"

" 'Cause she screams so much. When we leave she goes on screaming for days."

When Margareta left Susanne's she biked right home and threw her bike down on the gravel path leading to the house, rushing inside. Aunt Ella began to scold her, but when she heard about Daisy she went silent and turned her back.

You weren't supposed to talk about the specters. They'd go away if you just ignored them. They'd be all gone by the time the future arrived.

NOT UNTIL SHE was grown up did she realize that Christina and Birgitta had never shared her optimism, never believed in the future the way she had. Perhaps that was because their childhood specters were more tangible than hers. This hadn't really hit her until the day a few years ago when she'd called Christina to hear what Birgitta had been sentenced to for stealing that prescription pad and for the subsequent fraud and forgeries. Christina sounded doggedly pleased when she reported that Birgitta was already on her way to the women's penitentiary.

Margareta was disappointed. She'd hoped for probation, rehab and therapy. "The welfare state's eroding before our very eyes," she said.

"No great loss," Christina replied.

That tone of voice was enough to bring an old image into Margareta's mind. A tall building. A gray, concrete building in a muddy field. That was the welfare state in Christina's mind. And she suspected it was equally gray in Birgitta's; to her the welfare state was probably embodied by some frumpy little social worker's office. But in Margareta's mind, the welfare state would always be something else. A white house in a flourishing yard. A house where even lost children could grow up in security.

The industrial paradise.

"ARE YOU MY fare?"

The taxi driver is annoyed: he reaches across the empty passenger seat and opens the window. He must've driven all the way down to the end of Song Street, turned around and come all the way back to be heading out in the right direction without Margareta's having seen him.

She shoots him a smile. "Sorry. I guess I was daydreaming . . ."

Ten years ago a smile and a line like that would have made him melt, he would have shut off the engine, helped her with her bag, and opened the front door to be really sure she'd sit next to him. Now he just stares at her impatiently through the rolled-down window, and she has to carry her bag over to the car herself. He doesn't even protest when she settles in the backseat. Margareta smiles to herself. Not that she's ever played in the same league as Birgitta, but she's still spent several decades feeling as if she were wading through a swampy thicket of men's looks and hands. She's quite glad it's over, that she's finally made it out of the marsh and can stride through the open landscape without worrying about her skirt getting wet, even if she has to carry her own bags and be snapped at by crabby taxi drivers in exchange. Nowadays she doesn't have to be constantly on guard. She can sit, stand, and walk precisely as she pleases, with no risk of setting off any land mines of testosterone. But this transition may not have been quite as simple and straightforward for Birgitta.

The second Birgitta comes into her mind, she decides. All right. She'll drive to Norrköping after all. She'll even run Birgitta back to Motala.

Because Margareta's not afraid of the big bad wolf. Or of either of her sisters.

SHE GLANCES AT the dashboard clock as she leaves the garage: if she floors it she'll only be half an hour late.

On a day like today it's great to be in a rush, to speed along the narrow but sparsely trafficked road toward Motala, to open the window and let the warm wind ruffle her hair. The sky above her is clear and bright, the earth beneath her is damp and anticipatory.

Margareta's right hand searches for the car radio, and when she's turned the knob she laughs aloud in surprise. It's Claes's voice filling the car, she's driving along in Claes's old car listening to his voice! He's reporting in his usual staccato tone: the special language melody that seems to characterize foreign correspondents all over the world. It takes a few minutes for her to actually be able to listen to what he's talking about. They've found another mass grave in the Bosnian hills: forty-four bodies, probably men and boys . . .

She slows down, feeling for her cigarettes. Forty-four bodies. She can envisage their empty eye sockets, the grins on their bare skulls. And Claes, standing in their grave in his combat boots, microphone in hand.

He's coming home this weekend, she's promised to pick him up at Arlanda airport Saturday evening. They'll go out for a meal from there; he booked a table at their favorite neighborhood restaurant before he left. He'll sit there fiddling with his cutlery, talking without really telling her anything. Claes never tells her anything. He just fills the vacuum between them with words, without saying anything. Nothing really important. Nothing really true.

And she doesn't say anything, either, at least nothing really important or true. Because she doesn't know how he'd react. Just as he doesn't know how she would.

They comfort each other. But they don't trust each other. Not for a minute.

WHEN MARGARETA STARTED working at the Institute of Space Physics, she heard via the grapevine that one of the other researchers was the churchgoing type. Not that you could tell. He shouted and swore as much as the next guy, and when he made his semiannual trips to Svalbard to monitor his instruments, he was always sure to let it be known that he had a bottle of whiskey in his rucksack.

As if that weren't enough, his name was Viking.

At first Margareta had observed him with some concern. Churchgoers, like folksingers and poetry readers, can be an embarrassment at the most unexpected moments. But her concern was not unambivalent; she was also tempted to get to know him better. The advantage of those possibly embarrassing types is that you can let down your own guard in their company and be a little embarrassing yourself.

One evening at a surprise birthday party for one of the staff, she fell prey to her temptation. There had been a buffet dinner in the cafeteria, and later there was dancing. Margareta withdrew when the music began, scurrying up the stairs to her office as if she had suddenly remembered something really important she needed to finish, though all she actually intended to do was get her coat. As so often before, she was tired of this large gathering already and wanted nothing more than to be alone for a few minutes, enjoying a smoke on the roof of the lab.

She wrapped her down coat around her shoulders but went out without zipping it up or putting on her boots. She liked seeing her feet in her dress shoes with the pointed toes. They made it easy to believe she was someone else, a person who was simply surface and facade, who lived an entirely different, much fuller life than her own.

Getting onto the roof was easy. You just went up the stairs and out through a regular door, that was all. The roof had to be accessible, because it was covered with plastic bubbles, huge ugly ones, there to protect the cameras and instruments that were always pointed toward the heavens.

The moment she opened the door she saw the aurora borealis. It filled most of the sky that night and was of a color she'd never seen before. Ordinarily it was white or blue, but she had heard of the occasional night like this one, when deep purple waves rolled across the skies, billowing lines came and went, huge patches of lavender fluttered like sheets drying on a line in a windy dream. And the sky was mirrored on the ground. The snow down there was suddenly violet.

"Wow," Margareta gasped, enchanted and disappointed at once. After a couple of years in Kiruna she still hadn't gotten over her irrational feeling that you should be able to hear the aurora borealis, too, that the music of the spheres should fill the skies when the electrons of the sun danced in the atmosphere, that the curtains of northern lights should be accompanied by strings, that kettledrums and trumpets should sound when she saw the rays of a corona, that a gentle flute should ring out like a silver song through the heavens as the drama abated.

But of course you couldn't hear the aurora borealis, not even this kind of purple northern light. The color came from the fact that the high-speed electrons had penetrated the atmosphere more deeply than usual. Still, this violet satin curtain was a miracle, and no witness to a miracle can but gasp, put her hand to her heart, and turn her face to the heavens. Somewhere deep inside she must shout with jubilation but still be perfectly silent because even the slightest little sound is taboo.

Ah. She lifted her hand from her heart and rummaged in her pocket for her cigarettes. If there had to be perfect silence in the presence of a miracle, the whole planet should be so quiet you could hear a pin drop. Because what is this Christmas tree ornament of a planet if not a miracle in the great scheme of things? A neglected miracle, however, a noisy, dirty miracle full of forgeries and trivialities, of cracked bathtub duckies and outdated calendars, of panty hose with runs and acrylic sweaters with burls, of fatty junk food and stinky kitchen sponges? And perhaps we owe a debt of gratitude to that distracting rubbish, thought Margareta, because if we human beings were constantly aware that we are living a miracle, we might sail through life like New Age nymphs in a Walt Disney production, deadly serious, upright, and wrapped in mantles, oohing and aahing in endless wonder over the tiniest birch leaf and blade of grass. And would that be any fun? She was just asking.

As Margareta bent forward to light her cigarette, the door behind her was pushed open, shoving her a few stumbling steps forward. Viking's square face stuck out through the opening. "Gosh," he said. "Sorry."

Margareta regained her balance. "That's all right. Come on out, there's a great show on tonight."

"Yeah, I see," said Viking, rubbing his eyes. "Magnificent."

Not only did he have no jacket on, he'd also rolled his shirtsleeves up.

"Aren't you cold?" Margareta asked.

"Just the opposite. I need to cool down. It's so hot downstairs, and the party's just getting started . . ."

"You're asking for pneumonia."

Viking grinned and gave her a look. "That's all right. I believe in the afterlife."

Margareta giggled uncomfortably, crossed her arms over her chest, and stamped her feet in her dress shoes to see if she could still feel her toes. "Personally, I believe in coats, as you see."

"Mmmm. But not in boots."

"True. Some people are never willing to take that ultimate leap of faith. Not even when it comes to the thermometer."

There was a moment of silence. The northern lights arched above them.

"It must be nice to be a believer," said Margareta. "Does it simplify life?"

Viking gave a little sigh, and crossed his arms, too. "The correct answer is no. Religion is not a stimulant, not an aid in the search for the simple life."

Margareta waited for him to go on, but he said no more. In the end, she nudged him. "And what's the true answer? The noncorrect one?"

"The true answer is yes. It's nice to be a believer. It simplifies life. It gives you access to another language."

He turned toward her, squinting. "Am I correct in my assumption that you are a humanist who got lost in the shuffle?"

Margareta snorted. "That's right. I guess you are. More lost than humanist, however. If you know what I mean . . ."

"No. How did you happen to get into physics?"

Margareta inhaled deeply. Should she tell him? No. She might go to bed with Viking, if necessary, but she had no intention of telling him about the satellite dishes at Tanum. There are limits.

"Oh," she said. "You know what the seventies were like. Almost nobody applied for physics, everybody wanted to be a sociologist. The science departments accepted anybody who happened to walk past . . . and I happened to. I'd meant to become an archaeologist, really."

She leaned against the wall and stubbed her cigarette out on the sole of her shoe. For one instant the ashes hung on to the light leather, then they fell to the snow.

"Gravity." Margareta snorted. "Gravity, gravity, and more gravity . . ."

Viking raised his eyebrows questioningly but didn't speak. Margareta straightened up, stuffing her hands into her coat pockets, pulling her neck and chin in under her collar.

"And am I correct in my assumption that you're a traveler?" she asked. "A class traveler?"

He grinned. "Right. My father was a lumberjack. What about you?"

"Of course. Mamma was a home helper. And then a housewife."

"Aha," said Viking. "Well, and what have you seen and learned on your journey, my dear?"

"Oh, one thing and another," said Margareta with a wry smile. "About what we got and what we missed out on."

Viking clapped his arms around himself a couple of times; when he exhaled his breath billowed out of his nostrils in a white plume. "Are you talking about self-confidence? That universal aura of 'I'm the standard and everybody else is the deviation'? We sure missed out on that. And on the preconception that those who were born to prosperity deserve it, and everyone else deserves the poverty to which they were born."

Margareta made a face. "You're forgetting our advantages. The freedom. We have a kind of freedom they'll never have."

Viking put his hands in his armpits. He was freezing cold now and had forgotten all about the northern lights. "Maybe."

"You can see it especially clearly in the women," said Margareta. "They're pathetic."

Viking started jumping in place, his hands still in his armpits. "What do you mean?"

"So terribly well-bred. Never raise their voices. Never laugh with their mouths open. Never run. Never climb. Never have fantasies. Just sit there with their knees together, hoping they're not bothering anybody. Could be half dead."

Viking became thoughtful, jumping all the while. "Okay," he said. "I'll grant you that. Even for the men. The bourgeoisie demands conformity. But so does the working class."

Margareta started jumping too; she was cold as well but didn't want to go back inside. It was good finally to be having an honest conversation with an honest person. Their feet pounded the roof rhythmically.

"But class travelers like us are free," she said. "We don't belong anywhere. That's an asset."

Viking's sigh exited his mouth in a cloud. "I'm not so sure about that. It must be wonderful sometimes just to belong, spontaneously and without having to think about it."

Margareta shut her eyes and thought for the space of a few jumps. "I disagree," she finally said. "I prefer not having to belong."

"And you see no disadvantages? Nothing but freedom?"

Margareta stopped jumping and held herself tight. Viking stopped too; his breathing was heavy now.

"Sure," she said. "There's a disadvantage. But I'm too ignorant to know whether it's a personal psychological problem or an aspect of social mobility. I lack trust. I don't trust anybody."

Viking stared at her for a second, then put his arms around himself, too. "Trust?" he asked. "Why would anybody trust anybody anyhow?"

"You mean you don't trust people either?"

Viking opened the door and gestured as if to shepherd her back where it was warm. "In God I trust," he said. "But my fellow humans? I cannot see any reason to trust human beings. They're obviously capable of almost anything."

THE NORRKÖPING POLICE station crowns the North Promenade the way an exclamation point crowns a sentence. Margareta sees it from a distance, but when she finally gets there she has to go twice around the traffic circle to figure out how to get into the parking lot.

Norrköping hasn't changed. The sky still exudes a brass-colored light, the streetcars still rattle along the streets, and the people seem to be in as much of a hurry as they were thirty years ago. She likes this city. There's nothing of the rank and sour self-righteousness that can sometimes drive her bananas in Kiruna. Maybe she should trash her dissertation and move here, take advantage of her old teaching degree to get a job at some high school, find herself a lover. Maybe a farmer with rough cheeks and deep roots in the local soil. That would be good for her. Alternately, she could do as Hubertsson had done: go to the poor excuse for a dance at the Standard Hotel every Thursday and then spend Fridays looking like the Cheshire cat. Just like him.

Alas, however, that cannot be. If you were brought up by Aunt Ella, there's no way you can trash your doctoral dissertation. Margareta will have to finish what she's begun. There's no difference between Margareta's thesis and the runners she once embroidered. In both cases she was aware from an early stage that the results were going to be disastrous, but she had no alternative to finishing the project. Aunt Ella said she had to. Or God. Or the Higher Education Authorities.

She bangs the car door shut, locks it, and looks around. There's nobody outside the door to the police station, but maybe Birgitta's waiting inside. She finds her brush in her handbag, pulls it through her hair, straightens her jacket, and runs her tongue over her front teeth. You have to look presentable when you enter a police station, particularly if you are going to be associated with a person like Birgitta once you're inside. Margareta has a certain respect for authority. She thinks that both police stations and social welfare offices are essential and should be readily available for citizens in need, although she doesn't personally want to have any more to do with them than she absolutely has to. She suspects that policemen and social workers are like the badgers of mythology, they get their teeth into you and refuse to let go until they hear your bones crunch.

THERE'S NO ONE standing inside the door, either, no sign of Birgitta hanging around at all. Margareta glances at her watch; she's driven faster than she realized, she's only twenty minutes late. Birgitta should have had the sense to wait. Maybe she's sitting in the lobby.

It's crowded in there. There are people everywhere, sitting, standing, waiting around. Everyone has taken a number; they could just as well be waiting at the post office. Margareta takes one, too, repressing a groan. She's number 73, and the person who's at the desk right now is only 51. This may take all day.

She looks around the room: she hasn't seen Birgitta for a couple of years, maybe they just aren't recognizing each other. No. No one in this lobby even vaguely resembles Birgitta. Most of them are quiet, well-bred people, there's only one person muttering and swearing under his breath. That could have been Birgitta if it were not so obviously a man: he's got whiskers and a tattoo. Margareta would believe almost anything about her sister, but not that she's had a sex change. Birgitta's always enjoyed being female.

Suddenly she realizes.

Oh, no. It's happened again. Twice in twenty-four hours, she's been fooled into traipsing off somewhere Birgitta isn't. But this time it's weirder than yesterday. Christina might very well have invented the message from that phone call if, for some incomprehensible reason, she had the desire to spend half the night running from ward to ward at the Motala Hospital, but today Margareta had spoken with Birgitta herself. And it really was Birgitta on the phone. No question about it. Christina would never have been able to do such a good imitation.

What the hell difference did it make, though? She's fed up with this game. Whoever's playing it will have to go on without Margareta. She crumples her number and throws it in a wastebasket. Next stop, Stockholm.

She turns around so fast she bumps into a police officer who's just crossing the room, and before she can halt the impulse she finds she's put a hand on his shoulder. When he turns toward her, she sees how young he is. His skin is as smooth as his shirt, it's as if someone had steam-ironed him from top to toe.

"Excuse me," says Margareta. "I just have a quick question."

"Yes?"

She weighs her words carefully, speaking as she imagines a probation officer or a social worker might: "I was to collect a woman from Motala here, someone I think you were holding earlier today. Birgitta Fredriksson."

"And?"

"Well, I cannot find her. I was told she'd be waiting outside, but she isn't there."

The steam-ironed young man frowns. "Do you know what she looks like?"

Margareta hesitates. What would Birgitta actually look like now? "She's in her fifties. Heavyset. Loud."

The police officer sneers. "I think I know who you mean. We had to remove her with bodily force a while back."

Margareta's legs buckle with relief. Birgitta's really been here. That means she hasn't been fooled. She raises her eyebrows and looks inquisitively at the steam-ironed man. "Bodily force?"

He straightens up. "She was disturbing the peace, so we ordered her out. My partner and I saw to it that she vacated the premises."

Margareta wipes her forehead; she can just imagine. Sounds like fun. "Did you notice which way she went?"

"She headed down the North Promenade toward the train station."

THE FIRST TIME the light is green she doesn't make it any farther than the island in the middle. Impatient, she's suddenly in a great hurry, suddenly feels it's incredibly important to find Birgitta and see to it that she gets back to Motala.

She goes through the train station first, checking systematically. No Birgitta in the waiting room. No Birgitta in line at the ticket window. No Birgitta out on the platform. She can't have left, either, because there hasn't been a Motala train in the last two hours. Neither of the doors on the public toilets is locked, so she can't be in there. Well, actually, she couldn't really picture Birgitta paying to use a toilet. She'd better look inside.

A teenage girl in foot-high platform shoes stares suspiciously at Margareta as she deposits a coin in the slot of each door, opens it, and then closes it again. No Birgitta. Just the usual bits and pieces of toilet paper on the floor.

When she goes back out onto the station steps, she hesitates a minute, looking around. Maybe she should go over to the park, across the North Promenade. It used to be a hangout. And if she doesn't find her there, she'll get the car and drive over to Salt Flats. Of course she has no idea if the neighborhood is still what it used to be, but she does know Birgitta well enough to know that she's a creature of habit.

She glances across the street as she approaches the park, then stops in surprise: the Standard Hotel isn't the Standard Hotel anymore! Now she'll never be able to go there for the same purpose as Hubertsson and come out with the same satisfaction. Oh well. She kicks the gravel on the path and moves on into Karl Johan Park. That looks like a bunch of drunks on the benches over there. She squints nearsightedly: they appear to be men, but if there's one thing she's learned in life it's that young men and older women are confusingly similar at a distance.

No, this is a thoroughly male gang, that's clear when she gets close. Three seedy-looking middle-aged men, with one pathetic can of beer being passed from hand to hand. Well, maybe they've seen Birgitta, maybe they know where she is . . . no, forget it. Margareta's not going to ask them. Not that she's scared, but she knows once she starts talking to them she'll never get rid of them. So she gives them a wide berth and walks on.

A few minutes later she sits down on one of the broad steps leading to the waterfront restaurant in the park, formerly Norrköping's first nightclub. Looking out over the water, she feels at home. She and her girlfriends spent a lot of time on these very steps, staring at the water. And she'd once been to a graduation party at the restaurant, too. André had been there. With his wife.

Margareta makes a face and opens her bag to hunt for a cigarette. What a sonofabitch that man had been! He had seemed to get a kick out of having them both in the same room, of leading Margareta around the dance floor with his wife sitting alone at a table, opening and closing the clasp on her evening bag. And what a little fool she had been, too. Smiling and happy, wet and ready the minute he looked her way.

It's windy; she has to hold her hair back with one hand so it doesn't blow into the flame of her lighter, which makes it impossible for her to cup the flame in the wind, the result being that it flares up for only a fraction of a second and then goes out. Still, her hair is more important: she puts her chin to her chest, clicking her lighter again and again.

"So you turned up after all?" says a voice in her ear. "Un-fucking-believable. Got a smoke for me, too?"

BEING BIRGITTA'S LITTLE sister meant being her Raggedy Ann doll as well, tossed around with your eyes shut, never really knowing where you'd be the next time you opened them. That's how things always were in Aunt Ella's yard; in an instant, an ordinary game could turn into something very different; the currant bushes that were just the walls of a grocery store a minute ago could become the shelves of a pharmacy with no warning. Margareta would lean against the sun chair that was the counter and smile kindly at the customer who came limping across the lawn with her right hand hidden in her cardigan.

"Now I'm a professor," said Birgitta. "One of those nutty ones. And I ask if you sell snake poison at your pharmacy."

"Snake venom?"

"Right. And you say you don't."

Margareta tipped her head and curtsied. "I'm terribly sorry. We don't stock snake venom."

Birgitta's face was transformed into a horrifying grimace; she pulled her hand out from under her cardigan and shook a little vial in Margareta's face. "Ha-ha! Now's your chance. This bottle of baby snakes is for sale, madam!"

Margareta cringed, a wave of nausea rising. She couldn't see what was in the jar, but the very idea of those slimy gray things behind the shiny glass was quite enough. "No!"

Birgitta laughed, throwing her head back, really a mad professor now. "That's right. You say no and I am enraged. 'You have to buy my snakes. Pay me a thousand or I'll let them loose in here!' "

Margareta raised her arms to ward off her own fear. "No!"

"Right, you say no. And that makes me so furious I open the top and let the snakes loose!"

Margareta screamed, a sharp little sound that frightened a few birds out of the cherry tree. They rose like a shadow against the sky. She could see the spotted gray creatures slithering out of the bottle, winding and coiling around themselves when they landed on the counter, some of them falling to the ground, crawling, winding in her direction, one of them sliding up onto her foot, encircling her ankle. . . . She bent down, her arms flailing around her leg but not daring to touch it. "No!" she shouted. "Cut it out! No, no!"

"Crybaby," said Birgitta. "Let's see who can climb highest in the cherry tree." The glass bottle was on the sun chair. Empty. It had been empty the whole time.

MARGARETA WRAPS HER arms around her legs, observing Birgitta as she lights her cigarette. Birgitta counters with a quick look at her. There's a warning crouching inside that glance: I know very well what I look like. But if you say one word about it I'll knock you from here to kingdom come!

Her double chin is a loose, wobbly pouch. She has dark circles under her eyes. Her lips are chapped and cracked, her hair dull and wavy from a permanent that's outlived its time, hanging across her face like a half-open curtain. Her thighs are so fat the insides of the legs of her jeans are threadbare from rubbing. Her quilted jacket is ripped, the white synthetic filling is sticking out of a hole by one of the pockets and out of a tear on the sleeve. The red quilted fabric is visibly filthy, as if someone had sprayed dirt-colored paint evenly all over it.

"Took you long enough," says Birgitta. "I waited for ages. Then I gave up."

"My car was being repaired. I had to pick it up."

But Birgitta doesn't hear her. "The cops in this town are such goddamn bastards . . ."

"Oh?"

"You'd think there was a law against just walking along the streets. . . . I wasn't even drunk, but they locked me up anyway. I hadn't done diddly-squat."

"So what are you doing in Norrköping anyway? What brought you here?"

Birgitta inhales deeply, blinks. "Some party. I don't know exactly, I was pretty beat yesterday. . . . I was with a bunch of people, though."

Memory lapses, Margareta thinks. It won't be long till your brain is as full of holes as Swiss cheese, my dear sister. And you know it. "You don't remember?"

Birgitta gives her a sidelong glance, trying to make light of it. "Jeez, you know. One helluva party, lemme put it that way . . ."

She tries moving her lips to form a smile, then remembers her teeth. She turns her head and looks out over the water, blinking hard.

Margareta puts her arm around Birgitta and pulls her close. Birgitta's head falls to Margareta's shoulder.

ONLY ONCE DID Margareta violate the prohibition and answer the phone. It was late one winter evening, the year after Birgitta arrived. A Thursday evening.

At Aunt Ella's, Thursday evening was bath time, when the girls put on their robes and followed her single file down the basement steps. While Aunt Ella scrubbed one of them clean, the other two sat on the wooden slats of the floor waiting their turns.

This particular Thursday evening, however, Margareta had a temperature, so she wasn't allowed to have a bath. She was sitting cross-legged on her bed in the empty room reading Nancy Drew when the phone rang.

She perked up her ears. Aunt Ella didn't like it when Birgitta answered the phone despite her prohibition, but Birgitta still ran to the phone the minute it started to ring. If Aunt Ella was doing the dishes or had sticky hands, Birgitta would get there first, and she'd always be scolded afterward.

Now Margareta hesitated. Should she answer? Were they forbidden to answer even when Aunt Ella wasn't there? No. If the phone rings somebody has to get it, and right now she was the only available person. She pulled her knitted socks on quickly—it was also strictly forbidden to be out of bed barefoot when you had a temperature—and shuffled down the hall.

"Hello?" she said, raising the black receiver. It was so big she had to hold it in both hands.

"Schweetie pie," sniveled a voice in her ear. "I'm ssho glad you answered. . . . I was afraid it would be that mean old woman who's always hollering at me . . ."

"Hello?" Margareta repeated. "Who is this?"

The woman at the other end of the receiver sniffled. "Oh honey, don't you recognize my voice? Can't you hear who this is? It's your little mommy, your sweet little mamma. But you'll never hear from me again."

The voice rose to a howl. "That's right. Your little mamma won't be calling anymore, dearie, because now mamma's gonna die! I'm all prepared. There's a big jar of schleeping pills on the table right in front of me, and a knife alongside. . . . I'm going to take all the pills in just a little while and then slit my wrists, sweetie. I'm gonna diiiie! Diiiie because they won't let me have my little girl here with me. That'll teach them, I swear, those people who took you away from me, who won't even let you come here and help your mamma with the least little thing! They're gonna regret it!"

Margareta was so weak with fever that she had to support herself on the wall to remain upright. "Who is this?" she asked again. "Hello, who's calling?"

Her sniffles were quickly replaced by an angry hiss. "Don't you put on airs with me, Birgitta! You know perfectly well who this is!"

"Yes, but . . . this isn't Birgitta. This is Margareta."

The strange voice suddenly went stone-cold sober and crystal clear. "Oh my, well in that case . . . I see."

The receiver clicked. Birgitta's mother had hung up.

"Christ," says Birgitta almost right away, straightening up and releasing herself from Margareta's embrace. "We can't sit here, we'll freeze our asses off."

True enough. Margareta gets up, turns around trying to get a look at whether her sheepskin jacket's damp at the back.

"Have you had lunch?" she asks, standing tall.

Birgitta grins. "Lunch? No, lunch isn't usually a priority for me. I don't tend to take afternoon tea, either. And today I haven't had anything at all."

"Shall we grab a bite, then?"

Birgitta makes a disgusted face. "Not me, I'm not hungry."

"Well, I am. How about just a pizza or something?"

Birgitta shrugs, trying to extricate a cigarette from a pack of Marlboro Lights. It takes Margareta a minute to realize they're her cigarettes. Were. Birgitta's made them her own. Her body language makes it plain that this pack of cigarettes is hers now, and that if anyone else thinks she has a claim to it she will have her to deal with. Margareta's annoyed with herself for being such a coward. Why does she just stand there like an idiot instead of demanding her cigarettes back? She turns, sticks her hands in her pockets, and heads back toward Queen's Street.

Birgitta hurries along behind her, but loses her balance just as she catches up. "Damn," she says. "I can hardly walk in these shoes."

Margareta's eyes follow. Birgitta's got on an old pair of black heels, unevenly worn, and definitely too big. She wiggles her own toes. Securely packed into a pair of nice warm boots, new this winter, they're still pretty cold. It's still winter.

"All right, we can go eat," says Birgitta. "But you'll have to pick up the tab. I'm flat-out broke."

Birgitta wrinkles her nose about the pasta place on Queen's Street. She doesn't like spaghetti, it's sticky and yucky. But she approves of the combination pizzeria and steak house, even looks happy once they're inside. "Great," she says, her eyes playing over the line of bottles at the bar.

Margareta feels her mouth starting to pinch up. Still, she's made it pretty long this time. It doesn't usually take more than fifteen minutes in Birgitta's company for her top lip to begin to purse as if she were some Christina type. Today it's been almost half an hour. "Just a meal. That's it."

Birgitta makes a deprecating gesture. "Did I ask? Forgive me for living. Pardon me, madam."

The place isn't very crowded, but it still takes a while for the waiter to bring the menus over to their window table. Birgitta gives him an appreciative look. He's young, dark, and wearing a chalk white shirt. His response is a cutting glare. Then, hands behind his back, he stares out into the street. "Orders!" he barks.

Margareta puts on her snottiest teacher's voice. "We'll just have a look at the menu, please. Give us a minute."

"But we'll have a couple of beers while we look," says Birgitta. "For starters."

Margareta puts the menu down with a sigh.

WHEN WILL SHE ever learn? She's had enough acute attacks of philanthropy over the years to know better. Birgitta won't allow herself to be helped without a price tag. Honestly, she should have realized it the very first time. Although that time she had gone looking for Birgitta not to help her but to be helped.

A few weeks after Margareta graduated from high school, Margot lost interest in her. She'd set her heart on an old derelict manor house by the bay. Fourteen rooms! Ceiling murals! A private tennis court! And when Margareta wasn't readily persuaded to give up her plans to study archaeology at the university in Göteborg and instead allow herself to be transformed into the pallid maiden of the manor, Margot stopped talking to her overnight. Although she still set the dinner table for three, her body was tense and jittery when she passed the milk or the salt to Margareta. Now she was completely focused on Henry. Her desire for that manor was a laser beam aimed right at his mind.

Henry wasn't unhappy about this, that was clear despite his long harangues about women's total lack of business acumen. Though, he added, when it came right down to it, even the blind could strike gold, and that old mansion might not be such a poor investment, provided Margot was able to control herself during the renovation. He'd see to it that a good contractor was hired. At the most Margot would be allowed to choose the wallpaper; beyond that she would be expected to keep her mouth shut. Margot nodded eagerly. But couldn't she please book them a trip to London in August, so she could go to that wonderful wallpaper shop on Oxford Street while Henry was at his favorite pub in Soho? Henry nodded benevolently, and Margot clapped her pudgy hands with pleasure. Wonderful!

Which explains how Margareta found herself alone in the house packing her things to go off to the university. Her uncertainty was slowing her down, she couldn't decide what to do about all the presents she'd received from Margot and Henry. Three Christmases, two birthdays, and a graduation had made her jewelry box as heavy as a treasure chest. But was that jewelry really hers to do with as she pleased? Not to mention the problem of what she was supposed to pack her things in. When she'd arrived in this house she'd had only one little suitcase, which would barely hold a third of her present wardrobe. And what was she supposed to live on when she got to Göteborg? It would be weeks until her student grant came through.

She ran out of food the third day. Margareta sat looking at the last slice of bread, resting on the palm of her hand, and decided to consider the jewelry her own. She'd read enough novels to know what a pawnshop was, and she also knew there was one in Norrköping. She'd seen the sign one day last spring when she was supposed to be having a date with one of those Prince Charmings but was actually wandering the little streets down by the courthouse.

Walking into the pawnshop was like entering a novel; suddenly instead of the 1960s it was the 1910s, and she was a heroine, suffering from consumption, in lace-up boots and a baggy dress instead of a miniskirt and clogs. The man behind the counter was a period piece, too: his bent little body was enclosed in a threadbare black suit, his fingers so white they looked as if he'd never left this drab brown room, never seen any other light than that coming from the dirty yellow ceiling fixture. Silently, he examined the gold watch, the pearl earrings, and the necklace she'd decided to sacrifice, and named his price: 325 crowns. A small fortune. Margareta nodded mutely and reached eagerly for the pen to sign the receipt. Her imaginary tuberculosis had passed; she could feel her heart pounding in her young, perfectly healthy body, a body preparing to conquer the world.

She went straight to the department store and bought twin suitcases, then took the streetcar home, her hair blowing in the wind coming through the open windows. She stepped down at the stop and ran the rest of the way to Margot and Henry's Mexican-tiled home, taking the stairs to the second floor in three long strides: Yes! She was free! Finally.

Once her new suitcases were packed, she indulged in a concession to the past: she called André, although she knew he was on vacation with his wife and family. She stood stock-still for a long time, with the receiver pressed close to her ear and the cord twisted around her index finger, listening to the phone ring, imagining the sound careening off the walls in the empty house. Then she hung up and went and got her luggage.

She headed right for the station, although she hadn't checked the schedule. Sooner or later there would be a train.

SHE WROTE TO Margot and Henry a couple of times during the fall, but they never answered. Their silence worried her, so she wrote another, chattier letter, thanking them for having shared their home with her, describing her new life with great enthusiasm. She told them that although she hadn't gotten a dormitory room, she'd found a room with a family who lived right in the middle of town. She liked Göteborg, despite the rain and wind. She was enjoying her studies and expected to do well on her first finals. And of course she had to add one little white lie: she was making lots of new friends, and had loads of dates.

She wrote other letters, too, shorter and more truthful, but never perfectly honest. She never told anybody about the chasm in the pit of her stomach; she had no words for it. Instead, she wrote André about love and Aunt Ella about lonely evenings; Christina about her studies and Birgitta about how she fluctuated between fear of and longing for a family of her own.

Months passed without a single answer, but one afternoon in December, when she returned from a late lecture, there was a little postcard for her leaning against the lamp on the chest of drawers in the hall. Her landlady smiled when she saw Margareta's excitement about having mail, and she couldn't keep herself from revealing she'd read it as well. Margareta didn't mind. She skimmed the few lines and smiled back in relief. She wouldn't have to spend Christmas in her rented room: Christina planned to spend the holidays in Vadstena and wondered whether Margareta would like to share a room with her in the guesthouse at the cloisters and celebrate the holiday at the nursing home with Aunt Ella.

The week before Christmas, Margareta went to the pawnshop with a rhinestone ring and—after some hesitation—the second to last of her gold bracelets. The ring was worth more than she had expected. She stuffed the money into the pocket of the rabbit-fur jacket Margot had bought her the winter before and went shopping. She walked the main street for hours, looking for the perfect presents. A handwoven shawl from the craft guild for Aunt Ella, sheepskin-lined gloves for Christina. A soft pink lamb's-wool pullover for Birgitta.

Not until she was on the train did she realize that, of course, Birgitta wouldn't be spending Christmas with them.

STILL, IT TURNED out to be a Christmas of reconciliation. This Christina was different from the one she had seen off at the Norrköping station several years earlier. Although she was still pale and thin, she no longer looked ill but more—Margareta searched her mind for a word—silver-plated. The Christina of today would have fit right in at Margot's manor house. Maybe she should give Margot and Christina the idea, so Christina could get a summer job as Margot's maid of the manor and spend it sitting at an open window looking soulful, with her embroidery in her lap.

Their room at the cloisters was every bit as celibate as anyone might wish: a dim ceiling lamp, two narrow beds with hammocklike mattresses, a crucifix on the wall. Outside the tall window the world looked dusky although it was early afternoon; the snow whirled in the glow of a solitary streetlamp along the lakefront, and behind it the dark water of Lake Vättern gleamed. Margareta suddenly felt like crying: she put her brow to the windowpane and tried to blink back her tears. It didn't work. She had to stand perfectly still for ages, until she was able to wipe her cheek discreetly with one finger and turn back around.

Christina hadn't noticed. She was busy unpacking Margareta's suitcase for her and hanging her clothes in the closet. Like a mother. Or a real big sister. "At first I thought we could take her home," she said, stroking a white blouse. "Celebrate Christmas in the Motala house, like we used to. They would have discharged her for a few days, they let other patients go. . . . But it turns out that pike-jowled Stig has rented out the house and had all her things put in cold storage. He's her legal guardian now."

"But what if she gets better? Where will she live?" Christina turned around and looked at her. "Aunt Ella's never going to get any better. Didn't you realize?"

Margareta frowned. "I believe in miracles . . ."

"Forget it," said Christina. "There's no such thing as a miracle."

* * *

CHRISTINA HAD PLANNED everything. She'd spoken with the matron nearly a month earlier and arranged for them to let her prepare a real Christmas dinner and serve it in Aunt Ella's room; she'd persuaded the nuns to allow her to use the kitchen in the guesthouse late in the evenings. The night before Christmas she didn't get to bed until four in the morning. Somehow, though, she hadn't seemed the least bit tired when she opened the refrigerator and triumphantly showed Margareta her accomplishments: anchovy and potato casserole and marinated herring, ham and meatballs, red cabbage and spareribs, headcheese, almond pastries, spice cookies, and all the traditional Christmas fare. In addition to all those homemade dishes, she'd bought cheeses and pâtés, cocktail sausages and malt bread. Just enough of everything for three, all carefully packaged in foil and wax paper.

"Oh, Christina"—Margareta laughed in delight—"it's Aunt Ella's Christmas smorgasbord in miniature!"

Christina laughed back. "Right! I picture this as a sort of doll's house Christmas."

Aunt Ella laughed, too, when they arrived with the baskets of food: she began to act more like her old self, pinching Margareta's cheek and calling her silly at one moment and frowning at Christina and telling her to eat more so she'd finally put some flesh on those bones of hers the next. The nurse's aides had helped her decorate her room. A hospital vase on the table contained a few pine boughs with Christmas tree ornaments on them, and a wooden candelabrum from occupational therapy decorated the windowsill.

When they started to exchange Christmas presents, Aunt Ella got upset, however, and slurred, "If only I could still use my hands properly," apologizing as Margareta opened her gift. "I would have loved to make you something really beautiful . . ."

Margareta looked down to find a little necklace, round beads and long ones in a rhythmic pattern.

"Well, I love this," she said, pulling the necklace over her head. "It's very pretty."

Christina nodded, giving her own present a little squeeze. "It looks great with your dress. And it will be perfect on black tops as well."

She opened hers: a set of crocheted pot holders.

"I learned to crochet this fall," said Aunt Ella, smiling her wobbly smile. "I can do it one-handed. So next year you'll get bedspreads . . ."

Margareta laughed. "I'd like a yellow one, please!"

Christina said, with a gleam in her eye, "I'll take pink!"

AUNT ELLA HELD up well, but by ten she was fading. She gratefully accepted Christina's and Margareta's help in getting ready for bed. They removed her best dress and put on her nightgown, and she seemed almost happy as they sat there, one on either side of her bed. When she'd fallen asleep they rose quietly from their chairs and tiptoed out to the staff kitchen. Christina filled the sink with water while Margareta hunted for a dish towel.

"Wonder how Birgitta spends an evening like this," she said.

Christina shrugged. "No idea. Same as any other evening, I s'pose."

Margareta carefully set down the plate she'd just dried. "Not on a holiday evening, do you think?"

Christina's voice was still soft, but her tone was sharp. "Who knows how people in that world spend Christmas? Who knows what they ever do? I don't want to talk about it. It turns my stomach!"

IT WAS STILL snowing when they went outside. The cold stung Margareta in the gap between where her rabbit jacket ended and her boots began. Christina was more sensibly dressed, of course. Her coat reached nearly down to her knees, and she'd pulled on a pair of woolen trousers before they left. Margareta hesitated a minute, summoning the courage to ask the question she'd been working up to for the last hour: "Feel like going to midnight mass?"

Christina stared at her in surprise, pulling on her new gloves. They were the perfect color and just the right size. "Not really," she said. "What would we want to do that for?"

BECAUSE I NEED it, Margareta thought a while later, lying in the soft bed at the guesthouse. Because my eyes need to take in icons and candlelight, because I'm much too hollow, and need to be filled with the peal of an organ and voices singing hymns, because I need to forgive and be forgiven . . .

She squeezed her eyes shut, not wanting to remember. She'd erase it all from her mind, and a few years from now when she looked back on this fall, all she'd remember would be her studies and her kind landlady. However hard she tried, she wouldn't be able to recall the shame she'd felt when she first entered the university, a shame so heavy she was para-lyzed by it, so that she—loud, cackling, always flirtatious Margareta—hardly even dared introduce herself to her classmates; instead of going to the student union parties or potluck suppers, she'd wandered all alone through the city streets at night with her right fist clutching her abdomen, turning around to look strange men in the eye when they spoke to her. And three times she'd gone along with a stranger, relenting silently.

Could she whisper all this in the dark to Christina? Could she confess to her that she'd stood behind a building, leaning against the wall, her panties around her ankles, cheek to cheek with a perfect stranger? That she'd spread her legs to rough fingers at the movies? That once before she'd gone along with a man, whose name she didn't even know, to his shabby boardinghouse room? That she'd experienced a sort of relief at the time but had throbbed with anxiety afterward, slapping herself in the face as a punishment for having no peace of mind, as a punishment for the fact that nobody wanted her for more than a moment?

No, she couldn't talk about it. Not with Christina. But possibly with Birgitta.

I'm sinking, she thought. Somebody rescue me!

CHRISTINA HAD TO be back in Lund by the twenty-seventh. The snow melted in the rain, and Aunt Ella nodded eagerly when Margareta suggested a walk. The next few days were filled with long walks: Aunt Ella loved being rolled out into the fresh air, didn't mind the cold wind or the drizzle. She was perking up. In the afternoons she treated Margareta to coffee at the café on the market square, expecting her to stand quietly behind the wheelchair while Aunt Ella chatted with the ladies at the coun-ter, asking about the filling in every kind of cake and cookie. On the thir-tieth she ordered a big cake, and in spite of the freezing rain on the morning of New Year's Eve, she insisted on coming along to pick it up. She couldn't wait. It was very important for her to know that her cake would be on the table in the staff room at four, when the nurses had their afternoon cof-fee. On the way back, her teeth were chattering as Margareta pushed her wheelchair, and she started giving orders about how to cross streets and go up and down curbs so the cake wouldn't bump around too much in the big box on her lap. Margareta couldn't help but laugh. Her fingers were stiff with cold, her rabbit jacket matted and heavy with rain, but Aunt Ella's familiar scolding voice warmed her up.

Then the holidays were over and she had to depart. Aunt Ella stroked her cheek when Margareta came to say good-bye. Margareta leaned into her hand. "Please write me now and then!"

"Oh, my handwriting's so wobbly," said Aunt Ella, shaking her head. "You wouldn't be able to decipher it . . ."

"Oh yes I would," said Margareta. "Please, please, stay in touch."

Aunt Ella pushed her bangs out of her eyes. "All right," she said. "I'll write you, then. Since you seem to feel it's important."

SHE DIDN'T REALIZE she'd been planning it, but she found herself on the opposite platform from the one where the train would take her to Mjölby, to change for Göteborg. There was still one Christmas present at the bottom of her suitcase.

It was raining in Motala, too, and she stood in the waiting room at the station for a few minutes, looking out at the park hoping it might stop. Eventually she tucked her chin into the furry collar of her jacket and pushed the door open.

There was a wrinkled slip of paper in her pocket with an address on it; she'd wheedled it out of pike-jowled Stig before moving to Norrköping. She knew the street was a dark little alley in the old part of town, but she had only the vaguest idea of which building it was. Most of the houses down there were identical anyway, all equally ramshackle and damp-looking.

The past was being effaced in Motala, she noticed as she walked through town. Where there had once been derelict wooden buildings leaning against one another for support, there were now new apartment houses of brick and concrete. The future was on the way, and it was as critical as a mother-in-law, expecting everything to be neat and tidy when it arrived.

But the future hadn't hit Birgitta's neighborhood yet, had only sent a scout in the shape of a shiny new gas station on an old lot where a building had been torn down. Beyond that, things looked as they always had: broken fences along the sidewalks, wooden houses in dire need of a coat of paint.

Margareta opened the front door and looked up the stairs. The walls were brown boards, the floor covered with worn linoleum. There were no modern features at all, not so much as a little sign listing the names of the tenants in plastic letters. There were four old-fashioned mailboxes on the wall, though; maybe one of them would bear Birgitta's name. No luck. No Fredriksson. In fact, none of them had names on them at all.

"Take a flying fuck, you disgusting hooker!"

A door opened upstairs, a man's voice thundered, and one second later there were heavy footsteps on the stairs. Margareta backed up against the wall. He was pulling a black leather jacket on as he passed; the sleeve brushed her face, but he didn't seem to notice she was there, just kicked the front door open and left. She saw the back of his jacket as the door closed: it bore a picture of an enormous tiger. A kid, she thought. Birgitta's in a relationship with a little boy.

Now she knew she was in the right place. That was Hound Dog, a fatter, somewhat worse for wear Hound Dog than the one who had been Head Knight of the motorcycle gang's Round Table a few years ago, but still clearly himself. And wherever Hound Dog was, Birgitta was probably nearby.

A baby was wailing somewhere, with an undertone of desperation in its cries that gave Margareta gooseflesh as she headed up the stairs. She stopped on the landing. Behind which of these brown doors could she assume Birgitta was keeping herself? She picked the one to the right, for no particular reason.

The baby stopped screaming for a minute when she rang the bell but picked up again when someone crossed the wooden floor. "Yeah?" said Birgitta, opening the door roughly. "Waddaya want?"

THE APARTMENT WAS drafty and very old, with neither central heating nor hot running water. There was a space heater on the kitchen floor and a hot plate on top of the disused wood-burning stove. It took ages to heat up. Birgitta smoked three of Margareta's cigarettes while the coffee water was boiling. Somewhere that baby was still wailing, but more softly, less desperately now.

Birgitta was still very pretty: her hair was just as fair as ever, her skin just as smooth and silky, the curve of her lips just as soft. But her fingertips were still swollen, over nails bitten down to the quick, and her bangs looked greasy. You could see where the comb had been, she needed a shampoo. In fact, she needed a washing altogether: the gray streaks of dirt from her childhood were back, like an iron shackle around her neck.

Birgitta returned her critical examination with at least equally critical scrutiny as she poured their coffee. "You look like something the cat dragged in," she said, pushing a saucer of zwiebacks in her direction. "How did you get here? Swim?"

"It's pouring out there," said Margareta, helping herself. "And I walked all the way from the station."

Birgitta glanced out the window, as if she hadn't noticed the gray mist. She didn't seem to care, though, turned her back to the window and extended her legs, examining her thin calves and the black tights covering them. Somewhere the baby was gasping exhaustedly for air. When the screaming started anew it was thinner, frailer. Birgitta didn't seem to hear it.

"So what are you up to these days?" she asked, lowering her legs.

"I'm at the university. In Göteborg. I wrote you from there. Didn't you get my letter?"

Birgitta shrugged her shoulders and lit another cigarette. "What brings you to Motala, then, if you're living in Göteborg?"

Margareta extended the gift, trying to smile. "I came to deliver your Christmas present."

Birgitta just stared, dropped her extinguished match in the ashtray, but didn't seem inclined to accept the gift.

"Go on," said Margareta. "It's for you."

Birgitta took the package tentatively in one hand, then stuck her cigarette in the corner of her mouth and began excitedly tearing off the wrapping paper and ribbon.

"Wow," she said, exhaling a cloud of smoke from one corner of her mouth and holding the pink sweater to her chest at the same time. It was a V neck, which wasn't exactly in style, but Margareta had had a feeling Birgitta still liked being a vamp in a V-neck sweater and a tight skirt.

Birgitta put the sweater in her lap, took the cigarette out of her mouth, and exhaled a suspicious puff of smoke. "You came all the way from Göteborg to give me a sweater?"

Margareta raised her cup to her lips, momentarily embarrassed. "Not exactly. I spent the holidays in Vadstena. With Aunt Ella."

Birgitta's brow creased. "So the old lady's moved, huh? Lives in Vadstena now?"

Margareta took a sip of her coffee. "She's in a nursing home there."

Birgitta looked surprised. "She's still sick?"

Margareta nodded and looked down at the table. The oilcloth was cracked, threadbare under the plastic. "She's paralyzed. One side. She'll never recover."

Birgitta inhaled deeply, looking away, then said in a sharp tone, "It wasn't my fault."

Margareta looked down, speechless. There was a silence; the rain lashed the windowpane, the crying of the baby had faded to an exhausted background lament. Margareta stared into her cup, suddenly very tired. It was hopeless. She'd never be able to tell Birgitta what her autumn had really been like, and even if she could tell her, Birgitta would be unable to offer her either consolation or insight. She was too locked into her own life. The baby stopped for breath and then, one second later, its screaming rose to a desperate pitch.

"Damn brat."

Birgitta swept the coffee cup aside and got up, crossed the kitchen floor, and went out into the hall, disappearing in her stocking feet. Margareta heard her pull a door open.

"Shut up!" she screamed shrilly. "If you don't shut up I'm gonna kill you."

Margareta got up so fast her chair fell over behind her, suddenly aware that the baby was actually in Birgitta's apartment. She crossed the kitchen in three long strides, nearly lost her balance as the hall rug slipped under her feet, grabbed the doorframe.

Birgitta was standing in a dark little room. It must have been her bedroom. The shade was down, and there was an unmade bed on the far wall. On a mattress on the floor was a rumpled pile of blankets, in the middle of the floor was a crib. It smelled terrible: sweet and poopy at the same time.

Birgitta stood by the crib in a strange pose, as if at attention. Her back was rigid, her hands were pressed tightly to her body, and she was staring up at the ceiling. "Shut your mouth!" she screamed. "Shut your fucking trap or I'm gonna do something I'll regret."

A high-pitched cry rose out of the crib, a tiny hand was lifted.

Margareta took a dubious step into the room. "Birgitta?" she asked. "Is that your baby?"

Birgitta whirled around and stared at her. "Well, what the hell did you think it was?"

SHE MANAGED TO make it into a game, turned herself into the little sister begging her big sister to let her play with her doll. The baby was only three months old and felt virtually weightless on her lap, but she still imagined she could see a gleam of living terror in his eyes when she lifted him out of the crib and onto the bed. His buttocks were flaming pink, bordering on purple, as she could see when she used his pajamas to clean up his mess. They'd have to be washed anyway, the poop had long since overflowed the diaper and run down his legs.

She hurried out into the kitchen and wet part of the pajamas, using them as both a washcloth and a towel, finding a pack of diapers, and then changing him the way she remembered doing with her dolls, long ago. The diaper pants were old and dirty, the seams brown with dried excrement. She wrapped him in a blanket, then held him in her arms like a little stuffed cabbage leaf, still crying but less hard now, and with his eyes shut. His round forehead was beaded with perspiration.

Margareta stood in the kitchen doorway, cocking her head. Birgitta was at the table, smoking another cigarette.

"Is he hungry?"

Birgitta's top lip curled as she said, "He doesn't need to eat. He's just making life difficult."

"But, Birgitta, I've never given a baby a bottle. Couldn't I please?"

Birgitta nodded and looked away.

She had to find the formula herself, make it, and wash a dirty bottle. It wasn't easy. She couldn't get it really clean without hot water and with only one hand free. She didn't dare put the baby down; he was still crying and Birgitta was sitting there with her hands over her ears. God only knew what she might do if the baby was lying on the kitchen floor. But it was hard to mix the formula with him in her arms, and it came out lumpy.

Finally, she sat down at the table and offered him the bottle. He opened his eyes for an instant, looked vacantly at her, then closed them again and started to suck. Instantly the apartment was quiet. Birgitta was still leaning over the kitchen table with her hands over her ears.

"What's his name?" Margareta asked cautiously.

Birgitta took her hands away from her ears and shrugged. Her fingers fumbled along the oilcloth trying to reach the cigarettes, but she had no sooner picked up the pack than she dropped it again. "Hey," she said. "Could you maybe look after him for an hour? I really need to go to the store. And I have an appointment with my social worker, to get the money for a doctor's appointment."

Margareta hesitated, looking at her watch. Birgitta's voice grew eager;

she leaned forward. "I don't have a stroller, you see, so I can't get out un-less I have a sitter. And there's nothing to eat in the house. I really do need to go to the doctor, too, I'm in a lot of pain."

Margareta nodded. She felt sorry for Birgitta. She felt sorry for the lit-tle boy. They needed help. "But be back by five. I have a train to catch."

Birgitta was already on her feet, running a hand through her hair. "Don't worry. I'll only be a couple of hours. You're a really decent type, you know that, Margareta? You always have been."

Margareta looked down. Decent? Yeah. She guessed so. Actually.

Birgitta pulled off her black sweater, tossed it into a corner, put on the pink one, and scurried out into the hall. The next time she looked into the kitchen, her eyes were circled in black eyeliner and her lips smeared with pale pink lipstick. "I won't be long." She smiled. "Thanks!"

AT EIGHT THAT evening Margareta started to cry. By ten she'd stopped and was listing every invective in the book, pacing the kitchen floor and uttering one with each step. At two in the morning she fell asleep with the baby beside her. At six-thirty the next morning somebody shook her by the shoulder. "Shove over, dammit," said Birgitta. "This is my bed. And I'm beat."

"YOU DON'T HAVE to look like a thundercloud about it," says Birgitta, pouring from bottle to glass. "It's just a beer, you know."

Margareta looks away: once again she's wondering why she did it. She always wonders why she did it. The next time she gets the urge to be nice to one of her sisters, she's going to take herself aside and give herself a hard kick in the butt. Just as a reminder.

"I'm not getting drunk," says Birgitta. "I'm just having a beer. No need for hysterics."

Hysterics? Margareta snorts and opens the menu. "What're you going to have? Pizza? Or something else?"

Birgitta doesn't answer. She's closed her eyes and is downing her beer in long, lascivious gulps.

"I'll take the salmon, anyway," says Margareta, putting the menu down. "Broiled."

Birgitta lowers her glass, wiping a little foam off her top lip. "Salmon? No shit like that for me. I'm not even really hungry."

If she doesn't eat anything she'll get drunk, and if she gets drunk she'll be difficult. Margareta can envision the scenario: walking the length of Queen's Street trying to keep some semblance of order around a shouting, stumbling Birgitta. She has no intention of subjecting herself to that kind of humiliation. Both hands on the table, she leans toward her sister, hissing: "You'd damn well better order a meal. If you don't eat, I'm not driving you to Motala. You'll just have to get home as best you can!"

Birgitta looks astonished, but only for a fraction of a second. "Jesus, no need to overdo it. I'll eat, but I really don't like salmon. Which, I s'pose, is allowed?"

She looks at the menu, nursing what's left of her beer. "Minute steak?" she asks. "Is that like a flip steak?"

Margareta lights a cigarette, her hand trembling slightly. "A minute steak is all the butcher's leftovers scraped and pressed together and fried for a minute."

She bites her tongue and doesn't go on with what she was about to say: a minute steak is a dish specially designed for people like you, by others who hold people like you in contempt. Birgitta hasn't heard a thing anyway, not what she said or what she was thinking.

"With fries and gravy . . . All right, dammit, I'll take that." She raises her glass again, smiling across it.

"Jeez, you're really decent, Maggie. You're always there for me!"

THEY DON'T TALK for a while. Margareta looks out the window and feels the tension in her shoulders dissipate. Queen's Street is already getting dark. Nothing's changed. If it weren't for the fact that people dressed differently and the streetcars were now a different color, it might just as well still be the sixties. And she could perfectly well still be seventeen and in high school. At least on the inside.

"When I lived in Norrköping, I was having a thing with one of the teachers," she says, filling her own glass. She's surprising herself. Never before has she spoken with anyone about what happened with André. Birgitta, however, doesn't appear to have heard her. She's just staring in disappointment at the glass Margareta's raising to her lips. She must have been hoping for the other beer, too.

"We used to drive around in his car looking for somewhere to park in the evenings. We'd find a new spot every time so no one would recognize us. We did it in his backseat."

Birgitta's paying attention now, grinning. "Shit, I wouldn't have thought you were like that. Was he any good?"

"Any good?"

"Yeah. Was he a good fuck?"

Margareta sneers slightly. Oh, God. "I guess so. But that wasn't the main thing. I was lonely. I needed somebody . . ."

She stops talking as the young waiter sets down her plate. She stares listlessly at the salmon. Birgitta reaches for the salt shaker, salting her fries with wide, sweeping gestures.

Margareta takes a deep breath, then goes on. "What happened to Aunt Ella was so awful, I think I was in a state of shock for almost a whole year afterward."

Birgitta stops in mid-movement, her eyes narrow. "It wasn't my fault!"

"Who said it was?"

Birgitta puts down the salt shaker and reaches for the cigarettes, pursing her lips and clicking the lighter. "You've always blamed me! Always!"

Margareta stabs a potato on her fork, suddenly feeling the urge to be mean. "We saw you one night, my teacher friend and me."

Birgitta lowers her eyes, drops the lighter, and fishes around in her jeans pocket with her free hand. "Look," she says. "Christina must be nuts, she's harassing me. Isn't this the damnedest letter? She . . ."

She tosses a little piece of yellow paper onto the table, folded into a square. Her hands tremble as she attempts to unfold it. Margareta observes her with an odd little smile; she will not allow herself to be distracted. No more manipulation. She's done being decent. She's not even scared. "Well, as I was saying," she said. "We saw you one night, the two of us. You were waiting for a john down in Salt Flats."

Birgitta stares at her for one second, stubs out her cigarette on her minute steak, and retracts the yellow slip of paper. She gets up and fumbles for her jacket, which is hanging over the back of her chair. "You bitch," she hisses over her shoulder. "You fucking fake snob! I get it now—you and Christina planned this whole thing together, didn't you?"

Margareta looks at her coldly. Let her run, she thinks, I'll get to Stockholm that much faster. But she's not done yet: she wants to sink her teeth a little deeper into Birgitta's flesh, take a bite. She balances her chin in her hands, saying in her sweetest voice, "Was Hound Dog your pimp? And what about the kid? Was he conceived in the line of duty?"

Birgitta's got the jacket now and throws it over her shoulders. It flaps like a cape as she rushes to the door. Her shoes are definitely too big, they're gaping at the heels and she's having trouble keeping them on.

OF COURSE MARGARETA'S conscience begins to bother her, but not until she's finished her salmon. Her heart is pounding and she gobbles her meal. She chews and swallows, gaining confidence with each bite. It's a good meal, better than she had expected, and it improves even more once she's waved the waiter over and gotten him to take away the beer and bring her a bottle of mineral water. Margareta's never been a beer drinker. Beer turns her off, and people who reek of beer turn her off even more. It's a fact.

Her qualms come with the coffee; she leans over her cup, hand to her forehead, trembling. Who did she think she was? How could she have said those things? What did she presume to know about Birgitta's life? How could she be so sure she hadn't been just like Margareta, walking around with her hand clenched to her abdomen, as if she were dying of internal bleeding? Maybe for her, too, the encounters with complete strangers had been the only consolation. Maybe she, too, had just been looking for confirmation that she really existed.

Margareta rubs her eyes and straightens up. No. There is no similarity between herself and Birgitta. The time has come for her to forgive herself for almost having lost control during those first weeks in Göteborg. Things had changed radically quite soon, during the spring semester of her first year. She got a postcard from Vadstena every single week, with shaky letters and brief, telegraphic messages: "Spring's on the wing! Take care!" It was as if these postcards awakened her, got her to sit up and blink and look around, after a Rip van Winkle sleep. She wasn't so much worse looking than the other girls in her program after all, she just had to muster up some courage and start going to the student union parties and the potluck dinners. After which she became promiscuous in a more socially acceptable manner, having learned that she could use young men of her own age, too, to dull her anxiety.

She'd gone out with them, to the movies and to political demonstrations; she'd eventually even moved into an apartment with one of them. They'd lived together for nearly a year until, one morning, she'd left him in the same way she would later leave four other men. She'd gotten up early, packed her things very quietly, and left him sleeping in the premarital bed, moved into a rooming house, and rebounded into an affair with a graduate student. But, as opposed to Birgitta, she'd always taken responsibility, even when she was in her deepest crisis; she'd always been sure to take her birth control pills.

Still, she had no right to get on her high horse with Birgitta, no right to judge her. She couldn't know what would have happened to her if that anonymous mother of hers had stayed instead of having the good sense to leave, had hovered over Margareta's childhood like a specter instead of abandoning her in a laundry room. She should be grateful and thank God—whoever God was—for having taken her to Aunt Ella's and given her what she had. For not having put her in Birgitta's or Christina's predicament.

But there was one thing Birgitta was right about. They had always blamed her. When Margareta had accused herself, thinking she should never have opened the door to that phone booth and shown Christina the graffiti on the wall, another accusation had been crouching in the background: Birgitta! If only she hadn't been so ready to slip out of her panties in one backseat after the next. If only she hadn't been dumb enough to flaunt what others thought of as disgraceful. If only she had realized how lucky she was to have ended up with Aunt Ella rather than her own slut of a mother. And, most important: if only Birgitta had refrained from whatever it was she must have said or done when Aunt Ella confronted her, whatever it was that made Aunt Ella's heart race, her blood pressure rise, and a vessel in her brain burst, then everything—their whole lives— would have been completely different!

The stupid bitch!

Margareta pushes her bangs out of her eyes and picks up her coffee cup with trembling hands. Of course she's mad at Birgitta! She's been furious with her for thirty years, since the minute she walked through Aunt Ella's door and heard a shrill voice whining, "Not my fault, not my fault, not my fault!"

Even before she shut the door and crossed the little hallway, even before she saw Aunt Ella lying on the living room floor, she knew that life would never be the same again.

She had fallen on the brown Wilton rug and wet it; the odor of ammonia hit Margareta as she knelt beside her and took her hand. "Aunt Ella! What happened?"

Aunt Ella raised one eyebrow and moved her mouth; her nose had bled down over her top lip, and there were little bubbles of saliva at the corner of her mouth. She couldn't speak. Margareta looked at Birgitta, who was standing over by the windows all dolled up: her hair teased and sprayed, in a tight skirt and sweater. The contempt in Margareta's mind fused to a single burning point: You slut! She swallowed. "What's going on here?"

Birgitta put her hand to her mouth and whimpered between her fingers, "It wasn't my fault!"

Margareta's voice fell to a whisper. "Did you hit her? Did you fall so low as to hit Aunt Ella, you goddamn—?"

Birgitta pressed right into the wall, hand still to her mouth. "No! I never touched her, I swear. . . . We were arguing, she shouted at me and then keeled over. It wasn't my fault!"

Margareta frowned, speechless, and shifted her eyes back to Aunt Ella.

That creature wasn't even worth looking at. She let go of Aunt Ella's hand, went over to the couch, and returned with a throw pillow embroidered with a green-and-red pattern in the loveliest twist work, carefully raised Aunt Ella's head, and inserted the pillow under it. "It's all right, little mamma," she said, stroking Aunt Ella's hand. "Everything's going to be all right."

Christina walked under the arch to the living room at that very moment. Her whisper was so soft it was barely audible. "What happened?"

Margareta looked up, saw her sister, and finally burst into tears.

BIRGITTA'S SERVING a life sentence. And she deserves it.

Margareta reaches across the table for her cigarettes but realizes after a moment that they're gone. Birgitta may have been upset, but not too upset to remember to snatch them for herself. Oh, well. Now Margareta's made up her mind, anyway. She's going to find a florist's, buy a rose and a memorial candle, and go back to Motala. Alone. She'll go to Aunt Ella's grave and sit there for a while, tell her about the letters coming from heaven only knows where, about how everything is and how it might have been. That's it. She's going to tell Aunt Ella the things she's never told anyone, about André and about her first autumn in Göteborg, about her trip to South America with a man she walked out on the third day they were there, about the walks she took through Lima by herself, about the time she returned to the orphanage and found the bed empty.

"Where's my boy?" she had asked, turning to look deep into the dark eyes of the matron.

"Oh, señorita," the woman said with a sly smile. "He wasn't yours. His mother was here this afternoon. There was a lawyer with her. He got her five hundred dollars for the child. Would you have given more?"

Yes, she would have given more, she would have been able to give a great deal, because she had been given so much herself. The legacy she could pass down to an endless number of orphans would have been enough to outbid any American couple with deep pockets. But the boy was already gone, the matron refused to give her the lawyer's name, and thus Aunt Ella would never be at the head of an endless lineage of orphans, and Margareta Johansson would never have any descendants. She's nothing but a totally tenuous mix of particles that will dissolve and emerge again as thousands of other equally transient blends of particles, leaving not so much as a trace behind.

* * *

WHEN SHE LEAVES the restaurant, she walks on the sunny side of the street, turns her face to the sky, and lets the wind play through her hair. The air is cool and fragrant; she takes a couple of breaths, trying to identify the molecules ricocheting off the mucous membranes in her nose, smiling when she succeeds. *Spring is here, why doesn't my heart go dancing?* . . . True. Tomorrow's the spring equinox. The eve of the equinox is a perfect time to visit Aunt Ella.

She sees a florist's across the street and hurries to the crosswalk. Someone grabs her by the arm just as she's walking out into the street. She turns around and finds herself staring into Birgitta's ashen face, watching her baggy double chin tremble as she slurs, "It wasn't my fault. You've got to believe me, sometime you've got to believe me!"

Margareta doesn't answer, just pulls away and steps briskly out into the street. She has to move fast; the light turns red again when she's just partway out. A bus growls threateningly in her direction; she doesn't hear what Birgitta's shouting until she's on the other side. "She lied to me. She was a damn bitch! You have no idea what she'd done!"

That settles it. How Birgitta gets back to Motala is her own problem.

In the Balance

Oh self, thou lovely, glorious nature
What art thou but an ornate troll
Who murders and consumes thine own offspring
Deceiving them with cruel embraces first?
Thou who art grave and gravedigger at once
And guardian of the gates of heaven, a Sphinx,
With innocent face and body of a lion,
Pursuing with deathly smile and silence—
Ah, take me if thou must: but not without
An explanation: what was life all about?

Per Daniel Amadeus Atterbom

I CANNOT SWALLOW. I will never swallow again.

What does that mean? Where has this loss taken me?

The answer is simple: to the edge of the abyss of nothingness.

KERSTIN ONE HAS fluttered out of the room to phone Hubertsson. I could have told her that there was no point, that Hubertsson's gone for the day, but she's left my computer so far beyond my reach that I can't get at the mouthpiece.

Ulrika's still in the room. Her face has changed, the professional smile is gone. She's actually finished with what she had to do in here: she's put me in a clean nightgown and she's changed my sheets, washed my face with a soap-scented washcloth she dipped in lukewarm water, arranged the books on my nightstand by size so the whole pile won't come crashing down, yet she can't get herself to walk out the door. Instead, she pads around my bed in silence, straightening the sheet, which is already perfectly straight, refolding my honeycomb blanket with fastidious care.

She's scared. She's suddenly so young and frightened I wish I could comfort her. But my mouthpiece is too far away.

I mustn't be frightened. I know what's ahead, and that's exactly why I must not be afraid. Once you've lost the ability to swallow, there are only three treatment options. The first is to do nothing at all, in which case the patient dies of dehydration on the third day. The second is to put the patient on an IV drip: this gives the body liquids, glucose, and essential salts but no real nutrition, and so she dies of starvation in a matter of months. The third alternative is to insert a tube through the nostril, run it down through the esophagus to the stomach, and fill it with a nutritional solution once every three hours. In which case the patient can live forever and forever. Amen.

Praise the Looord
I've seen the Light . . .

Joyous voices are moving down the hall to Maria's room. For a fraction of a second I think maybe the heavenly gates have opened right up above the nursing home and the archangels, the seraphs, and cherubs are all enticing me with song. Then I recall that today is the day a choir was coming to sing. Their jubilations transport me to a place of perfect serenity. I look at Maria's angels. Are you longing for me to join you? Are you waiting for me? I'm coming. Soon.

But not quite yet.

MY NOTION OF the Almighty Trickster is a naïve one, I know. I've met enough hospital chaplains over the years to be clear about the fact that it's not exactly *comme il faut* to envision Him as the fairy-tale king of the kingdom of the spheres, a Jupiter with a white beard and a diadem of stars, a giant whose galactic throne hovers in the vacuum on the other side of the Milky Way and whose blue robes are decorated with white stars and supernovas, glittering clouds of antiparticles and dark, shimmering material. He's far more mystical than that, they say; he's the inherent mystery of existence.

Such a god is so abstract that he must be locked into his own mystery, deaf and mute, blind and disabled. Although I cannot imagine how one would address him, I would like to speak with the Almighty Trickster. Because who else can I argue with, who else can I hold accountable? But I am not a believer. There is no reason to believe. Today, physicists are in the process of discovering the answer to the triumphant ultimate question of all religions: how can anything come of nothing?

Matter can arise in a vacuum if the pressure is sufficient. That's been proven. So something—such as a universe—can come of nothing. Nevertheless, pressure should count as something. And possibly vacuums, too. Is emptiness anything? What about nonexistence? Who created the Almighty Trickster? Who created whoever created the Almighty Trickster?

You can go on and on like that. If you have the time. And unless you can endure thinking, instead, about what we already know: that anything can turn into nothing. Consciousness, for instance. Thoughts. Existence.

*　*　*

I SHUT MY eyes and sink into the Valium. This is a weird sort of exhaustion, not suffocatingly heavy as lead like Birgitta's, as she stands at a pedestrian crosswalk in Norrköping, not aching and alert like Christina's, as she closes her eyes in her office, not yawning and sleepy like Margareta's, as she waits her turn at a florist's. This is my own exhaustion, as airy and transparent as it is paralytic. It is as if I were resting in a swaying spider's web, unable to extricate myself, unable even to wish to extricate myself.

Well, all right. So I would have liked to extricate myself, if only I had been able to hope. The state I dismissed so disdainfully just a few hours ago now appears idyllic. Imagine sitting in bed having breakfast. Imagine the pleasure of lifting a trembling spoonful of oatmeal with applesauce to one's mouth; imagine pressing one's tongue to one's palate and delighting in the fantasies that arise. Autumn. Stalks of oats trembling with fullness, the scent of apples, the view of the enormous Östgöta plain.

A postcard, sort of.

OUT IN THE dayroom, the choir is starting up again, letting their silvery voices go:

Search me, Lord,
Shine a light from heaven on my soul
Search me, Lord,
I wanna be right, I wanna be saved
I wanna be whole . . .

No thank you. I don't necessarily want to be redeemed, saved to the safe side, I don't strive for that kind of eternal life. Yet I would like to stand before the Almighty Trickster after my death and sum things up. I'd like him to be sitting there on his galactic throne with a set of scales in his hand, making me atone for my sins. At that very moment I would open my own hand and there would be three small black orbs in the palm: one for envy, one for bitterness, one for not having fully multiplied my talents.

"Listen!" I would say as I set the orb of envy on the scales. "It is true, I have sinned. Every day of my life I have coveted what others have. I was envious of Tiger-Maria because her mother wrote to her, of Agneta because she was so sweet and easy to love, of Elsegerd because she could walk, even though she needed a crutch. I was envious of all of them because they got out of the cripples' home, each in her own way. But many years later, when I got out myself and was returned to the custody of the Östergötland County Council, I was still not satisfied. When I was in Linköping being the guinea pig of the neurosurgeons, I was envious of other patients because they healed. The neurosurgeons opened their heads up and poked around in them, after which everything was all right. I saw them get up from their beds, one after the other, and take their first faltering steps across the floor while I remained in my bed all the time, watching them through narrow slits. I wanted to walk, too."

I'd take one step backward and tip my head up so I could look him right in the eye. "Why did you make envy a sin, but not begrudging? It ought to be the other way around. It ought to be a greater sin to say *Don't let her have . . . !* than to say *I want some, too!* Why should the have-nots, who have been denied everything, not even be allowed to want?"

Then I'd set the second orb on his scales. "This is bitterness. I have committed this sin as well. I have no objection to this one, it is and should remain a sin. But allow me to explain it, allow me to attempt to show it as it really is."

Here I would lower my voice and say, in nearly a whisper, "Bitterness is an ancillary disease. It afflicts those who have not been allowed to grieve properly. And I have lived in an era when grief was not acknowledged, in a time when people looked for problems instead. Problems are easier to deal with, they can be solved, whereas grief must be endured. Moreover, grief is contagious and frightens others, and so they are prepared to go to extremes to prevent a person who has cause to grieve from truly mourning. They lie. They moralize. They shout and laugh in shrill voices to drown out the sorrow.

"I had great cause to mourn, and so I triggered their fear. They were angry with me because my situation was so desperate. So I was instructed first to be grateful that I was even being fed and clothed, second to accept my destiny and be realistic, to come to consider my disability as an impractical condition although not a tragedy in the great scheme of things.

"But it *was* a tragedy! It *is* a tragedy to be unable to walk and talk, it is infinitely more than an impractical condition. Anyone in this state should have the right to raise a fist to the heavens in the sight of all the world, to curse and condemn, to shout and struggle, to throw herself to the ground, kicking and banging her fists if she is able, crying until her eyes are void of tears. Not until then is one able to see the world. Not until then can one lie there, following the course of an ant with one's eyes, watching it carry a blade of grass, and not until then can one accept that life is never going to offer any more than this, but that this is more than enough. Not until then can one admit that it is a great fortune merely to be alive."

Once more I would look up at the Almighty Trickster, who would tug at his beard and look at me, nod to me to continue. And I would continue, because now nothing could stop me.

"And yet the fact that I was never allowed to mourn fully was not the only cause of my bitterness. There was more. I was never the favorite. Never, ever was I the favorite person in the world to another person. Not even when I was born, since, to Ella, Hugo's death was more important than my life. And as I never later met anyone on whom I could make a reasonable claim, there was no reason for me to be anyone's favorite. That's only logical; if you have never been the most important person in the world to your mother, you can never be really important to anyone else. Or really even to yourself."

The voice of the Almighty Trickster would resound across the heavens: "Hubertsson?"

I would look sternly at him; the fury of the microbe would strike the ruler of the universe. "Almighty Trickster, be silent and listen, just for once. I'll get to Hubertsson. In due course. But first I must set my third orb on your scales: the sin of not multiplying one's talents."

I will stand up straight and clasp my hands behind my back, clear my throat and continue: "I didn't come away entirely empty-handed. You gave me sharp sight and an operative mind. So why didn't I get myself a life, when push came to shove? Why didn't I become a Stephen Hawking, a world-renowned scholar? Or at least a mediocre university student? Why did I lay there in my bed begrudging my sisters what they had at my expense?"

He would nod. Right, why not?

"Just accompany me back to Linköping, to the years when I was the little guinea pig of the neurosurgeons, and a smart idiot. Oh, what a smart girl I was! Oh, how I loved being a smart girl—I shone like a sun when they praised me: Look at smart little Desirée sitting there in her wheelchair in the invalids' unit with the latest correspondence course on her lap. Now she's completed English. Now she's done a term paper on

Thomson and electrons. But now she'll have to put her books away for a while, because now we're going to take her back down to neurosurgery and cut into her skull again."

At this point I'd look back up at him. "Do you know how many operations I underwent, Thou omniscient Almighty Trickster? I don't know myself. All I know is I believed that all that surgery was a sign they were on the way to finding the magical little nerve ending that was the root of all evil, that they would be able to repair it with skillful fingers and instruments sharp as awls, after which I would be able to do things I had never even dared dream of. Sing. Dance. Run. I was preparing for a new life, that was why I bent my shaven head over those textbooks again just a few days after every operation, that was why I never complained when the incision barely had a chance to heal before they were collecting me from long-term care and taking me back down to neurosurgery for a new one. There was a life waiting for me."

I'd take a deep breath, to steady my voice. "Then my high school graduation day arrived. A representative of the company that sold correspondence courses arrived at the ward with my diploma and my white graduation cap. My fellow patients gave me flowers, and the staff had a reception for me, with cake and coffee. The local paper sent a team, too, and I was bolstered up in my wheelchair, surrounded by all my bouquets. A photographer took a picture while the reporter stood amiably in the background. . . . I was happy. For the first time I was truly noticed and truly happy. Lundberg arrived a few hours later."

Here, I would probably have to swallow deeply if I were to be able to continue at all.

"I suppose you remember Dr. Lundberg, the senior physician. Yes, of course you do, you are omniscient. So you also know what he said when he came, after having perfunctorily presented me with a book as a graduation present. He said he wanted to split my brain down the middle. He wanted to drag his scalpel through my corpus callosum and separate the hemispheres of my brain. He said he needed to do so in order to prevent further brain damage. It was all they could do for me, he hoped I realized that, because they could neither cure me nor give me a new body, they could merely prevent further damage. And although it was unusual to split a human brain in two, commissurotomy was a tried-and-true intervention and had been used in the United States since the forties."

Here I would lower my voice even further. "I shriveled up. That's what happens when you abandon hope. You shrivel up. I could feel it happen: it was as if my bones were voided of marrow in no time at all, as if I lost every ounce of what little strength and stability I still possessed. He planned to split my brain in two, separate emotion from reason, letters from numbers, consciousness from nonconsciousness. He planned to deprive me of my very personality to keep it from being further damaged. I set his present down and looked at him, suddenly realizing that he had never given me any promises, realizing that I had duped myself. That would never happen again. What did I have to hope for? Singing? Dancing? Running? No. A job as a filing clerk if I was lucky. Four or six or eight hours a day in the back labyrinths of a dusty library. If I was unlucky, endless unemployment. And it was fairly probable that I would be unlucky in the future as well. I gathered my remaining bone marrow, that last vestige of my strength into a single word: No. I was not going to let him split my brain. I refused to allow it."

Here I would look the Almighty Trickster in the eye again. "I was prepared to give up. To die. I stopped speaking and reading, stopped eating and drinking. I screamed my horror the moment I caught sight of a neurosurgeon. That made me useless, and the county council moved me to Vadstena for less expensive, less sophisticated care. Then life took a hairpin turn: Hubertsson crossed my path, and I found I was something more than I had previously believed. My soul took flight, if you'll forgive the paucity of the metaphor."

The Almighty Trickster would grunt. Get to the point!

"There is nothing to add. I had to become his patient in order to be near him. I flew out into the world by night and lay still in my bed by day and found it quite sufficient. And so I did not pursue my studies, and so I never became a Stephen Hawking."

Here, I would smile and perform my feat of magic: from a fold in my shroud I would draw out a fourth orb; a shimmering golden sphere, larger than the other three put together. "Look," I would say. "Lean forward and look into my crystal ball! I am going to put it on the other scale pan. Will it outweigh my sins?"

Here I would let the orb roll out of my hand and onto the pan of the scale. It would glitter and gleam, and even before it settled there would be no question that it outweighed all the Almighty Trickster's stars.

"Look," I would say, "see how the scales shift under the weight of my orb, how the metal pan is pressed to the breaking point . . ."

The Almighty Trickster would lean forward, put the vastness of his hand in front of me, and I would step toward Him, trembling and fearful but determined. Slowly I would rise through the heavens, in the hand of God I would be brought to the face of God. To his answer.

"I know," he would say. "You have loved."

KERSTIN ONE AND Ulrika are back in my room, I glimpse them from behind my heavy eyelids. Never have I seen them like this. Kerstin One's hair is disheveled, Ulrika's eyes are glaring and she is on edge. They raise the head of my bed even more, lift me up, and smooth my nightgown between my back and the sheet. That feels nice. Creases can be torture if you have to spend hours and hours lying on them.

"Desirée," says Kerstin One, in a very different, much deeper voice than her usual one. "Desirée! Can you hear me?"

I open my eyes and look at her.

"I can't reach Hubertsson. I've called the health center and his home, but he doesn't answer. Do you want me to call Dr. Wulf in the meantime?"

No. I don't want that. I have other plans for her. I shut my eyes and make a minimal movement with my head. For the first time, Kerstin One admits she has seen one of my nonspastic movements.

"You'd rather wait for Hubertsson? Fine, I promise to keep trying to reach him. And if I don't get him by the end of my shift, I'll inform Kerstin Two. Is that all right?"

It's all right. Perfectly all right.

I DON'T KNOW what I'm going to say to Hubertsson when he arrives. Decisions will have to be made. Promises kept.

We have, of course, discussed euthanasia, particularly in recent years, now that the word is no longer associated only with Nazism and concentration camps but also with new solutions in the high-tech era. The Netherlands isn't the only country where new things are being tried. In Australia, a new aid for the disabled has been invented. A death computer. You roll the wheelchair over to the computer, fill a hypodermic with a toxic substance, and insert a blocked needle into the arm of the victim.

A question comes up on the monitor and is repeated at thirty-second intervals:

"Are you certain you are ready to die?"

ENTER.

"Are you certain you are ready to die?"

ENTER.

"Are you certain you are ready to die?"

ENTER.

The question is asked three times, and you have to press ENTER three times, after which the needle is unblocked and the poison mixes with your blood. Simple and hygienic. No executioner, only a victim. And a substantial saving of the taxpayers' money.

The chorus out in the dayroom is on the finale; the singers are now in full, eager swing, the music possesses them. They are clapping the beat so loudly I can hear only fragments of the lyrics:

No one else can calm my fear . . .

I envy them. I'd also like to sing. I'd like to sing Hubertsson the very song they are now performing.

I KNOW MORE about Hubertsson than he thinks I do. I know how the skin on his tongue tastes, how the hair on his chest feels, how he shuts his eyes and opens his mouth at orgasm. But the memory is a fine, fragile one. I've hidden it away to make it last longer, been careful not to wear it out. Now, though, it makes no difference, the future is so short.

Only one single time did I follow Hubertsson to the Standard Hotel in Norrköping. It was a Thursday in January, right around the time my upward curve was about to take a dive, when my seizures started to be more frequent, when the sounds and grunts that crossed my lips had begun less and less to resemble words and sentences. At that time I was often irritated and impatient with my caretakers; I accused them of putting on airs when they didn't understand what I was trying to say and brought me an alphabet to point to letters on instead, forcing me to spell every single little word. Pointing was at least as difficult as speaking for me: my hands flailed all over the board, making my messages mysterious and incomprehensible, even to myself. In the end I tried putting the pointer in my mouth, but it didn't help much.

And so I went silent, turned inward, lay in bed almost all day every day, sleeping or pretending to sleep, sputtering with rage whenever anyone tried to get me to go out. The streets were snowy and the air was cold! Why on earth should I go outside?

After some time my caretakers grew accustomed to this behavior and settled into my living room with books and magazines, just tiptoeing over every now and then to peek in through my bedroom door and make sure I wasn't convulsing. They stopped addressing me, which was exactly what I wanted. Because if there was no risk of anyone speaking to me, I could go off.

I'd found an excellent carrier, an aging crow who had turned up in the evergreen tree outside my bedroom window sometime toward the end of November and had now made her home there. Her state of mind suited me; she was brusque and huffy most of the time, but fundamentally an eminently sensible creature. When she noticed me sitting behind her eye, she didn't panic like other crows tended to do, she made some quick calculations. Although I was admittedly stronger than she, she realized I needed her, and thus there would be some kind of fair balance. I reinforced the calculations to my advantage with a little puff of certainty through her bloodstream: if she did as I wished she would survive the winter, and when spring came I would leave her in peace to roost on her eggs.

I took it easy to begin with, just had her carry me over Vadstena a few times a day. I never forced her out over the lake. The dark water was visible between the blocks of ice along the shore, and it scared her, so I accepted regarding the lake from the turrets of the fortress and from the treetops in the lakeshore park. Later I had her take me to a tree outside the health center, where I would sit watching Hubertsson and Christina examine their patients.

After some time I grew bolder, abandoning the crow for a while to rest in a drop of water on a branch while she flew off to another tree. She never went far afield, and after a few days she began to arrive the minute my thoughts called her. But I still had some preparations to make, forcing my crow to fly in larger and larger circles over the Östgöta plain, stopping in woods and groves, then leaving her so I could ride a fox or a wild rabbit, to creep into a sleeping porcupine and dream with him, to comfort a freezing cold squirrel with memories of summer before calling her back. She came instantly, although I'd kept her waiting for hours. She was mine. Trained and ready for use.

On Thursday I always woke up uneasy: this was the day Hubertsson would rush off after a quick cup of coffee, and the next day he would arrive very late if at all. He never said much on Thursday mornings, already enfolded in the night to come. I didn't like it. I knew too little about his Thursday nights and his Friday mornings; I didn't even know if he went with the same woman every week or if he chose a new one each time. And believe me I had no intention of asking, that would have been violating every provision in our pact. Nor did I intend just to watch him from a distance, follow him with my own eyes as I already followed my sisters in those days. Nor did I want to see through Hubertsson's eyes. I wanted to be seen through them.

Finally the Thursday morning I had been waiting for arrived. Hubertsson raised his briefcase in an absentminded good-bye and disappeared through my door. I watched him go and made up my mind finally to take the risk. I was docile and obedient all day, even allowed myself to be taken out for a wheelchair walk to keep my caretaker calm. By five o'clock I was yawning and able to make her understand I was ready for bed. Around six a new caretaker came on duty—an eager young art student who peeked in through my door and was pleased to see I appeared to be sleeping soundly. He opened his sketch pad and took up his pen. He could get a lot done that night.

The minute I steered my crow northeast, she seemed to realize this was a special occasion, and rose high into the black night sky, screeching. I laughed back inside her head and drove her to a higher speed. Still, it was hours before we landed on a streetlight outside the Standard Hotel in Norrköping. The crow was exhausted, her head flopping from side to side; all she wanted was to nestle it under her wing. I held her back, needing her eye to find my next conveyor. There was no one outside the door; I had to wait nearly twenty minutes until a solitary latecomer arrived. This was a middle-aged man who didn't even notice me, just lurched briefly, as if my landing made him momentarily dizzy. In the cloakroom a woman passed him on her way to the lavatory. I barely had time to look at her before making the leap.

She had a pleasant body, light and soft to wear. Her lungs were pale pink, the cilia in her respiratory system floated like seaweed over the ocean floor, the saliva in her mouth was fresh and dewy as a child's. I made up my mind at once. This was where I wanted to be.

She'd had a couple of drinks and didn't even notice me until she was sitting on the toilet. She looked up from her white cotton panties, stared at the wall, and a question fluttered into being. Is someone there?

"I want to dance," I whispered.

She chuckled and repeated my words: "I want to dance!"

When we came out of the cubicle, I had a chance to check out her reflection in the mirror. Her coloring was good: blond hair and green eyes, but her face was youthful rather than really fully mature, her skin was smooth, her eyes round and wondering. She might be too young for Hubertsson.

But I want to be light under his weight, I thought.

She smiled at her reflection, cocking her head: "Light under his weight . . ."

One second later her hands shot up to her mouth and she was staring at herself. What's gotten into me?

"What's your name?" I whispered.

She raised her hands from her mouth and whispered: "Who are you?"

"A dream and a fairy tale. What's your name?"

Her voice trembled with panic. "Who are you?"

The door of one of the other cubicles opened, and a giggling girl stepped out.

"What's with you, Camilla? Talking to yourself?"

Camilla swayed slightly and laughed. Her laughter was crystal clear, shimmered like glass. Hubertsson would like her.

"I feel really weird. Almost as if I weren't the only one inside me . . ."

The other girl chuckled. "You're not likely to be for long . . . if you ask me."

What a vulgar type. Lucky I didn't pick her.

I HAD CAMILLA stand in the doorway to the restaurant for a while so I could get my bearings. Crystal chandeliers and subdued lighting, red-velvet curtains and a parquet dance floor. An amplified but sober quartet in black jackets onstage. Just about what I had expected.

Hubertsson was sitting by himself, leaning back, at a table by the window. His face was grave, his pose arrogant: legs crossed, right arm stretched along the chair next to his. He looked not really present, sort of unaware of the lights and sounds around him.

Camilla's girlfriend was halfway across the room, and she turned and beckoned impatiently. Camilla took a step or two in her direction, then I halted her.

Him, I whispered. The man by himself over there.

A foul-smelling wave of disdain flowed through her mind. That old guy? I hissed and expanded, her own self withdrew, intimidated, and she walked in the direction I had chosen. I fixed her green eyes on Huberts-son's and ran my fingers across his tablecloth, smiling a distant little smile as I passed.

It worked. At the very instant I sat down in Camilla's seat, he put his hand on my shoulder. I set Camilla's little evening bag on the table and got up. He took me by the arm and led me to the dance floor.

Oh!

At last to have the opportunity to dance cheek to cheek with Huberts-son, to smile as a little thrill ran through my nervous system, to be in a milky white body with strong sinews, to vanish into his embrace, to allow one of my thighs to glide in between his, as if by accident.

He was a good dancer; all I had to do was relax in his arms and let him lead. I didn't say a word, nor did he. He simply led me though dance after dance around the floor, silently. Camilla's friend danced past several times, raising her eyebrows in wonder, but I shut Camilla's eyes to close her out. The real Camilla had nearly dissipated. She was sitting some-where in a corner of herself, in a state of suspended disbelief, telling her-self she must be dreaming.

I had arrived late, it would soon be time for the last dance. Hubertsson laid his hand dictatorially on my back and held me close. I responded with a little laugh in the direction of his neck. Yes, I whispered, and my own voice as it would have been if everything had been different, sud-denly came out of Camilla's mouth: "Yes. Yes. Yes."

Hubertsson laughed and stroked my back. "Yes," he said, too. "Yes. Ab-solutely."

His hotel room was readied in a way that indicated he was accustomed to this. The bedside lamp was on, so there was no need to ruin the ambi-ence with the ceiling light, the curtains were closed and the bed unrum-pled. There were two little pieces of chocolate on the pillow; he tossed one to me nonchalantly. I caught it with an easy movement and laughed again. Camilla must have been good at ball sports.

On the table was a bottle of wine and two glasses. I was surprised at his attention to detail: these were no bathroom glasses but real, thin-stemmed wineglasses.

I remained in the middle of the room, feet close together as he uncorked the wine. I was suddenly nervous. Would what I had learned from books and television be sufficient?

"So tell me," said Hubertsson, extending a glass. "Who's this Camilla?"

I raised my glass, answering truthfully: "I don't know. And who are you?"

He set his glass down, removing his jacket in one smooth movement. His eyes were gleaming, this was a game he liked. "A stranger. Shall we keep it that way?"

"Let's," I said. "Stranger, what do you want of me?"

"Everything," said Hubertsson. "And nothing."

IT SURPRISED ME that he was so willing to be mine, that he was able to sit still in the only armchair in the room as I sat down on his lap, astride him, and unbuttoned his shirt, that he leaned back and closed his eyes as I allowed Camilla's fingers to run through the hair on his chest, then put her ear up close to listen to his heartbeat. All at once I was an animal, a lustful predator wanting to lick and bite, to chomp at his almond-scented skin with sharp teeth, until he began to moan. Then I slid off him, fell to my knees between his legs, and started working the clasp of his suit pants. I felt him raise his pelvis slightly, but I was in no hurry and made him wait a few seconds before I slowly undid the fly, allowing what was concealed in his white cotton briefs to rise.

"Ah." Hubertsson sighed hoarsely as I lowered myself upon him. "Ah, but who are you?"

ALL NIGHT I remained nameless, as I lay on the floor beneath him as if crucified, as we rolled from one side of the double bed to the other, two as one, as I stood howling like a vixen on all fours. The air in the room grew thick with our scents. Camilla's hair was matted and damp with perspiration, I stared at Hubertsson's face through the strands of it—wet lips, wide nostrils, eyes half shut—and showed my bestial teeth. Everything! Give me everything and nothing!

* * *

He never noticed when I left, sleeping like a log when I rose and picked up Camilla's things—an evening bag, a pair of panties, a bra, and a wrinkled dress—from where they were strewn. She was getting difficult now, whining and moaning in her attempts to get out. But I wasn't done. I pulled the sheet up around Hubertsson's naked shoulders and bent over him, kissed his whiskers one last time, and turned out the night-light before quietly closing the door of his hotel room behind me.

I didn't want Camilla to have to see the grumpy expression on the face of the cloakroom attendant, so I was dutiful enough to remain in command until I had collected her coat. She perked up as she stumbled out onto the sidewalk. I stopped her there and invoked my crow, who was sitting in a tree in the park by the station, at my beck and call, and who spread her wings instantly. I let go of Camilla and rose toward the sky, filling the crow with jubilation and angels' song. She responded with her hoarse cackle.

And outside the Standard Hotel in Norrköping, Camilla stood on the sidewalk, hugging herself.

A few hours later Hubertsson rang my doorbell, scaring my morning caretaker out of bed. "Where is she?" he asked.

"Who?"

"Desirée, of course."

"In bed. Where did you expect her to be?"

He set off for my bedroom door, the caretaker padding behind him in her thick woolen socks.

"She's sleeping. We weren't expecting you, you don't usually come around so early on Fridays . . ."

She put out a hand as if to restrain him. "Let her rest. She was really tired yesterday."

He pushed her aside, opened the door, looked into the room, and then turned on her. "She's in seizure! And you didn't see or hear!"

My night of lovemaking with Hubertsson cost me dearly: four days of unrelenting hurricanes, when the world ripped and crumbled before my eyes. Only with the greatest of effort did I manage occasionally to drag myself up to the surface of reality and gasp for breath before sinking again.

When I awoke on the fifth day, I was no longer at home. I was in a strange bed in a strange room. It took me some time to figure out that I was back at the nursing home where I had met Hubertsson. He arrived a few hours later, lumbering along, a far older man than the one I had last seen.

"Status epilepticus," he said, standing at the foot of my bed. "Close call. Do you know where you are?"

I tried to answer, but groans were all I could get out.

"Pardon?"

I extended myself, formulated the word in my head, rolled it through the labyrinth of my brain, let it ricochet off my vocal cords, and opened my mouth. A grunt emerged. Hubertsson picked up the alphabet board from my nightstand and inserted a pointer in my mouth; my head began to ache with the effort as I spelled out the three-letter word: y-e-s.

"Are you finding it difficult to speak?"

There was a heavy fire hovering over my brow, and it took all I had to keep my eyes open as I pointed to seven more letters: I cannot.

"Can't? You can't speak at all?"

I closed my eyes and fumbled for his hand, pressed it twice, and then let go: no, I could no longer speak. His hand fell limply from my own. He stood motionless by my bed for a long while. I heard the sound of cloth rustling and realized he was putting his hands in his pockets.

"We'll keep you here for a few more days," he said. "But then we'll get you back home. We just need to get your medications right again."

I neither opened my eyes nor reached for his hand. I had nothing to add, and my head was killing me. The soles of his shoes whispered against the floor; he was heading for the door. I heard him open it, but it didn't close. The seconds passed before he spoke, and I heard an odd little chuckle in his voice: "I dreamed about you Thursday. All night."

I smiled behind my closed eyelids. It had been worth the price.

THAT TIME, THEY let me out of the nursing home after just a week or so. This time it's more questionable. Hubertsson is evasive when I bring it up.

But I'd like to get back to my apartment just one more time. I'd like to sit in my sunny living room with a quiet caretaker—preferably the art student, it's very pleasant to be close to his concentration when he's drawing—beyond my field of vision and listen to Grieg. I like Grieg. He's neither tentative nor modest; he claims his space and asserts himself like a man, but at the same time he is an unusual enough man to be able to laugh at himself. Like Hubertsson.

My living room is pretty, far prettier than any of my sisters'. Not even Christina's pale blue paradise can compare. The light works in my favor, the bright summer mornings and sparkling winter noons. It may be the light, more than anything else, that has drawn Hubertsson to my apartment every morning for years. It certainly isn't my gorgeous curtains.

He was angry with me for a full six months when, after our annual visit to the museum of technology in Stockholm one year, I got him to take me into an exclusive handicraft and furniture store nearby. He felt taken advantage of, claiming I had only asked him to take me back to the diffusion chamber as an excuse to go to that disgusting establishment for the wealthy old biddies of the town. Hadn't I? In addition to which, he thought it was obscene to spend so much money on curtains. There were people in the world who had no food to put on their tables. Wasn't I aware of that? I just snorted at his rumblings. I'd been coveting those Josef Frank curtains ever since I moved into my apartment. A thousand times I'd imagined what it would be like to have a whole flowering garden wall, and I'd been saving up from my disability pension for years to buy them. What business of Hubertsson's was the price of my curtains? What business? Were Josef Frank and I taking the food out of the mouths of the needy?

I want to go home. To my curtains and everything else. I'd like to sit one last time in my living room early in the morning, smell the aroma of coffee wafting through the apartment. One last time I'd like to make a sign to my caretaker to push the power button on the microwave the minute Hubertsson rings the doorbell so the white rolls will be just right when he takes his plate.

Hubertsson and me. Our curtain quarrel. Our mornings with strong coffee and hot rolls. Our long silences and occasional conversations. Our trips to the museum of technology. Our one and only New Year's Eve, the time I raised a trembling glass of ginger ale, clinked it against his glass of champagne, and made a toast to the new year.

Perhaps it was a life, after all. The one I lived.

YES. I WANT Hubertsson to come now, just as the afternoon light begins to shift toward blue in anticipation of twilight. I want him to hold me in his arms and carry me across Vadstena to my apartment, lay me down on my red couch, smooth the white throw over my body so no one can tell it's a piece of driftwood, open the Josef Frank curtains partway and allow the dusk to slide in. Then we will sit there, hand in hand, for three days and three nights. All alone. But together.

Tomorrow's the spring equinox, but the *benandanti* will have to hold their procession without me. I want to stay in my body, I want to rest with my hand in Hubertsson's and spend my last few days giving him the only thing I have to give: a finished story.

None of my sisters stole the life that was meant for me. I have lived the life that was meant for me. But I cannot let go of them yet, cannot yet let Christina, Margareta, and Birgitta run off in different directions.

Hubertsson asked a question. Before it's all over, he will have his answer.

Mean Woman Blues

Sometimes being a bitch is the only thing a woman has to
hold on to.

Stephen King

A BUS PASSES, blocking her view of Margareta, and when it's gone Margareta is nowhere to be seen. Typical Margareta. Here today, gone tomorrow. She has the most astonishing ability to vanish, especially at times like this, now that she's made Birgitta want to explain and defend herself, now that she's irritated Birgitta to the point where she's finally prepared to dig up the memory of what happened back then. Margareta pulls out, runs off like an anxious rabbit with a twitching nose. She likes to insult you and imply things, but when push comes to shove she's afraid of what she might find out.

It hurts so much!

Birgitta puts her hand to her abdomen and leans against the traffic light. Shit. She's going to throw up, she can suddenly sense that little bubble of nothing rising in her stomach that always precedes a vomit attack. She feels it expand in her throat and force her mouth open. She stands still, spreads her feet, and bends forward, and in the midst of all the nausea a sober little question runs through her mind. Where the hell did those high-heeled shoes come from? And whatever became of her sneakers?

Margareta thinks she doesn't have a clue about anything, Birgitta could tell from the look in her eye a few minutes ago. But there are things about the previous day she remembers. Lying for hours on a mattress, numb and heavy as lead, for example, unable to get up and equally unable to sleep, while Roger lay there snoring on the floor. That sometime in the afternoon they had a fight; he lost it when she refused to bring out any more beer. Right. That was what happened. And then she finally had the satisfaction of kicking the bastard down the hall, opening the door and throwing him out.

Afterward she had been high from it. Really up. That should teach him, Birgitta won't be pushed around, never in her life has she let anyone walk all over her. Once the newspapers had called her the drug queen of Motala, and it was true, at least it had been, then. She'd never been just any boring old run-of-the-mill junkie chick, willing to spread her legs for anyone who'd give her a fix in return, she'd been a pusher herself, and in control of her own destiny.

That was the mood in which she had gone into town, where she'd met Kåre, an old junkie who was looking to buy roofies. She'd gone around with him from one drug lair to the next. Somewhere along the line they'd bumped into some creepy foreigner who had a car and the whole gang—Kåre and Sessan, herself and Red Kjelle—had gone off to a party someplace with him. In Norrköping. It must've been in Norrköping, since that was where she had woken up that morning, and where she still was right now. And sometime during the night some Minnie Mouse must have grabbed Birgitta's sneakers and gone off in them. There's a hole in one sole, as the woman in question has probably noticed by now. Hope her toes got frostbitten and fell off her feet like clinking ice cubes the moment she removed those shoes.

Oh, shit. Here comes the puke.

Birgitta gasps, then vomits with a force that makes it splash up from the asphalt. Her eyes tear, but she can still see there's a woman by her, waiting to cross the street when the light changes, who reacts by jumping several steps to the side. Snotty bitch!

It's not a very big one, all she has in her system is one measly little beer. Birgitta looks up, leaning against the post, closes her eyes a moment, and tries to remind herself that she's virtually sober. She's only had that one little beer to drink, so she's actually throwing up more because exhaustion has given her a stomachache. Jesus. If only she were at home, in her own place, if only she could just lie down on her own mattress with a shitload of beer within reach. She'd just lie there for hours without moving a muscle, just lie perfectly still staring up at the ceiling.

She's got to get home. And Margareta, that bad-tempered bitch, has to drive her. She promised, and she's not going to get away with copping out.

Birgitta tries scouting the street once again. It arches and shakes like the floor in the house of horrors, but she doesn't give a damn, it doesn't bother her one bit. She's always dizzy after she throws up. It will pass in just a couple of minutes; she can just stand here leaning against the post and wait, pretend she's a regular Fru Svensson who's suddenly had a dizzy spell but who's well-bred enough to wait to cross until the light is green.

But who's she really trying to fool? Herself. No one else would ever even imagine she was an ordinary Fru Svensson. There are so many Svenssons standing waiting for the light to change now, three women and two men, and they've pulled together in a little huddle, as far from her as they can possibly stand. In addition to which they are trying very hard not to look at her; they're all pretending to be waiting impatiently for the light to change. It's only a matter of time before the whole gang starts whistling, just to make it perfectly clear that they neither see nor hear her.

"Scumbags!" Birgitta mumbles, laughing as she sees a little wave of discomfort roll over the group. They're scared: all five of them are glowering straight ahead, the women clutching their handbags, the men pushing their hands even deeper into their pockets.

Birgitta snorts and gropes in her own pocket for her cigarettes. What do they imagine she's going to do? Gobble them up?

THERE WAS A time when she took pleasure in being rejected by the Svenssons, when it made her feel proud and reckless. Like the Midsummer's Eve when a whole caravan of them drove from Motala to Mantorp, with Hound Dog's Chrysler at the head of the parade. She had sat there next to Hound Dog in her new white jeans with a checkered brassiere à la Brigitte Bardot under her pink blouse. She was such a knockout! She'd tied a pink head scarf over her teased hairdo before she left the house, untying the knot the minute she shut the gate. And once she was out of sight of Old Lady Ella's, she'd also untucked her blouse from her jeans and knotted it just above her waist. When she stretched, her belly button was exposed, which was why she had raised her arm up over her head to wave when she saw Hound Dog waiting for her in his Chrysler a few blocks from Ella's. Hound Dog couldn't help smiling, which was unusual: he tended to keep her on a short rein. Especially early on, that first time they went together.

They took the Mjölby Road, even driving through the town, although it was out of their way, eight big souped-up cars in a long line parading from the outskirts toward the market square. At first no one noticed, the town was quiet as a Sunday morning in the sunshine; it was early in the day and no midsummer poles had yet been raised. The town looked as if it had been the object of an especially severe attack of dustcloths and floor mops by Aunt Ella and Christina. It looked like Christina had gone at the lawns with a fine-tooth comb and a nail clipper, and Old Lady Ella had personally scrubbed the housefronts with her vegetable brush and shined every single birch leaf with silver polish.

As they approached the center of town, more people appeared. Holiday shoppers. Hound Dog was driving with just one hand on the wheel; the other was resting, relaxed and self-assuredly, on the back of Birgitta's seat. Without embracing her, he was still showing all and sundry that that chick who almost could have been Marilyn Monroe belonged to him. Birgitta leaned back, letting her neck brush his arm. This was the life, this was how things should always be. If there were a heaven, it must be like an eternal morning before Midsummer's Eve, gliding through a little two-bit town in a newly washed convertible, with bottles of booze clinking on the floor of the backseat, comfortable in the knowledge that the day and night to come were going to be nothing but party, party, party.

There was, however, something missing. Hound Dog quickly realized what and set the turntable spinning in the elegant little phonograph in the Chrysler. Birgitta had bought it for him with her staff discount at the plant. He turned up the volume, and as the caravan glided out onto the bridge over the Svartå River, a familiar voice rolled across the water:

Well, since my baby left me
I found a new place to dwell
It's down at the end of Lonely Street
At Heartbreak Hotel . . .

It was as if that voice brought all of Mjölby to rigid attention. The farmers vending their wares on the square looked up from their fruits and vegetables and moved stealthily toward their cashboxes, men in mail-order summer shirts bought especially for the midsummer festivities cleared their throats and focused their gazes out on the street, while their fastidious wives with permanents and beige poplin coats were turned to pillars with boxes of early strawberries in their hands, suddenly unable even to put them in their shopping bags.

Birgitta and Hound Dog sat with the top down and their faces as impassive as their rank required, while the gang in the cars behind them had already opened their bottles and were warming up. They rolled down their windows, hanging out like bunches of grapes, shouting and singing, hooting and laughing. Hound Dog glanced in the rearview mirror and, seeing that the entire entourage had crossed the bridge, put on his brakes and halted at the market square.

Birgitta and Hound Dog got out first, Hound Dog throwing his keys a foot or two in the air and catching them again with the most sophisticated of gestures, Birgitta removing her scarf and puffing up her hair with her hand before they started walking.

"Do you think I could have an ice cream?" she asked, snuggling up close to Hound Dog and sneaking her arm under his. He was certainly looking good today: his hair was combed into an artistic Brylcreem swirl at the front, and he had on the shiny new black satin jacket he'd ordered from the Hollywood Company in Stockholm. He'd waited for it for weeks, and it had finally arrived just the day before. There was an eagle on the back. No one else in any gang in the whole county had a jacket with an eagle on the back.

"Well, why the hell not?" he answered, pulling out his wallet.

Birgitta stood on tiptoe at the ice cream stand. In the background there were loud voices and slamming car doors as the others got out, but she still knew that every single Svensson on the square was staring at her and her alone. At her and Hound Dog.

Hound Dog knew it, too, you could tell from the way he held himself tall as he leaned forward at the window, tossed a coin on the counter and said, "One Top Hat!"

Birgitta put her arm around him. "What about you?"

Hound Dog snorted. "Hell no. Sticky stuff's for chicks. . . . Want some strawberries too?"

Strawberries? Why would she want strawberries? Then she remembered. Hound Dog liked to look flush. They'd only been going together for a month at that point, but she had already learned that when he was in the mood to spend, it was best just to open your mouth and swallow. The other evening she'd had to stuff herself with three orders of frankfurters and mashed potatoes just to make him happy. When they did it together afterward she could feel the pickles and catsup coming up in her throat, but she'd held back her nausea and put a good face on it. It was easy to imagine how Hound Dog would treat anybody who puked pickles and catsup all over the backseat of his Chrysler. He hadn't yet really started hitting her, just given her cheek a slap with the back of his hand when she talked too much. That had sent a little thrill of desire shooting up her thighs, but she wasn't fool enough to imagine it would be much fun to take a real beating from his fists.

The inhabitants of Mjölby stepped aside when Hound Dog headed for a stall on the square, still holding his wallet. She came tripping along behind—in sandals with straps and stiletto heels there weren't many alternatives to tripping—licking the cardboard top from her ice cream meticulously clean. Every single man on the square stared at her, so she made her tongue particularly long and pointed, running it over the lid with slow, sensuous brushing movements, sweeping every little bit of chocolate covering and strawberry filling carefully into her mouth.

There was a whole flock of Svenssons in front of the stall Hound Dog chose, but everyone kindly stepped aside to let him go ahead with no grumbling. Birgitta wedged her way in after him, licking her ice cream cone.

"Strawberries!" roared Hound Dog.

The stallholder quickly grabbed a box of berries and extended it for approval. Birgitta turned around and inspected the nearby Svenssons apathetically. They'd begun to relax now, were talking softly and grouping together slowly. Right near Birgitta was a woman who looked a lot like Old Lady Ella: a gray cotton housedress with a flowered print stuck out from under a buttoned poplin coat. She had a head of tight little permanented curls, with a net over them. Putting a brown paper bag into her shopping basket, she extended it to a man on the other side of Birgitta. He reached out and took it quickly from her.

"Christ!" cried Birgitta. "Filthy scumbag!"

Hound Dog quickly turned around.

"He tried to feel me up!"

Birgitta pointed an accusatory finger at the man with the shopping basket, having already convinced herself it had really happened. Of course it had happened! Why would her voice be so shrill and loud otherwise, why would she be vibrating with fury inside?

"Who?" asked Hound Dog, pulling up the sleeves of his jacket. There were elastic cuffs, so he could expose his hairy forearms without having to turn up or wrinkle the black satin.

"That guy! The one with the cap!"

Red splotches appeared on the unknown woman's neck; she pushed past Birgitta, standing between her and the man. "Don't be ridiculous." She snorted. "Egon would never—"

"And how would you know, you old hag? Just look at you!"

That was Sigge Wasp. The rest of the gang was there now, the guys forming a little semicircle to contain the Svenssons. Sigge Wasp was in the middle, thin as a beanpole and sandy as a lizard, his arms crossed over his leather vest. The girls flapped with indignation in the background: Some dirty old man had tried to feel Birgitta up! Shit! He was asking for it!

"Shove over, old lady," said Hound Dog in his deepest voice, pushing the woman aside.

Like a movie, Birgitta thought. With Hound Dog everything is just like at the movies . . . and since this was a movie, she prepared herself to play her role, slipping both her arms through one of Hound Dog's, leaning toward him, and blinking again and again as if to hold back her tears. "Come on, sweetheart, let's get out of here! Don't give that disgusting old slob the satisfaction!"

"Fuck that," said Hound Dog. He pulled his sleeves up another inch, focused on the man, and threw a punch.

"Owwww!" his wife moaned, then collapsed.

BIRGITTA MAKES A face at the memory as she shuffles slowly across the street, digging around in her jeans pockets for a lighter. The flock of Svenssons had hurried across before her and then dispersed, she might have stopped one of them and asked for a light, if for no other reason than for the pleasure of seeing them flutter like frightened hens. But it's all right, her fingers have found what they were looking for in her pocket. She stops in the middle of the street, feet hip distance apart, cupping the flame in one hand, to light up and inhale. A car growls in irritation on her left; she exhales a little plume of smoke, glancing at the driver with annoyance. What's the rush, dammit? It still says "Walk"!

That business in Mjölby had marked her debut on the wrong side of the law, although she hadn't really done anything that time. Still, it was the first time she'd been inside a cops' station. Hound Dog had shouted to the gang to go ahead to Mantorp when they led him across the square with handcuffs and all, but he hadn't protested when they wanted to take Birgitta along for questioning. She'd been flattered, despite a nagging fear that somebody might find out about it back home in Motala, and that Old Lady Ella would hear Birgitta had been picked up by the police. She'd make a fuss for sure. Because although she'd smartened up a little the last few years—as could be seen by the fact that when Birgitta told her she wouldn't be coming to the family midsummer festivities this year and wouldn't be sleeping at home that night she'd just nodded mutely—she'd surely have a stroke if she found out any of her girls had been arrested.

Well, she ended up having a stroke anyway. By the time Hound Dog's case came up in court, months later, she was already done for. Somehow, autumn seemed to begin on Midsummer's Eve that year, and it was as if there was no question it was going to be a terrible fall.

But it started well. They let them go in the evening, and when they walked out onto the steps of the police station, Hound Dog grabbed Birgitta by the hand for a second, applied a little pressure, and laughed before taking his usual grip on her wrist. There was a beautiful sunset, the town was warm and still as a sleeping cat at their feet, but pastel colors and a peaceful atmosphere were the last thing Hound Dog wanted—he needed action. They had to get over to Mantorp ASAP and liven up the party.

THEY WERE WELCOMED like local heroes. The Motala gang cheered when they drove into the campsite an hour later with Elvis on at top volume. Hound Dog pushed his sunglasses onto his forehead and grinned; Birgitta laughed and readied a set of easygoing, nonchalant responses to the other girls' questions about what it had been like, what they'd done to her, what the pigs had said.

But after only a few hours the atmosphere shifted. Of course it was Sigge Wasp's fault, he could never keep his big mouth shut and just had to reel over to Hound Dog, throw his arm around his shoulders, and slur into his ear with wet lips: "Holy shit, Hound Dog the Lion-Hearted! Never in my wildest dreams did I imagine you'd be able to floor an old lady with a single blow."

This, of course, enraged Hound Dog, who stood up and pulled off his jacket. Sigge fell to his knees before him, clasping his hands beseechingly: "O master, do not strike me, please! Slug my woman instead!"

An instant later he was on his feet, quick as a monkey to run behind Anita, pretending to hide. "Strike her! Yes, do! She's fucking powerful. Or else we can go over to Skänninge tomorrow and find some feeble old man.

I swear I'll knock his cane out of his hand so you can sock him one as he falls!"

By that time Hound Dog's face was white with fury. He was so livid it had almost made him sober; he pressed his lips together and was breathing through his nose like a *toro,* opening and shutting his fists, then slowly bending his fingers in preparation. In one fell swoop he shoved Anita aside and threw himself at Sigge, grabbing the front of his shirt and lifting him by it, dangling him in the air, legs flailing for a while, only to let go and slam him with his fist. Sigge tumbled backward and lay there, motionless, staring straight up at the blue-gray midsummer sky, not seeming to be aware he was bleeding from one nostril. Slowly he raised one hand, wiped his nose and inspected the blood, then inserted his index finger into his mouth and wiggled one of his front teeth. He raised his torso, leaning on one elbow to spit in the grass—phlegm, mixed with blood. "Shit," he said, falling back to the grass. "I never guessed you were gonna take it like that, man."

Hound Dog was still standing over him, his fists clenched, breathing like a raging bull. One blow had hardly been sufficient to release his wrath; he wanted to hit more, to hit harder, but of course he couldn't hit a man who was already down, especially not after what had happened at the market in Mjölby. And Sigge knew how to utilize his power. He settled in, one arm across his brow, shaking his head in feigned sorrow so the little rivulet of blood under his nose quivered and changed course. "No siree," he said. "I would never have thought you'd take it that way, Hound Dog. A guy like you, with the fanciest Chrysler in all of Motala and the best lay in the city, too. . . . Shit, we all envy you, don't you know that? You've been lucky. If you hadn't turned up, every guy in the gang would have had his chance to get into Birgitta's panties. As it was, she only had time to let half of us in before you came along and shut up the shop. Christ, you've got to understand, there are so many of us who are still craving."

The pale evening light of midsummer night was extinguished. All the colors suddenly turned to gray: the grass, the cars, Birgitta's pink blouse. They were surrounded by silence, as if a bell jar had been lowered over Motala from the heavens, forcing them to stand in a circle, closing out all the other noises from other gangs at the campsite.

Somebody laughed. With one quick glance Birgitta knew it had been Little Lars. His new girlfriend filled in with a hoarse giggle. The circle drew tighter, and suddenly Birgitta found she was no longer part of it. She, Hound Dog, and Sigge Wasp were in the middle of the ring, the others now encircling them.

Hound Dog was still frozen in position, but his lips were no longer as tightly pursed and his hands hung open and defenseless at his sides. Sigge pulled up one leg and crossed it over the other, looking as if he were lazing on the beach. Once more he wiped his nose, scrutinized the blood for a moment, then lifted his other hand off his forehead and began to clap. *"Oh if I were . . ."*

His voice was soft, whispering, but the rest of the gang could still hear what he was saying and knew what he meant. In an instant the bell jar filled with rhythmic clapping, all hands suddenly in rhythm, all voices whispering the same lines, becoming a single voice that quickly rose from a slight breeze to a roaring wind:

> *. . . in Birgitta's shoes*
> *I'd fill my cunt with sticky glues*
> *And travel all over, far and near*
> *Screwing for nothing, there and here.*

Out of the corner of her eye, Birgitta saw Sigge get up slowly and find his footing, clapping all the while, never losing the beat, turning slowly around to start them repeating the verse, then moving around the circle grinning and almost dancing, urging the others to chant faster and louder, to continue until the bell jar cracked and smashed to smithereens around them. The circle dissolved, the one voice was suddenly many voices, eyes that had been clear and gleaming a moment ago were suddenly as turbid as they had been before the bell jar had descended. Sigge raised one arm in a gesture of victory, grabbed the neck of a bottle in his bloody hand, called out *"Skål,"* and guzzled.

Hound Dog and Birgitta found themselves standing there alone, staring at each other.

THAT WAS THE first time they broke up. That fall they saw each other at a distance now and then, but they never spoke. Still, when the case about the Mjölby business finally came to court, Birgitta testified in Hound Dog's defense, saying that the old woman had been asking for it, that she had been quick to get in his way the minute Hound Dog started jabbing at the air. Her testimony hadn't helped, though, and she'd ended up going home alone. Hound Dog was sent straight to the reformatory—amazing what a rush they were in to get him behind bars, despite the fact that he'd spent nearly six months hanging around Motala waiting for the case to come to trial. That may have been just as well: it would have been hell if they'd let him go and he hadn't offered her a lift home, if after the trial he had stared at her just as vacantly and indifferently as he had when she stepped down from the witness stand.

She'd behaved very strangely that evening back in Motala, as if she were high, in spite of the fact that at that point in her life she didn't even know there was anything called hash or amphetamines. She'd begun by making her way to Gertrude's old apartment and pulling at the locked door, somehow having forgotten that Gertrude was dead, not remembering until the moment the door was opened by a perfect stranger. She'd backed up and run down the steps and right to the bus stop, taken the bus to the outskirts of town, where Old Lady Ella had lived. Not until she had her hand on the gate did she remember that here, too, nothing was what it once had been. The only light in the house was upstairs: Hubertsson still lived there, but of course Old Lady Ella was lying someplace in Linköping, mute as a fish. Birgitta remembered that nowadays she had an apartment of her own, a freezing cold little hovel in the old town. She went there but couldn't get herself to go to bed and spent the whole night sitting at the kitchen table, chain-smoking and staring at the glow of her space heater.

The next day she stayed home from work, and because this was the sixth time she'd stayed home without calling in sick, she got the sack. So damned unfair. How could she call in sick? She didn't even have a phone.

WHEN BIRGITTA GETS to the other side of the street, she pauses on the sidewalk to look around. The street has stopped rolling under her feet, but it's so narrow and crowded it makes her claustrophobic. It's cold, too. With tall buildings on either side, the whole street's in the shade. Motala doesn't look like this, Motala's a bright, airy place. There aren't any streetcars in Motala, either. Birgitta doesn't like streetcars, they scare her. Somehow she thinks it must be much easier to end up under a streetcar than under a bus, has even imagined how it must sound when the metal wheels of a streetcar run over your body. Squish, squish, squish. Sticky, extremely bloody goop. But the things she sees in her head never really happen, so since she's imagined it she will never be run over by a streetcar—unless this particular vision breaks the magic spell. You never know. If you don't believe the things you imagine will really happen, maybe they will . . .

Shit. Best not to think at all.

So what became of Margareta? She can't just have gone up in smoke and floated off. She's probably trying to stay out of sight in a doorway or a shop somewhere nearby. That would be just like her.

Margareta is actually completely incomprehensible. Either she's a fake through and through or she's out of her mind. Christina is easier; she's more consistently snotty and vicious. You know what to expect of her. But Margareta can be sweet as sugar at times, the best friend anyone could have, giggling and laughing and talking and having fun, only to bare her teeth like some fucking rottweiler and bite, one second later. Hundreds of times she has persuaded Birgitta she'll be there for her, that there's nothing in the world she'd rather do than treat her former foster sister a little kindly, and then she has bitten—*snap*—and walked away with her nose in the air. But she knows how to do it: it's easy to forget how shitty she really is when she cocks her head and seems so incredibly decent.

What business is it of hers if Birgitta worked the streets of Salt Flats for a while? Does it have anything to do with her? And why did it upset her so much to talk about it now? It's ancient history, should be barred by statute. Somewhere along the line Birgitta's read or heard that your body is completely renewed every seven years, in which case there isn't a single fingernail or strand of hair, not a single patch of skin on her body that's the same as the girl who worked the Salt Flats. Suddenly she's furious. That's right! She's an entirely different being today; those snobs can't blame the Birgitta of today for what happened to Ella. And, anyhow, wouldn't the old lady have been dead long ago no matter what? Could they possibly imagine she would've lived forever if it hadn't been for Birgitta? Didn't Ella herself play any part in what happened? Yeah! But now she's going to tell Margareta the whole truth; now she's going to force the bitch to listen and to admit that it wasn't Birgitta's fault!

She stops outside a shop window and looks in. Maybe Margareta went into this fancy dress shop and is hiding in a dressing room. It's an expensive enough place to satisfy a snob; there's a blouse in the window for twelve hundred crowns. Birgitta can just imagine the look on the face of Ulla, her welfare officer, if Birgitta waltzed into her office in a blouse like that, but she guesses it's an everyday thing for somebody like Margareta. She can probably throw thousand-crown bills right and left, as if they were small change. Not to mention Christina: when she'd turned up in the courtroom to testify against Birgitta, she'd had on a suit that was literally shouting money, which didn't prevent it from being both dowdy and ugly. In addition to which she was wearing three heavy gold bracelets. Birgitta had stared at them throughout Christina's testimony, trying to figure out how much speed she could get if she hocked them.

She pushes the door open and takes a couple of steps into the shop. It's empty, there isn't even a salesperson. She stops and looks around. Where are the dressing rooms?

A drapery at the back sways, and a thin young woman emerges, hastily trying to swallow what's in her mouth. A typical harassed shop slave trying to get a quick bite between customers. But this one has the highlighted hair of a real upper-class bitch, and a spinal column so straight she's almost tipping over backward.

"Yes?" she asks, raising her eyebrows. It's clear she doesn't consider Birgitta a potential customer, she's talking with her mouth full. She doesn't even look frightened: her raised eyebrows are stuck as if they were glued there, half an inch below her hairline. Just at that moment Birgitta catches a glimpse of her own image in a mirror on the far wall. Her hair is straggly, her face ashen, her thighs heavy, thick as tree trunks.

"I'm sorry, but we don't allow smoking in here," the woman says without lowering her eyebrows. "And we don't normally accept requisition forms from the welfare office."

Birgitta opens her mouth to answer, but nothing comes out. Christ! Why the hell did she ever walk into this place? Margareta's nowhere to be seen. She twirls around, pulls the door open with a jolt, hears a little bell ring and the woman telling her to have a good day.

She's seasick again, the street is rising and falling under her feet. She has to lean against a building so as not to collapse, and suddenly all her energy seems to vacate her body. Her knees are buckling, and the rest of her would like nothing better than to go along with them, just fall, lie right down on the heaving street and fall asleep.

If she just weren't in so much pain! She presses her hand to her abdomen and stumbles on. It's good she's in pain, it's keeping her awake. This time of year it's dangerous to let yourself lie down and fall asleep out of doors, you can freeze to death. No one would come along and put a blanket over her or stick a pillow under her head, the Svenssons would just step right over her and pretend they didn't even see her. The only person she can count on is number one, so she leans her back against a shop window and rests against the glass with her arms supporting her. She's just going to stand here like this for a little while, then she'll muster her strength and go on looking for Margareta.

Someone opens the shop door next to her and comes out onto the sidewalk. At first Birgitta can't even get herself to open her eyes and look, but once it seems clear that the person isn't about to walk away, she peeks out through a little slit. There's Margareta, standing in front of her pulling on her gloves. There's a paper bag hanging over her arm. She's been buying flowers.

"Hand over my cigarettes," she says. "And by the way, it's no use putting on that pathetic face. I'm not going to feel sorry for you anyway."

FEEL SORRY FOR her? Had Birgitta ever asked anyone to feel sorry for her? Never. Not once, man.

And yet she's been treated like a factory reject all her life, as if she were lame or hunchbacked, deaf or dumb. Ella and Christina are actually the only ones who never felt sorry for her. And Grandma of course. Grandma spent her whole life in a rage, never feeling sorry for anyone, just laughing that little cackling snicker of hers and saying that life was actually pretty fair. Most people got precisely what they deserved. Particularly on the last leg of their journey.

Sometimes Birgitta wakes up at night and thinks she hears that laugh, but of course she's only imagining it. Her grandma's been dead for donkey's years, and Birgitta can't really conceive of her as a ghost. She always snorted with contempt at the ghost stories Gertrude came home with, and there was no reason to think she was any different after her death. She's probably sitting on some cloud, lips pinched, arms crossed over her chest: if she says there's no such thing as a ghost, there isn't, and she has no intention of riding a broomstick just because somebody tells her to.

Still, for all her bitterness, Grandma did a lot of laughing. Like in the mornings, when she stood in front of the mirror combing her hair: "And a very good morning to you," she always said to her reflection, with a laugh. "Don't you look young and chipper today?"

Birgitta used to watch her from the wooden kitchen settle. When she was really little, she thought it strange that Grandma considered herself young and chipper; she couldn't see anything chipper about that sagging body and that pale, doughy face. Not even her hair was pretty, although Grandma herself seemed so proud of it. When she let out her night braid and ran her hands through it, it just fell dull and flat down her back. It had no particular color. Many years later, when Birgitta was at some rehab center, she happened to turn on the TV and hear an American astronaut say that the strangest thing about the surface of the moon was that it wasn't any particular color, and the first thing she thought of was her grandma, a woman whose hair was the same shade as the surface of the moon.

Grandma never devoted much time to her hair, though. She just smoothed it over the top of her head and twisted a tight little bun at the neck. Then she pulled on her old boots and went out to look at the railway tracks.

Grandpa was a trackman, and they lived in a little red cottage right by the rails, somewhere in the endless farmlands of Östergötland, half a mile from the big road, and three miles from the nearest farm, which was more like a manor than a farm, really. The manor property extended all the way to their cottage fence. Grandma told her that the proprietor had children, but that she shouldn't get her hopes up. They didn't let their kids play with workers' brats.

She wasn't allowed to play alone out in the garden, either; it was too dangerous. She might wander onto the tracks any time, the way she had done once when she was little. Grandma had found her lying on one of the crossties with her nose to the tarred timber. The tracks were already humming; her grandma had grabbed her up just in the nick of time. Birgitta would've been a dead kitten if she hadn't had her grandma, who never let her forget it.

When they got back to the cottage that day, Birgitta spoke her first words, as Grandma often reminded her. First she'd had just as hard a licking as she deserved, after which she'd stood in the middle of the floor and screamed: " 'Gitta not bad!"

Grandma said she was an odd kid. She'd never heard of a child starting to talk like that. Most children said ma-ma and da-da for ages before they could put words together. But not Birgitta: she'd kept her mouth clamped firmly shut until she was more than three, and then had spoken full sentences from the very outset. And she was odd about walking, too. She just teetered around hanging on to Grandma's apron strings, until one day when Grandma got tired of stumbling over her and took her apron off. Birgitta didn't notice, she just toddled on across the kitchen floor, quick as a bunny, without falling down or hurting herself at all. But the minute Grandma took the apron away, she tipped right over and cried her lungs out. It was as if she didn't think she could walk without that rag to hold on to.

That was about all Birgitta remembered from her years in her grand-parents' cottage. It was almost as if she'd spent six years sitting in that wooden settle doing nothing. She didn't see much of her grandpa. He slept late in the mornings, and when he finally got up he was a busy man and didn't come home until supper. Birgitta imagined he spent all day rid-ing the rails on his inspection car. She'd would've liked to have gone along, but she wasn't allowed to—it was no place for kids.

Grandpa had three crooked fingers on one hand that he couldn't straighten out. Once he'd held Birgitta on his lap, and she'd grabbed his bent ring finger and tried to force it up, but she couldn't. His fingers had stiffened long ago; his hand was more like a claw. When Gertrude came to visit she whispered to Birgitta that the old man had only himself to blame, he'd severed the tendons in his fingers once when he was drunk and angry and had overturned the kitchen table. The floor had been cov-ered with shards of china and glass, and he fell down in the mess and cut himself. Grandma just let him lie there; it was precisely what he deserved.

Birgitta liked it when Gertrude came. It was as if the air and the light in the cottage changed the minute she appeared in the doorway, as if her blond hair made everything brighter. Once she had on a white suit, too, with a tight-fitting jacket down to her slim waist, and a long skirt, billow-ing like a princess's. She had a blue blouse under the jacket, and a little hat with violets on it. Birgitta thought they smelled like real flowers when Gertrude bent over to hug her. But Grandma didn't like Gertrude's new suit; she just glanced quickly at it and then turned back to the stove. "If you've got any sense in your head you'll change before your father gets home," she said. "He's not an idiot. He'll know right away where you got the money for that outfit."

Birgitta had slid down off the settle and was following Gertrude up the stairs to the attic room. Gertrude always slept in the attic when she came home, despite the fact that it was freezing cold in the winter. She didn't mind freezing if that was what she had to do to get away from those sour-pusses, she'd say, making a face that always made Birgitta laugh. But now it was summer and the room was hot, so hot the timber walls had begun to exude the smell of resin. Gertrude opened the window wide and sat down on the bed, lighting a cigarette. "Oh my God," she said, giving her little hat such a hard push it went askew. "Here we go again, back to the Middle Ages . . ."

Birgitta didn't know what she meant, whether there really was a different age here than in Motala, where Gertrude lived and worked, but she nodded eagerly and stuck her hands between her knees, sitting on the wooden chair next to the bed.

Gertrude tweaked her nose and smiled. "I'd never come here if it weren't for you," she said. "You're my little angel, you know . . ."

Suddenly she stuck her cigarette in the corner of her mouth and opened her arms wide. "Come here! I'm going to love you a bushel and a peck, and cover you in kisses!"

Birgitta had hoped Gertrude would put the cigarette out before she started kissing her, but she forgot. She even forgot to take it out of her mouth before embracing Birgitta. Birgitta gave a little yelp and cupped her hand over her cheek.

"Good grief!" said Gertrude with a laugh. "Did I burn you?"

"Just a little."

She'd hoped Gertrude would go on kissing her when she'd stubbed out her cigarette, but she didn't. Instead, she just got up off the low-slung mattress and unbuttoned her jacket. "I'd better change, then," she said, taking down a hanger from the hook on the wall. "Wouldn't want the old man to have a fit. . . . Look and see if he's coming!"

Birgitta got to her knees on the rib-backed chair and leaned out the window. The yard looked much nicer from above than from the kitchen window. From here you couldn't tell the lilacs were past their prime, they still looked moist and fresh. The last white petals of cherry blossoms fluttered like little butterflies through the air, looking really pretty and not at all as messy and untidy as Grandma made them out to be. On the embankment the wild chervil had begun to bloom, and if you squinted it looked like the grass was covered with lace. Birgitta liked wild chervil, but she wasn't allowed to pick it. Grandma called it a weed. If you picked it and brought it inside, the blossoms fell to the table, covering it with fine, white pollen. Grandma had enough to do picking up after Grandpa and Birgitta as it was, and she certainly wasn't about to pick weeds indoors on top of that.

It smelled good outside. The sun had heated up the crossties, and the whole railway line smelled of tar. Birgitta inhaled the perfume, nearly swallowing it to keep hold of it, but at the same time she felt the dull throb of a little headache starting behind her forehead. It was strange how she still liked the scent of the crossties, although it always made her head hurt.

"I don't see him," she said, turning around and plopping back down onto the chair.

Gertrude was standing at the little mirror on the wall, combing her hair, in nothing but her slip. The suit was on a hanger on the hook behind her, the skirt billowing along the wall like an upside-down blossom. That was it, it looked like a tulip in full bloom, a tulip with white petals that would soon fall off and blow away in the wind.

"Fine," said Gertrude, bending toward the mirror to examine her face, trying to get one of the curls on her forehead to behave.

"Sixes," she said, spinning around. "Do you like them?"

"I can't do numbers yet," Birgitta answered.

Gertrude laughed. "I mean the way my bangs curl. Can't you see it? I have two sixes on my forehead. The latest style."

Birgitta was ashamed. How dumb of her not to know that. But Gertrude didn't seem to mind, just looked back in the mirror, fluttering her eyebrows and giving her sixes a last slick. "Lennart thinks they're terrific, anyway."

Birgitta looked up. "Who's that?"

Gertrude raised her shoulders, as if her whole white body were cooing. "My new fellow. A real looker. Nice guy, too."

She sat back down by Birgitta and took her hand. "Can you keep a secret?"

Birgitta nodded gravely.

"It's top secret, not a word to the sourpusses, okay?" Gertrude whispered. "We're going to get married in the fall, me and Lennart."

Birgitta gasped.

Gertrude leaned forward, coming so close Birgitta could feel her breath on her cheek. "He already knows about you, I've told him. He says he doesn't mind, that he'd be happy to have you live with us when you get a little bigger. He likes kids."

She was quiet for a minute, listening as if she was afraid somebody was eavesdropping from out on the attic stairs. She lowered her voice even further. "He's going to get a divorce; they only have a few months to go on their waiting period. And he's going to keep the house; it's a real beauty, three bedrooms and indoor plumbing. He's even got a fridge."

Birgitta nodded. She'd seen pictures of refrigerators in *Look,* she knew what they were.

"I'll be a housewife, Lennart thinks that's best. He wants someone to look after him full-time. We're going to really live it up. You'll have your own bedroom, the tiny one behind the kitchen would be perfect for you . . ."

She let go of Birgitta's hand to light another cigarette, waved to extinguish the match, then spoke in a more normal conversational tone. "But it's all secret. If you so much as breathe a word of it to the sourpusses, you'll have to stay where you are. Got that?"

Birgitta nodded. Her lips were sealed. She got it.

ALL FALL SHE sat with her nose to the windowpane, waiting. She knew just what it would be like. One day Gertrude and Lennart would come walking down the path from the big road. Gertrude would be wearing a bridal gown with a tulle veil, Lennart would be wearing a tux. He'd be tall and handsome, with a white carnation in his buttonhole . . .

One day she decided to draw Gertrude's wedding; that wasn't tattling. Grandma muttered when she asked for drawing paper but eventually wiped her hands on her apron and gave her a pencil and a piece of stationery. Birgitta sat down at the kitchen table looking determined. She knew just how she wanted to draw it. She'd seen plenty of brides and grooms in *Look.*

But her drawing didn't end up anything like the pictures in *Look.* Gertrude came out far too large, and Lennart appeared very strange, she'd had to draw his legs apart so the tails would show, but he looked like he had a bag dangling between his legs. Birgitta threw the pencil to the floor and covered her eyes with her hands; suddenly she felt she was going to burst into tears.

"What kind of behavior is that? You pick that pencil right up!"

GERTRUDE CAME FOR Christmas, but not in a bridal gown. She wasn't even wearing her white suit, just a brown coat and a blue scarf. Maybe it was the scarf that kept the light from changing that time: the kitchen remained just as wintry and dim after her arrival as it had been before.

Birgitta went up to the attic room with her, but Gertrude hardly seemed to notice. She was cold, pulled her hands up into the sleeves of her cardigan as she sat down on the bed.

Birgitta hesitated for a moment before whispering her question: "May I see the ring?"

Gertrude pulled herself into a ball and stared dubiously at Birgitta. "What ring?"

"Your married ring."

Gertrude frowned and pushed her bangs off her forehead. Her sixes were straight. "Oh, that. . . . Didn't work out. He went back to his wife. They always do."

IN SPITE OF which, Birgitta got to move to Motala the next summer. She was going to start first grade, so she couldn't go on living in a cottage in the middle of nowhere, Grandma said. The nearest school was miles and miles away, and there was no school bus. "Besides which I've done above and beyond the call of duty already," she said, extending Birgitta's suitcase to Gertrude. "You'll have to take over yourself, now."

Gertrude didn't take the suitcase right away. Grandma just stood there holding it out to her for ages before she sighed and gave in.

"But I have such a tiny place," she said. "And I work at least three nights a week."

"Well, I guess you'll have to get yourself a different job," said Grandpa. He'd just filled his pipe and was meticulously folding away his tobacco pouch and reaching out for the matches across the kitchen table.

"GOD!" SAID GERTRUDE indignantly as they walked down to the bus stop on the main road. "The old man's nuts, if you ask me. He's still living in the nineteenth century."

Birgitta scurried along. The elastic in one of her socks was broken, the sock was sliding down and rolling into a little ball under her foot, but she didn't dare stop to pull it up. She didn't want to fall behind and have to go back to the cottage; she wanted to go along with Gertrude to Motala, in spite of the fact that she wouldn't have a room of her own. Gertrude had told her she had only a studio apartment with a little kitchenette. Birgitta didn't really know what that was. All she knew was that she'd rather live in a outhouse with Gertrude than anyplace else.

"Do you know what he said yesterday?" Gertrude asked, setting their suitcases down. "He said being a waitress was no better than being a cigar girl. And when I asked him what a cigar girl was he said it was a kind of a floozy they had in Norrköping when he was young. Can you believe it?"

Birgitta had caught up by the time Gertrude started walking again. Her shoes were already gray with dust, her high heels sinking deep into the gravel. "Cigar girl my eye! Next thing we know he'll be claiming I go around in laced boots and stays."

"Damn the old man," Birgitta whispered tentatively.

"Right you are," said Gertrude. "He's a damned old fool."

AT HER GRANDPARENTS' cottage, Birgitta wasn't allowed to be outside, in Motala she wasn't allowed to be inside.

"Can't you go out for a while?" Gertrude asked the next day when she got home from work and had kicked off her shoes.

"Go out?" Birgitta asked.

It hadn't occurred to her that it would be all right to go out alone in such a big city as Motala. She had spent the day while Gertrude was at work exploring the apartment. She'd opened every single dresser drawer and rummaged through the piles of underwear and scarves, nylons and necklaces. Then she'd opened every single cupboard in the kitchenette, stolen a few raisins out of a red box and two sugar cubes from the sugar bowl, after which she went into the bathroom because she needed to pee. She stayed in there for nearly an hour. It was fun to flush, almost like magic. She'd been in a water closet only twice before, and on both occasions it had been Grandma who'd pulled up the little black knob, and Birgitta hadn't really been able to see what happened. Today she'd floated little pieces of toilet paper, watched them swirl and dance, only to be sucked down the pipe and vanish.

Gertrude threw herself down on the bed on her back, and the bedsprings creaked under her. "Yes, go out and play, isn't that what kids are supposed to do?"

Birgitta's mouth hung open. "But where do I go?"

Gertrude frowned in annoyance. "Jeez! Go out in the courtyard. Or to the newspaper stand or something."

She dug through the pockets of her white jacket and fished up a coin. "Here you go! Buy yourself some candy!"

Birgitta had never bought candy before, but she knew what it was. Now and then Grandpa would bring rock candy home when he'd been to the liquor store, and Grandma kept a little bowl of hard candy on the top shelf of the pantry. But where was the newspaper stand? Out in the courtyard, she hesitated, looking around. There was no newspaper stand there, nothing but rubbish cans and a few clotheslines, heavy with white sheets. There were some children playing over by the archway out to the street, climbing on a gray metal frame. One of the boys pulled a lever on the side, and a pole rose and fell at the top. A little girl was climbing on something that looked like a lattice.

Suddenly a window opened in the building nearest the street, and a woman's face emerged. "Hey kids, get offa that carpet-beating rack! The courtyard's no playground!"

BUT A LITTLE while later they were all sitting on the carpet-beating rack again. Nobody went very far beyond Birgitta's reach, because no kid in the whole building had ever been given an entire crown for candy before. You were lucky if you could beg enough small change off your parents for a couple pieces of chocolate money, a handful of wine gums, or, on occasion, a little box of salted licorice. The salted licorice lasted longest, one of the girls said ecstatically as the whole gang walked down to the newspaper stand. You poured the tiny black drops right into your mouth, spread them out over your tongue, pressed your tongue to the roof of your mouth, and sucked. After a few minutes you could feel little strings of black saliva running out of the corners of your mouth—not much, it just looked like a little shadow. That was when you were supposed to swallow your spit, let the salty liquid flow down your throat. After you swallowed, you could start to chew. By that time the licorice was soft, almost a little slimy.

But Birgitta didn't buy any salted licorice, just marshmallows and jujubes, toffee and chocolate pralines. And now she'd closed up the bag and was holding it tight. The air was warm although it was already dusk, and the voices of the other children were mixing in her mind with the sound of a car out on the street. A little thrill of pleasure coursed through her veins. It was evening and she was outside, she was sitting on a carpet-beating rack in the middle of Motala with a whole bag of sweets on her lap.

She began to be confused, however, a little later when one window after another opened, in both the building on the street side and the one on the courtyard, and a woman's voice called out that supper was ready. She couldn't help but laugh at them—they looked like Grandpa's cuckoo clock as they leaned out the windows, each woman a cuckoo with a painted beak. One after the other the children climbed down from the rack and disappeared inside. Only one of the older boys dared stay a little while extra to see if she would give him one more piece of candy.

When he'd gone, Birgitta sat there for a little while longer, dangling her feet. Maybe Gertrude would open the window soon and call to her that supper was ready. It didn't matter if it took her a while. She wasn't hungry anymore.

GERTRUDE HADN'T BEEN able to afford a bed for her, so Birgitta slept in the easy chairs. Every evening they shifted the furniture around, then moved it back every morning; during the day the easy chairs stood on either side of a little brass-topped table—a real Turkish smoking table, Gertrude told her—but in the evening they put them together, foot to foot, making them almost like a little bed. Birgitta couldn't stretch out all the way, but she didn't mind. She liked sleeping in the easy chairs, she liked everything at Gertrude's.

Sometimes Gertrude didn't feel well. She'd come home from work with aching feet and in a foul temper. That meant some snotty guests had treated her badly, not enjoyed their meal or been showing off and sneering at her. The women were worst: no one was more horrid than a snobby woman, she wanted Birgitta to know that. But in reality they had no reason to turn their noses up at her; most of them were ugly as sin and their men were just like all men, pinching Gertrude's bottom and fondling her breasts the minute their old ladies were looking in the other direction.

When Gertrude felt like talking about things, she let Birgitta lie next to her on the bed. Birgitta loved that. Gertrude smelled good, like perfume and tobacco, and sometimes there was even a tickle of fancy liqueur on her breath. When Gertrude needed to dump her cigarette ashes, Birgitta would run across to the low, brass-topped smoking table and get the ashtray, and when it needed emptying she would take it over to the kitchen sink. Gertrude said she was a good girl then, in fact the only nice person she'd seen in years, except for Lennart perhaps, but he wasn't really nice because he'd let her down about marriage and gone back to his wife. Though, actually, Gertrude thought she still had him hooked, since he always turned such longing gazes on her when he brought his clients to lunch at the City Hotel . . .

They spent hours like that on the bed; then suddenly Gertrude would realize she had to be at work in a little while. Birgitta would help her get ready fast, put some water on to boil for her coffee and make her some sandwiches, while Gertrude ran around the room searching for a pair of nylons with no runs and a coin that would fit in her broken garter belt and hold her stocking up. Then she'd put on her white uniform jacket and her black uniform skirt, laugh at Birgitta's thick, uneven bread slices, have a quick cup of coffee, and rush out the door. After which Birgitta was on her own and could do as she pleased, as long as she didn't go dragging a bunch of dirty kids into the apartment and make a mess.

They seldom had a meal together. Gertrude would eat at work, and sometimes she'd bring a little container of something home to Birgitta. The problem was that since they didn't have a refrigerator, Birgitta had to eat whatever Gertrude brought right away, since it wouldn't keep. Sometimes Gertrude worked nights, and that meant Birgitta would have dinner for breakfast.

It felt a little weird to sit at the Turkish smoking table in her nightgown taking little bites of warmed-over brisket.

THE NIGHT BEFORE Birgitta's first day of school, Gertrude didn't get home until about three, she told her afterward. But the minute she woke up Birgitta realized Gertrude must have been ever so tired, because she'd fallen asleep in her clothes and forgotten to set the alarm. Birgitta was just lucky enough to wake up anyway at a quarter to eight and remember that she was supposed to be in the classroom for roll call at eight. She tried to wake Gertrude, but she seemed quite lost to the world—just turned on her back, threw one arm over her head, and started to snore.

Luckily, Birgitta was wearing her best nightgown, the seersucker one that almost looked like a dress. Grandma had made it from a remnant, which explained why it was only knee length and not long like all her other nightgowns. All Birgitta had to do was pull on her cardigan and put on her shoes and socks and she could rush right out the door like Gertrude.

She knew where the school was, all she had to do was run to the end of the street and turn right. Bosse had shown her. He lived in the building on the street side, and they were going to be in the same class. He must be the one walking ahead of her holding his mother's hand, though Birgitta wasn't absolutely sure. Bosse's hair usually hung over his collar like a little ducktail, whereas this boy's neck was nearly clean-shaven, his skin white and shiny under the little hair there was.

But she called "Bosse!" anyway, because by the time she got to the gate outside the school yard she was feeling a little uncertain. The other evening the school yard had been empty, the asphalt black. Now it was dotted with people. Birgitta had never seen so many people in one place in all her life, despite the fact that she'd been living in Motala for almost a whole month now.

The little boy in front of her with his mother was just turning in through the latticed gate. He turned around and looked at her.

"Bosse!" Birgitta shouted again, waving her hand, since now she was sure it really was Bosse, in spite of his haircut, and the white shirt and tie he was wearing with his shorts. His mother had a hat and coat on, and was clutching her handbag to her body, as if afraid someone was going to steal it. She glanced quickly at Birgitta and burst out: "Oh my God! You poor child!"

THAT WAS HOW it all began. Bosse's mother made the most of the situation, leaning conspiratorially toward other mothers and whispering anxiously, shaking her head in resignation when the teacher called Birgitta's name, and staying on in the classroom to exchange a few words with her as she pulled on her white gloves. She had a terribly ugly coat, huge as a tent and the color of lingonberries with milk. Birgitta had often had lingonberries and milk for supper when she lived with her grandparents, and she always had to shut her eyes to be able to get the last few bites down. The color was so ugly it made her sick. Bosse's mother was so ugly it made her sick, too.

Three days later was the first time Gertrude was one of the cuckoos in the cuckoo clock, leaning out the window like all the other mothers to call Birgitta. It was a little odd, in that she'd only just come home from work and told Birgitta to go out and play, saying she was so damn tired and had such a bad headache she had to have some time to herself for a nap. But when Birgitta opened the apartment door, she was putting on her shoes. That was unusual. She usually went around indoors in her stocking feet, since her feet were always so tender and swollen after work. Her hair was ruffled, too, and she cast a sullen glance at Birgitta before nodding toward the room and putting her finger to her lips. Birgitta wasn't supposed to say anything; she got that message, although she couldn't imagine why Gertrude looked so angry.

Birgitta leaned against the doorframe, looking in. There was a woman in one of the easy chairs, wearing a blue suit and a white blouse with the buttons done all the way up to the neck. She didn't notice Birgitta, was rummaging around in the brown leather briefcase on her lap. She extracted an eyeglass case and gave the glasses a thorough wiping before putting them on.

"How do you do, young lady?" she said. "You must be Birgitta. My name's Marianne. I'm from the child welfare authorities."

IT WAS BIRGITTA'S fault, Gertrude kept repeating afterward. If she just hadn't been dumb enough to go waltzing off to school with nothing but her nightgown on, that Marianne would never have turned up in their lives. As it was, she came around almost every week, and after some time she had the gall to start rummaging around in their drawers wanting to inspect Birgitta's underwear, or going into the bathroom to make sure Birgitta had a toothbrush of her own. Which she didn't. Gertrude said it was just a momentary lapse, that her old toothbrush was worn out and she was going to buy a new one any day, but it wasn't true. Birgitta hadn't brushed her teeth once since coming to Motala, and Marianne seemed to know it. She grimaced when she opened Birgitta's mouth to inspect it, saying she'd tell the school to give Birgitta priority for an appointment with the school dentist.

The dentist told her not to fuss when she recoiled from the Novocain needle. Then he pulled out three of her back teeth, stuffed something white into her mouth, and sent her back to school. The white stuff got all spongy after a while and Birgitta stopped and spit it out on the sidewalk. It wasn't white any longer but red with blood, and she felt more blood welling up in her mouth. She leaned forward and spit, but that didn't help; the blood just went on running and running. If she didn't want to stand here spitting blood forever, she'd have to swallow. The very thought made the sidewalk sway under her feet; she sniveled and bent forward again, picked up the bloody wad of cotton and put it back in her mouth. It was a little dirty now, but she didn't mind. At least it kept her mouth from filling up with blood.

That evening she refused to go out and play; her mouth hurt now that the Novocain had worn off. Gertrude just snorted, mixed some soda pop with vodka, and told her she only had herself to blame.

Still, she seemed to realize Birgitta was really in pain. She put the easy chairs together especially early and let Birgitta go to bed, even took the empties out to the garbage herself when it got dark. Birgitta always went to great pains nowadays to get Gertrude's bottles, even the deposit ones, out of sight. She didn't want Marianne snooping around in the cupboard under the sink and counting them, because she'd already mentioned the temperance board, though only in the vaguest of terms.

When Gertrude came in from outside, Birgitta took her thumb out of her mouth, shut her eyes, and pretended she was asleep. She'd made up her mind. The next day she was going to slug that Bosse right in the nose.

'Cause it was all his fault. His and his ugly mother's.

Birgitta blinks and blinks again, as if she's been woken up. "What cigarettes?" she asks.

"Mine," says Margareta, frowning. "The ones you pinched a while back."

Margareta straightens the shoulder strap on her bag and extends a hand. She's almost good-looking despite that irate face she's making, looks somehow firm and dependable. Like solid marble. Strange, really. When they were young Margareta wasn't much of a looker—flat as a pancake and pudgy-cheeked as a little girl until she was way into her teens— so how can she be better-looking now that she's pushing fifty? It must be the money, the fact that she can afford miracle creams and new clothes whenever she wants. Every stitch she has on looks new: the white collar on her sheepskin jacket doesn't have a single stain, her jeans still seem stiff. Birgitta likes stiff jeans, too, though you'd never know it. Hers are worn and shapeless.

A perfectly fresh memory flits through her mind. That reflection. What Birgitta saw in the mirror in that snotty shop was a welfare case.

Ten years ago you couldn't tell by looking at her. Not just because she was dealing then, she was already on welfare, too. In those days, though, if your jacket was getting a little worn, you just showed them your frayed cuffs and they let you get a new one. These days they make you go around in your old clothes until they're in tatters. Probably so everybody will be able to tell how absolutely splendid people like Christina and Margareta are and how phenomenally worthless other people are. Torn quilted jackets for the riffraff, sheepskin jackets and leather handbags for the snobs.

Birgitta's not a snob, though, she wouldn't wear ladylike suits or sheepskin jackets even if she were rolling in money. Instead, she'd buy a black leather jacket from that immigrant guy who has a stall on the town square in Motala on Saturdays. His jackets are great-looking and not expensive, either, but Ulla, her welfare officer, still refuses even to discuss the matter when Birgitta brings it up. She says there's no reason Birgitta can't mend her quilted jacket. Or wash it. Ulla's big boss has decided the time has come for some belt tightening, in case Birgitta doesn't know it, and Ulla—wimp that she is—always does as she's told. Consequently, Birgitta's belt has been in just about the tightest hole for some time now. They barely give her enough to put bread and butter on the table. But maybe it's one of those blessings in disguise Gertrude used to talk about, since the very thought of food has started to turn Birgitta's stomach. Though she wouldn't at all mind having a little extra cash for calories in liquid form. In fact, at this very moment she'd give her right arm for a beer.

"Well?" says Margareta.

Birgitta blinks again. What's she talking about? And why does she look so grouchy? Margareta takes a deep, impatient breath and leans forward, putting her face right up to Birgitta's. "May I please have my cigarettes?" she asks, enunciating every syllable with perfect distinction, as if there were something wrong with Birgitta, as if she were unable to hear or understand.

"What cigarettes?" Birgitta asks back, recoiling against the shop window and shutting her eyes. She's tired. Very tired.

"Cut it out!" Margareta hisses. "You took my Marlboros with you from the restaurant. I want them back!"

Oh, yeah. Now she remembers. Of course she will return this woman's cigarettes to her, she could probably never survive such a substantial financial loss. And if she did survive she'd be sure to harass Birgitta for another thirty years, plague her with police reports and anonymous letters, stand outside her apartment at night shouting: it was all your fault, it was all your fault! Naturally she will return her cigarettes.

Eyes still shut, Birgitta gropes around her jacket pocket, which also has a hole in it, but just a little one. The cigarettes are still there. She pulls out the pack and extends it, feeling the air for Margareta's hand but still too tired to open her eyes. Or rather, still not wanting to open her eyes and see that purse-lipped snob glower right in her face. She's sure Margareta's going to demand to be reimbursed for the couple of pathetic smokes Birgitta's already consumed. In which case Birgitta will have to propose a debt clearance plan, since she doesn't have the money to buy cigarettes very often. People like her have to make do with rolling their own, you know, if they're uppity enough to smoke at all.

Margareta snatches the pack, and Birgitta hears her unzipping her handbag and putting it away. Now she ought to walk away with her nose in the air, so Birgitta can open her eyes and look around, but she doesn't. Birgitta can still hear her breathing.

"Are you going to be all right now?" Margareta asks. Her voice is different, a little hesitant, not as shrill as a few moments ago.

Birgitta nods. She'll be fine, thank you, if Margareta will just be fucking kind enough to remove herself, her sheepskin jacket, her cigarettes, and her whole kit and caboodle faster than you can blink an eye. But Margareta doesn't get it, just places her hand on Birgitta's arm and gives her a little shake. "Hey," she says. "What's up with you now? You can't go to sleep right here on your feet . . ."

Well, you couldn't care less if I did, Birgitta thinks, but she doesn't say it, just stands there silently, eyes shut, back pressed to the shop window. The cold from the glass has started to penetrate right through her jacket and freeze her back. She shivers and changes position, pulling her hands up into her sleeves. Her fingers are rigid with the cold. And her feet are icy, too.

"All right, then," says Margareta with a sigh. "I'll give you a lift to Motala after all. But I don't want any fuss."

Birgitta opens her eyes. Who's gonna fuss? Does anyone intend to fuss? Not Birgitta Fredriksson, that's for sure.

No way, José.

MARGARETA IS RUSHING down Queen's Street as fast as her legs can carry her; Birgitta's loose shoes prevent her from keeping pace, so a little distance develops between them. And grows, fast.

Margareta's probably scurrying along like that intentionally, she probably wouldn't be caught dead walking alongside an old hooker. Birgitta snorts. As if Margareta was so much better herself. If she was wild enough to be letting a teacher screw her in high school, she must've had quite a few since then as well. Birgitta's been able to piece a few things together over the years; sometimes Margareta's phoned her, and every time she's talked about a man it's been a different one. She seems to have switched boyfriends about every six months, her whole life.

Margareta's already made it to the bridge before she notices how far behind Birgitta's lagging. She stops, takes a quick look around, then gets moving again. What's her hurry? Can't she see how Birgitta's staggering along like some damn Bambi in her Minnie Mouse heels? If she were as fucking nice and good-natured as she pretends to be, she'd let Birgitta wait on a park bench while she goes and gets the car.

Well, at least now she's waiting, over there at the crosswalk. Birgitta gets herself together to try to run, but she can't make it for more than a few steps. Shit. She's out of shape. It must be her goddamn liver. Or her lungs. Or her kidneys. Or her heart. When they let her out of the hospital a few weeks ago, the doctor said it was a miracle she could hold herself upright.

"It's thanks to my strong constitution," Birgitta had answered, since she couldn't say what she was really thinking. If she had, they'd have locked her right up in the nuthouse.

The doctor had laughed and turned toward his computer screen, pushed a button, and brought up her medical records. "I guess it is," he said, shaking his head. "But at this stage you need to think about taking things a little easier. At least if you want to get any older than you already are."

He was an unusually pleasant doctor, almost of Hubertsson's caliber, but he didn't get it, no more than any of the others had. Birgitta didn't plan on dying. Nor did she have the slightest intention of getting old, she didn't have a model for that. Gertrude hadn't even made it to thirty-five.

But there's no question about it, Gertrude never had Birgitta's constitution. You could tell by looking at her. She was so incredibly thin and transparent, she looked like that porcelain ballerina on Grandma's chest of drawers. That figurine was one of Grandma's most prized possessions. She'd boxed Birgitta's ears so hard there was a ringing in her head for hours the time she discovered Birgitta climbing up on a chair to touch it. It was not a toy!

Birgitta didn't even try to explain that she wasn't stupid enough to have wanted to play with the figurine, that all she wanted to do was look closely at the ballerina's china tutu, see what it felt like. She'd actually wanted to bite it, too, but there hadn't been time before Grandma caught her. So she just had to go on longing, in her total conviction that china tulle was as sweet as rock candy.

Once she'd wanted to take a taste of Gertrude, too. It was just before they moved her to Aunt Ella's, so she must have been in fourth grade by then. Gertrude didn't go out to work anymore; she'd been sacked from the City Hotel, and there was nowhere else in Motala that needed a waitress. Gertrude certainly had no intention of being a dishwasher at some greasy spoon, no matter how much Marianne and the other welfare dames harped on it. She was a professional waitress and proud of it. Not to mention the fact that she had marriage to Osvald in the pipeline. She was going to be a housewife in that two-bedroom apartment he was hoping for. And the first thing she intended to do when she got that ring on her finger was to tell Marianne and her whole crew to go straight to hell.

Birgitta was looking forward to the wedding, although she didn't like Osvald. He was such a big, clumsy type, the apartment felt too small for the three of them. And he had strange habits. He never said hello, and the minute he walked in the door he'd pull off his shoes and his sweaty socks and toss them over his shoulder, padding barefoot into their one room. He would sit down on one of the easy chairs and then not get up again all evening. But he still somehow had the most amazing ability to make a mess. Just a little while later there wasn't a clean glass in the house, all the ashtrays were overflowing, and the floor was rolling with empties.

Not that Birgitta was much of a cleaner in those days, either, but Osvald was a real pig, belching loudly and letting his ashes fall to the floor, grinning when he let out long, noisy farts that stank so much Birgitta had to open a window. In addition to which he never had the sense to leave, just sat on and on in that easy chair. Birgitta couldn't go to bed properly, had no choice but to make a little nest of clothes in a pile on the floor out in the hall and curl up as best she could. Osvald always woke her when he was leaving, pulling the pile out from under her, cursing because she was sleeping on his jacket.

When he left, Gertrude was always jumpy. She'd start sniffling and crying, hugging Birgitta and calling her her little angel, her only little friend in all the world. Everybody, even Osvald, the bastard, wanted to split them up, but Gertrude wasn't going to give in. She was a mother, wasn't she? He'd just have to accept that. And to a good mother, the love of her child always came before the love of a man. If Osvald wanted her, he'd have to take Birgitta in the bargain, because Gertrude couldn't survive without her angel, and Birgitta didn't want to be separated from her mamsi-mams, did she? Or maybe she did? Gertrude began to cry: yes, she probably did, Birgitta probably wished Gertrude was dead and buried. Because then Birgitta would be able to move in with one of those good families Marianne was always talking about, those families where she would be so well off, with a bed of her own and her own room and everything. And once she was there she would be quick to forget her poor little mamma and . . .

At that point Birgitta would not be able to hold back her own tears, they would well up in her eyes and start running down her cheeks when she blinked. She would sink to her knees, sniffling, alongside Gertrude's bed, hold her hand tight, and swear that she didn't want to be sent to any shitty foster home, that she didn't want a room of her own or her own bed. She hated them all, Osvald and Marianne, Bosse's mamma and her teacher. None of them understood how happy Birgitta was, that she had the dearest mamma in all the world. . . . Her body was racked with sobs, she spurted out the words along with big bubbles of saliva, but Gertrude didn't even seem to hear her. She just went on crying and screaming, pulled her hand out of Birgitta's and covered her face, her whole thin little body contorted with cramps.

"Oooooh yes you do," she would shout, kicking at the mattress, her head jerking this way and that. "Oooooh yes you do. You just want me to die, I know it. Everybody despises me! I know it, I know it. But I'll show you all, you'll see. Tomorrow when you go to school I'm going to kill myself, I swear it! I'll take the big kitchen knife and stab myself right in the stomach . . ."

Birgitta would throw herself at her, climbing up into her bed and putting her arms around her neck, as if to hold her down, as if to force her to remain alive. "Mamma," she'd cry, the words suddenly just rolling out. "Mamma, Mamma, Mamma . . . please don't die! Don't die on me, Mamma, please don't die!"

Gertrude would settle down when Birgitta pressed her damp cheek to her own and was crying just as hard as she was. Her legs would stop kicking, her head would stop jerking, and after a little while she wouldn't even be crying, just sniffling and shuddering every now and then, until her head sank slowly to the side and she fell asleep. Then Birgitta couldn't even sniffle herself, she had to swallow her tears, which formed a hard little lump in her throat. Otherwise Gertrude might wake up and be upset all over again.

Birgitta would lie perfectly still until she could no longer discern Gertrude's breathing. Then she would carefully untangle her arms from around Gertrude's neck and get up. She had things to do before she could

allow herself to go back to sleep. First she had to slice the bread for breakfast, then hide all the knives. They had only three, so that wouldn't have
been very hard to do if she just weren't trembling so hard. One she put
behind the water pipes in the cupboard under the kitchen sink, one in the
toilet tank, although it was quite hard to unscrew the flusher and remove
the top, the third one she hooked behind the mirror in the hall. One of
her first days at Old Lady Ella's she'd practically fainted when she opened
a kitchen drawer and peered down at eleven sharp knives—she'd counted
them in a fraction of a second—and the thought crossed her mind that
she'd have to find eleven different hiding places. But there was no need
in that house, of course. And at Gertrude's it gradually became a habit.
Gertrude herself never seemed to notice that the knives weren't there, or
that they turned up again when Birgitta got home from school.

Once she'd hidden the knives, she would clean up all the bottles, collecting them in a canvas bag she set under the coatrack in the hall. Every
morning on the way to school she would drop the bottles off at the
garbage can, then roll the empty bag up into a little ball and put it in her
schoolbag.

The women in the other apartments, who peeked out at her through
their shiny clean windows, undoubtedly thought she was throwing them
away, but she wasn't. She was just storing them behind the garbage cans
for the moment. They were worth money, and Birgitta wasn't enough of a
fool to let the opportunity to make some money pass her by. Because, although she loved Gertrude, she knew there wasn't much money in the
house, and Birgitta still craved candy from the newspaper stand. She had
such a sweet tooth she sometimes wondered whether there might be a
sugar mouse in her stomach, a nasty mouse with a long tail, demanding
to be fed, threatening and frightening her, declaring that he would sink
his gold teeth into Birgitta's intestines and tear them to bits if she didn't
nourish him.

Maybe it was the sugar mouse that drove her to take a taste of Gertrude one night. She'd just hidden the knives and cleaned up all the bottles, and she was standing by the Turkish smoking table rewarding herself
with a handful of sugar cubes.

Gertrude was sound asleep, had crept up over by the wall, one white
arm along her hips. Birgitta was watching her while the sugar cubes first
went all porous and then slowly melted in her mouth. The sugar mouse
hissed impatiently; it wanted something more, preferably chocolate, a

whole bar of milk chocolate, one that was sticky and soft after having been in the hot sun on the ledge of the newspaper stand. Or ice cream, yes, it would also be satisfied with vanilla ice cream, a whole carton of melting vanilla ice cream with thick waves of strawberry ripple, the kind that made the back of your mouth tingle with pleasure . . .

It was already getting light behind the window shade, the room was gradually getting lighter, too. The furniture and objects began to dissolve, went fuzzy and blurry around the edges, and Birgitta herself was no longer mistress of her body. She could feel her tongue exploring her teeth for the last crystals of sugar, her hands wiping away the snot from under her nose after all that weeping, her feet beginning to walk. It was as if she were walking through a sea, surrounded by water and light, everywhere, the whisper of waves driving her to walk to their beat, over to the bed.

Gertrude was sleeping deeply; she didn't notice when Birgitta lifted up her arm. Birgitta first stroked with her index finger along the fine, downy hairs on her forearm. The sugar mouse clawed anxiously at her stomach; every strand of hair on Gertrude's arm looked like cotton candy. She recalled the white fluff she'd been given once at an amusement park, and her mouth was suddenly full of saliva, her whole throat tickled and roared and itched with longing for something sweet . . .

Birgitta closed her eyes and let her tongue run right up Gertrude's arm in a wet caress, from her wrist to her shoulder. Then she carefully set her arm back down on her hip, straightened up, closed her eyes, and waited for the taste sensation that was sure to explode in her mouth any minute.

But Gertrude didn't taste of chocolate and vanilla. She tasted salty. Like salted licorice.

MARGARETA STARTS WALKING again the second Birgitta catches up with her; the light hasn't even turned green.

"Hang on," Birgitta pants, but Margareta's already halfway across the street.

Dammit to hell! Birgitta stumbles out into the street—fucking shit shoes! She tries to catch up again. Margareta's rushing on purpose, she's trying to get away from Birgitta! Because if she can't see Birgitta anywhere when she gets to her car, then she'll be able to just jump in and floor it without a second thought. Yes, that must be it, she can imagine it all, even imagine Margareta's vicious little smile a moment later as she drives right past a desperate, stranded Birgitta without a penny to her name, and pretends not to see her. She can even see Margareta wrinkle up her whole face in a look of surprise when Birgitta reminds her about it the next time they meet. What does she mean? She, Margareta, would never have broken a promise to Birgitta. She never would have let her down. Oh no, she'd waited and waited, but when Birgitta never turned up, she'd eventually had to get going. She was so, so sorry.

By that time Margareta has entered the park by the station, but Birgitta's still out there on the sidewalk. Her heart is pounding heavily, she feels like her chest is going to burst. Still, she has no choice but to rush on. This exertion may kill her, the little clot of blood that's been waiting to burst a vessel may be pumping right up to her heart or her brain.

Yes, that's it. She knows exactly what's going to happen, she can see it all: Birgitta Fredriksson puts her hand to her heart and stops in midstride, twirls around on one foot—the other is raised as if she were a dancer—stares for one instant up at the icy blue March sky, then crumples slowly to the ground. People gather from all directions, shouting with worried voices and wringing their hands. Is she dead? Oh, no, she can't be dead! She's Birgitta Fredriksson, who was once such a beauty! Birgitta, who would surely have become a famous photo model, a Swedish Anna Nicole Smith, if she had been young today. Ah, if only life had not treated her so cruelly!

SHE'S JUST TOYING with the idea. Actually, Birgitta doesn't believe in death. Not for a moment.

Of course she's imagined it a thousand times, the drama, the grief, the guilty consciences, the misery her departure from this earth would give rise to among the snobs and others, and still she is unable to believe that she will actually one day be dead, that she will cease to exist. Others may, but not herself. Birgitta Fredriksson will live for eternity, all else is inconceivable.

As a child she had attempted to explain this conviction to the grown-ups, but no one had taken her seriously. "I'll take a shovel with me into my coffin," she told her grandma. "And when everybody's left after the funeral I'll dig myself back up."

Grandma cackled her dry little laugh. "You won't be able to. Dead is dead, and can't do any digging."

"Oh, but I will."

Grandma threw her head back and laughed at an even higher pitch, which made the windowpanes in the cottage ring. This was obviously the funniest thing she'd heard in years. "You just wait and see," she cackled. "Just wait and see!"

Gertrude got angry. It was early one evening, she wasn't really drunk yet, and she raised herself from the bed on one elbow and hissed, "Are you out of your mind or what? What do you think's so damn special about you then? Why should you be the one to get away?"

Birgitta didn't answer. It was as if she had a little button inside, a little this-isn't-really-happening button she could push when Gertrude was angry. It never worked when Gertrude was crying and miserable, only when she was hissing and cursing. Like now.

"Chriiiist!" Gertrude shouted, sinking back to the pillow. "What did I do to deserve this? Tell me that. Here I lie in a pissy little apartment in a pissy little town without even enough money for the bare essentials, and on top of it all my kid turns out to be a loony! You just watch out, that's all I can say, because if you go around saying dumb things like that to people out there, Marianne will put you in the monkey house without a second thought. I just want you to know that!"

Old Lady Ella neither laughed nor shouted, just looked up from her lace-making pillow to stare at Birgitta for a moment. "Aha," she said then, looking back down, shifting a couple of bobbins at such speed that Birgitta's eyes couldn't even see what she was doing. "So you're immortal . . . how do you like that?"

Birgitta observed her through narrow eyes, waiting for her to go on, but she didn't. Ella just stuck a pin between her lips and bent closer to the pillow to see better.

"I'm going to keep one eye open," said Birgitta, "to see what happens."

Ella looked up and flashed her a smile. Birgitta cleared her throat impatiently. Stupid old woman! Say something already! She made a wicked face, raised her hands, splayed and crooked her fingers like a monster. "And if they try to bury me I'll howl like a banshee."

Ella took the pin out of her mouth and chuckled. "I don't doubt you will," she said. "But since you're not dead yet you might as well go wash up. Those hands of yours are filthy."

AND EVEN NOW, that's how Birgitta imagines death: a play in which she is both the heroine and the audience. She'll lie there in her coffin in full possession of her senses, her eyes just half closed so she can watch the people at her funeral, and when they've gone she'll open her coffin lid and sit up as if she's Dracula. She doesn't want cremation, as she's informed Ulla at the welfare office, but she has no high hopes that they'll respect her wishes. If Ulla's big boss tells her the local government's decided that all trash is to be incinerated, Ulla will see to it that they burn Birgitta up. That's why she's taped a note inside her closet door: "I want to be buried. Not cremated under any circumstances. Birgitta Fredriksson." She hopes the snobs will turn up at the last minute. Yes, she can just imagine it, imagine them finding the note, looking at each other with tears in their eyes—finally they realize how badly they've treated her—and then rushing to the crematorium at the cemetery, stopping the coffin just in time, as it's about to be pushed into the oven . . .

But it probably won't happen like that; Birgitta's sisters can't be relied on. And a few minutes from now, when people gather around Birgitta as she lies on the gravel path in the park as if crucified, there's at least one person who'll be conspicuous in her absence: Margareta. She'll probably just keep on rushing in the other direction. The fucking bitch!

Birgitta raises her voice, and from the depths of her lungs she gathers every noisemaking resource she possesses into one single roar: "HOOOOLLD IT!"

She hasn't shouted this loud in years, but she can still do it. It's as if she makes all of Norrköping come to a momentary halt, as if every engine ceases to idle, as if every conversation is disrupted for the few seconds it takes for the echo of her voice to ricochet between the old Standard Hotel and the community center. Birgitta leans forward, hands on her thighs, like a sprinter who's just crossed the finish line, and watches Margareta freeze to ice up there, watches her backbone straighten, watches her stand stock-still. Birgitta catches her breath, no it's more than that, she wheezes and her heart races so hard she feels the pulse in every inch of her body: in her head, her fingers, the varicose veins behind her knees. She can even feel her pulse in the lobes of her ears. You know you're tired when that happens. You've really earned a rest.

Now she hears Margareta's footsteps, hears the gravel rattle, hears the sound of the slush as she trips her modest snob's gait back toward Birgitta. "What is it?" she asks softly, as if she imagines she can lower the volume of Birgitta's scream retroactively by keeping her own voice down. "What are you shouting about?"

Birgitta's still there, hands on her thighs. She raises her head and makes a face. "Christ! What is this? The Norrköping-to-Motala marathon?"

Margareta tips to her heels a moment, looking away. "That might be good for you, actually. You seem a little out of shape."

What is with her? Can't she open her mouth today without uttering some cutting remark? She hasn't been this mean, when it comes right down to it, since the day Birgitta walked out of pike-jowled Stig's fancy home. Neither Margareta nor Christina had spoken a word to Birgitta during the weeks they had shared his rec room, and when Birgitta was leaving they didn't even answer when she said good-bye, just stared at her with vacant eyes. No wonder Birgitta was surprised a few months later when Margareta started writing to her. She thought they were enemies for life, but Margareta didn't seem to see it that way, since letter after letter, each longer than the last, started turning up in Birgitta's mailbox. Oh yes, now she remembered how Margareta had also turned up at her place in person, just a few months after she'd had the kid. Right. Now she remembered the whole thing, had a very clear picture of Margareta sitting at her kitchen table giving him a bottle . . .

Aha! That's why Margareta's being so bitchy today. She must've started thinking about the baby when they were sitting at that restaurant, that's it, she must have suddenly realized that Birgitta had everything she never got. Birgitta had had a mother, a husband, and also a baby, while Margareta had never had a single other person in the whole world. Nobody wanted her when she was little, and nobody wanted her now. There wasn't anything strange about that, since she was such a particularly bitchy menopausal hag. Margareta's simply jealous. But she'd never admit it, even at gunpoint, of course. When they were little, Margareta never wanted to talk about her mysterious mother, and she always turned away when Birgitta started talking about Gertrude. She was jealous then and she's jealous now. That's it.

Still. She really ought to understand that Birgitta feels hurt, that it's the awful things Margareta's been saying to her that have brought tears to her eyes and made her mouth tremble right now.

"Shit, Maggie," she says, straightening up. "I'm not very well, to tell you the truth, and I just can't run like you can. I've got cirrhosis of the liver, you know. . . . I've been in the hospital, just got out two weeks ago."

Margareta's face softens, but not enough for Birgitta to feel safe. It's possible Margareta doesn't know what cirrhosis of the liver is—and Birgitta certainly has no intention of informing her—so she might not understand the gravity of her situation. She has to strengthen her defense.

"It's my own fault, of course," she says, turning toward a park bench, dragging her feet so the gravel rattles. "Those of us who live on the other side of the law don't tend to live to a ripe old age. The doctor gave me six months, if I'm lucky . . ."

She sits down on the bench, casting a quick glance at Margareta. She's getting there. Margareta's opened her mouth and is staring at Birgitta, eyes glassy.

"But you know me," says Birgitta, laughing a bitter little cackle. "I just can't look after myself, couldn't even if I wanted to . . ."

Margareta shuts her gaping mouth and swallows. "Are you telling me the truth?"

Of course she is. What does Margareta think she is, after all? Does she imagine Birgitta would sit here lying? The doctor sure as fucking hell has told her she couldn't expect to live more than another six months or a year if she doesn't stop boozing!

"Of course I'm telling you the truth," she says, lowering her eyes to conceal the fact that she's lying anyway. Because of course she's lying. Birgitta Fredriksson won't die. She can't die.

THEY WALK SLOWLY out of the park and approach the station, Margareta holding Birgitta by the arm, supporting her as if she were an old woman. "You can just wait right there on one of these benches, and I'll go get the car," she says. "I won't be long, I parked over by the police station."

Birgitta closes her eyes and nods, allowing herself to be guided slowly across the street. She notices she's limping a little and stops. No need to overdo it: pickled liver doesn't make you limp. She ought to know, she's been in and out of the hospital with her fucking liver for a year and a half now, and she hasn't started limping yet. In fact, she never gives her liver so much as a thought, except now and then when she's puking. Then she peeks out from behind her eyelashes to see if there's any blood, because she knows that when she starts to vomit blood she'll have to let them hospitalize her, and she doesn't want to be hospitalized. Birgitta doesn't like being in the hospital. Truth be told, hospitals terrify her.

"Whoops," Margareta says when they get over to the bench. It's wet with slush. "Too damp and cold. Hang on a minute and I'll go buy a paper to put under you."

A second later she comes back and spreads a thick newspaper with several supplements across the bench. When Birgitta has made herself comfortable Margareta hands her a can of something. "In case you get thirsty while I'm gone. I won't be a minute, though."

Birgitta restrains a grimace: Diet Coke. Typical. What she needs is a beer. But if she says so, Margareta will just start barking like a rottweiler again.

"Will you be all right?" Margareta asks.

Birgitta nods, closes her eyes, then opens them right up again. "Maggie," she says with a pleading smile. "You wouldn't let me bum a smoke off you, too?"

It's a nice day, why hasn't she noticed it earlier? Birgitta leans back, turning her face up toward the sun and stuffing the pack of cigarettes into her pocket. Not bad, sitting here in the spring sunshine having a smoke.

Birgitta's always liked being outside, has always preferred being out-doors to being indoors, whether it's hailing or raining cats and dogs. Under other circumstances she might have turned out to be a real sporty type. The thought makes her snort with laughter. She can just see herself playing the rosy-cheeked scout leader with a basket over her arm and sun-shine in her eyes. Jesus Christ! Lucky she didn't suffer that particular fate.

Not that there was ever any great risk of it; her grandma had been highly suspicious of the great outdoors despite having spent her whole life surrounded by chlorophyll, and Gertrude had been a city slicker if there ever was one. Birgitta's actually only been on an outing to the countryside one time, and that was when Ella took all three girls mushroom picking, though she normally would never have set foot in the woods. But this was when pike-jowled Stig was about to turn forty, and Ella had promised to help with his birthday dinner. The appetizer was supposed to be vol-au-vents filled with wild chanterelles in cream, and because canned chanterelles cost a fortune and Ella was parsimonious, she figured it wouldn't be much trouble to go out into the woods and get them where they were free of charge. That was what she thought. In actual fact they never found even a morsel of edible mushroom.

But what a sight they must have been, as they paraded out through the gate and onto the road. Birgitta recalls it as if it were yesterday: at the head of the line was Ella in her rubber boots, her housedress, and her cardigan, followed by Christina, rushing to keep up and in similar garb, trembling as if she were afraid the road were going to open up under her feet and swallow her whole. Margareta tottered behind, unable to walk straight because she had smuggled a Nancy Drew book out of the house and started reading the minute Ella turned her back. She was really addicted to those books, had her nose in one constantly, heedless of the remonstrations of Ella, Christina, and Birgitta, who all rolled their eyes and told her it wasn't normal to be reading all the time, no matter where you were. It made no difference, she just went on wandering through life, always some new book in hand.

This time she reached out and held on to Birgitta so she wouldn't step into the ditch by mistake. Birgitta tolerated it, since she was in a pretty good mood that day. She'd put lots of paper bags for the mushrooms in her pockets, because she had no intention of donating any mushrooms she picked to the centenary jubilee of some old man, she planned to transform them into candy by selling them for good money. In addition to which she'd paid a surprise visit to Gertrude that day on her school lunch break, and Gertrude had been nearly sober and had promised to harass Marianne unstintingly until she let Birgitta move back home. Birgitta had now been at Ella's for nine months and twelve days. No one knew she was keeping such exact track of the time, no one knew she was counting the days, hours, and minutes as if she were a prisoner in her cell, and had been doing so since the very first day she arrived at Ella's.

Marianne was the one who'd brought her there. She'd come to school on a Friday, knocked at the classroom door during the last hour, and asked softly if she could speak with Herr Stenberg, please. He had waved the pointer threateningly and growled at the class to be quiet and stay in their seats before he went out into the hall.

None of the other kids in the class recognized Marianne, not even Bosse, who lived in the same building and who, just like all the other kids in the yard, would stare till his eyes were popping out of his skull when the woman from the child welfare authorities turned up in her beret, briefcase in hand, and tripped across the courtyard. They stared, not only because they were scared of the child welfare people, as Birgitta had understood, but also because Marianne was so strange-looking. No other woman in all of Motala wore a beret or carried a briefcase like that; only men had the privilege of making fools of themselves in that particular way. Today, however, Marianne was wearing a little hat instead of her beret, which was probably why Bosse didn't recognize her.

Birgitta had her science book open in front of her and had been about to turn surreptitiously from the chapter on hedgehogs to the substantially more interesting chapter on reproduction. Mind you, it was pretty cryptic and incomprehensible, but not sufficiently cryptic and incomprehensible to keep a person like herself—a young person with eyes and ears at the ready—from drawing certain conclusions about human behavior on the basis of descriptions applying to mammals. Birgitta was almost sure human beings were mammals. The book said that children came out of their mothers' bellies, although she couldn't really imagine how that happened. Gertrude's tummy was perfectly flat, she couldn't conceive of herself having spent any time in there. Gertrude would have burst, she was sure, and Gertrude's belly didn't look the least bit like it had ever burst. Maybe Mother Nature arranged for some kind of extra layer of skin, maybe babies lay in their mothers' stomachs covered by an extra layer of skin that looked something like a nylon stocking. That must have been it, yes. Nylon stockings were see-through, in which case the mamma would be able to see the baby and so she would know she was pregnant. Because if the kid was lying hidden among her organs someplace deep inside, she wouldn't even know she was going to have a baby . . .

Shit! She couldn't stand the suspense any longer, couldn't force her thoughts to be elsewhere for one more second. She slammed her science book shut and stood up, her chair scraping against the floor. The low voices and quiet whispers of her classmates were instantly silenced. Everyone looked at her; every single eye in the classroom was on Birgitta, wondering what she was going to do.

But Birgitta couldn't do anything. She was paralyzed. She stood straight as an arrow next to her desk, unable to place one foot ahead of the other, unable to walk over to the door and open it, unable to demand to know what Marianne was doing at her school. Because she already knew.

She'd forgotten the knives that night, had been sleeping like an idiotic log! And now Gertrude was dead, she'd finally stabbed herself in the stomach with the big kitchen knife.

Time stood still. Soon the earth would crack open.

"No, she's certainly not dead," Marianne was saying a little while later. "Wherever did you get an idea like that? You'll get to see her and say good-bye to her in a little while."

She was literally dragging Birgitta across the school yard, holding her tightly by the arm and pulling. Birgitta moved her feet only when it was absolutely necessary to keep from falling. Just a minute ago she'd tried to bite Marianne in that hand that was now gripping her own wrist like a handcuff, but she had failed. Marianne was stronger than she was and had anticipated her move, shifting her hand out of reach without letting go. It made no difference, though, because she was wearing thick gloves and Birgitta's teeth would never have cut through them. What she could do was kick her in the calf.

"You just stop resisting now!" Marianne shouted, pulling at Birgitta with such force that she stumbled and almost lost her balance. Stupid old biddy! Her new hat had slipped down over her forehead, she looked ridiculous!

The school yard around them was empty and bare; it would be ten minutes until the bell. They'd let her go early. Tomorrow was Saturday and they had school on Saturday, but Herr Stenberg had given her the day off to adapt to her new home. On Monday, however, he expected her back in her seat. Although there was another school closer to her new home, they were letting her stay at this one. The principal and the nice lady from the child welfare authorities thought it would be better for Birgitta not to have to switch classmates and teachers just now.

As if she cared. As if she gave a good goddamn about anyone but Gertrude!

The apartment reeked of vomit. The stench was so overpowering that even Birgitta felt nauseated when Marianne opened the door. But Birgitta was pretty used to puke—she was the one who wiped up Gertrude's throwups—so she could have stood it if the apartment hadn't been so transformed.

She just stood in the doorway staring. How had it happened? That morning the whole apartment had been like it always was when she went to school, maybe a little messier than usual, since Osvald had brought along some of his friends as well as a particularly rowdy lady when he arrived last night, but at least almost like always. Birgitta had overslept. Osvald and the others had apparently not bothered to take their coats when they left, so she was still lying in a heap of clothing in the hall. But it was late, she could tell when she tiptoed into the room to see if Gertrude was still there. She was. Sleeping like a baby. In fact, she'd been sleeping so deeply that Birgitta was a little worried, and after having found her clothes she leaned over Gertrude while she did up her stockings, just to be sure she was really breathing. She had been. No problem. Birgitta had grabbed her schoolbag, stuck a few sugar cubes in her jacket pocket, and rushed out the door. She hadn't taken the time to pick up the empties, but that didn't matter, she didn't think, since Marianne had been around just the day before. She never came two days in a row.

But this time she obviously had. And obviously she had redone the whole apartment. Nothing looked the way Birgitta and Gertrude usually had it. The shade had been pulled up, the curtains opened, and gray daylight was streaming into the room. It made Birgitta feel cold. Marianne had also lined all the bottles up on the floor, by the chest of drawers. They looked like they were waiting to be filled, waiting for the party to begin anew. Maybe there would be dancing. The rug was rolled up and pushed right against the wall, as if it were ashamed of itself. There was something else on the floor by the door; Birgitta had to bend down and see what it was. The bedspread. It was all wet, which made it look much darker than usual. Why had Marianne soaked the bedspread? And why was there a plastic bag full of Birgitta's own clothes next to it?

Gertrude was sleeping on the bed. Her face looked so strange, almost as gray and patchy as the pail on the floor next to the bed. It was their rubbish pail, the one that usually banged against Birgitta's leg when she took out the trash! Why in the world had Marianne put their rubbish pail in the middle of the floor instead of in the cupboard under the kitchen sink? Didn't she know where it belonged? Was she dumb or something?

Marianne put one hand on Birgitta's head, and whispered, "Your mamma's a very sick lady, Birgitta. She's asked us to take care of you so she can get better."

That was a damnable lie, and she got what she deserved for it immediately. Marianne no longer had her gloves on to protect her hands, they were bare and exposed.

Birgitta chose the right one, she was fast as lightning and sharp-toothed. She took pleasure in Marianne's loud scream.

IT WAS FUNNY going back to school on Monday; everything was the same and yet everything was different: the buildings, the street, her classmates. Even the classroom had changed over the weekend; she couldn't say exactly how, but it had something to do with the color and the size of it. It was as if everything, even the windows, had grown, yet everything was much darker than it had been on Friday. Maybe Stenberg had re-painted it over the weekend, to emphasize the enormity of the changes that had taken place, but if he had he wasn't a very good painter. The crack up in the corner of the wall was still there. And the light patches where there had been drawings the year before.

At recess some of the kids from her old building flocked around her. What had happened? Where had Birgitta gone? Did she know that when she and that Marianne left an ambulance had arrived in the courtyard and they had carried Gertrude out on a gurney?

Of course she knew. Birgitta tossed her head as if she had a really long ponytail to flip. And it was probably that fraction of a second of inattention that made her miss hearing who whispered that word, the word that suddenly flew through the air at her like a poison arrow and found its way into her ear: *lush!* She punished the person closest to her, grabbed at an arbitrary head of hair and pulled, not noticing that it was that chicken Britt-Marie until she heard her scream.

Ordinarily the others would have run into the staff room and tattled to Stenberg quicker than she could let go; she would have had a scolding and a demerit, and maybe even a rapping on the knuckles with the pointer, but not today. Gunilla, queen of the chicken roost and chief of the teachers' pets, put her arm around the weeping Britt-Marie and pleaded with the others not to tattle on Birgitta. They had to understand that she was a sad case. She'd never had a pappa and now she didn't even have a mamma! For a moment Birgitta considered throwing up into Gunilla's hair or scalping her with her teeth, but she didn't get a chance to do either. The bell rang, and in one second the flock had dispersed; the teachers' pets were rushing to the door, hearts pounding with fear of being late to class. She'd have to wait for the next break.

But she didn't get to go out at all on the next break. Stenberg called her name as she was heading for the classroom door with the others. He wanted a word with her, would she please come to the front of the room? He made it sound as if she had a choice, which was unlike him, he usually just shouted her name as if it were a command: Bir-git-ta! Sit still! Hush up! Wipe your nose and go out and wash your hands! Once he'd even called her a filthy pig, loud enough for the whole class to hear.

But now she wasn't just any old run-of-the-mill kid in the class, she could tell. Now she was a real uppity little girl, but an uppity little girl you still had to feel a little sorry for. Stenberg cocked his head like an old woman and put on that peculiar voice he normally reserved for little sweeties like Gunilla and Britt-Marie. It was nice to see Birgitta looking so neat and tidy today. She had new clothes, too, didn't she? Lucky her. Now she'd see that everything would work out for the best, now she would surely have more time and energy to devote to her schoolwork. Herr Stenberg just wanted her to know that he was sure that she, Birgitta, was a really clever little girl if she would only put her mind to it. There was nothing stupid about her, nothing at all. And surely she would put her mind to her schoolwork now that her life was a little better organized. Wouldn't she? Wouldn't she? Wouldn't she?

Birgitta curtsied and agreed, she wasn't so stupid as to talk back to Stenberg. She'd tried that once, and after the strapping he gave her she could hardly sit down. Gertrude had looked at the marks on her bottom and sworn she would report that old man to the school board, the medical authorities, and the diocese, but then she'd forgotten all about it. And when Birgitta reminded her, she was drunk and angry and told Birgitta she probably deserved what she got.

THEY WEREN'T ALLOWED to leave the school yard at recess, but nobody ever checked. The teachers must have been in the staff room stuffing themselves with cake; the rumor in the school yard was that cake with whipped cream on top and white rolls with cheese were served in the staff room every day. Nobody was able to check on that rumor, though, because the children weren't allowed into the staff room. If they wanted to talk to a teacher they had to wait in the cloakroom, which gave them only a quick glimpse of the luxury inside when the door opened and closed. The teachers had armchairs in there, Birgitta had seen that for herself. Big brown armchairs with little brown tables and coffee cups on them. So the rumor that the teachers gobbled up wonderful white sandwiches and cream cakes while the kids were sitting in the cafeteria eating rye crispbread and stewed liver certainly seemed to be true.

But today Birgitta didn't begrudge the teachers cake and cushy armchairs, and any other luxuries their hearts might desire, as long as it kept them out of the school yard. Quick as a weasel she scurried out through the gates and ran back toward her own street and her real home.

She hid in the archway to the courtyard for a while to be sure no nosy old ladies were beating their rugs and the child welfare authorities hadn't posted sentries to keep children from going to see their mammas. But the yard was quiet and empty; it was as if both the building on the street side and the one on the courtyard side had been vacated the minute Birgitta was dragged out to the sidewalk kicking and screaming. She didn't doubt that Gertrude was in, though. She'd probably had an operation at the hospital over the weekend and was all right again. She was probably walking around up in the apartment in her kimono looking for a pair of nylons with no runs. Because of course she had to have a good pair of stockings on to go up to Marianne's office and demand to have Birgitta brought home. She would be so happy to see Birgitta, happy she had come of her own accord! Birgitta knew she'd open her arms wide in that way she had done when she'd come visiting at the cottage, crying that she was dying to give her little girl kisses, kisses and hugs and a bushel and a peck!

Birgitta couldn't wait; she rushed across the yard so fast that nobody, not even Bosse's eagle-eyed ma, would be able to see her, pulled open the door, and stumbled up the stairs, falling and getting up again without losing momentum, although she'd scraped her knee, although it really hurt.

The door was locked, and no one answered when she rang the bell, but she still had her key. In the taxi on their way to the foster home she'd had the sense to pull the white elastic band with her key on it over her head and hide it deep in her coat pocket. Marianne didn't notice, she was quite preoccupied throughout the taxi ride examining her right hand, rubbing her index finger over the blue imprint Birgitta's teeth had left on her skin, sighing. No one, not even that old lady they'd put her with, had checked Birgitta's pockets. She'd laid out all Birgitta's clothes on the kitchen table when Marianne had gone, raised every garment to the light, scrutinized each one, sticking her finger in every hole as if wanting to make it bigger. But she'd neglected the coat, which had remained hanging out in the hall. That was what had kept Birgitta calm enough not to break every single object in the house. She had her key, she would be able to go back home.

She put the key in the lock but couldn't get herself to turn it. The little ounce of hope that had kept her going since Friday shriveled like a flower at twilight. She leaned her head against the door, holding her breath. Maybe she'd be able to hear Gertrude walking inside, humming as she searched for those stockings. But there was absolute silence on the other side of the door. A worry whizzed through her head, like a puff of wind: what if Gertrude wasn't there at all, what if she was never coming back?

Birgitta withdrew the key from the lock in one quick pull, rushed down the stairs, feeling her feet fluttering beneath her as if they didn't even touch the steps. She was being chased by ghosts and ghouls, she had to get away, out, escape, as fast as anybody could go . . .

NEVER IN HER life had Birgitta seen such a scaredy-cat, such a wimpy type as Christina. It was awful. That damn little louse was so cowardly she didn't even seem able to talk out loud; it was as if a whisper was all she dared to utter. But most of the time she said nothing at all, just stared at people with those solemn gray eyes of hers. She was enough to drive you crazy.

She deserved a beating. Or two. But on Monday afternoon all she got was a knock on the back hard enough to make her fall down face first on the gravel path in the yard and ruin her stockings.

That's life. For a scaredy-cat.

AT OLD LADY ELLA'S the girls were commandeered out of bed at a quarter to seven in the morning. Birgitta was then expected to wrap herself up in some damn bathrobe and put slippers on her feet like the others—never before had she needed a robe and slippers, what good were they, anyway?—and march out into the kitchen. Old Lady Ella would be at the stove, as always. She seemed unable to tear herself away from that stove, it was as if she spent all her time there, day and night, stirring whatever was cooking. She'd ladle some slimy oatmeal into Birgitta's bowl, with instructions that in her house you didn't leave the table until your plate was clean. Birgitta would glower at her from under her bangs and refrain from making trouble. She'd already realized that there was something sacred about food in this house, that you could raise a ruckus about your clothes or having to wash and make your bed, but you were never allowed to make a fuss at mealtimes. If you did, the Old Lady would probably knock you upside the head with the porridge ladle. So Birgitta ate up her slime, but not until she'd shoveled a little mound of sugar on top. That mouse was howling in her belly; after just these couple of days at Old Lady Ella's it was as starved and raging as a beast of prey. Birgitta just couldn't figure out where she was going to get the money to placate its needs; she'd already had a look in both the broom closet and the cupboard under the kitchen sink, but she hadn't found one single bottle. She'd have to figure out some other way.

The other girls gobbled up the oatmeal as if it were delicious. Ella sat down next to Margareta, who was apparently the sweet little apple of her eye. Christina was on the other side of the table, fingering the tablecloth nervously with one hand, spooning the porridge into her mouth with the other. Ella gave the breadbasket a little shove in her direction, and they exchanged smiles. Strange ones, as if they were both grown-ups, as if Christina hadn't been just as much of a ten-year-old kid as Birgitta was. But Christina was still as obedient as a child. She set her spoon on the edge of the bowl and took a roll.

"Fresh?" she whispered, still with that wisp of a smile glued to her wisp of a face.

"Mmmm," said Ella. "Aren't they still hot?"

Christina nodded. Ella put an arm around Margareta and gave her a squeeze. "Would you like a whole-wheat roll, too? They're still hot."

Margareta nodded with her mouth full, reaching for the breadbasket. When the butter started to melt on the hot roll, she put out her tongue, quickly licked up a big blob, then spread on some more. Ella laughed and pinched her cheek. "Silly!"

Ah, so that was how you were supposed to behave in this house. Either you had to be as cute as a button, like Margareta, or play at being grown-up, like Christina. In addition to which you had to stuff yourself to the brim.

Those girls were traitors. Ella wasn't the mother of either of them; they must have real mammas someplace, but they had apparently forgotten all about them. Birgitta, however, was no traitor. Nor would she ever be.

ELLA DIDN'T LIKE Birgitta, didn't even really want her in the house. Birgitta could tell from the very first day, by the way Ella dragged her down to the bathroom in the basement and started scrubbing her so hard she almost rubbed away her skin. She never even smiled, just wrinkled her forehead and issued curt orders about turning around and raising her arms so she could get at every part of her. Birgitta had said that she could bathe herself, that she was, in fact, accustomed to taking her own baths and not to being bathed like a baby, but the old lady had just snorted at her, muttering that to look at Birgitta you wouldn't know she'd had a bath in years. But that was a damned lie, Birgitta had certainly bathed in years. One day last summer she'd gone all by herself to the beach at Varamo and taken a dip in Lake Vättern. Who cared, though? Nothing gave the old lady the right to skin her with that rough brush.

Ella was one of those people who could bear a grudge forever. It was as if she would never forgive Birgitta for what happened the very first day, when Birgitta refused to drink up the orange drink she'd prepared, saying it looked too much like piss to drink. From then on she jumped at Birgitta for the littlest thing, scolded her all the time, like when she accidentally knocked over a little china figurine in the dining room, or because she shouted too loud or ran too fast when the girls were playing, or for not realizing you couldn't go around in dirty clothes or that you had to brush your teeth every single day of the week, twice even. Now and then she'd collapse from her own irritation and her nose would bleed. The other girls got all riled up when that happened, as if the world were coming to an end or something. Christina would rush out into the kitchen and get a bowl of water to wipe Ella's brow. Margareta would get some cotton for the old lady to stuff up her nose and then crawl up and sit on her lap. They'd both stare at Birgitta as if it were all her fault, as if she were the thing that made the old lady's nose start bleeding.

Other than that, Margareta was okay. She was a little prissy sometimes, but nowhere near as damn cringing or ingratiating as Christina. She liked to run around the house, she liked to play, unless she had a new book, of course, in which case there was no point trying. At times like that she'd just curl up on her bed in the empty room, oblivious to everything, not seeming to have any idea how disgusting she was when she picked her nose while reading. She was a fast reader, though, and the minute she finished a book she'd hurry out to find Birgitta. She always wanted to play whatever adventure she'd just been reading about, especially when she was reading a Nancy Drew. Birgitta went along with her sometimes, but only if she got to play George. Which was the only way to do it, anyhow. Margareta could never be George, no matter how hard she tried.

It took almost the whole summer for Ella to start treating Birgitta normally, by which time it was too late, in a way. It was as if she were suddenly deeply impressed because Birgitta managed to climb to the top of the cherry tree, so Birgitta never bothered to explain that she'd climbed a lot higher than to the top of that old tree in her day, that there was a time when she and her friends had gone off to the beach at Varamo in the fall to fill their pockets with fruit from the gardens of the summer places out there after the owners had closed up for the season and gone back home. Ella got so excited she even took a picture of Birgitta at the top of the tree. The other girls were in the photo, too, and afterward Ella had it enlarged and hand-tinted. Then she bought a shiny frame and set it on top of the chest of drawers in her bedroom.

Birgitta liked knowing it was there; she'd often sneak into Ella's room all alone and look at herself. She actually looked real cute in her pink dress and with her blond hair.

ELLA MADE HER clothes nowadays, and Birgitta honestly couldn't complain about them. Ella let the girls pick out the patterns and fabrics themselves, even Birgitta got to choose her own. If you asked for something really wild, like winter shorts or summer scarves, she'd chuckle and refuse, but otherwise you basically got whatever you wanted. Which explained how Birgitta came to have the nicest dress in the whole class for the last day of school in fourth grade. It was white with pink rosebuds and a frilled skirt. Not a single one of the teachers' pets had rosebuds and a flounce.

That showed them. Finally.

AND YET THAT dress ended in disaster.

One day at the end of May, Bosse told her Gertrude was back. His eagle-eyed ma had seen her the day before, dragging her suitcase across the courtyard.

Luckily he told her at lunch break, just as they were heading down the steps to the cafeteria. Otherwise, Birgitta would have had to play hooky. This way all she had to do was step stealthily aside, walk over to the gate, and then set off at a run.

She didn't have her key, which she'd buried under a bush in Ella's yard as soon as the ground had thawed. But that didn't matter. Gertrude was home now and would open the door for her. It was great to be alive!

After that day, and for what remained of the spring semester, she never once went to the cafeteria at lunchtime. The minute the bell rang she rushed across the school yard and out to the street. After a few days she even stopped taking precautions, would have been prepared to mow down both the principal and Herr Stenberg if she had to. All she wanted was to go home and be with Gertrude.

Gertrude was as usual on her bed, just like before, yet she wasn't really the same. Her face was rounder, but not in a way that made her look healthy; she had gone ashen, somehow. Everything about her seemed to be pulling downward: her hair, the lines in her face, her breasts sagging listlessly beneath her kimono. But she always smiled and said she was happy when Birgitta arrived, sent her right down to the newspaper stand for smokes and sweets, magazines and soda pop. Birgitta got to eat her candy while she was at Gertrude's, but Gertrude herself never even leafed through the magazines while Birgitta was there, never poured herself a drink. She would just lie on the bed and smoke and talk.

Gertrude hadn't had an easy time of it the last few months. First she'd been in the hospital for weeks, then they'd sent her to some damn home, an awful place run by a gang of particularly nasty, hypocritical Salvation Army soldiers. At that home Gertrude had had to eat soup with dumplings in it and spend her days with a bunch of drunks. And it was all Marianne's fault; that woman really didn't have all her marbles, and Gertrude rued the day she had come into her life and destroyed it. Only a real moralist like Marianne would ever have had the idea of putting Gertrude into a home.

When Gertrude got to the part about the day Marianne had come into her life, Birgitta would sit on her hands and glance at the alarm clock. It was almost time for her to go. "Sorry," she'd say, gliding off her chair, "Stenberg'll whip me if I'm late."

Gertrude's bottom lip would start to tremble; she'd shut her eyes. "Off you go, then," she'd say. "It can't be much fun for you to sit here listening to your little mamma's litany of complaints . . ."

Birgitta would find herself standing by the bed, hesitant. It was as if she didn't dare put her arms around Gertrude anymore. She'd just reach out and touch Gertrude's forearm lightly. "When can I come home?" she'd ask. Her voice was a little choked up; she had to swallow. "Have you asked Marianne?"

Gertrude would cover her face and hiss, "I will! I told you I'd ask her soon, didn't I?"

ON THE MORNING of the last day of school, Old Lady Ella kept apologizing for not being able to be at two schools at once, but there was no way she could make it from Christina and Margareta's school to Birgitta's. She was ever so sorry. She seemed to think Birgitta was going to be all upset about it, but Birgitta had no intention of being the least bit upset. On the contrary. Only wimpy kids brought their parents on the last day of school, and if there was anything Birgitta wasn't, it was a wimp. In addition to which, if Ella had been hanging around, she wouldn't have been able to go by Gertrude's afterward.

She was almost used to ringing the bell at Gertrude's now. She'd dug millions of holes in Ella's yard one afternoon without turning up her key, and in the end Ella had marched out into the yard and told her enough was enough and she couldn't go on playing mole any longer. Gertrude had promised her a new key, but so far she hadn't had the money to get one. And Birgitta didn't want to nag about it; Gertrude had enough troubles of her own.

No one answered when she rang, but she could hear voices on the other side of the door. Gertrude was at home, but she must have had company. Birgitta hoped maybe one of Gertrude's old girlfriends had decided to pay her a visit, in which case there would be two people there to clap their hands and exclaim about her pretty dress. She straightened the skirt a little, then rang the bell again. When no one answered she tried the handle.

It wasn't a girlfriend. It was Osvald.

As usual, he was sitting in one of the easy chairs, but this time Gertrude was on his lap. They both had glassy eyes, and one of Gertrude's stockings had slid down and was hanging from the knee like a veil. Gertrude's lipstick was all smeared around her mouth, and she didn't seem to have noticed that Osvald had slid his big hand under her skirt. Both of them blinked at Birgitta, turning their heads to look when she entered the room. Then they just sat there, perfectly silent and still for a moment, staring at her. The dress had rendered them speechless.

"Is that you?" Gertrude asked, leaning forward for her cigarettes. Osvald pulled back his hand and fumbled in the air over the Turkish smoking table for his glass.

"Mmmm," said Birgitta.

"And all dolled up from top to toe," said Gertrude, squinting and exhaling the smoke from her first puff. "Where the hell did that outfit come from?"

"Aunt Ella."

"Ella? Who the fuck's Aunt Ella?"

"The lady where I live."

Gertrude made a face and got up, walked over to the bed, one stocking falling down around her ankle, to sit down. The springs creaked, as usual. Everything was as usual. Definitely. Nothing had changed.

"So she can afford to buy you fancy dresses, can she?" asked Gertrude, baring her teeth.

Birgitta didn't know how to answer that, but it didn't matter, Gertrude just went right on talking. She knocked the ashes from her cigarette into her cupped hand and chortled. "Well, I sure as hell hope she *can* afford to buy you dresses. . . . I guess she makes a tidy little fortune taking care of other people's kids. Don't you think so, Osvald?"

Osvald grunted in agreement from the easy chair.

Gertrude stuck the cigarette between her lips, taking a close look at Birgitta. "Holy shit, you really are done up to the nines. A real little Shirley Temple, a person might say. . . . I guess you're real happy about that. I guess you'd like nothing better than to stay at that Ella's house. Where you can wear silk and satin every single day."

Birgitta clamped her mouth tight and just shook her head. No! All she had ever wanted was to come home and live with Gertrude. Hadn't she told her a thousand times? What if she'd been talking too softly, what if Gertrude hadn't heard her? She wished her flowered dress would split at the seams and fall from her body in rags; she wished she could make herself move and speak. But no, the dress just stayed on Birgitta, who was petrified. She couldn't even open her mouth.

"What's the old lady like anyways?" Gertrude asked, leaning back and supporting herself on the pillow with one elbow. She'd forgotten about the ashes in her hand; they made a little gray stain on the bedspread. But Birgitta didn't have to worry; the ashes weren't hot, and the minute she could move again she'd clean it up.

"Do you know her, Osvald?" Gertrude asked. "D'you know what that person Birgitta's living with is like?"

Osvald took a swig of his drink and belched. "Sure," he said. "Ella Johansson, you know her, too. Who takes in foster kids. She must have three or four of 'em by now."

Gertrude's brow drew up into a crease. "Which Ella Johansson?"

"Widow of Hugo Johansson. Local bigwig, you know, the guy who died about ten years back."

Osvald chuckled, took another swallow, scratched his chest. "She must be one sly woman, too. Twenty years younger than him if she was a day.

They hadn't been married more than a year when he kicked the bucket. There she sat with his house and his money . . . and he wasn't exactly penniless."

Gertrude sat right up in bed. "Was it a tumor? Did he die of a tumor?"

Osvald shrugged. How the hell should he know? But it didn't matter, Gertrude had already answered her own question.

"Jeez, yeah! Now I know who she is. A little woman, kind of square build. . . . Oh, yeah!"

She inhaled deeply, squinting at Birgitta. "You tell her I say hello. Tell her I remember her and her monstrosity very well. We happened to be in the same maternity ward once upon a time, her and me."

"Nice car," says Birgitta once she manages to get the seat belt fastened.

Margareta laughs, as if it were a joke. "Not really. Showing its age, actually. Exhaust system gave out yesterday. That was why I had to go get it from the shop."

Had her car been in the shop? And is Birgitta supposed to be aware of it? Sounds that way, sounds like Margareta thinks Birgitta's in the know. People keep doing that to her, she's noticed. There must be some general conception about Birgitta Fredriksson's being able to read people's minds. If she doesn't want to make a complete fool of herself, she'd better change the subject. "Did you drive all the way from that Lapp hellhole?"

Margareta shakes her head. The tip of her tongue protruding from between her lips, she looks like she's trying to steer the car with her tongue as she zigzags into the traffic circle in front of the police station. "Nope. I flew from Kiruna to Stockholm. This isn't my car, it's just borrowed."

Birgitta gropes in her pocket for the cigarettes. "Whose is it?"

Margareta smiles again. "A guy's I know. A guy named Claes."

Birgitta raises her eyebrows as she withdraws a Marlboro Light from the pack. There aren't many left. "Nice fellow?"

"He's all right. Well, yeah. Thoroughly nice, now that you mention it."

"Gonna marry him?"

Margareta bursts into laughter again, funny how jolly she's become in the last little while.

"I doubt it. Neither of us is the *mariage d'amour* type."

What the hell is with her now? Can't she just use plain speech? Birgitta's forgotten the very little French she ever learned at school, has no idea what Margareta meant by that, but definitely doesn't intend to reveal her ignorance just because Margareta feels like showing off. So she just lights up and says nothing.

"I'll take one, too," says Margareta, reaching toward her but not taking her eyes off the road.

Birgitta looks down into the pack. "I don't have many left."

One second later she realizes she never should have put it that way. She's awakened the rottweiler.

"Dammit, those are *my* cigs!" Margareta shouts, pulling the pack out of Birgitta's hand.

IT'S PRETTY GREAT getting a ride in a car, even if the chauffeur could be pleasanter. Birgitta yawns and stretches. Hell, as soon as she gets back to her own place and has a few beers under her belt, she's gonna lie right down and sleep the sleep of the dead. And when she wakes up tomorrow she will have forgotten all about the anonymous letters, the snobs, the whole spiel.

"Tired?" Margareta's voice has a sharp little edge to it; she's clearly still pissed off, although she's got the pack of cigarettes next to her now, way out of Birgitta's reach. In addition to which she has one between her lips, so she could at least sound pleased with herself instead of so grumpy.

Birgitta's not going to answer her, just leans back and shuts her eyes. Margareta, however, doesn't seem to get it, doesn't seem to realize she's planning to take a nap. She just goes on talking: "I'm pretty tired myself. It's questionable whether I'll have the energy to drive all the way to Stockholm tonight. Might fall asleep at the wheel if I try."

Oh, how exciting. Fascinating. But Birgitta just has to sleep now, she's got her hands full with her own troubles and couldn't possibly be less interested in Margareta's. And incidentally, which one of them is it who is more or less dying and who therefore has the right to a little bit of extra consideration? She can't help but wonder, although it's sure not a question she's about to open her big trap and ask out loud. If she did she'd probably be rottweiler stew before she could say Johnny Appleseed.

But Margareta just won't stop: "You see," she says, in her same sharp voice, "we had quite a night last night. Didn't get a wink of sleep. As I guess you know."

What? Birgitta opens her eyes again, blinking hard. "What do you mean by that?"

Margareta is leaning forward over the wheel, her eyes still glued to the road. Birgitta must actually have catnapped a little; they're on the high-way now, almost halfway to Linköping.

"You can't fool me," says Margareta. "You know perfectly well what I'm talking about."

Birgitta pulls herself upright. "What the fuck is this?"

Margareta must be flooring it, the speedometer's quivering somewhere around eighty. A sudden vision of the Fateful Road Accident flutters through Birgitta's mind, but she pushes it aside. She doesn't have time for the movies right now. "You think so?" she asks. "Well, I really don't know what the fuck you're going on about."

Still staring at the road, Margareta stubs out her cigarette in the ash-tray with perfect precision, lighting up a new one right away. "Well, what I'm talking about is that little game you were playing last night."

What little game? Birgitta doesn't remember any game; all she has is some vague recollection of some kind of party someplace. In Norrköping. Right, it was in Norrköping.

"I'm talking about the fact that about eleven-thirty last night Christina got a phone call," says Margareta, her voice heavy with portent.

"A phone call?" croaks Birgitta. "So?"

Margareta doesn't appear to have heard her, just goes right on talking: "It was from someone who claimed you'd been assaulted and were on your deathbed in Motala Hospital. You'd said you wanted to see us one last time, and we actually went, Christina and I. That's how gullible we are. And when it turned out you weren't at the hospital, we spent the rest of the night running around Motala trying to find you."

She takes a deep drag, closing her mouth as if she intends to swallow the smoke. She fails, though, and it seeps out through her nostrils. When she begins again her voice is softer, almost as if she were talking to herself. "A couple of hours ago, I was pretty convinced the whole thing was Christina's doing, some loony idea, but when you went into that song and dance about being so sick, and even got me to leave you resting on a bench in the sun while I picked up the car, I realized the truth. It just took a while for the penny to drop. You really ought to vary your methods, you know. You can't expect to be felt sorry for one day because you've been battered half to death and the next because you're dying of pickled liver. We're not complete nincompoops, you know, Christina and I."

For just an instant, she takes her eyes off the road to glance at Birgitta.

"Jesus Christ," she says a moment later, shrugging her shoulders.

"You're a boozer and a junkie. You're a liar and a thief. You deal and you cheat. You once even put a bag full of your own excrement on Christina's desk. Shit! What did she ever do to hurt you? And now you're into anonymous letters and mysterious phone calls. Haven't you ever thought about growing up?"

She sits silently for a while, smoking in quick puffs, then removes the cigarette from her mouth and puts it out. "I'm only driving you to Motala because I had decided to go there anyway and take flowers to Aunt Ella's grave. Consider this my final service to you. Because when you get out of this car, I never want to see you again. You make me sick."

Birgitta shuts her eyes. She's a different age and hearing a different voice by the time Margareta stops talking.

"IF YOU HAD behaved like an adult you would have been treated like one," Marianne said, setting her pale hand on Birgitta's kitchen table.

Birgitta screamed at the top of her lungs, and one hundred percent honest-to-goodness tears ran down her cheeks. "But it wasn't my fault! Why should I be punished for it? It was Hound Dog who did the hitting, not me!"

Marianne leaned forward, rapping her knuckles on the table. "Hound Dog hit you, not the baby, as far as I know. He will be convicted for his wrongdoings, both that one and others. And we couldn't very well have left the baby lying here all alone in the apartment when you were taken off in the ambulance and Hound Dog was taken off by the police, could we? We had no choice but to take him into our custody, you must realize that."

Birgitta slammed her fists on the table, hammering a loud drumroll and screaming. "But now I want him back! He's my kid!"

Marianne leaned back in her chair, shaking her head. "Cut that out, Birgitta. It won't do you any good. Think a minute. The baby is eight months old but weighs no more than a baby half that age. He had bruises on his thighs and terrible diaper rash when we placed him in foster care. And he was dehydrated. They call that child abuse, Birgitta. Neglect. Possibly even extreme cruelty. The foster mother's a nurse, and she could see that he needed immediate hospitalization to prevent permanent damage. He's still hospitalized, and his foster parents visit him every single day. In fact, the mother spends all her time at the hospital."

Birgitta put her hands to her beehive hairdo and pulled at it, her voice suddenly cackling like a witch's. "She's not his mother. You'd better get that through your fucking head, you stupid bitch. I'm that kid's mamma and I always will be. Me and only me!"

Marianne looked like she might burst into tears any minute; Birgitta could see it from somewhere deep inside her fury. This was the first time in all these years Marianne from the child welfare authorities had reacted with anything other than factual arguments and moral judgments. She opened her handbag to find a tissue and wound it around her index finger, as if she were some kind of damned duchess!

"They're fine people, Birgitta. They love him. You and Hound Dog haven't even gotten yourselves together to give him a name, so they've named him. They've named him Benjamin."

Benjamin! What a fucking shitty name! He was supposed to be called Steve. Or Dick. Or Ronny. She and Hound Dog had decided that while he was still a bun in her oven. What the hell business was it of Marianne's if they hadn't made a final decision yet?

"Birgitta, please," Marianne went on, wiping her nose with the tissue. "I know you're upset and disappointed, but you're only nineteen years old. You have your entire life ahead of you. In a few years, you'll know this was right. It's not good for a little baby to grow up surrounded by fighting and shouting, and you and Hound Dog haven't been getting along for the last year or so, if I'm rightly informed. Moreover . . ."

Marianne lowered her voice and leaned forward, knocking gently on the tabletop. "Moreover, rumor has it that you go down to Norrköping sometimes. To Salt Flats. That you're literally following in your mother's footsteps. It's not against the law, I know that, and there isn't much the welfare authorities can do about it. But leaving an infant alone for more than twenty-four hours constitutes severe cruelty and gross negligence. And according to your neighbors, that's what you are guilty of, that's what you've done over and over when you've gone to Norrköping. In which case we have no choice but to intervene, for your little boy's own sake."

Now she leaned back again, putting her hanky back in her bag and shutting the clasp. She must have been done with her sob story, then. Her eyes were perfectly dry now as she looked up and said, "Let him stay where he is, Birgitta. He'll do well there. You don't want him to grow up to live like you, do you?"

* * *

BIRGITTA HAD EXPECTED them to take her to the lockup afterward, but the pigs drove her to a nuthouse in Vadstena instead. Women who used physical force were considered nutcases in those days; no one could imagine that a girl who could punch somebody in the nose could also be in full possession of her senses. And Birgitta had given Marianne a couple of good socks, had managed to floor her and then to spit on her and kick her in the face. They said she'd been given a disability pension after that round and left town. Maybe it was true. At least Birgitta had never seen her again, which was one helluva relief.

It's going to be nice to be rid of Margareta, too, sanctimonious bitch. She'll give her a punch or two before they part as well, or at least a shot below the belt. It wouldn't be very smart to lunge at her driver in the middle of their trip. But a burst illusion can sometimes hurt just as much as a broken jaw. Ask Birgitta. She knows, she's tried both.

"What are you grinning at?" Margareta asks. "Is there something funny about all this, do you think?"

Birgitta drums her fingers on the dashboard, humming softly to herself. The cigarettes are on Margareta's far side, but she might be able to reach them if she took off her seat belt.

"What the hell do you think you're doing?" Margareta asks edgily when Birgitta undoes her seat belt. Birgitta doesn't answer, just calmly reaches across the steering wheel for the white pack. Margareta brakes so hard she almost goes into a skid, her voice rising to a scream: "Are you out of your mind?"

Birgitta still doesn't say anything, just slowly and quietly puts her seat belt back on.

"You must be crazy! We could have swerved off the road."

Oh my God. She sounds like a crackpot herself. Getting hysterical.

There's only one cigarette left. Birgitta lights it and inhales with satisfaction, then crumples up the pack and tosses it to the floor. She's being provocative, showing Margareta in no uncertain terms that she's claimed the last cig, wanting her to feel the frustration of it.

"Oh yeah," says Birgitta, stretching a little. "Speaking of anonymous letters . . . I had the privilege of receiving one myself. Christina sent me one, too. Her name was even on it."

"Well, hell, it wasn't anonymous if her name was on it," Margareta spits. "The definition of an anonymous letter is the absence of information with regard to the sender."

Listen to that. The lady's taken up cursing. If Birgitta had had a Magic Marker on her, she would have made a great big exclamation point on the ceiling of the car. She reaches out and draws a quick invisible one with her index finger on the white vinyl, but Margareta doesn't notice. She leans heavily into the steering wheel, flooring the accelerator with even greater determination. Now she's certainly doing over eighty. If the pigs catch her, she's seen the last of her license. For the first time in her life Birgitta thinks she'd be prepared to sacrifice one or two cans of beer to see a cop car in the rearview mirror.

"Let me tell you how it is, in fact, possible for there to be names on anonymous letters," she says in her calmest voice, weighing her words with great care, sounding almost as cold and calculating as she always does in the courtroom. When it comes right down to it, she's learned a thing or two in her day; in some circumstances staying calm helps you hit harder.

"Christina hadn't signed the letter. She hadn't written her name, but she'd written the letter on one of her own prescription forms, that asshole!"

Shit! She's got to restrain herself. She shuts her eyes and takes a deep breath, makes a fist, and pounds it lightly on the windshield a few times.

"And?" says Margareta.

What does she mean by "And?" Birgitta snorts and takes a deep breath, then blows the smoke right at Margareta. It works. Her eyes fill with tears and she starts flailing with one hand. Sensitive type. Especially for a smoker.

"Seems to me you'd like nothing better than to have us end up in a ditch," says Margareta.

"Shut up," says Birgitta. "Your fucking bitching is giving me one helluva stomachache, I just want you to know that."

It's true. Somebody's claws are tearing at her innards. Maybe it's that old sugar mouse who's finally decided to turn her insides out. But candy hasn't been exactly what it's wanted for the last thirty years. Its taste has become more sophisticated, just like Birgitta's.

"I can't believe you can be bothered," Margareta goes on. "You can't fool me anymore, don't you get that?"

Birgitta doesn't answer, just leans forward and throws up between her spread feet.

THE NEXT TIME she looks up, the car has come to a halt. Margareta's stopped at a rest area and is pulling the rubber mat out from under Birgitta's feet, hissing, "Would you please just lift your legs at least?"

Birgitta raises them a little, letting them drop back down the minute Margareta's got the mat out. Shit. She's never been quite this tired in her whole life. Not even when she's been in the hospital, getting IVs and injections and all.

Margareta's standing by a tap a few steps away rinsing the mat. The door is open. Birgitta raises herself with one hand on the dashboard, and turns so both her legs are out of the car, then levers herself to an upright position with great difficulty. She just has to lean against the car while the dizziness passes. Then she can start to walk.

"Where do you think you're going?" Margareta calls out to her back.

Birgitta's only reply is a dismissive gesture as she shuffles toward the service station. Isn't a person even allowed to go to the rest room anymore?

There's hardly anybody inside, not a single customer. Just one guy behind the counter, and he's on the phone and barely glances in Birgitta's direction. She's straightened up, her posture is erect and her mouth is closed. From a distance she must look almost normal.

The rest rooms are all the way at the far end, and the path to them is like Paradise, with a tall pile of six-packs at hand. Birgitta looks quickly at the attendant. Yes, there is a God! Because the attendant is just turning slowly around, receiver to his ear, leaning out the window to see what's going on out there. So he can't possibly see her, there's no way he can see Birgitta's left hand sliding out of her jacket pocket to seize a six-pack as she advances slowly into the ladies' room.

MARGARETA'S STANDING AT the counter paying for something when Birgitta comes back out. She turns around and says in an almost pleasant tone of voice, "Oh, there you are. Feeling better now?"

It's a rhetorical question, Margareta's only asking it so the attendant will hear how considerate she is. So Birgitta doesn't bother to answer, just nods and holds back a belch. Yes, in fact, much better. The weak beer they sell at places like this is just piss, of course, but it's one helluva lot better than that Diet Coke Margareta forced on her in Norrköping.

"Want something to drink?"

She certainly isn't offering beer. She means soda pop or some other kind of soft drink. But she can cut it out now; the attendant has undoubtedly already recognized her sister's outstandingly noble personality, she doesn't need to put on such a damn show. Birgitta just shakes her head again and walks slowly out the door. She's neither rushing nor being conspicuously sedate, just walking to the car at a perfectly ordinary pace.

When Margareta comes out, Birgitta's sitting straight up in her seat with her seat belt buckled. Margareta looks pleased with herself, too, as she drops a pack of Marlboro Lights in Birgitta's lap with a grin. "One for you," she says. "And one for me."

Aha. So what's she supposed to do now, burst into jubilations and praise the Lord? Or get out and roll around in the slush and oil spills out of pure gratitude? It's true that Birgitta had an asking price in her day, in several respects. But she's not that cheap, nobody can buy her forgiveness for a pack of Marlboro Lights.

Disgusting! She knows who's disgusting. And who's the best liar, to herself and to others.

SHE DOESN'T PULL a can out from under her jacket until they're past Linköping. Because she guzzled the first four in the toilet cubicle, she's not in dire need. Now she can allow herself to really relish the last two, to let the taste sink into her palate, to lick the foam from her top lip.

The car swerves when the opener on the can pops. Margareta stiffens at the sound, forgets to look where she's driving, and her hands steer the wheel where she's looking instead. For a few seconds they're headed right off the road. Luckily there's no one in the other lane.

"Watch it!" says Birgitta. She doesn't shout, her voice is dull and muffled.

Margareta straightens the wheel and slows down, wiping her forehead with one hand. "And where did that beer come from?" she asks, her voice trembling so much you'd think she'd witnessed a natural disaster or something.

Birgitta nods out the window. "This is where you turn. Didn't you see the sign? Or aren't you heading for Motala anymore?"

Margareta glances hastily in the rearview mirror and clicks on the blinker. There are beads of perspiration on her upper lip. That woman really is a menopausal hag, and her expensive clothes and miracle creams don't help. Birgitta smiles to herself as she raises the can to her lips. Oh, that aroma! You might even mistake it for the king of bottled beer instead of service station piss. But as long as it will hold the sugar mouse at bay until they get to Motala, it's good enough for her. If you haven't baked any bread, you have to make do with zwieback, as Old Lady Ella used to say.

Margareta pulls to a stop as they turn onto the Motala Road. It's completely empty, not a car in sight, but Margareta doesn't drive on, just lets the car stall out and doesn't even bother to turn the key in the ignition. She sinks down over the steering wheel moaning, "You stole them! You went into that gas station and stole beer from them!"

The next time she looks up, her face is all blotchy. "I'm sure you realize I'll have to stop at that service station and pay for your beer on my way back to Stockholm. You do realize that, don't you? I'm going to have to walk in there and tell them that for the millionth time I let an old junkie pull the wool over my eyes."

She shakes her head slowly. "Never in my entire life have I ever been so humiliated. Never!"

Birgitta doesn't answer, just takes long, pleasurable swallows of her beer, waiting for Margareta to start the car.

THOUGH SHE COULD tell her a thing or two about humiliation, if she wanted to.

For instance, she could tell her what it feels like to be called a whore. She could offer comparisons, sermonize on the distinction between being called a whore when you're a virgin of fourteen and being called a whore when you're seventeen and actually are one. She could even describe what it's like to be called an old hooker, so ugly that a man has to cover your face with his hand to keep his cock from going soft.

What's worst? Well, it may be a matter of taste, but in her personal opinion Birgitta's inclined to think the worst thing is actually being a whore rather than just being called one. You can hold your head high and convince yourself that what's making the air thick with whispers behind your back when you walk along the shop floor at the plant is nothing but the soured lust of dirty old men, even if you know they're jiggling their balls and grinning behind your back. You know what you are: fourteen and a virgin, with full breasts and a lily-white complexion, a blossom all the men in the world dream of picking and, for that reason, that you have power over all the men in the world.

It's worse a few years later, when you know you're a whore, know it in your mind and see the evidence collecting in your wallet and in your underpants, sticky with clap discharge. You take your penicillin like a good girl, you wash and wash and wash, and yet you never get clean enough to be loved and forgiven by the one you really love. You're not allowed to say that all you really want is to nestle your head to his chest and listen to the beating of his heart. And so you have to provoke him constantly instead, you have to bounce your naked tits in front of his face, grab at his hand and stick it between your thighs when you're sitting next to him in a car, let him feel that you're really not wearing any panties under your tight skirt. And that's why he sometimes bellows in desperation and frustrated desire, makes a fist and slams it into the hooker's temple at the very moment she thought she was safe and had almost forgotten where she was. She must never forget. He must never forget. That explains their love-hate relationship, their arguing and fighting, day after day, year after year, until the fateful day he OD's and leaves her alone with her guilt. Because it is her fault, she drove him to death by being what she is. A whore.

And when you're an old whore, so ugly that . . .

Well. Now and then you head right into the whole world, horns lowered like a bull, spit in the face of a cop when you have the chance, throw out some little worm of a john who's been lying there doing nothing for a quarter of an hour too long, and punch anyone who makes you want to cry right in the nose. Then you have a beer, because nothing is a better cure for humiliation than beer. And it tastes good, too.

BIRGITTA WIPES HER top lip, knocking a little foam off with her hand, and looks at Margareta out of the corner of her eye. She's started the car again but is driving more slowly than before. Wonder if her little pink ears would fall right off if Birgitta told her, if she had to listen to the story of what real humiliation is?

Probably. Birgitta sticks the can of beer between her legs and starts fumbling with the pack of cigarettes, ripping at the cellophane to open it. She doesn't know where the words are coming from, why they suddenly gush forth, rolling out and not letting themselves be halted: "Bitch. Hooker's kid. Shitface. Damned brat. Filthy pig. Dirty dog. Scumbag. Sewer rat. Rubbish dump. Ugly creep. Troublemaker. Problem child. Lush's girl . . ."

Margareta turns her head. "What the hell is with you now?"

But Birgitta can't tell her, there isn't room for any words in her mouth other than the ones that have been forced down her own throat for years and years and that are now bubbling right up by themselves. It's like puking, she just can't control it.

"Tart. Hooker. Filthy cunt. Shitty pussy. Easy lay. Slimy screw. Slimy fuck. Fuckass. Fucking fanny. Stoned floozy. Junkie hooker. Pusher tramp. Junkie's girl. Speed cunt. Fluff fuck. Loose-loose-loose-loose cunt."

"Shush," Margareta hisses. "You just shush up now!"

But Birgitta can't hold the words back. They're pushing and shoving in her mouth, making her fumble with the cigarettes, as if the pack were theft-proof. She rips and tears at the cellophane, but she can't do it, can't even open a pack of smokes anymore. Her hands are trembling too hard, and her mouth won't be silent.

"Witch. Viper. Sucking lush. Pig. Sicko. Floozy. Wino hag. Soused bitch. Betrayer. Fake. Welfare case. Beggar. Slut. Con. Thief. Killer. Murderer. Liar! Liar! Liar!"

Margareta's almost screaming: "Quiet down! Can't you just quiet down?"

And Birgitta does quiet down; she leans against the seat and shuts her eyes. The words are out of her, her hands have stopped trembling. Finally she's arrived at the truth.

THE HOUSE WAS unusually quiet that morning. Ella, Christina, and Margareta were sitting at the kitchen table, ruffled as a cluster of freezing cold sparrows, when Birgitta stuck her head in through the kitchen door to say good-bye. Only Ella mumbled a response, Christina and Margareta just nodded. Tired, of course. Tired, though all they did was go to school, and though they didn't have to get up half as early as Birgitta.

It was drizzling, the autumn air was cool and easy to breathe, but the bus puffed a stinking fume in her face when it arrived. She frowned and turned her head, like everyone else at the stop. It was just the usual crowd: old man Nilsson and old lady Bladh and a couple of others. They all worked at Luxor; if you worked at Motala Engineering you had to take the earlier bus. Old man Nilsson usually sat next to Birgitta if she let him. He'd read his paper, never letting on that he was also pressing his thigh against hers. Birgitta let him have his way most of the time, despite the fact that he was disgusting, despite the fact that his lips were always wet and he had tobacco stains on his front teeth. Because he was the fore-man, he had control over the hours and the minutes, over the time clock and over docking.

He gave her a little grin when she took a window seat, leaving the aisle free.

"Mornin'," he said, sitting next to her. He opened the *Motala Daily* across his lap, pressing his thigh against hers as she had expected. Birgitta just sat there, immobile, unsmiling, but without pulling away, either. She just read his paper with one eye for a few minutes, then averted her face, looking out at the rain and the gray mist for a while until what she'd read sank in. She leaned back over his paper again; the old man gasped for breath when her jacket opened to reveal the cleavage at the top of her blouse, and the space between her breasts. Yes. She'd seen right. Today was the fifth of October. Three years since Gertrude's death. To the day.

"Hey," she said softly, carefully putting her own hand on Nilsson's thigh underneath the newspaper. He blinked and glued his eyes to the paper as if he'd just seen something really important, some extremely interesting article that was about to change his life. Birgitta's hand gave a little squeeze. "Do you think you could arrange for me to get off work a little early today? Without anyone knowing?"

Nilsson grunted and turned the page, not looking at her, but with his eyes bulging out of their sockets. Birgitta drew her hand across his thigh in a light caress before withdrawing it. "Thanks," she whispered. "Great. I won't forget the favor."

WHICH WAS HOW it came about that she was able to go to the cemetery in the afternoon, before dark. The previous year she had had to go after work, had rushed through the factory gates as if she were being chased, hurried into the florist's, and then stood there, paralyzed with indecision between red and white roses for so long that she began to weep with stress. And by the time she finally came out with a tube of flowers for the grave, all the streetlights were already lit and it was nearly dark. She heard a key turn in a door behind her and realized the florist was about to close. All the stores were closing.

Darkness fell as she walked to the cemetery. The streets of Motala were black; she could hear her footsteps echo between the buildings, see her own shadow grow and recede in the light of each streetlamp she passed. Her heart was pounding, and it was as if she were unable to take a really deep breath.

In the end, it was so dark she hadn't dared enter the unlit cemetery. So she just stood there at the gate, her bouquet pressed to her chest for a long time. Suddenly she thought she heard a laugh, a feminine little laugh penetrating the darkness. It was as if someone in a grave were laughing at her, enticing her with a glimmering silver voice, someone with a knife concealed in her shroud.

She'd tossed the flowers over the wall and run away. Behaved like a complete idiot. But this year it would be different.

NILSSON NODDED AND turned his back to indicate that she could go, at least he'd see to it that her time card was punched as if she'd worked all day. She knew he might demand reimbursement in a toilet cubicle one day, but it was going to be worth it. All he would want was her body anyway.

She ran across the square to the florist's. This year she wasn't going to hesitate, already knew what she wanted. Red roses. There was no question that red roses were the right thing for Gertrude's grave.

She'd been dead for three years now, but Birgitta still sensed her presence daily. She would glimpse her in the nape of a stranger's neck on the bus, in a passerby's way of walking, in a distant laugh. Time and again she would feel her hope fanned, turn her head, and be let down. Gertrude was dead. She wouldn't be back.

She stopped for a moment outside the cemetery gate, taking a deep breath. It wasn't dark yet, but it was a gray, misty afternoon. The trees looked like shadows, the clouds had descended upon them and were preparing to dissolve and annihilate them.

Not that it mattered. The clouds could annihilate Birgitta, too, when it came right down to it. She was going to Gertrude, no matter what. She was going to lay her red roses in the yellowed autumn grass of the memorial grove, stand there for some time with her head bowed, and remember.

ELLA WAS SURPRISED when she came home. She was sitting in the living room embroidering as usual, and when Birgitta appeared in the archway she looked up, peered over the top of her eyeglass frames, and let the embroidery hoop fall to her lap. "You're early today!"

Birgitta nodded, untied her head scarf, and began to unbutton her jacket as she replied, "Yeah. I left work early."

Ella frowned. "With permission?"

Birgitta removed her jacket, dangling it from her index finger while she walked out into the vestibule to hang it up. She could tell from the smell it was going to be stuffed cabbage for dinner. She went back into the living room, smoothed her teased hair, and sat down on the couch. "It was all right. Nobody minded."

Ella had raised the embroidery hoop toward her eyes and begun stitching again, pulling the thread to a tight red line in the air between each stitch.

"Will you be docked for it?"

Birgitta shook her head. No. It would be all right. But Ella didn't take her eyes off her; it was as if her hands were embroidering on their own while she stared over the tops of her eyeglasses at Birgitta. Boring right into her with that gaze. Wasn't that the word Margareta read out loud, about that kind of look?

"So, why did you leave early?"

Birgitta looked down at her hands, suddenly realizing she was sitting on the edge of the sofa cushion, as if she were a guest who was just about to depart. "I wanted to go to the grave. It's the three-year anniversary today. I went after work last year, and it was too dark. I really wanted to go while it was still light out this year."

Ella nodded but went on glaring at Birgitta. "Did you buy flowers?" she asked.

Birgitta nodded.

"What kind?"

What business was it of hers? Wasn't that between Birgitta and Gertrude? And yet she had to tell her, in this house you always had to answer when you were asked a question. Birgitta sat on her hands and replied, "Roses. Three red roses."

Ella nodded. Approved, obviously. Passed inspection, no objections.

THE ROOM WAS silent for a few minutes, except for the ticking of the clock on the wall. Birgitta sat back on the couch, looking around. Not one stick of furniture had changed in this room in all the years she'd been living here. Everything was as it always had been, every plant, every piece of furniture, every bit of bric-a-brac was in its usual place. The clock was ticking with the same regular beat as always, despite the fact that time had stood still. The rain was pattering on the window as it always pattered.

Ella straightened her glasses and groped for the embroidery scissors, cutting the thread and inspecting her work. Undoubtedly perfect as usual. No reason to imagine otherwise.

Suddenly Birgitta was desperate for a smoke. There was an almost full pack of Lucky Strikes in her purse, but she didn't dare go out in the hall to get it. She'd never smoked here at Ella's, although it wasn't expressly prohibited. Maybe she could sneak out into the yard and take a few puffs over in the far corner. She put her hands on the sofa pillows to raise herself up.

"Where are you going?"

"No place. Just to the empty room."

Ella set the embroidery hoop and scissors aside, removing her glasses. "Hang on a minute, young lady," she said, putting her thumb and forefinger to her face and rubbing at the spots where her glasses pinched. "I need to speak to you."

Birgitta straightened up. "Talk to me? About what?"

"Your behavior. I've heard things that aren't very nice. What were you doing last Saturday, for example?"

Birgitta clamped her mouth shut, biting her lips until they hurt.

"Well?" asked Ella.

Birgitta squirmed. "I didn't do anything special Saturday. Have Margareta and Christina been saying nasty things behind my back again? Shit, they're always bugging me, they lie about me, and they constantly pick on me. I can't see why—"

Ella took a deep breath and interrupted. "No, Birgitta, no one's been talking behind your back. Just calm down now. I've heard one or two things, from the girls and from others as well, and I want to know if those things are true."

Birgitta bent forward, still with her hands under her thighs, her voice soft as a whisper. "What did you hear?"

Ella cleared her throat, rubbed once more at the marks from her glasses on her nose. "I was talking to Marianne at the child welfare office today. She said your name was making the rounds. Literally. That there's a little rhyme about you turning up all over the place. Christina and Margareta knew, too, but they refused to tell me what it was about, or to recite it for me."

She lifted her thumb and index finger away from her nose, let her hand fall to her lap, took another deep breath, and looked down. "Uncle Stig called this afternoon. He'd heard that rhyme, too, even knew it by heart. He also told me you'd gone all the way with three different boys on Saturday. He'd spoken with a girl who was there. He was driving her to a home—she's in child welfare, too. He said she'd told him all kinds of things about you on that ride. Especially about Saturday. That you'd had too much to drink and just lay there in the grass out at Varamo and let it happen, let one boy after the next . . ."

Her voice choked up. She put her hand to her throat, unable to continue.

* * *

BIRGITTA HAD CURLED up in the far corner of the sofa and was crouching there like a threatened animal, preparing to leap. She hadn't moved, though. Hadn't moved or spoken at all yet, although she could feel a little hissing sound starting to leak out from between her front teeth.

Marianne! Pike-jowled Stig! Christina and Margareta! Some damned little reform school tramp with a mouth she was unable to keep shut. When the fuck would she be free from all these stupid assholes who had made a mission of ruining her life, just like they'd ruined Gertrude's once upon a time? They just wanted to kill her, all of them! They wanted to tear her to bits, as they had torn Gertrude to bits with their malice and slander, with bureaucratic decisions from the temperance board and the child welfare authorities! Why couldn't they leave them in peace? Why couldn't they have let Gertrude and her live in peace, why had they had to tear Birgitta away from the only human being she really wanted to be with? It was their fault Gertrude had been left all alone, and had died all alone in her apartment. If Birgitta had been allowed to go on living with her, if they hadn't dragged her away to Old Lady Ella's and forced her to stay there, it would never have happened. When Birgitta was there, she would turn Gertrude over when she was sick and vomiting. Ever since she was a little girl, she had known that when Gertrude had had a drink or two she needed to lie on her stomach, couldn't be on her back. But Birgitta hadn't been there. They'd killed Gertrude by taking Birgitta away from her! And now it was Birgitta's turn, now she was the one who was going to be torn to shreds!

Now the words came to her. At last. Birgitta could feel them rising. At first they came out hoarsely and jerkily, then gradually they began to flow: "You! Killed! Her!"

Ella recoiled in her chair. "What are you talking about? Who's been killed?"

Birgitta grinned. The plug in her throat was pulled, now the words were pouring right out: "Don't play dumb with me, you old bag. Gertrude, of course. You killed her, you and your whole damn crew. You and Marianne and Pike-Jaws!"

Ella blinked. "What are you trying to say? Killed? Pike-Jaws?"

Birgitta got up off the couch, she could literally feel herself growing. Soon she'd hit the ceiling, she'd burst right through it and just go on growing, her body would push right up through Hubertsson's apartment and on up to the attic, she'd make the damn roof fly off this damn house!

She planted herself in the middle of the floor, feet as wide apart as they would go in her tight skirt, pointing an accusatory finger at the easy chair. Her voice fluctuated, like a teenage boy's, from the deepest bass to the shrillest shriek. "Shut your mouth, hag! I'm so damn tired of you and your crew. If you and pike-jowled Stig and Marianne hadn't stuck your damn noses in other people's business, Gertrude would still be alive today. If I had been able to stay with her, to be with her, to take care of her like I wanted to, she wouldn't have died. I would have seen to it that she'd stayed alive!"

Ella went pale, only to go red and then pale again. At the same time, and as laboriously as an old woman, she got up from the chair and opened her arms. "Oh, my dear! My dear little Birgitta, I had no idea . . ."

Birgitta thrashed, not wanting to be touched by those hands. Let anything else happen, anything but that! No, those hands were the last thing Birgitta wanted on her. Let anyone else in the world touch her, other people could use her body however they pleased, but not her. Not her! Never, ever her!

Now the old lady had started to blubber, too. Big tears ran down her cheeks as she stood there, hands extended. "You poor little thing," she whispered. "Poor, poor Birgitta! Of course we would have let you move back home, if only your mother had wanted it. I spoke to her myself, though, and she told me she didn't. She said she wasn't up to it."

Liar! That fucking bitch was standing there casting a bold-faced lie in Birgitta's face! She could see it. Birgitta could literally see the lie come streaming through the air, like a white-hot ball of fire. Her arms flailed all the more, but it didn't help; her eyes were blinded and scorched to ash, her skin was burning, charred in one instant.

Oh, the pain! Birgitta's hand flew to her abdomen; she bent double and howled, bellowed straight out, just a sound with no words, with no meaning. She was bursting! Now she really knew what it meant to be torn to pieces, soon she would fall dead to the floor. . . . Escape! Escape! Escape!

But she didn't die. She could feel the first savage pain ebb, the screaming go silent. She rose slowly and looked at Ella. The old lady just stood there, though she had dropped her hands; they were hanging slack and open at her sides. The tears were still running down her cheeks, and a little streak of blood was seeping from her nose.

"You're grieving so," said Ella, shaking her head. "I hadn't the slightest idea you were still mourning her death . . ."

She stepped forward. Birgitta recoiled, backing toward the windows along the wall, raising her arms to protect herself and hissing, "Don't you touch me, I'm warning you! Do you hear me? Don't you dare touch me! Because I know what you are, you pious hypocrite!"

Ella halted, reeling, a gleam of caution rising in her eyes. "What are you saying?" she asked, wiping the tears from her cheek with her wrist. "What is it you're saying, Birgitta?"

Birgitta took one more step backward, spitting on the floor at her feet. "You better believe I know."

The streak of blood under Ella's nose had begun to coagulate, and every second her face seemed to stiffen more, the more she extended herself to sound impassive and innocent. "You just calm down now, Birgitta. What exactly do you know?"

Birgitta wiped at her own nose, sniffling. "The monstrosity! I know all about that deformed monstrosity of yours!"

Ella was ashen. Birgitta saw her blanch; it took only a fraction of a second. Ella swayed where she stood but said nothing.

Birgitta cackled. "Gertrude had the bed next to yours, you stupid old bag. She knew what kind of a person you were the whole time, that you'd abandoned your own spastic monster just because it was difficult to have something like that in the house. You were too lazy. And too stingy. You preferred healthy kids. Ones you would be paid to look after."

Ella stood there, immobile. Birgitta took one further step backward, away from those hands that were no longer open to her, and leaned against the wall. She laughed again, loud and crystal clear this time, and suddenly laughter was just pouring from her. She laughed until she was shouting, until her stomach began to ache and tears came to her eyes. She had to gasp for breath and wipe her eyes before she was able to speak again. "And you've walked around here all these years like some kind of frigging saint! With Margareta and Christina swishing around you, kissing your feet and licking your ass. Because you are so damn wonderful, you aren't the least little bit like their own filthy mothers. And I've known it all the whole time. . . . I've known all this time that you were exactly like their mammas!"

Birgitta laughed once more, unable to stop. She laughed until she had to cross her legs to keep from wetting herself. She laughed and laughed, felt her legs buckle, and had to shut her eyes and hold herself up against the wall so she wouldn't fall over. She was barely able to speak, really had to force herself. "And I've known all the time!" She panted, wiping her nose. "For all these years I've known what a shit you really are. . . . That there's nothing you wouldn't stoop to!"

She opened her eyes and looked at Ella. The old lady'd had one of her nosebleeds, and the blood was smeared on her face. But now she wasn't moving, was just standing perfectly still as she whispered, "Yes. But . . ."

That was all she got out before her eyes appeared to be popping out of her head and she moaned. She reached out, fumbled the air with her hand, searching for invisible support. Then her legs caved in and she collapsed.

HOW LONG DID Birgitta stand there, pressed up against the wall, staring at Ella's body? A couple of minutes? A couple of hours?

She doesn't know. She only knows that when she became certain, the certainty filled every cell in her body, the certainty that there was no hope, that a life sentence had been pronounced. She could hear it whispering and hissing from the walls and the ceiling, the voices of invisible judges mixing with the ticking of the wall clock, with the patter of the rain on the windowpane: Guilty, guilty, guilty! It didn't help to try to defend herself, didn't help that she raised her arms to protect herself, tried to vanish into the wall, whined with a shrill voice: "Not my fault! Not my fault! It wasn't my fault!"

"You're lying," says Margareta, downshifting.

Birgitta doesn't answer, just sighs and opens the second can of beer. Of course she's lying. Naturally. She's never done anything but lie, has she? What she had really done that time was to pull a viper out of her bag and scare little Aunt Ella so badly she had had a stroke. Of course. When Birgitta took that night-school course in General Revulsion, that vocational training for professional bitchiness, they'd taught her to keep a viper in her bag at all times, just in case she should bump into someone it might be fun to drive around the bend. Right. Unless, of course, a phantom suddenly passed through Ella's living room and scared the living daylights out of her. Or maybe she just happened to trip over the upturned fringe on a rug and fall head first to the floor. That must have been it. Any old explanation will do. Who says you have to make do with the truth?

The road's gone narrow and dark, with woods on both sides. Soon it will brighten up again, the fields will open out and the road widen. Then they'll be approaching Motala. Birgitta can now safely guzzle the last of that near beer. Soon she'll be home and can dig up a real one from her reserves.

"So you expect me to believe that Ella had a baby of her own once?" asks Margareta, shaking her head. "It can't be. She never said a word about it. . . . Nobody did, actually."

"Maybe not," says Birgitta, gazing out at the woods. There's still white snow under the trees. "But she did have a kid, I can tell you. A kid she abandoned."

Margareta pinches her lips together and shakes her head, saying nothing for ages. The next time she opens her mouth, her bottom lip is bleeding a little. "Maybe the baby died," she says, quickly licking away the blood. "If it was so deformed."

"The baby didn't die," says Birgitta. "Hugo died, but the kid didn't."

Margareta tosses a condescending look her way and picks up speed. "And you know all this?"

Birgitta nods and wipes her mouth. Yeah, that's it. She does know. "I even know her name."

But Margareta doesn't ask for names, just takes a cigarette, puts it in her mouth, gropes for the lighter, and drives even faster. This is definitely getting dangerous, and Birgitta leans forward and lights her cigarette for her in a moment of pure self-preservation. She really doesn't feel like being wrapped like a Band-Aid around a fir tree now that she's so close to home sweet home. Soon she'll be free to curl up on her mattress and relax in the dark. She'll take that blanket Roger pulled down off the window when they were arguing yesterday and hang it back up. Even though it's starting to get dark out, Birgitta wants that blanket in place so she won't be woken up when it gets light in the morning. She wants to sleep for days.

She sees that it's suddenly lighter on the road and is glad for that, anyway. The woods are thinning out, they're approaching the plain, which means they'll be in Motala really soon. Birgitta leans back. She's tired. Very tired. She could fall asleep here and now.

SHE OPENS HER eyes just as they drive past the old community center, reaches for the beer can, and gives it a little shake just to see whether there might be a swallow left. There is. More than she thought. The can makes a promising sloshing sound.

"Left," she says, wiping her mouth after the first swig, "but not quite yet. Left on Charlottenborg Road. I live up in Charlottenborg."

Margareta says nothing. She's put on her schoolmarm look while Birgitta's been sleeping and is sitting there with her nose upturned and her face utterly rigid. Well, if that's how she wants to spend the last few minutes they'll ever have together, Birgitta doesn't mind.

"HERE'S LOOKIN' AT you, sister," says Birgitta, raising her beer can in Margareta's direction. "It's gonna be great not to have to see you again. Left here!"

But Margareta misses the intersection and just goes straight on. Shit! Birgitta pounds a fist on the dashboard. She doesn't want any trouble now that she's almost home! "You missed the turnoff, idiot!"

Margareta turns her head, gives Birgitta a quick glance. "No I didn't. I did not miss the turn."

"Waddaya mean? I said I live in Charlottenborg, and that's off to the left here. What the hell do you think you're doing?"

Margareta turns quickly toward her again, giving her a really friendly smile. "Well, we aren't actually going to your place right now. We're going to Vadstena. I thought you'd better tell your story to Christina. For once, you're going to take the consequences of the stories you tell people."

THIS IS A hijacking, no question about it!

Birgitta pulls at the door handle when Margareta has to stop for a red light, but she can't open it. Margareta steps on the accelerator impatiently, making the engine growl again and again. She doesn't even look at Birgitta. "No use pulling at the handle," she simply says. "You'll just break it. I've locked all the doors from here, so you won't be able to get out, no matter how hard you pull."

The light turns and the car starts moving. Margareta seems to know the way, turns left here as if she did it every day. Not so strange, really, she walked this way to school every day for years. They're close to Ella's now.

Margareta shoots a glance at the house as they pass, as if she imagined she could see more than a pale shadow at this speed, then squints straight ahead at the road again. She's driving like a car thief. A fucking near-sighted car thief. Birgitta is going to be happy if she gets to Vadstena in one piece, in spite of the fact that Vadstena's the last place she wants to go, and a confrontation with that other frosty-eyed snob is the last thing she wants to have.

"You're hijacking me," she says indignantly, raising her beer can for the last swallow. "I'm gonna report you tomorrow."

Margareta chuckles. "You do that. We'll just have to see whose word the police accept."

After that, there doesn't seem to be anything left for them to talk about, and the car quiets down.

IT'S GETTING DARK fast now, the night appears to be rising right out of the earth. The fields and the sparse groves of trees on the plain are black as pitch, although the sky above them is still pale. It's the color of withered lilacs. Birgitta smiles a little at the memory. At Grandma's, the lilacs always paled before they withered, turning almost white.

* * *

MARGARETA'S FEATURES HAVE gone fuzzy. Birgitta can't see her eyes or the expression on her face any longer, she's nothing but a shadow. Birgitta squeezes her beer can until it buckles, looking out into the darkness. She, who never has any compunction about lying, is now having second thoughts about having told the truth. Not because of having been kidnapped, she can live with that. It's not the end of the world to have to make a trip to Vadstena, but, for once, reality is giving her a shock. For one instant—right when she started to tell—she was foolish enough to imagine that she would be believed and that the truth would make a difference. But now the truth is out and nothing is any different anyway. Her sentence has been confirmed. There will be no clemency.

Birgitta snorts and lights a cigarette. As if she would have wanted clemency from them! That shitty pair of snots.

WHEN THEY GET to Vadstena and Margareta stops the car in front of some old house, Birgitta doesn't get out. This must be Christina's place. Margareta rang the doorbell first and now she's going into the yard, around to another door. How can she be bothered? It's obvious there's no one at home, all the windows are dark and shiny.

Birgitta leans back in the passenger seat, suddenly feeling a strange kind of warmth spread throughout her body, like when a flower blooms, opening its petals at sunrise. She feels her shoulders slouch, her fists relax, her heartbeat slow. It must be the silence. Vadstena's such a quiet place; she doesn't hear a sound. No car engines. No human voices. No birdcalls.

The world hasn't been this quiet for a long, long time.

The little dome light goes on. Margareta's back and is tossing her bag into the car. She opens her mouth to say something, but when she sees Birgitta, she stops. Just sits in the driver's seat and turns the key without a word. Before she starts to drive, though, she turns toward her sister and strokes her cheek lightly.

The Procession of the Dead

How quickly your cheeks turn to dust!
Come, kiss me with liquid lips.
See the gulls create as they must
Their nocturnal poem with wingtips.

Stig Dagerman

A LITTLE DRUMMER boy makes his way through Vadstena as darkness rises out of the earth. He is all concentration, his eyes nearly shut, the tip of his tongue protruding between his lips, his mouth changing its shape to each beat of the drumstick against the drumhead. He's gifted, despite his youth; he can't be more than ten. But his pudgy fingers hold the drumsticks in a firm, adult grip, and he beats the rhythm with determination, with no hesitation. In his mind, a rhyme goes round and round, a simple poem that helps him keep the beat:

> *Life. Life. Live.*
> *Life. Life. Live.*
> *Life. Life. Life.*
> *Life. Life. Life.*
> *Life. Life. Live.*

He's learned his drumming at the local music school, but that's not where he got the rhyme. He's a *benandante,* though he doesn't know it. All he knows is that early in the evening he crawled up into his mamma's lap and leaned his curly blond head into her chest. He doesn't do this very often anymore. He's a big boy now, he's wearing a black T-shirt with an Iron Maiden decal on the front. But he felt so strange. As if all he wanted was to sleep. His mamma put her lips to his forehead, said he felt a little hot and maybe he needed to have an early night.

She sat on the edge of his bed for a while holding his hand and looking at the pictures on his wall, smiling gently at their garish dreams of masculinity. Kiss. Iron Maiden. AC/DC. Leather. Studs. Frowns. She looked at his chubby hand, resting in her own, stroked his soft skin with her index finger, thinking about the big man's hand that was developing inside. What kind of man would her son be? A good man, she knew that, because he had a good heart. He and his little brother were both born to a life of music and stories, songs and pictures. She stood up, patted his forehead, and smiled once more. He was perspiring in his sleep, as he had done all his life.

Even when he was an infant she knew everything was going to go well for him: he was born to the caul.

AND NOW THIS boy, who doesn't yet know he is a *benandante,* is walking the streets and lanes of Vadstena with his drum. He thinks he's dreaming, he thinks he's still in bed, that he's really asleep under the guardian eyes of his hard-rock heroes, and that the shapes he glimpses now and then behind his closed eyes are nothing but dream shapes. He doesn't know why he is playing his drum. He doesn't realize he has a mission, that he is the one who is calling the *benandanti* and all those who have died an early death to the procession. Tomorrow is the spring equinox. Tonight the dead will celebrate life.

I HEAR HIM very clearly, although I am still in my body. Just now there's no wind; my convulsions are the only things that make me jolt now and then, and between them I can lie here observing the world, quite still in my bed, relaxed and listening to the beating of the drum.

Maria's back in her room, and that makes her happy. She's sitting at the table, enveloped in a cone of light from the reading lamp, humming to herself as she cuts out yet another angel wing from recycled county council cardboard. Dusk has crept into the room, is sweeping like a shawl around her shoulders. The angels on the wall have taken a step backward, cocked their heads, and are looking at her, smiling and waving as they sink slowly into darkness.

But it's not quite night yet. The sky outside the window is still almost the same color as Birgitta's wilting lilacs. That's how it always looks as the last day of winter is extinguished, slowly, slowly. So I lie here in my bed and can still see the world out there. With my own eyes, I look at the parking lot and the health center. The maple tree on the lawn is stretching, as if it had just woken from a long sleep and wanted to touch the heavens with its black branches.

The air must be lovely to breathe. I saw Kerstin One and Ulrika stand still for a few minutes in the parking lot as they left for the day. They just stood there breathing, neither smiling nor speaking, then slowly waved and parted.

Kerstin Two has arrived. She's looked in on Maria and me a couple of times, to be sure we are all right, that no new storm has racked either of us. The last time she opened the door she was carrying a cup. Coffee for Maria and the aroma of coffee for me. When she'd put it down on Maria's table she came over to me, raised the head of my bed a little farther, bent me forward, and wiped my back with a warm, wet washcloth. It felt nice. I was very sweaty.

"We're still trying to reach Hubertsson," she said softly. "He's not home yet, but I'm sure it won't be long. As soon as we reach him he'll come to see you. You know that."

I nodded. He'll come. Of course Hubertsson will come.

RIGHT NOW I want to stay in my own body. I don't have the energy to catch a gull or a crow and fly out over Vadstena to locate Hubertsson. Moreover, it's probably not too easy to find a decent gull or crow right now, since in apartments and houses all over Vadstena men and women—all once born to the caul—are standing at their windows silently enticing potential carriers. Now their birds are sitting on naked branches and windowsills, cleaning their feathers and waiting for the arrival of night, so they can carry their masters to the market square. Experience tells them it's an easy task. As soon as they get to the square the *benandanti* change their guise, leaving the birds and becoming their own shadows instead. Only one single bird will get to be a carrier all night, only one single bird will get to hover over the Procession of the Dead. Mine. But tonight I won't be there. The *benandanti* and those who died an early death will have to walk the streets and lanes without me; they will parade out of town and into the countryside for the first time in many years without a black bird flying overhead screeching about the lean years of the olden times. It doesn't matter. They'll be so pleased with that little drummer boy they won't notice I'm not there. They haven't had a little drummer boy for a long, long time.

It has always surprised me that Hubertsson's not a *benandante*, since he, too, was born to the caul. But I've never seen his shadow with the others. Every time I have seen him his contours have been equally firm, whether I've looked at him through my own eyes or through those of others. Otherwise, he would have been an excellent *benandanti* captain, though. I can imagine it, imagine him arranging the ranks on the market square, imagine him giving orders to his subordinates among the *benandanti,* putting his arm around those who had died an early death, comforting them as if they were his patients.

They are always very surprised, those mutilated victims of traffic accidents, those pale suicides, those who have died of cancer and heart attacks. They look around, wide-eyed, not really understanding what they are seeing. Nowadays, when people tend to live so long, the knowledge that we all have our time has been lost, and that even the dead are not allowed to leave the world until all the years they should have lived have passed.

Ella took it quite well. She wasn't frightened. She just looked around in surprise, smiled briefly, and gave what had once been her arm a little pinch. She didn't grow serious until a bird began screeching overhead, a black bird crying out the story of the lean years in the olden times.

She never found out who I am. And now she's no longer of this world.

I THINK MARIA hears the little drummer boy, she's started humming his rhyme: *Life. Life. Live. Life. Life. Live. . . .* She hasn't said a word to me since she came back from the dayroom, but now she turns toward me with a little smile, lifting up her latest angel for me to admire. I nod, and raise a hand to wave. It is a very nice one. Somehow she has made the gray county council cardboard glitter.

Christina's still at the health center, I know that even though I've stayed in my body since I left our mutual sisters outside the Post-Industrial Paradise. I haven't bothered to shut my eyes and see her, but the light in her office is still on. Come to think of it, though, all the lights are still on at the health center, Hubertsson's office light, too, and he's not there, as Helena has repeatedly assured both Kerstin One and Kerstin Two. Helena may have turned on his office light and gone in there to straighten his desk. She's definitely still at the center. I saw her just a few minutes ago when she locked the front door. Although they're closed for the day, Helena is in no hurry to get home. Nobody's waiting.

I RECOGNIZE THE sound of the engine. Even before I can see them, I know Margareta and Birgitta are arriving. It took them longer than I thought, though. Maybe they had trouble finding the way, although Birgitta has been to Christina's office and to her desk before, and although

Margareta should remember the way to the building where Aunt Ella died.

The filthy snowdrift at the edge of the parking lot comes to life and starts to sparkle in their headlights. Margareta does a lousy parking job, as if she were suddenly in a rush, and opens the door before even unbuckling her seat belt. Birgitta is still leaning back in the passenger seat, but she clearly doesn't intend to sit in the car while Margareta goes to find Christina. Her seat belt's off, and she opens the door and raises herself heavily. For one second it looks as if this might have been too much for her. She bends forward, rests her arms on the roof of the car, and lets her head sink.

In the distance the little drummer boy is beating his rhythm. Maria hums in time.

"CAN I HELP you?" Margareta asks.

Birgitta looks up, shaking her head. "I just felt dizzy."

"Are you all right now?"

Yes, she's all right. Birgitta nods and shuts the door. Margareta locks the car.

"Do you think they'll be open at this hour?" Birgitta asks hesitantly. There's something different about her now. Whatever else you might say about Birgitta, whatever else you have said, *hesitant* was not a word you would use to describe her. Not even when she's frightened. No, she never charges more savagely at an enemy than when he truly frightens her.

"No, but I bet Christina's still around," says Margareta. "Erik's away, so she doesn't have to be home at any special hour."

She stands in a little square of yellow light, hands pushed deep into her pockets. It's the reflection of Hubertsson's office light on the tarmac. There seems to be a weight holding Margareta's head down, she looks really beat. More than twenty-four hours have passed since it all began, and it's not over yet.

Birgitta waits in the lot while Margareta walks up the steps to the door of the center. She suddenly realizes she's in the light from another window and melts back, like one shadow among so many others.

As expected, the door is locked; Margareta pulls at it a couple of times before starting to knock on the pane of glass. No one seems to hear her, despite her quick crescendo from knocking with her index finger to pounding with her whole fist. She bangs at the door for a long time, but not a soul appears in the lighted hallway. "Anybody there?" Margareta shouts. "Anybody there?"

And finally somebody comes.

HELENA OPENS THE door just a crack. Her eyes are red and her skin is blotchy. Maybe she's getting a cold; maybe a little virus jumped from the skin of a patient over to Helena's.

"We're closed," she says thickly. "If it's an emergency, you'll have to go to Motala."

Margareta smiles her polite smile. "Excuse us, but we're not patients, we're Christina's sisters. She wasn't at home, so we figured she might still be at work."

Helena stares incredulously at Margareta. "Christina's not here." She sniffles.

Margareta frowns. "We must have passed each other on the road then. We'll just have to go back to her place. Thanks, anyway."

She's just turned around to head down the steps when she hears Helena say, "Christina won't be at home. She wasn't going home."

Margareta turns back in surprise. "So where is she?"

Helena bursts into tears as she opens the door wide. "In the waterfront park. The police called to say they'd found Hubertsson there. Dead!"

Margareta rushes down the steps, running across the parking lot. Birgitta emerges from the shadows and follows her. Helena's lament cracks the air behind them: "He's dead. They said Hubertsson was dead!"

No!

That wasn't supposed to be what happened! Hubertsson wasn't supposed to die, not now! He was supposed to sit at my bedside for three days and three nights, sit with me to the bitter end and follow the story of my sisters as it scrolled down my screen, with a smile on his lips.

He can't die! He can't leave me! How can I live for three more days if Hubertsson is dead?

THE FINAL WINTER storm sweeps in across the Östgöta plain from the north, and it's freezing cold. The soil freezes to ice in a moment as it passes; the shoots of green hidden under leaves and old grass wither instantly and die. Leafless branches and bushes crouch down and curl up, but the cold wind just laughs at them and presses them flat, only to tear them upward again and shake them, breaking their fragile shoots and leaving them hanging, like broken promises. Leafy trees bow down and beg to be spared, but this is a storm that spares no one and nothing; it shakes and bends them, tosses them aside and breaks them in two, exposing the green wood in their trunks. The wind halts then, to spit at them, to toss earth and sand and whirling cobweb-thin leaves from last autumn on their wounds, only to take off again and rush, like a furious giant, in among the conifers.

The fir trees stand mute and tall as soldiers at attention, refusing to beg for mercy. The storm laughs at their stiff pride, laughs and mocks them for a while, then tosses them aside, one by one, tearing them up by their roots and overturning them, revealing the thousand creatures hiding in the ground underneath. And none of these creatures lives for more than a few seconds after that; the frost lags behind only to pinch them with icy fingers and crush them to death as the storm gallops onward across the plain, in the direction of a town and a nursing home.

It stops briefly, catches its breath, and gathers its forces, turning its renewed force on the yellow building, shaking it by the foundation, ripping at the roof tiles so they clank against one another, so the walls moan and groan, so the windowpanes press inward in an arch, preparing to smash . . .

Maria's wailing. She's standing by my bed, trying to hold my jerking hand, crying because it's so difficult to grip, and because my whole body is convulsed. Maria knows what it's like to be swept away by a storm, to be torn like a dry leaf from its branch, to be tossed hither and yon in the vacuum, only to fall to the ground through the empty air.

"Kerstin!" she shouts. "Come, Kerstin, come!"

And Kerstin Two comes.

I LIKE KERSTIN Two. I like her because she's robust and solid, because she seldom smiles but often laughs, because her laugh sounds like a little dove is nesting in her throat, because she sometimes squints down at me over the frames of her eyeglasses.

But now she's not laughing, no little dove is cooing in her throat. She's thrown her arms around me, is biting her lips and pressing me tightly to her. She's suffering. She cannot give me any more Valium than I've already had, and there is no doctor at hand to decree an IV drip. Christina's left the health center, and Hubertsson's nowhere to be found.

Time stops for a millisecond between two seizures; the storm settles and my body is no longer being tossed and turned. In this hole in time, I lie with my head against Kerstin Two's white coat, suddenly able to hear her heartbeat. Every clock in the world has stopped, every electron in the universe is frozen in position, but Kerstin Two doesn't mind. Her heart just goes on beating steadily. And suddenly I realize there is no longer any reason to hang around. I can leave the nursing home at this very moment, go wherever I please. Other hearts will beat for me. There will always be hearts to beat.

I shut my eyes and let go. The storm passes.

NO GULL WITH bright white feathers awaits me in the maple tree, no shiny black raven with a golden gaze, not even a crow with irises of steel. Just a little gray birdie. An anxious little house sparrow with a ruffled coat of feathers.

But how this bird does fly! She lifts me high above the streets and lanes of Vadstena, higher than I've ever flown before. Laughing, she takes me in wide circles up through the air, higher and higher, until we nearly touch the clouds, the clouds that are now whiter than the heavens above them. Far off to the west, where the sun has just set, the Hale-Bopp comet glimmers like a shiny silver fireworks display. This is a night of celebration; the last night of winter is a night of festivity every year. The darkness extends itself one last time, yet we are surrounded by light, my bird and I. The skies above us are starry, as is the earth below us—in Vadstena and all the other towns, the lights are now on.

For one moment I hang suspended between heaven and earth, for one moment I have a choice between them.

I choose earth. I will always choose earth.

NOW THE LITTLE drummer boy has reached his destination. He stands erect, at attention, on the market square, beating his drum, as the shadows deepen around him and a thousand whispering voices join his rhythm:

Life. Life. Live.
Life. Life. Live.
Life. Life. Life.
Life. Life. Life.
Life. Life. Live.

Not one single *benandante* sees me fly over the square. I'm nothing but a quiet little sparrow, no big black bird am I. I am no longer screeching the story of the lean years.

MY SISTERS ARE in the park by the lake, standing in the dark. The light from the streetlamps doesn't reach in under the trees, not even the blinking blue light on the ambulance out on the street reaches them.

They're standing close together watching the paramedics lift Huberts-son's body onto a gurney. None of them is crying, none of them is speaking, but Margareta suddenly bends forward and tucks the blanket closer around him, as if she thought he was lying there feeling cold. When she straightens up, Christina takes her hand and squeezes it gently. Margareta looks at her and quickly takes Birgitta's hand in her other one. And suddenly it's as if a thought ran through their arms and hands and, for one moment, united them.

"He was the last one," says Christina. "Now there is no one left who was a grown-up when we were children."

"No one remembers Aunt Ella like we do," says Margareta.

"I'll bet he knew more than we thought," mutters Birgitta.

Margareta tries to extract her hand, but Birgitta won't let go. Christina doesn't notice this struggle.

"I would have liked to get to know her," she says. "On equal terms. Adult to adult . . . Sometimes I dream about us having coffee together at a café. But I'm doing all the talking. She never says anything."

Margareta's hand has stopped twisting in Birgitta's. "There was that empty room," she says softly. "And someone else who really should have lived in it."

A smile crosses Christina's face. "How could they have? We filled the emptiness."

Birgitta bends forward slightly, spitting in the gravel. "Some emptiness can never be filled," she says. "No matter how hard you try."

The three stand there silent for a moment as the paramedics carry the gurney with Hubertsson on it to the ambulance. They nod to the three women as they pass. Birgitta releases Margareta's hand, and Margareta lets go of Christina's. They do not look at one another.

"Why don't you two come along to the Post-Industrial Paradise for tea and sandwiches?" Christina asks, pushing her bangs out of her eyes with a pale hand, her cape following her movements. She turns her back and heads for the street before continuing, "You'll need something to eat before you hit the road."

Margareta laughs and starts to walk in the same direction. She gets the hint. "Yes, thank you," she says to Christina's back. "If it's not too much trouble."

Birgitta stands still a moment before following the others. She kicks at the gravel as she walks, annoyed over the gaps in her Minnie Mouse heels. Shit! Fucking tea and sandwiches! Leave it to Christina! What she needs is a beer.

HUBERTSSON'S SITTING IN the shadows on a park bench. His face is solemn, but his posture arrogant. He's extended his legs and crossed them at the ankles; his right arm is stretched out along the top of the bench. He can't see me yet. He can't see me as I would have been if everything had been different.

Over at the square, the little boy beats his drum. The sound is powerful now, it thunders through streets and lanes, it echoes off the roofs of cloisters and churches, roars like a spring wind across the lake.

But Hubertsson doesn't respond to the call, he doesn't get up and head for the market square. He just sits calmly on his bench, waiting for me to emerge from the shadows.

About the Author

MAJGULL AXELSSON is the author of four works of nonfiction as well as one previous novel, *Far from Nifelheim,* for which she was awarded the 1994 Moa Stipendium. The 1997 publication of *April Witch* in Sweden earned her the prestigious August Prize. She is married, has two children, and lives in Stockholm.

PART I

The Covert No Destroys Love

Chapter 1

Does Saying No
Belong in Love?

Does saying no belong in a relationship informed by love? If so, we must learn to say no in a way that does not destroy but rather aids love. What we initially experience as given to us in the spontaneous blossoming of love for another is an unconditional response of "Yes!" to one who was so distant from us and now suddenly appears so close, so intimate. The "Yes!" that was a mere feeling in the initial infatuation can become a vow by which one gets married. Then the happiness of two persons appears to depend on whether or not the mutual yea retains unlimited validity. Each "Yes, but . . . ," to say nothing of each "No," goes against the grain, disrupts harmony, announces something nasty: conflict, infidelity, separation, divorce. If, almost against one's will, one nevertheless says no, one is ready to do a fast about-face: "But, naturally, I didn't really mean it that way." One cannot distinguish between a refusal that signifies merely the delimitation of boundaries necessary in every bond and a refusal that, above and beyond limit-setting, is intended to expel the other from one's life. We have not yet learned to say no within the context of a love relationship.

The paradisiacal state of the unconditional yea often lasts only a few weeks or months, in spite of the most intense infatuation. Its most notable feature is that it can suddenly turn into its opposite; out of the absolute yes comes the absolute no. The smallest occasion may suffice to put an end to the sweet feeling of unity in which all differences melt away and to let the antithetical feeling of strangeness arise in one. After unbounded harmony without delimitation in shared love, the two individuals stake out two territories in isolation when they first break out of love. If the two get back together following this first no, fright permeates their bones so long that they begin to form an "arrangement." The uniting yea of the first, "happy" time imperceptibly turns into a mutual stance of making demands that separates the partners emotionally. Both sit at the same table and both want to be taken care of. Each would like to have his or her own needs satisfied. That one of them should take care of the other at the same time complicates the matter and incessantly stirs up little power struggles and every more sophisticated verbal agreements about who sets the terms when skirmishes are fought with or without words. The initial yea has slipped out of the center and now lies on the surface as the legalization of a care-taking institution that both partners operate together.

Whoever does not learn to say no to the other in order to establish his or her boundaries within the love relationship is likely to withdraw into a "welfare marriage." The absolute yes easily leads to the absolute no. Two lovers experience this after only a short time. In order to save the relationship from such a turnabout, some partners renounce love altogether and become merely parties to a contract. They suffer the disappointing loss of the bond of love because they have gained no skill in saying no in love. Fearing the word "no," the two partners can no longer say yes to one another either. Then, because they cannot create boundaries between themselves, they can no longer encounter one another. Because neither can say, "I have my own domain that I do not share with you—my own capacities, interests, and passions," they can no longer meet one another in the common middle ground.

An index of this is the sad fact that married persons often neglect and even give up earlier friendships. Yet it is just these very friendships, and new ones as well, particularly of women with women and men with men, that would further the appreciation of and nurturing of individual uniqueness in contrast to what binds two lovers together. Without other friendly relationships, the powerful yea of love deteriorates into dullness, convenience, and infantile need-satisfaction.

The feeling of oneness in which lovers initially experience the meaning and the joy of life evaporates. They avoid the uncertainty between yea and nay and flee into a relationship that differs from that of the child to its mother in one regard only: The child now has to take care of mother, too. There is a tendency to get one's partner to feed one all sorts of "treats," material and spiritual. Calmly, reluctantly, or angrily, according to situation and temperament, each partner counts the cost of his or her feeding of the other.

What gets lost is the possibility for each to develop a broader personality. But every person who is in love hopes precisely for this transformation. When one is seized by the god of love, the boundaries drawn about the ego by temperament and training become permeable, perhaps for the first time. Crossing this frontier makes one dizzy. In the fairy tales from *The Thousand and One Nights*, man and woman often swoon at the moment they fall in love. The woman breaks into the man and the man breaks into the woman, and after the dam is broken a new, strange world flows into the lovers—potentially the entire world. There follows a feeling of complete unity. One has the impression of being organically united with the entire world and of becoming part of a whole.

To dismiss this condition as transitory infatuation is not entirely to the point. It is true that mere infatuation is short-lived if it does not become conscious devotion.* It is likewise true, however, that each person really is part of a whole such as one experiences when in love. Physically and spiritually, all people have common roots. Thus the expansion of the ego when one loves a Thou corresponds to the objective fact of our ties to the world. This experience is so valuable that we must not abandon it. Feeling oneself united with the world is the highest meaning of life; life without this feeling is senseless. Initially the feeling of oneness is simply given to one who falls in love. The question becomes: What does one do with this gift? Does one consume it with keen appreciation, or does one enter into a love-inspired confrontation with the beloved person? In the first case the emotional yea soon turns into an equally emotional nay—the death of love. In the second case one learns to distinguish oneself from the Thou and to say no, in order to be able better to perceive and accept the Thou—to say yes. It is enlightening to observe how one person, as a consequence of love for another, can enlarge his or her personality. This is the first step in making clear the need for limit-setting between two lovers, the need to say no.

As an individual, each person embodies only a small segment of

---

* In the original German, the author uses the term *Hingabe*. *Hingabe* derives from the verb *hingeben*, meaning: 1) to hand or pass (something to someone); 2) to give away; 3) to give up or sacrifice (one's life for someone or something); 4) to devote or dedicate oneself; 5) to abandon oneself (to a pleasure or to despair); 6) to surrender or yield (to one's dreams; to another person). Hence *Hingabe* has the sense of (loving) devotion, dedication, abandon, sacrifice, and surrender. In the following text, *Hingabe* has been rendered either with devotion, surrender, or both; yet the reader should keep in mind that all these shades of meaning are present simultaneously, although now one may predominate, now another. —Translator.

what is possible for "the human being" and what, in part, is already being lived out by others. The ego—the center of consciousness—pays a high price for its boundaries and its solidity by renouncing the rest of the world. However, if the ego has attained a certain degree of strength, it no longer tolerates the limits. One experiences this at every difficult threshold of personal development. Thus, for example, the young person gets the feeling that other people—parents and teachers—have forced unsuitable limits on him or her. This feeling is a sign of growing ego strength. He or she begins to transgress these limits, first by reactions of defiance against adults, then more and more by acquiring his or her own knowledge, skills, and friendships outside the range of adult influence. In such initial attempts at breaking out, the possibility of retreat within the previously established boundaries still exists.

Not so when a person is seized by love. Now the limits of the ego are relativized, and the lover feels himself or herself to be potentially one with everything. In this mythic feeling of unity, the experience of oneself is expanded to the limits of the world. The beloved person is the portal through which the world, previously excluded by the ego, begins its influx.

The excluded external world corresponds to the soul's excluded inner world that we call the unconscious. The unconscious is our inner system of readiness for all humanly possible experiences. In order not to be extinguished in its identity, the ego must lock out many of these fundamentally possible experiences. Consciousness develops between the extremes of curious openness to vital impulses from the unconscious and their exclusion. In a similar manner, the experience of the external world moves between curious penetration—for example, into new areas of knowledge—and delimitation for reasons of self-protection; between the extremes of a fragmentation lacking a standpoint, and the boring retreat into one's shell. Just as the excluded external world embraces realms into which we have not yet set foot in our personal lives and in part never will—foreign cultures, for example—so, too, the excluded internal world embraces possibilities of development that we have not yet developed and in part never will develop: inner experiences of that which comprises human nature.

When we are in love, the intimation of this much greater world that we have in common with all other human beings permeates us, the intimation of a new inner and outer world revealed thanks to a Thou. When in love, we feel ourselves to be vitally connected with both: with the Thou as with a foreign realm of the external world, and with the Thou as a mirror of the inner world that is foreign to us.

In love's first dissolving of the boundaries, however, we easily commit two mistakes. First, we confuse the initial spontaneous experience of love with an expansion of our concrete living space guided by consciousness and will. Thus we believe that being in love suffices to transform us into a new person. And second, we close ourselves off against the insight that this Thou, who releases such pervasive and boundless feelings of love in us, is also "merely" a concrete and limited piece of the world and that we must exert some effort in order to discover him or her step by step.

The success of love depends on correcting these two mistakes. It has to do with transforming the *gift of love* into the *giving of love*, into the devotion and surrender that expresses itself in the effort to understand the Thou and take an active part in his or her blossoming. Hence the inner coming to terms with the Thou is redeeming. Paradoxically, this means that after the first phase of falling in love, we should again create some distance and return to the old ego in order, from the old standpoint, to take a good look at the new point of view that has seized us so powerfully. We should look at the new Thou from the vantage point of view of the old ego. Fusion is replaced by the tension between two persons who certainly are different but who are matched to one another as in Plato's well-known image of the two halves of a sphere.

This is the essence of saying no *in* love. One must say, "I am not Thou," but one must say it from within love: "Little by little I will endeavor to extend my narrow limits toward you." Love itself is the guarantee that this risky undertaking makes sense in terms of one's own life. More precisely than any marriage test, the mere presence of love reveals the path to oneself in the beloved, or at least a piece of that path.

Countless love relationships that perhaps were by no means mistaken choices of mate (as the post mortem devaluation would have it) have come to grief because lovers have not been able to say no in time. The opportunity to become "more human" and to come closer to the inner personality pattern that aims at development is then squandered and does not return again in the same form, nor can the loss of emotional energy be redeemed.

The nay must be said while the binding, instinctive yea of first love is still strong enough, otherwise this yea gets replaced by the separating nay without love, from which there is no return.

Earlier generations found it easier to say the live-saving no of delimitation within the love relationship. The firm, socially prescribed assignment of roles between man and woman took effect from the first moment of becoming acquainted and found its fixed form in the division of responsibility between husband and wife. The roles gave the ego a fixed standpoint from which it could distinguish itself from and come to terms with the Thou. The relationship between yea and nay was socially prescribed.

The increasing loss of husbandly and wifely roles imposes on the individual a task that society previously took care of. Today the individual must assume the very difficult responsibility for concurrent bonding and delimiting. The no that delimits I from Thou creates the precondition for actualizing the deepest human longing, namely the longing for unity that is more than the need for just some sort of relationship. It is obvious that more than a few successful or unsuccessful marriages depend on this. The vision that we have of ourselves and of the world depends on the success of setting limits in love— either the vision of a dismembered world threatened by chaos as a consequence of the absolute nay against love, or the vision of a world in whose dismemberment and chaos we can create a bit of unity and order as a consequence of the nay integrated into love. Visions are active in themselves and form the world just as much as they copy it. How we see the world is how we shape it. Whether or not we can deal with setting limits in a love relationship has direct consequences for the way in which we see the world and intervene in its events.

The force of destiny that finds expression in the story of Romeo and Juliet, the young lovers from Verona, has gripped people since the Italian author Luigi da Porto wrote the novella and Shakespeare recast it as a drama. Even though in industrial societies there are no longer hostile clans that could thwart the marriage of two young people, the love motif of Romeo and Juliet retains its general validity and truth. Why is this so? Because it shows that being seized by love breaks the rigid structures with which the ego has heretofore identified, be they of the more familial and social variety or of the more individual sort. However, love leads to self-destruction if the lovers do not succeed in giving their bond a structure of its own that is stronger than the structures that would separate them. Otherwise the relationship shatters because of social resistance or as a consequence of the ego's return to its earlier paths. The new river bed that the stream of love carved out dries up and turns desolate again.

The modern Romeo and Juliet no longer founder on the opposition of their hostile families, but rather—following a phase of the most intimate merging—on their own resistance against granting the Thou a right to live in the concrete everyday world. After the great yea to merging, they come to grief on the great nay against common transformation. Thus they kill the decisive possibility of life in themselves;

that is its suicide. The resistances that shatter them are less external than internal, even if now, as before, social factors are of significance for the success or failure of a love relationship.

Even today Romeo and Juliet need a structure for their relationship. Even today each partner must be able to say, "I am not you, and yet we belong together." Differentiation between them can no longer rest on the traditional division of roles, whereby the husband earns the money and the wife takes care of the children and the household; or the husband has reason and the wife has feeling; or the husband is active, decisive, leading, and aggressive, and the wife is passive, long-suffering, protective, close to reality, and maternal. The differing biological functions of man and woman no longer necessitate rigid assignment of roles. Indeed, the unaltered attraction between the sexes shows that, independent of the momentary understanding of roles, there is something specifically masculine and specifically feminine, but it is as though in our times the burden has fallen to each Romeo and every Juliet to discover what uniquely completes him or her as well as their common wholeness without being able to lean on a generally valid model of man-woman relationships. Very few people are up to this new task. Through this book, I hope to offer aid in mastering it.

There are already many offers of help, but they are usually superficial. For example, one is told that partners play their favorite complementary roles and cling rigidly to them. A man may adopt his favorite role of being mothered and a woman her favorite role of mothering. One is told how these roles "interact," and then it is shown how a more flexible assignment of roles, with an occasional exchange of roles, can relieve relationship problems.

Although such descriptions do accomplish something useful, they do not penetrate to the essence of love. Whoever follows these prescriptions may perhaps save his or her marriage, but will not have won that vitality and freedom that he or she had sensed like a prickling promise when first in love. One delimits oneself from one's mate and is at the same time nice to him or her: Nay and yea are part of the rules of the game in the social contract called marriage. But one has lost the most important thing—the inner feel for the Thou, the meditative savoring of the other in one's own heart, the delight at the sight of that particular person and devotion to the beloved. Perhaps one has never consciously experienced this most important thing, but one's unconscious knows it to the extent that one was at least once in love. If, however, two partners merely function together, they fall victim more and more to boredom and disgust.

Superficial descriptions of role problems omit asking after the *meaning* of two human beings' completing each other in a relationship. Does completing each other consist *only* in dividing up the work and the responsibility, similar to how the male and the female among lower mammals assume biologically different tasks and thereby complete each other? In that case an honorable partnership would be merely the most expedient form for a person's realizing his or her social talent by striving for a more flexible division of roles. Neurotic fixations would be almost unavoidable, since the dyadic relationship would permit both partners to remain their old selves even with new roles. The wife, for example, might be a dependent but industrious "father's daughter" and the husband a "courageous hero" in his professional life but a timid "Mama's boy" in the marriage. The dyadic relationship becomes a real hindrance to self-actualization if its goal is seen only in a distribution of social roles, for roles alone do not bring about a transformation of personality.

As a matter of fact, the dyadic relationship does block self-actualization in many instances, yet this is not its meaning. The meaning of love lies not only in the completion of two persons living together, but also in two separate individuals becoming whole. The origin of Eros lies in the longing of two persons, I and Thou, to become more complete and more human, in himself or herself but also in the company of the other. Love for the other is supposed to stimulate the development of "the other" in one's own soul. Above and beyond I and Thou, the child that is born in a love relationship symbolizes a third: the new human being, the new person. Thanks to being together with the other, each partner can become just such a new person.

The fundamental experience of love consists in overcoming the isolation of the individual. This experience emanates from the overwhelming feeling of being one with the Thou, and through the Thou, one with the entire world. In this experience, the ego is not stabilized but is relativized; it is not tied down but is set in motion toward a greater Self. What ultimately motivates every love is the shadowy presentiment that one can become a new person through devotion and surrender to a Thou. That love often turns into hate does not contradict this assertion, but rather indicates the considerable difficulties that are bound up with the process of devotion and surrender to a Thou. The major difficulty probably lies in perceiving in the Thou something strange and different and yet at the same time very close, something of one's very own in the deepest sense of the word: "I am not you, but you are an image of that which I lack on my path to reaching my own Self." Bringing together this—"No, I am not you" and this—"Yes, through your very being you reveal to me things that

I must also actualize" is an art that must be learned. That is the message of this book.

By and large I am limiting myself to the description of the love between man and woman, the most common form of love. Other forms of love, such as homosexual love and love of one's neighbor, would, of course, be suitable for relativizing the too exclusive love expectations between woman and man, but unfortunately we have largely lost the art of cultivating these other forms of love. Yet to open the heart to other forms of love would be part of the unique dynamics of every love relationship. In general, a love that secludes itself from the rest of the world in egotism cannot last. It will fall victim to its inner contradiction.

There are three developmental stages of an emotional relationship. The first is *fusion*. Fusion informs the relationships of natural man, the child—and also those of the lover. The distinction between I and Thou does not exist or is not yet possible. The confluence of I and Thou is intoxicating and, depending on the situation, is experienced as an increase or as a loss of strength.

The second stage is *projection*. Unconscious parts of oneself are erroneously cast out onto an object in the external world—onto the lover, for example—so that one's perception of him or her is distorted. In political life, images of the enemy are just such projections. Admittedly, there are usually "hooks" in the object that fit the projected contents, but they are exaggerated. Judgments that are shaped by projections have something absolute about them. The external object is reduced to a common denominator, and we no longer perceive the differentiated features of its whole being.

The third stage is *reflection of the guiding image*. This is the most complete form of emotional relationship. The person whom I love becomes a guiding image for me that reflects my own heretofore unknown possibilities of living, the dynamics of my development. Reflection of the guiding image is a realistic perception both of the partner who already embodies such characteristics in his or her personality, qualities that I still lack, and also of my Self in a facet of personality unknown to me up until now. "Reflection" could be associated with cool distance and egocentric vanity, but here, on the contrary, I mean that vision into the depths of the Thou of which only the one who loves is capable. Only with strong mutual feeling can two people reflect each other so deeply that they become guiding images and not merely external, perhaps unfitting role models for each other. In the person whom I love a new picture appears at each new meeting, a picture that bursts the narrowness of my usual way of experiencing and seeing and heralds a heretofore undiscovered aspect of my own nature. Through this, my partner now becomes a potent guiding image for me. In the course of this and of the following chapters, I will fully develop the various characteristics of reflection of the guiding image. To help the reader get an initial feeling for the reality of the reflection of the guiding image, I want to illustrate the concept with a brief example.

A twenty-five-year-old man had experienced all the events of his life up until then—friendship, completion of professional training, death of close persons—with a cool, detached, observing distance. He was never "in" these events, hence he could never be fully and completely happy nor could he fully and completely mourn. "Life roared past me," as he expressed it. Then he fell in love with a woman about his own age who, in contrast to him, was totally "in" everything that she felt, thought, and said. She was quite at home in her body, too—again in contrast to him, who often felt his body as foreign, as not belonging to him when he looked in the mirror as he shaved in the morning. The young woman whom he loved spontaneously awakened in him a new feeling for life. Often he was able to delight and to mourn, just as she was. In the course of many years he learned no longer to be dependent on her company in his new, more direct manner of experiencing. For him the woman became an inner guiding image that worked autonomously in him, even when he was alone, and bestowed upon him the gift of a previously impossible level of intensity of experience. That is reflection of the guiding image. It enlivens our developmental dynamics.

In this book we are always talking about *mutual* reflection of the guiding image. In love, two persons become mutual guiding images for countless separate developmental steps.

Fusion, projection, and reflection of the guiding image are not three discrete developmental steps. It is a question of three shifting centers of gravity in the development of the soul that we always experience simultaneously, although with different intensities. Hence it is an aspect of the health of the soul to plunge into complete merging with the external world from time to time throughout the whole of one's life, be it in an intense experience of love, be it in dance or when listening to music. One who understands how to emerge again at the right moment feels refreshed and reborn. The creative person, too, is allotted phases of fusion—for example with the fates of other people or with a landscape—before he or she can give form from within the Self to what experienced in the fusion. The work of the artist presupposes merging with what he or she expresses. In the act of creation, however, the fusion is overcome and a unique union is acheived between the object depicted and the personality of the artist. If it remains at the level of undifferentiated emotional fusion, the result is kitsch.

The same thing can be said of projection. Without projection there is no new self-knowledge. What delights or irritates us in our partner has to do with *us*. Recognized projections are glimmers of dark, unknown parts of our own personality. Every strong affect that we feel toward another person is a certain sign of a projection. Projections indicate our emotional vivacity. As long as we are under way and there are new, unknown realms of the soul to be discovered, we initially project every bit of new emotional territory onto the outside world. Usually we do not examine our projections voluntarily. We submit to a serious investigation of them only when communication with our partner is disturbed by our unrealistic projections because the partner continually feels misunderstood and begins to protest against our projected assertions.

However, our emotional relationships should be informed progressively less by merging and projection and progressively more by reflection of the guiding image. Admittedly, every relationship is a mixture of these three forms of relationship. Let us assume that after the initial infatuation in a love relationship, in which I felt entirely fused and identified with the other, there follow violent projections of infidelity that get so disturbing that I withdraw them and assume responsibility for them—that is to say, I admit that I myself felt like having an affair. Let us assume, moreover, that I succeeded in withdrawing these projections. Actually, one might then expect that the strong affect and the intense interest in the partner would diminish, but this is not always so. In this example, the Thou has characteristics that fascinate me: her sureness of instinct, calmness, rootedness, and imperturbability. These characteristics occupy me in even greater measure than did my previous projections of infidelity. In the case of these particular characteristics, it is obvious to everybody that this is not an issue of my subjective projections but rather of her actual characteristics. Why do they occupy me so very much? Because I still lack them and because I am emotionally ready to develop them in myself. The beloved person is the guiding image that incites me to become what I see in her. Of course, I will never succeed in becoming so instinctively certain and so calm, so rooted and imperturbable as the woman I love. Thus the polar tension between us in this relationship will never abate. But gradually I can develop these characteristics to the extent that I need them in order not to get regularly into situations that overtax me because I am not up to them.

After I have experienced a reflection of a guiding image, a new, more authentic relationship can begin. Each of us sees modeled and reflected in the other the parts of ourselves which, thanks to this perception, begin to live in us too. In the love relationship, the overwhelming feeling of being one, which we know from the initial merging with the Thou, now arises afresh, but is carried by the realistic perception of what the partner really is: one's guiding image.

The meaning of saying no in love emerges from this survey of the three developmental stages of the love relationship. In merging there is only the complete "yes" of affirmation and the complete "no" of separation, either identity with the Thou or panic and destruction. Merging with the external world is the state of being of the animal. So long as an animal can use its instinct, there is only the unbroken, unconscious yea to the surrounding world. But if an animal panics—think of a suddenly startled horse—it falls into a total contradiction with the surrounding world that often leads to destruction and self-destruction to the point of suicide. Of course, in the instance of the animal we can speak of yea and nay only as an analogy to the human being. In the unconscious condition of merging there is no delimitation within the context of love, no conditional, constructive demarcation from the beloved Thou. There is only the yes *to* love and the no *against* love.

With reservations, the same holds true for the person who is projecting. So long as we project a negative characteristic—for example, one's own unconscious avarice—onto our partner, we say no to him or her and place ourselves outside of love: "I cannot love you the way you are." Admittedly, this no does not have to be absolute, since perhaps we also have positive, realistic insights into the Thou that appeal to us in a good sense, along with such negative projections. If we are able to take back our projections, we delimit ourselves from the Thou in a new, conscious way. Then we say, for example: "The miser that I thought you were is me. But you are no miser." Consequently, the withdrawal of a projection, leads to the nay of conscious delimitation: "I am not you." The delimitation now arises from the insight into one's own boundaries, not the boundaries of one's partner. They follow voluntarily from within, not by coercion from without. The real coming to terms with the Thou as he or she actually is begins only in the phase of reflection of the guiding image. Only actual qualities in the Thou—not fictitious characteristics that we project onto the Thou—can awaken intensive and enduring love.

Moreover, we can enter into reflecting the guiding image only with regard to those facets of a person that concretely inform the way he or she shapes life, for only those facets make possible the conscious coming to terms with the Thou. In reflecting the guiding image, the yea of union joins the nay of delimitation—"I am not you"—that follows from the withdrawal of projections. "Such as I am in my concrete being—a man with more intuition than a feel for reality, with more feeling than intellect—I differ from you who are more realistic and intellectual than I am. But the entire movement in the present phase of my life is tending toward being more like you and better developing my intellect and my reality sense, without, of course, becoming like you. Ultimately my identity, like yours, has been strongly shaped by temperament and early influences. In you I perceive, as in a mirror image, how a new personality begins to live in me in union with my old personality while I contemplate you and as my interest turns toward the precise thought and the details of everyday life that I have neglected until now. I see that through this I am becoming more complete than I previously was."

In the reflection of the guiding image, the nay—the delimitation of I from Thou—finds its place in the love relationship because it is included in the dynamic context of the development of the individual into a more comprehensive personality.

In *The Myth of Sisyphus*, Albert Camus describes the total feeling of strangeness and uninvolvement that suddenly came over him while he rested in the arms of a woman. Every inner connection with this woman and with the world was severed. This sense of strangeness and isolation is not the ultimate possibility of the human condition. The encounter we experience when our guiding image is reflected to us can dynamically unite what is other and what is one's own, the nay and the yea, in a relationship of love. In the reflection of the guiding image, it becomes possible to experience the truth that the world of the soul and the world of matter cohere in all their parts. This experience makes possible a special development. Wherever I take interest in a bit of the external world, this can become for me a guiding image of a part of my own personality hitherto unknown to me.

Love is the expression of the strongest possible interest. It is certainly a sign that its object—the human being—signifies something essential for my subjective development. This way of seeing by no means reduces love to an egocentric contemplation of one's navel, for only real, unselfish devotion to a Thou gives rise to insight into the self.

Chapter 2

The Tragedy of the
Happy Couple

The essence of tragedy is that under certain conditions a tragic fate is unavoidable. The so-called happy couple fulfills all the conditions that destine a human relationship to disastrous failure, among them the following articles of belief:

- In the first affirmation of love, the happy couple declares their allegiance until death.
- The happy couple does not fight and does not suffer.
- For the happy couple a serious no is not permitted either in the other's personal realm, which each partner must respect, or as criticism—and certainly not in the form of infidelity and betrayal.
- The happy couple can be recognized by the happy impression they make in public. Before other people they are always of one opinion, the opinion of the happy couple.
- For the happy couple, sexuality is a regular part of their relationship and is satisfying for both persons. The partners spoil each other.
- The happy couple is the most efficacious prescription against loneliness and the uneasiness caused by personal questions and problems.
- The happy couple knows only couples who are also happy couples.
- In the happy couple, the man and the woman complement each other harmoniously.

• The happy couple has happy children. With their happy children, the happy couple construct their own happy world.

For decades these myths of the happy couple have appeared relentlessly on billboards, in engagement announcements, on the screen, and on television. It is the ideal image of the middle-class marriage. Every couple, married or not married, is exposed to this pressure. At the same time, the happy couple embodies in exemplary fashion the manner in which the unconscious resistance of the repressed and hidden no of two persons toward each other destroys love. The tragedy of the happy couple lies in this: No right of residence and no place at the hearth is granted the devil, this "nay-sayer from the outset." Consequently, the devil is nowhere more devilish than in the happy couple. Whenever conflict, criticism, and aggression are considered inappropriate and are consequently banished from the life of a couple, negative feelings secretly grow in each partner. Only their concealment makes them really evil and destructive.

Probably the most fateful dogma concerns the supposed harmonious complementarity of two partners. We even find it in marriage manuals that are not part of the popular literature. The statement that man and woman really complement each other harmoniously, that by nature they are well matched one to the other like a key to a lock, creates pressure to be gallant and to strive to be attuned to the other. This compulsion to complementarity leaves neither the woman nor the man the possibility of openly sharing their own innermost thoughts and feelings with one another.

Love consists in the active devotion to a Thou, in sharing with a Thou. Whoever lets himself or herself be guided by a need for harmonious completion conceals the most interesting and most unsettling sides of his or her own personality. Two lovers should start from the point of view that they do not complement each other in any sense, yet nevertheless they love each other. This also holds true in practice for the actual complementarity of two lovers lies at such depths in the two personalities that it can never be completely examined—certainly not in the first years of a relationship. The pressure to complement the other not only hinders mutual disclosure, but also obstructs the self-actualization of each individual within the relationship.

The assertion that love is a mystery should not be dismissed as sentimentality or romanticism. It remains a mystery why precisely these two people love each other; most of all it remains a mystery for the lovers themselves. "Love is a mystery" has a practical significance: It keeps us from linking love with certain ideas of typological.

complementarity and thus with certain "objective" conditions such as, for example, "We love each other because you are extraverted and I am introverted." Even when such typological ideas are refined, they are still nothing but attempted explanations of the inexplicable, rationalizations of love that nonetheless depend on entirely different factors of which at most we can perceive only vague intimations. Psychology becomes a mortal sin whenever it blocks vital processes by "explaining" them.

Whenever a relationship goes on the rocks, similar typological ideas are adduced in order to demonstrate to oneself and to the world that "this relationship could not have worked anyway." Yet even when lovers part company, the mystery of a now dead love is not revealed—now least of all.

The image of the inevitable complementarity of two lovers arises from a world not of idealistic but rather of materialistic ideas: Each lover provides the other with what he or she does not have. The same quantitative thinking underlies the question, "Who loves whom more?" This question has something of extortion in it and inevitably carries in its wake hypocrisy and lies. In love there is no measurable security, not even in the love of the beloved person. For these reasons lovers should abstain from institutionalizing the mutual satisfaction of needs such that the other knows ahead of time, "Today I get chocolates" or "Today is Saturday; we'll sleep together."

Just so in marriage it is difficult to resist the propensity to create harmony and thus to institutionalize the regular mutual satisfaction of certain needs. By this term I do not mean the performance of the small duties of everyday life by dividing up roles in the common household, but rather experiences that actually can be enjoyed only when they are unplanned, such as a sexual encounter or playing a certain record or reading to each other a passage from a book that fits the situation. Such shared unplanned experiences permit love to revivify in all its nonrational vitality.

As wrong as it is to set up a marriage as comfortable, superficial complementarity, it is nevertheless right to give answers to each other's existential questions that an individual is incapable of answering alone in his or her finiteness. That I am capable of giving and receiving such redeeming answers—not only words, but also gestures and actions—gives me a feeling for the vitality of this love. To call it mere complementarity would be to trivialize it. Answers do not always lead to wholeness and harmony, but just as often they lead to conflicts, helplessness, and inner fragmentation. Even my partner's momentary coldness in answer to a specific behavior on my part has the right to a place in a relationship informed by love. Possibly a cold response can set more in motion in me than a calculated "complementary behavior" to which the other forces herself or himself "with good will," against her or his own cold, rejecting feelings.

Even members of a "happy couple" can be unfaithful, in spite of their professions of faith. Then they play down their turning away from each other by calling it a "harmless escapade," even if as a result of it they feel alive again for the first time in years. They do not want to admit that the "harmless escapade" is the expression of a real no, a no that secretly has set its stamp on the relationship to his or her "life's companion" for a long time already. The betrayal is much older than the escapade. That is why the suffering of the "betrayed" gets stuck on the surface—perhaps despite noisy scenes—and is dealt with in terms of practical considerations.

Even in a lively emotional relationship there can be infidelity and betrayal. In such a relationship infidelity and betrayal come less unexpectedly than for the happy couple, because in shaping the partnership the nay has been said openly from the beginning. The infidelity of the one can indeed cause great suffering and bitter hurt for the other, yet the chance to comprehend and work through this delimitation with each other in mutual love is greater for the honest than for the happy couple. Perhaps it even turns out that an extramarital affair of one or both is indispensable for the vitality of their partnership. Yet this can never be known in advance and be planned. Such considerations also should not be misused as a justification for entering frivolously into an extramarital affair instead of responsibly continuing the struggle to come to terms with one's partner. Of course there is always the risk that saying no to an extramarital affair ultimately turns into saying no to love in the partnership that has existed until now.

Returning to the problem of partners' complementing each other brings us to the question of why I expect decisive impulses from this particular person, why I take a passionate interest in the life of just this one person and even take his or her side when I am furious at him or her. This question cannot be answered easily, no more easily than the question of whether or not I will react in a similar manner tomorrow or day after tomorrow, much less twenty years hence. To be sure, the chance of this happening increases to the extent that the authentic activity of each lover increases within the partnership: making decisions, shouldering responsibilities, undertaking conscious struggles, caring. Emotion as such and by itself is passive. What looks like the activity of emotion is merely spontaneous agitation. Love as mere emotion has no permanence. Only the agreement of one's own activity with the emotional tone one feels makes the latter into a supporting feeling that can, perhaps, ensoul us to our life's end.

The ideology of complementarity proceeds from the premise that, with good will and honest effort, life à *deux* always gets "more positive" and that "positive experiences" predominate. On this premise rests the paradisiacal world view in which destruction and death are only chance occupational hazards: Everything in the world "really" could be good and harmonious and constructive. Such wishful ideologies of paradise can appeal only to persons who do not know of their own conflicting emotions. How many outrageously enlivening, but also how many destructive, emotions are awakened in two persons who are related to each other with body and soul! In a love relationship confused, crazy, and evil emotions also exist, along with the problem of what we do with them. Destructive inclinations do not necessarily have to be lived out, yet we must acknowledge them. In the tension between yea and nay, good and evil, constructive and destructive, and life and death, energy, strength, and meaning flow into the lives of two people who love each other.

The happy couple makes no room for such contradictory experiences. They incorporate the yea into a properly organized cohabitation. The nay, however, cannot be wished away. It creates secret pockets of resistance. The more happily the partners in the happy couple smile at each other, so much the more doggedly do they erect unconscious barricade after unconscious barricade against each other. Emotional coldness, disdain, and hatred thrive within them. The bourgeois living arrangement is all appearance and disguise. Exclusion of the nay from everyday life—of aggression, criticism, and delimitation—gives frightful dimensions to the nay in one's own soul, so that the yea of love finally suffocates.

In every happy couple love is destroyed, even if in different ways. Let us consider the example of a woman whose husband suffers from stomach troubles. With greedy anxiety she decides for her husband what he may and may not eat, and with missionary zeal oversees his diet in all details. She appears to love her partner very much and to be interested in his continuing to live. It is noteworthy, however, that by her behavior she aggravates his stomach problems because she upsets him and from time to time provokes him to eating binges. What is that, other than that she unconsciously *wants* to worsen her husband's suffering, that she nourishes a powerful, destructive negativism toward him that is harbored like a poisonous serpent within her! Nowhere are there more murderous hostilities than in happy couples.

The happy couple appears to want to live according to a noble

ideal, the ideal of a partnership in which no conflict clouds their harmony. But in reality the partners are caught up in materialistic attitudes: In a shared life the partners should take care of each other,
confirm each other, possess each other. Love is functional. The current sad image of "strokes" that one gets and gives vividly reveals
the functional attitude toward love; one can "give strokes" without
giving oneself. Love is measured in "stroke and orgasm units."

Functionality, however, has nothing to do with the moving experience of love. Love leads to an inner change in the personality of the
lover. Marriage as an institution has obscured this ancient truth.
Marriages, like all other love relationships, should be entered into "in
the spirit," that is, endeavoring to devote oneself to the Thou and to
one's own soul and not merely ratifying a functional agreement. That
in their shared life lovers must also assume functions and roles is
understood as a matter of course and it is often also difficult to do.
Lovers understand how to confuse functions and roles from time to
time, to shake them up and divide them anew. There is something
refreshingly chaotic about this, and such lovers do not bend to the
same role pressures for long.

The open structure of such a couple also expresses itself in their
attitude toward friends and acquaintances and to social and political
problems. Each person in the couple has a circle of persons whom
he or she likes and who interest him or her. The one's circle of
friends overlaps that of the other only in part. A person's friends and
acquaintances, of course, make that person's uniqueness
conspicuous.

Yet in that area where both circles of friends coincide—the common circle of mutual friends—a meeting of a special sort also takes
place between the members of the couple. Each of the mutual
friends underlines and strengthens qualities in me and in my partner.
With a certain friend, for example, I can let myself go more than with
someone else, and my ability to let myself go in the company of my
friend is revealed to my partner and can arouse him or her. My circle
of friends enables me to communicate things about myself to my
partner, and vice versa, things that would not be possible in the
exclusivity of a dyadic relationship. Again and again the common
circle of friends throws light on new facets of both of us, luring us into
a life where mutual communication and reflection of the guiding
image—our self-perception in our perception of the Thou—continue.
There also ought to be a few problematic and odd sorts of people in
our circle of friends; after all, we both do have problematic and odd
aspects to our personalities, too, through which we also want to
relate to each other.

Similarly, social and political questions must no longer be warded off as threats to "our happiness." It is necessary that lovers' mutual devotion and surrender radiate into both the proximate and the more distant environment and that it come to encompass devotion to concerns that go beyond the couple's own immediate interests. Whenever two persons are overly occupied with their relationship, they create for themselves and for each other as many problems as they would experience in relation to those from whom they both withhold themselves in their "egotism à *deux*." They squander their energy on superfluous constant frictions instead of standing up productively for those outside their relationship whom they have excluded. "Egotism à *deux*" is a sign of the happy couple who cannot face the realities of partnership, which involves the necessity of dealing not only with their own relationship but also with relationships to others.

Chapter 3

Merging and Resisting

Merging—the purely emotional, unconscious feeling of oneness with a Thou—is almost irresistibly attractive to most people. The attraction can go so far that one person might seek a symbiosis with another, a "growing together in life," through all of life, perhaps until death. The motives for seeking symbiosis are fear of isolation, meaninglessness, indifference, boredom, and responsibility for oneself. Even when a symbiosis of hate has led to separation and divorce, one continues carefully to cultivate the symbiotic relationship in one's own soul until death, as if it were one's most valuable possession.

In a certain sense it is, for hate is the one thing that keeps such a person alive, the one thing through which he creates an emotional link to the outside world, the only doorway to the world and into his own soul. Oneness with that which the ego, within its narrow confines, is not—the strange, alluring world outside and the strange alluring soul inside—is in fact the meaning of a human life. Like every other symbiosis, the symbiosis of hate also keeps one young because it perpetually channels new life to the ego.

Like suckling infants, symbiotic persons have an inexhaustible source of energy. The beloved or hated person is for them the eternally young maternal breast.

Moreover, the emotional nay of hate always gets mixed up with the emotional yea of love. If the unconscious yea and nay are mingled, and if I and Thou both go deep enough, we gradually grow together into a single form, neither good nor bad, we exist less and less as individuals. Love and hate are related not only as emotional opposites, but are identical at the deepest level of the soul where the light of consciousness, with its distinctions between good and evil, yea and nay, no longer penetrates. Paradoxical events give us some intimation of this, as when two persons, separated because of the most horrid quarrels, and who were for years possessed by one single emotion—their hatred for each other—meet again to spew forth their hatred and "tell each other off." They get rid of their hatred, but entirely differently than they had anticipated: They fall passionately in love again. They wanted to hurt each other, yet they rediscover one another in an embrace. Likewise, in our dreams we often find love turning into hate and hate into love. The most beloved person appears to us with his or her face distorted by hate, and the most hated person exerts an irresistible erotic attraction on us.

Involuntary merging with a person, through whatever emotion, stirs us up so much because in merging, all the values, boundaries, and distinctions that heretofore have given our life structure and have protected it from destruction are torn down. If we remain at the level of such an unconscious merging, we pay a high price, the price of a life shaped by free individual decision. The irresistible force of destiny that radiates from symbiosis makes it impossible to shape one's life in freedom. Indeed, the mere emotion of oneness—if it does not become the conscious reflection of the guiding image, with the differentiation of I and Thou peculiar to it—keeps one young, but we cannot grow older and more mature that way. Personal development via active submission to a Thou does not take place in symbiosis. Consequently, it is understandable that after a while, the healthy human being feels resistance against every merging, regardless of how necessary it may be at first—resistance that motivates him or her to abandon this condition and seek a new, more conscious form in which to become one with a Thou.

Such resistance is unconscious at first. It can find expression in terrifying visions. For example, the wife of a man suffering from cancer cannot shake the fantasy that on the day he dies, she will die, too. This fantasy has a historical background, namely the custom practiced in some primitive patriarchal societies of cremating widows, a ghastly consequence of the first vow of love: "My life and your life are inseparably joined to the very death."

Similar terrifying visions that have as their goal the awakening of our resistance against symbiosis are found both in the fantasies of individuals and in the collective fantasies of myths. Young people who are in a love bond for the first time often justifiably fear giving themselves over to their partner and thereby losing "body and soul," their autonomy and freedom. They have terrifying visions such as those depicted in the Greek myth of the lamia, a woman who sucks the blood of young men. The lamia has an additional destructive side: She kills the children of other women because her children were killed by the goddess Hera. The union of these two evil qualities in the lamia shows that, for the autonomous ego no "children,"— no fruitfulness, no possibilities for individual development, can come out of a blood-sucking, destructive bond to the partner. On the contrary, they are, strangled. Resistances, motivated by justifiable visions of horror, bear the meaning of dissolving the sterile fusion with one's partner.

Again and again we get into the very sort of symbiotic dependence that we really wanted to get rid of. Thus a girl falls in love with a certain young man in order finally to get away from the influence of her hated father as well as from the inner dependence on father, from her own father complex. She regards her boyfriend as a symbolic parricide, as the hero who is able to dissolve her fusion with her father. However, because she expects this important developmental step to arise not from herself but from her boyfriend, she jumps from the frying pan into the fire: Her boyfriend soon assumes the authoritarian father role in her life. For the second time she has walked into the trap of symbiosis with a man and has herself smashed her longing for freedom to bits.

Such a development can be foreseen in the Greek myth about the love union of Perigune and Theseus. The hero Theseus kills an older man, by the name of Sinis, in a most gruesome way. He bends two trees down, ties one of his victim's arms to the top of one tree and the other arm to the other tree, and lets the trees snap upright again so that Sinis' body is rent. After this, Theseus falls in love with Perigune, the daughter of Sinis. From her father's murderer she hopes for liberation from her inner dependency on her father—liberation from her father complex and authority complex. By loving Theseus, Perigune installs him in her life as her father's successor and grants him the same property rights over her life that her father had, all of which is totally unconscious. But that is the symbiosis of man and woman that is typical of the patriarchy. Theseus and Perigune fall in love, thus carrying on the old patriarchal symbiosis of father and daughter.

Sinis' murder would have been superfluous if Theseus had not wanted to take his place. Neither Theseus nor Perigune notices this in their first transports of love. On the contrary, Perigune sees Theseus—so we could fantasize the myth continuing—as the hero who differs from her hated father in all things, and Theseus is convinced he is no authoritarian dictator, but rather a "democratic partner."

This view is maintained until suddenly this positive estimate turns into its opposite and Perigune begins to criticize Theseus as an authoritarian, inconsiderate father and Theseus begins to criticize Perigune as a dependent, spoiled daughter. The Greek myth, completely caught up in the patriarchy, cannot yet describe the salutary resistance against the patriarchal symbiosis expressed in such mutual criticism. From this point on we must continue to spin the myth ourselves. One thing is certain: man and wife cannot really love each other so long as they are united primarily symbiotically. Indeed they may be in love initially, but in time unconscious resistances, irritations, fault-finding, and pointless bickering gain the upper hand.

A different terrifying vision of the symbiosis of husband and wife that is common in our times rests on realistic experiences. This is the terrifying vision of death by heart attack. We find this especially often among men who stand in a relationship of passive dependency on their wives. Perhaps they perceive this dependency only as separation anxiety. Such men chronically compensate for their dependency on their life's companion with excessive accomplishments in their profession and in sports in order to feel independent and strong. Stress overload can result in premature occlusions of the coronary arteries. The terrifying vision of death by heart attack exists justifiably, even if we must be on our guard against the opposite inference, that every death by heart attack is the consequence of such passive dependency on one's partner compensated for by accomplishment, or that such dependency necessarily must lead to a heart attack. The significance of this terrifying vision is that of awakening resistance, of opposing the unconscious yea of dependency with a conscious nay of independence.

In this chapter we are not yet concerned with conscious, constructive "saying no in love." For the time being we are limiting ourselves to becoming more familiar with the still unconscious forms of resistance against merging with one's partner.

Nothing at all changes in the emotional equation if the man of achievement we are speaking of assumes the role of hero for a young ladyfriend and displays "manly" strength and autonomy for her benefit. It happens that such a man suffers a heart attack precisely when his wife separates from him because of his love affair.

There is something treacherous about examples like those described above. They can awaken crippling guilt feelings and anxieties in the reader who thinks he is in a similar situation. Therefore we must add here that not every extramarital relationship, not even that of an older man with a younger woman, is merely a flight from one's own problematic situation. Furthermore, none of these relationships can be considered from this viewpoint only. Examples have the advantage of being concrete, but they must never be confused with a more differentiated picture of a particular situation.

The last example should show above all that over-compensation, like the mania to be outstanding and to accomplish, is incapable of dissolving the fundamental symbiotic dependency and can degenerate into self-destruction. Once again we have gotten into a blind alley with the merely unconscious nay to symbiosis in the form of resistance. We suspect that the only way out of symbiosis would be the conscious nay *in* love, the realistic differentation from the person whom we love the most. People who incline toward merging generally harbor resistances against a deeper relationship, since they justifiably fear that it could lead to captivity. And yet avoiding a real relationship is the wrong way to deal with the problem of symbiosis. Only in a conscious relationship where yea and nay have their place can the personality develop structure. Such persons often have the feeling up into old age that "real life" comes only later and their life heretofore is merely a provisional, preliminary skirmish. That one can indeed grow old and die with this feeling of always having led a provisional life is not at all clear to many; and when they do see it, their previous optimism easily turns into depression.

People who have just entered a relationship and are already dreaming of the next one—and with this trick avoid every relationship—always seem to wait longingly for the ideal partner or the ideal outer situation that would make their provisional life more binding. They are people who on the first superficial contact appear entirely open to a change. In every encounter they present themselves as if they were just about to shed their emotional virginity and surrender. Yet it rests with this unfulfilled promise. Because they expect everything and give nothing, they remain throughout their life like a door closed to the outside.

The contradiction between luxuriant relationship fantasies and the fear of a real relationship; between melting away in sentimental oneness with everything and cool, rigid delimitation against the "demands" of one's fellow man; between passive openness to the world, filled with longing, and stingy refusal to make a concrete gesture of surrender—this contradiction blocks the soul's development. It constitutes the conflict in which the Greek youth Narcissus finds himself.

I do not mean that this conflict is typical for the narcissistic person, for the concept of narcissism has undergone such an inflation and has become so imprecise that it can scarcely be used any longer. And yet it is not by chance that the concept of narcissism has been freighted with downright religious significance. It expresses something central in the condition of contemporary man, who feels isolated in human society and in the world about him in general and who counterbalances this isolation with merger fantasies. Perhaps the origin of the narcissism concept in the Greek myth of Narcissus can reveal the core of meaning of the collective drama that we call narcissism.

The fateful turn in the life of the heretofore happy young man Narcissus begins when he sets out to hunt a stag. This is a common motif in myth and fairy tale that expresses the young man's instinctive search for his own autonomous "masculinity." His search takes place primarily "up in the antlers," that is, in the realm of spirit. He must develop ego strength, the will to do battle, endurance, courage, and the ability to stand his ground—characteristics that, in the history of mankind, were initially developed more strongly in the male and hence are seen as specifically masculine, although inherently man and woman have them in equal measure.

In his search for his own masculinity, Narcissus does not differ from his age-mates. And what now follows does not at first differ from what is depicted in many fairy tales that treat the development of a young man, or from what young people, both male and female, experience up to the present day in their search for autonomy and independence.

Narcissus finds the opposite of what he sought. Instead of the stag, he finds the nymph Echo; instead of proud, invulnerable autonomy that excludes feelings and sensations, he finds woman and Eros. At this point in the lives of most young persons a spontaneous shift occurs. They relativize their heroic striving after pure autonomy not "contaminated" by Eros, a striving for surrender in love to a Thou, and paradoxically just in this they experience themselves for the first time in their own identity, including their sexual identity. Thus they can comprehend and accept what has fallen to them as being what they need. After having taken the lead in hunting the stag, they now let Eros lay hold of them. In this they demonstrate their permeability and openness to what simply takes place from within them in their corporeal-spiritual humanness. They let go of their ego, and the Thou gives them the gift of themselves. This decisive transition causes them to awaken as adults in the midst of the real world of joy and sorrow, love and hate, life and death.

Perhaps many erotic relationships preceded this transition, but they expressed more the "stag hunt," that is, they served the goals of self-assertion and ego strength and were not a real surrender to a

Thou. Only devotion to a Thou grants identity: "He who loses himself will find himself."

Narcissus, however, cannot accomplish the emotional shift of which we are speaking. He remains fixated on the stag, on his proud autonomy, and feels it threatened by Eros. The fact that he believes the woman to be an "Echo Nymph," that is, an echo of his ego, shows his rejection of Eros who binds the I and the Thou. The name Echo for the possible beloved is itself Narcissus' apotropaic magic, since he is intent only on preserving his untouchability and his independence.

At the sight of the nymph Echo, that fateful moment when he really should have let Eros seize and transform him, his "manly" courage forsakes him. The "strength of the stag," the undaunted, proud readiness to do battle, is not at his command because he is so fixated on it. If he could renounce the strength of the stag in surrender to a Thou, he would gain it for the first time, but by fixating on it he loses it before he has found it. We can experience only the power that flows out in surrender. The power that withholds itself from the Thou is experienced as powerlessness.

The myth says that Echo could only repeat the calls of others. It is interesting that the meaning of the words that Narcissus calls to her is turned into their opposite by Echo's repeating them. In the echo, of course, only the last words that one says are audibly repeated. Narcissus calls out: "I would sooner die than lie with you!" to which Echo imploringly replies; "Lie with you!" What Echo expresses is the innermost longing of Narcissus himself. However, in his self-consciousness of ego Narcissus silences Echo's voice, so he cannot hear the paradoxical truth of his soul in the reversal of his own words and thus he cannot open to the guiding image that Echo mirrors.

Instead of seeking the fulfillment of his tensed hunting drive in relaxation with Echo, Narcissus flees. The hunter becomes the hunted, the seeker is sought. The flight from Eros is the flight from his own soul, flight from transformation and from becoming adult.

And yet Narcissus, like every human being, still has the longing for Eros, for becoming one with a Thou. Having evaded the real Thou, the sole "object" remaining for the satisfaction of this longing is his own ego. Narcissus doubles his ego in the reflection of it, and thus that love which in accordance with its nature would be directed toward another person now flows toward himself. This is the opposite of mirroring the guiding image. He does not yet know that the beautiful youth whom he loves is his own mirror image. Only when this dissolves each time that he attempts to embrace and kiss it does he realize that it is not two beings who love each other, but rather only one who loves himself: Narcissus.

Now Narcissus becomes conscious of the unsuitability and impossibility of his ego infatuation. He would like to burst the bounds of his ego through love so that from two a greater whole might arise, yet he loves his own ego instead of a Thou, and thus he remains imprisoned within his narrow limits. The circle is perfect. There is no escaping it; there is no longer any future. As a reflection, his ego awakens in him a longing that only a Thou can quench, hence all that is left is suicide. Narcissus plunges a dagger into his breast. Ego-infatuation in place of surrender to a Thou means death of the soul.

The seer Tiresias had predicted that Narcissus would grow old if he never knew himself. Now that Narcissus knew the ego-infatuation that excluded emotional growth, he had to draw the inevitable conclusion from his knowledge and seek death. Originally Narcissus was probably a vegetation deity. He becomes a tragic figure only when the human individual rises above the flower-like, unconscious, cyclical blossoming and withering of life and at the same time senses the danger of again falling back into this cycle, and then recognizes with the instrument of consciousness, created for surrender to the world, his own inability to surrender.

Like Hyacinth, Narcissus was a Cretan hero of spring. Spring flowers blossom and wither after a short time. During a certain developmental stage in every person, Narcissus has meaning and a right to life. In this, boys and girls scarcely out of childhood have something hermaphroditic in their appearance. I and Thou, man and woman, unconscious and conscious appear to become one for a brief time. The glance of such young persons shows both self-consciousness and a melting oneness with the world, a union that is seldom possible later. In this phase no resistance to the Thou beclouds the yes said to ego. The merging with ego is at the same time a merging with the unknown world within and without. It is the true hour for Narcissus. The creative person experiences a reflection of this hour when, in the blossoming of a new work, he or she no longer distinguishes between I and Thou, self and world.

However, if Narcissus attempts to prolong his hour unduly, his ego becomes ever more narrow, anxious, and hard, and his resistance against union with a Thou grows. Simultaneously he becomes more and more dependent on the world around him by repulsing it and shutting himself off from it. His unexamined resistance to merging gives rise to that very merging. The dreams of a Narcissus grown old show how threatened his autonomy is and how greatly he is overwhelmed emotionally by the world around him.

So long as we waver in a relationship between compulsively passive dependency and resistances against it, there can be no love for a Thou, for love is freedom that finds expression in active surrender, care, interest, and joint responsibility. Passive resistance against the Thou is the opposite of the actively affirmative stance.

This inability to love manifests, among other places, in the case of the impotent man who is emotionally so dependent on his wife that he must express resistance against this symbiosis with his sexual impotence, perhaps the sole nay to dependency on his wife that is available to him. This incapacity to love appears also in the frigid woman who in her life with her husband can develop no life of her own, and who expresses her nay to her dependency in sexual insensitivity. Impotence and frigidity illustrate how the hidden nay to the Thou prevents loving surrender.

Chapter 4

The Self-Destruction of the Stronger Partner

When we are in a couple relationship, we have a hard time resisting the pressure of mere functionality that more and more exclusively governs the relationships among people today. Whoever thinks and acts in the categories of debit and credit at work from morning till night finds it difficult to develop in his or her free time the capacities for inner experiencing, delight, and savoring, without which no love relationship can germinate and grow. Our economic mentality rests on the presupposition that if something is entirely mine, it cannot be yours at the same time. This mentality is ubiquitous, so that most of our contacts have the commercial character of barter: Whoever gives something, gets something else in return.

In mature love, however, debt and credit, getting and giving, are identical. In giving we get as a gift exactly what we give. If we give happiness, we receive just this happiness as a gift; we become happy when we make someone happy. In giving, the giver experiences his own vitality; in the Thou to whom he gives, he perceives the unknown possibilities of his own soul. He who is accustomed to thinking in economic terms can hardly get a sense of the paradoxical correspondence of giving and getting.

We must call this to mind when we attempt to understand the self-destruction of many people in our society. At best, many people feel themselves to be fully alive at the beginning of a love relationship. For a period of time they protect the special experience of love from the barter mentality that informs their other relationships, but in the long run they cannot retreat from the terror of the trader's mentality into their love relationship. Perhaps at the beginning of the love relationship they have already apologized to colleagues at work for the important place that their new relationship assumes in their life, as one apologizes for some sort of childish foolishness. With the apology, they begin to devalue Eros: Love is an excusable weakness that one must permit oneself now and again in the face of the hard realities of life. Thus love has no reality; it is a mere fiction. On the basis of this mentality, love gradually becomes less and less important to them. They ascribe this to habituation. While their feelings are growing cold, they govern their life with their partner according to the time-tested economic model: As far as possible, each does as much for the other as the other does for him or her.

Men in positions of leadership are especially susceptible to this self-destructive process. Since they represent the ideal in our civilization, nobody is safe from the dangerous wake they create. Among women, too, the tendency toward devaluing Eros increases to the degree that women subject themselves to the masculine striving for achievement.

Men of achievement deal poorly with their talent for love. Their ability to perceive feelings as inner reality and to structure their own feeling world in devotion and surrender to their partner remains undeveloped. With their emotions they do not engage a Thou, but rather an unsuitable object. Like Narcissus who, contrary to nature, guided his emotions back into his own ego rather than toward a Thou, the man of achievement invests his profession or his favorite sport with the energy that should be intended for love, rather than devote and surrender to a Thou.

If the energy intended for love finds no connection with a Thou, excessive pressure builds up in the ego. One creates outlets to let off steam—for example in sexual fantasies and experiences without real interest in a Thou—or else the pressure makes the ego ever more taut, inflated, and aggressive on all fronts. The emotional and physical circuit gets perpetually overloaded and exhausted. With an impetus that could find its natural meaning only in love, the man of achievement hurls himself into work. Perhaps the same misfortune then overtakes him that overtakes the electric razor that is connected to too high a voltage. For a while it functions more efficiently than another razor of the same make that is connected to the right voltage, but in a short while the motor overheats and is irreparably damaged. Similarly, a man of achievement can actually die of a broken heart. His love has not found the path out of the ego and into a Thou.

If finding a Thou is prevented, finding one's Self is impossible, for only in the guiding image of a Thou can the ego, as in a mirror, perceive, enliven, and actualize its own readiness to develop emotionally. Whoever does not find access to a Thou does not find access to his own inner core, either, the care that we call the Self. Without Eros we do not we feel alive. Even the hermit can unfold his soul only if, in meditation or prayer, he relates to the world—to the "redemption of all creatures," as the Buddha says. The man of achievement suffers from a surcharge of the energy that should be intended for discovery of Thou and Self.

In marriage the man of achievement appears to be the stronger: He decides how the practical side of living together should be structured. However, this strength is only a supposed one, not only because he is addicted to maternal care from his wife, but above all because he exposes himself to the same unnatural pressure to achieve in the family that he expertences at work. Consequently, one day his power will unavoidably turn into powerlessness.

The man of achievement has a dark, unsettling knowledge of these interconnections. He has excessive fear of illness and of death. In the family and at work he becomes ever more rigid and tyrannical in order to protect himself against this fear; thus his isolation increases and the pressure that will some day tear him apart builds up.

One does not expect a sensibility for nature from the man of achievement. For him, protection of the environment means nothing more than additional bundles of laws. He is insensitive to the messages of his body and his soul, to the warning signals of the initial signs of bodily wear and of his ominous, apocalyptic dreams and fantasies. Indeed, he does take note that his wife is wasting away beside him, but he has no real feeling for this, just as he lacks any feeling for the wasting away of his own soul.

The self-destruction of the man of achievement proceeds step by step, and his fateful nay to life that initially disguises itself in the enthusiasm to achieve gradually kills all growth and finally flows into the total nay of self-destruction. If the energy of the soul that is intended for Eros is habitually turned back into the ego—into ambition and accomplishment—*greed* takes the place of Eros. The erotic gradient from the I to the Thou and from the Thou to the I is replaced by influence on other persons, which the man of achievement greedily seeks to strengthen. He takes as much as possible for himself: money, success, power, sexuality. Because greed only demands and gives nothing, it never leads to truly relaxing satisfaction. It never comes to rest. Life runs mechanically and compulsively at too fast a pace.

Greed always negates what it wants to have. Greed totally lacks respect for its object because greed is intent only on incorporating it. "Devouring" or "scavenging" other people is the source of pleasure for the greedy person. We must beware of persons who only "crave" us, for their greed could annihilate us. If we ourselves are greedy for a person, our sense of responsibility should bolt the door of our greed.

In contrast to healthy need, greed is never of the same magnitude as its object. Greed seizes the object improperly and misuses its autonomy and uniqueness. In contrast to the yea of devotion and surrender, greed is the nay of destruction. Greed does not lend itself to being united with love nor with a natural relation to things. For the greedy person, money loses its significance as barter value for the acquisition of desirable goods and becomes an end in itself. The greedy person draws pleasure from "being stuffed," as a popular new expression in Switzerland profoundly designates material riches. His "being stuffed with money" replaces his erotic potency. One keeps one's money to oneself, grants oneself and others little, and feels powerful and strong in one's greedy avarice. The refrigerators in the villas of the greedy are often almost empty, for the greedy person does not collect wares that are intended for immediate consumption, but rather amasses things of lasting worth with which to "stuff" oneself.

Greed differs from the beneficial influence of one person on another, an influence that comes without special exertion from the natural aura of the personality and that has the effect of making the person be heard and taken seriously. Such a beneficial influence stands in the service of Eros, of the feeling bond between people, of reflecting the guiding image, and of enriching communication. The greedy man, however, attempts to cripple and immobilize other people with his influence so that they cannot turn their gaze from him and so that every shred of independent life in the other petrifies. The greedy man does with other people what he does with his own soul, whose need for freedom and devotion he stifles. He continually neutralizes the suppression of his own feelings and his vivacity by suppressing other people; the one allows him not to feel the other. His hardness toward himself acquires a perverse meaning in his hardness toward others: self-contempt in contempt of mankind. To be at war on all fronts gives the greedy person the illusion of fullness and of pulsating life. Something is always afoot for the greedy person, but he is never relaxed because he shuns Eros' easing.

For the greedy man sexuality is not overflowing vivacity in physical-emotional surrender to a Thou, in ecstatic bursting of ego boundaries, and in becoming one with the beloved. For him it always has compulsive character. Orgasms are tallied like cash receipts. The Thou remains distant; it is hardly perceived. At most he is nice to his partner in order that she will help to increase his own pleasure.

The reactions of the greedy man to external stimuli and demands are exaggerated. To a superficial observer the greedy amn is a vigorous person with superior vitality; yet on closer inspection he is obviously an impostor. His muscles contract more than necessary for the task at hand; his exertion for a given concern seems inappropriate; he fights where he should play, hits the table with his fist without external cause in order to add emphasis to his opinion. In the confusing stir he creates about him, only one thing is lacking: the feeling tone, the good-natured relationship, the warmth-giving Eros. As a busily tense impostor, he continually overtaxes both his environment and his own energies.

In Buddhism, desirousness is the cause of all suffering. Our Occidental concept of suffering is not entirely comparable, yet the man of achievement illustrates the Buddhist saying that greed stands at the beginning of a chain of suffering that ends with death.

In fact, the man of achievement cannot indulge his unbounded, limitless greed decade after decade. After a time it begins to show its true face: It is essentially a nay to life, self-destruction from lack of love for Thou and for self. Initially the man of achievement can still shut off his "achievement motor" at will and take a break. But it can suddenly happen that after the conclusion of a satisfying business deal, or after a successful orgasm, he turns the key of his vehicle to the left and instead of being shut off, the motor howls and continues to run. He can no longer shut down. Against his will, the man of achievement gets "on a roll" with his greed. His heart continues to race when it ought to be quiet. His thoughts continue to spin in his head even after they have already attained their goal. These are the consequences of the excessive character of the greedy lifestyle.

The man of achievement has split his feeling for life. Contrary to his intention, his ostentatious resistance to a Thou seizes his ego. The greedy person is frightened that the weapon in his hand turns more and more often and uncontrollables against himself and threatens him. The personal burden in his profession, which up until now he has sought, gets out of hand, not primarily because it has become greater but rather because he can no longer control it and it is no longer the object of his greed. He feels *aversion* toward this threatening subjective feeling of overload.

Now the running amuck of greed is checked. Greed finds itself in conflict with the inner aversion against the overload that the man of achievement did, after all, seek and create himself. The sole pleasure that he knows—the pleasure of devouring, of stuffing himself full, of retaining—is spoiled. He feels helplessly wedged between the old greed and the new aversion. Now he can get rid of his inner tension even less than he could before. If, unexpectedly, yet a new burden is added to the old ones—for example, an unexpected complication in closing a deal—his aversion and his tensions become insupportable.

Until now the man of achievement has not yet lost all sense of his own autonomy and power to act. Indeed, he does feel split between the yea of greed and the nay of aversion, but the hope of ultimately mastering the burdensome problem has not yet deserted him. However, that changes. A process of repression imperceptibly begins in the man of achievement. He represses the fact that it was his own greed that incited him to assume these burdens, that he himself wanted to take them on. This repression is understandable, since he experiences his greed less and less positively as triumphal pleasure in conquest, and more and more negatively as displeasure resulting from being overburdened. We are inclined to repress our own responsibility for unpleasant experiences. By doing this, they gain even greater power over us and can no longer be tamed.

Through repression, the man of achievement loses all power to control his life. He who spoke his great nay to Thou for the sake of a limitless yea to his ego increasingly falls into a defensive panic, much like Narcissus, who refused Echo's embrace for the sake of his independence and is put to panicked flight by Echo's demands. The man of achievement no longer feel himself to be his own master, but is delivered up. Gone is his greedy grasping of the world. His emotional energy, intended for devotion and surrender but perverted into egotistical greed, now is his *defense*: It is the fault of those others whom he greedily exploited that he is overburdened. They want more and more from him and overtax him. His repressed greed appears in projection on others and is directed against himself: They had it in for him; he himself is weak and defenseless.

In this paranoid idea the longing of his youth is fulfilled. Finally he has again found the connection to Thou. The Thou cannot be excluded. If we do not seek it in devotion and surrender, it demands access to us and becomes our persecutor. Warding off the Thou reveals our yearning for Eros.

For the first time since the infatuations of his youth, a strong emotion lays hold of this man: panic fear and defensiveness, the revenge of Eros scorned for decades. He feels ravished and exposed. The many whom he has ravished have banded together against him, or so his projection believes. Gone is the freedom of the hunting predator. Now he works so that the others will not devour him; now he lets himself be devoured by work.

It is pointless to defend himself against the spirits he has summoned. The man of achievement has never learned to see the Thou other than as a competitor and thus as a potential persecutor. From this perspective, there can be no relaxation. However, in Eros the aim is purposeless relaxation, otherwise we overtax ourselves. For the man of achievement, there ultimately remains only *powerlessness*. He still holds his old position; he still makes decisions, beats the competition, holds his ground against the burdens that have now become so foreign to him, but his life has turned into mere defensiveness. Thought and action no longer proceed from him himself, but are as if directed by remote control. Everything storms in upon him from outside. He has ceased leading his own life. Out of habit he continues to earn money and maintain his position but he does so without pleasure. His sexual drive also seems to be burned out: There is scarcely a prickling in his body when he meets an attractive woman.

In addition to this, he makes more and more errors in his work, errors that previously he would never have made. His colleagues begin to take note of changes in his personality. The routine gets worse. Others want to push him aside to take his place. Now he actually *is* beset from without. This serves to confirm in his mind that not he but the others were and are guilty for his harried life. He had always been right to be wary of other people and to resist the sentimental wishes for friendship. He should have paid even closer attention; now he has become fair game.

Longing for death takes hold in him. The sole living thing that remains for him is the only thing that no one threatens. Having suppressed Eros in the course of his life, having neutralized greed and impotently surrendered defensiveness, a sweet weariness and indifference permeates him. He is still on the job—he decides, organizes, and plans—but his life is no longer there. Nor is his life that of the others who now openly plot intrigue against him. His life is in his waiting for death. He feels almost as he used to feel when he could still love. He is almost happy that the stranger within him is destroying itself.

Chapter 5

Pursuit and Flight without Love

Many people are shocked to recognize themselves in the tragedy of the stronger partner who destroys himself. It holds an element of truth not just for a few business leaders, but for most people in our society. Denaturing Eros results in egotistical greed, then the splitting of greed into a need for achievement and the aversion to the burdens associated with achievement, followed by the repression of the knowledge that these burdens were freely chosen in the "greedy phase" and the defense against the demands erroneously believed to be assaulting one from without. The feeling of powerlessness and the longing for death form the final stages of a tragedy of the soul in which most people in our times—especially men—see themselves mirrored. But we are particularly shaken by the fact that the entire chain of suffering of the man of achievement has one single cause, namely, the unconscious nay to Eros. The uncanny, hidden loss of the erotic connection to the world rightly unsettles us. Today a great degree of conscious effort is needed to escape the embrace of a merely functional view of the world, because such a view informs all public life.

We must go even further. If we are no longer able to enter into bonds of love, if we no longer actively experience our potency and vitality by actively becoming one with a Thou, opening ourselves to a Thou and thus gaining insight into our own Self, there remains for us no other way than the tragedy just described. Where, then, is the energy of one's soul supposed to go when it finds an insurmountable obstacle to the erotic path that leads outward into a Thou and the mystical path that leads inward into Self, if not into the ostentatious ego and its achievements? What is then left to us but extravagant self-centeredness?

The consequence of this is the feeling of threat from within and from without. Whenever the mystical opening to the Self and the erotic opening to the world atrophy, we are persecuted by what we scorn—by the depths of our own soul and of the external world. Persecution dreams and unjustified existential anxieties can be the consequence. Because we shun contact with these two poles of our existence, we are oppressed by them, for the connection with them is the commandment of our nature. What we refuse becomes evil, what we accept becomes good. The lover sees no enemies, neither in his or her own heart nor in the surrounding world. If the lover encounters people who view him as an enemy, he does not let them poison him emotionally, even if they do him harm. Only through the conscious erotic stance can we avoid the paranoid mental attitude of our civilization. Indeed, the growing threats are a terrifying reality— the risk, for example, of a military error with catastrophic effects and destruction of the world about us. But the paranoid mental attitude stands in the way of a realistic policy that could reduce these threats. In contrast, the attitude of Eros lets us see more clearly the possible steps toward protection and growth of all living things.

Insofar as it lays claim to absolute truth, Christianity inadvertently succors the paranoid mental attitude. By proclaiming the person of Jesus to be the historically unique and total revelation of God, Christianity incites a defense against all insights into human nature that arise outside its own walls. Love of neighbor is tied to the conditions of the true faith or the true morality. The courageous basic stance of Eros toward the world atrophies into a musty warmth in one's own stall. The search for the "God in us," as the Christian mystics called the Self, turns into an apology for articles of belief that, because of existential anxiety, are held to be true. This Christianity aids the stronger partner who destroys himself by confirming his paranoid feeling for life. Christians who have fallen victim to the claim to absolutism are, as human beings, either as restive as goats or as tame as lambs. They ward off or they submit. Therefore they never break through to the fundamental attitude of Eros that alone can redeem us for community with our fellow creatures from both the evil enemies and the good fellow travelers. They allege that they love Jesus, but whoever really loves does not need to protect himself from the world. Only he who doubts his own love and defends himself against these doubts surrounds the beloved with dogmatic fences. The stronger partner who destroys himself is not only a child of the functional mentality, but also of Christian intolerance.

Politics in our century has been and still is being determined to a significant degree by nonerotic individuals who are ruled by the egocentric feeling of threat. Thus they increase the actual political threat. From this there is no real exit other than to turn away from self-destruction and to return to Eros, and thus to reverse the tragedy sketched out. With all the strength of consciousness and of will that is at our disposal, we must take the side of Eros and let Eros, as the active core, shape lives. This is no new edition of the flower children who, like Hyacinth and Narcissus, fade as quickly as spring. An Eros that is moved more by passive merging than by active devotion and surrender cannot intervene directly in the events of the world.

I speak expressly of Eros and not of love of neighbor. To Eros belongs the physical bodily desire for one's neighbor, be it a gentle shared resonance or be it sexual union. Without bodily pleasure in one's neighbor, the love of neighbor—Christian charity—is something feigned and unfruitful. Without practice in erotic love, love of neighbor loses the characteristics of love and becomes merely functional thinking and acting "for a good cause." Unerotic "love of neighbor" can indeed relieve pain and heal wounds, but the cause of the pain and the wounds—the inability to love—remains.

Of course I do not mean that we should strive for a sexual relationship with all the people we get close to. On the other hand, without a total sexual partnership with *one* human being, it is difficult to find one's way to a generally erotic fundamental stance that is not to be confused with an aesthetic "oceanic feeling" for God and the world. Thanks to such a partnership, sexuality resonates in all one's relationships.

The more intense and intimate a human relationship becomes, the more difficult it is to divide responsibility one-sidedly, to see oneself as good and the partner as bad. However, the further away a relationship is from the erotic central element, from the experience of inner oneness and of surrender to the Thou, the less sensitive the partners become to their own responsibility. In the most primitive marital quarrels, it is hard to believe that partners hit each other over the head with as many lies and unfounded reproaches and impute as many evil intentions to each other as do politicians in an election campaign, where the hostile camps appear clearly separated. The risk of destruction in our relationships—the triumphant, annihilating nay—increases the farther we distance ourselves from the proximity and intimacy of erotic love. The risk of being destructive grows more and more monstrous in us as our distance from the erotic central element increases. Only the conscious practice of Eros by many individuals can save us from destruction.

The contemporary man of achievement resembles the Greek hero Heracles who, with "the club of his willpower," storms from heroic deed to heroic deed, but lacks the reverent, erotic relation to the world. After completion of his ten labors, Heracles rages onward. The blood that he now sheds is meaningless. He kills because he cannot stop swinging his club. After he has completed the useful deed of cleaning Augeas' stables, he cleans the world to death and leaves the cadavers lying on the edge of the earth. As punishment, he is sold as a slave to Queen Omphale, whose lover he becomes. In three years of love service to her he is healed of his insanity. True, this is not without complications, because in the first phase Heracles, sick of his heroic masculinity, turns into a womanish man and puts on women's clothing. In our time, similar complications between woman and man are unavoidable as they struggle for Eros. Yet our fear of the entanglements of love must not frighten us away from entering Eros' school. Three years of a human life are not enough for learning the inner and outer union of man and woman, of masculine and feminine. In three years one can at most give one's own life a new erotic orientation; Eros, however, demands our whole life.

Today a school for Eros would probably have to begin with uncovering the destructive forces of the nay that inform a merely functional partnership. In such a partnership the lovingly disguised defense against the partner takes the place of Eros that bonds and binds. The first step in learning Eros is the insight into the violence that can hide behind anxious caring and a considerate attitude.

Superstitious practices give us astonishingly precise information about the destructive "guerrilla skirmishes" between people in the underground of their unconscious. Take, for example, the practice of *countermagic*. In the middle ages people often felt themselves to be pursued by the magic of a witch—by her spells and tricks. They believed that witches could sow misfortune and death. In this, they projected their own unconscious need to destroy onto certain women who were called witches. If someone felt himself or herself to be threatened by the magic of a witch, he or she sought refuge in the corresponding countermagic: certain spells, gestures, rites, and potions that were supposed to neutralize the evil magic. The battle between magic and countermagic, in which each maintained that he or she was not indulging in offensive magic but only in defensive countermagic, takes place at all levels of human relationship, from the dyadic relationship to the relations between political factions.

Magic and countermagic can most readily be discerned and understood in an intimate relationship and can then be transformed into a play of love. In an intimate bond, the ruling emotion of a merely functional relationship—namely, the nay to one's partner—cannot so easily be concealed as it can be in a relationship where the participants keep their distance. In an intimate relationship the nay of taunting, of aggression, of suppression, and of hatred comes to light more candidly and demands a settlement. If one does not want to risk a divorce, one ultimately has to come to terms with the nay that separates.

A school of Eros would have to address the question of how magic and countermagic interact in marriage and in other intimate relationships. Each partner believes his or her magic is only countermagic; the other's magic is the origin of necessary countermeasures. Viewed from a neutral vantage point, however, both parties are indulging in both kinds of magic.

The superstitious practices of the Middle Ages were, of course, not created to deal with the conflicts between married people. But applying them to marriage is psychologically justified and informative. First of all, I will give an example of an alleged witch's spell in order to elucidate the psychological motives of defense. Let us picture a gruesome scene that was acted out in many houses in the Middle Ages. A mother looks at her infant and is profoundly horrified. She no longer knows her child; it must be a different child. A demonic power, a witch, has stolen her baby and laid another in its place, a so-called changeling. The psychological explanation of the belief in changelings is, in most instances, the fear of an abnormal change in the child. Yet occasionally there were reports of changelings that were completely healthy. How could this superstition have arisen?

Today when parents say to a growing child who is becoming independent, "You are not our child," they really do mean it, for they can no longer identify with the child. How is this total turnabout of feelings possible? It presupposes that previously the parents were completely merged with their child and that they had not been capable of perceiving the child's uniqueness and individuality. Now they no longer believe their child is their own, for to them having a child means nothing other than being as identified with the child as with an organ of their own bodies. Something similar must have taken place in the Middle Ages when a mother suddenly believed the child who was externally identical to her own was a changeling. Because she discovered something unique, different, strange in it that was no longer identical with her, its mother, she could no longer maintain the old identification. A changeling was threatened, for example, with being shoved into the heated oven, that is, back into the now deadly womb of symbiosis. Hence, instead of supporting the uniqueness in the child, the mother refused to see this "other" child as her own. The destructiveness was thereby transferred to the child; among other things, it was said of a changeling that it would suck four to five women dry.

A thoroughly comparable emotional process can also come into play between two adults after a period of loving merger. A minor expression of independence often suffices to change the beloved into a stranger. The partner's expression of autonomy is experienced as an attack that must be repulsed. This is the first decisive threshold in every love relationship. During the initial merger, the Thou unconsciously broke in as something other and strange. The ego was put out of commission for a period of time in order to make it possible for its narrow boundaries to expand: This necessary operation took place, as it were, under an anesthetic. Infatuation benumbs the old ego, but without changing it into a larger whole.

But now the old ego again perceives its function as an organ for delimiting the conscious personality. Arrived at this threshold, we ought to grasp that the ecstatic merging with the Thou holds a profound truth and that it was caused not only by the drive for surrender, but simultaneously by the drive for self-realization, which really is the same thing. This insight can set in motion the mirroring of the guiding image through which we actively seek what we have previously passively felt, namely, the Thou as a still hidden, undeveloped truth in our own soul. This way the devotion and surrender to one's partner also becomes devotion and surrender to one's personal truth. With this, the threatening feeling of being delivered up to foreign magic falls away, as does the compulsion to repulse this supposed magic by an effective countermagic.

But let us return to the maneuvers of countermagic between two lovers. Countermagic is a defense against new bonding, a defense against the transition from a passive "oceanic" feeling to a realistic, active, responsible devotion and surrender to the Thou. In the Middle Ages, defensive magic against the threat of one's own child's being replaced by a changeling lay in the anxious and scrupulous care of the child. Experiencing another person as strange or foreign can take place only when devotion and surrender are lacking.

In the Middle Ages people made lots of noise and commotion as an effective countermagic to drive witches away, just as still happens today on Shrove Tuesday to drive out winter. Likewise, a married couple's "getting into a row" serves the purpose of repulsing the

Thou. By thundering, shouting, making a racket, and roaring at each other, we don't let the other get close. We close ourself off from the other's influence, from what the other might perhaps be able to tell us about our own hidden truth. The barking of dogs provided a desirable intensification of this acoustic countermagic in the Middle Ages, just as today "snarling at each other" helps to keep the other off our back.

Another form of countermagic lay in making ugly faces at the demons, be it with tatoos or masks. Married people, too, make the most horrible faces at each other in order to keep the other from being attracted, and thus finally to have some quiet. One's own turf is aggressively defended with grimaces that often sneer just as stonily as the gargoyles on Gothic cathedrals. The defensive magic of ugly faces often finds its high point in a divorce in which the two persons mutually put each other to flight with the fiercest faces they have at their disposal so that they can have some peace. Often one partner does this intentionally and the other, the one "abandoned," involuntarily.

The same purpose is served by the stench that one makes. Ill-smelling substances, even human excrement, were used against demons. It is known that deep-seated defensiveness against one's partner is often sweated out as a foul body odor. But if the defensiveness changes into erotic attraction, people can tolerate or enjoy each other's smell again. An obtrusive perfume worn at the wrong time can also serve an unintentional defensive function. The overly intense erotic signal indicates the secret fear of sexuality and consequently puts every potential partner to flight.

A more concealed but no less effective form of countermagic was common in the Ardennes. Whenever someone believed demons were following him as he walked, he tore paper into small shreds. The demons had a good time collecting the scraps of paper and thus forgot the walker. This form of activity therapy sometimes fulfills a thoroughly desirable purpose for married couples, too. When the atmosphere between them is loaded and a bad quarrel threatens, they divert themselves with trivialities. They tell each other banal things: what's in the paper, what their friends have told them, or how the weather is in Rome, although they aren't going there until next year. Meanwhile they both relax, and the possibility for a rewarding coming-to-terms with each other is again open. Two people who continually live together need such countermagical tricks now and then. However, if they make it the habitual style with which they deal with each other, it turns into a sly, slick sort of defense.

This is the way partners in the happy couple are nice to each other; it is an escape maneuver in relationship.

A school of Eros would also have to address how two people live together who both feel exploited and threatened by the other. Here I will confine myself to observations in which it is especially clear that defense on the part of both partners is always a cooperative matter of active threat and passive flight. Together, gestures of threat and of flight make up the nay that can destroy love. I am not yet suggesting any solution, but am rather limiting myself for the present to awakening a sensitivity to the antithetical perspectives of such partners.

As a starting point I propose the example of a man who is overworked in his occupation and of his wife who is underworked in their contemporarily furnished, small household. Gradually this man comes to suffer from being the only wage-earner, provider, giver, and the one responsible in the family. Earlier his devotion to his wife and children had made him feel alive and happy; now he sees himself as exploited. Gradually his discontent intensifies until he feels threatened. Once he dreamt that his own flesh was being cut off his body with the carving knife intended for the Sunday roast. More and more he personifies the threat in the person of his wife: She is exploiting him, taking advantage of his money in various ways, including carrying on another relationship for which she has the necessary leisure and relaxation that he does not have at his disposal. His earlier love for his wife suffocates in his feeling of being threatened. Seen from his viewpoint, he is the persecuted and his wife is the persecutor.

But his wife sees the situation the other way round. She feels delivered over to an authoritarian, tyrannical, moody man. In his presence she feels as if cut off from life, crippled, without initiative. When they have company, she is usually silent and lets him do the talking. If he were not so domineering, she would have more strength to pursue interests other than just the household; possibly she would even have a part-time job. In her feeling of being threatened, her love for her husband suffocates. From her perspective she is the persecuted and her husband is the persecutor.

This collapse of love between a man and a woman was typical in a patriarchal society and is not just a modern phenomenon. It is scarcely possible to preserve the central element of love in this constellation of partners. Through a new division of roles relating to job and family such as is possible today, two people could prove that they really regard their love as the supporting central element in their lives, and that under all circumstances they intend to save this in spite of the social difficulties. But the fundamental problem lies deeper than the division of roles. A more flexible redistribution of roles and obligations often alters little in the loss of Eros if the patriarchal self-image of a husband and wife has not changed.

The situation is similar to that of child rearing. Parents who themselves are constricted and unfree can nonetheless rear their children according to the latest psychological findings, but internally the children become constricted and unfree. The unconscious of the parents is more influential than their consciousness. Parents must rear *themselves* to freedom so that their children become free persons. Likewise, only a new self-concept on the part of marriage partners can save love.

There is a Greek myth that describes the typical stance of man and wife in the patriarchy. It deals with the married couple Laius and Jocasta. Laius, King of Thebes, refuses to sleep with Jocasta because the oracle at Delphi had prophesied that his son would slay him. Jocasta saw no other way to "lure Laius into her arms" than to get him drunk. Nine months later she had a son.

The relationship between Laius and Jocasta must be considered on two levels: the visible social level and the hidden intimate level. Outwardly, King Laius certainly determined how the couple's life together would be governed. He also took it as a matter of course that if he so chose, they should be sexually abstinent against his wife's wishes. In the myth there is no mention of any discussion of this issue. He was the ruler, she the ruled. Jocasta saw herself as disadvantaged and threatened in her right to sexual pleasure. This is the external appearance of the patriarchal marriage.

Inwardly, however, in wordless concealment, the inverse relationship took its course. In the image of the husband who sleeps while he sires a son, we recognize the dependency hidden even from him. Seen superficially, the husband is the father to his wife, but in secret the wife is also mother to her husband. As such she controls his male procreative power—she can make him dependent on her through sexuality.

Actually, only the oracle is guilty of the fate that ultimately overtakes Laius, since it caused his son Oedipus to be abandoned and hence incapable of recognizing his father. Had Oedipus recognized Laius as his father, they would not have come to mortal blows. Thus the oracle must be included in our understanding of the patriarchal familial constellation.

The oracle is to be found in Laius himself. His fate, which seems to depend on an external oracle, is realized in word and deed when Laius himself fulfills those conditions that the myth cites as the facts of his life: he fears losing his masculinity and being weakened by sexual intercourse with his wife; he compares his masculinity with that of a younger man, his son, instead of experiencing and strengthening it in devotion and surrender to his wife; he "unconsciously" sleeps with his wife in spite of his defense, and thereby deepens his symbiotic dependency on her; he ultimately represses the younger, potent son from his consciousness, thus making the latter the truly more potent one. The oracle is not to be seen outside of these four conditions. It is, rather, identical with them to the extent that, taken together, they must necessarily lead to that fate which finally befalls Laius: the loss of Eros, and his son's depriving him of political power.

Modern soothsaying practices also reveal the seeker's deep anxieties and hopes, which later are often fulfilled. The trip to the soothsayer often reveals a fateful basic attitude: the belief that destiny is assigned us. Precisely this passive attitude brings it about that our destiny is fulfilled as our fears of or, in the favorable case, our trust in propitious stars dictates. "Fate" arises from our passive acceptance of what transpires in our life without our involvement. Many myths depict such courses of fate. Eros as devotion and surrender to life is the power that can effectively intervene in fate so that our life ultimately becomes an unmistakable mixture of fateful preconditions and our own conscious choice.

Oracles make clear the constraints of fate, emotional sequences that can come about thus and not otherwise because no redeeming consciousness can intervene in them. It is part of the fateful constraints of the patriarchal marriage that outwardly the man rules and inwardly the woman rules, not only in the house but in the soul, too. In social behavior the patriarchal value system prevails: The man rules the woman and the woman lets herself be ruled by him. But intrapsychically she rules the feeling atmosphere in the marriage. In the patriarchal world women have more inner power then men.

So Oedipus had a father who was outwardly strong but inwardly weak, and a mother who was outwardly weak but inwardly strong. It is easy to understand that, because of the attraction exerted by the feminine in this parental constellation, the son bonds beyond all measure with the mother against the father, up to the point of incest with the mother and murder of the father. As the son of both, Oedipus thereby reveals in himself the hidden inner power relationship between man and woman in the patriarchy that mirrors the external social power relationship. As the murderer of his weaker father, he is also the tool of his stronger mother and, like his father, under the power of the feminine. Moreover, as the husband of his mother he unconsciously chooses the fate of his father, who secretly was his wife's son.

The self-concept of husband and wife in the patriarchy is the birthplace of the Oedipus complex. This self-concept makes mutual devotion and surrender in Eros impossible. The Oedipus complex belongs not just to the nature of the male; it contains the history of Laius' and Jocasta's marriage, the history of marriage, in the patriarchy from the man's perspective.

Chapter 6

Heterosexuals' Homosexual Fantasies

In spite of liberalization of the public attitude toward homosexual love, the defensiveness against homosexual love, particularly among men, has not diminished in recent years. Wherever there is talk of homosexuals, tension increases. Defensive reactions can be observed: embarrassed grins, smutty comments, demonstrative poses of one's own heterosexuality, attempts to change the subject. Among young people the topic often arouses feverish overreaction. Hardly ever does the provocative word "homosexuality" meet with lack of interest and indifference. Once uttered, it sets unexpected ideas and fantasies in motion for many people, including people who experience their capacity to love only in heterosexual Eros.

In each person the word "homosexuality" mobilizes emotional energy to varying degrees. Homosexuality has a certain degree of energy charge in every psyche. It is thus astonishing that homosexual Eros scarcely appears in public life. It is one of the most noteworthy contradictions of our culture that, on the one hand, individuals show strong reactions to homosexual stimuli, and, on the other hand, homosexuality, seen from outside, seems hardly to exist in the lives of most persons and in public life.

But emotional energy cannot simply disappear, nor can it be redirected at will. It is only partially possible to divert homosexual attraction into heterosexual love. Indeed it is true that for many people growing up, an intense phase of homosexual love is replaced by the conclusive heterosexual orientation. But it is not the same emotional energy that was first in the one, then in the other. It can be observed that the homosexual inclination in young persons diminishes to the extent that they come to resemble, in many characteristics or even in physical appearance, their same-sex friend who attracted them and to a lesser degree still attracts them. The emotional energy that was channeled into homosexual love now empowers newly developed aspects of their own personality.

A simplified example of this is the anxious teenager who has fallen in love with a spirited comrade and who loses his infatuation to the extent that he becomes spirited himself. For heterosexuals, the mirroring of the guiding image between members of the same sex leads to a higher degree of "becoming Thou" in their own Self than does mirroring between contrasexual partners who, in their physical and emotional polarity, remain more distanced from each other, even if each is able to actualize in his or her own life much of what the other imparts. It was in the context of same-sex relationships that I first observed the phenomenon of mirroring of the guiding image.[1] At that time I called it the phenomenon of mirror communication. Subsequently I investigated it in terms of the confrontation with religious images[2] and in the love relationships of men and women. The emotional energy of homosexuality flows in part into impulses for the development of one's own personality and in part into continuation of same-sex fantasies.

Heterosexuals who knew same-sex Eros in their youth still experience same-sex fantasies that could lead to sexual encounters, particularly in phases of emotional turmoil and transition. If heterosexuals ward off and repress their homosexual inclinations, personality development is blocked because the transformation of homosexual attraction into impulses for development cannot take place. What happens with the homosexual inclination in such a case? To too great a degree, it intermingles with both the heterosexual inclination and the aggressive drive. The same-sex Eros disguises itself with heterosexuality and aggression and is no longer easy to identify. In order to avoid proscription by society and by one's own conscience, homosexuality submerges in these intermingled impulses, which result in something new. This is an unconscious process of which the individual has no knowledge at all.

If too much same-sex Eros vanishes into intermingling with contrasexual Eros and with aggression, it becomes destructive. A limited intermingling of heterosexuality, homosexuality, and aggression, on the other hand, is natural and necessary and does not arise from

---

1. Peter Schellenbaum, *Die Homosexualitt des Mannes* (München: Kindler Verlag, 1979).
2. Peter Schellenbaum, *Stichwort: Gottesbild* (Stuttgart: Kreuz Verlag, 1981).

repression. Still, a potential for same-sex Eros, varying from individual to individual, should be freely available to consciousness. That is, we ought to admit same-sex fantasies and enter into the corresponding feeling relationships. Otherwise something destructive creeps into both man-woman relationships and the aggressive stirrings.

This destructiveness finds expression as exaggerated defensiveness that inhibits Eros in the relationships of man and woman. While an appropriate intermingling of contrasexual and homosexual Eros in the meeting of man and woman favorably strengthens the gender-specific and individual qualities in the two partners and tends to increase the erotic attraction, the excessive cathexis of contrasexual Eros via repressed homosexuality leads to defensive reactions vis-à-vis the partner, to deficiencies in tenderness, to genital fixation, and often even to sado-masochistic behavior. I observe this regularly in heterosexuals who have repressed their homosexual tendencies.

The same holds true of the connection between aggression and same-sex Eros. When intermingled to an appropriate degree, they lead to pleasurable assertiveness, playful competition, joy in confrontation and dispute, and talent for group formation and social tasks. However, the excessive cathexis of aggression due to repressed homosexuality results in a relentless competitive spirit, rivalry, fear of members of the same sex and compulsive comparison with them, lust for power, a self-destructive mania for accomplishment, and feelings of powerlessness and depression.

The threshold at which the constructive intermingling becomes a destructive one varies from individual to individual. Theoretically, little can be said about this. It is more important to develop a sense in each individual case for when this threshold has been crossed. This always happens when the destructive symptoms mentioned above appear in the Eros between man and woman and in aggression. Then the task is to liberate the same-sex Eros from its unnatural bondage and make it conscious. Often the mere insight into these psychological interrelationships is helpful. However, bringing homosexuality to consciousness can be a difficult, anxiety-ridden path. When it is traversed successfully, a stronger need for friendship between women and between men can be observed. Perhaps we find our way back to friends we have lost sight of for years; perhaps we form new friendships.

In old myths, especially the Greek and Babylonian tales, we find many examples of same-sex Eros. Even Zeus, who deceived his spouse Hera with many other goddesses, nymphs, and women, loved two youths, Ganymede and Phaeneon. I suspect the Greek myths depict about the same proportion of contrasexual and homosexual relationships that the average human psyche has of contrasexual and homosexual components. The basis for the open homoeros in Greek myths lies not in a lesser valuing of heteroeros, as is often maintained, for no myths are richer in contrasexual models of relationship than the Greek. The opposite would be closer to the truth: Because the Greek myths did not put a taboo on same-sex love, compulsiveness and inhibition are absent from contrasexual love.

This can also be observed in our time as well. A heterosexual who also has hearty friendships with members of the same sex and does not anxiously ward off homosexual fantasies is more empathic, richer in fantasy, more tender, and more lively in his or her devotion and surrender to the contrasexual partner. But whoever gives up earlier friendships with members of the same sex and permits only "acceptable" feelings between man and woman finds in time that his or her Eros goes lame in contrasexual relationships.

The repression of homosexuality effects the suppression of "the feminine" in the male: feeling, the capacity for empathy, inner strength. Likewise in the woman it suppresses "the masculine": persistence and self-assertiveness in professional life and in public generally. This is not surprising, for in same-sex friendships the division of roles is not gender-specific as it is in contrasexual relationships. For example, we can observe that a woman together with another woman develops initiative which, in her marriage with her husband, she leaves to him, and that a man together with another man can listen and hear better than when he is with a woman. The fixation on culturally conditioned, gender-specific patterns of behavior is loosened in same-sex relationships. This is probably one reason for the fascination that homosexual men and women exert on contemporary society, which has come to a standstill with the old role assignments. In the mirror image of the homosexual, the heterosexual can see the possibility of letting his or her own contrasexual components live. On the other hand, the fear of and aversion to the homosexual signifies fear of and aversion to the contrasexual side of one's own soul: of the woman in man and the man in woman. The homosexual is the sign that genderspecific role fixations are breaking down. Thus the homosexual has, since ancient times, fulfilled a valuable, irreplaceable task in society. The male shaman, who in the exercise of his function wore women's clothing and cultivated homosexual contact, had access to the demons and spirits. He was the witness to a more comprehensive humanness.

The fundamental erotic attitude is genuine only when it embraces persons of the same sex as well as those of the opposite sex. A real erotic aura touches both men and women with its warming, enlivening, and heartening power.

In recent decades an entire culture of same-sex friendship has been lost. Its most recent zenith was in the period of Romanticism and in the German youth movement called the *Wandervogelbewegung*. Such books as *Le Grand Meaulnes* by Alain-Fournier (1913) and *The Little Prince* by Antoine de Saint-Exupéry (1943) haven't been written for a long time. But has contrasexual Eros grown stronger and richer in exchange, as the antihomosexual ideologies maintain? By no means. Contrasexual Eros atrophies to the same degree as do man-to-man or woman-to-woman friendships. Eros cannot divide humanity into two halves, for the essence of Eros is devotion and surrender and becoming one.

How impoverished the history of humanity would be if homosexuals were stricken from her annals! Plato's simile of the two half-spheres as a description of the mutual attraction between two persons cherishing the goal of becoming something whole, something "round," would not exist. Neither would the paintings in the Sistine Chapel nor the Mona Lisa, for the artists who created them were Michelangelo and Leonardo da Vinci—homosexual artists embodying the union of male and female in the individual with gripping clarity. The men they depict are indeed thoroughly masculine and the women thoroughly feminine, but these figures all radiate a secret: They burst gender-specific limitations. The reverse of this is emotional fragmentation. In our time, homosexual artists like Pasoline and Fassbinder mirror with unmistakable directness every heterosexual or homosexual human being's soul rent by conflicting strivings.

My intention is not that of explaining same-sex Eros as the cause of the genius of these and of other artists, for then I would fall victim to the error opposite to that of placing homosexuality in the proximity of pathology and crime. Homosexuality is the cause of genius just as little as is heterosexuality. But homosexuals make a specific contribution to elucidating what it means to be human. We cannot simply bracket out the homosexuality of a homosexual. This would be to veil a significant statement, as happened in the case of the Sistine Chapel frescoes after Michelangelo's death when the genitals of the human figures depicted were concealed with flowing veils. The personality of the homosexual is informed by homosexuality in all areas of life. To exclude it means to misunderstand the Eros specific to this person, that is, to completely misunderstand his or her own particular relationship to the world and to the soul.

It also means that the heterosexual misses the chance to perceive his or her own male-female wholeness in the homosexual's mirroring of the guiding image. Above and beyond this, the homosexual is in general an image of our own otherness. This otherness is precisely what creates fear in the heterosexual—and in the homosexual, too. The experience of otherness is the experience of one's own unmistakable identity. In every person, there is something unadapted, in conflict with the norm, strange and different, and precisely this is the distinctive mark of one's own individual self. Overcoming our defensiveness against homosexuality also means finding the courage to express our otherness, the courage to be an individual, and that in all realms, not just the realm of sexuality. Every person, not just the homosexual, suffers from ultimately being different from others. To deny this suffering by insipid adaptation to the norm would have as its consequence that one's own way of the cross to the Self would be missed and one's delight in being human would be lost.

PART II

The Overt No in Love

Chapter 7

Delimitation

Love aims to overcome separateness and to establish union. Hence love stands in the service of life. Love is life energy, for life arises from the union that love seeks. From the union of woman and man, the child grows out into the world—and the transformed human being, who has overcome the polarity of woman and man in the experience of the polar Self, grows into the soul of each individual. Life does not flow so long as the ego remains caught in its isolation. The ego must seek to lose its power outwardly in the Thou and inwardly in the Self in order to be born anew.

As I discussed in the first part of this book, two extreme behaviors, merging and defensiveness, impair both love and self-actualization—often to the point of destruction. They always appear together.

In merging, the ego makes a short circuit. It gets lost in another person and in its own unconscious. Whoever identifies with the world around him and sacrifices his ego to it believes he is saying yes to life. But in fact he says no, not only to himself by surrendering himself, but also to the world around him because he will avenge himself for his loss of ego. This vengeance is the second extreme that destroys love: defensiveness. Merging and defensiveness impede the conscious working over of the communications that we receive. We remain fixated in symbiosis or rejection, and justifiably suffer from the feeling of isolation. We have already spoken in detail of this concealed nay that destroys Eros.

Love presupposes an ego that has a firm grip on itself and is at the same time open to devotion and surrender to a Thou. The ego must be both solid and permeable. It needs to establish open, flexible boundaries between itself and the outside world. The nay of delimitation must be bound to the yea of love.

We should get used to seeing and addressing a person not as "half of a couple," but rather as an individual. Likewise, the person whom I love most of all is not only my partner, but first and foremost is an individual who is somebody even without me. The "couple perspective," from which married persons in particular regard themselves, cripples both partners and hinders both in developing from an "outer couple" into an "inner couple," a psychic whole. The compulsion to be a couple ultimately makes a mere community of interest out of two persons. From time to time in every shared life a line must be drawn through the illusion of the many supposed commonalities of which we boast for the sake of preserving our warm nests. Usually life itself involuntarily draws this line in the form of conflict, disappointment, or infidelity; then we must also agree to draw it. The cosily boring affirmation, "But we do belong together!" is now passé. We do not belong together and yet we are together—a paradox that lets a realistic tension arise and casts us into the uncertainty that belongs to all life. We are again surprised by each other and in this surprise we again learn to love—maybe. More bored couples get divorced than conflictual ones.

From time to time married persons ought to imagine simply living together without being bound by the institution of marriage and by children. They should pose themselves the question, as if for the first time, "Do I really want to marry this person?"

I have described mirroring of the guiding image as the way in which to discover the Self—new, richer possibilities of life—in the Thou. Even in the most fortunate instance, this path is not continuous. Here and there it consists of individual leaps of progress, between which lovers mark time. The sudden transitions always have the effect of a surprise. They happen at the least expected moments, when I have acquiesced to the complete foreignness of the other and to our being stuck. When something unprecedentedly important and essential for me rises resplendent from a word or an action of the Thou, and I see in a flash what I have long struggled to understand in my finiteness, then I must look this guiding image of my own hidden soul squarely in the eye and carry it into myself so that from within me it will emerge as form. Such a leap always contains a nay to the old ego, to the previous feeling for the world and for life. This is why our language often expresses the effect of surprise with exclamations that are negations: "Incredible!" "Unheard of!" "Impossible!" or simply "No!"

Let me offer an example of this: An architect who has quite reasonable but somewhat rigid views cannot get along with a colleague who is likewise an architect. In working out shared projects they often get into insuperable differences of opinion. This architect, whose marriage also has been stagnating for some time, comes home one evening. His wife is on the telephone, and he follows the conversation, at first absentmindedly, then suddenly with amazement and attention. His wife, who is a teacher, is talking with a colleague of hers about whether or not a certain pupil ought to be promoted to the next grade. His wife is in favor of it, her colleague against it. The architect recognizes how his wife receives all of her colleague's arguments with genuine warmth and takes her time to weigh them so that the impression arises that she shares the views of the other teacher. But then she executes a reversal by evaluating the arguments anew and in a positive sense. This moves her colleague to reevaluation and finally to agreement.

Of course, in listening the architect did not first and foremost get a good method for carrying on a conversation but rather he got a glimpse of the inner, essential nature of his wife. With astonishment and gratitude he perceived her anew, and for the first time in several months his Eros was set in motion. Out of an inner impulse he embraced his wife after her phone call. The leap into a deeper relationship had taken place.

At the same time he leapt into a new phase of his own development. The next morning, he was able, for the first time, to come to an agreement with his colleague. He had taken into himself and integrated a certain image of his wife. Now it lived from within him. This is a graphic example of mirroring the guiding image.

The polar tension between lovers does not diminish on account of an instance of mirroring the guiding image; on the contrary, it becomes capable of being experienced. Characteristics that we develop only at a later hour in our lives never have the stability and familiarity of characteristics that have informed our personalities since childhood and youth. In order to keep and to unfold new possibilities, we are dependent on mirroring of the guiding image.

It is never certain whether a given mirroring of the guiding image will not be the last with one's partner. We have no guarantee that the other will ever again step out of her or his otherness and foreignness toward us. Then there still remains for us the possibility of devotion and surrender to this unknown person in spite of her or his otherness—of loving a secret although it does not reveal itself to us, in the hope that one day a bridge will again materialize. In this way a new mirroring of the guiding image can be realized. The Thou is practically as inexhaustible as the Self, yet there are phases in which access to the one as well as to the other remains closed, and the belief in a new breakthrough is nourished only by the memory of past "times of fasting" and the following "days of Easter."

Besides, love is often kindled by just such puzzling qualities in the Thou. A man will perhaps never fully grasp, in spite of all his understanding of psychology, why he loves this particular woman, this Amazon for whom profession and social contacts are more important than the erotic bond. Whenever we can no longer make headway with such questions, we are well advised not to ask them for a while and to come to terms with our love. The worst thing we could do would be to work tyrannically on converting our partner until we "understand" her or him. This would be to deny the nay uttered by the suchness of the other's delimitation and thus also to deny the possibility of entering into a paradoxical relationship with this nay. Not only the Thou, but also one's own unconscious soul is, in its most valuable parts, a nay to the ego.

So let us learn to welcome the unwelcome, to seek what cannot be found, to love what is separated from us. The small ego must become more magnanimous, up to the very borders of insanity.

Nor can we do justice to other people, not to mention our life's companion, if we view them merely from the "couple perspective," let alone the "married couple perspective." We have the inclination to pathologize people who do not fit into the world of married couples and their children. Why, for example, should it not be acceptable for the sibling relationship to be the most important and most valuable for someone, without his or her risking the verdict of unlived life and, for fear of that epithet, submitting joylessly to the yoke of marriage? Why do people mutter behind the back of a successful business-woman that "She's only doing that because she can't find a man"? Perhaps this woman understood how to draw the boundaries that are right for her, boundaries that were more fundamental for her path in life than marriage would have been. And why see the pitiable victim of Church discipline in a celibate man who has taken holy orders? Perhaps life among his fellow brothers truly corresponds to his inner calling. For "enlightened" people of our time, the theory of neurosis exerts a social pressure similar to the constraints imposed by the Ten Commandments on the "less enlightened." Unfortunately for many, psychology has more normative than analytical character, in which case the Ten Commandments are preferable.

But let him who lives his Eros in no institution, and perhaps not even in a sexual relationship, beware of being declared sick and of falling ill. Today men are astonished to note that there are women who want to be mothers, but not partners in a permanent erotic relationship. With what right does one assert that such a woman lets "the most important thing" in the human being perish, namely the relationship between woman and man? What do we really know of such a woman's most important individual concerns in life?

Eros is also respect for another person's limits that are incomprehensible to us. Thanks to the fundamental erotic attitude, we experience human society as a community—not in a comfortable, harmonizing manner but rather in the paradox of the most incomprehensible contradictions. In this respect, Eros is belief: In spite of all obvious boundaries, the lover senses unity. In addition to the multiplicity of the earth's plant and animal kingdoms, there are also the manifold ways of being human expressed in the individual, which in turn enrich the human community as a whole. The multiplicity of different persons reflects and reveals the potential multiplicity of each single individual. Therefore it is also in our personal interest not to let humanity be reduced to a common denominator.

The psychological vocabulary for characterizing persons has, unfortunately, entered popular speech. The exuberant person is called an hysteric, the sad person, depressed; the reflective person is labeled schizoid; the elitist, self-satisfied and narcissistic; the conscientious is branded compulsive, the persecuted stigmatized as paranoid. For this reason I have made an effort to avoid the technical language of psychology in this book. When an individual says no to the world around him or her and wants to live according to his or her own nature or momentary disposition, the drive to follow the lead of his or her uniqueness is often held in check by a deprecating value judgment drawn from the theory of neurosis. At least the old system of morals refrained from scientific disguise when it disciplined the individual. Respect for the limits that another person sets for himself or herself commences with scrutinizing the words with which we characterize people.

To want "the whole truth" about a person at all times is disingenuous. Under the pretext of a rounded image of humankind we close ourselves to developments in society that, like all developments, begin one-sidedly. We may properly speak of neurosis only when a person is stuck in conflict between two contradictory inner strivings of approximately the same strength for an extended period of time. Consequently, it is wrong to call creative persons neurotic. Their lives have a powerful gradient, even if "only" in *one* domain—for example, in music.

That which is different and unique in a person is, of course, not to be confused with the role he or she plays in differentiating for the role of his or her partner in a relationship. The natural boundaries between I and Thou have little to do with the division of roles. There are also roles that should no longer be assumed by anybody. For example, it is by no means desirable that women let themselves be devoured by their professions, as many men have done. This is hardly to be avoided in the instance of a woman who works for a male boss. Therefore women should perhaps create feminine institutions in this time of transition in our civilization, in order to let feminine alternatives to the male world of work germinate and develop.

Authentic delimitation leads into the unknown. For example, if a woman who has cooked for her husband every evening at the same time simply goes out one afternoon, "leaves him on his own," and comes home around midnight without explanation, she is signaling not only her wish for a new distribution of roles—that is, for a husband who once in a while helps around the house so she can again take up her previous profession—but rather signals to her husband and to herself a puzzling and unsettling departure from the spirit of their entire decade-long life together and the intimation of a new, necessary, difficult freedom.

This example shows that no reasonable conversation, no mutual respect, no ability to empathize with the other—practiced for decades—can spare them the painful necessity of perhaps once or several times delimiting themselves from each other, contrary to all the rules of courtesy and consideration, and thereby making a symbolic gesture that both of them will struggle for many years to understand. Just when everything seems to be lost in these most difficult hours, everything can begin anew—but only perhaps.

Whoever has left her partner alone like this or has been left alone has re-experienced something forgotten: the value and the necessity of being alone. Only the person who is lonely at heart can love. Only the person who feels different from the other in his or her heart of hearts, and hence feels the lack of the other's support, is capable of Eros. A jack of all trades cannot love, because while he is at home in all trades, he is not at home with himself. It is not primarily sexual distress that preoccupies the hermit in the desert with glowing fantasies of love, but rather the hellish torment of separateness and loneliness. Whoever is certain of his partner can no longer love her, for in his certainty he overlooks the abyss that separates him from her. The awareness of otherness, of strangeness, creates the emotional precondition for love. Love suffocates so soon in marriage because it runs out of the oxygen of freedom, autonomy, uncertainty, and loneliness. The meaning of marriage as an institution should be sought no further than in the everyday division of tasks and sharing the rearing of children.

It is important that lovers be able to be alone with themselves from time to time. Even when they have children, phases of solitude must be organized for each partner. There are problems a person has to deal with alone. If, however, both lovers are almost constantly together, they run the danger that problems are played out perpetually within the same division of roles, as if on the stage, instead of their solution being sought in quiet reflection and re-evaluation. Mythic battles should be fought out not with one's partner, but in inner combat with oneself. By mythic battles I mean conflicts between diverging parts of one person's personality, battles such as are depicted in myths. The ego takes the role of the hero; inner and unconscious forces are represented by other figures.

Thus the Greek hero Perseus fought the terrifying Medusa, who had gigantic teeth, an extended tongue, and snakes instead of hair. Whoever looked directly at her turned into stone. Perseus protected himself from petrifaction by gazing at her reflection in a mirror and thus was able to chop off her head. The Medusa embodies all those forces from one's own unconscious that can overpower the ego: overly powerful emotions, instinctuality, lack of distance, passivity instead of active devotion and surrender, lack of responsibility, and the desire to be a child. Whoever succumbs to her is petrified, that is, loses the possibilities of movement and development. Perseus wards off her direct influence with a mirror. Just as a mirror deflects the direct radiation of the light, the power of the Medusa is also turned aside. Perseus can behead the Medusa and rob her of her dangerous autonomy because he fixes his eye on her without surrendering to her influence: He maintains the emotional distance necessary to close in on monstrous problems.

Similarly, objects in the external world lose their threatening aspect when we demask them as mirror images of parts of our own personality. If I feel myself completely paralyzed, petrified, and robbed of all my own initiative by another person, if I cannot look at this person without losing my power, then this has to do in the first analysis with my own Medusa that I project. The task is to employ the mirror of perception as a weapon against being overpowered. What do I see in this mirror? Perhaps a mother who devalues me, who hasn't a good word to say of me, who denies that I am good at heart—a mother who is in me, nourished by a memory image. If I look at her hard enough, she dissolves like a ghost in the morning mists and I have become stronger—a person who also has caring, maternal characteristics.

Many marriage partners experience each other as the Medusa that cripples and petrifies. One can free oneself only through insight into the momentary projection.

There are phases in which we, like Perseus, feel ourselves cornered by the Medusa of a crippling problem. The temptation to withdraw into passivity is great. Now we must be alone more frequently. Mythic battles belong in one's own breast, not at the dinner table. It would be unjust to make one's own wife into a Medusa and always to deprive her anew of her power, devouring, as if she were the Great Mother. The repressive, authoritarian man often confuses his wife with the Medusa in his soul. He who fights at the wrong place fights phantoms. Even today Perseus must withdraw into his inner solitude in order to turn his mirror toward the appropriate object; his own soul. This delimitation is indeed a nay to the Thou, but it makes possible new inner freedom and hence, ultimately, renewed devotion and surrender to the Thou. But men often behead their wives and let the Medusa continue to rampage in themselves undisturbed.

Being alone also means withdrawing from the sphere of influence of the beloved person. Primitive anxieties perhaps rise up now: If I withdraw from the power you exert over me, if I rebelliously break your magic spell, if I no longer move like your marionette, then you will no longer take an interest in me and will no longer love me. In making such fears conscious I must expose myself unavoidably to the solitude that sets boundaries. Only then do I notice how passively dependent I still am on the other person and how little I can actively love him or her. My passivity makes the other into a Medusa, a mirror image of my horrifying lack of love. Differentiation from her, and disempowering and slaying her by insight, changes me into a person capable of love.

Chapter 8

Hate and Love

People who think in moral categories are disquieted by their occasional eruptions of destructiveness. Guilt feelings plague them because they hate where they think they should love; because they take secret pleasure in the sufferings of others; because they cannot suppress sadistic fantasies and even death wishes against others; because they are not at all sad but rather are happy that others have a hard time, even when it relates to those they love most of all.

The guilt feelings demand explanation. Why am I so evil? Who infected me with these destructive stirrings? Where does this nay come from, this negativism that regularly gets underfoot and makes me and my efforts on behalf of my fellows stumble? The need to understand underlies the readiness to accept every plausible theory of human destructiveness as an Aha! experience. But the relaxation of tensions does not last long, for the obvious explanation has not diminished the evil tendencies. Thus a new explanation is sought that again eases the burden for a limited time.

The explanations of human destructiveness can be traced to three basic models. The first model posits that destructiveness arises out of the realm of instinctual drives that threaten the moral strivings of the ego and therefore are experienced by the ego as evil. In this explanatory model, destructiveness is not "curable" because it belongs to the instinctual structure of the human being. The second model holds that destructive fantasies and patterns of behavior derive from traumatic experiences in childhood. A child who was victimized by the sadism of the persons who reared him or her has sado-masochistic stirrings as an adult. According to this second explanatory model, there would be no evil adults if there were no evil persons rearing children. According to the third model, destructiveness belongs to the physical-emotional constitution of mankind and of all living creatures. Life continually creates and destroys itself. Destructiveness cannot be eradicated.

None of these three basic models for explaining human destructiveness is capable of helping the person plagued by guilt feelings. This is because none offers a new emotional attitude toward one's own destructiveness. These are models useful for momentary relief, nothing more. They change nothing in us, least of all the fact of aggressive, hate-filled, sadistic impulses.

Only observing destructiveness in relationship to love can help us to move onward. I shall make a strange assertion: Love is the meaning of destructiveness. Or, formulated differently: Destructive behavior wants to create the emotional precondition for love, and often actually succeeds in doing so.

This assertion presupposes the third basic model: Destructiveness is something given by nature. But in addition, it says that love is the only emotional attitude that completely corresponds to the natural fact of destructiveness and gives the latter meaning. Expressed in terms of the theme of this book: In the loving yea, the meaning of the destructive nay is fulfilled. This nexus of meaning mitigates our inner strife between love and hate, love of life and longing for death, good and evil, God and devil. Why?

In order to answer this question, let us turn again to the protagonists of this book, to lovers. There are phases in which the wedge of hatred drives them apart, phases in which their love turns into hate and each would like to wound, hurt, or strike the other, and perhaps even does so.

Here I am not speaking of partners who have long since grown apart, but of lovers whose love has fallen asleep. What change can come about in the wake of such an escalation of hatred in their bond? First of all, it is like an awakening. A condition of calm and stability has come to an end. They had a good relationship together, or at least a comfortable one, and did not need to reflect on it much. They had gotten a bit sluggish, a bit dull and bored. Now that is as if blown away. Wide awake, they stand opposite each other, and between them lies the malice with which they have destroyed their pleasant togetherness. Nothing of love is felt, only this alertness— the activation of emotional energy, the attentiveness, perplexity, and confusion such as follows a natural catastrophe. Quickly and sharply, they scrutinize the situation and assess the damages and the chances of a new beginning. Without noticing it, they attend to each other in an extraordinarily sensitive manner, perceive each other's every glance, tone of voice, and posture. Without knowing and without intending it, they have begun actively to tune in to each other and again, for the first time in a long time, to love. Hate drove them apart and placed them into relationship with each other again. Hate created the precondition for a new beginning in love.

Why did these two not ultimately turn away from each other following their outburst of hate? Why have such waves of aggression in their relationship, unintended by them, become a rite of renewal of love? Why did their consciousness suddenly become wide-awake and the highest possible degree of interest appear precisely at the zenith of their hate? Finally, how did hate pair up with devotion and surrender?

The occasion for the hate-filled confrontation was probably banal. Perhaps the wife merely said, "You have been looking tired for weeks," and he, without understanding it himself, answered in full rage, "You can sleep an hour longer in the morning than I can." Then one word led to another and both of them wounded each other for half an hour, and piece by piece they demolished their life up until now. From rage arose hate that came from the heart of hearts. Of course, we can understand this eruption as arising from the couple's problematic division of roles, and up to a point that would be correct. Yet it seems as though even partners with satisfactory divisions of roles actually seek occasions to break out in rage and hate from time to time.

Both partners wanted to overcome their dullness and complacency and become alert. For this to happen, they must again become complete strangers to each other. What is strange engenders hatred because it relativizes and threatens what is one's own. Destructive stirrings arise in us if something strange or overpowering assails us, casts us out of accustomed pathways, and disorients us. We must penetrate deeper yet in our search for an explanation of how a ludicrous cause has made our partner a stranger to us. Strangeness has laid hold of us, shaken us, rent us, taken away our honor and self respect; it hates us. Defenselessly, we are destroyed. What is destructive is more powerful than we are. It is not destructive in itself, but in relation to us. Destructiveness is a form of relationship: Something stronger penetrates something weaker and rends it from within.

And this is precisely what has taken place between the two lovers. For each of them, the other is the intruder, the hater, the destroyer—and the beloved. They feel nothing of love while they hate. But were they now not still lovers in secret, they would leave each other after the conflict, each in his or her otherness and strangeness. The opposite happens: They have never been closer, never more attentively and sensitively attuned to each other—to the one who hated, who destroyed, the stranger, the other. This other is the goal of their present devotion and surrender.

Both begin to attune themselves to what destroys them, for the destruction does not cease. On the contrary, it proceeds faster and faster. The more intensively and concentratedly each of them focuses on the Thou, the more radically the heretofore existing structure is dissolved and destroyed in each of them. Afterward what is strange remains strange, it continues to destroy, but the attitude to this work of destruction has mutated. Defensiveness has turned into devotion and surrender—devotion and surrender to one's own destruction, to the destruction of the ego and to its creation anew in the mirror image of the Thou.

This is what it means to say that love as the meaning of mankind's destructiveness. How could love create a new person if love did not simultaneously imply devotion and surrender to the destruction of the old? Perhaps at its deepest level destructiveness is always devotion and surrender to a process of transformation. Whoever does not know this interconnection runs the risk of destroying without transforming; then destructiveness has not fulfilled its purpose.

Let us return to the moral person who is plagued by guilt feelings. He experiences pangs of conscience for harboring his hatred. In fact he *is* guilty, but not because he hates. His guilt lies in the fact that he does not hate enough. He cannot devote and surrender himself to what he hates, to what hates him, because he is too egocentric. He never lets go of the reins. He does not let his hatred lead him, hatred that really would like to show him the locus of his devotion and surrender—the Thou.

Often at the end of a shared life it is scarcely possible to say what qualities of the Thou, obviously important for and to me, were the ones that made me consent again and again to the destruction of the ego, nor is it always possible to say in what respect I was always deeply transformed. Much that I could say about "the change of my character under the beneficial influence of the Thou" would be trite attempts at explanation that would pass over the essential elements in silence. Yet one thing I can say without hesitation. Ultimately we experience this dawning, this rejuvenation and vivification, the joy of creation and rebirth, nowhere more strongly than in devotion and surrender to the destruction of the ego or—which is to say the same thing—in devotion and surrender to the Thou: to its life, its blossoming, its unfolding, its liberation, its smile in unexpected awakening.

Although one can never say with certainty what it is in our partner that actually motivates us to take a developmental step, and hence to embrace the destruction of the old ego, and although what lures one into following the mirroring of the guiding image always remains mysterious, one must still attempt to unveil this secret. Is it perhaps the everyday reality sense that I lack, or the inner calmness for which I yearn?

Immediately after a hate-filled conflict such as I have depicted, each partner must seek to comprehend what really sought destruction in himself or in herself. Was it, for example, the aestheticizing lack of obligation with which I handle people and ideas? Or was it my drivenness?

If we do not ask such questions, we run the danger that hate will remain destructive and will not turn into love. Destructive ideas and actions threaten to lay hold of the whole person if we do not comprehend their specific meaning in the given situation. The unconscious is totalitarian. If we are guided by it, we become totalitarian in everything we think and do. Then we destroy not only a particlular long-outdated attitude—for example, the juvenile aestheticizing lack of commitment mentioned above— in favor of a new attitude that is appropriate to the present developmental phase—for example, fidelity and reliability—but also, we destroy much more than we want to, for example, a relationship whose potential is by no means exhausted. True, it is a sign of vitality when from time to time in transitional phases of our lives and our relationships we are completely seized by unconscious emotions—even by destructive emotions. But then we must, as soon as possible, enter into mirroring of the guiding image with the partner in order to find out what now wants to live out of us anew. Persisting in a destructive emotion is just as unnatural as persisting hedonistically in aesthetic emotion. On the other hand, it is natural to seek the meaning of the destructive emotion. What is it in me that wants to destroy itself and what wants to grow out of me? Mere transports of emotion must lead to concrete comprehension and to a new step in development.

In the now conscious devotion and surrender to my own destruction, my image of the Thou that destroys me changes. It becomes worthy of love. Thanks to my active devotion and surrender, my partner becomes a person who approaches me and with whom I can bond, for active devotion and surrender means empathy—becoming Thou. This is the opposite of mere imitation. The Thou as image of my Self is a symbol; the familiar features of my partner place me in contact with my own unknown possibilities. How the Thou ultimately lives out from within me no longer has much to do with the reality of my partner. My real partner would not recognize himself or herself in the manner in which I let "him" or "her" live out from within me. He or she is spared the discomfort of being imitated.

Reflecting the guiding image happens only with the "image behind the image," that is, with the partner as the symbolic figure of my Self, with the emotional image that I discover when I step into the image that the loved person throws out to me (not throws back to me as in projection). The person I love is, in the reflection of the guiding image, not merely a hook for a projection, but is essentially what I perceive in him or her. Yet he or she is not merely a photograph of my unconscious soul, either, but a late symbol of what now wants to come forward in me and take on shape and form. Thus, reflecting the guiding image is not to be confused with the common psycho-therapeutic technique of mirroring. The latter consists in the thera-pist's imitating the client—for example, by repeating a sentence word for word or by assuming the same posture—in order to facilitate the client's becoming conscious, via mirroring, of what he or she is actu-ally saying and doing. Reflecting or mirroring the guiding image leads into a deeper realm, the realm of what one does not yet say or do, the realm of what the dynamic of one's soul now intends for one to say or do.

When one *consciously* surrenders to one's own destruction, the destructive power is limited to that area of the personality that really must be destroyed and transformed. This is the sole defensible use of our destructiveness. Even though with this attitude we cannot impede the manufacture of atom bombs nor their possible use, we should exercise this surrender so far as it is possible. If people with strong eros were guiding the history of civilization, the destructive-ness in humanity would be set free from its isolation and redirected into its natural union with love and the enhancement of life. Without such strong people, however, it could happen that the image of the cycle of total destruction and a total new beginning, so deeply rooted in human nature, would not be interpreted as a symbol, but would be acted out in totalitarian fashion. Instead of a meaningful partial destruction of old patterns of behavior, as, for example, in the exploitation of the environment that no longer befits contemporary humankind and its problems, it could ultimately lead to total destruc-tion in a global catastrophe. Then the Indian god Shiva, the creator and destroyer, would cease to dance—at least on our Earth.

The natural interconnection of destruction and love, as I have interpreted it, does not imply that we should seek our own destruction. That would be masochistic. What we should seek is the Thou: its strangeness, its otherness, its native land at the other end of the world. And yet it is necessary to know that devotion and surrender to the Thou embrace the more or less radical destruction of the ego. It is this knowledge that can curb the hesitation and wavering in our surrender, our reservations and retreat maneuvers. It is necessary to be devoured by the Thou, but to leave it at that contradicts our natural need for freedom. Whoever consents to being "emptied out" can hope for new fulfillment.

Let us then not boggle at this temporary loss of ego, lest we waver endlessly between loving surrender to the Thou and destructive impulses against the Thou. If that happens, we run the risk that the hate impulses against the Thou become stronger and more totalitarian, and we take the path toward separation.

One misunderstanding must be cleared up. It is impossible completely to bind one's own destructiveness via devotion and surrender to a partner. However, insight into the interconnection between ego-destruction and surrender to a Thou hinders the quantum of destructiveness that cannot be transformed in surrender from becoming greater than our love can "digest."

The stronger partner who destroys himself, as I described him earlier, takes his stand outside the life-affirming interconnection of active surrender and ego-destruction. In him we find greed that exploits and devours the Thou, instead of surrender. Thus in the case of the stronger, instead of consent to the destruction of the I, we find destruction of the Thou and of the world about him in general. In his case, this leads to unintentional destruction of his own personality. The natural and meaningful destruction of the ego would entail the consumption of one's own energies in the service of devotion and surrender. But the stronger partner who destroys himself lets himself be swept into an ever more feverishly spinning whirlpool of self-destruction that does not correspond to his "inner clock," to his natural rhythm of dying and becoming. This chaotic destruction bars his entry to a meaningful life that, through devotion and surrender, would consume him in a way that would make him happy. His death is senseless. The death of the stronger partner who destroys himself is the antithesis of Jesus' death on the cross, which is the expression of devotion and surrender to one's own calling.

In showing the natural interconnection between love and destruction, I have no intention of playing down destructiveness. Destructiveness remains a gruesome law of nature. The destructive potential that is not bound by love and does not lead to something constructive—to a new step in development—is terrifyingly large in many individuals, as well as in human society as a whole.

What stance can we take toward this element of destructive potential that remains destructive? The most mature attitude would be that of consenting to all unavoidable suffering with active devotion and surrender. This devotion and surrender would be active to the extent that we register the destruction of our selves with a wide-awake consciousness and thereby impart to it a paradoxical meaning, the meaning of a conscious process of life. Perhaps this might even be the meaning that the conclusive destruction of the planet could hold for some.

These are not speculations derived from a periodic eruption of an apocalyptic mood, but rather these are realistic liminal experiences into which every one of us can fall once or several times in the course of life. If surrender to the unavoidable facts of the situation miscarries—surrender that cannot be substantiated objectively, but is subjectively necessary—destructiveness will ultimately prove to be the only fundamental law ruling the world. Then we could no longer say that love is stronger than death, but would have to say that death is stronger than love. Whether one will be devoured by a rampant cancer, or will lose the arms that want to embrace one through the death of the most dearly beloved, or will be extinguished in an atomic catastrophe—the question of the meaning of one's life will be decided ultimately by the extent to which we meet this work of destruction alertly and actively, or with panic and passivity—if such a meeting is still possible.

Something similar also holds true for the process of aging and the natural decline of one's partner. The decline of our powers and possibilities for living as we grow older acquires meaning only in emotional surrender to this process. Emotional surrender to the process of aging involves actively employing our diminishing powers and experiencing our vitality right up to the moment of death. Now our Self becomes something indestructible, which Buddhism compares with a diamond. The experience of the indestructibility of the Self grows out of the destruction of the ego. Even if we are destroyed, we are indestructible as long as we perceive our destruction with undivided alertness and affirm it in its inevitability.

In the relationship of two people who love, the predominant attitude—acceptance or rejection of destruction of the ego—gradually crystalizes out. Either the two succeed in remaining related when they place their firmest attitudes and habits in question, even feeling themselves threatened and hated, or the sterile hate of defensiveness and the destruction of love itself predominate. One thing or the other grows: either surrender to the Thou and with it diminution of the ego, or destruction of the Thou and hence of one's own Self.

The relationship informed by Eros is the natural place where surrender to the Thou and the partial destruction of the ego can be practiced, for nowhere else are partners closer and farther apart at the same time. Nowhere else are love and hate more intimately distributed. Nowhere else do the "just me" and the "just you" oppose each other more irreconcilably and nevertheless seek to unite. The attitude toward surrender that a person attains via the bond of Eros imprints itself on his or her relationship to world and to the Self. Either we practice love until death—active surrender in the death of the ego—or we die from love—we are initially satisfied with the passive, sweet feelings of love, but later we more and more actively hate what we once passively loved without knowing it.

Often we encounter persons who, in a seemingly liberal but, actually cynical, manner, acquiesce in the observation that love and hate, surrender and destruction are two fundamental forces that determine the fate of the individual and of the world. Now the one predominates, now the other. One simply has to accommodate oneself to it. This frame of mind serves to disguise and rationalize the person's own hard-heartedness. This attitude is held by people who let others struggle through ticklish situations. It corresponds to the third basic model used to explain human destructiveness, which holds that the world cannot be rid of destructiveness. Of course, I share this view, only I don't leave it at that. Rather, I look for the meaning of destructiveness.

Thus I come to the fourth fundamental model: Of course the world cannot be rid of destructiveness, but it does not exist totally without relation to the forces that further life. One part of destructiveness acquires its meaning in surrender to life. It signifies the painful separation from outgrown parts of the ego in favor of a Thou who, like a guiding image, mirrors a still-unlived new development and makes it possible, thanks to this mirroring. Only this fourth fundamental model grasps the positive dynamic that is peculiar to human destructiveness.

Greek myth also connects destructiveness and love by uniting as lovers Aries, the god of war and destruction who fights on both sides, and Aphrodite, the goddess of love. The precise interpretation of this myth is not that surrender and destruction correspond in the human couple and in the world and mutually cancel out each other— that love dissolves hate and that hate dissolves love. Ultimately, Aries and Aphrodite, destruction and surrender, are lovers. In a love relationship, love and hate are united—in surrender they attain a common meaning. Not only the meaning of love, but also the meaning of hate lies in surrender. Aphrodite finds the meaning of her life in her love for Aries, but Aries, too, finds his meaning in his love for Aphrodite. To be reborn in the ego and in the Self is the meaning of surrender in Eros. Even the masochist draws his pleasure in his own self-destruction from the unconscious longing for transformation that, admittedly, is not to be fulfilled through the means he has chosen.

A natural harmony arises in our lives from the pair of opposites called Aphrodite and Aries. Aries' and Aphrodite's daughter is named Harmoneia. She must have been a mature personality, for together with Cadmos, her husband, she had one of the few marriages with a mortal in Greek myth that ran its course happily and without irreparable separations and blows of fate, and ended at an advanced age with the death of both partners. Through surrender to the Thou and through the corresponding consent to the destruction of the ego, we too would become harmonious personalities, but no flesh and blood human being achieves such a complete marriage of Aphrodite and Aries as happens in this exemplary myth.

Chapter 9

Love Relationships without Sexual Intimacy?

It befits our civilization, with its emphasis on economic values, that many people limit their practice of love to that area of sexuality that, contrary to nature, can be reduced to a mere technique for the creation of sensations. However, in contrast to this reduction, it is possible through sexuality to express inclination, affection, surrender, and oneness with one's partner in a unique and all-embracing manner, both in body and soul, and to experience the outflowing of one's own energies into the beloved as potency, as giving of one's self, and as being given to. But in a similar way, the soul can withdraw from sexuality as from loveless, greedy eating and drinking. For many persons it is possible to have a complete orgasm that sets the entire body vibrating, that pleasurably tenses it and then lets it sink into blissful relaxation, without loving, respecting, or benefiting his or her partner. Such people arrest love in sexuality and prevent love from blossoming.

Reflexively inferring a soul's capacity for love from the capacity for sexual enjoyment and reflexively inferring a capacity for sexual enjoyment from the soul's capacity for love are ideological prejudices. Whoever one-sidedly views the individual in terms of the body does the one, and whoever regards the individual one-sidedly in terms of the soul does the other. Body and soul are neither separated from one another nor are their interactions fully comprehensible. Indeed, the soul always expresses itself bodily, and the body reacts to all movements of the soul. But an awkward sexual encounter can, under certain circumstances, express the soul better and grip it more powerfully than the most successful orgasm. On the other hand, perhaps we can enjoy sexuality very well with a person to whom we are indifferent. It accords with mankind's natural dynamics to strive for the greatest possible unity of body and soul, but the path to that unity is long and by no means unproblematic.

This view that love and sexuality are identical exerts great pressure especially on persons who have subtle feelings. Such persons are often so radically shaken by the attraction felt for another that they cannot perhaps express themselves sexually for considerable periods of time. Their overpowering emotions make them unsure of themselves in every respect, and they are easily upset and hurt. If it happens that, from those around them and particularly from the partner whom they love, they start to sense the erroneous view that sexuality always and necessarily belongs to love and that a successful or unsuccessful sex life quickly determines whether or not two people suit each other, either they flee forward into a sexuality without surrender in order to strengthen their sense of self worth and keep their partner, or instead—which is more common—they pull back believing they are incapable of relatedness and love. In both cases they confuse sexuality with love.

Those persons with sexual anxiety that can be mastered neither by deadening their feelings nor by fleeing into sexuality prove that they regard sexual surrender as a holistic opening of self to another and a penetration of one another's body and soul. Were this not so, they would have as little anxiety with regard to sex as they do with regard to eating and drinking, as mere satisfaction of needs. Without knowing it, they have the correct view of sexuality; through their anxiety they prove they have a greater talent for love than do others who have never noticed this anxiety. They not only see the erotic surrender more correctly, but also the difficulties associated with it. They cannot outmaneuver these difficulties with a split-off sexuality directed one-sidedly toward bodily excitation and relief, but must now begin to practice surrender to the Thou in manifold forms, including sexuality.

Confining Eros exclusively to sexuality is completely unerotic. The nature of Eros is to become one, and that in all areas where people encounter each other. We know how love changes the lover's functioning in body, soul, and spirit. For example, metabolism is accelerated; the capacity to associate, to create spontaneous connections between various mental contents, is improved; logical thinking, on the other hand, is impaired; all emotions and feelings, not only those of love, are intensified.

This applies not only to the first phases of being in love, but also to all other phases in which love is revivified. And the cause is not always physical—say, one's own sexual need or the partner's particular attractiveness at a given moment. The hook can also be emotional: an intense reflection of the guiding image. Or it can be spiritual: a shared insight. Usually physical, emotional, and spiritual elements interact.

Through these changes in body, soul, and spirit, we actually unite involuntarily with the beloved. Many energies, not merely sexual arousal, are mobilized for surrender. In Eros the individual reveals himself or herself in his or her entire complexity. On the other hand, it would be an ideological prejudice to maintain that all these changes serve only as preparation for coitus. Every change reveals a particular aspect of erotic unification.

There are people—more than is commonly supposed—who have not only an initial but an enduring, seemingly insuperable timorousness of sexual intimacy. It is wrong always to equate sexual timorousness with the incapacity to love. Such people see in sexuality such an intensive fusion with another person that they fear getting caught in it and losing every trace of themselves and the freedom of their souls. They have a dark premonition that in a sexual union they would give up something that constitutes their particular value—the very thing of which they could make a gift to the beloved person.

To exemplify this I recall an active, imaginative woman who, in a series of several sexual affairs, had become apathetic and dulled. She feared that this would happen again in the future. Initiative and imagination are exactly the gifts with which this particular woman can love and make people happy. For the sake of preserving this capacity to love, she renounces intimate relationships. She regards this boundary as her personal fate which, despite various attempts at therapy, she cannot alter.

Such people are very familiar with the sacrifice of the ego in surrender to a Thou. Their weakness lies not in surrender, but rather in their losing themselves in love, in fusing with and making themselves subservient to their partner. Some—like the woman in the example above—have already had this experience in sexual relationships; others fear it, sometimes justifiably, more often unjustifiably. Usually letting oneself fall into sexual surrender brings about the exact opposite of what was expected and feared—not a weakening but a strengthening of one's autonomy. But there really are persons who must avoid every kind of fusion with another person, because their loss of ego has something dangerously final about it and does not lead to a rebirth in a stronger personality enlarged by the Thou. Their surrender lacks alert consciousness. They need greater distance from others in order to maintain their standpoint and in order to be able to love other people with a clearly delimited personality. For their own sake and the sake of their capacity to love, they avoid all forms of surrender that, to them, would signify loss of identity in fusion. Often such people choose a service profession in which they can unite surrender with delimitation.

For them it is vitally necessary to free themselves from the social pressure to have a sexual union. Here it helps to be conscious that "I have been right in the choice of my lifestyle, and for the time being I need alter nothing about it." Freed of the pressure to have a sexual union, if conditions permit, they are able to fall in love more intensely than before and can even consent to the "violation" of their previous attitude by entering a sexual union. Thanks to their new freedom, they have become stronger and are ready to give themselves fully while still maintaining their autonomy. This can (but does not have to) happen when the compulsion to have a sexual union is alleviated. Possibly such a person will live a long time, perhaps his or her entire life, without a sexual union.

It is the nature of Eros to manifest different forms of love in different individuals and to reveal humanity to be a community in the interplay of all these forms of love. Even in Eros there are many callings. Were Jesus, Francis of Assisi, and Buddha pitiable, cramped, and neurotic persons because they had no sexual liaisons? Do not all of us have limits to our creativity, necessary restrictions and "specializations" that reveal precisely what is individual about us? Certainly an individual is limited without sexual union, but his or her limitation strikes us merely because it is not our limitation. The limitations that we notice least of all are those that we share with most of the people around us.

Persons who do not express their Eros in a sexual union but instead express Eros in a "platonic" love relationship or in devotion and surrender to a social, cultural, or religious task are not, for this reason, asexual. On the contrary, they often radiate a strong sexual energy. In intense periods of their particular form of surrender, their bodies mobilize the same hormones as the body of a person preparing for a sexual encounter. Everybody can have the experience that the most varied forms of surrender—for example, active aid, artistic expression, engaged conversation, and sexuality—call forth in him or her similar enlivening feelings of flowing oneness, if it is really surrender that moves him or her and not merely self assertion. Nonsexual forms of surrender expressing Eros are not detours of the sexual drive but authentic variations of the one surrender. Someone who entirely excludes the sexual bond from his or her life must, of course, chose a very powerful different form of surrender that is at least comparable to sexual surrender in its intensity. Otherwise the ego will ossify.

There is no standardized, "normal" path along which Eros develops. I recall a man whose nonsexual relationship with a wise woman positively shaped his development for two decades. I also recall a woman who likewise for many years had a spiritually and emotionally fruitful relationship with a significant fatherly man. A woman like that must not be immediately saddled with a "father complex" that she absolutely must "work on," nor a man with a "mother complex." So long as such "unorthodox" relationships get life flowing, they embody the "good direction."

If Eros calls one to a special vocation, it is important to cultivate contact with other people who live their Eros in different relationships, for example, in a family. The formation of sectarian groups and ghettos weakens Eros even if the group members intend to protect one particular expression of Eros. For example, in a cloister that sees itself as a ghetto, the mystical expression of Eros is weakened. Likewise Eros is impoverished in the homosexual ghetto. A group that closes ranks against "the evil world" and on behalf of its own lifestyle does not let Eros flow in from the rest of the world, with the result that the love in the ghetto group atrophies in the course of time. People whose greatest passion is not the love between man and woman but rather a social task should not submit to the pressure to marry unless they can live this passion together with their marriage partner. Two culturally creative persons, for example, can experience themselves relating in Eros more to a third thing—their cultural task—than to each other. Marriage serves the end of strengthening their mutual surrender to a goal outside themselves. Their lives may thrive while the lives of countless others who live a conventional married life without being called to marriage may come to nought.

Love relationships without sexual intimacy all have something in common. They are neither entirely "penetrating" nor entirely "receptive" relationships. They are, to continue the body symbolism, relationships of "friction." The partners resemble two bodies that rub against each other and create energy in that way. They need clearer boundaries than other people, and they believe they cannot afford the fusion of the sexual act. Their optimal distance from each other is greater than that between other lovers. The manner in which they approach each other and in which each perceives and receives the other resembles a kind of "rubbing." By rubbing their external surfaces against each other they charge themselves with energy. But if they were to unite with one another in the center and the depths of their Selves, they would perhaps lose their unique character without gaining a new one. In order not to succumb, they make a sacrifice of the most intimate form of human encounter, sexual intimacy. They set a higher value on the ego and its autonomy. In many cases the sacrifice is worthwhile; after a period of abstinence, they too are ready for a sexual relationship, but it almost always is entered into with a new partner. Under the most favorable circumstances, the previous partner is kept as a friend and forever after symbolizes something they cannot renounce, namely, the mutual respect for each other's "territory."

The lives of persons who sacrifice their sexuality embody for other people the meaning of sacrifice. Every meaningful sacrifice is intended to save some important value, for example, human dignity and the integrity of the ego. In order to rescue this value, other values must be sacrificed temporarily or permanently because no one person can actualize all that is humanly possible. The capacity for integration is limited. Often we distinctly sense the limitations of our possibilities as a warning, be it in diminishing physical powers or in slackening emotional vigor. Then it would be presumptuous, perhaps even suicidal, to hand ourselves over to what overpowers us and for which we are no match. Indeed, it is difficult to renounce a beckoning goal, but with this sacrificial renunciation we place ourselves in the service of a patient, organic process of growth that does not overtense the bow. Thus, paradoxically, it is precisely the sacrifice that sets limits that can take us furthest. Often what we have sacrificed is unexpectedly given us because we have sacrificed it. This can also happen with the renunciation of a sexual relationship. Perhaps it creates the very precondition to our becoming capable of a sexual union in freedom.

In all cultures, periods of sexual abstinence have been institutionalized. Even today in Buddhism many people regularly withdraw into cloisters. People who temporarily or permanently renounce sexual relationship give witness to other forms of love. Moreover, such a reuunciation is a sign of the necessity for limitation in every person. There are areas in every individual where he or she must set limits. Athletes must not run their hearts out, but must know their physical limitations. Every individual must sacrifice the "limitless growth" that, even in the realm of the soul, can lead only to destruction. Often we do not choose such a sacrifice voluntarily; it chooses us. When an emotional barrier compels us to sacrifice, the first thing to do is to comprehend the meaning of this limitation and actively undertake the sacrifice to which we have been passively forced.

Impotent men and frigid women often do not know the meaning

of their lack of sexual reaction. Probably without suspecting it, they associate sexual merging with another form of merging that they want to avoid: a certain dependency on their partner in thinking and feeling. Materially dependent women often seek the autonomy of their souls in frigidity, and impotent men do so with an overly strong need for a mother. Often the insight into this interrelationship is healing in itself. The independence that previously found expression only in the symptomatic nay of involuntary sacrifice must be learned in all areas of life. Then the sexual reaction can return little by little. The impotent man and the frigid woman need an affirmative attitude toward their lack. They need to feel that the absence of a sexual reaction is not something inferior, something of which one must be ashamed, but is rather the most valuable thing for them at that particular time. In it a personality is revealed that is unconsciously ready for the sacrifice of sexuality in order not to be sacrificed itself. In this realistic reevaluation of sexual impotence and frigidity, the ego finally takes itself seriously. Freedom is in fact a greater good than the capacity for sexual reactions in a relationship.

The partner should attempt to comprehend in this manner the unconscious fundamental concerns of the impotent or frigid other partner. He or she should forgo pressuring the other, as perhaps has all too often happened, as it places the other's autonomy in question. It is highly probable that the one is co-responsible in bringing about the other's impotence or frigidity. From that one a surrender is now demanded that is truly intended for the Thou. The impotent or frigid partner should take note that the other's love is not linked to the reward of sexual gratification.

It is dangerous to interpret incipient impotence or frigidity as a diminution of love. Usually the absence of sexual reaction indicates the necessity of delineating oneself more clearly within the love relationship and of tending a domain of one's own, for example, an activity that carries just as much responsibility as does the partner's. If this concern is met, energy begins to flow again into all areas, including into sexual feelings.

Chapter 10

Becoming More Feminine, Even as a Man

The two sentences "Surrender to the Thou presupposes a strong ego-standpoint" and "Surrender is the dissolution of the ego in the Thou" reveal a contradiction, since the first conceives of love as tension in the polarity of two different persons, and the second sees love as the abolition of this polarity in oneness. These are not only two differing viewpoints from which to reflect on love. Above all, they are two experiences in love that grate on or repulse each other, that never give each other rest. They embody an attitude of yea to the loss of ego in merging oneself with the Thou in order to feel and to think as the Thou, and hence an attitude of nay to miserly self-preservation and to the inclination to withhold oneself from the world. And, in spite of this, these two experiences of love comprehend yea to one's uniqueness, difference, to the irreplaceable otherness in the ego, and an active nay to symbiosis and to dependency. Theoretical commentary can postulate the difference more easily than can two lovers in their experiences of love. Love simultaneously drives two persons together and apart, unites and sunders them.

This contradiction cannot be resolved, because we are fully in it; we ourselves *are* this contradiction. Ultimately it is the contradiction of all polarities of which the world is made: life and death, love and hate, dissolving and erecting boundaries, I and Thou, unconsciousness and consciousness, woman and man. These polarities cannot be canceled out with a mitigating "both-and," with superficial concessions, adaptations, and "normal" compromises. In the soul of humankind there is no normalcy, because the polar opposites never reach equilibrium in a "normal midpoint." The midpoint between the opposites lies at a different place for every person; there are no generally valid midpoints. The "average" person does not exist. The longing for "the average person" is the longing for paradise lost, for the unconscious past in which the opposites had not yet been perceived. The need for statistics and their ideal product, "the normal person," draws its energy from the yearning for paradisiacal unconsciousness. An attempt to construct the "normal person" signifies the refusal to live consciously—that is, to live with contradictions. We must resist the temptation to construct a "normal" image of man or woman if we want to find a clue to the meaning of nay-saying in love.

After having pursued the paradox of surrender to one's own destruction in the chapter on "Hate and Love," we were concerned in the chapter on "Love Relationships without Sexual Intimacy" with the delimitation of the ego as something of highest value that must be employed if surrender is to lead to the collapse of the polarities of I and Thou, and thus to love. The temporary sacrifice even of the fullest possibility of becoming one with another person through coitus illustrates the function of delimitation. In this chapter we now turn from delimitation to the other side, to the capacity for surrender and "conception"—to a traditionally feminine capacity.

Until recently delineation—the demarcation of limits—has tended to be more a man's affair than a woman's. The woman experienced her identity more strongly in accepting, absorbing, gestating, enduring. Her danger lay—as it still does in part—in surrendering herself; she risked loss of self in devotion and surrender. Whereas the woman must now learn to delineate and to set boundaries, the man's task is to practice devotion and surrender. But this does not yet say the most necessary things about man's and woman's inner experiences of themselves.

Man and woman both live in a world that was created by the male. In this patriarchal world the setting of boundaries, confrontational encounters, rigid ego-standpoints of individuals and of the collective, and the exploitation of nature have reached a critical level. In a growing number of men the feeling of helplessness and powerlessness is increasing. They see that their world—the world of the male—is running in an increasingly dangerous direction. In their love relationships, more and more men are renouncing the affectation of impressiveness, of one defending one's turf. In this they also lose the artificial vivacity that sprang from seduction, conquest, and coercion. No new source of vitality has taken the place of this egocentric one. Uncertainty and retreat have set their mark on the behavior of many sensitive men in our time.

Not infrequently, such men slip into apathy, passivity, and depression and thus share the symptomatology of many women in the patriarchy. They know that theoretically they are making a meaningful sacrifice by giving up their overly tensed masculinity, but they do not take pleasure in their sacrifice. Rather, they are ruled by the impression of defeat—not defeat by an external opponent, the woman, but defeat by the existential feeling that has given power to the man for millennia: the existential feeling of superiority, of aggressive optimism, of delight in expansion in all realms. In his distress, man is on the lookout for woman, no longer to subjugate her and to celebrate his masculine potency in the triumphant progress of masculinity but, on the contrary, to find direction in woman, who is "at the other end of the world." He seeks the route to "the middle of the world," to his own Self, as well as to find hints on how to behave toward nature—the world without and the world within.

Men and women with differing concerns are now faced with a common task. The man's concern is to learn to approach, perceive, and take into himself the woman in her different nature, as well as people and problems. Thus he would like to enter into a relationship of mirroring the guiding image with the woman. By carefully contemplating the woman, he would like to raise potentialities of his own darkly intimated things from within his depths into the light of consciousness. Such efforts on the man's part tend to make the woman's situation more difficult, for she herself had only just begun to find her way into the patriarchal world's "masculine" professions, politics, and culture. In working with men, she is also working to become familiar with a way of being that, up until now, was the man's domain—the way of being characterized by boundaries and delimitation. Yet today women, too, live in a world in which respect for nature, the relativization of ideological boundaries, empathy, and oneness have become survival tasks for all. Hence it is a world in need of traditionally womanly qualities. Women are thus faced with a double task. They have to take possession of and further develop a world created by men, including the values that inform this world— the values of penetration and confrontation, of conquest and self-differentiation, of comprehending and defining. Since these are values just as befitting a woman as a man, values that become destructive only as outgrowths of an extremely masculinized society, the woman cannot forgo developing these values. But since at the same time she lives in a world that, for the sake of its survival, has need of the values that heretofore have been exercised almost exclusively by women— particularly the holistic capacities for empathy and adaptation to natural rhythms and facts—she now must come to terms with

the difficult task of pursuing feminine concerns within male structures, in part using male methods. To this extent the woman must
become more feminine *and* more masculine.

Do women's and men's new understanding of themselves have
any effect on their love relationships? There are two dangers inherent in considering this question. First, instead of working through the
differences between the sexes that, in part, arose historically, women
and men are tempted to override them. In denying the differences
between men and women, in making light of them, or in accepting
them as immutable facts, men and women become colorless, emotional mongrels. Blandness and lack of interest in working through
actual relational problems are nothing other than modern defensive
magic with which a person wards off problems. Whenever two persons do not express their antithetical views to one another, the individuals and their relationship are emotional hermaphrodites,
monsters in which the organs are awry, in each other's way. Here I
use the words "mongrel" and "hermaphrodite" to indicate the
unconscious mingling of gender-specific emotional opposites in the
individual; I am leaving out of consideration the other, equally important meaning of these words: the conscious, inner relationship and
fertilization of woman and man in the individual, be this individual
male or female. Dull stagnation pervades such a sterile partnership.
The premature retreat from conflicts is defended with bogus wisdom:
"If it doesn't work between us, then we simply don't belong together.
We converged once; now we have grown apart. That's too bad, but
it can't be changed."

In place of the previous assignment of roles, husband and wife
tacitly agree to the lowest possible degree of mutuality, a condition
under which people can just barely live together, so long as the situation does not get complicated. An unexpected illness or financial
troubles can overtax such a minimalist partnership. Then both feel
themselves to be just as helpless together as each one feels alone.
Mutual caring almost completely falls by the wayside.

By retreating from all gender role differences, man and woman
come to resemble each other, thereby creating a hybrid of woman
and man on the basis of a minimal consensus. The man is no longer
so masculine and the woman no longer so feminine as men and
women used to be. Of course this is gratifying, but wife and husband
do not get inwardly closer to one another when they avoid confrontation and dispute about their previous gender roles. This leveling of
the differences between the sexes arises out of defensiveness
against conflicts. True, from time to time there are conditions that
lure them out of their reserve—for example, when one feels taken

advantage of by the other. Then the colorless man suddenly becomes primitively masculine or the colorless woman primitively feminine, as if they wanted to caricature the old gender roles. At the same time, the man gets tyrannical and whiny and the woman obstinate and wild but ultimately ready to subordinate herself. Thus they distort those characteristics that man and woman have selectively developed in the last millennia: the man's ego-strength and separateness, and the woman's devotion, surrender, and empathy. In such outbursts they prove that they are not a single step farther ahead than their ancestors were.

When the crisis is past, husband and wife again find themselves in their undifferentiated monotony. In both of them the capacity for ego-strength and differentiation atrophies to the same passive reacting to the other, and the capacity for devotion and surrender and empathy shrinks to familiar passive experiences of fusion, be it in sexuality or in conversation. In talking they let their linguistic expression become impoverished in order to exclude their partner's taking a controversial position in a conversation. What is shared is only the intense feeling of belonging fatefully together "in spite of everything." In appearance, dress, and mannerisms, such partners approximate each other more and more. The emotional mongrel appears clearly—not only the concealment of gender-specific characteristics in contrast to, say, the fashion of the extremely masculine and the extremely feminine, but also the mingling of all individual differences in mutual adaptation. Each one avoids letting his or her uniqueness show. When, in spite of this, one or the other does take a stand or show initiative, it is immediately made to look unimportant by a banal tone of voice or a deprecatory gesture. The other's suggestions and initiatives are seemingly accepted with a gentle indulgence, but in reality they are neutralized.

This husband and wife resemble a couple from Greek mythology: Endymion and Selene. Endymion was asleep when Selene saw him and kissed him for the first time. He has still not awakened from this sleep. The reason given for this "sleepy" relationship is that Endymion does not want to grow older and that Selene prizes tender kisses more than passion. They are related to each other by their restraint. They do not put themselves into their love relationships, and thus they prevent aging, the maturation of the personality.

It is possible for the plight of the emotional mongrel to be merely a phase in early adulthood. Considering the difficult transitional situation in man's and woman's self-understanding, it is easy to grasp why young people "lie out in the weeds" longer today. If undisturbed by other persons, they can collect their energies for later confrontations. But it is rather striking that for many people the mongrel relationship rigidifies into a permanent way of life.

The second pressing danger to the love bond between man and woman is emotional gender switching. Like every turn from one quality into its opposite, this, too, is a passive, unconscious process. The partners do not ponder their previous gender roles and do not feel themselves to be thrust into the opposite sex. The man turns into an inferior woman and the woman into an inferior man. The man is subject to changeable moods and emotions, and the woman puts forth unsubstantiated opinions and thus determines the spiritual climate of the relationship, such as I have described in the situation of the emotional mongrel under particularly trying circumstances. This form of reaction is also found among older couples. It consists not in a retreat into behavior that lacks differentiation according to gender, but rather in primitively living out the characteristics of the partner.

Turning into the opposite is not to be confused with that playful exchange of roles that couples undertake in order to develop new talents and capabilities, in which there is no rigid either-or and each promotes the other in his or her newly discovered possibilities. A man who for many years has developed his musical talent for playing the piano now stimulates his wife to learn to play an instrument. With their flexible understanding of roles in all realms, including sexuality, such a couple vivifies themselves and stimulates each other. To be sure, they are by no means stable, and again and again conflicts threaten their life together, but even outsiders sense that they are lovers who seek a common path, even if they squabble more often than others.

I want to further illustrate in detail how a husband and wife relativize their one-sided, gender-specific roles in mutual mirroring of the guiding image and how they can gain insights into fallow parts of their personalities. Having dealt with two current dangers in the self-understanding of man and woman, I will limit myself here to the question of how the man can become more feminine, that is, can develop traditionally feminine qualities in himself.

Many men are afraid of losing their masculinity if they get intensely involved with women, especially if they get involved with their own "inner woman," that is, their undeveloped feminine side. Although they are glad to get rid of their earlier role as breadwinner, as the partner with sole responsibility as "head of the family" they are still afraid of becoming womanish and tend to cling stubbornly to the old ways.

It is true that the man does not know what he is letting himself in for when he gets involved with a woman. But this is the essence of the adventure of genuine development—its outcome is unforesee-able. If the man does not risk this adventure and does not get involved with a woman, exactly what he fears happens to him: he becomes womanish, which means he becomes dependent on a woman of whom he takes possession as mother. Rigid masculinity is always coupled with womanish dependency, and the man who really won't get involved with a woman knows least of all about just this relationship. He can overcome his womanish dependency on woman only by promoting mature femininity in himself. If he does not become more feminine himself, he remains his wife's child. Then his wife has to be "feminine for two." If he does not promote "feminine" values in himself—such as the capacity to perceive, acknowledge, and incorporate new signals and impulses; to think about problems not only in his head but also to "weigh them in his heart"; to be patient and steadfast in feeling; and to have inner strength in difficult situations—he will remain dependent on his wife in all these impor-tant areas of life. He will want to be accepted, loved, cuddled by her, he will perpetually appeal to her patience and her irrevocable fidelity. Instead of actively putting himself in his wife's place—which would be the place of devotion and surrender—he passively begs for atten-tion. He is a womanish man because he perseveres in his rigid masculinity.

There is nothing more invigorating for a man than to frequent the company of women, being open to the uniqueness of a woman and to this woman in particular. This is the opposite of the compulsive masculine reflex of seeing oneself confirmed as a man by being involved in a "successful" seduction of a woman, for example. The easy, cheerful sort of interest, free of design or intention, involuntarily sets body and soul vibrating so that the rhythm of the woman is united with the man's own and the woman within him thinks with her, feels with her, converses with her. In the fluctuation and the exchange, both figures flow back and forth. One moment he sees her form clearly as his own, then he senses how she steps out of him. In the interplay of opposites, they are simultaneously relaxed and alert. Different from sexual surrender where I and Thou fuse in giving and taking and yet remain wholly themselves, this happy play is a gentle trial exchange and mutual savoring of both partners in their first approach to each other.

There is no better way for a man to become more feminine than by being with women often, just as there is no more sure way for a man to become womanish than by being only with men. After losing Euridice, Orpheus shunned all contact with women and therefore found his death among women at the hands of the maenads, who tore him to bits. He lost his masculine identity because he fled from women. His lack of relationship to woman was already heralded when Euridice was slipping away from the underworld and he looked back, thus losing her forever. The glance backward to the timeless realm revealed his uncertainty in relation to Euridice and his woman-ish dependency on her.

This way of becoming more feminine by no means resolves the polarity of the sexes for a man. On the contrary, the tension between him and the woman only becomes really palpable when he becomes more feminine—not in the grim battle of the sexes but in a gaily bright and deeply inward interplay in which he has the feeling of creating his world anew. Among the most apt depictions of this interplay of man and woman belong those that portray the union of the Indian divine couple Shiva and Shakti. These two figures, completely related to each other in sexual union, resemble each other in a certain sense. The masculine Shiva has a "feminine" suppleness and grace and Shakti a "masculine" resoluteness and strength. And yet, it would never occur to one to call Shiva womanish or Shakti manish. The gods' concentrated and liberated vital energy, fully conscious of itself, is imparted to the viewer. The antithesis of masculine and feminine has, as an alternative, completely lost its object, and yet Shiva is an unequivocally masculine figure that exerts his effect from within more powerfully than Michelangelo's or Rodin's statues of men. It follows that Shakti, like Shiva, is a fully related figure and hence appears as Shiva's own vital energy.

Contemplation of this divine couple gives one an intimation of how the union of man and woman in one's own soul comes about. Here the man's becoming woman and the woman's becoming man has nothing forced and artificial about it. They impress the viewer as the most natural creatures in the world, and indeed they are, yet in his or her own concentrated awareness the viewer senses intimations that here something has found perfect expression, something that has overcome the primeval history of the most horrible and most desperate battles between man and woman. Indeed, those delightful hours of interplay between man and woman are the fruit of decades of coming to terms with each other. How many petrifactions precede the flexible and composed agility, how many cunning embraces precede the freedom of play, how many illusions must disperse before the mirroring of the guiding image can take place!

Becoming more feminine means playing this game unerringly, even under difficult conditions in which people are put to the test. It means encountering a woman's smile in the midst of dogged effort, and immediately smiling that same smile in one's own soul! It means getting stuck in work and then releasing the feminine figure from within oneself; relaxing one's contorted face in the mirror of a woman; running up against one's limits and nevertheless surrendering oneself and awakening transformed! How beneficial it is for the man, aware of the woman, to open himself, to take her within himself; to bear, to sustain, to nourish her and let her grow and then to give birth to her! It is also healing for him to receive the seed instead of only implanting it; it makes his own soul fruitful.

In order to further the growth of his own feminine side, a man should open the pores in his soul's skin in all meetings with women. Every individual woman contributes, in her own uniqueness, to shape the woman in him. Her image awakens his power to give form. Alertness is surrender; the sleepiness of Endymion, on the other hand, is refusal. In the presence of a woman, a man can overcome the nay that wants to let him rest in his maleness and the yea that seeks the child's level of dependency. There is no ugly woman; there are only limits in a man's surrender to the reality of the woman and of his soul.

The play of fantasy can also strengthen and shape the feminine in a man. Let him not be afraid to spend entire days dreaming of women, yet let him try to remain alert in these dreams so that the fleeting image of the feminine becomes the permanent shape of his soul. Fantasy play is not merely chance good fortune that appears in leisure hours. It can be learned and practiced; helpful rules of the game can be discovered. Play becomes binding form, past and present. For the man, becoming more feminine is the path to his own vitality.

PART III

Must One Choose Between I and Thou?

Chapter 11

The No of Separation
and Divorce

Indifference, cynical devaluation, not taking one's partner seriously, continual hostility, and stubborn hate: this attitude of absolute no can change two persons who once loved each other into bastions of self-defense between whom the spark of mutual enlivenment and communication is no longer alight. The nay no longer serves to build up the tension in love. The natural wave rhythm of up and down, closeness and distance, hope and disappointment, union and differentiation has congealed; each is fixated at a point of resistance against the other. Instead of envisioning shared future with the other, each sees a coming-to-myself and keeping-to-myself because of separation from the other. This has become the only goal. The nay has gone beyond the point where it could still serve loving unity.

Now it is too late—and yet it is too early to ask how things could have gone differently, how the escalation of the nay could have been prevented. Now it is not even a question of seeking a new path, but simply a matter of leaving the old path, cutting off the dead branch. Parting is forever.

Truly, this nay no longer has any place in the love for the Thou, but little by little it should lead to love for oneself. It is not the separation and divorce from another person that causes the greatest damage, but rather the separation and divorce from oneself. This is so because being one with the other always means respecting oneself, trusting oneself, and being one with oneself. The mistake of believing there is an indissoluble bond of fate between two persons is a common erroneous belief among those who have come to grief in a relationship. Gretchen's words to Faust, "If I don't have him, life is a tomb. For me the whole world is spoiled," hold true not only for the partner who has been abandoned, but often for the one who took the initiative in separating, too. It holds true as well for the one who no longer loves but now can only hate. Without the other we feel cut off from life. The nay to the Thou comes to mean a nay to oneself, often even for the partners who comport themselves reasonably and calmly and part from each other by mutual agreement. Such feelings of loss are frequently experienced even by someone who leaves a partners in favor of a new relationship, although they may not surface until long after the time of the separation.

When I separate from a partner whom I have loved and who has loved me, it becomes clear that not everything humanly possible is possible for me, but that my possibilities are limited. I was not capable of realizing Eros, of becoming one, in this failed relationship. Nowhere does one come up against the limits of what can be realized with greater impact than in the situation of separation. My inability to save this relationship gives me the pervasive feeling of powerlessness. It is difficult for me to resign myself to what I cannot prevent.

That I have changed from a lover to a hater is the most painful confession of my limitations. I sense that the Thou was also a part of myself, otherwise I would not have loved, but my surrender was limited—my surrender to the Thou and to that part of myself that corresponded to the Thou. I extended my hand and then let it fall; I took the Thou within me and than cast out the Thou. This part of my world was too foreign for me to be able to unite with it permanently in Eros. And my influence on the Thou was also limited. The Thou was free to withdraw from the mutual reflection of the guiding image. My power over the other is limited. I do not stand in the other's place and cannot determine the other's thoughts, feelings, and actions.

It is easy for me to mistake my present inability with complete impotence. I generalize my experience with one person to all possible experiences with other persons. Fear paralyzes me; I fear that I cannot love and that I am not worth loving, that I am not a loveable person.

These two fundamental fears—the inability to love and the inability to inspire love—beget resignation. This passivity can only be overcome by actively practicing surrender, but it is no longer surrender to my partner from whom I have parted. I must surrender to the inner person I had hoped to become—even if unwittingly—in the course of the failed relationship. The inner coming to terms with the once-beloved person must begin as soon as possible so that the nay to the Thou can become a yea to myself and to a new development; later perhaps even a new love will be possible. Thus the relationship that has come to grief realizes the potential that it always had.

Following a separation, we should exert ourselves in two directions by turning away from the outer Thou and turning toward the inner settlement with him or her. In what follows we are concerned with this dual effort.

The turning away from the other does not, of course, end on the day we give up our common dwelling or when divorce is pronounced legally. It began long before and has not yet come to completion, even though the actual turning away can only begin on this day. The first task is to call to mind by force of will and in detail all those differences in viewpoint between the just-separated partners—differences that made a life together, and particularly a bond of love, impossible. In calling to mind these differences, even banal details can play a symbolic role. Perhaps the person just divorced is as happy as a child to sleep again with the window open because the partner who could sleep only with the window closed is no longer there.

Differentiating oneself from the former partner gives a feeling of relief and of release: "I have lost something but I have also won back something." While I am pondering the differences between my former partner and me, perhaps I realize how seldom I reflected on this theme in the course of the relationship; little by little my firm standpoint got lost. Thus I make up for something that was left undone in the relationship. Completing this task also gives me a good feeling.

In the first period following the separation, those horrible, wounding, final conversations keep going round and round in my head. How much malice, disappointment, sadness, and despair I have felt in those conversations, in myself, and in others! But just these negative feelings make it easier for me to turn my back on the past. The wounds to my soul were necessary to shake me awake and make me take flight. The wounds we inflicted on each other help me actively to will the separation that my partner initially forced on me. At first I hesitated, but then there was no turning back.

Moreover, the aggression and hatred that broke forth from me at that time was already in me, secretly, before. Now I remember it very well. Something in me wanted the separation for a long time, but I left it to my partner to demand separation on my behalf, too.

Two fairy-tale motifs give us hints about how we can turn away emotionally from our previous partner. The first such motif is the *refusal to accept nourishment.* In the North American tale of "Ititanjang, the Man who Married the Wild Goose," the woman refused to accept even the least morsel of food from her husband.

Often the dependency of one person on another goes so far that finally she can think only with her head, work with her hands, and eat with her mouth. Then rescuing one's own individuality is the highest commandment. Now she must refuse any and all nourishment—spiritual and material—in order to gain the sense of what she is in herself, much as anorexic adolescents express their need for autonomy by refusing nourishment.

The material dependency of many women on their divorced husbands is a severe psychological problem in this regard. On the one hand they have a right to his support and are dependent on the money. On the other hand it is difficult to distinguish emotional from financial independence. If because of children a woman is limited in pursuing her career, she must put all her efforts into making this distinction and attaining emotional independence in spite of material dependence.

The most important refusal of nourishment refers to the projections with which one partner has fed the other until one could no longer distinguish one from the other. A woman is perhaps not such a good housewife as her husband's wishful projections desired, but neither is she such a bad businesswoman as her husband's devaluing projections tried to make her believe. The fasting cure of refusing emotional nourishment helps her to find her way back within her own boundaries, in that she learns to distinguish herself from the carrier of projections into which her divorced partner had made her.

A second helpful fairy-tale motif that promotes active separation is the *liberating sacrifice*. In many fairy tales a woman flees from a dangerous lover while throwing objects behind her over her shoulder. The objects grow larger and become obstacles for the pursuer. Thus a hair brush turns into a mountain; a pinch of salt becomes a salty sea. As in the case of refusing nourishment, the woman makes sacrifices here, too. She forgoes the less important things in order to save her bare skin, that is, her identity. The previously common practice of interring with the deceased such implements as the eating utensils used in life has a similar significance. Under no circumstances might they continue to be used by the survivors. Likewise, following the death of a relationship, the material dependency must be dissolved so far as possible in order to lighten the emotional dependency. We have already investigated the motif of the meaningful sacrifice in the chapter "Love Relationships without Sexual Intimacy."

What makes one tend to postpone the day of separation is the many comforts that were shared together but must be given up when one is alone again. After all, the money of one household must suffice for two after the separation. And despite all the conflicts, there was something comforting about knowing there still was another person at home.

The inner settlement with the ex-partner and the connection with that realm in oneself that the ex-partner maintained by proxy for one cannot begin until the inner turning away from the ex-partner has been completed to the extent that he or she is no longer seen as a poor devil or as the devil incarnate. In fairy tales this is expressed in the motif of the *quest*. In the search for a princess, for example, the hero encounters and overcomes so many obstacles that he becomes a mature person. The description of the goal is less important in fairy tales than the description of the way that leads to it. Children to whom a fairy tale has been told reveal this. After hearing the fairy tale they remember individual episodes of it exactly, but they often forget the ending, although they had burned to know it as the tale was being told to them. The episode they remember best always has something to do with their own development. In the language of images, that episode shows the child how it can take the step in its development that is now indicated and necessary. Thus the child's primary interest is in the quest itself, just as an adult no longer recalls the end of a movie, but the complications and their resolution.

Consequently, the quest is concerned less with an external process with, say, the tricks a young man uses to marry above his station in life—than with the inner path to oneself. In order to find himself, the male hero must enter into relationship with his own femininity, relationship to the "inner woman" who balances the man's one-sidedness. The "marriage" with the "inner woman"— the union of masculine and feminine elements—means that I now bring contrary realms in my nature, such as aggression and contemplativeness, into relationship, and as an individual I become, as it were, a "couple," a whole in which the opposites are united.

Following a failed relationship, it is of primary importance to develop insight into one's own projections that had little to do with one's partner. Certainly the relationship was very strongly shaped by unrealistic projections, otherwise it would not have come to the point of ever more misunderstandings and finally to separation. Obviously, realistic mirroring of the guiding image hardly took place at all. It is now too late for this. Mirroring of the guiding image makes sense only with a person with whom one is bonded in love and with whom one wants to live, therefore in what follows we will be concerned exclusively with insight into the projections on to the divorced partner. This insight is the goal of our quest. It is the highest value in the present phase of life, a treasure that we absolutely must unearth.

What did I seek in my previous partner but did not find because I really wanted to find it in myself, and not in him or her at all? To take a new example, did I want to become just as active as the image that I initially projected on to him or her, the image of an active, imaginative person? We should dedicate much time and attention to these questions. Truthful answers determine whether we can transform the failed outer relationship into a successful inner one, whether our nay to our partner can or cannot ultimately, in a deeper sense, turn into a yea to what we projected onto him or her.

I want to make some suggestions regarding the path of inner critical appraisal with the outer partner. In doing this, I shall not consider the important problem of the children of this marriage. Marriage and family are not the theme of this book. Let me say only this about the problem of children: They do not provide their parents with an adequate reason for remaining together. Children enjoy a more favorable development with only one of their parents than if they were pulled back and forth between their parents in their parents' conflicts.

Grown stronger as a result of decisively turning away from the previous partner, the separated person now attempts to get closer to that person—or to what was seen in him or her. As a *first question* let us ask: "What is the *major reason* I generally give for the collapse of my marriage?" In answering this, let us remember what reasons we give in everyday conversations with acquaintances and friends, and let us choose that reason which we state most often. As examples I will mention four answers that are often given. A first answer might be: "The relationship collapsed because I entered it only to get away from my parents. My partner was actually incidental, although of course I was in love." A second typical cause that is made responsible for the collapse of a marriage goes like this: "I was too young. I didn't know what I was doing." A third reason: "Back then there was no sex without marriage. We were just sexually compatible." And a fourth: "I didn't know him (or her) well enough. He (or she) was good at playing a role."

I have intentionally cited the reasons that are made responsible for the collapse of a love bond in their simplest form in order to reveal the superficiality of the reasons given. Whoever "runs off at the mouth" this way is still misusing the former partner as a scapegoat. He or she still does not have the courage really to go into the question concerning the collapse of the partnership. In the first phase of parting and inner turning away, we cannot afford to feel the old feelings that have bonded us to this partner for years. But we must realize how defensively superficial our answer to this most important question is if we are to be startled into asking the *second question* and, in our attempt to answer it, taking the second step.

What *tacit expectation* is revealed in each of the four reasons that were given? It must have been that very expectation that formed the sore point in the relationship, that is, the most vulnerable point that finally led to the collapse of the relationship.

Recall the first answer: "The relationship collapsed because I entered it only to get away from my parents." This reveals an unconscious expectation of the partner: "You should be my father or my mother." This is no contradiction. Whoever enters a marriage or marriage-like bond in order to get away from the parental home is seeking another parental home. Alone, he or she cannot get away. The partner is now supposed to be father or mother or both. Behind the second answer, "I was too young and didn't know what I was doing," is concealed another expectation of the partner. "I would like you to be responsible for me." This goes together with the later reproach, "You are responsible for our marriage, so you are also guilty for its collapse." The third reason given was: "We married only for sex." The underlying attitude of expectation here is obvious: "I would like for you to take my sexuality in hand. You are supposed to give me pleasure and satisfy me." And the fourth reason given— one's insufficient knowledge of one's partner—reveals this expectation: "Be intelligent for me and make all the decisions that have anything to do with us. Put your maturity and power of judgment to work for me."

Of course, none of these expectations or similar ones is expressed spontaneously in this way. Stating them this way would break the spell that such expectations evoke. Unconscious expectations of this sort are expressed in the first vivifying phase of a relationship as *positive projections*, revealed in sentences such as "You are absolutely reliable" or "You always do the right thing" or "I just know that you are the only one who will never disappoint me." The absoluteness, generalization, and unsubstantiated certainty prove such assertions to be merely projections. All positive projections contain the identification of the partner with one's inmost expectations: You are in fact just as I secretly want you to be. As early as 1913 Marcel Proust wrote, "Whenever we are in love with a woman, we simply project our emotional condition on her." The subjective feeling of being in love is confused with how our partner really is. It transforms the Thou into an image of our own unconscious soul, similar to the way in which the evening sun with its golden radiance is able to transform landscapes and faces into an image of one's soul so that suddenly the world appears as a revelation. Feeling resembles a certain coloration of light. Whatever receives the glow of projection becomes a revelation. In fact, the lover sees the "enchantingly beautiful image" of the beloved as a revelation, only he or she does not know that it is a revelation of his or her own soul.

Positive projections are bridges reaching out to the Thou. But if we remain standing too long on the bridge, we are pulled back to the old river bank again. We lose the relationship that we found through the projection and demarcate ourselves from our partner before we have gotten to know him or her. Then the vital feeling in the relationship turns into its opposite: Our unconscious expectations express themselves as reproaches in *negative projections* that contradict the earlier positive projections. Such affect-laden reproaches as "You're totally unreliable lately" or "At the decisive moment you always do the wrong thing" or "I just know you'll disappoint me in the end" are always negative projections. Their meaning is that of throwing us back on ourselves to accomplish what we expected from the other. But if we are ruled by disappointment over the expectations our partner did not fulfill, we remain on the same side of the river and do not find the way to the other side, to our partner as he or she really is. This happens in all love relationships that end in disillusionment.

For Paul Claudel, woman is a promise that she cannot keep. Consequently he ascends higher in his projections right up to God, from whom he expects the fulfillment of the promise that the woman made to him. Another person never can fulfill the expectations that we place on him or her when we are in love. If we take these expectations into our own hands—that is, see through our projections—the woman becomes the guide for the man and the man becomes the guide for the woman to "God in us," as Christian mystics call the Self, the dynamic center of the whole person that spontaneously regulates the interplay of the opposites, including those that are gender specific. The relationship becomes the medium for experiencing and actualizing oneself. Opposites that previously were separated between me and my partner as I saw him or her become bound to my life by my taking my expectations in hand. The Chinese book of wisdom, the *I Ching*, saw the goal of human life in the wisest possible union of opposites: hard and soft, vehement and gentle, creative and receptive.

However, so long as we reproach our partner for not having kept his or her original promise, the path to self-knowledge is barred. In a certain sense, our partner remains a supernatural figure—angel or demon, god or devil—from whom we expect salvation or fear or perdition. In many fairy tales such fateful partnerships are depicted with supernatural players. As long as we project our expectations, we are not yet married to the real partner but to an unknown inner figure of our own. As an inner reality, such "projection marriages" often outlive the outer separation and divorce.

If people have the courage after a divorce to examine and to formulate their earlier infantile expectations that found expression first in positive, then in negative projections, they have already begun to assume a more active, more responsible stance. Perhaps for the first time they overcome the passivity that finds expression in such expectations.

In the first transports of love and merging, it happens as a matter of course that we fulfill the expectations of our beloved so far as possible. However, when the time for delimitation arrives, the passive expectations of one partner cause resentment and aggression in him or her because he or she does not get everything wanted, and in the other because that partner has the feeling of being exploited.

The infantile attitude of entitlement, however, is usually present in both partners, and this in mutually complementary fashion. Thus a man expects from his wife: "Be my nurse, even on my good days," and complementary to this the wife expects from her husband: "Firmly guide our common destiny." The invulnerable hero and the nurse—the projections cross. The one's passivity runs athwart the other's passivity. Each fights for his or her own irresponsibility, and this replaces their common surrender. The most cunning weapon in this battle is the reference to one's own supposedly unalterable weakness that demands sympathy: "That's just the way I am. Do help me!" Passive expectations that the other will act replaces acting oneself. Presumably the failed relationships we have been discussing ran aground primarily on this shoal. The partner was not a guiding image for one's own unfolding, but rather a stopgap.

The meaning of a passive expectation lies in this: It signifies a need to apply myself to my own activity. This is the *third step* in the inner critical appraisal and settlement with the partner from whom I have just parted: taking into my own hands responsibility for my initial expectations. Now I know that the energy of my expectations is aimed at their fulfillment through my own activity and development.

In the first example, it is a question of leaving the parental home, the childlike, passive safety, emotionally as well as physically. The protagonist in the second example assumes responsibility for the collapse of the marriage and thus also the responsibility for his or her own future. Living one's sexuality not only in one's own passive enjoyment but also in active surrender to one's partner's pleasure is the goal in the third example. Finally, in the fourth example it is a question of strengthening one's own power of judgment.

If the last step succeeds, we experience the past relationship less and less as a collapse and more and more as the precondition for our present autonomy. Through it we have gained the freedom to desire only what we can attain for ourselves. Now we are able to live even without our former partner; hence, we are capable of a new partnership. In devotion and surrender to what we can no longer receive from other persons but can only develop within ourselves, our energy begins to flow again. It is no longer separation, but bond-forming Eros that now sets its mark on how we shape our lives.

Chapter 12

Surrender and Discovery of Self in Sexuality

In sexual union one experiences the direct interconnection of surrender and discovery of Self. Here the cleavage between Thou and I, oneness and delimitation, yea and nay can dissolve into one single movement. Let us now attempt to describe the *experiential path* of sexual union, not in order to analyze it, but to make it more accessible to consciousness.

This experiential path begins in fantasy. Children, adolescents, and adults fantasize and dream over and over of approaching attractive persons, of meeting, touching, and connecting with them. They glide back and forth between their inner images and the outer persons who constellate the images, between fantasy images and concrete persons in the world about them.

It is impossible fully to distinguish between the two; the real woman whom I love becomes an inner image for me and is my own creation. At the same time, the image that I have of this woman gives her vital energy so that she comes more and more to resemble my image of her. Who are you and who am I? Fantasy knows not and cares not. The world that fantasy creates for itself is simultaneously an inner and an outer world; yearning drives us to seek in the world what our soul has long known only dimly. In the wedding of fantasy image and Thou, we step out of the old realm of ego into the more complete Self and out into the broader world. As we do this, opposites are united. In our fantasy's sketch, we become more complete persons.

In fantasy the outer and the inner are united, world and soul.

Their interplay transforms both, just as the child sees the image of its mother and develops toward it. The mother loves her child, and in doing so becomes the image that the child sees in her. Lovers see in and with the heart and are mutually transformed. The world creates the soul and the soul creates the world. The one does not come earlier nor the other later. Surrender and finding Self are equally primary. The human being develops out of the simultaneity of both. Fantasy is our creative power.

The young person growing up has ever more glowing fantasies and finds in them the unification of the inner and the outer world. Fantasies of sexual fusion give him or her the intense feeling of oneness with everything. Abundant images of how people crowd in on and merge into each other surge incessantly just beneath the surface of even the most banal occupations. Such images give the adolescent boy wings, even when he is rushing to school, and make his eyes shine even when he is doing math homework. The most varied women move embodied in his visions: ethereally delicate, reticently gentle girls; challenging young women; warm women with soft breasts and spread legs; dangerous women of ill repute; women in distress awaiting rescue; abysmally sad women; wise, superior women; women of effervescent gaiety and vivacity; and many more—a greater diversity than he will ever be capable of loving in his entire life. Never will his arms be able to embrace so many and such diverse women, but his fantasies embrace them all. Outwardly he is closed off and often motionless, but he gazes inward and his contemplation spurs on the dance of female figures.

In his first love relationships he usually cannot perceive his actual girlfriend and his inner, glowing image of woman as a unity for very long. Enraptured in surrender, he is soon lonely again in separation. His girlfriend is close to him and then distant and foreign, according to whether or not he can hold this fantasy world and the outer world together or whether he lets them fall asunder.

From time to time the grown man, too, feels himself a foreigner to the woman he is close to. His fantasy takes leave of her and plays its own games. This has to do with the fact that no outer relationship ever attains the richness of the inner fantasy. Therefore every person must, from time to time, withdraw into himself in order to feel this vitality again in a manner different from that possible with his partner. Everything I have said about the adolescent boy and adult man can easily be applied to the adolescent girl and the woman. From their perspectives, women paint similar pictures.

In growing older, many persons forget this enlivening interplay. They fixate on one person and let their fantasy life atrophy. Then the outer bond becomes functional, and their souls dry up. The sexual union with the Thou bcomes lifeless; it no longer leads to their own vitality. The life of such a person no longer flows together with the life of a Thou. It moves quietly and stunted in the background. The Thou is also impoverished because it receives too little nourishment. Fantasy as the force that unites both has rigidified in functional thinking. Thus both the individual's development and the relationship to the partner, which is no longer a lover relationship, stagnate. Neglect of fantasy and loss of the talent for Eros are one and the same thing. Collective fantasies in films and novels do not take the place of one's own fantasies, but they can stimulate them. (Here I am not talking about the real danger to many people of getting stuck in the noncommittal nature of fantasy and of avoiding the step to the committed shaping of life.)

No book on body awareness and orgasm can replace the role of fantasy. Where fantasy is lacking, sexuality becomes unerotic. On the other hand, where fantasy again begins to play, even incomplete sexual experiences become fresh, not to mention the successful coital union of man and woman.

Since all possible women arise out of the man's fantasy and all possible men out of the woman's, we need manifold contacts with the outer world, too. Many real women and men whom we know mirror facets of our unknown soul and spur our inner figures to life, preventing us from remaining caught in mere fantasy. Whatever wants to move in the inner world depends on related movement in the outer world, and what moves outside becomes an emotional reality only in inner movement. It is an error to believe that the uniqueness of a central love relationship would be endangered by enlivening friendships with other people in which sexuality also plays a role. The central love relationship is, on the contrary, endangered if the soul withers away while rigidly staring at only one person. Fantasy needs the outer world in order to maintain the interplay between soul and Thou.

The sexual relationship suffers in the long run if two lovers dovetail in a falsely understood, anxious fidelity and dare not smile at a person other than their partner. It should be possible to speak to each other about other women and men with heartfelt sympathy without awakening jealousy. By finding pleasure in my partner's fantasy, I affirm her life. This, too, is surrender. What you fantasize makes you richer, and what I fantasize makes me richer. If we can accept that, our shared sexual relationship will also be richer.

With this attitude, men and women become more gentle with each other. The oft-lamented lack of tenderness on the part of men, in particular, derives from a lack of fantasy. Tenderness of feeling and gesture grows out of the inner person's touching the Thou, and this inner touching presupposes fantasy.

In sexual surrender we experience our vivacity as a simultaneous giving and taking. The man senses this as he penetrates and the woman as she receives. Yet both the man and the woman experience penetrating and receiving, giving and taking, in equal measure thanks to their intimate union in which the penis belongs not only to the man but also to the woman, and the vagina belongs not only to the woman but also to the man, and above and beyond this the woman can give with her vagina and her entire being and the man can also take with his penis and his entire being. Giving and taking are equally primary in each and act in concert in the same way. In both modes I experience myself as an individual: in the way I enter life and the way I receive life. Loving penetration of another person, brings about my taking him or her into myself. And by lovingly receiving another person I penetrate her or his being.

The sex act, consequently, signifies the same thing in the realm of body and emotion as does mirroring the guiding image in the realm of emotion and spirit. Both penetrate the Thou and take the Thou into one's own center. Whereas in sexual union bodily sensations make oneness possible, the same union arises out of the holistic perception of the Thou when the guiding image is mirrored. Moreover, the sex act is, in the sense described, also an emotional-spiritual perception of the Thou; it cannot be clearly distinguished from mirroring the guiding image. And mirroring the guiding image is also a bodily process: The eye seizes on a figure in the outer world. Inseparable from the physiological process, I perceive a symbolic form: the mirrored guiding image of something still unlived that, at the instant of being perceived, begins to live. Eye, intuition, understanding—body, soul, and spirit—are bound together in this one perception. Each mirroring of the guiding image also has effects on bodily functions. This likewise points to the relatedness of sexual union and mirroring of the guiding image.

In coitus, two persons engage each other physically and emotionally. In contrast to this, mirroring the guiding image as an emotional-spiritual perception presupposes a certain distance from the Thou, the "optimal mirroring distance" from which one contemplates his mirror image. In sexual union the double movement of penetrating and receiving, giving and taking, stands in the place of the mirroring distance of two persons gazing into each other's eyes.

Let us take a closer look at the natural dynamics of experience of sexual union. First of all, both partners transmit their excitement to each other. Then follows a phase in which the physical processes of tenderness, sexual union, and coital movements are still partially guided by the conscious will. Little by little, however, the woman and the man fall into an involuntary common rhythm of movement that they do not determine from their heads but simply allow to take place. However, it is in their most lively and most active movements that they feel as though they are moved. My movements are given me as a gift, and yours are given you as a gift. In my own movement, I experience the Thou imparting himself or herself. But this imparts something about me, for the gift of movement given me is fully and wholly my own movement. In orgasm the unity of giving and taking, Thou and I, world and Self is complete, ecstatic reality.

I express the experience of sexual union in the following maxim: moved from the center, moved by the Thou. I experience both sides of that equation in interaction. The more active and "self-forgetful" my surrender to the movements of the Thou is, the more distinctly I sense the autonomous movements of my central personality. And the other way round: The more I move spontaneously from out of my own dynamic—from my pelvis, my middle, my Self—the more I am identical with my surrender, that is, with the Thou to whom I surrender and with her movement. Here, too, neither is more primary than the other, and each exists only together with the other. If isolated, both would degenerate; self-realization would turn into pleasure that is "made" by the will with the help of a technique, and the surrender to the Thou would become *a faire la charité*, that is, a "Christian charity" that is likewise "made." The meaning of both is revealed only in their simultaneity and their union, hence in a third thing: in moved movement or—which is the same—in moving movement, in the experience of Self and of Thou as a unity.

My depiction of sexual union is the description of an ideal that corresponds to the dynamics of body and soul. It is less important to realize this ideal fully than it is to hold it "in one's feelings." It is unavoidable that one or the other of the partners falls out of the common movement from time to time, and it is by no means unsettling if I regularly catch myself in the "sin" of "made" pleasure or "made" Christian charity. This is to be seen not as a lack and a weakness, but rather as an expression of our being historically en route. Nevertheless, my description of an ideal remains valid as a description of the natural *dynamics* of the human sexual act. As such it avoids the risk of being understood as only an ideal and hence as not binding. In *every* sexual act the experience described can be sensed and traced out as its most inner and genuine goal, even if it is experienced only in intimations. It is a question of a model, not in the sense of "normal" sexual behavior, but rather as the expression of the dynamics of body and soul.

The "normal" person has the need for things to be unequivocal, for a clear either/or. The normal person cannot sustain a tension of opposites in thought or in life. The "erotic" person, by contrast, seeks out this tension precisely where it is the most intense. The equally strong orientation to Thou and to Self causes erotic surrender.

I have already described the kinship between the physical-emotional act of sex and the emotional-spiritual act of mirroring the guiding image. Tantrism, the Tibetan version of Buddhism, set itself the goal of uniting these two. I will conclude this chapter by describing tantrism from the viewpoint of this union.

The artistic representation of tantric couples depicts them vividly. Man and woman are seated and fused together in the sexual act, yet simultaneously their torsos and their heads maintain a distance, making observation of one another possible. Both are completely at one, yet nevertheless at the same time each perceives the other. They utilize the energy animated in the sexual union for percieving the Self in the mirror of the Thou. Mutual attentive perception is to be observed in all tantric lover couples. The image of the other serves the formation of the image and its inner elaboration in the one contemplating. Sexual union generates the dynamic for this "inner work." The partners strengthen each other by "holding the heat fast," that is, by prolonging the sexual act as long as possible with relaxed attention. The man reserves his semen for a long time or even entirely. Thus the union of bodies can become a union of souls; two persons permeate and receive each other into their essences. This "holding back" demands a high degree of surrender: The shared coital movements are entirely internal and restrained. There is no "mechanical" substitute for love. As mere physical activity, the coital movements ultimately fall away entirely.

The increase in emotional temperature produces fantasies. In the mirror of the woman sitting astride and vis-à-vis the man, the Buddhist tantric devotee sees an "inner maiden" who ascends his spinal column. She is his ascending emotionality vitality.

In yet another respect the tantric experience of Eros touches on the conceptions of Eros that I have presented in this book. I discussed earlier how surrender to the Thou is also experienced as destruction of the I. In himself, the tantric devotee develops consciousness of the death aspect of erotic surrender. In the woman, he loves not only the "goddess of creation," who promotes life and growth, but also the "goddess of destruction," Kali, with her protruding tongue and her mouth full of fangs dripping blood. He often honors her by performing the sexual act among corpses.

Surrender to the destruction in the world means that when we have run up against our limits resisting evil, it is time to become one with life's countermovement, that is, the movement of death. I understand evil to mean all that diminishes and destroys life: illness, stupidity, failure of one's powers, hate, war, cruelty, natural catastrophies. Every sort of destruction and death is present *in nuce* in the "little death," as the French call the transitory loss of ego in orgasm—not as an experience of anxiety, but rather as unquestioning surrender and acceptance. Extreme situations test whether our erotic attitude is superficial and "manufactured" or is our central dynamic. Tantrism teaches that the basic erotic attitude can be singularly strengthened by the sexual act, which also mirrors the guiding image, precisely in the decisive affirmation of unavoidable destruction and death.

Sexual union is the fount of energy and central model for surrender to our life in all possible situations. Ecstatic sexual union makes it possible for us to experience the union of the opposites between which we stand: of potency and of strength consumed, of delight in an object of the world and in our destruction by it, of synthesis and of fragmentation, of life and of death.

Chapter 13

Thou Art an Image of my Secret Life

Perhaps we have spent many years—half a lifetime—telling another person with or without words, "That's the way you are. I've got your number. I know who you are." Good points and bad, we "simply knew." True, we couldn't substantiate it, but one really ought to trust one's feelings more than one's reason. Without noticing it, a great power emanated from us: the power of an image. Instead of seeing the other, we saw an image, and the more tenaciously we clung to it, the more the other truly became this image—the image of our projections that commanded: "You must be this way! You must be the mirror image of the environment that is manipulating you, the environment which we are." This suggestive projection was perhaps our sole creative act in the relationship: The other became the creature of our image. This was the common belief that bound us together.

Projection as disguised oppression has been described often. It does not let the other grow. A cool power emanates from our projections, even from projections of ardent amorousness, for by the projected image we separate the other from himself or herself; from insight into his or her own nature. We cut the other off from the world instead of furthering his or her ties to it, because we allow him or her no standpoint of his or her own from which to venture into the world. Thus we have the other in the palm of our hand. Now the other is dependent on our projection as a substitute for his or her lost identity.

What drives us to estrange a person from himself or herself to this extent? First of all, we are driven by the fear that nobody would voluntarily enter into a union with us. But we are especially motivated by our inability to love. Relationships that consist primarily of projections exclude love. Instead of forming a oneness with another that would be love, we cast an image over him or her like a disguise. We bind ourselves not to the other, but to our image of him or her.

Not all the images we have of people derive from projections. It happens occasionally that I meet someone whose personality is exactly what still slumbers in my soul's unconscious. Then the need stirs in me to connect with this person so that in being one with the other I learn how to develop the still undeveloped sides of myself that the other lives consciously and openly. If I, as a man, love a woman, this has to do with that fact that for the growth of my soul as a man, it is important to be more feminine. If I love this particular woman more than all others, this means that I want her especially to lead me on the path to my femininity, not in order to become just like her but rather to become as I myself must be through my inner confrontation with her. This is mirroring of the guiding image: I communicate with the other in this realm that already constitutes a mature, central domain of his or her personality, which is timely for me to develop just now. I communicate with the other as in a *mirror*, because I see mirrored in the other's personality this realm of which I knew little or nothing up until now. This is not noncommittal, merely aesthetic perception, but my awakening to a concrete development that is already under way in me. At the moment of perception, my partner already functions as my *guiding image*.

Every profound love rests on mutual mirroring of the guiding image; each sees something else reflected in the other, namely his or her own decisive secret. Consequently, we further our own development when we affirm the person we love. In contrast to projection, no one wants to change the other when mirroring the guiding image. Rather, each one wants to change himself or herself in the confrontation and in coming to terms with the Thou. I exert no force on the Thou to be as he or she should be according to my views, but rather I expose myself to the image that the Thou presents to me. Mirroring the guiding image is characterized by the feeling of freedom. I am free of the compulsion to change you and free to enlarge my emotional living space together with you. In surrender, I receive myself as a gift in a new, truer image of myself.

Mirroring the guiding image shares with projection the experience of being gripped by feelings; with a merely functional relationship it shares realistic, conscious perception. In contrast to projection, however, mirroring the guiding image knows no coercive intent, but only liberating feelings. However, this description of mirroring the guiding image is artificial to the extent that we are never totally free of projections. Phases of deeper transformation always begin with projections that we should, as soon as possible, redeem as mirroring the guiding image, but complete separation of projection and mirroring the guiding image is never possible.

In connection with trantrism, I explained that the energy of mirroring the guiding image is love. I do not subjugate you to my will, but rather I attempt to feel and to think from your point of view. I want you to be confident that you are lovable as you are, and I attempt to grant you the freedom to be as you must be. At the same time, I awaken to just that image which, from among countless women, spoke to me from within you. Initially my wishes and fears are mingled in this image with the reality of who you are, but because I love you, I perceive the signs with which you tell me ever more distinctly who you really are. Your image does not take the place of my life, but combines with it. I can unfold in the back and forth between you and me. You are your reality in yourself, but in me you are a dream figure with whom I create my life anew in my waking moments as if with a form that imparts shape—that is, with a guiding image. Thou art the image of my secret life.

Permanence indwells in this bond. Even with increasing familiarity, the mirroring between us can continue. In place of the drivenness of the first time together, there appears a vivacity that embraces all possible good and bad feelings. This vitality between us and in us is the stuff of love. It needs time to blossom. I hope we have that much time.

Often when I have grown tired, I lose my inner image of you. Then I feel like Orpheus, who lost Euridice to the underworld and never again found his way to another woman. The torture of the separation I now suffer is the first feeling I have had in a long time. It is a gift to me and spurs me on to concern myself anew with you and with your image in me. It was never true that we had nothing more to say to each other. If, nevertheless, we have this impression, the reason for it is to be found in our having loved each other too little. The borders of the Thou are farther away than I can ever travel. Whoever no longer loves builds a boundary in order to give up. The borders of my surrender always lie closer to me than the borders of your personality. Your land is larger than my eye can comprehend. "You bore me" really means that my surrender lies below your measure. I have become half-hearted in love. That is why there is no longer any mirroring of the guiding image between you and me.

Lovers have more important things to tell each other than perpetually to repeat their same views on mealtimes, sleep habits, friends, acquaintances, and politics. Of course, they cannot continuously carry on profound conversations. The back and forth of mirroring the guiding image can be casual, easy, and light, but it takes place across open boundaries. The soul's permeability to the Thou decides all. The same theme, approached with closed or open boundaries, leads either to disgust at the carping and to defense of turf, or to the pleasant increase of erotic temperature. In order to penetrate yet deeper into the meaning of mirroring the guiding image, let us now turn to the mirror as a symbol.

What is a *mirror*, really? What does it signify in an extended sense as an image in the soul? The image of the mirror is one of the richest images there is. Here I will limit myself to three meanings that are important in shaping a love relationship, namely, the mirror as emptiness, as defense, and as an oracle.

In contrast to a painting hanging in a museum, a mirror has no reality of its own. If the reflected object disappears, there is no longer a mirror image either. Consequently, in the "diamond vehicle" school of Buddhism the mirror is a symbol of *emptiness*. On the occasion of his ordination, each monk is handed a mirror that serves to remind him that the external world exists not in itself but only as a representation of his soul. By means of the mirror, he is guided out of the external world and into the inner world. The world is an empty mirror, a dream of the soul.

Knowing the meaning of the mirror as void is also helpful to lovers in conflict. For example, when they get entangled in a situation with each other, it helps to say to one another, "You are only my mirror image. I must get in touch with myself in order to see what is getting me upset in this fight." Thus I learn to dissolve fixations on my partner in critical situations and to turn my attention inward. My projections gradually become weaker, and I prepare myself to see the reflected guiding image again. After all, my partner's significance is not merely that of a dream I happen to be dreaming at the moment. My partner is not just a projected figure a reality in his or her own right with whom I can communicate, even if only to a limited degree. It is for this reason that contemplation of the mirror as a symbol of the void has something liberating about it. It guides one back into one's own soul and promotes delimitation when we are too one-sidedly taken up with the external world.

The mirror as image of the void leads next to the mirror as a symbol of delimitation and of *defense*. "Defense mirrors" against evil powers were and still are customary among many peoples. Let us recall Perseus and the Medusa. By carrying a mirror that weakened the Medusa's power, Perseus was able to behead her. Weakening the Medusa's power came about only in that he denied her any reality of her own. He saw her in the mirror of his own soul.

When I am in conflict with my wife, I can detoxify the atmosphere if I realize that I am not really fighting with my wife but with the evil harpy that is on a rampage in me at the moment. Now the evil harpy is beheaded. It has lost its power over me; I have calmed myself. The defense mirror has fulfilled its function by leading to the necessary differentiation between my wife and me.

The defense mirror signals, "Keep away from me!" But it is addressed not to the partner, but rather to one's own projection. Now I must withdraw behind my borders for a while before I can again make the attempt to enter into realistic contact with my wife, without disruptive projections so far as possible. Thus I prepare myself to listen again to the secret that she can impart to me.

The symbol of the mirror, therefore, signifies mediating insight into the process of projection as this becomes distinct in the image of the void and of the defense mirror. Above and beyond this, however, as *the oracle* and *the magic mirror*, it acquires the significance of deep, hidden knowledge of reality. In this third meaning, the symbol of the mirror corresponds to the mirror of the reflected guiding image. The oracular mirror imparts what I have not previously known and what can now give my life a new direction. Alexander the Great was said to have a magic mirror through which one saw with "the eye of spiritual perception," which is here and everywhere and recognizes everything. And in the Greek Patrai there was an oracular mirror which the priestesses of the fertility goddess Demeter queried concerning the possibility of ill persons recovering their health.

Oracles usually gave dark and puzzling answers and thereby stimulated the imagination to find the solution that was sought. Likewise, our life's companion is a dark and puzzling answer to the question of which of the soul's developmental stages I am just now traversing and what is to be done. I must take pains to understand her. The more I try, the greater is my surrender to my partner.

The oracle's sayings are symbolic. We do not understand them if we take them literally. We must step into the mirror and penetrate its depths—a common fairy-tale motif—in order to understand the oracle. The oracle is a symbol and must be interpreted. But in reference to me, my beloved is a symbol who must be interpreted. If I see my beloved only superficially, I get no answer. Love motivates me to step into the mirror of my beloved and plunge into my beloved's depths. Because I love, I am ready from the outset to take all my beloved's words as meaningful and to seek their meaning. A simple sentence from a person I love gives me a more profound answer than an entire book with which I have no connection. Love draws me into the depths of the Thou and into my own depths.

Having pursued the significance of the mirror in the love relationship—the mirror as void, as defense, and as oracle—a physical observation can still be made that is itself an image of mirroring the guiding image: If I look carefully, I discover my own miniature upside-down mirror image in the pupil of my counterpart's eye. This observation stimulated fantasies even in antiquity. In the figure in the pupil of the eye one saw one's own soul: the "pupil-mirror-soul." In the language of mirroring the guiding image, the concrete Thou as counterpart is a paradoxical image of my "mirror-soul," an "image of my secret life."

Why not return playfully now and then to the physical foundation of mirroring the guiding image by "gazing deep into each other's eyes" after the end of a conflict, not in order to destroy ourselves with the "evil eye," but rather to seek together our own mirror images in the other's eye. If we are successful, this optical mirroring of the guiding image will give us the impetus for an emotional mirroring.

This chapter on the partner as the "image of my secret life" would be incomplete if I did not say a few words about a form of relationship that seems to contradict what has been said so far, the sado-masochistic relationship. There seem to be fateful, destructive bonds between some men and women that lack all emotional growth but that nevertheless are love relationships. It is hard to grasp how people who have cut each other down decade after decade in their attempts to express life and have inflicted wound upon wound on each other remain together to the end of their lives as if they had a mission to fulfill, a life-and-death mandate. I intentionally depict this sort of relationship as one-sidedly destructive. It is intended to serve as an extreme model for the thesis that the meaning of each human life lies in establishing a relationship to the world and in surrender to a Thou.

Usually we find that sadistic persons were involved in the rearing of such destructively bonded persons. Without a doubt, both partners in such a relationship are compelled to repeat the pattern in the senseless hope of finally being able to break the circle of destruction by actively repeating the passively suffered cruelties. This explains why they are entangled with each other and cannot break free.

But why are these two persons lovers? What enigmatic meaning does each one seek to fulfill through love for the persecutor or victim? Is it only a sick form of surrender, the only one possible for such persons? Sado-masochism as a detour to love? Why do they surrender themselves to each other? What is the goal of their surrender?

Without going into these questions, I have to charge myself with having depicted a predominantly bright world of the soul's growth. While it admittedly includes a spectrum of crises extending from relatively minor upsets up to separation and divorce, they stand in the service of a new beginning and ultimately of success. But for the sado-masochistic couple, nothing succeeds but destruction: malice, cruelty, rage, hate. When one dies, the other does not heave a sigh of relief but also dies or leads a dull, shadowy existence. With the death of the other, life has lost its meaning because nothing has vitality any longer. Had they been divorced, they would have already "died" this sort of death. Destruction is rooted too deeply in their lives; since earliest childhood their fate of a life lived in cruelty has been too influential for them to have been able to get free of it through divorce. Each is the victim of the other, just as he or she was a victim in childhood. For both of them, being destroyed was the only form of vivacity "given" them.

Why don't such people kill themselves? Here I am thinking less of suicide than of tragic accidents or illnesses that come "as if summoned." Obviously they want to live. Whence do they draw the strength for such a life? How is it possible to surrender to such a life?

To this one could answer that they do not want only to be destroyed by the other as a victim, but they actively destroy the other, too, and their pleasure in this awakens and nurtures their greed for life. But in the last analysis, each of them experiences himself or herself only as the victim that persecutes the persecutor out of a feeling of self-defense. Hence we must repeat the same question: What motivates and impels them to surrender to such a life?

To this there is only one answer: Eros. In these lovers the power of Eros reveals itself even more clearly than in persons who succeed in neglecting love for extended periods of time. These two need Eros—the unceasing affective relationship to a Thou—in order to be able to accept their life, a life of progressive destruction, in order to affirm the countless cruelties of which their life consists. They love each other in the only language they understand, the language of destructiveness. To love the other means to destroy him because saying yea to his being is saying yea to his destructiveness. Being destroyed by the other means that he loves me just as I am. Destruction is part of the bargain because relationship comes with it.

For these two people, love truly is stronger than death, although, or precisely because, it brings death. They live in destruction, yet also love. The price of destruction and of death is not too high a price to pay for love. There is no growth, only destruction and dissolution, and nevertheless there is surrender, attachment, the oneness of two who destroy each other. For them the meaning of life arises only from the fact that they mutually surrender to their life, to their destruction.

Do these kinds of fateful, destructive components belong only to other people? Is everything in us capable of development and forward striving? Are there no death places in us where nothing grows, no foci of the fires of destruction? Does everything in us strive for resurrection and a new beginning? We should be wary of a person who sees fateful evil only in others, for nobody could damage us so radically as that person. We all have an irreversible, unredeemable devil in us to whom we are bonded with a deep, hopeless empathy. We love him as a mother loves her deathly ill child. In our experience, it is the opposite image of the highest value, of the good most worth striving for. It does not enter the play of our principles; it is, as it were, a "counterself," autonomous and sterile. Its existence alone is a sign of total destructiveness.

I have never met a couple that was so exclusively given to destructiveness as the model couple I described; I know no absolutely evil people lacking all possibilities of growth. But I was concerned with making clear the thesis that surrender and relationship are vitally necessary for every person, if not for their own growth, then for assuming a tragic fate. This is the opposite of mirroring the guiding image, whose goal is that of promoting the soul's growth. Both are surrender—the one in a negative, the other in a positive sense. Both are Eros because they seek relationship with a Thou. This tragic couple is not only terrifying in their destructiveness, but also exemplary in their total surrender. Note well: They do not destroy outside of their relationship. They avoid this at all costs, because there would be no meaning in it. They live à deux as in an oasis of cruelty, which offers them the sole possibility of breaking out of their isolation.

In loving our partner, do we also love our partner's dead areas where no life sprouts? And do we feel ourselves loved by our partner even with our "counterself"? One could easily understand if these questions were answered in the negative, and yet the negation would be the expression of a decisive, fundamental failure in the partnership. Something in us would be like a deathly ill child that is loved by no mother, and like a mother who deserts her deathly ill child. We should assume a maternal attitude toward irreversible, destructive aspects of our personality. The mother accepts her deathly ill child and cares for it, but she does not let herself be drawn into death. She loves her child and sets a boundary between herself and the destructiveness that it embodies. This is possible for her because she has something other than destructiveness in her. People with possibilities for growth must enter into mirroring the guiding image for these possibilities and unconditionally set boundaries against their own destructiveness. But the possibility cannot be excluded that persons with overwhelming destructiveness, which cannot or can no longer be modified, are capable of entering into relationship with each other only through their own destructiveness.

Conclusion

The Attitude of Eros

To say no within the context of a love relationship means, first of all, to say nay to the hegemony of the ego. Secondly it means to say yea to the relativization and transformation of the ego in surrender to a Thou. I have attempted to set this concept forth in this book. Nay said *in* love serves to strengthen the fundamental attitude or stance of Eros I have often mentioned wherein we are linked in a feeling of oneness not only with the Thou whom we especially love, but also with people in our proximate or our more distant environment, as well as with the rest of animate and inanimate nature.

Our concern now is to illuminate from a different angle and to summarize the things already said. These reflections are intended to facilitate realization of the message of this book.

Our attitude to life in general is revealed in our central love relationships. From them can be seen whether our fundamental stance is grounded in Eros as well as what still separates us from a fundamental stance of Eros. Therefore the theme of this book has been primarily the love bond between man and woman. The viewpoint taken here excludes the possibility that these bonds of love can become a substitute for responsibly living in the world. A dyadic relationship that shuns the world thereby reveals that it rests not on love but on projections. Projections separate people emotionally from their surroundings, although they seek a connection with them. Love embraces the world about us precisely where active devotion is most necessary. Social responsibility are furthering of people from our immediate surroundings not relativized by a love relationship and crowded into the background. On the contrary, a love relationship is a focus of energy for the attitude of Eros in all areas in which we live; it promotes our surrender to all the tasks we face.

If the attitude of Eros were only a sensation, we could not call it an attitude. To be sure, in the love relationship the attitude of Eros is initially set in motion by sensations, but whether it can turn into an enduring attitude depends on whether our understanding and our will accord with our sensations of love and whether we are capable of building Eros into our day-to-day life. Consequently, the question that a lover often asks—whether he or she "still" feels love—is asked one-sidedly. More comprehensively and correctly posed, the question must ask whether or not in the lover's surrender to the Thou he or she has come so far that the development of the Thou is furthered and the lover experiences and furthers himself or herself in the process too. The very fact that the lover poses the question in this one-sided form reveals that his or her surrender is faulty. When the attitude of Eros is solid, the temptation to ask "Do I still really love my partner?" falls away.

The fundamental attitude of Eros unites two opposing stances that are usually mutually exclusive: the permanent, conscious relation inward to one's own soul, and the conscious, permanent relation to the external world—introversion and extraversion. The either-or of extraversion and introversion makes access to the attitude of Eros more difficult. My concern has been to sketch concretely their interplay as two lovers mirror the guiding image for each other. The major difficulty lies in finding a place and a meaning within love for the nay to the beloved—delimitation from him or her, resistance to and defensiveness against him or her—and in grasping the nay to the beloved as a yea to one's love for him or her. This interpretation of the nay to the beloved as a nay expressed *within* love—thus as a yea *to* love—lays bare the inner dynamics of the attitude of Eros and promotes that attitude.

Yea and nay. In order to grasp the peculiarity of a love relationship, our language must move back and forth through the middle range between identification and delimitation, experience and conceptual thought. Besides, a book on psychology runs the danger of getting away from the vivacity of the soul by erecting a rigid conceptual framework. I took pains to resist taking the easy road and "clicking into" rigid concepts and patterns of thought. It seemed to me that the credibility of my statements depended on my making them from within the attitude of Eros.

Consequently I decided to refrain from mentioning even those writers to whom my thought and feeling are most deeply indebted.

This was the result neither of presumptuousness nor the need for originality at any price, nor am I ashamed of my sources. It was the result solely of my fundamental concern with mirroring the guiding image: with a wish not to "settle" views and opinions with a one-sided objectivity and external logic, nor to refer the "truth" back to merely subjective experience. By employing the most realistic mirror image possible of the external world, hence also by reflecting my intellectual and emotional "teachers," I was intent on sharing insights that are my own because they lie close to my heart. My asceticism in forgoing a technical language—excepting the concept of mirroring the guiding image, the validity and vitality of which I trust because I coined it myself—and my asceticism in not citing other writers to whom I feel myself indebted are meaningful only in terms of my efforts at authenticity.

The following final observations pertain properly to the attitude of Eros. At the beginning of a love relationship, unbounded hopes awaken in us for the other as well as for changes that the other will bring about in our life. In a single stroke the horizon of expectations for our life is broadened. But little by little, due to daily experience with our partner, we see ourselves forced to accommodate our hopes and expectations to "the real facts." And yet, the initial boundless feeling that promised freedom and the expansion of the range of our life was no illusion; we only interpreted it wrongly. We assumed erroneously that it signified an almost unlimited number of new objective possibilities of development through our bond with this person whom we love. But, strictly speaking, the object of our feeling was not boundless, for every person's possibilities of development are limited. Our feeling was boundless; our earlier narrow attitude to life opened up and became an attitude of Eros.

It is important to see these interrelationships when, little by little, our expectations of our love relationships shrink back to everyday dimensions. Now we can remain lovers only if we cease trying to cling to illusory ideas that finally some day perfect harmony with the other will prevail, or that he or she will again lay aside the characterological weaknesses that have been appearing clearly for some time, or that I will turn into the happiest of all people, thanks to this partnership.

What we have actually "promised" each other was the unrestricted feeling of love. But a merely passive feeling cannot be maintained permanently. It is devoured by the banalities of day-to-day life. Feeling must become active in order to attain permanence. It must become a conscious attitude: the erotic attitude of surrender. The meaning of the "boundless feeling" is the attitude of Eros.

By "attitude of Eros" I do not mean the unrealistic overvaluation of one's own capacity to love—say, the heroic dream of redeeming someone from all the sufferings of this world. I mean the fundamental openness to the Thou that consists in our anticipating vital impulses from the other even in "stuck," blocked phases in the relationship, even from the other's sadness, his or her crushing defensiveness or childish behavior against me. To say, "I won't have anything to do with that; that's not my problem" is to betray the attitude of Eros. Everything that touches the Thou is significant for me and can tell me something. Not that I should take responsibility for the other's moods and difficulties, but the person whom I love is, even in his or her repugnant and burdensome aspects, still "an image of my secret life." On the one hand this is so because my particular love for this person instead of for another points to my own inner personality with which I must form a bond, and on the other hand it is so because nothing except love can ever motivate me to come to terms with the unpleasant and painful facts of life rather than avoid them.

Only in the relationship of love can we learn little by little to extend our boundaries. Who besides our beloved would dare to challenge us regularly? Whence other than from love do we get the necessary energy to loosen entrenched habits and views and to include foreign territories in our personality?

Indeed, many persons can care for others untiringly, even without a central love relationship. But nobody succeeds in fundamentally transforming his or her personality from within unless he shares his life with another person whom he loves. That is the limit of Christian charity that does not have its roots in love informed by Eros. In uncommitted love relationships we often fall victim to the temptation of seeking the reflection of the guiding image only so long as a good vital feeling warms us. In decisive situations, however, we refuse the challenge to become someone else.

In contrast to this, I am bonded to this person in a stubborn devotion and surrender that makes it impossible for me to evade unpleasant facts. Half-consciously I regularly help build up tension between us in order to test the power of devotion and surrender once again and to cast light on one more dark side of my personality through confrontation. For example, I am indeed deeply hurt that my partner has stubbornly and hard-heartedly refused me all attention for three days only because she is annoyed by my messiness and indifference; but at the same time, my fantasy is working at high speed. What does this stubbornness and hardness of heart mean for me? Is it perhaps meaningful? In one respect or another, must I perhaps lay aside my messy indifference that is the opposite of my partner's stubbornness, not only because it does not suit my partner but also from an inner necessity? Am I letting myself go, although the need for order and clear goal-setting is also in me and is especially strong in recent days? Is that what my Self mirrors in the Thou as in a guiding image? Does her stubbornness and hardness of heart also relate to my own determined resistance against coming to terms with my nonchalance in the future? And is her unyielding, rigid stance an extreme guiding image for the clear structuring of life that I lack?

If this inner dialogue came only from my bad conscience and from a childish need for love, I would not feel so open, relaxed, and enlivened, as a result of it. I would not have this feeling of a new freedom that lets me seize the initiative in my work or in other relationships. This inner dialogue was actually a reflection of a guiding image. In the symbolic image of the Thou, I actually perceived a side of myself that has to be developed, namely, the order and structure that I have lacked up until now. If I had merely adapted myself to the other, I would now be crippled and dull. Of course, adaptation for the sake of peace is something I also know. At best one then feels relieved, but not really free. Adaptation for the sake of peace lacks the curiosity and the openness to everything that moves and wants to live from within me, as well as the inner evidence of a new development belonging to me and the pleasurable connection to it. It lacks the attitude of Eros, but this is precisely what I have regained.

This last example is intended to illustrate what is meant by the openness and the permeability characteristic of the attitude of Eros, and how this can set in motion a fruitful mirroring of the guiding image. The attitude of Eros implies turning one's attention from the I to the Thou, trying—with the love set free by love—to perceive that symbolic guiding image in the Thou that one is now in need of. If you look closely, it will start to take shape in you. It enters into a new union with the ego you have known up until now and shapes your new personality that is closer to the Self.

Bibliography

Bächtold-Stéubli, H., editor. *Handwörterbuch des deutschen Aberglaubens*, vol. 1 (Berlin, 1927).

Barz, Helmut. *Stichwort: Selbstverwirklichung* (Stuttgart: Kreuz Verlag, 1981).

Buber, Martin. *I and Thou* (New York: Scribner, 1970).

Cardinal, E. *Das Buch von der Liebe* (Hamburg, 1971).

Franz, Marie-Louise von. *Projection and Re-collection in Jungian Psychology* (La Salle, Ill. & London: Open Court, 1980).

Freud, Sigmund. "Some Neurotic Mechanisms in Jealousy, Paranoia and Homosexuality (1922)," vol. 18 of *The Standard Edition of the Complete Psychological Works of Sigmund Freud* (London: Hogarth Press, 1953-74), hereinafter referred to as S.E.

———. "Three Essays on Sexuality," S.E. vol. 7.

———. "The Taboo of Virginity," S.E. vol. 11.

———. "Some Psychical Consequences of the Anatomical Distinction between the Sexes," S.E. vol. 19.

———. "Inhibition, Symptoms and Anxiety," S.E. 20.

Fromm, Erich. *The Art of Loving* (New York: Harper & Row, 1956).

Glasenapp, H. von, editor. *Pfad zur Erleuchtung* (Düsseldorf & Köln, 1980).

Guggenbühl-Craig, Adolf. *Marriage Dead or Alive* (Dallas: Spring Publications, 1981).

Hillman, James. "Betrayal," *Loose Ends* (Dallas: Spring Publications, 1975).

Jung, C.G. *Psychological Types*. In *Collected Works of C.G. Jung*, vol. 6 (Princeton: Princeton University Press, 1971).

————. *Mysterium Coniunctionis*. In *Collected Works*, hereinafter referred to as *Collected Works*, vol. 14 (Princeton: Princeton University Press, 1970).

————. *Aion: Researches into the Phenomenology of the Self*. In *Collected Works*, vol. 9, pt. 1 (Princeton: Princeton University Press, 1959).

————. *The Practice of Psychotherapy*. In *Collected Works*, vol. 16 (Princeton: Princeton University Press, 1966).

————. *The Development of Personality*. In *Collected Works*, vol. 17 (Princeton: Princeton University Press, 1967).

————, and Richard Wilhelm. *The Secret of the Golden Flower* (New York: Harcourt, Brace & World, 1962).

Kerenyi, Karl. *Die Mythologie der Griechen*, 2 vols. (München, 1977).

Lao Tzu, *Tao Te Ching* (New York: Knopf, 1972).

Lemaire, J. *Les Thérapies du Couple* (Paris, 1971).

Lowen, Alexander. *Love and Orgasm*.

Moser, T. *Stufen der Nähe: Ein Lehrstück für Liebende* (Frankfurt, 1981).

Nell, R. *Traumdeutung in der Ehepaar-Therapie* (München, 1976).

Neumann, Erich. *Zur Psychologie des Weiblichen* (Zürich: Rasher Verlag, 1953).

————. *Amor and Psyche* (Princeton: Princeton University Press, 1956).

Paul, N. and P. "Homosexuelle Phantasien, Partnerwahl und eheliche Harmonie," in *Zeitschrift Familiendynamik*, ZL 4-1, 1979, Stuttgart.

Ranke-Graves, R. von. *Griechische Mythologie*, 2 vols. (Hamburg, 1980).

Rawson, P. *Tantra* (Munich, 1974).

Richter, H.E. *Flüchen oder Standhalten* (Hamburg, 1978).

Schellenbaum, Peter. *Die Homosexualität des Mannes* (München: Kindler Verlag, 1980).

————. *Stichwort: Gottesbild* (Stuttgart: Kreuz Verlag, 1981).

Shah, Idries. *The Sufis* (Garden City: Doubleday, 1964).

Theweleit, K. *Mnnerphantasien* (Hamburg, 1981).

Wiederkehr-Benz, K. "Scheidung—Stirb und werde," in *Neue Züricher Zeitung*, 28/29 November, 1981.

Willi, Jürg. *Die Zweierbeziehung* (Hamburg, 1980).

————. *Couples in Collusion*. New York & London: Jason Aronson, 1982).

Zimmer, Heinrich. *Indische Mythen und Symbole* (Düsseldorf & Köln, 1981).